The House of Baric

Part Three:

Widows and Weddings

A novel by

Jillian Bald

HILLWALKER PUBLISHING

A NOTE FROM THE AUTHOR

The world was a troubled and dangerous place in the 17th century. Not all the residents of Baric Castle understood how fortunate they were, living in their orderly, mannered community. I didn't want to write about all the bad things that happened, but I thought you would want to know the whole story.

I have grown fond of all the people in the House of Baric. Each has their own charms and flaws, but I picked a few of my favorites to follow more closely in *Widows and Weddings*. I wanted to reaffirm that the women in these novels were more than playthings in pretty dresses, although the men might not have agreed with me.

These House of Baric women, real yet fictitious, faced different dangers compared to the soldiers I focused on in the first books. Like the men, they are warriors. But instead of wars, they fought for a tolerable place in a man's world. In the pages to come, you will understand what I mean.

If you need to be reminded what happened in the first books, I put a synopsis for each on my website: JillianBald.com/synopsis.

In *Part Three: Widows and Weddings*, we will be leaving the House of Baric and traveling to Venice to celebrate Stephan's wedding. Resi was so looking forward to that. But once our friends leave, Resi, Ruby, and other favorites will realize how Mauro's indulgence of their opinions does not extend beyond the sheltered castle walls. Some are in for an awakening and will long to be back at the House of Baric. Other friends might never return to Baric Castle. They have different journeys ahead of them.

Widows and Weddings begins where I left off in *A Brother's Defense*— Jero and Ruby are on their way to be married, escorted by their sellsword friends. With good roads, good weather, and gold in their saddlebags, their spirits are high, and they are looking forward to a happy reunion in Thessaloniki. What could go wrong?

Let's join them and see.

~*~

Widows and Weddings

Part Three of

The House of Baric

Chapter 1

Ottoman Territory, 23 July 1649

It should have been an easy journey to Thessaloniki. The seasoned mercenaries had crisscrossed the Balkans with no troubles in the past. The days were still long at the end of July, and at night, sleeping under the stars was bearable. They had food, money, and rested horses. They were Salar Nassim's lucky six.

Jero Baric was sore and sunburned from the long days of riding on the hardened dirt highway. Still, he could think of no place he would rather be than in the company of Ruby Spiros.

If Ruby felt the same road-weariness, she did not complain. This was the price to seal their love, and it was a bargain. After a year of secret mutual admiration, Jero and Ruby believed they would marry once they got her father's permission, even though Ruby was already promised to a man handpicked by Angelos Spiros. Angelos had said so in his last letter and had asked Patrik Kokkinos to bring Ruby home to marry.

Thessaloniki was still days away, and Jero and Ruby let themselves become lost in the sameness of the scenery as the days turned into a week of traveling south along the Croatian coastline. Glimpses of the glistening Adriatic and its archipelago of rocky islands lingered reliably to their right. The bobbing of fishing boats held their attention as watercraft sailed on the sparkling sea.

Their four escorts were not immune to the monotony of the ride. They, too, became lost in private thoughts as their horses clopped along the well-traveled route.

While fighting far from the sea in the heart of Europe, Patricius Kokkinos—or Patrik as he preferred to be called—had ached for a glimpse of it. Now he wished to be winding through shadowed mountains again, past the endless Adriatic, closer to Thessaloniki, his home.

Bem Tavares rode next to Patrik. He, too, was in a hurry to be south again. Bem's young wife had been taken from him in Egypt, kidnapped by her former mistress. Bem's search for Fatina had been futile without money to pay for information, but he never gave up on finding her. With pouches of gold in his pockets from selling his sword in distant wars, Bem could finally hunt for Fatina in earnest.

Salar Nassim had two reasons to journey south again: Hafza and Emine. The sellsword was Persian, as was his first wife, Hafza, who lived on the island of Rhodes with their sixteen-year-old daughter, Shirin. It had been years since he had traveled so far south to see them. Usually, he went no farther than Athens, where he had left his Ottoman wife and his true love, Emine. But he had a duty to both, and with gold in his saddlebags, Salar Nassim would travel to Rhodes after helping his friend find Fatina.

Soren rode at the rear of the group. The heat of the southern lands didn't bother the Dane, but Soren had no plans to linger here. He would stay in Athens only long enough to help Bem. After that, Soren was determined to leave the continent altogether, at least for a few years. At twenty-six, Soren had seen enough of warring to fill a lifetime. He had decided to sign on with a merchant ship, as he had once done with his now-dead brother, and sail away.

A week after their departure from Baric Castle, they finally crossed the Venetian border and found themselves in the fortified city of Ragusa. Under other circumstances, the gang might have lingered in the bustling port town to learn the news of the world and add a few coins to their purses. But they continued on after resupplying, turning east and crossing into Ottoman territory.

The new route led to a swampy plain beyond the sight of the sea. Despite the oppressive humidity and biting insects that fed on every patch of exposed skin, the six rode hard through the swamps to put the miles behind them. This lowland route was a quicker way to Tirana, albeit a miserable one.

Tirana had been a quiet trading stop along the caravan crossroads for centuries until the Ottoman Army transformed the sleepy Albanian village into a burgeoning town. The ruling Turks in Constantinople were fools to believe Tirana was firmly under their authority just because they set up a military post there. Ethnic tribal lords infiltrated Ottoman governing offices, keeping their dominance over the locals.

Despite the inhospitable geography of the old caravan route, it was well used by other travelers, merchant traders, and, now and then, gangs of sellswords. One such gang would change the six's fate.

~*~

Salar Nassim urged his horse up a grassy knoll to assess the road ahead. Bem followed him.

From their elevated perch, they noticed the beginnings of a forest and a meandering river crossing the landscape. Small carts and pairs of travelers could be seen at a distance, going in both directions.

Salar Nassim was more interested in finding water and shelter for the night than who was on the road with them. He pointed out, "The highway follows the trees at the edge of the valley. There might be a stream there where we could camp."

Bem scouted the landscape, looking back in the direction they had just come. "Do you remember those three at the water hole?" he asked.

Salar Nassim turned to where Bem was looking. He could see the outlines of horses to the north and recognized the colorful garments of the Ottoman riders in the distance. "What about it?"

Bem pondered out loud, "Why have they not passed us? They aren't loaded down like we are."

Salar Nassim was troubled by their shadowing. "We have better horses."

Bem continued to watch the group to the north, then shook off his doubts and asked, "How far do you think it is until we reach Tirana?"

"I have never been this way, but the map shows it's between two mountains. Probably those two on the horizon. My best guess is we still have two nights on the road."

"Two nights, three days. We are low on supplies."

"Let's camp while we have good light. We'll fish for our dinner, and maybe you can set some traps, too."

Bem nodded with a smile. "Trout and roasted rabbit. That sounds like a feast compared to our bread and dry cheese of yesterday."

They turned their horses to tell the others of the plan.

~*~

Duties were not assigned, but a routine naturally fell into place in camp each evening. Jero went for water; Ruby searched for kindling; Bem tended to the horses; Salar Nassim cleared a site for their bedrolls; Patrik and Soren scouted the vicinity for threats.

Ruby had been given favorable consideration at the end of a tiring day. She was not required to hunt or even cook the meal, and she was the first to be offered a plate at the fire. Not because she was a woman, but because she was an outsider, both she and Jero were, and the mercenaries did not require their help in setting up camp.

They ate their hard-earned dinner in cheerful conversation that night. Happy to be rid of the mosquitoes and biting flies that swarmed in the lowlands, the companions enjoyed their roasted catches while stretched out on their bedrolls. Under the starry sky around the flickering fire, the four sellswords had an easiness together after years of shared nights like this one. Even Soren added a tale to the fireside conversation that night.

Ruby was the first to wrap up in her blanket and fall asleep at Patrik's side. She slept in what she had worn that day. There was little privacy for a young woman traveling on the open road with five men, but that did not trouble her. She was too worn out by the time the darkness could give her cover to strip down to wash. So, like the others, she gave up on worrying about her appearance.

Jero sat quietly by the fire. He was grateful his four escorts had accepted him. The mercenaries did not have to honor Baron Baric's request to take Jero along with them to Thessaloniki. Even though he was now a nobleman with a leisurely life waiting for him upon his return, Jero would do whatever task was asked without complaint. His escorts found no fault in the man or his quest to marry the woman he loved.

The more time Jero spent with Ruby, the more he could not keep his eyes off her. As Ruby's assigned guardian on the trip, Patrik had not made it easy for the lovesick couple to have any time alone. They were already separated on their horses each day and slept at opposite ends of their camp each night. That had been their routine day after day, and Jero woke each morning to the same disappointing sight of Ruby wrapped in another man's arms.

~*~

Jero was the first one up on that unseasonably cool morning. His woolen cape and blanket hadn't kept the dampness of the nearby woods from crawling under his clothes in the deep of night. The campfire was long extinguished, and a chill hung in the emerging sunlight.

His boots crackled on the sandy ground, and the horses stirred. Bem would be up soon. Their shifting to be untied would wake him.

For now, Jero was alone in his movements as he carefully stepped around his companions. The sight of Ruby nestled against her childhood friend at the end of the row of sleeping bodies made him uneasy. Patrik's strong arm was around her waist, keeping her warm. Standing over the slumbering couple, Jero could not tell where one body stopped and the other started.

Jero had exercised the gentlemanly control that Patrik required of him and had not crossed any lines of propriety. He had quelled his urge to touch a wisp of Ruby's hair, resisted holding her hand while walking or wrapping his own arms around her to keep her warm at night. Jero cringed at Patrik's betrayal.

Before Jero could decide whether to kick Patrik or just tap his shoulder to quietly remind the Greek that he was too close to the woman Jero loved, a firm hand grabbed the ankle of Jero's boot.

Jero looked down in surprise.

Soren was awake next to Patrik and had watched Jero's indecision. "I will talk to him," Soren whispered, still cocooned in his blanket.

After a second look at his competition, slumbering against his future wife, Jero agreed to let the Dane settle his grievance. Jero pushed through the bushes at the edge of their camp to revive his pride at the cool stream.

Patrik opened his eyes with a questioning scowl as Soren unpeeled Patrik's arm from Ruby.

"Come on," Soren whispered and then walked away from the cradled couple.

Thinking it was urgent, Patrik slipped out from under the blanket and followed him.

"What is it? What is the matter?" Patrik asked.

Soren glared disapprovingly and said, "You are the matter, Patrik."

"What did I suddenly do in my sleep to offend you?"

"It is not sudden, and I should have brought it up before. Look, Patrik," Soren explained crossly, "it is becoming clear that you don't want Ruby to marry Jero. We are not yet too far from Ragusa. If you are going to block Jero's way with her father, then say so now, and he can catch a boat for home."

"Block his way? What gives you that idea? I am not against Jero. I like him. He is a good man," Patrik grumbled defensively.

Soren rubbed his brow and shook his head. "You don't see it, do you? Jero was standing over you and Ruby this morning with a very different view. You sleep with her like a lover. If she were my bride, I would have stood over you with my drawn sword, not with my clenched fists."

Patrik let out an exasperated sigh. "She took my blanket in her sleep. It got fucking cold, and she is like a little furnace under her covers. My covers! She doesn't seem to mind my heat, either."

"Jero minds your heat, and I am beginning to agree with him. Why are you keeping Ruby from him, anyway? You are like a jealous brother. Let Jero have his courtship with her and arrive with real determination to sway her father's opinion."

"All right, Soren. You've made your point. Maybe I am a little overprotective," Patrik said with annoyance.

Soren scoffed. "A little?"

"Fine," Patrik conceded. "But I want to clear one thing up before I back off."

Soren shot him an encouraging smile. "I will hold you to your word. Have your say, but make it quick. The others are up now, and we won't linger long this morning."

~*~

Patrik found Ruby coming up the path from the stream. "Good morning, Ruby. Did you sleep well under my blanket?" he asked.

"Did I take it again? I will try to leave you alone tonight," she said with a chuckle.

"I will not give you the chance," he said unexpectedly.

"Oh?"

They reached the camp clearing together, and he looked around. The others were busy with their morning chores. "I had forgotten how fond I am of our old friendship," he told her. "I cannot help but want to take care of you, Ruby."

"I told you, Patricius—"

He interrupted her with a gentle shush. "What I wanted to say was, well, it has been pointed out to me by a certain Dane that I have been too protective of you, Ruby. I have decided that Jero is equally capable of watching over you. He will be your protector for the rest of the trip."

"Do I need a guardian? I feel quite safe with all of you."

"I am glad you feel that way, Ruby dear. Then maybe Jero doesn't need to sleep at your side in my place."

A smile spread across her smudged face. "Is that what you mean by 'protector'?"

"Indeed, but with one stipulation." His poker face cracked into a mischievous smile when he added, "Be quiet when you sleep with your lover. We will still be close by."

Ruby was not amused. "Do not even jest about something like that, Patricius Kokkinos. I would never put myself in such a compromising position. I will be sleeping just the same as before."

"That is not reassuring, my little blanket thief. Promise me I don't have to worry about your virtue."

Ruby looked down the path to be sure they were still alone. "Of course, I promise. And so does Jero."

"And are you certain that you love him?"

"I am very sure I love him."

Patrik nodded approvingly. "With your solemn promise, I release you to Jero Baric."

She squeezed his hand in gratitude. "If I had a brother, I would have loved for him to be like you, Patricius."

He brought her hand to his lips and kissed it. "I am at your service. Now go make yourself useful and pack up your things. We will not stay long after our breakfast."

"Is there enough time to bathe before we go?" she asked.

A toothy grin crossed his unshaven face. "You didn't worry about your smell when you slept next to me."

"Yes, well, we could all use a good washing. You especially," she declared.

"I think Salar Nassim is anxious to go."

"I noticed that the stream pools in a hidden spot just off the path. Tomorrow there might not be such a spot. If I go now, I can be done before you are even finished with breakfast."

Patrik was suddenly her protector again and warned, "You are not going alone."

"Are you going to bathe with me?"

"Didn't you just tell me I needed a washing?"

She laughed at his logic. "I will leave my pot of soap, and you can take your bath after. I will be quite fine by myself."

"I will tell the others the change in plans. But be quick about it."

"Thank you, Patricius. I will go get my bag."

Patrik saw Jero walking toward them, having just filled the water jugs. "I will talk to Jero about the change in sleeping arrangements," Patrik told her. "Hurry along now to the stream and get started. I'll bring your bag to you."

"As you wish, Patricius. But don't change your mind about tonight."

Chapter 2

He set the satchel on the top of a boulder that blocked his view of the stream.

"Can you unpack my pot of soap, Patricius? And my linen?"

He opened her bag and found what she had asked for. "It is me, Ruby, not Patricius. I will just leave it on the rock where you can reach it."

Ruby heard the crunching noise of his footsteps as he went away.

"Jero!" she called out. "Stay! Did Patricius talk to you?"

Jero leaned against the boulder and replied, "He did."

"Come around to the water's edge so we don't have to shout over the rocks."

"I . . . um . . . Patrik made quite a list of demands just a moment ago. I do not think he would approve."

"I won't tell him."

When Jero walked around the barrier, Ruby's back was to him. She was not nude in the waist-deep water, but her gauze shift and long auburn hair were drenched.

"I'll take that soap now," she said.

"I'll leave it on the shore and turn my back."

She lathered herself from head to foot as she contemplated her companion. "Do you want to come in?"

Jero averted his eyes. "The others are eating now, but we will take your advice and wash up when you are done."

She sank in the water to let the suds on her body lift away. "Have you eaten already?"

"I am not so hungry," he said, locking eyes with his betrothed.

"I am ready to get out now."

Her eyes dared him to watch her leave the water, and Jero's dilemma showed on his face. He let out the breath he had been holding. "I'll just wait over here," he mumbled and retreated to the cover of the boulder again.

Ruby was upbeat when she called over, "Have you been practicing your Turkish with Patricius?"

"Do you want to hear?"

"I do," she said eagerly from behind the rocks.

Jero cleared his throat and focused on his accent when telling her, "I be Jero Baric, and I love and admire your girl. I will marry and take her to Solgrad after me."

Ruby laughed.

"I may have mixed up a few words. Is it right?" Jero asked.

"Mostly right, but I think you shouldn't be so direct about your intentions. You must first flatter my father, say wonderful things about his family, and especially about him."

"Those were all the words I could put together so far, and my Greek is even worse."

"I admire you for trying," Ruby said. "Why don't you just say what you want in Latin, and Patricius can translate for you?"

"I want to impress your father."

"Then you must practice, night and day."

"You can teach me the words I need. We'll start tonight, while I hold you in my arms," he told Ruby.

"That sounds wonderful."

She emerged from the bank with her hair wrapped in linen, wearing a long tunic and a belted vest over men's leggings. The collar of her tunic was open, and her pale skin was still rosy from the cold water.

"You look lovely," Jero breathed out.

"Dressed as a man?" she joked shyly.

"Anyone would know that you are not a man."

He held out his hand, and she took it in hers. It was warm and comforting. He picked up her bag, and they walked back toward the camp.

"Something smells good on the fire. I am suddenly starving," Ruby said.

"Bem's traps must have worked."

A man's voice answered, "They did, Jero, and the rabbit is delicious. We left you some." It was Bem. He emerged from the underbrush, followed by Salar Nassim, Patrik, and Soren.

"The camp is packed up and the horses are saddled," Patrik told them.

"We will leave shortly. The sun is already hot," Salar Nassim added.

"I'll just go get my things," Jero replied.

Soren held up Jero's pack and said, "We already thought of that."

Ruby took her bag from Jero's grip and said, "I know the way from here."

He squeezed her hand and then followed the others back down the path to the stream.

~*~

Ruby had not been alone in the two weeks since leaving Solgrad, and she savored the solitude while she searched her bag for the comb she needed. She could hear the distant sound of her companions carried by the wind to their camp. She hummed, joining their muffled conversation.

After she couldn't find what she needed in her satchel, Ruby went to the horses for her saddlebag. She smiled to herself when she saw the last pair of clean stockings at the bottom of it. As she bent over to take off her boot, the linen wrap on her head threatened to come loose.

When she stood up to re-tuck the ends of the cloth, something caught her eye. The morning sunlight reflected off the scattered boulders at the other side of the camp, and an odd shadow next to Zeus's leg stretched under the beast like a spirit.

"How strange," she said to herself.

She was fixated on its movement when she realized it wasn't a shadow at all but a pair of tall black boots. White trousers appeared. A man, or at least the bottom half of a man, was now clearly visible next to Jero's horse. A gloved hand reached up, unfastened a strap on Jero's saddle, and took down a bag.

Did one of her companions forget his change of clothes? She called over to the shadow, "Jero, is that you?"

The boots quickly disappeared. He did not hear her at that distance, she thought. But if they were already coming for their clothes, then they would soon want to leave, and Ruby had little time to braid her hair.

She quickly unwound the linen and dragged a comb through her tangled locks. The hair on the back of her neck tingled with instinctive dread. She stopped.

A new, longer silhouette stretched ahead of her. Before Ruby could turn to meet the shadow, a strong arm grabbed her around her waist. She let out a screech as the man's grip tightened painfully.

"Aren't you a pretty thing?" a gruff voice whispered in her ear.

The man had spoken in Turkish. His hot breath assaulted her senses like uncovering a round of moldy cheese. Ruby struggled to pull free from her assailant, but his arm was clamped firmly around her middle.

"I thought you were a boy traveling with your elders," he hissed, "but I can feel you are definitely a woman."

The abductor wasted no time carrying her away from their camp. His horse was behind a clump of low trees near the road where two other riders waited impatiently.

Ruby dug in her heels, dragging her feet to slow his hasty strides, but her unbuckled boot caught on the stony ground.

The brute heaved her up onto his hip to keep her off her heels. He half-carried, half-dragged her past where her own horses were tied. Fatina neighed loudly at the stranger's intrusion.

Despite being tipped nearly upside down, Ruby caught a glance of the second man. He wore tall black boots and white trousers: the shadow thief. He called over to her captor, "We have what we wanted. Leave the bitch, Gorgi."

Ruby was clenched in the arms of trouble. She struggled to make a noise, but the man clamped his stinky hand over her mouth when she tried to cry out.

"She's mine, Kuj," he called back. "And when I am done with her, she'll still fetch a good price with the trader."

A third man held Gorgi's steed by its reins and said, "Get her on your horse. We've lingered too long."

In desperation, Ruby reached her leg out and kicked hard against Cairo's haunch as her kidnapper hobbled by.

Cairo did not disappoint her and let out a long, loud whinny in protest.

Ruby prayed it was enough.

Gorgi dropped her to the ground. "You are quite a handful, girl," he said with irritation. He wound her tangled hair in his fist and pushed her along. Her attacker was Ruby's height but had a stocky build and the strength of a young man.

Mismatched but not helpless, Ruby could not let herself be taken away. She dropped to her knees onto the rocky ground to trip up her assailant, but her action only made him tug cruelly on her hair.

Her world spun in slow motion as Ruby felt her strength give way. Still, Ruby saw the two riders' panicked faces through her tearing eyes. She could not see what they saw coming, but she could hear the sound of boots running.

A thump vibrated against her, and Ruby's assailant fell, dragging her down with him. Salar Nassim's dagger had hit its mark on her kidnapper's back.

"Ruby!" Jero untangled her hair from the dying captor's fingers, then lifted her into his arms and carried her away from the chaos.

The two thieves on horseback didn't wait to learn their friend's fate but galloped away, leaving a trail of dust behind them.

Bem and Soren did not wait, either. They swiftly mounted their saddled horses and gave chase.

Patrik ran up to where Jero held Ruby and cried, "I knew we shouldn't have left you alone! Are you all right? Tell me you are all right!"

Ruby stared blankly with shock.

Salar Nassim retrieved his knife from the dying man's back and then shoved him over with the toe of his boot. He walked over to the others. "Bem had a bad feeling about them. We should have expected something like this," he said.

"Expected that fucking thieves and rapists were hiding in our camp, right under our nose?" Patrik shouted.

"Walk around, Patrik," Salar Nassim said. "You are of no use to me like this."

Patrik stomped off to the tethered horses to calm himself.

Jero had carried Ruby to the downed log where her bags lay open. The fall had cut the side of her face, her hands were scraped from bracing herself under the man's weight, and she was covered in dirt. But she was alright.

"Is the man dead?" Ruby asked no one in particular.

Salar Nassim gave the bleeding man a vengeful kick and replied, "Almost."

Patrik had regained some self-control and knelt in front of Ruby. She wasn't crying or yelling, and he worried about her.

Patrik took her bleeding hand in his and said softly in Greek, "Talk to me, Ruby. Tell me nothing is broken. Are you hurting anywhere?"

She looked from him to Salar Nassim to Jero, all watching her with concern. "He wanted to take me, Patricius," she answered. "I tried to call out to you. I tried to fight him."

The horror finally set in, and she began to weep.

"You did good, Ruby. We heard you. We all came. The men are gone. Everything is going to be alright."

He turned her hand over as he held it and gently brushed the pebbles from the bleeding scratches. "Jero is going to take you to the stream to tend to your hands."

Patrik put her hand into Jero's.

"Go with him, Ruby," Patrik said soothingly. "It is all over. You are safe now."

Jero wrapped his arm around Ruby, and she leaned into his strong embrace. "You are safe with me," Jero said softly.

Patrik waited until the two were well down the path before he grumbled, "This is a fucking mess."

Salar Nassim surveyed the camp. "The man's horse is still here. I'll check his pack to see who they were."

Patrik kicked the dead man back over again so he didn't have to look at his face. The red jacket he wore was too faded to mask the crimson blood that had spread across the fabric where the knife had plunged into his back.

"Where should I drag his body? I don't want Ruby to see him again," Patrik said.

Salar Nassim looked up from his search, rummaging through the dead man's pack. "Put him in the brush for the scavengers. If they are drifters, his death will not matter to anyone."

After Patrik had disposed of the body, he checked their horses for what might have been stolen. "They took the bags off Zeus," he reported.

"Jero's things. He won't be happy about that," Salar Nassim said offhandedly while he read the document in his hand.

Patrik looked over Salar Nassim's shoulder with interest. "Did you find anything of importance?"

Nassim shrugged. "If these are the dead man's papers, he was called Gorgi Zogolli. He didn't pack much—a change of clothes, a little food, and some money, too. They were robbing us for the sport of it."

"And for Ruby," spat Patrik.

Salar Nassim pointed to the road. "Here come Bem and Soren."

"Alone," Patrik added.

"Could you catch up to them?" Salar Nassim called over to the two.

Out of breath from the chase, Soren explained, "They had too much of a lead, or maybe they know where to hide. Either way, they are gone."

"Then they probably won't be missing this," Salar Nassim said. He strapped the dead man's saddlebag onto the open spot where Jero's stolen satchel had been tied.

Bem looked around the empty camp and asked, "Where is Ruby?"

"Jero has taken her to the stream to clean her hands," Patrik replied.

"I'll put her bags on her horse," Bem offered.

Salar Nassim added, "We should leave as soon as she is fit to ride."

"Our things are still at the stream," Soren reminded them.

"I'll go with you to get them," Patrik said.

~*~

Jero tore strips of cloth off the bottom of his last clean shirt to wrap around Ruby's bleeding hands. He wound the linen over her cut palms as he muttered, "I should have stayed with you, Ruby. We should have known those men were close by."

"You couldn't have known the men would want to do us harm. Do *me* harm," she said quietly.

His sympathetic eyes spoke the words he could not, and she replied with a shy smile.

With the last unused strip of his shirt, Jero carefully wiped the dirt from her skinned cheek. "There, Ruby—all cleaned up. How do you feel?" he asked.

"I'm still a bit shaky, but I think I will be alright," she said tearfully. "Did you at least get your bath?"

Jero smiled at her misplaced worry. "If it makes you feel any better, we were nearly done washing up when we thought we heard voices. Then we heard the horses."

"I kicked Cairo," she said.

"That was clever of you. We knew right away something was wrong and came running."

Ruby tried to pick up her comb, but her hands were too thickly wrapped. "Poor Cairo," she said absently. "I knocked him pretty hard, but I knew he would make the most noise."

Jero took the comb from her and began to unknot her locks.

She suddenly flinched when Jero tugged on a strand, and tears leaked from the corners of her eyes. "My head hurts as much as my hands," she whispered.

Jero put the comb down and wiped the tears from her cheeks. "I'm so sorry, Ruby. What can I do to help?"

"Perhaps you can bind it, and I can comb it out tonight."

Jero found a leather cord from his own bag and wound it around her matted hair. "I admire you, Ruby," he finally said. "You were very brave."

"I was frightened. I've heard tales about what men do when they kidnap a woman," she said miserably. "I did not want that fate. I would have been lost to you forever, Jero."

"They would never have succeeded," he declared. "I would have searched for you forever, to the ends of the earth."

He wrapped his arms around her, and she sank into his embrace.

"I will not let you out of my sight again, Ruby Spiros." He gently stroked her cheek with his fingertips and touched her lips. Then he kissed them.

Patrik and Soren appeared through the thicket and startled the entranced lovers.

"I am sorry," Patrik said. "We've come for our clothes."

Jero awkwardly moved away from Ruby and busied himself, gathering his scattered things.

"Did you find the men, Soren?" Ruby asked.

Soren shook his head guiltily. "I am sorry, Ruby. They got away."

"They stole the two bags strapped onto Zeus," Patrik reported grimly. "Your gifts were in those bags, weren't they, Jero?"

Jero plopped down on a boulder and groaned, "Everything was in there: The gifts for the Spiroses, things from Terese for her family, my wedding clothes. . ."

"We will get them back," Soren assured him.

"It doesn't matter, I suppose." The sight of Ruby's bruised face and bandaged hands reminded Jero of what did matter. "It is a fair price for being rid of the criminals."

Patrik's face mirrored Jero's at his misfortune, but the young Greek had learned that a man could not dwell on bad luck. He grabbed his packed bag, along with Bem's, and said, "We should go now."

Salar Nassim had killed the kidnapper, but they would not be accused of stealing his horse. They left the animal tied near the road as they left camp. If his companions came back for their friend's body, they could take him on his horse's back. If not, another thief would surely claim the abandoned beast.

Once back on the road, the six riders met with only friendly travelers for the rest of the day. They kept a constant watch that night as a precaution, but by morning, they were in agreement that the thieves had moved on with their spoils. They had put the fateful encounter entirely behind them by the time they reached Tirana on the third day.

Chapter 3

The two Albanians had outsmarted the foreigners. They could not ride faster than Bem and Soren, but they did know where to hide to make their escape. Because of that, the two locals arrived in Tirana the night before the mercenaries.

Ardi and Kujtim Zogolli were Gorgi's first cousins, and the two thieves had not put his death behind them. The three cousins were inseparable—young and brash, only twenty and twenty-one, and unable to get ahead under the confining tribal order. They roamed the countryside, looking for an easy way to make their mark in the world. As a result, neither Ardi nor Kujtim had held a real job or taken responsibility for their futures beyond stealing what was not tied down. But now, tribal duty required them to seek vengeance for their dead kin, Gorgi.

The Zogollis were not a powerful clan in the Albanian region of the Ottoman Empire, nor a wealthy one. But they were a proud and extensive family, one that took care of their own. In Ardi's and Kujtim's minds, their cousin had been murdered, so they formulated a plan to assure retribution for it. They sought the help of another first cousin, one who happened to work at the local jailhouse.

~*~

Vigan Zogolli had come of age with his three reckless cousins but had more sense than all of them put together. Vigan had enlisted as a soldier under the Ottoman regime and took his occupation responsibly. But like his cousins, he, too, put the Zogolli family above all else.

The two thieves found Vigan at his post outside the small jail on the edge of town.

"Vigan! We've been looking all over Tirana for you!" Ardi hollered.

"Ardi! Kujtim!" the soldier greeted them happily. "This is a surprise."

Kujtim reached him first and embraced his cousin. "We didn't know you were a guard now," he said.

"Not just a guard, I am a sergeant. I have my own squad—can you believe it?"

"Congratulations!" Ardi said as he wrapped his big arms around his cousin in greeting. Then Ardi's tone became serious. "Hey, can we have a word? In private?" he asked.

"We bring bad news," Kujtim added.

Vigan led them away from the soldiers of his squadron, looking on at the front of the building. He stopped at the edge of the prison grounds and braced himself for the worst. "Is someone in my family dead? I was just there last month."

Kujtim quickly explained, "Gorgi got himself killed."

Vigan grabbed the fence for support. "Killed? Where? How?"

Ardi sneered when he described the circumstances. "We were on the highway. A coward put a knife in his back. Some foreign bastard."

Vigan kicked an imaginary stone in his way and groaned, "Poor Gorgi, the little shit. Did you bring him home?"

"We couldn't, but we know where to find him. He isn't going anywhere," Ardi said.

Kujtim added, "We want revenge, Vigan. We thought you could help us."

"I'll try. Did you track his killers?" Vigan spoke as a sergeant now.

"It was easy enough. A group of six riders can't hide on the open road."

Vigan was outraged. "Six against three? That's not a fair fight!"

Ardi and Kujtim had already debated whether they would divulge their own crime, and they came clean with their cousin.

"Um . . . we were taking a few bags off their hands while they were swimming in the river, but Gorgi got it in his mind to take their woman instead," Ardi explained.

"Shit! Gorgi was always thinking with his prick," Vigan mumbled.

"Yeah, well, she was a pretty one. Hard to pass up," reflected Kujtim.

Although they were alone, Ardi leaned in and whispered, "But we were thinking, Vigan, that there might be a way to profit from Gorgi's mistake."

"Profit? How so, Ardi?"

"Well, we think one of them is a Venetian. There were expensive items in the bags that could only come from there."

"Sell them and you've got your profit," Vigan advised his foolish cousins.

Kujtim nodded to Ardi to go on.

"Yeah, but Kuj and I were thinking you could put him in jail to get some bond money from his friends, too. You know, arrest him and then let him out when they pay up."

Vigan considered Ardi's plan but shook his head. "It won't work. A man has the right to kill a man for stealing his woman—even a Venetian. The charges won't hold up in trial."

"It doesn't matter. The Venetian knows he can run home once he is out on bond. Besides, if you don't put it in your arrest book, we can split the bail money, just the three of us."

"What if he can't pay?" Vigan asked.

"His friends' horses are loaded. They must have money," Ardi asserted.

"Easy pickings for all of us. There is nothing to lose." Kujtim added, "And it settles the debt for Gorgi's death. That's what it's all about. Revenge for Gorgi."

Vigan scratched his head, considering the foolish ploy. Vigan was in charge of the soldiers who policed the town center. His commanding officer had been called away, and there were not many other pressing tasks for his squadron. Perhaps Kujtim was right. There was nothing to lose.

"How do I find them?" Vigan asked.

Ardi and Kujtim exchanged hopeful glances.

"We saw them ride through town just a bit ago. They stabled their horses near the market," Ardi said. "If they have a meal and resupply, you will have time to make your arrest. It is almost too easy."

A smile spread over Vigan's tanned face. "Almost," he agreed.

"No harm will come to them," Ardi told Vigan.

"Alright, I will gather a few soldiers and bring the Venetian in. I'll let his friends bail him out with a promise to be on their way. Come find me tonight for your cut of the bail money," Vigan told his cousins.

"We'll do it for poor, dead Gorgi."

"Yes, Kuj. For poor, dead Gorgi," Vigan said.

Chapter 4

Tirana, 3 August 1649

Tirana was most inviting on market day. Stalls with colorful carpet awnings stood in rows along the cobbled road that led to the central square. There, more merchants hawked ordinary wares next to exotic goods of every origin. The mercenaries were not interested in shopping, but they were glad that the busy crowds of locals, travelers, and foreign traders took the focus off their arrival on their over-laden steeds.

The smell of meat roasting over crackling coals and rounds of soft bread displayed at makeshift shops made their stomachs beg to be fed.

"I don't know about the rest of you, but my empty middle tells me we should stop to eat," Patrik said.

"Let's stable our horses," Salar Nassim said, pointing out a tall plaque on a barn just off the town square.

They walked their horses down the alley toward the building.

"I'll stay with the horses and guard our things," Bem said.

Salar Nassim insisted, "We'll draw straws."

Soren drew the short straw that day. He unburdened their packhorse and said, "Don't linger too long. It is sweltering in this barn."

"I will swap places with you after our meal," Bem offered.

Patrik pulled the saddle off his horse with a grunt and stated, "This looks like a lively town. Maybe a man can get more than water to drink around here." He called over to the stable groom. "Boy, is there a tavern nearby?"

"A tavern?"

Patrik flipped the boy a coin to help him think.

"Oh, yes, sir. Old Isaak sells ale at his lodging house just around the corner."

Patrik raised his brow and asked, "Are you up for a drink, Jero?"

Jero brushed the road dust from his clothes and replied, "Gladly."

"A mug of ale might be nice, especially if the food is bad," Bem affirmed.

The boy interjected eagerly, "The food is good, sir. And the prices are fair."

"With such a recommendation, point the way, young man," Salar Nassim said.

~*~

The sign outside the vine-covered veranda of Isaak's inn was in Turkish and Greek. Under the canopy of hanging fruit were several empty tables, but the mercenaries continued through the double doors of the old stone building. It was a welcoming dining room that catered to both locals and travelers. They served Ottoman specialties and Turkish coffee to Muslims, along with an assortment of ethnic dishes and fermented beverages for the Christians traveling through.

A few customers were seated at the tables adjacent to the stairs going up to the guest rooms. Those men paid the newcomers little attention when the five sat down at a round table near the entrance.

The proprietor himself came to welcome them to his establishment. For generations, Greek immigrants had run the lodging house, and the current patriarch was Isaak Linos. His loose, white shirt was belted over his billowing black trousers, and a black canvas cap covered the top of his neat graying hair. His polished low boots clicked as he strode across the worn stone tiles to the table. Only his dirty red apron, tied tightly across his middle, signaled that he was in charge of more than just talking to the customers.

After salutations in several languages by their waiter, Salar Nassim ordered lunches for those at the table and another one to be brought to Soren in the stables around the corner.

"Zerina!" Isaak called out pleasantly.

A young woman came through the kitchen door at the back of the dining room.

"Is your boy about? I have an errand for him."

She left through the door again without a word.

Isaak turned back to his customers with a friendly grin. "We will send your friend his meal right away. What will you be drinking, gentlemen?"

"A round of ale," Bem ordered.

The proprietor eyed Ruby skeptically. "For the lady, too?"

"For the lady, too," Salar Nassim confirmed with a confident nod.

After a short while, Zerina carried out a large tray with platters of sliced meats, boiled greens, steaming couscous, and a bowl of the same grapes that dangled over the terrace. The spicy smells that floated from the food were mouth-watering. A second serving woman brought a stack of flatbread on her tray along with the mugs of ale and then left the strangers to their meals.

As the mercenaries filled their plates from the platters of savory offerings, they quietly signaled to each other that they, too, had noticed the soldiers that hovered at the doorway and scanned the dining room.

Two more soldiers came into the restaurant through the kitchen door. One spoke briefly to Zerina, who shook her head in answer to his question and then disappeared into the kitchen again. Those soldiers joined the others at the front of the restaurant.

It happened now and then: interrogation of travelers for no other purpose except intimidation and perhaps a cash payment. Patrik and Salar Nassim, who sat facing the soldiers, braced themselves for the expected questioning. They had their cautious answers ready.

Sergeant Vigan Zogolli approached their table with authority. "Are you traveling through today?" he asked, addressing no one specifically.

Salar Nassim answered, "Yes, Officer. We plan to be on our way before evening."

Vigan looked from chair to chair. Ardi had told him there were six riders. He asked, "Is this your whole party?"

"Is there a problem, sir?" Patrik interjected with annoyance.

Vigan Zogolli considered that this man, with his bluish eyes and fairer skin, might be the Venetian, except he had spoken in perfect Turkish.

"Yes. There is a problem," the sergeant answered dryly. He studied each face when he added, "There has been a report of a murder."

The mercenaries didn't flinch, but Vigan knew his man now.

Bem spoke up, "We have only just arrived in Tirana. We would not know anything about a murder."

"And you, sir?" Vigan asked Jero directly.

Patrik shook his head ever so slightly, and Jero answered with a clear "no" in Turkish.

"Then you understand what I am telling you?" the sergeant asked Jero point-blank.

"We all understand you, but you are not clear about the reason for your visit to our table, Sergeant," Salar Nassim said boldly. "We have told you we are in Tirana for a meal and supplies. Is that so unusual? Is there something else you want to know?"

Vigan asserted, "There is a Venetian among you."

"Since when are Venetian travelers not welcome in Tirana?" Patrik asked in his best imitation of Turkish with a Latin accent.

Vigan's stare moved from Patrik to Jero again. "Oh, Venetians are welcome, except when accused of committing a crime. Take him!"

The accompanying soldiers grabbed Jero, locking his arms behind him.

Jero's friends stood up to defend him and blocked their leaving.

Ruby spoke up for the first time as the chaotic scene unfolded. "Why are you arresting him? On what grounds?" she protested.

The sergeant sneered victoriously. This was the pretty girl Gorgi had lost his life over. "For murder, miss," he said with contempt.

Jero stopped his struggle and faced his accuser. On the outside chance the man might understand him, Jero argued in Croatian, "I should be asking you to arrest the thieves who stole my bags and kidnapped my bride."

The sergeant was taken aback for a moment. He had never met a Venetian, but he didn't expect one would speak to him in Slavic. Perhaps Ardi and Kujtim had been wrong. He would figure out the facts later at the jailhouse.

"You will come with me," the sergeant replied in his crude Serbian dialect.

"He has done nothing wrong," Patrik shouted after them. "There are laws in this Empire against false arrest!"

Helplessly restrained by the soldiers, Jero was pushed along until Patrik's shouts were lost behind him.

Vigan and the last of his armed force blocked the mercenaries at the door. He informed them, "Your friend stands accused by reputable witnesses. You can state your defense at the jailhouse."

With no choice but to do as the sergeant required, they left their uneaten meal on the table.

Salar Nassim stopped long enough to say to the proprietor, "Send your boy to tell our friend where we have gone." He dropped some coins on the counter.

Isaak had, of course, observed the confrontation. It was better not to take sides, so he pocketed the money and grimly nodded.

"Aleksander!" the Greek shouted.

The scrawny boy crouched by the door had witnessed everything as well. He hopped up without needing an explanation and ran to the stables to tell the big man from the North that the police had taken his friend to jail.

~*~

Sergeant Zogolli ordered Jero locked in a jail cell for good measure. He did not plan that the Venetian would stay there long, but he wanted to be sure Jero's companions paid what the sergeant would demand.

Zogolli read Salar Nassim, Bem, Ruby, and Patrik the charges against Jero while his soldiers looked on. He highlighted Gorgi's importance to his village and the loss his clan had suffered. "The man that your friend murdered was a cousin of mine. He had a mother and two sisters that need to be compensated."

When Zogolli finished reading the charges, it was clear to even the lounging guardsmen what this was about.

"How much compensation do his mother and sister need to set our friend free?" Patrik asked with disdain.

"Twenty gold coins," the officer replied defiantly.

"Twenty!" Bem exclaimed in disbelief. "You are just as much a thief as he and his friends are."

"Return what was stolen from us, and we will give you your ransom," Salar Nassim offered. "But ten coins are more than sufficient payment."

"Fifteen should settle it. And I know nothing about your stolen goods," the sergeant lied.

Patrik grumbled under his breath but agreed to the price. He counted the coins from his bag, dropped them into a small pouch, and then pushed it across the table. "Now, release our friend and let us be on our way."

With a satisfied smile, the sergeant told his guard, "Emir, get the prisoner. He is free to go."

Around the room, the soldiers came to attention one by one. In the middle of the jailhouse entrance stood a uniformed man. Captain Poljani had not been expected back in town until the end of the week.

"What is going on, Sergeant? Who are these men?" the captain asked from across the room.

Zogolli saluted his commander. "Sir! I . . . um . . . I didn't know you were returning today," he said with genuine surprise.

"I can see that, Sergeant. Are you having another party in my absence?"

Zogolli gingerly slid the pouch of payment out of his commander's sight as he made light of the accusation with a nervous chuckle. "No, Captain, sir. We are just releasing a prisoner to his companions here. His small offense has been settled."

"More petty disputes over market prices?" the commander queried. "I hate market days," he added under his breath.

"No, Captain, just a case of mistaken identity. A Venetian nobleman traveling through was accused of a crime by one of our locals. We jailed him as a precaution, but his friends have cleared his name satisfactorily. They are leaving with him now," Zogolli explained.

"What crime was this Venetian accused of?" the captain asked.

Zogolli cleared his throat as his commander came closer to the desk. Vigan didn't want to call attention to his farce, but it was too late. Emir had mistakenly recorded Jero's supposed offense into the logbook, and it was on the table for Captain Poljani to plainly read.

The captain's expression darkened, and he looked hard at the Baric group. "Murder, Zogolli? And you are letting the Venetian go?"

Ruby took Patrik's hand, hearing the intense scorn in the commander's voice.

"Like I said, Captain, it was a mistaken identity. His papers state he is a Venetian aristocrat from the Croatian territories. That is not who we were looking for, sir."

"That is curious," Poljani said slowly. "A Croatian noble, you say? What is his name?"

Sergeant Zogolli picked up Jero's identity documents lying on the table, ready to be returned.

"Uh, let me see . . . family name is Baric, son of Baron Lorenc Baric . . ." he began reading with his thick Ottoman accent.

"Did you say Peric?"

Vigan did not hear the difference between the two and repeated, "Yes, Captain. Peric is the man's family name on the documents. Jero, son of Lorenz Peric."

The commander's interest in the prisoner puzzled the guards, and they shifted uncomfortably as Captain Poljani paced the room with obvious delight.

"Well, well, well. This is indeed excellent luck that I returned early."

Poljani turned to his first officer and said, "Rahmi, tell Emir he is not to release the new prisoner. This Venetian owes me a debt."

Rahmi pushed open the heavy door that separated the holding cells from the front room and disappeared from view.

Patrik wrapped his arm around Ruby as she began to sway.

Salar Nassim spoke up, "Captain Poljani, sir, we can attest that our friend Jero has spent his entire life in a village called Solgrad. How could he owe an Ottoman anything? You must be mistaken."

"And you must want to join him in his prison cell," Poljani hissed. "Guards! Show these visitors the way out."

Sergeant Zogolli was as panicked as the mercenaries—worried that his deceit would be discovered. He intervened and said, "Captain, sir, the Venetian has been cleared of the charges. What shall I record?"

"A blood debt, Sergeant."

Chapter 5

Patrik kicked a pile of straw in anger. "A fucking blood debt? Are we not in the Ottoman Empire? Do they not follow laws in Tirana?"

Patrik's continuing rant had scared the stable boy away, and except for the horses pacing in their stalls, the five had the barn to themselves.

Patrik's shouting hadn't helped Ruby's panic. She leaned against a railing and tried to take a needed breath. He took Ruby into his arms to calm both of them and rocked her tightly while the others contemplated Jero's predicament.

Soren hadn't had the benefit of witnessing the bizarre accusation, and he reasoned: "Even if the captain holds to this crazy notion that Jero's father wronged him, Jero cannot be convicted of a crime. There are no witnesses, no perpetrators, not even a victim. A blood debt may be possible in tribal law, but the magistrate will rule by civil laws. As much as I hate this Empire, their courts generally respect the written laws. They will have to release him."

Salar Nassim agreed, "The crime Lorenc Baric is accused of would be a consequence of war. We have all killed someone's brother, someone's father. Jero will be let off."

"There will still be a trial," Ruby added shakily. "Even the best defenses don't always end well."

Bem considered their options; then he reflected, "Maybe with enough money there will be no need for a trial or a blood payment. Cyro left us his gold. It is enough to buy a man's freedom."

Salar Nassim reminded Bem, "We have already paid the sergeant plenty. Besides, if we buy Jero's freedom, there will not be any left for Fatina's freedom."

Ruby was frantic to find a solution to her lover's fate. "Mauro Baric will pay whatever the captain wants to free his brother," she said with certainty. "The soldier said the traveling magistrate isn't coming before the twentieth. That's almost a month away. We can send a message to Solgrad for help."

The men exchanged nods in a silent vote.

Salar Nassim announced, "That is what we will do, Ruby. That should give Baron Baric plenty of time to come in person to negotiate this. In the meantime, Patrik can take you home."

"No!" she protested.

"This will take a while to resolve, Ruby," Bem said soothingly. "It is not safe for you to wait here, and your family is expecting you."

"He's right, Ruby. I can bring you home and be back in time for the trial," Patrik assured her. "Soren can go with us."

Soren nodded.

"And Jero stays imprisoned while we all go about our lives?" argued Ruby through fresh tears.

"We have no other choice at this point. The jailor made that clear," Bem said.

"Jero can hold out for a few weeks, Ruby. Mauro will come and pay their father's debt, real or not," Patrik added.

"Don't worry. I will stay here until we get him out," Bem told her.

Soren took a horse blanket from the rail. Patrik followed his lead and sorted his and Soren's reins from the others on the peg.

"What are you doing, Patricius?" Ruby asked anxiously. "We are not leaving right now, are we?"

He heaved the saddle onto Fatina's back. "We need to put this place behind us, Ruby, before they change their minds and arrest all of us."

"No! I need to talk to Jero first. I need to tell him what is going on."

Salar Nassim warned, "They will not let a woman in to see him, Ruby. You know that. Go with Patrik and Soren and wait for Jero in safety, back at home. We will explain everything to him. Jero will understand."

~*~

The guard named Emir had taken Jero through a long dim corridor, past two other crowded jail cells that came to life with protests for food and relief. Emir led him to the end room and wordlessly shut the barred door behind Jero.

Despite the shock of his new surroundings, Jero was glad to be locked in with only three other men. It was at least quieter than the other cells, and he needed quiet right now.

Mildewing straw was strewn over the muck on the filthy granite floor. There was no furniture except a stone slab built into a wall. Jero suspected it served as a bed. Yet the men curled up on the stone platform were not asleep but rocked and swayed with pain. The one chamber pot in the corner overflowed with their sickness.

"Guard! These men need a doctor," Jero shouted through the bars into the empty corridor. The guard had already shut the heavy door between the prisoners and the rest of the world. Jero crossed himself and said a short prayer to God, begging for this to not be a plague they suffered from.

Jero paced the front of the barred chamber, as far away from his miserable companions as possible. He was sure Patrik and the others would try to secure his release. Jero strained to hear any voices at the end of the stone hallway, but he heard only the moans of the men behind him.

He had nearly given up on his friends when the same guard came to his door, smiling this time and carrying a ring of keys.

Jero smiled at the young soldier in return. No real harm was done, he thought. The misunderstanding had been cleared up, and they would be on their way soon.

The soldier had just opened the door for Jero and waved him out when another soldier hurried behind him and shoved Jero back in through the cell door.

"The captain is back, Emir. He said this man is guilty. Poljani said he is to remain in his cell until the trial."

The keeper of the keys did not argue. He shrugged at Jero and clicked the lock closed again.

Jero shook the bars in disbelief. "Wait! There is a mistake! Who is this captain? Come back," Jero pleaded.

The two guards walked away without a glance back.

~*~

Jero went over the scene in his mind a dozen times. He had no idea what had happened after they left the inn, but he was sure his friends had done their best for him. Minutes passed, and then an hour, then two. Jero began to face the fact that the nightmare was real.

Tired of standing, Jero picked the driest straw scattered in the middle of the floor and piled what he could against the wall under the window for a chance at some fresh air. He sat on the dirty mound of straw to wait.

Jero had nearly dozed off when a deep voice called over to him: "So, you are the new prisoner. I am Captain Poljani, the commanding officer of this jailhouse."

Jero opened his eyes and stared at him blankly.

"Do you understand me, Venetian pig? You only speak Latin, I suppose."

Jero had understood a few words. 'Captain' was one of them. His Slavic had worked before, so Jero wasted no time in pleading his case.

He stood up and confronted his accuser, telling him, "A grave mistake has been made. I demand to be released."

The officer took a step back from the iron separating them and laughed.

"You demand? This is not one of your castles, your lordship," Poljani said with mockery, "and I am not your servant to be ordered. You will await your trial like the other lowly criminals locked up here. We prefer to hang our prisoners quickly, but you should settle in. The magistrate won't be back in Tirana for a month."

Jero let out an audible sigh of distress. "Why am I being held? Can you not see how this is a mistake?"

"There is no mistake. A crime was committed. I witnessed it myself."

Dumbfounded, Jero began, "But I never—"

Poljani interrupted, "Not the son, but the father. I was there. Your father killed someone important, stabbed him point-blank. As his son, you shall be tried for his crime of murder."

"You cannot be serious, sir! My father has been dead for two years. And before that, he never battled this far south. He only fought the Habsburgs, never the Ottomans. You would have never met him," Jero argued.

"Oh, I am certain that I have. We take these crimes very seriously in this part of the world. A killer must pay. A family must pay."

"Even if my father did kill this, this . . . important man, those were times of war. People die in wars all the time."

"He did not just die. He was murdered. I was there." Poljani paused to conjure the memory of the horrific scene. "My brother was a commanding officer. His regiment fell to the Venetians, and the battle was over. He was unarmed, his hands held high, and he asked for mercy for his troops. Your father showed them none. Our soldiers were lined up, and the Venetian soldiers shot them. Then, perched on his horse like a coward, your father ran his sword across my brother's throat. My regiment survived the attack, and when I asked who my brother's murderer was, the others were certain of the commander's name. It is burned into my memory. Lorenz Peric."

Jero shook his head at the name. "My name is Baric, sir, and my father was never there."

"Liar!" the commander's shout echoed through the stone cell block. "I have waited years to avenge my brother. You shall pay this debt and die a painful death!"

Jero took a deep breath. "I am sorry about your brother, but my father did not kill him," he said in quiet contrast. "I said you have the name wrong. I am not this man's son."

"That is for the magistrate to decide. Until then, watch yourself, Venetian. You do not want to end up like the others."

The commander pointed toward the wretched prisoners on the stone bed.

Chapter 6

Salar Nassim and Bem appeared as shadows moving in the corridor. Daylight had faded from the small window above Jero's head, and he thought his mind was playing tricks on him until one of the shadows spoke.

"Are you all right, Jero?" Bem asked. The question seemed almost comical once it left his lips.

"All right?" Jero repeated as he rushed to the barred door. "No, I am not all right, Bem. An Albanian madman told me I am to be tried for a crime committed in some distant battle. He says I owe him for his dead brother. Have you come to tell me it is all just a bad dream?"

Bem and Salar Nassim exchanged worried glances.

"I'm sorry, Jero," Bem said grimly. "We talked to them again just now. The charges are very real."

Salar Nassim explained solemnly, "Captain Poljani is the Albanian commander pressing charges. He arrived just as we arranged with the sergeant to get you out. The Albanians may run the local prison, but the Ottoman officials will follow the laws. Whatever crazy accusation he has against you, at least he agrees you will get a trial."

"Yes, but he said the magistrate has already come and gone this month," Jero fretted.

"They told us the same, Jero. You will have to wait," Salar Nassim said.

"Can't you pay a bond and bail me out?"

"We tried. We paid the sergeant for his dead cousin. I really think he meant to release you. But this Captain Poljani is different. He cannot be persuaded today," Bem explained.

Salar Nassim added, "We have sent a courier to your brother to come help you. Every man has his price, Jero, and with time Poljani might change his mind. I asked the baron to bring enough money to be certain he can match any demand."

Jero breathed a sigh of heartfelt relief. "Yes, Mauro will come. He will know how to convince Poljani that it is not our father he wants."

Bem noticed the sleeping men behind Jero and asked, "What is their story?"

Jero glanced back and shook his head. "Maybe it is the food. The chamber pot is overflowing with their vomit, or worse."

Bem grimaced when he saw the source of the stink. "Will the soldiers not empty it?"

"It seems not, and the window is too high to dump it out."

"Keep away from them if you can, Jero," Salar Nassim advised.

Jero nodded unhappily.

Bem pulled a small round of bread from his jacket pocket. "You must be hungry. We will bring you some food and a jug of drink each day until you are out." He pointed to the dying men. "I would not eat anything they offer you. That might be how they reduce their prison population."

"Will you wait in Tirana until the trial?" Jero asked.

Their guilty glances were unmistakable, and Jero slumped against the bars.

Bem tried to smile when he assured him, "Of course, we will wait, but Patrik and Soren already left this afternoon with Ruby."

A groan escaped Jero's lips. "Yes. She cannot stay here. I understand that."

"None of us will abandon you, Jero," Salar Nassim promised. "Soren and Patrik will come back after they deliver Ruby to her family. By then your brother should be here as well."

"Thank you," Jero whispered.

A guard broke the awkward stillness when he yelled down the corridor, "Your time is up!"

Salar Nassim quickly said, "We have taken a room at the lodging house where we ate our lunch. We will ask around, find out what we can about this commander."

"One more thing, Jero," Bem said urgently. "Your ring."

Jero looked down at the ancient gold ring his uncle had entrusted to him.

"They might take it," Bem warned. "Shall I hold onto it for you?"

Jero slid it off his finger. "It means a lot to me," he said.

Bem nodded. "Then put it in the toe of your boot."

"I said it is time to leave!" the guard shouted.

"We will see you tomorrow," Bem assured the wretched prisoner.

Every part of Jero's being ached as he watched them walk away into the shadows. Then the door shut between the worlds, and he was alone again.

A trembling voice coming from behind him made Jero jump.

"Is that bread?" someone asked.

Without thinking, Jero hurried to the plagued men on the bench. "Can you eat a bite?" he asked the one with open eyes.

"I'll try," the near-corpse whispered.

Jero tore a piece off the fresh loaf and put it into the filthy outstretched hand. The man chewed hungrily.

"Easy, or you will not keep it down."

When the man finished, Jero asked, "What is your name?"

"Roman."

"I am Jero."

The man put another pinch of bread into the corner of his blistered mouth and whispered, "Thank you, Jero."

~*~

Pausing on the prison steps, Bem and Salar Nassim considered their next move after leaving Jero.

"I think it is time I went to pray," Salar Nassim told Bem.

Bem reflected on what that meant. "Someone at the mosque will have answers for us. I noticed there is also a bathhouse in the town center. Steam also loosens lips," Bem said.

"We will visit there tomorrow," Salar Nassim agreed. "They will be calling everyone to prayer soon. I will leave you to find your way back to the inn."

Bem nodded. "I will be waiting there."

~*~

Bem sat alone on a tall stool at the long bar in the dining room. The servant girl was stacking washed mugs on the other side of it. He watched her methodical movements as he sipped his ale. Her name was Zerina, Bem remembered.

Zerina finished her sorting and then focused on her other paying work. "Where is your friend?" she asked Bem.

Bem stared at his mug. "He is a good Muslim, so he answered the call."

She studied him for a moment. He was not black and not white, nor did he look like the other Ottomans who traveled through.

She asked, "And what are you?"

Bem answered quickly, "I am nothing."

She cocked her head in amusement. "The same as me," Zerina said.

Bem finally looked up and considered the young woman across from him. Her eyes were a soft brown, trimmed with long black lashes that quickly caught a man's attention. She would have been beautiful if not for the deep, ragged scar across her cheek that deformed her wide smile. She wore an embroidered white blouse and a pleated black skirt, plain and full in the ethnic style of the Albanians, not the loose robes of the Turks. Her shiny black hair was skillfully twisted and pinned at the base of her neck; her colorful, embroidered cap was perched prettily over it. She was thin from her hard chores but did not look fragile. This was a woman who had been through untold ordeals. She was a survivor, Bem could tell. He liked her.

"Zerina is your name, isn't it?" Bem asked.

Zerina considered him, too, and gave him a crooked smile that shone in her lovely fawn eyes.

"Do you want company upstairs while you wait for your friend?" she asked shamelessly.

Bem should have said yes. He had the time, and he could use the distraction. Instead, he said kindly, "Maybe another day, Zerina. I will just take my drink outside for now."

Zerina went back to her sorting, and Bem went to the front door to find a seat on the terrace. Before he could get out of the way, Isaak's servant boy ran in and knocked Bem's mug from his hand. It crashed onto the floor.

Isaak saw the collision from across the room and hollered, "Aleksander, you good-for-nothing little brat! Zerina!"

The skinny boy ran through the restaurant and out the back kitchen door.

Zerina frowned in his direction. A mess of scattered shards lay on the floor. She hurried with her tray to pick up the pieces as she told Bem, "Take a seat outside, sir. I will bring you a new one."

Bem was about to do just that when the front door swung open again, and two men with greasy aprons frantically searched the room. Bem left the frenzied scene to wait for his fresh ale out on the terrace.

"Where is he, Zerina!" the older of the two shouted. "Where has your little lice-bitten bastard gone to? He has been stealing from my stand again. You owe me!"

"Aleksander has never stolen anything from you, you old stinking oaf!" she shouted back. "If you minded your shop and didn't leave it in the hands of your own cracked son, maybe things wouldn't go missing!"

The men pushed their way past her and out the back door, the way the boy had gone.

Zerina shook off the encounter and went behind the bar to pour Bem a new drink.

Galena took it from her hand with a smirk. She was Isaak's youngest daughter, a plain, skinny girl with dull brown eyes. Her thin black braid hung unadorned down the back of her gray linen blouse. Galena was of marrying age, but her father needed her to help in the restaurant more than he needed another son-in-law. She resented that, and she resented Zerina.

"Stop trying to flirt with him, Zerina. You are too ugly," Galena said with an unmasked loathing.

Zerina leaned across the counter; her cleavage exposed itself conspicuously above her neckline. "My face may be ugly, Galena, but at least I have something to offer a man under my blouse. That is why they invite me to join them, and not you."

"Go back to the gutter where you belong, slut," Galena spat out with disdain.

Isaak had seen the two go at it before. He hurried over and stood between the girls with his arms crossed in displeasure. Zerina was his best worker, and he needed her just as much as he needed Galena.

Zerina defiantly pried the mug from Galena's grip and said, "It is my job to serve the men tonight."

Galena raised her thin arm to take a swing as Zerina passed by, but Isaak put his hand up to stop her. "Do not start this again, Daughter," Isaak warned.

She lowered her arm with a pout as Zerina walked out the door to serve the handsome foreigner.

~*~

Salar Nassim came back to their room from the morning visit and told Bem, "Jero made a friend overnight."

"One of the dying men lived?" Bem asked with surprise.

"It seems so, and Jero asks if we could bring enough to sustain him as well."

Bem shook his head with amusement. "I wish I'd had a cellmate like Jero when I was imprisoned back in Egypt."

"He was in better spirits, too, now that he knows we will visit him twice a day."

"Will you go to the mosque again this afternoon?" Bem asked.

Salar Nassim considered it. "I think there is little to gain by it."

"Shall we go to the bathhouse?" Bem asked.

"Yes, let's give that a try. There might be some answers for us there."

~*~

It was easy for Bem and Salar Nassim to lose themselves to the rituals of the elegant bathhouse. They began their afternoon session in the heat of the sweating chamber. It was surprisingly welcoming since the temperature outdoors was nearly as hot. The washing that followed, and the invigorating massage after that, almost made them forget that they were there to help their friend.

This bathhouse had a tea service, and when the two were fully relaxed from the solitary rituals, they ordered a pot of the hot, sweet liquid and lounged with the fellow bathers at the edge of the final cooling pool.

Salar Nassim struck up a conversation with three local merchants about the history of Tirana. In their discussion, he learned how the Ottoman authorities policed their town. He hoped to piece together information that could be useful in getting Jero freed.

After a time, the three locals politely took their leave, and Bem and Salar Nassim were alone at the edge of the pool until a group of young men appeared in the domed room. The mercenaries paid them little mind as the men settled in at the far end of the communal bath. Soon, however, one man from that group noticed Bem and openly stared at him.

After a short time, the newcomer approached Bem at the pool. He was tall and muscular in his towel drape; his curly black hair was combed back off his bearded cheeks. He stopped and asked, "Bem Tavares?"

Bem looked up at the stranger standing over him and tried to place the face. He soon grinned in recognition. "Ahmad Hassan?"

Ahmad laughed with delight. "I would know you anywhere, Bem, but meeting you here is truly unexpected. How long has it been? Almost three years?"

"Three years sounds about right. You have a good memory, Ahmad."

Ahmad nodded politely to Salar Nassim at Bem's side.

"Oh, allow me to introduce my friend, Salar Nassim. Ahmad was with me in Egypt," Bem explained.

"May peace be upon you," Salar Nassim greeted.

"And unto you peace," Ahmad replied politely.

"What are you doing so far from home, Ahmad? Have you been demoted?" Bem teased.

Ahmad chuckled and said, "On the contrary, old friend, I have been earning my warrior reputation these past few years. I am now captain of my own squadron."

"Captain? Congratulations! Join us for a while."

Ahmad glanced back at his companions before he slipped into the water. "I am glad to see you are doing well, Bem. I had heard that you were in some trouble after we left you in Egypt. I am glad you could clear your name of that."

Bem admitted, "You heard right. I was jailed, but falsely so. Between you and me, it was my jailers who let me out before my trial. I doubt my name was cleared, so I hope you aren't under any obligation to arrest me."

"Is that why you left Egypt?" Ahmad asked.

Bem let out a troubled sigh. "No, there was another reason. I don't know if you remember, but I had married just before your regiment moved."

Ahmad smiled at the memory. He and Bem became good friends while working together with the cavalry horses. "Yes, of course. You married that pretty little handmaiden. What is her name again?"

"Fatina. And do you remember the general's daughter, Alimah?"

"How could I forget?" Ahmad said, grinning. "We all wanted a chance to catch the eye of the general's daughter. In the end I think she was matched to General Sadik. He is head commander in Skopje now."

Bem could not believe his luck. "How do you know all of this?" he asked eagerly.

Ahmad shrugged. "I worked under him last year while he was still in Constantinople."

Salar Nassim clasped Bem on the shoulder and said, "God is good, Bem."

Ahmad was puzzled by Nassim's reaction and looked to Bem. "Were you looking for General Sadik?" he asked.

"I am looking for my wife. Alimah was her mistress, you know, and she took Fatina with her when she sailed to marry Sadik. I have been crisscrossing Europe as a mercenary soldier trying to earn enough money to buy Fatina's freedom, but I had no idea where to look for her. Now I do, my friend, thanks to you!"

The young captain seemed distressed to learn of Bem's plight. "I am sorry, Bem. I had no idea she had been taken from you. I saw her once or twice in Constantinople and thought I recognized her from somewhere, but I didn't place her as your bride."

"Do not be sorry. This is happy news you bring me. I never would have looked for her in Constantinople. And now you say General Sadik is in Skopje. That is only a few days' ride, is it not? You have given me so much hope."

Ahmad laughed nervously. "Well, I am about to give you even more."

"Tell me."

"Do you remember Gamal Bahur?"

"Yes, of course. He was a sergeant with the cavalry," Bem recalled.

"He is now a captain, too, and will be stationed in Tirana with me. He moved with the regiment from Constantinople to Skopje. He worked closely with the general until this new promotion."

Bem was beyond himself with excitement. "Where can I find Gamal?"

"Not so fast, Bem," Ahmad said with a chuckle. "He is on patrol right now. I don't know when exactly they will return, but a squadron never stays away more than a week at a time."

"So, where can I find Gamal? At the military headquarters?" Bem turned to Salar Nassim and added, "We passed that building on our way into Tirana."

"I remember," Salar Nassim said.

"I wouldn't go looking for him. It would be easier for him to come see you. You can talk more openly that way," Ahmad advised. "Where are you staying?"

"We are at a small inn on the west side of the market. Isaak Linos is the proprietor."

"I know the place. When Gamal returns, I will not let a day pass without sending him to you. I cannot guarantee that Fatina has moved with Sadik to Skopje, but Gamal might know whether she is at the residence."

"You are indeed a godsend tonight," Bem said with a boyish grin. "Tell me, Ahmad. Are you here alone? You must come have dinner with us."

"I will tell my friends to go back without me, and we can catch up on everything."

Chapter 7

The next three days were agony for Bem while he waited for Gamal's return. He and Salar Nassim continued to visit Jero to bring him food and hope each day. With no real change in their situation, neither shared the details of Bem's encounter at the bathhouse. They would wait with that optimistic news.

On the fourth day, Isaak escorted a uniformed captain upstairs and urgently knocked on the mercenary's door. "There is an officer here to see you," Isaak announced.

Bem's reaction to the intimidating military man was not what Isaak had expected. The innkeeper bowed and left with a new respect for his lodging guest.

Bem had immediately recognized his old friend from his horse-training days in Libya. He opened the door wide. "Gamal, come in, come in! This is indeed a treat. Let me introduce my friend, Salar Nassim."

The two strangers exchanged polite greetings; then Bem showed Gamal to the small table by the window where he sat down across from him.

"When Ahmad told me you were in Tirana, I did not believe him," Gamal began.

"I was just as surprised to see him, too, after all these years. I wish it were under other circumstances."

Gamal seemed to sense the urgency in his voice and got down to business. "Ahmad already told me a little about your life the last few years. I do not envy you now."

Bem laughed nervously. "Did you envy me once, Gamal?"

Gamal laughed with him. "I did! Mostly because of your pretty wife if I may be truthful." With a new seriousness, he added, "Did you know it was reported that you had died in jail? I believed you were dead, and Fatina must have believed it, too."

"Have you seen her?" Bem asked hopefully.

Gamal's expression remained solemn. "I have, Bem, but you will not be happy with the news I bring you."

Bem looked away. "Is she dead, Gamal?"

"To you, yes."

"I don't understand. Is she in Skopje or not?" Bem demanded.

It was apparent Gamal had uneasy news. He took a visible breath and reported, "Fatina is in Skopje, but you will not get her back. General Sadik has taken her as his concubine."

"Stolen twice," Bem said with anguish. "How is this possible?"

"I told you. They said you were dead."

Salar Nassim understood the graveness of Sadik's attachment to Fatina but offered encouraging words: "She is still your wife, Bem. Another man cannot claim her when it is clear that you live."

Bem's mind was reeling. "Is General Sadik married to Alimah?" he asked.

"Alimah is still his only wife," Gamal assured him. "Your wife serves her, and him. It is known the general has other mistresses besides Fatina. They are all in Skopje now."

Bem stood up, agitated. "Have you seen her? Does she look well, Gamal? Is she cared for?"

Gamal brought some good news to his troubled friend. "I saw her two months ago, Bem. She looked very well. She is more beautiful than ever, which is the reason I noticed, if you want the truth."

Bem was not appeased. "Does he flaunt my wife as his mistress?"

"She is not in public often. I saw her at their apartment by chance. But Sadik has made it clear that she is his alone. That is how it works for those with money and power."

Bem sighed in frustration.

"Do not let her go so easily," Salar Nassim urged.

"You are right, Nassim. What was this all for if not to see it through? I will save her from Sadik."

~*~

After going over Bem's plan of action, the three went downstairs to share a meal and reminisce about happier times. They compared battle stories and escapades until well after dark. When Gamal finally took his leave, Bem and Salar Nassim remained in the empty dining room to contemplate how they would break the news to Jero.

"We cannot leave Jero to rot in his cell. He will, you know, without our visits," Bem fretted.

"Patrik will be back in ten days, maybe less. Baron Baric will be here by then, too. Jero will not starve in that time," Salar Nassim reasoned.

"He is a part of our gang now, our family. We owe him our loyalty. I cannot leave Tirana yet. Who will bring him clean water, at the very least?"

Zerina quietly approached their table and took their empty plates. "Will you be wanting anything else tonight?" she asked. It was late, and she wanted to lock up.

Salar Nassim smiled up at her. "Come sit with us, Zerina," he said.

She looked around to see if Isaak was watching, but they were the only ones left in the restaurant. Hesitantly, she did as he asked and sat down next to him. Zerina had already spent time alone with Bem in his chamber a few nights ago. The handsome Persian had been kind to her during his stay, and she would willingly go with him upstairs, too, for a price.

Their eyes met, and Zerina said, "I cannot leave the dining hall right now if that is what you are wanting. Perhaps in an hour?"

Salar Nassim trusted the serving girl would keep his confidence as he would keep hers. "I am asking for a different service, Zerina, and I will pay you just as well."

She was puzzled by his riddle.

Bem caught on to what Salar Nassim would ask and said to her, "You know we are here because our friend is in jail."

"The Venetian man," she said.

Salar Nassim replied, "Yes. Jero Baric is his name. We have an errand that will take us away from Tirana tomorrow, and we need someone to bring Jero food and water. Someone we can trust. Someone who will be rewarded generously for such care in our absence."

"How generous?" she asked.

Salar Nassim went on to explain, "Jero's brother is a wealthy man. We have written to him, and he will be here for the trial. When he arrives, he will pay you for caring that his brother survives."

Zerina considered the request. "How can I trust this brother?"

"You will have to take my word for it. He is a Venetian baron—a gentleman in his world," Salar Nassim told her with emphasis.

She was puzzled. "I don't know what that means to be a baron. Is it like a prince?"

Salar Nassim smiled at her question. "It is something like that, yes."

"Is the man in jail a prince, too?" she wanted to know.

"Jero is not a baron, but he is a wealthy man, like his brother," Salar Nassim assured her.

Bem urged, "Both are good men, Zerina. They will not betray you when it comes to your reward."

"Can he take me away from here?"

Surprised by her question, Bem and Salar Nassim contemplated a truthful answer.

Nassim finally said, "I do not think he can take you with him, Zerina. Jero must continue on to Thessaloniki. He is to be married. His bride was the girl you saw at our table on that first day."

"I remember her. She had pretty red hair."

"Yes, and she is waiting for Jero to return to her. But we cannot let him starve in jail while she waits."

"No. That would be wrong," Zerina agreed.

"Will you do him this service? We will pay you for the food now. And his brother, the baron prince, will pay you whatever you want when he arrives in Tirana."

She searched their faces for a clue of deceitfulness, but she saw only pleading in their eyes.

"Just that? I don't have to do anything else?" she asked.

Zerina had given Bem a glimpse of what was behind her protective shell while in bed together. He drew on that when he asked again, "Can you help us, Zerina? Just food and water each day. That is all Jero needs from you."

Salar Nassim reached into his pouch, picked out several coins, and then put them in her hand. "Will this be enough to feed him for ten days?"

She counted the coins by feel before she dropped the generous payment into her apron pocket. "It will be enough."

Salar Nassim said, "We are leaving in the morning."

"Leave with no regrets," she assured them. "I will take care of your friend for you. Jero will be fine."

~*~

It was just after dawn when the guard dragged his club against the iron bars. "Wake up, Venetian scum. You have visitors."

Jero sat up bewildered on his straw bed. It was too early for Salar Nassim's usual lone visit. But he wasn't alone that morning.

"Is there news?" Jero asked hopefully.

Bem shook his head. "I am sorry, Jero. There is no change in your situation. But I have received good news. I have found Fatina."

Jero hurried to the barred door. "Is she here, in Tirana?"

"No, but she is not far, either. I met an old friend of mine by chance. He was stationed in Skopje, and he saw her there not long ago."

Jero forgot his misery for a fleeting moment. "Skopje? Yes, that is not far at all. I am very happy for you."

"You will not be happy when we tell you the rest," Salar Nassim added.

Jero needed no explanation. He could read the rest on their faces. "You are both leaving, aren't you?"

"Fatina is still a servant to her former mistress. I can finally get her back, but I will need Salar Nassim's help."

Jero swallowed the lump in his throat and said, "Then you must both go."

"Do not despair, Jero," Bem urged. "We have arranged to have a serving girl from the inn bring you food. Zerina will come each day until Patrik returns, or until your brother arrives. We have left both of them messages with the innkeeper. It shouldn't be too long now."

"Is this a goodbye, then?" Jero asked. "Will you be back?"

"We won't be back, Jero," Salar Nassim answered solemnly. "This is goodbye."

Jero could not hide his melancholy, but he tried to be brave from the wrong side of the bars. He reached through and shook each of their hands in turn. "I had hoped it would be a happier occasion when saying goodbye. Thank you. I thank you both for everything."

Both Bem and Salar Nassim felt the gravity of their farewell.

"This will be resolved, Jero. Patrik and Soren will take you the rest of the way to Thessaloniki," Bem promised.

"Yes. Yes, of course," Jero mumbled. "Will they not follow you to Skopje?"

Salar Nassim shook his head. "We must all part ways one day. We have written our goodbyes to them, as well, and asked that they not come after us," Salar Nassim explained. "In the end, who knows where we might have to go. Bem's wife might not be in Skopje after all."

Jero took a deep breath to keep back his tears. "May God watch over you, my friends."

"And over you, Jero Baric. Peace be with you," Salar Nassim replied.

Bem slipped a jug of water and a folded cloth filled with some bread and a few hunks of roasted meat into Jero's hands, holding them in his own before finally letting go.

Jero watched his companions leave down the corridor for the last time and then looked down at the food his friends had brought him. Roman came to his side at the bars, and Jero gave half of his bounty to his companion, who nodded his humble thanks.

They ate in silence for a moment before Roman warned, "Be careful of the girl, Jero. Your friends were fooled if they are counting on her allegiance to you."

"Do you know the serving girl they spoke of?"

"Zerina is one of the few women the guards let into the jailhouse. There is a reason for that. She is a whore, in service to these soldiers. Your friends were wrong to trust her. She will spend the payment and leave you to starve."

Jero leaned against the bars of their cell, no longer hungry. The words of his Uncle Vladimir resonated in his thoughts: trust no one. He sulked back to his dirty straw bed and sat down to wait for one more day to be over.

Chapter 8

Thessaloniki, 7 August 1649

The sun was low in the sky above the city. Ruby stopped her horse at the edge of the road before the descent. An empty ache of longing washed over her.

They should have hurried to the gates before the night watch shut them, but Patrik and Soren stayed by Ruby's side to watch the torches light up along the miles of commanding stone walls.

Hundreds of Ottoman soldiers stood guard at their posts where thousands had stood for a millennium, protecting these same bricks and stones. Thessaloniki was a city like no other. Whether under the rule of the Romans, Byzantines, Normans, Venetians, or Turks, Thessaloniki had defiantly held her guard on the baked hills above the Aegean Sea.

The dozen mosques within the walls sang out, calling the men to prayer. They loomed above Salonikan homes and businesses. Beyond the tiled rooftops were imposing seawall towers. Boats and merchant ships, big and small, were anchored in the sparkling water the protective seawall held back. A few of those boats belonged to the Spiros and Kokinnos families.

Perched on her horse, Ruby searched the city within its perimeter walls. Her family's house was only four blocks away from the largest marketplace, just inside the entrance gate by the harbor. Her tiny street was one of many meandering alleys in the cobbled neighborhood. In her mind, she saw herself walking those narrow streets with her sisters, guiding them home from a visit to friends or on an errand for her mother.

Home. Her home. The last time Ruby had seen her beloved city was when her carriage to Solgrad traveled along this same road. That final fleeting glimpse of home was more than a year ago. She had been filled with dread then, traveling with Resi into the unknown, but it had been the best decision of her short life. With this homecoming, her hopeful future was in jeopardy.

Patrik's future was also in jeopardy. His father would ask questions and give advice Patrik would ignore, making his parents unhappy. But he had made his decision, and he was ready to face them.

Patrik broke the silence on the hill and said, "We need to go. The gates will be closing soon."

Ruby urged the horse down the cobbled road behind Soren. She wanted to hurry now, be in the comfort of her family home, and tell them about her breaking heart. Her father would understand how wretched she felt without Jero. He would not make her marry Nikko in Jero's place. Her mother and three sisters would take her side. She was sure of it. And when Patricius returned with Jero in a few weeks, they would be married.

Her distracting thoughts made her almost miss the turnoff Patrik had chosen.

"Why are you taking the higher entrance?" she called over. "The Golden Gate is the most direct way to my house."

"We are going to my father's house first. We can unpack there and stable our horses," Patrik replied.

"I wish you would have asked what I wanted. I am eager to be home."

"It has been a long time since they've seen you, Ruby," Patrik pointed out. "Not that I don't think you look lovely, but I thought you might want to clean up before I take you home. You wouldn't want to give them a shock now, would you?"

Soren's sympathetic smile convinced her that Patrik was right. They had ridden hard from sunup to sundown each day and had slept on the dusty ground in their same clothes each night. If Soren and Patrik looked like vagabonds riding next to her, then she must look the part as well.

"I suppose your mother will have a clean change of clothes for me," Ruby said with a tired sigh.

~*~

Ruby Spiros's family lived at the end of a block of modest residences on a street near the harbor. The Kokkinos family lived higher on the hillside, where wealthy merchants owned freestanding homes with walled gardens. The muffled sounds of children's voices could be heard as the three riders approached the open gate of the Kokkinoses' courtyard.

Six small children lived in Demetrius and Celine Kokkinos's house. Three were Patrik's siblings: Hector, Lander, and Phyllis. Castor, Patrik's oldest brother, had an apartment at the back of the family villa where he lived with his wife, Alexis, and their three young children.

The playing siblings were surprised by the strangers riding through the gate into their walled sanctuary. It had been so long since they had seen Patrik that they didn't recognize him at first.

"Who's that?" the smaller of the two boys asked the other.

Patrik grinned at the sight of his brothers. "Do you not know me?" he asked Lander.

"It's Patricius!" Hector shouted excitedly. "Ma! Come quick! Patricius is back!"

Patrik slid off his saddle and embraced Hector, forgetting all about his earlier homecoming worries.

Lander, now seven, ran to take Hector's place.

Patrik knelt on one knee and held out his arms for his brother. "Look how you have grown into such a little man," he said when he picked up the boy and hugged him tightly.

Despite being squeezed in the folds of his brother's embrace, Lander managed to ask, "Where have you been so long, Patricius? Have you been fighting the bad men? Did you bring us presents again?"

Patrik chuckled at the little boy's honesty. "Of course, we brought you presents." He set him back on the ground and then picked up his sister, who had shyly followed her big brothers.

"Look who has come with us," Patrik whispered to little Phyllis.

"Ruby!" Phyllis cried, reaching out to be held by her. Ruby had often visited the children before leaving for Croatia and was missed.

Across the way, Celine Kokkinos wiped her tears with the sleeve of her tunic as she stood at the front door. She had not dared believe Hector until she saw them with her own eyes.

She hurried to greet them, with Alexis following her across the courtyard.

"Ma, look who has come," Lander shouted happily. "It's Patricius. And he brought Ruby and the yellow-haired man. Did you bring Resi with you, too?"

No one answered the little boy's question. They were too busy tearfully embracing each other in the dim torchlight of the courtyard.

Celine finally stepped back and gave her son a long looking-over. "Oh, Patricius, you have worried me these past years. I am happy you've made it home. Settle your horses and come in, my dear ones."

Alexis called out, "Children, come along now and let Patricius and Soren unburden their tired horses."

Celine led Ruby inside. "You must be exhausted, my dear girl. You will stay the night with us tonight and rest. There will be so much to tell when you arrive home, so many questions to answer."

"I am bone-tired, Mother Kokkinos, but I want to sleep in my home tonight. I would like to just wash up and change before I go again."

Celine patted Ruby's hand and said, "As you wish." She then called out, "Melissa!"

A servant girl appeared at the kitchen door.

"We will need water heated for washing."

The girl nodded and hurried away as Alexis came into the kitchen.

"What an adventure you have had, Ruby. How long were you on the road?" Alexis asked.

Ruby thought for a moment, then realized she did not know. "What day is it today?"

"It is the seventh of August," Celine replied.

"Then we have been riding nearly a month. We were a party of six when we left, but three—"

Ruby could not finish her sentence without crying.

Celine guided her to a chair at the kitchen table, where Ruby crumpled into sobs.

"Shhh. Everything will be all right, Ruby dear," Patrik's mother assured her. "Take your time and tell us what happened."

Patrik and Soren had entered the kitchen as the two women and children gathered around Ruby to hear her tale.

Patrik answered for her, "The other three are waiting for us there, Ma."

Celine looked puzzled. "Waiting where, son?"

He took a deep breath. Patrik would have to explain everything soon enough. "We ran into some trouble in Tirana. Do you know who Jero is?" he asked.

Celine and Alexis both smiled at the mention of Jero's name.

"We know plenty about Jero, Patricius." Celine turned excitedly to Ruby and added, "And I have good news for you, Ruby, my dear."

"We could use some good news," Patrik interjected.

Celine told them with a warm laugh, "Angelos was overwhelmed with correspondence out of Solgrad this summer. Your letter, Patricius, along with several from Ruby and Resi, all arrived at about the same time as the one from Mauritius Baric. His letter described Jero's fine qualities and love for Ruby. It was a request for a match between Jero and Ruby. Is that right, dear girl?" she asked.

Ruby nodded eagerly.

"Well, your father considered it seriously."

"And the good news?" Ruby held her breath.

Alexis eagerly shared the rest, "Angelos had an awkward conversation with Omiros Areleous. Omiros was angry, of course, that your pa would even consider rejecting his son after it had all been decided. But then Nikko confessed that he had fallen in love with your sister, Kallisto, after meeting her last year. So . . ."

"Yes?" Ruby prodded anxiously.

"So, the two fathers agreed to change the bride, and Kallisto is willing to marry him. What do you think about that?"

Ruby was stunned. "Kallisto will marry Nikko? But she is only seventeen."

"Seventeen is a bit young," Celine agreed, "but you know your sister and her infatuation with boys. She is already lovesick over him!"

"Tell her the best part, Celine," Alexis said urgently.

"Angelos has agreed that you can marry the Venetian. He wrote back to Resi to tell her so."

Ruby began to sob even harder than before.

"Why are you not happy?" Alexis asked with dismay. "Do you no longer love him, Ruby?" Celine and Alexis looked to Patrik for an answer.

He put his arms around Ruby's slumped shoulders to comfort her, and he said with a sigh, "I will tell you what Ruby couldn't. Jero rode along with us. He was going to ask Father Spiros for Ruby's hand in marriage, but we had to leave him in Tirana."

Celine covered her mouth in shock. "You left him?"

"Like I said, Ma, we had some trouble. Jero was arrested by the authorities there. Salar Nassim and our friend, Bem, stayed behind with Jero. He is to stand trial in two weeks. Soren and I will return in time for that. We've sent a message to Mauritius Baric. He should arrive there in plenty of time to clear his brother's name."

The children fidgeted restlessly, not following the serious talk. Phyllis tugged on her mother's robes to be picked up and held, but Celine focused on Patrik. "Why was Jero arrested? What did he do, Patricius?"

Ruby found her voice and answered, "We were robbed along the way, and the thief was killed. They blamed Jero for the man's death. They called it murder, and they took him away."

Celine and Alexis could barely breathe, stunned at the news.

"I will bring him home, Ruby, and all will be well. You will see," Patrik assured her. Then he picked up his little sister, who was clinging to her mother, and kissed her on her brow to soothe her.

Lander came to his side and leaned against his leg. He, too, wanted to be held by his brother again, and Patrik scooped up the little boy with his other arm.

The girl shyly eyed the Dane, and Patrik asked her, "Do you want the yellow-haired man to hold you, Phyllis?"

She nodded that she did, and Patrik passed her to Soren's open arms. The toddler fingered his blond curls as if she were twirling a security blanket.

"I think you have a new friend," Patrik told Soren with a chuckle.

Ruby felt better just watching the Kokkinoses' reunion. "Where are your little ones?" she asked Alexis. Her voice was steady again.

"Already tucked in bed," Alexis replied. "Shall I rescue you, Soren? Phyllis is up long past her bedtime, too." She stretched out her arms to take the girl, but Phyllis held Soren tightly around his neck.

"Shall I carry you, Phyllis?" the Dane asked sweetly, and without waiting for an answer, he told Alexis, "Lead the way."

Patrik set Lander down. "Take this little man, too," he said. "And you, as well, my other little man."

"I am ten now," Hector pointed out. "I am old enough to wait up for Pa."

"Not tonight," his mother said with a warning glare.

The boy hung his head but dutifully followed Soren down the corridor to the children's sleeping chamber.

Alone now with his mother and Ruby, Patrik asked, "Is Castor away at sea?"

"No, all our ships are in the harbor being loaded. I expect Castor and your father will be coming from there shortly."

Celine got up and poured glasses of wine, then put a plate of bread and olives down in front of them.

"While we wait, tell me about your visit to your sister, Patricius, and what you think of her new husband," Celine said with a renewed cheerfulness.

Patrik set his cup down with a grin and said, "Ah, well, that will take me all night to explain her husband. Wouldn't you agree, Ruby?"

"I think they are well-matched. But you are right, Patricius. There is a lot to tell about life with the Barics. It is hard to know where to start."

Celine picked up her glass and told Ruby, "Start with Jero if you like."

Chapter 9

Tirana, 9 August 1649

Roman leaned against the barred door and watched Jero pick up a piece of straw on one side of him and then set it to the other side. "She's not coming," Roman said. "She is keeping the money and leaving you to starve, as I warned."

Jero's stomach growled with hunger, but he dared not eat the pan of food the guard had brought at midday.

Daylight was nearly gone in their cell, and there was nothing to do once darkness took over but to wait for the next day.

"I'm going to sleep now. If you like, you can share the straw with me. I think both of your friends are finally dead," Jero said.

Roman's buddy Erol had been dead for at least two days. His corpse was beginning to decay next to Ilker's dead body. Despite Jero's emphatic protests, the guards would not take them away.

Erol and Ilker were two parts of a trio of wandering street entertainers. Roman was the third. They had performed crowd-pleasing acrobatics, juggled fire, sang popular songs, and sometimes even sold a homemade concoction they claimed could cure many common ailments.

One week ago, Roman and his pals had done just that in Tirana's market square, and the crowd of eager shoppers happily bought up bottles of their cure-all potion.

Tirana's marketplace had been so profitable for them that the trio greedily lingered a second day at their makeshift stall. The trio should have run for it when some customers came down with worse pains and afflictions than they had started with.

One unfortunate customer was Captain Poljani's brother-in-law. Before Roman could load up their donkey-driven cart, a squad of Poljani's officers arrested the three.

Roman and his pals swore there was nothing tainted in their potion. If taken by spoonful, as they had instructed, the sweet elixir was harmless.

As proof of their defense, the sergeant made them drink the rest of their profitable medicine—all of it.

Erol was the first to turn green from the deadly overdose. The bottle he had been forced to drink was an especially strong brew. Soon after, Ilker was doubled over in pain next to him. Roman had been able to spill a good portion of his allotted drink while the guards dragged them to the cell, or he might have succumbed to the same fate as his two friends. The food and water Jero had shared with Roman had helped him recover.

Roman was already asleep on the straw when Jero noticed a light flicker. The night guards did not leave torches burning in the windowless corridor, so the approaching lamp shone brightly in their black cell. When a soft voice called out his name, Jero imagined for a brief moment it was Ruby. He rushed toward the small figure holding the oil lamp between the bars.

"Did I wake you?" she asked.

Jero could see her face now, maimed yet beautiful in the soft light. "You are the serving girl?" he said.

"Yes, I am Zerina. I will bring you food, but I cannot come until my work is done in the restaurant."

Jero wondered out loud, "They let you in here this late?"

"I know the night guards, and they don't mind a little female company."

Jero shifted uncomfortably. "Do not go out of your way for me. Do not do anything—"

"Immoral?" she finished his thought.

"I did not mean to insult you. I . . . um . . . thank you for coming."

His accent was sweet, and his innocence was obvious. Zerina no longer regretted the deal she had made. "Your friends already paid me to help you, Signor Jero, and I will keep my word." She opened her shoulder bag and took out a folded cloth and a crock of water.

Jero eagerly took the food she passed through the bars. She had included grapes and dried dates with the bread and sausage. "I am truly grateful to you, Zerina."

She watched him in the lamplight as he hungrily ate. She did not remember Jero from before, at the lunch table with the others. His friends had exotic features that readily caught her attention, but she studied the prince's face now. He was dirty and unshaven, like an ordinary man. She noticed, though, he had made an attempt to keep his hair neat and tied. His cravat was orderly over his collar, and his waistcoat seemed finely made. Jero looked up from his food for a moment. His unusual green eyes looked kind and intelligent to her. "They say you killed a man," she blurted out.

Jero shook his head. "I did not kill anyone. The captain here says my father did, and I am to pay his debt. But he is wrong."

Jero pulled the grapes off their stems and savored the sweetness before continuing, "Captain Poljani has a vendetta against a man he calls Peric. My name is Baric. He does not seem to notice the difference."

"I must warn you, Jero Baric, to not anger the captain. He is unpredictable, like a cornered serpent. Poke at him, and he strikes. Leave him be, and he leaves you alone. He is not to be trusted."

Jero replied with the same seriousness, "Thank you, but I do not need that warning. I already know he cannot be reasoned with."

She looked down the hallway. The guards had opened the heavy door that led to the office, where they were waiting for her.

"I am sorry to hurry you, Jero, but you need to drink the water. I will take the crock back with me, but you can keep the cloth. Do they let you wash up in here?"

He pointed to the stone bed. "The stench is coming from our dead companions there."

Zerina held the light toward the bunk in horror. "Animals! I will talk to the night watch."

Jero drank the last swig of water and handed back the bottle. "Thank you for everything, Zerina."

"I will come again tomorrow."

As she left with her lamplight, Jero shook Roman awake to share the rest of his dinner.

~*~

When Jero opened his eyes next morning, they met Captain Poljani's glare.

"The night guards said that your delicate Venetian nose was offended by the smell in here."

Jero shook off his sleep and said, "Have you no respect for the dead, Captain? Even Christian souls must be put to rest, not left to rot on a bench."

Captain Poljani sneered and hollered, "Get up!"

Jero hesitated.

"You and your new friend—up!" Then the captain called down the corridor, "Emir!"

At the doorway, the guard left his place and hurried obediently to his commander's side.

"Take the prisoners outside for some fresh air and clean up this place," Poljani said with a mocking pleasantness.

Roman came to life at the shouting, and he pleaded, "Captain Poljani, sir, we are fine here. There is no problem with the smell. I smell nothing at all, sir."

Jero remembered Zerina's warning and realized he had poked the snake. "Yes, Captain, sir," Jero added to Roman's plea, "we do not need to go outside."

"No, no, gentlemen. I insist," the captain said in a honeyed tone that was chilling. "We have no garden to stroll in, Lord Peric, but I think the sun will do you wonders to clear the rotting stench from your senses. Emir, take his lordship and the clown out into the sunshine, please."

"No! Please! We want to stay here!" Roman begged.

It was futile. Poljani had given the order. Jero and Roman were marched outside to the prison courtyard, stripped to the waist, and then tied firmly to the crossbars of a post with leather straps.

Roman had witnessed prisoners tied in front of the jailhouse before; the whole town had. The simple rack on the south side was an easy form of torture for unruly prisoners and sent a clear message to the citizens.

The morning sun shone mercilessly on the stone pavers. By late afternoon, the radiating heat had burned prisoners' feet through their boots and blistered their exposed torsos. Without water, it was nearly unbearable, but the greater part of the punishment was the taunting throughout the day.

When word got out of the spectacle at the jailhouse, an occasional passerby quickly multiplied into a rowdy crowd. The unpredictable mood of the horde could have easily ended Jero's and Roman's lives that day. Jero prayed that no one would begin to throw stones.

The guards dragged Jero and Roman half-conscious back to their cell at dusk. The July sunshine had turned their pale skin a painful shade of scarlet from the top of their heads to their belted waists.

Zerina's customers had told her of their torture, but she could not bring herself to go see them on the racks. That night, she found them on their backs, softly moaning in misery.

Zerina paid the night guard one of Salar Nassim's coins to unlock their cell so that she could tend to them. She had packed more than just food with her. She took her time and spread a thick salve over their blistered skin. Then she knelt next to Jero and put the water jug to his lips to force him to drink. "I warned you," she whispered.

Jero's lips were cracked and swollen. It took all his effort to form the words, "Does not matter."

"The bodies are gone," she reported. "The men are wrapped in shrouds outside, ready to be buried. You got what you wanted."

"I know," he said with effort. "They laid . . . them . . . next to us . . . in the sun . . . so we . . . remember . . . why we . . . were there." Jero lifted his head to accept another drink. "Roman?" he asked.

"He looks no worse than you. I put some sleeping powder in your water, Jero. The powder, and time, will cure your pain. I will make Roman drink some before I leave. Hold still while I put this ointment on your lips."

"You are . . . an angel. Thank you." Jero shut his eyes and let the drug take effect.

Chapter 10

The painful blisters overwhelmed their senses, and the two men descended into delirium. Zerina tended their burns each night. Jero and Roman could hardly move for three days, and it took all their strength to feed themselves with the food Zerina left under their straw. Slowly, they recovered.

The prison had a predictable schedule, and the sound of the big door swinging open at the end of the corridor meant it was noon. The occupied cells down the hall came to life for a short time while guards brought the prisoners their daily meals. Jero didn't know how many men remained in those adjacent chambers, but their husky voices and the creak of iron doors opening somehow reassured him that he was not alone in his misfortune.

As the routine went, a guard would walk to the end of the corridor, look in on Jero and Roman in their cell, and then walk away. He no longer bothered to bring them plates of food that went uneaten. Although the soldiers had cleared the stone bunk of Roman's dead companions, the two still sat on their straw bed in the beam of light every day, all day.

On this particular day, it was not Emir who came to check on Jero and Roman. Captain Poljani himself stopped in front of their iron doorway. He glared at the two prisoners for a long moment before he asked Roman, "Is it true that your friends were Christians?"

Roman took a gamble and told the truth, "They were, sir."

"That is precisely why we did not bury them. When we lack a Christian prisoner to give another Christian a proper burial, we let the vultures dispose of them. But you are a Christian, aren't you, Peric?"

Jero held his stare. Whatever he answered would be wrong. He said nothing.

The captain brushed off Jero's open disrespect and reflected, "I thought you might say a few words of prayer over the bodies before they are interred. Wouldn't that be a proper Christian thing to do, Peric? Isn't that what your father offered the dead after he murdered them?"

"Erol and Ilker were not so faithful, sir," Roman interjected. "As a matter of fact, I don't think I ever heard them pray."

Poljani ignored Roman and shouted down the corridor, "Guards!"

Two soldiers arrived at the captain's side.

"Take our Venetian friend to the graveyard. He is going to lay a few Christian souls to rest. That is what you wanted, isn't it, Peric?"

Jero blew out his breath for courage and stood up to meet his punishment. Roman defiantly joined Jero at the doorway.

The soldiers escorted both of them out of their jail cell, but before they left the prison block, Poljani ordered, "Lock the clown in with the others."

Roman struggled against his jailers, but they managed to unlock one of the cells and shove him there. The half-dozen miserable men shouted obscenities at the guards in solidarity with him.

Roman rushed back to the bars and called out, "I will see you later, Jero. All right, friend? Keep your head up."

Jero needed that reassurance, and he nodded in reply.

The sunlight was harsh outside the jailhouse. They passed the posts in the courtyard where Jero and Roman had been tied. Seeing them, Jero struggled to breathe as a wave of panic came over him. And then he saw a cart and the wrapped, rotting remains of the street entertainers heaped on its low bed.

His two armed guards wrapped scarves over their noses and led Jero to the front of the cart. Still, the awful stench was more bearable than the swarms of biting flies that covered the stained shrouds.

Emir, one of Jero's escorts, informed him, "The Christian cemetery is outside the city gates. You will bury them there."

Jero asked, "Am I the beast and the grave digger?"

Emir gave Jero a shove to the front of the cart.

Jero slung the rope meant for a donkey over his shoulder and began to drag the cart down the road, flanked by his two guards. This time he was not jeered at or taunted by the onlookers. He was just another prisoner going about his work.

The cemetery was a long twenty-minute walk from the jailhouse. The guards directed Jero to the back of the graveyard. They stopped in front of an arched gate with an iron cross over the entrance. Inside the low-walled enclosure were the tombs of respected Christian citizens, lined up in straight rows, their names carved in the rock. Behind the rows of the elite dead, low mounds of broken rocks were lined up for those who had no one to pay for their deaths. No gravestones memorialized their passing.

In the cart with the rotting bodies was a spade. Emir handed it to Jero.

"You can dig one trench for both," Emir said. "It doesn't have to be deep. Take the rocks from the tops of the older graves to seal it. Those men are bones now and don't need cover."

The sun was high in the sky, and Jero had no hat to shade him. He buttoned his sweat-stained collar up to his chin and used his filthy waistcoat as a turban on his sunburned head. Then Jero picked up the spade and began chipping away at the packed dirt while the guards made themselves comfortable under the only tree in the cemetery. They had a long wait ahead of them.

~*~

It had been dark for hours when Zerina came to the cell door. "Are you awake, Jero?" she whispered from the hallway.

Jero rolled off his straw bed and hobbled, bent over, to where she stood.

Zerina moaned with worry. "Dear God! Have they broken your back?"

Jero painfully straightened up to ease her concern. "My back will be fine," he assured her. "Just not today."

She set down the lamp and said, "Let me see your hands."

He put them through the bars and turned them over to reveal what she had expected to see: cuts and blisters. Zerina then pulled a cloth and a pot of ointment from the bag slung over her shoulder. She spread the thick, greasy mixture over Jero's open cuts.

"Ahh," he groaned. "That is both agonizing and comforting. How did you know?"

"Two of Poljani's soldiers came to the restaurant this evening. They told everyone how it took you all day to dig one hole, and how you scavenged for rocks bare-handed to cover the grave. They joked that such labor shredded your soft Venetian skin. I imagined they were right."

"I suppose they had a good laugh over it," Jero murmured.

Zerina looked around and asked suddenly, "Where is Roman?"

"They put him into a different cell earlier. The corridor was already dark when they brought me back here."

She was out of time and hurriedly wrapped a cloth around Jero's first palm. "I didn't know princes could work so hard," she found herself saying.

"Who said I am a prince?"

"Bem and Salar Nassim told me your brother is something close to that, and that you are also a rich man. Were they your guards?" she asked.

"Bem and Salar Nassim? No, they are my friends. I was traveling with them to Thessaloniki. I am supposed to marry someone there."

She tied off the second wrapping and patted his hand. "Will you live in Thessaloniki?"

Jero pulled his hands back through the bars. They felt better, and so did he now that he had company, someone kind to talk to. "No, Ruby and I planned to sail back to Croatia. That is where I come from."

"Ruby was with you in the restaurant that first day, right?"

"Yes. My other companions took her home."

"This home you have back in Croatia—do you have servants there?"

Jero thought for a moment. His home was now the Baric's abandoned villa house. Ervin and Vilma would stay on as groundskeepers, and Mauro would arrange for more house servants for Jero upon his return.

"Why do you ask?"

"We have heard stories about the Venetians, that they are a pitiless people, selfish and cruel to others. But you are different from what I imagined. I bet you would make a good master."

He smiled at her misunderstanding. He had never been a master before and explained, "I have great respect for both servants and masters. I do not think being Venetian or Ottoman makes one cruel or kind, though. It is the person himself. I have never been treated more cruelly than here, yet I will not say it is because they are Ottomans. The woman I will marry is an Ottoman. You, too, have been exceptionally kind, Zerina. Why are you helping me?" he finally asked.

She held his handsome gaze in the lamplight and said, "Your friends paid me to help you."

He studied her jagged scar and sad doe eyes and maintained, "I do not believe that is the reason. I am here behind bars on trial for murder, and you have your purse of coins." He pressed his question again. "Why are you helping me, Zerina?"

She let out the breath she had been holding. "Maybe because I know what it is like to be treated unfairly. To have done everything right, but be punished for it. Cruelly."

"Is that how you got your scar?"

She met his eyes again and explained, "I don't like to tell that story. Most people think I deserved what I got. I am hideous now, but I have lived with this ugliness for a long time."

"You are not ugly, Zerina. Beauty has nothing to do with scars."

Flustered at the unexpected compliment, she reached into her bag and took out a tattered, folded cloth and a corked crock. "Hurry now, Jero. I'll leave the food, but drink the jug of water. I must be going."

Jero took a big swallow and felt the cool liquid fill his veins. He took a bite of the bread before he drank the rest, and Zerina slid the jug back into her bag.

"What day is it today?" he asked.

"It is, um, Tuesday."

"No. What is the date?"

"Um, the twelfth, I think."

"The magistrate will be here on the twentieth?"

"That is what they said."

"Someone should be coming soon."

Zerina was suddenly concerned for him and warned, "Keep out of Poljani's way until your friends get here. They told me you will not be convicted of this crime. You will go free, Jero."

He took an audible breath. "I know. Thank you again for everything."

She picked up her lamp and watched him slouch away to his dark corner to finish his meager meal. Before she left, she held the lamp to her face and warned, "Please. Be careful, Jero."

Her light disappeared down the corridor, and Jero looked up and whispered, "Thank you, God, for my angel."

~*~

Zerina and her son, Aleksander, had shared a small room at the back of the kitchen ever since she began working for Isaak eight years ago. Before that, she had wandered from town to town trying to start a new life, but nothing had stuck for long. Old Isaak was the first man to give her a real job despite her being the mother of a bastard baby.

Isaak took a chance on her for selfish reasons. He had just lost his beloved wife, Agathe, and urgently needed a kitchen maid who could also cook. He thought his Agathe would have approved of his taking in Zerina. His wife liked three-legged strays, and she regularly caged broken-winged birds until they mended.

Agathe would have been angry over the senseless maiming of a pretty fifteen-year-old girl. Zerina's new husband had flaunted his prized young bride in front of his first wife until the jealous woman cut Zerina's face from ear to lip with a boning knife.

Zerina's husband of three months left her for dead at the steps of a hospital in Sophia. She surprised everyone and survived the horrific wound, but the oozing stitches made her too grotesque for her husband to want her back.

Alone, she healed but struggled to make a living on the streets of Sophia. Her son, Aleksander, had been fathered by one of her many customers. With no one to care for her baby, she went home to Tirana and begged her family to take her in again. Isaak took her in as a kitchen maid instead.

By the time she was back in the warm room behind the kitchen, the oil lamp she had carried to and from the jailhouse was nearly spent. She blew it out and slid under the covers next to Aleksander.

"Was the prince all right?" her son asked sleepily.

"He was not hurt too badly. He is a strong man. Go back to sleep, Sasho."

"Did you ask him, Mama?" Aleksander whispered urgently.

"Not yet, my sweet. Shut your eyes now. It is late."

"I don't want to leave you," he confessed.

She held him tightly. "I don't want you to leave me, but there is nothing for you here. If the prince takes you back to his castle, and you work very hard and save all your money, then you can come back and take me away from here. Will you do that for me?"

"I will, Mama. When I am big and strong, I promise I will."

"You are a good boy, Sasho. You just have to remember to do as the man asks. Learn everything you can, don't talk back, and you will do well."

"What if he doesn't take me with him?" Aleksander fretted.

"I will tell his prince brother that taking you is my payment for caring for Jero. He will have to do it."

With new resolve, the boy asked, "When will I leave?"

"Shhh. Not until after Jero's trial. We have a whole week together, my sweet son. Let us not worry about leaving now."

Chapter 11

The way to Skopje was well-traveled by caravanning merchants, and the three-day journey went quickly for Bem and Salar Nassim until the last day. As they galloped along, the road dramatically climbed and meandered through an isolated canyon. Its deep abyss seemed to open to an underworld shadowed by high cliff walls, eerily quiet, despite the river rushing deep below.

Although the two riders were not superstitious, the legend some fellow travelers had told of the mysterious landscape was incentive enough for the horsemen to hurry through without stopping. Neither Bem nor Salar Nassim had been in this part of the Balkans, so they were surprised when the mountainous road suddenly opened onto a broad river valley, flanked by two distant mountain ranges.

This defensive plain was first settled by a people long forgotten, then ruled in turn by the Roman, Byzantine, Bulgarian, and Serbian Empires before the Turks conquered it almost three hundred years ago. Skopje had always been a desirable holding by empires, called by different names at different times.

The strategically built city was perched on the highest point of the surrounding foothills. Its imposing limestone fortress warned visitors of its might. The Vardar River defended the stronghold on its western side, and deep trenches protected the rest of the high walls. Bem and Salar Nassim could see more walls within the pentagon exterior, with lowered drawbridges linking them, as they traveled by.

General Sadik was an important military man to have been chosen to govern this city's defense. He would likely have a command post at the fortress, but where did he house his wife and servants? That was what Bem needed to learn.

Arriving from the western side of the river, the two crossed an immense stone bridge that led to a bustling covered market. The city was home to numerous goldsmiths and silk traders, who did a lively business under the tiled roofs of the enclosed bazaars.

While meandering through its busy streets, Bem and Salar Nassim passed mosques with high turrets and ornately tiled entrances, welcoming the faithful. In the center of Skopje was a grand bathhouse that would rival any in

Constantinople. Aqueducts supplied the many bathhouses with unlimited water for the men and women who took delight in the city's decadent offerings.

Riding farther, Salar Nassim and Bem crossed a smaller river crowded with women washing laundry on its banks in the afternoon sun. Men on flatboats in the middle of the waterway hauled goods to small docks along the banks, where dockworkers stood ready to unload them.

It was a prosperous city filled with commerce and a population of many ethnic origins. If Bem and Salar Nassim had not come with the urgent mission to find Fatina, they might have enjoyed their stay here.

Having now taken in the layout of Skopje, the two assessed where they would best find lodging for themselves and their horses. Both understood it could take days, perhaps weeks, to find and rescue Fatina. In the end, they decided on a centrally located inn near the main mosque and took a room there.

After settling in, the mercenaries went shopping for new clothes to match the charade Salar Nassim would play to gain information. Tomorrow was Friday, and he planned to spend the day praying with influential men who, he hoped, could help them in their quest.

Mingling with bathing patrons had been successful for them in Tirana, so they decided it would be a good start in Skopje. With their purchases done, Bem and Salar Nassim spent the rest of their day at the grand bathhouse they had passed earlier.

For three days, they struck up conversations in cafés, visited local shops, and socialized in a steam bath every day. Islam forbade gambling, but men still enjoyed a competitive match of Mancala or Checkers without wagering money. Bem and Salar Nassim took the opportunity to play a friendly game whenever they found an empty seat at a game board. They sipped tea at street vendors in the afternoons and lingered in restaurants after their evening meal for a chance to gain information. Bem and Salar Nassim made their search for Fatina known.

They were doing just that when three men in matching robes approached their table. Two taller men flanked a shorter one. All three were strikingly handsome, with smooth features, like painted portraits. Their deep brown eyes were lined with kohl, and their tan faces showed no stubble of a man. Only the wealthy had such ornate gold detailing on their robes. Only guards of the rich had such expensive, curved blades like the ones secured in embossed sheaths on the men's brightly colored sashes.

"Bem Tavares?" the tallest man asked in a gentle voice.

Eunuchs.

"Who are you?" Bem asked in reply.

"You are to come with us," the eunuch ordered.

Both Bem and Salar Nassim stood up.

"Just you," the guard told Bem.

"Who sent you?" Bem wanted to know.

"Alimah, the wife of General Sadik. She is waiting in a carriage around the corner," he answered.

Salar Nassim sat down again. This was what they had waited for. Bem would have to risk going alone.

Bem followed the three strangers around the corner of the lodging house. An enclosed carriage was indeed parked on the edge of the dark street there, as they had said. Oil lamps on each corner of its low roof revealed its shape, and lamplight glowed around the edges of the window covering.

The smallest of the three eunuchs wordlessly waved Bem to step up into the carriage.

Bem did as he was told.

A veiled woman was seated on one of the two bench seats. She motioned to Bem to sit down across from her, and the smaller eunuch climbed in behind him.

"Leave us," the eunuch instructed the veiled woman.

Without protest, she rose, climbed out of the carriage, and then the eunuch took her place across from Bem.

The man removed his headdress, revealing his coiled hair, and smiled at Bem's puzzled expression. "I heard you have been asking about Fatina."

Bem stared hard, disbelieving his own eyes. "Alimah?"

She laughed softly. "You did not recognize me? That is good to know."

"Why did you disguise yourself?"

"I dress like a man so I can see the world again. It is the only way I can get out from behind the walls of my husband's house. Skopje is a beautiful place, would you not agree? When he is gone, like he is this week, I visit the city."

"I compliment you. You succeeded in fooling me," Bem replied, still trying to find the young woman he remembered under the makeup.

She held his stare. "I do hear things behind my husband's walls. Word has come to me that you have been making many friends here, asking many questions. Especially for a dead man," she added.

He sat up tall, taking control. "As you can see, I am not dead. And, as you may have heard, I have come for my wife. Where is she?"

Alimah leaned back on her bench. "Do not be so hasty, Bem Tavares. What makes you think you still have a right to her?"

"She has never stopped being my wife. I have every right."

"She believes she is a widow. Perhaps it is best to keep her as a happy memory and not complicate the present."

"Give her back to me, Alimah. You can find another servant. I will buy her back, if I must."

Alimah laughed, but there was no amusement in her tone, only disdain. "I would gladly give you back your wife, Bem. Believe me; I would include a pouch of silver to have you take her away."

"Then do it," Bem demanded.

"There is one problem that we share. My husband has formed an attachment to Fatina. She is not for sale."

"I heard that. But he has not married her, so he has no claim. She is still mine, and I will take her with me," Bem asserted.

"Before you challenge my husband for Fatina, which I would not recommend, perhaps you would like to ask her yourself."

Bem jumped at the idea. "Please, Alimah. Where can I find her?"

Alimah took a folded paper from her robe pocket. "Unlike me, Fatina does not leave the walls, but she walks the garden every morning after breakfast. Come to the door at nine. I will see to it that you are let in. Here are the directions."

Bem read the parchment. He knew the street. "And you will not stop me from taking her?"

"I will not stop you, Bem."

He hesitated. Alimah had tricked him before. "You knew I was looking for her. Why not just bring Fatina with you tonight?"

"I did not think she would come."

"What have you done to her, Alimah?"

"Meet her yourself tomorrow, Bem. Then you will know."

Alimah knocked on the carriage wall, and the door opened for Bem.

Before he stepped out, he turned to say, "Nine o'clock. I will be there."

The veiled woman climbed into the carriage again, and it rolled away.

Chapter 12

Bem easily found General Sadik's villa from Alimah's instructions. The luxurious home befitted a man of Sadik's high rank in the Ottoman government. Unlike at the other mansions on the broad cobbled street, guards stood before the solid doors that blocked the view into the walled compound. Only the second floor of the building was visible over the garden wall. Iron balconies adorned several upper windows, where one could step out for fresh air.

Looking up at them, Bem willed his wife to walk out onto one of the landings. He imagined her linen robes fluttering carelessly in the light morning breeze. Sadly, Bem could no longer conjure her face in his daydream and longed to see her again. Only a few moments now, and he would hold her in his arms in the garden.

The two soldiers at the street entrance held their long spears in a warning. Bem approached them and announced, "I am Bem Tavares. I believe I am expected."

The guards lowered their weapons and pulled on the iron rings that opened the heavy doors.

Bem walked through in nervous anticipation. He still did not trust that Alimah would just let him take Fatina away after two years of enslavement.

More guards were stationed at the end of the walkway that led to the front of the house. As instructed, Bem didn't go to the house but turned from the main path and disappeared through a hedge of oleander. Nobody stopped him as he continued into the private oasis of General Sadik's walled garden. There, Bem passed servants burdened with yokes of well-water on their shoulders, but he saw no one else on the gravel pathway.

The lush garden had nooks and secluded corners that added to the illusion of space. Bem looked in each one before making his way toward the back of the house, where the flower-lined walkway ended at a stone terrace. In the middle of it was a percolating fountain ringed with marble benches. A veiled woman sat alone there, holding a bundle in her arms.

Bem walked closer and knew this was his lost wife. "Fatina," he breathed out.

The woman set the bundle on her lap and lifted her pale green veil to better see the stranger approaching her. The baby resting on her knees began to fuss. She hastily put it against her shoulder again and stood up to walk away.

Bem could not believe she did not know him. "Stop, Fatina! It is Bem. I have come for you."

She strode toward the back door, but he followed her. "Go away," she warned.

"It's me, Fatina. Chidubem," he called out.

She turned to look at the stranger more closely. He wore ordinary clothing: a simple, belted blue tunic over pleated black trousers. His hair was longer than he had kept it in Egypt, and it was tied tightly with a black cord under his unassuming black cap. He no longer had the windblown curls and rugged beard of the young desert horse trainer that she had fallen in love with. But those dark pleading eyes, they gave him away. She knew they belonged to Bem. Her beloved Bem was alive.

"They told me you died in prison," she said without emotion.

"They put me in prison. Are you not happy to see me alive?"

She held her head high and said, "When they told me you were gone, I stopped thinking about you."

"I have not stopped thinking about you, my love. I have not stopped looking for you. I have not stopped loving you. And now that I have found you, I will take you away from here."

"Away?" She shook her head at the impossibility of it. "No, Bem. I cannot leave."

Bem stepped in front of her and touched her pale face, highlighted in a way he had never seen. Her eyes were lined and shadowed to emphasize their natural beauty. Her lips were tinted a pale red to attract attention to their fullness. Strands of gold and tiny pearls decorated her throat, and clusters of pearls dangled daringly from her ears. The sheer silk over her black hair did not hide the beauty of the intricate braid.

And then it hit him. Fatina really was a pampered concubine, decorated and adorned to please another man, and Bem could hardly contain his agony.

Frustrated that he had lost her, Bem blurted out, "Did you marry him, Fatina?"

"No, but that didn't stop him from having me."

The baby squirmed in her arms, and he asked, "Is the child yours?"

She looked down adoringly and said, "Ahmeti is mine. He is almost seven months old now. He is my whole life."

Bem touched the beautiful boy's brow. "Is Sadik the father?"

"Does it matter, Bem?"

Tears welled in the corners of Bem's sad eyes. "It does."

"I didn't choose to be his plaything, his whore, but that is what I am now. You could never love me again, the way it used to be. Your Fatina is dead, Bem. You need to accept that and leave me in peace." She wiped the tears that escaped her long lashes and steeled herself.

"I won't just walk away and leave you, Fatina."

"You are a fool, Bem, grasping at memories. Our life together is over. It can never be the same again. My life is here now."

"You are wrong, Fatina. Alimah says I can take you with me. She said you can go."

Fatina threw back her head in frustration. "Alimah cannot decide that. Sadik decides," she cried.

"Alimah knows you are still my wife, Fatina. You are not bound to Sadik. You are bound to me."

The baby in her arms began to cry from the shouting.

Fatina rocked him as she paced in front of the fountain. "Forget about me," she pleaded.

Bem came to her side, touched her, and whispered, "How can I forget that the love of my life is enslaved, and I alone can free her? Come with me, Fatina," he begged.

She pushed him away. "Do you know why Alimah wants me gone? She wants Ahmeti. She cannot have him."

Bem wrapped his arms around his wife's waist and held her tightly until he felt her tension ease. He whispered into her scented hair. "I understand that you will choose your son over me. But answer me one question, and then I will leave you to your new life."

Fatina stiffened again under his hold. "Do not make this any harder," she said.

"No," he whispered into her ear. "It is not hard." He took a breath and said, "Tell me that you don't love me, and I will walk away."

She took a step back from the man she once loved more than life itself.

"Do you love me still?" he asked her.

"You were once easy to love, Bem, but my heart has hardened toward men. I don't think I would know how to love you now."

Bem saw Fatina look up at the balcony windows. He turned to see what had distracted her. There was a figure there, behind a thin curtain.

As if that were her signal, Fatina walked away. "Go, Bem. Do not come again," she said without looking back.

At the balcony window, the shadowy figure was gone.

Bem let her leave and was filled with despair when he arrived at the wall's entrance a few moments later.

"Open the door for me. Let me pass," Bem ordered the guard who was blocking his way out.

"The mistress wants you to wait here for her."

The soldier pointed toward the house at Alimah, who descended the front steps. She was elegantly dressed as a woman this time. Her beaded robes surpassed the beauty of Fatina's and confirmed Alimah's status as the first wife of a wealthy general. She wore no makeup or head covering. She had left the house in a hurry to catch him.

Bem met her halfway along the path.

"I was certain you could convince her," Alimah chided. "What happened?"

"She loves the child more than me."

Alimah scoffed. "I told Fatina that I will care for him like my own. I warned her to go while she could."

Bem rubbed his aching temples. "You warned her I was coming today?"

"Yes," Alimah admitted.

"Then why did Fatina not know me?"

"She didn't believe I had seen you and said I was sending an impersonator. She was sure you were dead."

"I am dead to her."

"Now you know your wife is a fool. She missed her chance, and so have you. Goodbye, Bem Tavares," Alimah said.

Bem grabbed her hand as she turned to leave. "Before I go, I must know one thing."

Alimah braced herself.

"If Fatina gave your husband a son, why didn't he take her as his second wife?"

"I will not be usurped."

Her stance seemed daring, and he questioned her reasoning, "If Sadik is the ruthless husband you portray him to be, why should he care what you think?"

Alimah held her head high at the insult. "My adoring father is the reason. Mehmed is where he is because of my father's influence. I would divorce him before I let him take Fatina as a wife, and then Mehmed would have to explain to my father why I hate him so much. Mehmed knows he would fall far in his ranking if my father spoke badly of his former son-in-law."

After listening to the spoiled woman's troubles, Bem had just one more question: "So, you don't love your husband, and your husband may not love you. But tell me, Alimah. Does your husband love Fatina?"

Alimah's sudden laugh caught him off-guard.

"Love?" she repeated with disdain. "Sadik does not love anyone but himself. Of course, he desires to sire sons with her, but I could give him sons if Fatina left," she reflected cunningly. "I can be Ahmeti's mother, and my husband will come to my bed instead."

"Is that what you gain from all this?"

She met his unwavering stare. "Yes, Bem. Is that so hard to understand?"

Her callous expression softened, and she said, "I loved Fatina once, you know that, Bem. But knowing all of this, the question I ask of you is this: could you still love Fatina?"

"I cannot fault her for bravely carrying on," he maintained.

"She has been used by another man, Bem, loved in twisted ways. Can you stomach that?"

"We all do what we have to do. You yourself must understand that, Alimah."

Her voice was icy when she demanded, "Take her away, Bem."

"She refused, remember? We both lost today."

"So, what will you do? Leave Skopje?"

"Yes. I have my answer, and I will travel on. Tell them to open the door for me."

"Give me until tomorrow. I know I can convince her."

Bem shook his head with pity. "I will not come back, Alimah. It is over, and I am leaving."

"Yes, leave, but give me one day. Please. If I succeed, Fatina will be at the stone bridge at noon tomorrow. Look for her then."

Bem shrugged with dismay. "Do you hate her so much?"

"I do hate her."

Hate was a force that could be relied on, and Bem began to believe that Alimah might succeed. "I will stay until tomorrow and look for her on the bridge. Twelve o'clock."

Alimah waved, and the guards opened the way out for him.

Within a quarter-hour, Bem was back in the city center. He hardly noticed the midmorning shoppers in the narrow streets as he pushed through the crowds, reliving the last hour again in his thoughts.

Salar Nassim was waiting for Bem outside the lodging house. He was sitting on tall cushions on the veranda and smoked a hookah in the morning sun.

"Bem," Salar Nassim called out when he walked past him.

Startled back to the present, Bem sat down on the cushion next to his friend.

Salar Nassim imagined it had not gone in Bem's favor from his friend's expression. He asked, "What happened?"

Bem stared ahead at the men mingling at the shop across the alleyway. "It is more complicated than I expected."

When Bem did not explain further, Salar Nassim prodded, "Complicated?"

Bem bowed his head and heard himself say the words he dreaded, "Fatina will not come with me. She has a child now, and her life is better here than what I could ever offer her. I think she does not even love me anymore."

Salar Nassim drew another long drag from his water pipe and asked, "Is this child Sadik's?"

"Yes. A baby boy," Bem said miserably.

Salar Nassim handed Bem the pipe and said, "The son belongs to the father. To go with you, she must give up the boy."

Bem breathed in the burning smoke and breathed out a part of his anger with it. "She has chosen him."

"It is hard to compete with a baby for a woman's love, Bem."

"Now that I have seen her again, I want her so badly."

"I am sorry, Bem. You tried so hard. I thought it would have ended differently."

Bem inhaled again. The fragrant smoke worked to ease his sorrow and clear his troubled mind. "There is one more chance," he said.

"You have done your best, Bem. Do not torture yourself."

Bem explained, "Alimah thinks she can convince Fatina to leave the child with her and escape with me. If she succeeds, Fatina will meet us at the stone bridge tomorrow. If my wife is not there at high noon, then my quest is over, and we will ride on to Athens without her."

Salar Nassim nodded solemnly at the proposal. The water gurgled as he inhaled deeply. He handed the pipe to Bem and said, "It is in God's hands now."

Bem leaned back on the cushion and blew the vapors from his lungs. "That is what I am afraid of."

Chapter 13

Tirana, 15 August 1649

Jero stared at the bars, mournful that his nightmare persisted. But the misery was real, not a dream. Jero's peeling skin and aching hands were proof of it.

He opened one fist and slowly unwound the tattered strips of filthy cloth. His exposed flesh stung painfully as he examined the cuts and weeping blisters the spade and stones had caused. These wounds would heal with time, like his burnt and blistered shoulders had.

He tightened the bandages with a sigh of self-pity. How had it all gone so wrong? It seemed like a lifetime ago since he had seen Ruby. She, Patrik, and Soren would have made it to Thessaloniki by now. They promised to come back. Mauro would have gotten the unfortunate news by now, too, and his brother would be on his way to Tirana. Jero took comfort in those thoughts and shut his eyes to think about pleasant things.

The *click-clack* of boots on the swept stone floor at the end of the corridor woke Jero from his meditation. The steady steps of his guard came closer. Jero didn't bother to look up for the inspection. Emir came every day to his cell, stood in front of the bars, nodded, and then left again.

On this day, the footsteps stopped but did not walk away. The figure that darkened Jero's doorway was not Emir but Captain Poljani. He held a wooden platter and slid it under the bottom bars.

"Get up, Peric," he said in his Slavic dialect.

Jero rose from his straw bed to face the commander with a straight back, his stinging hands locked behind him for support.

"I heard you managed to bury the Christian corpses. Your God will judge you well for that, when you meet him after your hanging. That must give you some consolation."

"The magistrate will find no reason to hang me," Jero replied defiantly.

Poljani did not argue the point. Instead, he quietly paced in front of the bars and contemplated his prisoner. "My men and I will be away for a few days. In the meantime, I suggest you get used to our meal offerings here." He pointed to the dish of lumpy brown lentils with a triangle of flatbread covering them. The platter sat in the middle of the dirty floor between the two men.

The captain added, "I have reminded the soldiers that they are to take their whores on their own time, not during the night watch. Enjoy your meal, Lord Peric."

He turned and walked away with the same steady clack of his hard soles against the stone.

In a rush, Jero grabbed the bars and shouted after him, "Baric! B-A-R-I-C!"

Captain Poljani was not a man whom one taught a lesson, spelling or otherwise.

He walked back to the cell doorway. "Are you unhappy here alone in your cell, Peric? Do you need some company?" the captain asked with a mock-friendliness. "Shall I have the guards take you out to keep you entertained today?"

"When I am released, Captain, you will be very sorry if you arrange one more punishment for me."

"Do you not see these bars in front of you? You are hardly in a position to make threats, Peric."

Poljani was perplexed when Jero ignored the threat and began to drag the heel of his boot in front of the doorway.

Jero formed B, A, R, I, and C slowly, letter by letter, in the soft muck on the cell floor.

Then, in the same mocking tone Poljani had used, Jero said with an ominous glare, "My name is Baric, sir. I have only had the name a short time, but I have spent my whole life looking upon the spelling of it. And I am certain you have it wrong."

Captain Poljani sneered as the two held their contemptuous stares. Then the captain walked away, and Jero went back to wait out the long, solitary day on his pile of straw.

~*~

Patrik and Soren left Thessaloniki after only a few days despite the protests from his family to stay longer. Demetrius and Celine tried to convince them that Bem and Salar Nassim, with Mauro's help, could win Jero's freedom. But Patrik had promised Jero that he would defend him at his trial, and he could not break that promise to his new friend.

While at the Kokkinos' villa, Patrik and Soren had managed to settle their personal affairs. They sold all their weapons, except their favorite swords, and stashed their hard-won silver and gold in legitimate and illegitimate places, taking only enough to see them through the next month or two. When they finally said their goodbyes, they knew in their hearts that it would be a long time before they ventured that way again.

In contrast to the difficult departure, it was an easy ride back to Tirana. This time, their load was light, and they had good weather on good roads. They did not pack much in the way of supplies and treated themselves to a real bed and tasty meals each night on their last journey through Ottoman lands.

As they waited for their dinner one evening, Soren voiced what he had been thinking for days: "What if Baron Baric is not at his castle when the courier arrives? Were they not planning to travel to Venice soon?"

"Resi said they were leaving at the end of August, and I am confident Mauro would drop all other plans to help his brother. He will be there when we arrive."

"I hope Salar Nassim is not too disappointed in our decision," Soren added.

Patrik shook his head. "Nassim knows we have to say our goodbyes sometime. Bem will find his wife without us, but I owe this to Jero, and to Ruby."

"Will we get to France in time?" Soren asked with worry. "Two more days of traveling, then five days just waiting for the trial to begin. I hope this magistrate is not delayed somewhere."

"I think you need a drink, Soren. Maybe they have a bottle of wine in a cellar somewhere for us Christians."

Patrik waved to get the serving girl's attention. The house's patron came to their table with a corked bottle and filled their two cups.

"We will toast to good fortune all around—for Jero's trial to happen quickly and for our smooth sailing," Patrik said.

Soren held his glass up and agreed, "To happy endings and new beginnings."

~*~

Restless, Jero had not yet fallen asleep. He thought his eyes were playing tricks on him when he noticed a glow growing brighter in the dark corridor. He hurried to the bars when he recognized who was coming.

"How did you get in here?" Jero asked in a hushed voice. "Captain Poljani said—"

"Never mind what he said," Zerina interrupted anxiously.

Zerina had been visiting for a week now and had always been so kind, so soothing. Tonight was different. She was afraid.

"What did you do to anger the captain?" she demanded.

"I, um, I could not help it," Jero said guiltily.

"Have you no sense of self-preservation?" she hissed. "Are you Venetians too arrogant and pigheaded to keep yourselves alive?"

Defending his actions, he whispered back, "I will not be persecuted by a madman."

"Not even to save yourself?" she pleaded.

Jero was tired, aching, defeated. The last thing he wanted now was to be lectured. "It's easy for you to say this when I am the one stuck behind these bars."

She held the lamp to her face. "I have my own personal bars, Jero. Children are scared of me. Women turn their faces, pointing out my shame. But I don't lash out. I stay quiet. Why is that so hard for you?"

Jero leaned against the bars, no longer hiding his hopelessness. "I am sorry, Zerina. I know you are only trying to help. I will ignore Poljani next time."

"I am afraid it's too late," she said. "I caught part of what some soldiers were saying at the restaurant earlier. You are in serious trouble, Jero."

"My trouble cannot get more serious, Zerina. I am in jail, remember?"

"Things happen to prisoners," she warned.

"The captain cannot hang me without a trial; too many people are coming to my defense. Until then I will go without food if I must, to keep him from poisoning me."

"You could hang yourself while waiting. Or fall on a knife and bleed to death. Or provoke the guards so they must kill you."

Jero held Zerina's stare in the lamplight. She was dead serious.

"I won't do any of that," he answered cautiously.

"It only matters whether Captain Poljani said you did, Jero."

She looked down the hallway. All was dark and quiet. "I have decided I am going to help you," she said.

"Help me? How?"

"I am going to help you escape."

He laughed under his breath. "You and I both know the only way out is through the front office, and it is guarded."

She quickly explained, "The local regiment was called away for some sort of military exercise. The usual guards have gone with Captain Poljani. I know the two soldiers on duty tonight. They are brothers—Bamir and Bashkim. They let me in just now."

"What are you saying? That these soldiers will let me go? I doubt that."

"I am saying they won't see you go. I told them I needed five minutes to bring you food, and then I would pay them."

"With the money Salar Nassim left you?"

"With sex, Jero," she told him unashamedly. "My face may be repulsive, but I know ways to distract men with the rest of me."

"But there are two guards."

"They like to do things together," she maintained. "You will have to trust me that my plan will work."

Jero shook his head. "No, Zerina, you don't have to—"

"I am sorry if you thought I was somehow something else, Jero—something better. It is the only currency I have to help you. I am counting on your brother to pay me back for my deeds tonight. Will he?"

"Yes. Mauro will reward you, and he will not care how you did it. Nor will I." He rattled the bars. "Do you have the key?"

"Shhh!" She turned to check if they were still alone. "I will get you the key, but you must first promise something in return."

"Anything."

She put her small hand through the bars and took his bandaged hand in hers. "You must swear to me, Jero, that you will not change your mind once you are out."

Jero squeezed her hand. "I swear to God."

She smiled her rare smile and said, "Here are my terms. My, um, brother Aleksander will unlock the door for you. But you must take him with you."

"Why?"

"Because Aleksander is clever and knows all the secret ways out of Tirana. He will help you get your horse and then lead you to the road to Thessaloniki."

"Is my horse still in the stables?"

"Yes," she whispered. "Your friends took care to pay in advance. I checked today, and the horse was there."

"I will be glad for your brother's help but just to the crossroads. I will be quicker on my own with only one horse."

"He is small, just a boy. He can ride with you," she argued.

Jero regretted his hasty promise. "I don't know, Zerina."

"That is my one condition. It is your share of the payment for getting you out. He is a good boy. Take him back to your castle, and he will serve you well."

"No, Zerina. I am not going to Croatia. I am—"

She held her ground. "Please, Jero. There is nothing but dishonor for him here. He has no parents and will take to the streets. That is a terrible life for a boy. Please. Promise me."

What did the promise matter if Jero did not believe the plan would work? He gave in.

"I will take him back to Croatia with me. I promise."

She squeezed his hand in thanks. "Now, it might take a few minutes, so do not worry. Aleksander will come soon."

Zerina hurried down the corridor to the waiting guards, leaving Jero alone in the dark again.

Chapter 14

Aleksander had come as far as the front door of the jailhouse with his mother. The boy waited under the shuttered window that flanked the entrance and watched through the slats for the room to empty.

Aleksander knew his mother worked for the soldiers at night. Even at the young age of eleven, he understood the shopkeepers' names for Zerina: whore, slut, prostitute. She told him the extra money she earned was to buy him an apprenticeship when he turned thirteen. But Aleksander didn't want to learn to lay bricks under the hot sun or weave carpets in a dark room somewhere. He wanted to run free.

Old Isaak paid a few coins each week for Aleksander's help at the restaurant, but Isaak gave that directly to his mother. Other times, Aleksander would hustle on the streets. Although his mother had forbidden him to run with the orphans, Aleksander liked their adventures together and the extra money he made just for himself.

While waiting for Zerina's cue, the boy contemplated her last words of advice. She had warned that the rich foreigner seemed to be a kind man while locked up, but he should not be counted on for kindness once he was free. "In the real world, wealthy people look upon poor people with contempt," his mother had said. "Do as he asks, do not complain, work hard, and then come back to me one day." He promised his mother that he would. But if he did not like his new master, he had already decided he would simply run away.

~*~

Bashkim and Bamir were farmhands who occasionally filled in for the night guards at the jailhouse. Bashkim was the older of the two and was a handful. Zerina had met him years ago when Bashkim did odd jobs for Isaak at the restaurant. He still came around after payday to buy her services. Zerina preferred his brother, Bamir, a quiet man who was easily satisfied with just a quick lifting of her skirts.

"There she is!" Bashkim said to his brother. "What took you so long, Zerina? Did you feed him by hand?"

She managed a smile and answered the oaf coyly, "He was asleep and, uh, I had to rouse him. It took a while."

"Well, I'm already roused. Let's get on with this, darling." Bashkim took her by the waist and pulled her toward the desk.

Bamir sat at the same desk and watched his brother grope at the ribbons that held Zerina's blouse closed. He never minded watching and waiting for his turn.

Zerina pushed Bashkim's hands off and took a step away. "Not in here, Bashkim," she cooed. "I think we need some privacy."

He laughed at her suggestion and unfastened the opening to his trousers. "It is past midnight, Zerina. No one will come in. Bamir! Clear off the desk."

Bamir carefully moved the quills and ink off the desktop. It was the elder brother that Zerina had to persuade to follow her. Bamir did what he was told.

She flirted and said, "I have something different to offer tonight, but it needs privacy."

"Do tell, sweetheart!" Bashkim growled. He rubbed his hand against his trousers to get himself in the mood again.

Zerina moved toward the commander's office. "Do you remember the time I was with both of you at once? I think you especially enjoyed that, Bashkim."

"And if I remember right, I think you did, too, darling." He said to Bamir, "You can go at her from behind this time. I'll stand in front of the bitch."

Bamir was eager to get into the action. With loosened trousers, he stood behind Zerina, rubbing against her skirt.

She had to slow them down.

"Oh, that is nice, Bamir. But let's go into the captain's office," Zerina insisted. "We'll shut the door, just to be sure."

She tugged on Bashkim's hand to make him follow her, pretending to be eager to please the horny guards.

He pulled her to him and asked, "Why there? You can't make too much noise with me deep in your throat."

She reached inside his loose trousers and reminded him, "I am not supposed to be here. Poljani's new orders, remember? But if someone does come in, I can stay hidden away in the office, and then we can start right back up again."

Bamir was the stupid one, but he could be counted on to follow the rules. "She's right, Bashkim. Poljani will make eunuchs of us if word gets out that we disobeyed his orders on the first night. I want to keep my prick."

Bashkim seemed to consider the possibility.

Zerina pulled on Bashkim's arm to get him moving. "Come on, lover. It'll be fun. We'll do it on Poljani's desk."

"I'm all about fun, Zerina, darling," he gruffly agreed. "Why don't you open that blouse of yours and get us in the mood again."

Bamir followed the half-dressed couple into the captain's office and shut the door behind them.

Aleksander had to hurry now. He opened the door a crack and slipped through, scurrying across the open space on all fours, afraid that some unseen night watchman would detect him.

His mother had told him that the ring of keys was on a peg at the side of the desk and that Jero was alone in the last cell.

With keys in hand, the boy opened the massive door to the cellblock and crept down the dark corridor, past the sleeping men in the first barred chambers.

Jero didn't know why he was so surprised when the small figure appeared at his cell. Wordlessly, Aleksander tried several of the thick keys on the ring until one clicked in the lock. He gingerly slid the iron latch back. Just as quickly, Jero was out the door, and the boy shut and locked it again to cover the escape. Together, they slunk down the hallway, past Roman and the other unaware prisoners. Jero wished he could do something to free them, too, but there would never be time for all of them to get away.

Once in the lamplit office, Aleksander hung the ring back on its peg. He peered out the front entrance to check that no one was in the courtyard before opening it to leave.

Jero glanced back in the direction of the captain's office. Muffled noises could be heard from behind the door, grunts and moans that filled Jero with guilt.

Beyond the jailhouse, there was no light from the surrounding buildings to guide them. Jero would have been helplessly lost in the dark, but Aleksander easily found the way to the stables.

The boy hurried Jero along and led him through a narrow alleyway to a low door at the back of the stables. They listened for movements, but it seemed even the horses were asleep.

"Wait here," the boy said. He came back a minute later and whispered, "I opened the front gate for the horse. If we hurry, we won't be seen. The groom is asleep in the hayloft."

Creeping through the stables, Jero looked for Zeus, but his friends had left him Cairo.

The quarter moon shone enough light through the open doorway to find his tack hanging on the hook, and Jero prayed the skittish horse would not protest being bridled. With no time to spare, he left the saddle behind.

Jero whispered soothing words to the fickle beast as he fixed the reins. To Jero's relief, the horse seemed eager to get away from his imprisonment as well.

While leading Cairo, Jero fixed his eyes on the small boy as Aleksander scurried down the unlit streets. When they reached the last building on the edge of the town, the boy finally stopped.

"We can ride now. The main road is in this direction." He pointed to the east, where a ribbon of gray light touched the edge of the black horizon.

Jero told the boy what he needed to hear himself, "Morning is near. We will ride until the sun breaks and then find a place to hide for the day. They will surely be looking for me."

"I have some food," Aleksander said proudly.

Jero hadn't noticed that his new companion had a bag slung over his narrow shoulder. "That is a good boy. What is your name, again?"

"Aleksander."

Jero quickly lifted the boy onto Cairo's bare back and then heaved himself up behind him. "Aleksander," Jero repeated. "Is that what they call you? That is a grown-up name for a little boy."

"I am not a little boy," the child protested. "I am practically, um, thirteen." He remembered what his mother had said about his manners and added, "Sir."

Jero sized up the skinny boy in front of him. "Practically thirteen? I beg your pardon, Aleksander."

"Well," the boy reflected as he settled in on the horse's back, "my mother calls me Sasho."

Jero held the reins carefully around his passenger. "That is a good name for a young man. If it is all right, I will call you Sasho, too."

"That would be fine, sir."

The boy's formality made Jero smile. "You do not need to call me 'sir.' We are friends now. Call me Jero." He flicked the reins and nudged Cairo. The horse seemed as eager as Jero to put Tirana behind him.

Jero leaned in and asked Sasho, "Is this a good road for horses?"

Sasho seemed to not understand what the man meant. He had never ridden on a horse on any road. "I think so. It is used by carts and wagons every day."

"Then hold on tight, Sasho. We need to put some distance behind us." Then Jero told the stallion, "You better be up for this, Cairo."

Jero kicked the horse's sides with the heels of his worn boots. Cairo did not disappoint him and sped down the road toward the sunrise while Sasho clung to the beast's neck with all his strength.

~*~

The packed-dirt road led them into the countryside, where they eventually came to cultivated fields flanked by dense woods. A ditch filled with diverted water for irrigation had been carved into the landscape. Jero stopped to get a better look at their surroundings.

"We'll hide in these woods before any travelers see us on the road. You can sleep a bit if you are tired," he said to Sasho.

"I am, Jero. I don't think I can hold on like this much longer."

Jero dismounted and helped the boy down. "You did well, Sasho. Now let's find where this water comes from and get a good drink ourselves."

They ventured deeper into the dark grove of trees on the edge of the roadway and found a spring. The adrenaline from his escape was long used up, and Jero lumbered with exhaustion. He looked around the tranquil woods for a soft place with grass where they could rest.

"Here is a good spot," Jero told Sasho.

Sasho put his bag against a tree and plopped down next to it. He opened the flap and assessed what was in there. "Do you want to eat, Jero? I don't have much. Just a haunch of roasted lamb and a round of bread I took from Isaak's kitchen. At least I am not there for him to beat me when he finds the food missing."

Jero hobbled Cairo in some moist grass and sat down next to Sasho. He assured the boy, "No one will beat you. When I take you back home, I will pay Isaak for the meal."

"My mother said I am not to come back," the boy declared. "She said I am to go with you, and you will give me a job."

Jero was puzzled. "Your sister told me you do not have a mother."

Sasho frowned when he said, "I don't have a sister."

"Zerina is your sister, is she not?"

Sasho laughed at the foreign man's mistake. "No, Jero. Zerina is my mother."

Jero slumped. His promise to Zerina weighed heavily on him now, but he was grateful to have company—even that of a burdensome boy.

Jero took off his tattered jacket, rolled it into a ball, and leaned back against the tree. "We will talk some more about your mother, but first we need some sleep. We will eat your feast of lamb and bread when we wake."

The boy was already sleeping.

~*~

The thick canopy of branches protected the weary escapees from the hot sun. While they slept the morning away, other creatures were on the prowl. Feral dogs sniffed their way into Jero and Sasho's camp, emboldened by the enticing smell of a quick meal. Jero and Sasho slept like the dead while sharp fangs bit the canvas bag with the savory joint and bread. It only took a moment for the crafty dogs to drag their dinner away.

Cairo had been grazing in a small square of green grass where Jero had hobbled him when the scent of the predators made him whinny nervously.

Jero heard Cairo's warning, but he convinced his tired mind that it was not his problem.

Sasho woke in a panic when he heard the growls of the dogs fighting among themselves in the underbrush. "Dogs, Jero! They took my bag!"

The growls of the feral pack were frightening. Jero was on his feet after the boy. "Stop! You won't get it back."

The boy collapsed against the tree again. "I am hungry. What will we do for food, Jero?"

"For now, have a good drink of water to fill your belly. I saw a farmhouse not far up the road earlier. We can ask if they have some bread and broth to spare. How does that sound?"

Sasho nodded eagerly at the plan.

Jero shook out his jacket and slipped it on, and then he untied Cairo. The sun had crossed to the west, revealing that they had slept the day away before the dogs ruined it. He considered his plan again. Even though the turnoff to the farmhouse was not far up the highway, Jero was worried they might encounter soldiers searching for them. Still, they would have to take their chances.

~*~

A dirt trek crossed the farmer's field for a quarter-mile from the main route before reaching the stone farmhouse. A lone woman with a baby strapped to her back was digging up roots in her kitchen garden.

The woman looked up in surprise when she heard a horse trotting toward her. Her husband and sons were working in the back field and would not be back until sunset. She cursed under her breath that she had not brought a spade from the shed. Soldiers had visited their farm a few hours earlier and had warned the tenants about the escaped murderer. And now, there he was.

Jero and Sasho dismounted and approached the garden fence. "Hello there, miss," Jero called over in Turkish.

"Please, don't hurt me!" she called out.

Jero looked to Sasho to translate for him. "Tell her we will do her no harm. We just want some bread to take on our way."

Sasho went toward her and repeated Jero's plea.

The farmer's wife backed away and pointed toward her house. "Inside, on the table. Take what you want and be gone," she shouted.

Her obvious fear shook Jero to his core. Somehow, even on this isolated farm, this woman knew he was hunted. But hunger prevailed. He gave the horse's reins to Sasho and then dashed to the front door.

The woman began to shout again, this time waving to a man running across the open field. "Help, Fatih! We are being robbed by the murderer!"

"No," Jero found himself shouting back, "it is all right."

But it was not all right. The farmer had a sickle in his hand, ready to defend his wife and child.

Jero ran and called out, "Bring the horse!"

Sasho was already on Cairo's back, and in no time, the two were galloping empty-handed down the dusty road.

When they were at a safe distance down the highway, Jero slowed his horse and said, "It is going to be a difficult journey to Thessaloniki. We have no food. No money. And now we know the soldiers are searching for me."

"We can hide, like we did earlier. And we can hunt or fish. Look, there are plums on that tree over there. We can eat some of those. That isn't stealing, is it, Jero?"

"Plums will not sustain us, Sasho, and we have no line to catch fish or rabbits. And even if we did, making a fire to cook them will be difficult with no flint or dagger."

Jero lifted the boy off the horse's back and set him on the ground. "It is too dangerous for me to take you along, Sasho. Take some plums and go home, boy. It is maybe two days on foot, or you might come across a merchant who will let you ride in his cart. You cannot come with me."

The boy remembered his promise to his mother and said, "I am not hungry. Really, I'm not. Let me stay with you. I will help you get to Thessaloniki."

"It will not be easy, Sasho."

"I don't mind."

"We will have to hide in daylight and ride in the dark until we are far enough away from here."

"I am good at hiding. Don't send me back," Sasho pleaded.

The child's bravery uplifted Jero's spirits. He slid off Cairo. "Quickly then, before anyone comes by. We will fill our pockets and find a good place to hide."

The two companions took their bounty of plums and rode another half hour until they came upon a rocky outcropping along the road. Jero scouted it out and said, "We can rest here. There is shade from the sun and a little grass for the horse."

Their hiding place behind the tall boulders proved to be a good spot for the day. They couldn't be seen by any soldiers searching for them or travelers passing by, like Patrik and Soren. They unknowingly rode within shouting distance of their friend's hiding place that same afternoon. The two mercenaries would learn about Jero's escape soon enough.

Chapter 15

Tirana, 17 August 1649

After a night of camping on the outskirts of Tirana, Patrik and Soren rode in early to join their friends for breakfast.

The streets were waking. Merchants propped up canopies outside their doors to shield their stores against the coming rays of the August sun. Their eyes followed the mercenaries as the two took a turn from the main street and rode down the familiar alleyway to the stables.

Henrik, the stable master, was not to be found, but the groom was there, watering the horses.

"That is odd. Nassim's and Bem's horses are gone," Soren remarked to Patrik.

Patrik asked the boy, "There should be three of our party's horses in your care. Did our friends already take them out this morning?"

"Not this morning, sir," the groom answered anxiously. He set his bucket down and left out the back door.

Patrik shrugged off the boy's rudeness. They would check for Bem and Salar Nassim at the inn.

~*~

The inn's dining room was empty at that early hour. Only Isaak's daughter was there, sweeping the stone floor. She hurried off through the kitchen entrance when she saw Patrik and Soren take a seat at a table near the bar.

The old patron himself came out to greet them. "You've come back. Welcome." There was a surprise in his voice the mercenaries did not catch.

"We would like to order breakfast," Soren said in his best Turkish.

"Have our friends already eaten?" Patrik asked casually. "We didn't see their horses in the stables. Did they mention where they were going?"

Isaak cleared his throat and replied, "Yes, well, I believe they have gone for good."

"When was this?" Patrik demanded.

"Um, I don't remember the exact day. There has been so much going on."

Isaak went behind the bar and began searching a shelf there. "They left you a note. Salar Nassim insisted you would want it, so I put it somewhere safe. Let me think." He scratched his head with worry.

Soren interrupted Isaak's search when he asked, "Was the Venetian with them?"

"The one in jail? No, sir. But he is gone, just the same," Isaak replied. He hastily pulled out a small wooden chest from under the counter and rummaged through some papers. "Here it is!"

Puzzled, Patrik asked the innkeeper, "How is he gone? Did the Venetian's brother arrive and bail him out?"

"The Venetian escaped," Isaak said as though he expected Patrik to know this already.

Patrik and Soren exchanged anxious glances.

"Did Salar Nassim and Bem go after him?" Patrik asked urgently.

"Your friends actually left a short time after you did. They weren't here when the Venetian broke out of his cell. That was only two days ago." Isaak put Salar Nassim's letter on the counter and said, "This might explain it."

Patrik broke the seal, and Soren read along with him, looking over Patrik's shoulder.

"That does explain it. They found Fatina," Soren said.

Patrik turned again to Isaak and asked, "The letter says Bem got information from a visitor. Who called on him, do you know?"

"I am just an innkeeper," Isaak said, "so how would I know who visited your friend?"

Patrik was growing impatient. "Because it is your inn, Isaak."

Soren slid a coin across the table in front of Isaak. "Think hard, now."

The innkeeper pocketed the money and recollected, "An army officer visited their chamber the day before they left. He seemed to be an old friend of Bem's. They had dinner together."

"Then they left? Just like that? It seems strange they did not wait for Mauro," Patrik wondered aloud.

"Is he the Venetian baron?" Isaak asked. "They left him a note as well."

Patrik asked, "But he hasn't arrived?"

"No, I would have heard talk of it if he had."

"Bem and Nassim wouldn't abandon a friend in need," Soren reflected. "There must be something more to it."

"Oh, then I should explain," Isaak said, fidgeting anxiously that he would upset the two sellswords with his news.

Patrik and Soren stared at him.

Isaak went on to tell them, "Your friends took care that the Venetian was fed. They paid my servant Zerina to bring him food. I didn't even know about it until she was arrested. It was my food, of course," he added with annoyance.

"Arrested? Did she help him escape?" Soren asked.

Isaak took off his cap and scratched an imaginary itch. "I don't know how she could have. The cell was locked, and the keys were with the guards the whole time. But your guess is right. The jailers believe that she did."

"Maybe it was a sympathetic guard," Patrik reasoned.

"I don't know, except they needed to blame someone."

Patrik groaned. "If Jero had just waited two more days."

Isaak leaned in and confided, "If he had lasted."

"Lasted? Was he ill?" Soren asked.

"Only from his punishment. But I heard he had been recovering from that."

Patrik demanded, "Tell a straight story, will you? What punishment?"

Isaak sat down at their table and explained, "Rumor has it that the Venetian got under Captain Poljani's skin. It was your friend's arrogance, the soldiers said. They thought the captain was planning something to keep him in his place, maybe even something . . . lethal. But then the squadron got called away for some ceremony in Sophia, and that night your friend disappeared."

Patrik asked, "Did they send out a search party?"

"In all directions, yes," Isaak reported. "His horse was gone from the stables. Still, there are only two ways out of town for miles, and he only had a few hours advantage. Curiously, no one up or down the highway remembers seeing his horse go by. They decided his horse must have stumbled in the dark, and he is dead in a ditch somewhere. The soldiers called off the search."

Patrik blew out a breath of relief. He nodded to Soren, who had reached the same conclusion. Jero would surely have been heading east to Thessaloniki. If he had been dead in a ditch, Patrik or Soren would have noticed along the way, or they would have recognized his horse on the road if someone else was riding it. With a rested horse and his wits about him, Jero seemed to have escaped his hunters.

Patrik took some coins from his pouch and put them into Isaak's hand. "This is for Jero's food and for your troubles," he said. "Tell Baron Baric the same thing you told us, and keep his note safe until he comes."

Isaak nodded that he would.

"Jero has been spared his trial," Patrik reflected. "He will find his way to Ruby. He is on his own now."

"We should be going," Soren said.

"We haven't had our breakfast," Patrik protested.

Isaak warned, "I would leave Tirana before someone hears you are looking for your friend. The police may decide to jail you in the Venetian's place until Poljani returns. I'll have Galena pack you something to take with you."

He shouted toward the kitchen door, "Galena!"

"I heard!" Galena hollered back.

Isaak shrugged and remarked, "Daughters can be a bit headstrong."

While they waited for their food, Soren asked Isaak, "Do ships sail to the Mediterranean from your coastline?"

Isaak thought for a moment. "The nearest port is three hours away. A few ships leave from there, but it depends on which direction you are going."

Soren shot Patrik a sideways glance and said, "What if one is going west to France?"

Patrik shook his head and chuckled. They had not yet agreed on France, but he would not argue about it just now.

Isaak answered as best he could, "Bigger ships sailing west all leave from Ragusa, but you could catch a ride from a local fisherman. They come and go from that port often."

Patrik asked, "And if we wanted to sell our horses, what would you recommend?"

"Ah, yes, I forgot you have horses. Fine ones, too, I am sure," Isaak noted with a clear interest in the outcome.

"We would expect a fair price for them," Soren said, emphasizing 'fair.'

Isaak rubbed his bearded chin, deciding how he would answer. "Henrik at the stables will buy them from you. You may have to haggle a bit, but Henrik is a fair man."

Galena approached the table with two cloth bundles and shyly set them down. Her father nodded his thanks, and she hurried away through the kitchen door again.

Each man added a sack to his shoulder bag. "Thank you, Isaak," they said in unison.

"Good day to you, sirs, and good luck in France," Isaak replied.

When they had left, the innkeeper went to the bar and put the wooden box back in its hiding place. He found the corked bottle of wine he had been selling to his Christian customers and poured himself a full glass, drinking it down in one long gulp. Isaak then counted the coins the mercenaries had left him. After such a payment, he would honor his promises. But if anyone had seen him talking to Jero's friends that morning, he might hang before he could spend his growing cash coffer.

Chapter 16

The granite boulders cast long shadows over the landscape, covering Jero like a cold blanket. The chill woke him from his dreamless sleep. He felt dazed. Where was he? What was he doing lying in the dust? It took him a moment before he remembered that he was running for his life.

Jero gave Sasho a nudge with the toe of his boot. The ring he had hidden there rattled, and that gave him purpose. "Time to go," Jero told the boy.

"Is there water?" Sasho asked hoarsely.

"We will find some. Come on. Let us put some miles behind us before it is full dark."

They traveled for two days in this new rhythm: sleeping during the day, riding all night, always heading east, waiting to find some sign that they were on the right road.

So far, the turnoffs were marked with the names of the villages in each direction. Jero anxiously waited for the marker directing him south to Thessaloniki. Where else would this road lead, if not there, Jero thought.

Sasho proved to be a good traveling companion. He didn't complain about the jarring ride as he sat in front of Jero on the horse's shoulders, nor about the missed meals that could hardly be replaced with the stolen pears and figs they found growing along the roadway.

But on that third morning, Sasho's gnawing hunger, and a mistimed encounter, would ruin their chances of finding their way home.

~*~

It was daybreak. The two had just settled in their new hiding place off the road beyond some sparse woods when Sasho heard the bleating of a goat. His stomach growled loudly to match it.

"Milk," he whispered to himself sleepily, "that would fill my belly."

He glanced over at Jero. His chest moved up and down rhythmically. Asleep.

Sasho tried to sleep, but he couldn't ignore the distant yammering of the nanny goat. Lying there, Sasho imagined he could catch the goat, drink his fill, and maybe even bring some milk back to share with Jero somehow. With his hunger satisfied, he would be able to sleep away the day.

With that plan in mind, the boy crept in the direction of the noise. He broke through the tangled underbrush and found himself at the edge of a gypsy camp. Three caravan wagons were parked in a triangle, two horses and several mules were tied to the nearby trees, and a dozen people were gathered around small tables in the center of it all, eating their breakfast.

The bleating goat was within sight of the gypsies. He could not risk it.

Disappointed, Sasho turned to sneak away through the bushes again, but a new temptation made him look back. A stack of freshly made flatbread sat on the window ledge of one of the wagons. The smell was delicious.

While the Romani were in an animated conversation, Sasho slunk ahead and slipped two rounds off the stack. Crouched down, he was sure the Romani had not noticed him from their tables. But the boy had not counted on someone coming into camp from the woods. The moment he took flight with the bread under his arm, Sasho ran right into the family patriarch himself.

Chavdar was a trader, a businessman, a Romani gypsy—clever and sly, corrupt perhaps—but he had never been a thief. And he would not be robbed in his own camp, not even by a hungry boy wanting only a round of bread to fill his aching middle.

~*~

Sasho's distant cry for help pulled Jero out of his slumber. He jumped up and looked around for the missing boy. After not finding him in their hidden enclave, Jero followed the voices coming from the edge of the woods. Jero was terrified that something awful had happened to his little companion, and he was right.

Jero rushed through the opening between the tall wagons to find a shocking scene. "Stop! What are you doing? Release the boy!" Jero shouted in his Slavic tongue.

The entire Romani family was gathered around a fallen tree, where Chavdar held Sasho's arm against it, and a second man gripped a small ax above it. He was ready to let the ax fall when the surprised audience all turned at once toward the new intruder.

"Let him go!" Jero repeated in Turkish as he pushed his way to Sasho.

"Are you the thief's father? Did you put him up to robbing us?" Chavdar bellowed.

The middle-aged man with a balding head and bushy beard seemed robust, and Jero decided he might lose to him in a fistfight if it came to that. So Jero didn't challenge him except to demand, "Robbing you of what?"

A hunched-over white-haired woman held up two rounds of bread. "Hard work ground this flour, and tired hands baked this bread. It does not come from nothing. The boy stole these, and the debt must be repaid."

Jero pleaded, "He is just a hungry boy who's not eaten in two days. You have your bread back, madam. Give me the boy."

"So he is yours?" the younger man with the lowered ax inquired accusingly.

More calmly this time, Jero replied, "I am his guardian, yes. His mother entrusted his care to me. Let him go now."

"The boy must learn a lesson about thieving," the ax man maintained.

"And your lesson for his misdeed is cutting off his hand? You have lost nothing. The punishment does not fit the crime."

The burly patriarch declared, "It is my right under the law."

"I will pay you for the bread," Jero pleaded.

Chavdar liked the sound of that, and he let the boy's arm go.

Sasho ran to Jero's side, and Jero held him protectively as he hastily surveyed the mismatched family. There were the two middle-aged men; the old woman who had baked the bread; another woman, who could be the wife of one of the men; and the rest were children—girls from marrying age on down to a few little boys, newly in breeches. One adolescent boy tried to look fiercely in Jero's direction, but the girls were openly in awe of the events happening around their breakfast tables.

Now that he had Sasho by his side, Jero felt more confident that he could talk his way out of the misunderstanding.

"I will pay you for the bread," Jero repeated in a humbler tone. "But I am afraid I have no money."

Chavdar did not laugh, as many men might have. Every man had something to bargain with, and he considered Jero's offer. They were on their way to help a cousin with the rye harvest before continuing on to Bulgaria for his daughter's wedding. He could use the extra wages from the man's labor to pay for a better ceremony.

"Yours is an empty proposition, stranger, but I have one for you," Chavdar proclaimed in his thick Bulgarian accent.

Jero waited with dread at what he might say.

Chavdar took his time deciding. He crossed his thick arms over his broad chest and critically sized up Sasho.

"How old are you, boy?" the patriarch asked him directly.

Sasho still rubbed his rescued arm and could not find his voice with all eyes staring at him. "I am, um . . ."

"He is thirteen," Jero answered for him.

"He is a puny boy for thirteen," the other man scoffed.

Chavdar considered Sasho again. "He looks strong enough, Boris. Three days of labor would pay his debt for stealing our bread," Chavdar announced sternly. "What say you?"

The Romani clan considered his penalty and nodded in agreement. Daylight was burning, and the women returned to their tables to finish their cold breakfast, leaving the details to the men.

Jero was not so sure. "What sort of labor do you require? Chopping wood? Building a shelter for the season?"

Chavdar became animated again and chuckled long and loud. "We are gypsies! We need none of those things. But each year we help harvest our clan's fields. The boy will pay his own debt by working as a thrasher. Your labor will be expected, too, if you want to stay with him."

Before Jero agreed, he asked, "Where are these fields?"

"Not far at all. Just a day's travel from here. If God is willing, we might be there tonight," Chavdar declared.

"Will we travel east or west?"

Jero's anxiety over the direction did not go unnoticed. Chavdar exchanged a glance with the old woman before answering, "We are heading east. Is the payment agreeable?"

Jero took a deep breath. He regretted this already. "All right, sir," he said. "We will follow you and help with this harvest. When the boy's debt is paid, we will continue on our way."

"Agreed," Chavdar said with a hearty shake of his bald head. He dropped his stern expression and became a jovial host. "What is your name, stranger?" he asked.

Jero hesitated. "My name?"

Less cheerfully, the other, Boris, insisted, "You do have one, don't you?"

Sasho blurted out, "He is Isaak and I am Sasho."

Jero nodded, relieved that Sasho had invented an easy alias.

"You are quick with your hands and quick with your tongue, boy. Be careful of that, as well," Chavdar warned.

Then he laughed at Sasho's panicked expression and added, "I'm not going to cut out your tongue. Let us be friends now, shall we?"

Jero tried to make the best of their predicament. "And what is your name, sir?" he asked.

"Me? Of course! Where are my manners?" The man removed his cap and tipped it in a welcoming fashion. "I am Chavdar. At your service," he said cheerfully.

The rest of the group came to attention as he called out their names, "This is my brother-in-law, Boris. My mother is called Granny by everyone. Irina, there, is my lovely sister and Boris's wife—my wife is no longer with us."

The family bowed their heads respectfully for their dearly departed.

The moment quickly passed, and Chavdar became animated again when he said, "I have four daughters: Lilyana, Jasmina, Roza, and Violeta. My youngest boy, the tall one there, is named Andrei. My oldest son is already married and lives with his wife's family in Bulgaria."

"Those are a lot of names to remember." Jero then said directly to the girls, "I hope I can remember which face goes with each flower."

The sisters—aged twenty, seventeen, fifteen, and thirteen—were immediately fascinated by the unusual stranger and began to whisper among themselves.

Boris pointed to the children scampering around the camp and said, "The little ones are mine. Toma, Dragan, Eva, and Petya."

Chavdar nodded and said, "Well, Isaak, now that you know everyone, sit down and eat with us. We were just finishing our meal, and then we will be on our way. We have a long day ahead."

Jero was stunned at his offer. "You almost took the boy's hand for wanting some bread, and now you invite us to your table?"

"Ah, well," Chavdar exclaimed dramatically, "is it so hard to understand the difference between taking and giving? One is a punishable crime, the other is a choice. My choice! Remember that."

Jero shivered as though a sudden chill blew over him in the morning sunlight. Jero would not forget.

The menacing tone was replaced with an inviting one. "Come, Isaak. Join us."

Sasho had already claimed an empty stool with the children, but Jero had other responsibilities. "Thank you, Chavdar, sir, but first I must retrieve something from the woods, just over there."

"Another boy?" Chavdar joked, nudging his brother, who laughed along with him.

Jero forced a smile. "No, sir. I must get my horse."

"You have a horse, but no bread and no money?" Boris asked suspiciously. "How is that possible?"

Jero stalled and said, "Yes, well, it is a long story. We did have a sack of food, but some scavenging dogs found it while we slept. We have been without for a few days now."

Irina spoke up for the first time, "Then you must both be starved. Fetch your horse, and we will ready a plate for you." She called out to one of the girls: "Jasmina, get a plate and cup from my caravan for Isaak."

Sasho got up to follow Jero back to their hidden camp, but Chavdar grabbed his arm. "The boy will wait here," he said with a false smile.

Jero assured Sasho, "I will be right back." He would have to come back now.

Sasho shook his arm free from the gypsy and said, "Can I at least go take a piss? Or do you want to hold my arm for that?"

Chavdar laughed heartily at Sasho's defiant expression until he realized the sparkle in the boy's eyes was not from warmth.

Chavdar released his grip and warned, "You need to learn some respect, boy. Go ahead, but through those bushes instead."

When Jero walked past Jasmina at the caravan, he asked her, "Might I bother you for a knife, miss?"

"For your horse?" she challenged, doubting he had one.

"I would like to shave my beard, is all, but I have no blade."

"Why would you want to be rid of your beard?" she asked skeptically. "All men wear beards."

"To be honest, miss, my beard itches with vermin, and I cannot seem to wash them away."

She looked him up and down. By the state of his dirty attire, she believed him. "If your beard is crawling, then your clothes will be crawling, too. Granny will not have that in her midst. Irina might have some discarded clothes. I must say, Isaak, yours are barely fit for the rag pile."

It was true. Jero ran his hands over his shirt and embroidered waistcoat, ruined while he had carried the stones. "Forgive me," he said, "but I have been away from home for a long time now."

She shook her head with pity and pointed to a bucket by the wheel. "There is a stream through those trees. You can put your dirty things in the pail to drown the lice until the girls get a chance to wash them."

"I can wash my own clothes, miss."

"Ha! That I would like to see!" Jasmina exclaimed. "But you will be busy in the fields tomorrow. The girls will wash them." She waved a knife and added, "Dragan and Toma will take this to you at the stream. I don't want you wandering away with Irina's best blade."

"You will have my horse in a minute, miss. Is that not collateral enough for your knife?"

She was unaffected by his reasoning and said, "I don't have a need for your horse, but I need the knife again. And one last thing: I am not a miss. I don't know what sort of gentry you are used to bowing down to, but we are plain folk here, and we talk plain to each other. My name is—"

"Jasmina. I remember." Jero bowed with his head high and then walked away to find Cairo.

As he disappeared into the bushes, she said under her breath, "What a strange man."

~*~

Granny watched the stranger walk away from their camp, too. She took her cane from the chairback and hobbled to her son's side, then whispered, "A bearded man on a horse. No coat. No hat. Is he the escaped prisoner the soldiers were looking for yesterday?"

"It crossed my mind, yes."

"Will you not turn him in for the reward, Chavdar?"

"I might, but he may be of use to us in other ways. He wants to head east; we will take him east. For now, I need another laborer for the fields. I'll decide what to do with him afterward."

"They say he was jailed for murder. Are you not worried for our safety, son?"

He flashed a confident smile. "How many men have you known in your lifetime accused of a crime they did not commit? One? Twenty? I will keep an eye on Isaak, but I am not worried."

"The soldiers didn't say anything about a boy. What will you do with him?"

Chavdar looked across the camp at Sasho coming up the path. "The scrawny boy might be worth something to us," he replied.

"A trade, you mean?"

"Ludvik might be willing to take another boy."

Granny was pleased, and it showed on her wrinkled face. "You seem to have already thought this through. I will say no more about it."

"No, you won't. We will keep this between us. The others did not hear what the soldiers came looking for."

Chapter 17

Alimah was to blame for keeping Fatina's life in limbo, and her once faithful lady's maid had turned against her because of that. General Mehmed Sadik had showered Fatina with gifts of jewelry and furs the winter she bore him his first son. But it was Alimah who had said he could not marry her and give her a secure place in his house.

As a mother to his son, Fatina was bound to Sadik, but not to Alimah. He was master over her, so Fatina could not refuse him when he called for her each night. But he did not intervene if she refused Alimah's orders. And Alimah despised her for it.

After Bem had left yesterday, Alimah formulated a plan. With the aid of the servant girls, she would change Fatina's mind. Alimah chose the girls that Fatina confided in, saw as her only friends in the household, but Alimah still had control over them.

Alimah coached the handmaidens on how to pester Fatina for letting her handsome husband leave. Fatina's maids were ordered to bring up the subject each time they were with her—during the meals that she took alone in her room, while they bathed her, while they dressed her, while they cared for her precious baby. The girls were to remind Fatina over and over that if they had a heroic husband who had come to take them away from servitude, they would not hesitate to go with him.

~*~

When Fatina rose the following day, she knew what she would do. She took nothing from her time in Sadik's house. All her fine silk robes, chains of gold, and strings of precious stones still hung in her wardrobe. Dressed in simple linen robes and a gauze headscarf, Fatina went to Alimah's private chamber to tell her she was leaving.

There Fatina found her mistress sitting in front of her looking glass, outlining her deep brown eyes. Alimah was still dressed in her flowing morning robes, but her maid had already pinned her black hair with golden clips and strands of glass beads.

Alimah set her stick of kohl off to the side when she saw Fatina approach her in the reflection. The former slave crossed the room dressed in dull gray for traveling. A satchel was slung over her shoulder with her essential possessions. Alimah wondered if Bem could still be in love with such a simple wife, so very different from the lavishly dressed woman he had wanted yesterday morning.

Fatina spoke first, "I have reconsidered, Alimah. Perhaps I was too hasty yesterday. I am going with Bem. He is my husband, and I still love him."

Alimah remained aloof and told her, "I cannot promise that he will keep his word and be at the stone bridge. But once you leave, Fatina, you may not come back. I will forbid it."

"You do not have to worry about that. Farewell, Alimah."

Alimah rose from her grooming table, thinking they could be civil in the end. "You were once my favorite, Fatina. Shall we not part as friends?"

She held out her hands, expecting Fatina to take them in hers, but Fatina did not embrace her mistress.

Alimah let her arms drop and tried to smile. It did not matter because the reward was hers, with or without Fatina's love. "Where is Ahmeti?" she demanded.

"I left him with Havva. I just nursed him, so he will sleep a few hours."

Alimah nodded. She trusted that her new son would be in good hands with Havva, the wet nurse for Sadik's other child, a newborn daughter from another concubine.

"I will care for Ahmeti like he was my own," she told Fatina.

"I know that," Fatina said sadly. "Goodbye, Alimah." She clutched her satchel to her side and left the house for the last time.

Alimah went to the window and stood behind the thin curtain to watch the guards open the gate for Fatina. Content, she retook her seat at her grooming table and stared into the glass. A victorious smile crept across her pale lips. She took up the pot of rouge and painted them a daring red. With Fatina out of her life, she could seduce her husband again. In the meantime, she would get to know her new baby boy.

"Korinna," she called out.

A small woman, barely out of her teens, came from an open doorway within the apartment. She was dressed simply but richly in a long gauze tunic and flowing silk jacket belted high under her ample breasts. The robe's shades of orange and red complemented her newly dyed hair.

The servant bowed submissively and said, "Mistress."

Alimah cocked her head at Korinna's changed appearance and asked, "Is there any more henna?"

"I thought you did not want to dye your hair, mistress."

"I want my hands decorated, so my son will see how special his new mother is when I hold him."

The servant flattered her ego and agreed, "That will please the little boy, and he will love you like his own. I will get the pot."

Soon after, the handmaiden went to work marking an intricate design on her mistress's skin while Alimah lounged on her cushions. In the corner, a girl strummed a melody on a small harp to entertain her.

The women were jolted from their quiet session by the sharp echo of heavy boots and husky voices at the end of the corridor.

Alimah sat up in a panic. "It cannot be," she said. "Did he not say he would be gone two weeks?"

Korinna held Alimah's hand tighter so her hard work would not be smudged. "Yes, mistress, that is what he said."

The footsteps became louder at the open door, and General Sadik strolled into his wife's private chamber.

"How God curses me," Alimah said under her breath.

Her husband assessed the room, and then he strode across the carpet to where the two women lounged in the light of the window. "Alimah, my wife, I have been looking for you."

Alimah forced a dutiful smile for her unwelcome husband. "Mehmed! I did not expect you home for days!"

"Is that so? I see you are making yourself very pretty. Is it not for me?" He took her hand to admire the lacy patterns down her fingers and across the top.

"It is to please you on your return, Husband. And it is an entertaining distraction for Korinna. She is a simple girl and gets bored easily."

He stroked Korinna's cheek with his fingertips, and the maid smiled coyly at her master.

"Korinna does beautiful work and is not so simple," Sadik said. "Perhaps it is your company that she finds dull."

Alimah's fury at the insult went unnoticed. His eyes had not left the pretty servant girl's face.

Alimah calmed her flash of anger, telling herself she would punish Korinna later for provoking him.

"How is my new little daughter, Korinna?" the general asked the handmaiden.

Korinna lowered her eyes humbly and said, "She is more beautiful every day, General Sadik."

"Like her mother," Sadik praised her. He touched her henna-dyed hair and said with a smile, "I will come find you later."

Alimah swallowed her pride and did not lash out at his brazen compliment to her slave girl. She pursed her red lips and sweetly asked, "You said you were looking for me, my love. Shall I send Korinna away?"

Sadik gave his wife a stern look while wondering what her new game was. "She may stay and finish your hand," he said. "I was looking for Fatina. I thought you might know where she is."

Alimah needed to hit something, to scream to the world that she was his wife, not the other whores.

Instead, she got up and went to the window to ensure Fatina was indeed gone before she answered, "How should I know? She does not serve me any longer."

Sadik went to her side. She flinched as he leaned in and whispered, "As my wife, you are given the one task to manage the women of my house. Find her for me."

Her eyes sparked with hatred as she said, "Whatever you desire."

Alimah then called out to the harp player, "Jozefa! Bring Fatina to my chamber."

Sadik added, "And bring my little boy!"

The girl bowed obediently and hurried down the hallway on her hopeless errand.

Alimah filled the unbearable wait with feigned interest in her husband's affairs. "Was your meeting in Sophia canceled, Mehmed?"

"The boy sultan cannot make up his mind again. We were told along the route that his council has been detained in the capital. They will come here instead of Sophia," he reported.

"My father is coming here? Mehmed! Why did not you tell me that?" she rejoiced.

"I just did, Alimah. They won't arrive until next week."

Jozefa returned and stood next to her master, biting her lip anxiously while waiting for him to acknowledge her.

"What is it, girl?" he asked curtly.

"I am sorry to interrupt, General Sadik, but your son is not in the nursery, sir."

Sadik was unconcerned. "Fatina will bring him to me. Did you tell her to come here?"

Alimah shut her eyes in anticipation of her husband's explosive temper.

The servant girl told her master, "Um, Fatina left this morning, General Sadik."

The general looked directly at the girl for the first time. "She left? To where?" he asked.

"To her husband, General, sir." Jozefa bowed her head as the bearer of bad news, bracing to be struck.

Sadik looked to his wife and demanded, "What is she talking about?"

Korinna got up from her place on the piles of cushions and took Jozefa's hand. She hurried the girl into the adjacent chamber and shut the door behind them.

Alimah was alone with her husband and met his coming wrath. "It is true. She left this morning," she said.

Sadik raised his hand to slap her, but her defiant stand made him reconsider who would get the satisfaction from the blow.

He walked away and paced the room, his heavy steps muffled by the thick carpets. The betrayal was too great this time. "You lounged here, pretending to know nothing, yet kept this from me the entire time!" he bellowed. "What other secrets have you kept from me? Where has she really gone?"

Alimah reminded herself that she was not to blame for Bem's arrival in Skopje. It was fated that he took Fatina back with him. If anyone was to blame, it was Fatina. She was the cause of all their misery.

"I have done nothing!" Alimah protested. "Her husband appeared on our doorstep yesterday, like a phantom from the past. He was reported as dead, but he is not dead, Mehmed, and she has gone with him."

Sadik was furious. "Why didn't you stop her?"

"Stop her?" Alimah shouted back. "You kept her like a slave, but she has been a free woman this whole time. I guess she was tired of warming your perverted bed, and she chose her husband over you."

"At least she knew how to warm my bed, Alimah."

The silence that followed sat like a weight upon Alimah's chest, and she struggled to breathe.

At last, Sadik demanded, "Where is my son?"

"She left him with Havva," Alimah said. "I will be Ahmeti's new mother. Fatina doesn't care about him."

"Liar! Admit that her leaving was your doing, Alimah! You are to blame."

"You are wrong, Mehmed! She couldn't wait to get away from you."

He pointed to the door. "Leave my sight!"

"We'll see what my father says about your twisted love for whores in front of your own wife!" she shouted.

"Your father will realize your treachery in my house and will not help you this time," he hissed through gritted teeth. "I will divorce you myself for such deceit."

Sadik stormed into the corridor and roared, "Guards! Find me Havva!"

Chapter 18

Bem scanned the stone bridge from high on his horse. It was hard to spot one lone woman with so many people and carts coming into the city. Salar Nassim had warned that Alimah might not be able to persuade Fatina, especially after his disappointing reunion yesterday, but Bem held out hope that his wife would be waiting.

He rode slowly across the wide bridge one more time. At first Bem didn't recognize Fatina. She was not the adorned woman in bright silks from yesterday. She looked ordinary again in her traveling clothes, like the Fatina he remembered.

"Thank you, God," Bem said under his breath.

Salar Nassim joyfully nodded when Bem pointed her out in the crowd.

When Fatina saw the two horsemen approaching, she waved with a look of genuine relief.

Bem dismounted and rushed to her side. The two embraced like the lost lovers that they were—until Bem felt the baby stir between them. He stepped back. "What have you done, Fatina?"

Fatina opened the flap to look into her little boy's wide eyes. "He is mine, Bem. I cannot leave him."

Passersby walked around the richly clad horseman as he threw up his arms in frustration. No one interfered with his rightful dispute with a disobedient servant girl who stood her ground in front of him.

Salar Nassim got down from his horse when he realized what Bem saw in her shoulder bag. He made his objections clear, "We talked about this, Bem. She cannot choose both, and neither can you."

Fatina closed her satchel flap and clutched it to her side protectively. "Who is this man?" she asked Bem.

"This is my friend, Salar Nassim. He helped me find you. I owe him everything, and so do you."

Fatina's glare softened when Nassim bowed before her and said, "I am happy to finally meet you, Fatina, but you must reconsider what you have done. Even a free woman is not free to take a son from his father. Sadik will come after him," he warned. "Take the baby back. Leave it at the gate. We will wait here for you."

Fatina did not waver. "It's alright. General Sadik has gone to Sophia. Too much time will have passed when he returns. He will never find us."

Salar Nassim shook his head and spoke directly to Bem, "I say no. You will be looking over your shoulder wherever you go. Do you want that?"

Fatina took her husband's hand and pleaded, "We can disappear somewhere, Bem. Sadik will not know where to even start looking."

Bem sighed and squeezed his temples, reeling with indecision. Salar Nassim was right, of course. He always was. But now that he had Fatina back with him, he could not risk her walking away.

He took a deep breath and told Salar Nassim, "I think she is right. We can start a new life somewhere outside Ottoman lands. The world is big enough to escape him."

Salar Nassim reluctantly backed down. "If you are confident, I will not interfere. Shall we part ways here, then?" he asked solemnly.

Bem was more lighthearted than Salar Nassim, now that Fatina was with them. "Let us ride together for a while. At least until I can come up with an idea where we might go. We will head south with you for now."

Salar Nassim was encouraged by his friend's happy mood and said, "I will be glad for your company until then, and yours, too, Fatina. Let's put this place behind us."

Bem helped his wife up onto Zeus and settled in on the saddle behind her. "Can you hold the baby tightly?"

She moved the fabric that covered Ahmeti's face to see that he had fallen asleep again. "I can. You will see that the baby will not be a burden to you at all. I hope you will grow to love him."

Bem looked down over her shoulder at the peaceful baby boy. "Your burden is my burden, Fatina. Of course I will love him, just like I love you." He put his arm around Fatina's waist to hold her steady and urged the horse on.

The men trotted away from the merchants and travelers, crossing the river into Skopje. When the tall fortress was out of sight, they spurred their horses on.

~*~

After several hours of steady riding, Bem stopped his horse and looked around.

Salar Nassim stopped next to him. "Should we take a break?"

Bem said, "I was thinking this would make a good camp for the night. It looks like there is a small river down beyond those boulders for the horses."

"It is a bit early to make camp. The sun is still high. I think we should ride on, Bem."

Bem said what his slumped wife did not want to acknowledge, "Fatina is not used to riding, and the baby needs to be properly fed."

Salar Nassim looked up the well-traveled road and back down from where they had come. The trodden dirt made a straight line through the countryside that seemed to go on and on until it finally disappeared over a distant hill.

Salar Nassim conceded, "This is probably the best spot for miles." He got off his horse and remarked, "It is going to be a slow journey to Athens riding like this. We'll have to find her another horse. You have too much gear on yours."

"If Fatina can hold out the week, then we can stop in Thessaloniki and take back my horse. Ruby won't need my mare any longer."

Salar Nassim said with a smile, "You mean Fatina?"

Bem nodded at the irony of it.

Salar Nassim agreed, "That is a good plan, Bem. We can easily be there in a week." The Persian looked down the dirt bank and added, "I will scout the area before we settle in. You can let her feed the baby."

Bem took the satchel with the baby from Fatina's lap and helped her to her feet.

"I am sorry if I am causing any trouble with your friend," Fatina said.

"Salar Nassim is not troubled, he is cautious." There was a twinkle in Bem's eyes when he said, "Do not worry, Fatina. He may not show it, but I think Salar Nassim likes you already."

Bem took little Ahmeti from his wet blanket with a skeptical frown, and the baby stared with wide eyes at the stranger who held him.

"Here is your mother, little man," Bem told him sweetly, then passed the baby on to Fatina's outreached arms. "He is cute, but very smelly."

"That is what babies do, Bem. They eat and make messes. I will clean him up first at the stream," she said with a chuckle. "Can you hand me the smaller bag?"

He did and assured her, "I will be right here. Don't get lost."

Salar Nassim came back to the road on foot. "There is a good spot for a fire and bedrolls just beyond those trees. Where is Fatina?"

Bem pointed beyond them, down the slope. "She went—"

Salar Nassim instinctively held up his hand. The ground rumbled with the beating of horse hooves. "Soldiers!" he exclaimed. "Take Zeus away!"

Bem pulled on the reins to squeeze the horse through the underbrush, but it was too late. Their horse had been seen. Bem had one shot loaded in his pistol, and he pulled it from its place on his saddle.

"No," Salar Nassim hissed urgently.

Bem put it back in its holder and stood by his friend, reins in hand.

General Sadik did not know what Fatina's husband looked like, and he had no idea whether he would be traveling alone or with others. But Bem and Salar Nassim knew that this man dressed in officer's garb and surrounded by cavalry could only be General Sadik. The advantage was theirs.

Salar Nassim and Bem bowed respectfully when the agitated horses stopped in front of them.

Sadik looked at Bem's laden steed and the weapons hanging from the saddle and demanded, "Who are you?"

"My name is Salar Nassim, General. My friend and I are mercenary soldiers, traveling through to our next job."

Sadik's expression did not change, and Salar Nassim breathed a low sigh of relief that the general did not recognize his name.

"Where is your second horse?" the general asked.

"I hobbled him down by the stream to drink. We were just assessing our map. Is there trouble, sir?"

"Have you passed a man riding with a woman along this route?" Sadik asked impatiently.

"We have passed many travelers. Some were with women."

"They would be on horseback," Sadik added.

Salar Nassim looked over at Bem, who shrugged and shook his head. "Not that we recall, General."

Sadik gave the two one last, hard look. "Which direction are you heading for your next assignment?"

"North," Nassim said. "We thought we would stop in Skopje first. Is it far?"

"You will be there before dark," the general briskly informed them. Then Sadik clicked his heels, and his horse took off, followed by the line of soldiers.

Fatina had heard the horsemen and had hidden just beyond the boulders to listen in. She had left little Ahmeti on his blanket, and the child finally noticed his mother was gone. He let out a long wail to call her back as the riders thundered away.

Salar Nassim heard the babe, and so did the last rider in the line. The soldier stopped his horse and shouted, "General Sadik."

The two mercenaries reacted and pulled the lone rider from his horse with precision. Salar Nassim's chokehold silenced the man, but the damage was already done. One by one, the riders ahead turned their horses.

"To the stream!" Salar Nassim shouted, and Bem pulled Zeus along the narrow path after him.

Fatina came running to their side, carrying her crying child. Bem's chilling look stifled any excuse for his outburst.

Salar Nassim whipped the rope that tied his horse free and was riding in one smooth motion. "Down the stream! Quick!" he called out.

Bem grabbed Fatina by the waist and heaved her up in front of his saddle.

The baby somehow understood the danger it was in and quieted, but Fatina began to sob uncontrollably. "I don't know what happened, Bem. Sadik was in Sophia. How could he know I was gone?"

Bem ignored her babbling sobs and followed Salar Nassim through the shallow water. He looked for a low bank to escape to on the other side.

A pistol shot rang out from the roadside, then another from the water's edge. The soldiers had followed them, led by the general himself.

"Don't shoot the girl," General Sadik ordered his bowmen before lowering his arm.

A half-dozen arrows found their way to Bem and Salar Nassim but were short of their mark and fell into the water next to Bem's horse.

Fatina pulled on the horse's reins and shouted, "Stop, Bem. It is over. I don't want you hurt. He has won."

Salar Nassim had already made it to the top of another bank, and he looked back at Bem and Fatina stalled in the middle of the stream. He did not call out to Bem to hurry but waited at a distance on his horse.

The air was still and quiet again as the opponents assessed their next move. Sadik shouted from the riverbank, "Give me the girl."

"She is my lawful wife!" Bem hollered back.

Sadik countered, "She is a thief, and she shall pay for stealing my son."

"*My* son!" Fatina exclaimed.

She clutched Ahmeti against her, and the jostled baby began to cry again.

Sadik offered more calmly, "Ahmeti belongs in his father's house. All will be forgiven if you come with me now, Fatina."

Bem's questioning eyes bore into Fatina's heart.

"You have to choose," he whispered.

"I cannot," she whispered back, holding her crying baby tightly.

"Then I will choose for you."

Bem jumped down into the shallow water. He walked his horse to the sandy bank. All eyes were upon them as he held his arms out to help Fatina down.

"Go to him," he told her. "We are not meant to be together."

"No!" She shook her head in despair. "I don't love him, Bem. I love you."

"And the baby?" Bem asked in anguish.

Fatina clutched Ahmeti tighter.

He took Fatina by the waist and lowered her to the ground. She did not fight it.

Bem kissed her lips and whispered, "Go, Fatina."

Her back was to the soldiers when she slid Bem's pistol from its holder and shoved it into her pocket. The men watching the scene could only see Bem's expression while they allowed his wife to say her goodbyes to him.

Fatina's eyes narrowed in determination, and she pleaded, "Do not stop me, Bem."

It did not matter to Bem if she shot him or planned to shoot Sadik. He was dead inside already. "I will always love you," he said mournfully.

She dried her last tears with the hem of her baby's blanket and took a breath for strength before she walked wordlessly in the direction of Sadik and his men.

In front of the soldiers, she kissed her son and offered him to his father for the last time. With both hands freed, Fatina pulled out the pistol and pointed it at Sadik.

But the soldiers raised their bows and pointed their arrows at the brave mother.

"Don't be stupid, Fatina," Sadik warned her with a noticeable tremble in his voice. "If you kill me, then you are dead."

"I will give you my Ahmeti, the greatest love of my life, and in exchange, you will not kill my other love. Bem is my husband of almost three years, and I will shoot you dead if I do not have your promise that we can go free."

Sadik looked as though he believed she would do it. "You are hysterical, Fatina. Put down the pistol and come home."

"I have given you what you wanted, Mehmed, and with it, my heart is ripped from me. I have no love left for you."

She turned the pistol on herself and held it under her chin. "I would rather die than go back."

Sadik waved his arm, and the soldiers lowered their arrows.

Fatina kept the gun at her throat, her head held high and confident.

Beyond her, standing on the bank, Bem did not waver while watching his wife do what she thought would save him.

Sadik stroked the cheek of the babe in his arms, then turned back to Fatina. "You have gone mad. Ahmeti will never know you were his mother. Go! Be out of my life!"

Sadik was not only ruthless but also a liar, and she held her ground. Fatina cocked the pistol and pointed it at him again. "Promise me that Bem goes unharmed."

Sadik shouted, "Guards! Ride on."

The soldiers didn't question their commander's judgment, and they turned their horses up the slope and disappeared on the road again.

"Are you satisfied?" the general asked her mockingly.

She waved the pistol toward the road. "Now you, Mehmed. Leave me before I kill you."

He unbuttoned his jacket and tucked the swaddled baby inside it. Then Sadik shouted to his rival, "Keep this bitch out of my sight and away from my boy."

Sadik kicked his horse's flanks and rode away from them.

When the sound of the rushing water could be heard again, Fatina dropped the pistol and collapsed onto the soft ground. Bem ran to her side, and through her trembling tears, she told him, "I chose life, Bem. My life. With you."

Bem held her tightly and kissed her wet cheek. "You will not regret it," he promised.

Hand in hand, they walked back to Zeus. Bem scanned the far bank for Salar Nassim.

The Persian was lying facedown next to his agitated horse.

"No!" Bem cried. He bolted across the stream, his wife at his heels.

Bem cradled his friend on the ground as a growing spot of blood stained the back of Salar Nassim's jacket.

"He is shot," Fatina cried. She covered her gasp with her hand.

Salar Nassim was as still as death. Bem rolled him over and saw that the blood had soaked the front of his jacket, and a trickle of crimson flowed down his lower lip.

Fatina stepped back to give Bem room to lay him down. "Is he alive?" she asked.

Salar Nassim's vein pulsed against Bem's hand, and Bem exclaimed, "He is!"

Bem quickly opened Salar Nassim's jacket and unbuttoned his tunic. The wound he found was only a small hole between the ribs, but it bled steadily.

"We'll get you all fixed up, Salar Nassim. Hang on for me," Bem urged.

Salar Nassim opened his eyes at Bem's voice. It took all his breath to wheeze one word, "Lung."

Bem had seen this before on the battlefield, and he went to work saving his friend's life. "Fatina! I need mud from the stream. Hurry!"

As ordered, she ran to the river bank and returned with two fists full of the sticky mud. "What will you do with it?" she asked.

"The bullet has gone through his lung and out the other side. I might be able to seal the holes so he can catch his breath again."

Bem wiped away the blood oozing from his friend's ribs and smeared the silt over the wound. Bem carefully turned his friend to patch the bleeding hole in his back.

"The musket ball went out the other side. That is good, isn't it?" Fatina asked. "He'll be alright, won't he?"

Bem searched for other broken bones from the fall; the rest of his friend was whole. Then he checked that the packed mud was still covering the tears in the flesh before wrapping the ribs tightly with Nassim's tunic.

With great effort, Salar Nassim tried to gulp air, but it only gurgled in his throat. He choked out the words, "No breath."

Bem propped Salar Nassim up against a rock to make breathing easier for his friend. He covered his friend's mouth with his own and gave him a puff of his breath. Nothing helped.

Salar Nassim signaled with his finger for Bem to lean in.

Bem put his ear to his friend's lips to hear the words: "Death found me."

Bem hung his head in grief. "It is all my fault. I dragged you into this," he wailed.

Salar Nassim gasped to fill his lungs. "God's will. No stopping," he whispered. His lips were turning blue. Salar Nassim took a labored breath through his nose. "Live. Love her."

Through falling tears, Bem begged, "How can I help you? What can I do?"

Bubbles of scarlet blood foamed in the corners of the Persian's mouth, and the word "Shirin" escaped. He sucked in a breath and exhaled: "Tell her."

Bem pulled Salar Nassim's failing body close to him. "Tell her what?" Bem urged.

The words Salar Nassim whispered were faint, then nearly incomprehensible. The dying man willed himself to finish what he had to say, but he could not muster another breath. He looked into Bem's pleading eyes. Salar Nassim smiled at something that Bem could not understand and then let go. The sparkle in his deep brown eyes faded to an empty blackness.

Bem held Salar Nassim's limp body tightly in his arms and sobbed.

Fatina dared not comfort her grieving husband, for she was sure that he blamed her for his friend's death.

Bem was numb when he finally looked up and saw his wife standing helplessly before him. Somehow it didn't make any sense. "Are you a phantom, Fatina? Am I surrounded only by death and ghosts?"

"No, my love. I am real. We are here, but your friend is dead." She wrung her hands and begged her husband, "Can you ever forgive me?"

"Forgive you?" Her question seemed so out of place.

Bem held out his arms, and she collapsed at his side on the ground. He stroked her soft hair and found comfort in her warmth as they wrapped their arms around each other in gloomy sadness. The two were alone in the world now.

Bem tried to overcome his misery and take comfort in his friend's words. He told his wife, "Salar Nassim always spoke of death as a part of life and believed all things are fated. He would not want me to be angry over what God had planned for us today. Salar Nassim faced death bravely. But I am not strong like he is, Fatina. I am angry that he should have to die while I go on living." Bem took a deep breath to stop his sobs. "I don't know why I keep losing so many loved ones. But somehow I have found you again."

"What will we do now, Bem?" she moaned.

Bem stroked Salar Nassim's peaceful face and gently closed Nassim's eyes. "First, I will bury my friend."

He stood up with effort and looked around the rocky outcroppings. "There must be a good place near here where he can lie undisturbed. And then I will honor his final request."

Bem held out his hand and helped Fatina to her feet. She asked, "Can you tell me what Salar Nassim said to you?"

"He said I must go to Rhodes."

His answer surprised her. "That is a long journey. What must you do there?"

"Salar Nassim has a daughter. Shirin. She lives there with her mother. I am to bring her his hard-won fortune, along with one other thing more important than his gold."

"What was so important to him, Bem?"

Salar Nassim had often talked about his daughter in the last few weeks. He had confided his worries to Bem, and Bem was sure those were his final, faint instructions.

Bem told Fatina, "I will tell her why."

Meanwhile . . .

Chapter 19

Baric Castle, 15 August 1649

A lone rider trotted up the castle road on his borrowed horse. To his disappointment, no one opened the way for him as he neared the wall, so he stopped his horse at the lowered gate and looked around to see who was on duty.

The rider took off his wide-brimmed hat, shaking off the road dust. He squinted to see the crossbow pointed at him from the ramparts. Unfazed, he set his hat carefully back on his raven hair and smiled at the young guardsman who peered through the gate bars at him.

"It seems Lord Baric has increased his security after last month's events. Will you grant me entrance?" the rider asked.

The guard's eyes widened. "Captain Carrera!" he exclaimed. "I am sorry I didn't recognize you, sir."

"I think I recognize you, soldier. You were in my last group of new recruits, were you not? Bernardo, right?"

The new guard was proud that his former captain remembered him—almost. "Bruno. Bruno Lombardo, sir. Baron Baric hired me on after my training."

"Well, Bruno Lombardo, did they teach you how to open the gate?"

"Oh! Sorry, Captain, sir." Flustered, Bruno turned the cogged wheel, and the heavy chain raised the iron bars.

"Where is everyone?" Fabian asked as he leisurely walked his horse through the wall's high entrance into the empty courtyard.

"It is noon, sir. The men have just gone to lunch in the Keep," Bruno replied. "The rest of the Baric household went with the baroness to Mass. It is the day of Our Lady, you know. Father David gives a special sermon each year."

"Does he? I am sorry to have missed it," Fabian said with nostalgia. "I suppose the baron is at the church with his wife."

"No, Captain Carrera. Lord Baric stayed behind, but I haven't seen the baron come out today. You might find him in the manor house," Bruno said.

Fabian tipped his hat in gratitude for the information. "I will look for him there."

Despite all that had transpired that summer in Venice and here at Baric Castle, Fabian had the sense that nothing had changed. He had stopped his horse hundreds of times on that very spot, and it felt like he was home again.

Josip, the stable master's eldest son, had seen the rider cross the courtyard from inside the stables, and he came out to take his horse.

"Captain Carrera!" the young groom exclaimed when he realized who it was. "Welcome back, sir. Are you here for good?"

"For a few days, at least," Fabian told him. "You can settle in my horse, Josip."

Fabian unstrapped an overstuffed saddlebag and slung it over his shoulder. He handed the reins to the grinning groom and then strolled with familiarity toward the elegant manor house at the far end of the courtyard.

A strange feeling came over Fabian as he walked past the old oak shading the walkway. It was quiet, too quiet. There should be noise—not like the bustle of Venice, but at the very least, there should be servants clipping and digging in the vast gardens, or soldiers going about their duties. But he only heard the crunching of his heeled shoes on the fine gravel. Fabian breathed in the pleasure of it.

The manor's double doors loomed in front of him. Intricately carved into the thick oak panels was the story of Mauro Baric's ancestors. As usual, Fabian bypassed the formality of knocking and simply opened the smaller door within the arched doorway and went in.

Fabian was met in the foyer by Mauro's manservant, Davor. Dressed for duty in his attractive green-and-gold valet uniform, Davor momentarily forgot his place.

"Lord Fabian! Lord Baric did not say he was expecting you." Davor shut the door after the nobleman and waited to offer assistance.

"I suppose since I am now a visitor, you should find the baron and announce my arrival," he told Davor with a wink. Fabian motioned to Mauro's closed study door and asked, "Where is Lord Baric hiding today?"

Davor, who had lost track of his master, had to admit, "I cannot say for certain if he is still there, but earlier his lordship was reading in the garden." Davor motioned toward the doors across from the study and suggested, "If you would like to wait in the great hall, I can find Lord Baric for you."

Fabian chuckled and said, "I enjoy a good hunt. I will have a look around for the baron myself. Thank you, Davor."

Fabian continued past the grand marble staircase to the end of the foyer. He didn't think Mauro would be in the sitting room on such a pleasant summer day, but he peeked in through the open door anyway. The sofas were empty, and no one was at the writing desk by the terrace.

He continued around the corner of the foyer and opened the door to the kitchen. There, he was reminded why he loved Mauro's house so much. His senses were bombarded with the aromas of freshly baked bread and roasting meat.

The Baric's cook, Nela, and the kitchen maid, Ivana, were quietly eating their noon meal at the long servants' table in the center of the room. The surprised women nearly fell off their stools when they noticed him.

"Excuse the interruption, ladies," Fabian said with a bow, "but I am looking for the baron."

Ivana self-consciously straightened her starched cap that had gone askew while Nela greeted the Venetian like an old friend of the family, which he was.

"Lord Fabian! You are the last person I expected to walk into my kitchen today! Welcome back, my lord," Nela told him gleefully. "What can I offer you?"

"Ah, well, has lunch been served for the house?" he asked. "I would not intrude on your meal, Nela, but if you could set one more place at the baron's table . . ."

"Yes, yes, of course, sir. But the baron wants lunch served late today, after he returns with Lady Baric," Nela informed him. "It is all prepared, though. Would you like something now, Lord Fabian?" Nela signaled Ivana to ready a tray.

"The smells are indeed enticing, but I can wait. Davor said the baron might be in the garden, but if he has gone for the baroness–"

Ivana interjected, "Davor is right, Lord Fabian. Lord Baric is reading by the grape arbor."

"Then I shall continue my search there. Thank you, ladies." Fabian strode out the back door of the kitchen.

Sitting down to their meal again, Ivana speculated on the Venetian's unexpected visit. "What could have brought Lord Fabian back to Solgrad unannounced?"

"A gentleman like Lord Fabian doesn't have to announce his arrival. He must have important business with the baron, though, to come all this way."

Nela ate a spoonful of her cold soup and then added, "I suppose we will find out soon enough."

Chapter 20

Mauro pulled at a clump of juicy grapes dangling by his shoulder and set them on his plate. The shady spot at the edge of the garden was already heating up, and it wasn't even noon—or was it? Mauro absently loosened his lace cravat, unbuttoned his high collar, and then turned the page of his book.

A voice shouted behind him, "Mauritius Baric! When did you become a sedentary man?"

Mauro turned to see if it was really Fabian he had heard.

"What are you doing here, Fabian? You could have just written, you know." He hurried over and embraced his best friend.

"I have not run away again if that is what you are thinking," Fabian replied with a laugh. "I got your letters, Mauro, but every time I sat down to answer one, my plans seemed to change. So, here I am to tell you my news before it becomes old again."

Mauro moved his jacket from the chair across from his own. "Sit down, have a drink, and tell me everything," he replied cheerfully.

Fabian settled in, grinning from ear to ear. He put spoonfuls of broken sugar into the dark coffee Mauro poured for him and leaned back to savor it.

The Venetian aristocrat was dressed for travel in plain broadcloth breeches, but he was not unassuming. The informal cloth expertly matched the dye of his red-leather doublet. His black buckled shoes showed little wear except for the dust of the horse ride from the ferry docks, and his embossed shoulder bag was of the same high-quality craftsmanship as his footwear.

Mauro commented on Fabian's newest acquisition, "Do you know how I am certain you made it to Venice after you left here?"

"Tell me," Fabian said serenely.

"By your fantastic hat! You look like a tall bird with those rose-colored plumes."

Fabian carefully set his prized hat on the bench next to the table, along with the saddlebag that he carried.

"This hat was a gift from my wife," Fabian explained casually, waiting for the words to sink in.

Mauro rewarded him with a baffled grin.

"How could you not write to me with such news? I thought there would be a glamorous wedding next month," Mauro protested.

Fabian made light of it and said, "Do not look so let down, Mauro. It was a very small affair with just our families."

"Since when do the Carreras have small affairs?"

"Well, the truth of it is that we were married the same week my bride arrived in Venice." Fabian's voice had an odd calmness to it that Mauro saw right through.

"There is more to it, isn't there? Why are you here and not on some glorious honeymoon in Rome or Paris? Is married life so terrible that you have already left your new wife?"

"My new wife was tired of traveling," Fabian said. "She wanted to enjoy Venice for a while. She is very agreeable and let me go off on my own for a few days."

"Is that the only reason for your visit? Because your wife agreeably let you come?"

"It is nice to get away from Venice, but I needed your advice and a letter would not do."

Mauro sat up with interest.

Stirring his second cup of coffee, Fabian declared, "Along with a very large dowry, my new father-in-law has given us a small country villa as a wedding gift."

Mauro choked on his own coffee as he listened. "Who is her father? That is quite a gift."

"Indeed."

"But wait. I thought you were going to join the senate. Wouldn't you need a home in Venice instead?"

Fabian shrugged off his concern. "We will keep an apartment in my parents' villa, and I will train there, but the official post I have been offered is with the territorial representatives. Here, in Croatia."

"In Croatia?" Mauro repeated in disbelief.

"Are you not happy about that?"

"I am very happy but also a little confused. There is only one villa for sale that I know of."

Fabian leaned back and smirked. "Exactly!"

"Fabian . . . you cannot be taking on the Dubovic estate?"

"Are you not happy? We will be neighbors!"

"But it is enormous," Mauro said.

"They have split the barony. My new father-in-law has some influence in Venice, and he took first choice before the sale was announced. It is the smallest of the three parcels, but it borders your land."

Mauro ran his fingers through his hair and tried to digest the bombardment of news. "So your bride is Venetian after all? Why did I think she came from another kingdom?"

"Because *I* thought so! Everyone told me she was traveling, so I assumed she was leaving her home to come to Venice. But she was returning from abroad. From the territories. From Croatia."

Mauro sat back in his chair and shook his head. "I would have guessed that your new wife is Isabella Valli, but that would be impossible."

Fabian laughed with delight. "The match was supposed to be a punishment to both of us. Can you believe my good luck?"

"For you, Fabian, but what did Isabella say when she was forced to become the new Signora Carrera? You had quite an angry farewell."

"I will admit that she was somewhat opposed to marrying me at first," Fabian said sheepishly. "After she threw a fit and locked herself in her chamber—thanks to your wife's example in her bathhouse—our parents decided to forgo the excessive wedding plans and have the ceremony over and done with."

Fabian sighed happily and continued, "I have loved Isabella one-sidedly for so long that even after we said our vows before the priest, I still expected her to walk away from me. But it turns out, Mauro, that she can love me as much as I love her. It has been pure bliss, this past month."

"Congratulations, Fabian. I truly mean it. That is quite a turn of events."

Fabian pulled some grapes off the cluster on the plate and was the old, animated Fabian again.

"Speaking of turn of events," he said between bites, "how is the lovely Baroness Baric?"

Mauro could not hide his joy in complimenting his wife. "As lovely as ever, maybe even more so."

"Are the reports true? Did Terese and Jero come charging through the darkness with arrows and pistols and dogs and God knows what else they found, to defend themselves? Rumor has it that they went through a crack in your castle wall and killed four intruders in the process."

Mauro laughed heartily. "Is that what they are saying?"

"Is that not what happened?" Fabian said with disappointment.

"Well, Resi and Jero were certainly brave and heroic. I think they might have even used those weapons against Dubovic's men. I am sorry I could not bring myself to write the full description in my letter to you. While you are here, we can drink a nice bottle of my uncle's wine, and I will tell you all the gory details."

"I have a better idea," Fabian said excitedly.

He searched the large pocket of his bag and brought out an opaque glass bottle. "I would like very much to hear the whole story, but we can drink my father's cognac instead. Happy birthday, Mauritius!" Fabian handed it to Mauro.

The heavy bottle was labeled in French. "This is the good stuff! How is it that you never forget a birthday?" Mauro remarked.

Fabian chuckled and said, "We all have useless talents, Mauritius." Fabian suddenly looked around them and asked, "By the way, why are you here all alone on your special day?"

"You know how I feel about my birthday."

Fabian frowned and said, "You could have done something out of the ordinary and gone to Catholic Mass with your Ottoman wife to get your mind off the day."

Mauro returned the scowl. "I did agree to make a brief appearance at the end of Father David's service."

Fabian looked up at the sun overhead. "Should you not be leaving soon?"

Mauro stood up to fix his cravat. "Yes, it seems late. Have you eaten? You can join us for lunch when we return."

Fabian eyed the empty pastry plates and cheese rinds on the table with regret. "I came straight from the ferry. To be honest, I am starving." He tossed a few more grapes into his mouth.

"I'll tell Ivana to bring you something," Mauro said.

"Don't bother yourself. I will get a morsel or two in the Keep. You didn't give my room away, did you?"

Mauro raised his brow and asked, "Why would I do that?"

"Well, I see you have put your new recruits into action, so I thought perhaps you had hired a few new officers, as well."

Mauro took the jacket slung over the chair back and slipped it on. "I will have to at some point," he acknowledged. "I lost Stephan, you, and now Simeon."

Fabian's smile faded when he asked, "How is Simeon? When you wrote that he was not eating or accepting any help, I was worried for him. I would not have expected him to be so hard on himself."

Mauro shrugged. "It has been over a month since the accident. He can get around with his crutches now, but he has not yet left the Keep."

"Simeon has been in bed this whole time?" Fabian asked.

Mauro sat back down at the table and explained, "He could not manage the stairs, so we moved him down to the sleeping quarters with the soldiers. They have been patient and helpful."

"That is encouraging," Fabian said. "From your letter, I was expecting worse."

"I think Simeon was at his lowest when I first wrote to you," Mauro said. "He will never walk without crutches, but at least we have convinced him that he is not an invalid. When the stump is fully healed, I will have a wooden leg made for him. Alberto thinks he can make some adjustments to Simeon's stirrups so he can ride again." Mauro pointed to the book on the table. "I was just reading about chariots and had a brief, crazy notion that we might rig up a low cart for Simeon to use instead of a saddled horse."

Fabian picked up the book with interest and flipped through the illustrations.

"*Greek and Roman Antiquities.* I have not seen that book in your library before."

Mauro perked up when he told Fabian, "Cyro had it sent from Venice for my wife. He studied the antiquities, you know. They had that in common, and he thought she would enjoy it."

Fabian set the book back on the table. "Very thoughtful. I must admit I have warmed up to my new brother-in-law."

"Did you meet him again while he was in Venice?"

"Oh, yes, how could I avoid it? Cyro arrived with an impressive Duarte entourage: his father, three advisors from Genoa, and half a dozen guardsmen."

"Did the wedding already take place, then? Resi has not heard from Caterina since she left, and my wife is in suspense. We all are."

"It takes time to negotiate the final financial exchanges and promises. My father was impressed with their terms and their obvious wealth. He liked the quality of the wine they brought him as well as their political connections."

"See, Fabian? I told you Cyro would be a good match for your father, if not your sister."

"I agree with you," Fabian said smugly. "The contract papers were drawn up, and then the Duartes left again. They should be back in October. Caterina cried for three days."

Mauro hid his amusement behind his hand. "Poor Caterina. She's had her ups and downs with her courtships. Did Lord Duarte approve of his future daughter-in-law?"

"Cyro's father did not scrutinize the bride's beauty or her devotion to his son. He was negotiating a political alliance rather than a love union. That is my father's main reason for rewarding Caterina with her desired mate. Politics."

"At least they are honest about it," Mauro said.

"Yes, well, it is no secret that the empire needs to work with the Republic of Genoa in the future, and this may be an opening for the council to do that."

"When will the wedding take place?"

"The *when* part has not been decided. If Cyro had understood my sister better, he would have already taken her back to Genoa with him."

Mauro was not so skeptical. "It has only been a few weeks. She cannot find another fiancé in that time. Can she?"

Fabian poured the last drops of the black coffee into his cup and replied, "Caterina falls for every man who bats his eyes and flatters her with sweet compliments."

"Your mother will keep her in line. Locked in her room, perhaps?"

Fabian chuckled at the reality of his sister's plight. "She is sequestered, but my mother unwittingly brought in a pet for her."

Mauro scowled. "A pet? I thought your father forbids dogs in your home."

"Yes, well, Monsieur Jean-René Vincent is a different sort of pet," Fabian explained. "He is a clothes designer my mother met in Lyon last season. He is staying with us while he negotiates silk purchases with my brother. Caterina has latched on to the Frenchman, and she is his Venetian muse."

"That is unlucky for Cyro."

Fabian set his empty cup down with a chuckle. "Oh, I think she is safe from being seduced. Jean-René is recently widowed, but he seems to be peculiarly—well, you can judge his character for yourself when you meet him. Mother says his indulgent flirtations are completely harmless. I find him quite irritating."

"How long will he be staying?"

"Until he is asked to leave, I am sure. He has already been with us two weeks."

"Does that affect our invitation?" Mauro wanted to know. "I planned to bring Davor and Verica. Hugo and Vilim will also come to Venice for the wedding festivities."

"Mother insists you stay with us. I am sure your servants can be accommodated with ours. Hugo and Vilim might have to share a room, but you and Terese will have Michele's apartment upstairs. He moved into his own house this summer."

"How long are you staying here?"

Fabian thought for a moment. "It depends. When were you planning to leave for Stephan's wedding?"

"There is not a lot that requires my attention this time of year. Nestor can easily handle the estate accounts, so I suppose we could leave any time," Mauro decided right then.

"Most of the social affairs will take place before the wedding ceremony," Fabian explained. "Unfortunately, I must wait until the end of the week to meet with the architects. Why don't you leave next week, and I will go back with you?"

"What do you need done at the new house?"

"Well, as you might know, we bought the parcel with the old hunting lodge. We hear it is a bit dreary and old-fashioned. Isabella wants it renovated into a villa, of course. That will take months to complete."

"Will you live in Venice until it is finished?"

"That is another question I came to ask in person. Is your country house available?"

Mauro said lightheartedly, "I must not have mentioned that I gave Jero the old villa house as his new home. He and Ruby might be back at the end of the month, so that will not help you with your lodging problem."

"Well, it was just a thought. Which reminds me . . ."

Fabian fumbled in his saddlebag again and took out a sealed scroll and a packet of documents from one of the pockets. "It is for Jero from my father."

Mauro took the skin-wrapped scroll from Fabian and asked, "His new registry documents?"

Fabian tapped the scroll for emphasis and said, "I believe Jeronim Lorenc Baric has been officially added to the Venetian nobility. And the second envelope contains his exoneration papers for the murder of Baron Sebastian Dubovic. Open them!"

"Just so you know, it was not murder," Mauro said. He untied the bindings and looked over the first page.

"Dubovic was a vile man out to ruin you. I was told the details of your claim about your father's poisoning, too. So it was all Dubovic's doing?"

A shadow crossed Mauro's pleasant features as he explained, "Patrik and I were hidden inside the doors of the great hall when Dubovic met his death. We heard him try to convince Jero to betray the House of Baric. He told my brother I was dead. Jero put a sword through his throat after Dubovic admitted he had set up the ambush that should have killed me."

Fabian shivered despite the heat of the day. "Maybe I never said so, but I always thought there was a particular strength locked away in Jero. I am not surprised he is a Baric. And he went with the mercenaries to Thessaloniki?"

Mauro said happily, "Yes, and he should be a married man by now. He and Ruby planned to sail back with Castor for the next rendezvous with my ship."

"Tell me, Mauro, did Jero ride Bacchus to Greece?"

Mauro set down the parchments and chuckled. "Do you miss your horse?"

"I do."

"I have good news, then. Bacchus is still in my paddock, causing trouble."

"Jero did not want him?"

"He knew you would want your wild stallion back," Mauro said with a laugh. "Bacchus did take a liking to Jero, though."

"My horse is a good judge of character."

"Jero is very likable," Mauro agreed.

Fabian said thoughtfully, "Do you think Jero was able to charm Ruby's father? I understand she was contracted to wed another man."

"Resi got a letter from Angelos Spiros after Jero and Ruby left. It turns out the Greek groom prefers Ruby's sister to Ruby."

Fabian reflected, "Ruby is a natural beauty, but maybe her sister is stunning, and he couldn't help himself."

Mauro shook his head with a chuckle. "I am sure any sister of Ruby's would be pretty, but the letter explained that, given a choice, he preferred to marry the girl he was sure he liked."

"The man got lucky in his wish."

"For a while, it didn't seem that way. Ruby is the eldest daughter and must marry first. Jero has solved that problem for everyone, and her sister is willing to marry this man in her place."

Fabian said thoughtfully, "I am glad it worked out for the pair, but if they sailed with Castor, Branislav should have brought them home by now. It is already past the quarter moon."

"Branislav had a few deliveries along the coast after the rendezvous with Castor. He has not sailed home yet. We are still hopeful that Jero and Ruby can join us in Venice."

"Maybe they will stay in Thessaloniki awhile. I am sure the Spiros family will want to get to know their new son-in-law," Fabian reflected.

"That is a good point. There has been no correspondence from Jero or Ruby, so we will know for sure when Branislav is back," Mauro said.

Fabian leaned back in his chair. "It has been quite a summer for marriages," he said. "I expect Stephan's will be the event of the season. Mira and her mother are going all out."

"You know, when I first met Stephan, we were only seventeen. Even then, all he talked about was how he wanted to marry Mira," Mauro maintained. "I would not miss seeing his happy union for the world."

"How will you get there? Will you take your ship?"

"We will have to," Mauro said with a laugh. "The maids have been busy sewing new gowns for Resi with the wonderful fabric your mother sent her. We could never take so many trunks with us in the wagon."

"And you, Mauro?" Fabian asked with a new seriousness.

"Me? Well, I can get by with only one trunk," he joked sheepishly.

Fabian could not hide his genuine concern. "Can you endure a water crossing?"

"I will manage. I have made peace with Neptune, but just in case, Resi is bringing a heavy bottle to knock me out," Mauro said with a smirk.

"She is a resourceful woman."

"Isabella would do the same for you," Mauro insisted. "They both have that in common."

A strange expression of clarity came over Mauro, and he announced, "I don't know why I did not think of this earlier."

"Think of what?"

"Your lodging problem. You and Isabella will stay in our house during your renovations," Mauro offered enthusiastically. "I know Resi would be thrilled to have your and Isabella's company again. It has been far too quiet since you all left. And we have been talking about having Resi's portrait painted. Isabella can bring her paints and canvas, and my wife can be her first model."

"Are you sure?" Fabian asked hopefully. "We might have to live here a few months. We would not want to impose."

"Of course, I am sure. I will be glad to have you here again for as long as I can, Fabian. I am convinced now that there is no better lucky charm than you," Mauro said.

Fabian nodded emphatically. "I don't mind keeping an eye on you, and Isabella will love the idea. We will sail back here with you after Stephan's wedding."

Davor quietly appeared at the table and cleared his throat to gain the baron's attention.

Mauro had lost all track of time. "Oh, dear. I should have already left, isn't that right, Davor?"

"Your horse is saddled, sir, and waiting in the courtyard. And I brought your hat, my lord." Davor held it out to his master.

Mauro stood up for the second time and set his unadorned hat over his short hair. Fabian put on his feathered one again and grabbed his lightened saddlebag. They walked toward the courtyard together.

Mauro remarked, "There is so much to tell you still. Are you sure you do not want to come with me to the church, Fabian?"

"You go to Mass so rarely, Mauro, I would not want to steal your villagers' adulation of you by having the attention focused on my sudden arrival."

Mauro glanced at his friend and asked, "Was my plan so obvious?"

Fabian nodded. "You are the village patron. Accept the adoration of its citizens!"

Mauro chuckled at his friend's open arrogance.

Fabian ignored him. "Anyway," he continued, "I wanted to freshen up in my old chamber if my trunks are still in there."

"Everything is as you left it. And when Resi and I are back, we will open your father's fine bottle of spirits and properly toast your new marriage."

"And your birthday," Fabian added.

Josip was waiting by the well with Mauro's stallion.

"Do you no longer take an escort with you?" Fabian asked with concern.

"Since Dubovic's passing, I am happy to report the threat to my life has greatly diminished."

Mauro nudged his horse to be on its way to the village, and Fabian crossed the courtyard to the Keep.

Chapter 21

The Venetian eyed the Keep tower's outside stairs that led into the dining hall. His stomach rumbled about his missed breakfast. He would surely find a hearty bowl of something while waiting for the Barics to return from the village.

Fabian opened the heavy door with anticipation. For this man who had spent his childhood eating under crystal lamps at gilded tables covered with embroidered linen, seeing the torchlit granite walls and waxed plank tables felt more like a homecoming.

Mauro's guardsmen were scattered around the big hall in pairs and small groups finishing their noon meals. The remaining Baric officers—Hugo, Eduard, Daniel, and Vilim—were eating together at a table near the back stairwell.

Heads turned when the man in red with the extraordinary hat entered their realm.

"Fabian is here!" Hugo exclaimed, pointing across the room.

Vilim stood up and called over, "Lazar told us you were here at the castle, but we did not believe him. Welcome home, Fabian!"

"Thank you," Fabian called back with a broad grin. "Let me grab a bowl, and I will join you."

Fabian carried his sloshing fish stew with Milan's special dumplings over to the crowded captains' table.

Eduard picked up his empty bowl to make room. "Take my stool, Fabian," he offered cordially. "It is high time to round up the men, but I am curious what brings you back so suddenly."

Vilim started right off, saying, "No one has heard a word from you since you went back to Venice, Fabian. We thought you had met your end. Have they run out of quills there?"

"Maybe his new bride wasn't new at all. Did they match you with an old spinster?" Hugo wanted to know.

"Di-di-did you rrrun awway again, F-fabian?" Daniel asked.

Fabian nodded guiltily and took the offered seat. He swallowed a spoonful of his steaming lunch and enthusiastically admitted, "I plead guilty to all charges, except I did not run away this time, Daniel." He set his spoon down and paused for effect. "This time they caught me! I am a married man now!"

"Did you hear that, men?" Eduard bellowed to the room. "Captain Carrera is a married man!"

A roar of cheers echoed around the common room.

"Is the match so terrible that you have already left her?" Hugo teased.

"It is at my bride's bidding that I return, but it is not due to lack of chemistry," Fabian replied with a jovial wink. "If you can wait until dinner tonight, I will explain everything to everyone."

Hugo raised his mug and said, "You always like to build suspense, Fabian."

Vilim added, "We'll toast your good fortune properly tonight, then."

"And a few glasses of wine always helps you with your storytelling," Eduard interjected.

Fabian's eyes rested on quiet Simeon at a table in the corner. The once burly soldier was barely recognizable as the same person. "You are looking well, Simeon," Fabian called over to him.

Eduard would no longer coddle his best friend. He told Fabian, "Go ahead and say it. Simeon is as pasty and thin as a ghost."

"We rigged up a pulley outside the stairs so he wouldn't need his legs, but we cannot get him to leave the Keep," Hugo said.

"I saw the chair hanging from the barrel hoist. Is that for you, Simeon?" Fabian asked loudly.

"It w-w-works grrreat," Daniel said with an enthusiastic nod.

Hugo added, "We all tried it out. The guards even had a contest to see who could pull themselves up and down the quickest."

Vilim reported with a laugh, "Teodor won that one!"

"I came in a close second," Hugo bragged.

Fabian could see the enthusiasm in everyone's faces, except for Simeon's. He asked the men at his table, "Who came up with the pulley idea?"

The officers looked awkwardly at each other, unable to take credit for it. Eduard finally admitted, "Idita did."

"Idita?" Fabian repeated.

"The crane has always been there for hauling up supplies," Eduard explained. "She thought to add a seat and rig it with ropes that could be pulled from the chair itself."

Fabian called over, "That is fantastic for you, Simeon. But you do not like it, do you?"

Simeon fidgeted on his stool. "What I don't like is making a spectacle of myself, like some people around here," he said directly to Hugo.

"It wasn't a spectacle. So, I fell off a few times, but it works perfectly now," Hugo argued lightheartedly.

Eduard crossed his arms and insisted, "Tell Fabian the real reason you won't go out, Simeon."

Fabian raised his brows with curiosity, but Simeon was mum.

Daniel replied for him, "F-f-franja."

"Of course," Fabian remarked. "You were going to marry her, weren't you? What happened, Simeon?"

"May I tell him?" Vilim asked Simeon directly.

"It isn't a secret," Simeon grumbled.

Vilim began, "Franja tried to visit him in the Keep, several times as a matter of fact, but Simeon would not see her. Then, when he finally agreed to let her in a week ago, she refused to visit. She said she would wait for him to come out, instead."

"Then Idita came up with the chair idea," Hugo explained.

"They are both beyond stubborn," Eduard remarked. "Simeon won't go out now, and Franja won't come in."

"One could say they deserve each other. They did think so once," Vilim pointed out.

Eduard nodded and said, "Franja probably would have still taken him as her man if his pride hadn't gotten in the way. Are we telling it right, Simeon?"

Simeon's glumness grew as the men bantered back and forth about his failed marriage proposal.

Fabian ventured to ask, "Did you ever give Franja the ring you had wrought for her?"

Simeon breathed out heavily with regret. "I proposed marriage to Franja on the night before the ambush. I never got my answer."

Fabian was suddenly hopeful. "Well, there you are! Hoist yourself down and go get it!"

Simeon shrugged him off. "I don't want her answer now."

Eduard shook his head pitifully. "The topic of Franja has been through the wringer more than once, Fabian. Best leave it be." He then shouted to the guardsmen, "Come on, men! The day is only half over! There is work to do!"

Before he walked away to his duties, Eduard leaned into Fabian and whispered what he had been saying for weeks: "Simeon will come around."

Chapter 22

Resi's nightgown slipped off the mattress and onto the stone floor. Mauro picked it up and went to the window to open the shutters. The stale air stirred again with the breeze. He stared out at the shadowed mountain and said, "Thank you for a wonderful birthday, Resi."

"I can only take credit for part of your day," she replied serenely.

Feeling a sudden chill from the draft on her naked skin, Resi slipped her arms through the wide sleeves of her dressing gown and tied the robe shut across her round middle. She joined Mauro at the window and put her arms around his bare waist, leaning into his warm back. The musky scent of sex, mixed with the lingering lavender soap on his skin, smelled lovely, and she let out a contented sigh.

Mauro turned and kissed her. "You spoil me, Resi," he said. "Through all your pampering tonight, did I mention how much I love you?"

She melted into his tall frame, listening to his heart's slow, rhythmic beating. "I love you, too," she whispered.

It was long past sunset, and the day had to end sometime. Mauro told her, "Why don't you crawl back under the covers?"

She squeezed his hand and went back to bed, stretching out on the disheveled sheets. She watched as Mauro rummaged through his open trunk for a fresh shirt. "It is nice to have Fabian here again. He always energizes a party," she remarked sleepily.

"What would you say about having Fabian and Isabella live in Mother's old room while their new home is being renovated?"

"Really?" she asked in surprise. "I love the idea, Mauro. Now that Ruby is gone, the house feels empty. Lady Isabella is such an interesting woman—so full of life and curiosity. I think we can be good friends."

"Ruby and Jero will be back soon, and you will have plenty of female company again."

"You are right," Resi said dreamily.

Mauro was dressed for bed, but he continued to search in his trunk.

"What are you looking for, Mauro?"

"This." He held up what seemed to be a cloth square.

"What is it?" she asked.

He came back to her side and set it on her lap. "A gift for you, Resi."

The cloth object was a green velvet bag. His wife stroked the delicate fabric and said, "But it is your birthday, Mauro."

His smile made it to his green eyes. Mauro liked surprising her.

"It has nothing to do with birthdays. I came across it in my mother's trunk a while ago, and I knew you should have it."

Resi untied the gold satin cord holding the velvet shut and pulled out a small ivory box. She ran her fingers around its smooth sides, admiring the workmanship. The letter B was skillfully engraved in the center of the lid.

"Thank you, Mauro. It is lovely."

"Open the box," he said excitedly.

Mauro had already given his wife a splendid bathhouse, a beautiful mare, and an extraordinary emerald ring. He had allowed books for their library and all the comforts of a home Resi had only read about in fairy tales as a girl.

"You know I need nothing else," she protested.

"Don't be stubborn," he said with a chuckle. "Let me have the pleasure of giving you something special."

She took a deep breath and lifted the lid. Under a small silk pillow was a holy cross the size of her finger. It was gold, inlaid with blue enamel, the color of the Adriatic Sea. The edges were faded, worn from being touched over the years. In the center of the cross was a brilliant square emerald. It came from the cave outside her bedroom window, like her emerald ring.

"It is meant to be worn on a chain," he pointed out.

"It is beautiful, Mauro. I am overwhelmed that you are entrusting me with your mother's pendant."

Mauro took the jeweled pendant from its box. He turned it over and told his wife, "It was my grandmother's first. Her initials AGB are engraved on the back: Anika Giorgina Baric. It's strange that I know almost nothing else about my grandmother except her name. My grandfather must have loved her very much. He never remarried after she died."

"She died in childbirth, didn't she?" Resi asked.

"Oh, Resi, my love, I did not mean to bring that up again." He reached over and lovingly stroked her belly. "Let us not talk about it, alright? You are strong and healthy. You will easily have this child."

She put her hand over his and attempted to make light of her condition, "I am not worried about the actual birth, Mauro. I am more worried that I will become too large to be attractive."

He kissed her protruding middle. "I promise, even at the end of your pregnancy, I will find you enchanting. I like enormous women."

"Mauro! I said large, not enormous!"

Changing the conversation back to his gift, he said, "Here, let me see how this looks on you."

Mauro lifted the strand of braided gold around Resi's neck and clipped the cross pendant onto it. "It looks pretty on your chain," he said.

She held the pendant up to admire it herself. "I see why the enamel is worn. It feels nice to hold. I will indeed treasure it, Mauro, but it is too precious to wear to bed." Resi lifted the chain over her head and put it back into its ivory box.

Mauro blew out the candles, and Resi sank deeper under the covers. Her eyes adjusted to the starlight coming in through the open window, and she let her mind wander.

"You know, Mauro. We haven't had a dinner party since the others left for Greece. I know I said differently before, but I must admit I do enjoy a party."

"Are you saying you want to host another ball?" Mauro asked.

"Maybe not *such* a big party again so soon," she said with a chuckle, "but I miss the company of friends. I guess I didn't realize how much I would miss Ruby these past weeks. Of course, Fabian brought back all the memories of this summer when he talked about Caterina and his life with Isabella."

She sighed. "I can't stop thinking about the happy news. It was always obvious to me that Isabella loved Fabian, and that they were good together. And Caterina gets to marry Cyro . . . It is such a fairy-tale ending to this eventful summer."

"The summer is not yet over, Resi. We will leave for Venice in a week. Are you looking forward to that?" Mauro asked sleepily.

"I truly am, and also happy we will all be together at the Carrera's."

Mauro mumbled, "They will take good care of you, my love."

She nudged him and asked, "They? Where will you be? Will we not spend time together?"

Mauro sleepily rolled toward her and explained, "Of course, we will spend time together, but I have not seen my old soldiering friends for a long time, and I will be required to join them."

"So, you will be gone all day with your friends, like here?"

"You will be so busy at all the parties you wanted that you won't even miss me. If I know Mira, there will be a few ladies-only parties that Isabella will want to take you to."

"But we only have three weeks, Mauro. Will there be time to visit museums or go to the theater? Fabian talked of the many art galleries we should visit."

"Whatever you like, my love."

"Are you even listening, Mauro? You told me you don't like art galleries."

Mauro pulled her closer and whispered, "But Caterina does, and you can go with her. I will show you off in other ways. Take you to the opera and . . ."

His voice trailed off, but Resi did not notice.

"The opera? Yes, that sounds grand. I am glad the girls were able to finish my new dresses. I don't want to embarrass you, Mauro."

She stroked the curly locks around his temple and whispered, "Are you asleep?"

He mumbled, "Have no worries, my love. People in Venice wear all sorts of costumes. You could never be out of place there."

"I have one more worry."

Mauro opened his eyes and focused on her troubled expression. "Tell me just the one, and then we will sleep."

"I didn't mention it before, but I gave one of the bolts of fabric to Verica to make herself a new gown. Do you think Lady Carrera will notice? I don't want Fabian's mother to feel insulted after going to all that trouble to send me such lovely cloth."

Mauro assured her, "Lady Carrera will be pleased with how generous you are, my love, and how fine the dress looks on your lady's maid."

"I am still hopeful that Ruby and Jero will be back in time to sail with us."

"Resi, I have committed to a field exercise at first light. I need to sleep now."

"I cannot help but worry," she whispered.

"It is a whole week away, my dear. If they are not back in time, they can take the ferry and meet us there."

"Will they know where to find us?" She leaned in close, stroking his cheek, needing his assurance.

Mauro let out a chuckle and said, "There is only one Carrera family in Venice. They will find us."

He moved her hand from his cheek to his lips and kissed it in the dim moonlight. "Now I insist you stay awake and go over all those thoughts in your pretty head, my dear, and I will sleep for both of us."

"All right, Mauro," she told him dreamily.

Resi rearranged the pillows to get comfortable with her ever-growing baby stirring within her. She listened to Mauro's steady breathing next to her as she stared up at the timbered ceiling. After trying not to sleep for a few minutes, she shut her eyes one final time.

~*~

Faithful to his duty, Mauro was long gone when the clattering of silver against porcelain stirred Resi from her deep slumber.

It was Natalija who woke her. The maid set the baroness's table each morning with the stealth of a mouse, but today she moved the dishes and spoons from the tray to the table with a frustrated clumsiness.

Resi pulled the covers down from her chin and asked good-naturedly, "Are you having a bad morning, Natalija?"

Natalija jumped from her daydream and apologized emphatically, "I am sorry I woke you, Lady Baric. I will try to do better, but I am indeed a bit anxious today."

Natalija knew everything that went on in the manor house. Resi sat up with interest and asked, "What are you anxious about? What has happened?"

"Oh, well, my lady, it is nothing terrible, I suppose. Except I have to tell Verica, and she will be very upset. And when she is upset, then she will not be good company for you, mistress. And, well, she might be angry at me, although it is not my fault, but she is my best friend, so it is my place to tell her the bad news."

Natalija sniffed back her tears and curtsied at the door. "I apologize, Lady Baric. I will leave you to your breakfast."

She opened the door and walked out.

"Natalija!" Resi called after her.

The maid peered back around the door. "Yes, Lady Baric?"

"What is this news that will make Verica so upset?"

Natalija inched her way back into the room and disclosed, "I, um, went home after Mass yesterday. I found out it's been decided that my brother Luka is going to marry the butcher's daughter from the neighboring village. Everyone is very happy with the match. My mother says she will get the best cuts of meat now."

Resi plopped back on her pillows with a groan and said, "You are right, Natalija. Verica will be very upset. She thinks she loves Luka, and she won't be consoled by your mother's good fortune for her dinner table."

Natalija hung her head.

Resi said urgently, "Do not tell her the bad news until we come back from Venice. Will you promise me?"

Natalija frowned, twisting her apron strings in distress. "What will I say when I see her, my lady? I cannot keep this from her for so long."

"It is only a week. Say everything to her but that! Promise me, Natalija."

She dropped the bunched apron and unhappily curtsied her agreement. "I will do my best, madam."

The servant girl went to the door with her empty tray, but turned around once more. "Is it true, my lady, that Lady Isabella will be returning?"

"I think so. She will stay in the same room as before, but this time with Lord Fabian until they can move into their new home."

"Will I be her lady's maid again?" Natalija asked with a frown.

"Oh, well. I had not thought about that."

Natalija unwittingly held the tray against her like a shield. It was clear to Resi that other arrangements would have to be made.

"I expect Lady Isabella will bring her own lady's maid this time since she will be staying more permanently."

Natalija blew out a sigh of relief, and Resi held back a grin. "You are disappointed?" Resi asked kindly.

Natalija shook her head and said, "I do like her ladyship very much, but the Venetians change their minds quite often, Lady Baric, and I had a hard time keeping up with what they might want next."

"I understand. Perhaps you can just bring Lady Isabella her breakfast while she is here."

Natalija grinned broadly and said, "I do know what she likes to eat in the morning. Thank you, Lady Baric."

Resi swung her legs over the edge of the bed as Natalija curtsied to leave. Verica crossed paths with her at the door, and she didn't look happy.

"I have news, Lady Baric," Verica announced uneasily.

Natalija blurted out, "Who told you already?"

Verica eyed her friend curiously and answered, "I met Geoff downstairs in the kitchen. He was told by the guards returning from the port."

"Why would the guards at the port even be bothered by the news?" Natalija wondered aloud. "Can no one keep a secret around here?" she asked and left the chamber.

Verica looked questioningly to her mistress.

Resi assured her, "I think Natalija was thinking of some other piece of news. Go ahead and tell me the rest."

"Well, madam, the morning guards told Geoff that Branislav docked the ship this morning. Jero and Lady Ruby were not on board."

Resi took a sip of the steaming tea Natalija had poured to calm herself and said, "I was counting on them coming."

"I am sorry, madam. The guards said your brother Castor had been at sea for two weeks before meeting Branislav. He left before Ruby and Jero even arrived in Thessaloniki. Castor promised to bring them directly with the next sailing," Verica reported.

Resi moaned, "That is a shame. I was hoping they could come to Venice with us. But at least Jero can spend some time with Ruby's family and know Thessaloniki better."

Verica curtsied and said, "I will leave you to your breakfast, Lady Baric."

"When you come back, Verica, I would like to try on all the gowns again to make sure there is enough room stitched in the waist to get me through September."

Verica hovered by the door and said, "I was wondering, my lady . . ."

"Yes, Verica?"

"I am almost done making my dress, but I am not sure if it is right. I was wondering if you could tell me what you think of it, madam."

"I would love to see what you have designed. Go put it on!"

"Oh, thank you, Lady Baric!"

Resi ate her boiled egg and finished her tea. Then she stood in front of her looking glass and wondered how long her fitted gowns would be useful.

She held her robe against her middle with a sigh and said under her breath, "I am growing like a harvest pumpkin. Three more months, and they will have to roll me down the stairs."

The door opened, and Resi's focus turned from her own blooming body to that of her young handmaiden.

"Oh, my," were the words that left Resi's lips.

Suddenly self-conscious, Verica smoothed the light fabric of the skirt to minimize its full effect. "Is it not good, Lady Baric? Do you not like it?"

"No, I'm just . . ."

Resi circled her maid, studying the gown. "Tell me, Verica. What inspired you to design your dress like that?"

"Well, um," Verica began awkwardly, "I loved the gowns the Venetian ladies wore when they were here." She took a deep breath and added, "And I do love the flowing sleeves and soft layers of your robes, Lady Baric."

Resi smiled and said, "I see it now."

"Is it too presumptuous?" Verica asked worriedly.

"The dress suits you, through and through. You have grown into such a woman right before my eyes this year. Somehow I am shocked at how the dress accentuates that. I love it, though. You look sophisticated and feminine. I wish you had saved that design for my dress," Resi said in praise.

Verica smiled sheepishly.

Resi continued, "I don't know if I can let you out in Venice in such a lovely gown. You will turn heads, for sure."

The maid giggled. "Please, say you are teasing me, my lady because I cannot wait to wear it in public. I have no use for such a gown in Solgrad. Luka doesn't care so much about how I dress, but I feel extra light and pretty wearing my new gown."

Resi cautiously advised, "You know I think Luka is a fine young man, but perhaps you need to look beyond him. You are too clever to be just a tanner's wife. Not that I ever want to lose you, dear Verica, but there is a man out there, perhaps even in our courtyard right now, who will appreciate how special you are, how beautiful."

Verica looked at her feet in embarrassment. "Thank you for your kind words," she said. "I will go change now. My servant's dress isn't glamorous, but I feel very much at home in it."

Verica's brown boots showed under the ornate lace hem of the gown as she glided out the door.

Resi called out, "We will have to take a quick ride to the village and find you some prettier shoes to match your gown."

Verica turned back with a beaming smile and said, "I dared not ask, my lady, but I was thinking the same. I truly cannot thank you enough for everything. Going to Venice will be the trip of a lifetime for me."

"For both of us," Resi agreed.

<h1 style="text-align:center">Chapter 23</h1>

Venice, 25 August 1649

The sea was in a gentle mood that day, and the bow of the *Margaret* easily parted the clear azure water of the Adriatic. The ship's crew worked the canvas sails through the steady wind while waves rhythmically splashed the sides of the wooden sailing ship. Resi didn't mind whether they were sailing on a placid sea or one rolling with white caps. She was glad to be on her way to Venice finally.

Mauro owned two sailing ships, captained by Branislav Tomsic. Each month, his crew ferried the baron's goods in the Baric's smaller ship to his customers across the Adriatic. Once the deliveries were handed over, Branislav and his crew would sail back with Mauro's provisions.

Since business was combined with pleasure on this journey, the larger ship, the *Margaret,* was loaded with the usual delivery of salt, skins, and produce from the tenant farms, as well as nonstandard cargo: the seven passengers from the castle with their trunks and baggage.

The Empire's capital seemed a world away, and it was. Even the larger Baric ship needed a whole day to reach it. Mauro was not entirely cured of his fear of deep water, so he kept to the captain's quarters at the stern of the ship to avoid a panic attack on the open sea.

Resi had joined him in the little cabin at first, but with so much happening on deck, she was restless in the small space. Her fidgeting made Mauro even more anxious in the close confines, so Fabian exchanged places with the baroness and kept Mauro's thoughts off the rolling sea.

When Resi stepped out onto the ship's deck again, no land could be seen on any horizon. Verica and Davor were wrapped in their cloaks just outside the cabin door. They had settled on the lid of a storage compartment to keep out of the sailors' way while the crew busily worked the ropes and surveyed the ship's sides for hazards.

Verica had never been on a boat of any size before and had talked nonstop to the other maids about how excited she was to sail on one. Once on the open sea, the excitement of the excursion waned, and Verica unpacked her needlepoint to pass the empty hours. Davor sat comfortably next to Verica in solitary quietness. They had already discussed all there was to say in the first hour, and now Mauro's valet contentedly read the book he had brought with him.

Resi faced the salty breeze with a satisfied smile, moving from port to starboard, watching the crew at work and the sea rushing by. She was a sailor's daughter, and she found much to hold her interest during the monotonous crossing. Hugo and Vilim, too, took an active interest in the operation of Mauro's ship and lent a hand where needed. She was pleased to see the two enjoying themselves.

By mid-afternoon, a sandy shoreline was visible in the distance. While in Branislav's cabin, Resi had studied his map of the Venetian lagoon that was unrolled on the table. It showed how the long dunes shielded the lagoon's low islands.

Ships that crossed the narrow entrance into the lagoon without a map like Branislav's risked the peril of meeting hidden sandbars in the shallow marshes of the bay.

The capital's protective geography was one factor in the Empire's strength, but its wealth came from commerce, and commerce in Venice revolved around mastery of the waterways. The Venetian Republic traded with the whole world, but crossing this lagoon was the only way into its capital city.

The baron's crew knew the channel markings as well as any Venetian sailor, but the *Margaret* required more care in navigating them. Branislav shouted orders into the wind as he steered the big wheel of the rudder.

The renewed activity on deck made Resi think of her own seafaring family. She pictured her father shouting orders as his merchant ship left the docks of Thessaloniki for distant waters. If she had been given the same chance as her brothers, Resi would have chosen to stand at the wheel of her father's ship like Branislav stood now, his hair blowing wildly in the breeze.

Resi would have also preferred to leave her hair loose to blow around freely, but she was now a noble lady governed by expectations. Verica had carefully pinned her long hair before they left, then tied her hat with a wide scarf to keep her curls from blowing loose and tangling during the voyage. The broad-brimmed hat shaded Resi's eyes as she searched the horizon for the city itself.

Fabian strolled toward Resi, who stood at the railing. He was not a sailor's son, but he was a true Venetian. Fabian had acquired sea legs at a young age and managed well on the rocking deck. He held his own wide hat with his hand to keep it from taking off like a kite.

"We should be there soon, Terese," he shouted in her direction.

She leaned in to be heard and said, "I pictured Venice differently. It is all so flat. I cannot make out the landmarks."

Fabian pointed along the horizon. "There is the dome of the Basilica," he said. "Do you see the bell tower next to it?"

She scanned the water as the ship moved briskly toward its destination. "I can see it now. And what island is this ahead of us?" she asked. "The church seems to float in the sea."

"Ah, yes. That is San Giorgio," Fabian leaned in to explain. "The church there is fairly new. I hear it is magnificent inside."

"Is it a monastery?" she asked.

"It is, but they allow visitors. I doubt Mauro would enjoy the boat ride there, but I would gladly escort you for a visit, Terese."

"I would love that, Fabian," she said.

Their ship quickly approached the bay in front of the Basilica of San Marco, and the men reefed the sails to stop their momentum.

Other ships, large and small, were anchored in the water on the city's edge. A flurry of small boats and gondolas busily transported people and goods to and from those ships.

Branislav shouted orders, then expertly turned the *Margaret* to lay anchor among them.

It suddenly occurred to Resi that Mauro had not come out to join them. "Is my husband still in the cabin?" she asked Fabian.

"Well, Terese," Fabian said, hesitating, "I actually came to tell you Mauritius is quite unconscious."

"Oh, dear. That might be my fault," Resi awkwardly confessed. "I poured him a special tea Idita made to help him relax. He must have drunk too much of it."

Fabian began to laugh. "I, too, put something in his mug. I suppose our combined concern has put him completely out. He is going to be angry if he has to be carried off the ship," Fabian said with amusement.

Resi pulled on a rope tied to the railing and found what she had expected. "If you help me dip this bailing bucket into the water, I will see what I can do to wake him."

"A dunk of cold water should do the trick," he said. "I'll carry it to the captain's quarters. Perhaps we need not tell Mauritius why he was asleep the whole journey."

Resi agreed with a hearty nod.

As Branislav and his crew completed the final preparations and secured the anchor, a man in a flatboat shouted up to Fabian at the railing, "Ferry service to the shore, sir, at a fair price."

Fabian hollered back, "Thank you! You can talk to the captain about transporting the goods to the docks. Baron Baric and his wife will need a gondola, as will I and my companions. There are several trunks to be transported as well."

"How many passengers, sir?" the oarsman asked.

"Five gentlemen and two ladies. One gondola must be canopied for the ladies' comfort."

"I'll arrange that right away, sir. Where will you be going?"

"To my home, the Carrera villa, halfway down the Grand Canal."

The oarsman perked up when he realized he had been addressing an important nobleman. "Yes, Lord Carrera, sir. I know exactly where that is."

A second flatboat paddled up to the first, and the two gondoliers exchanged instructions while Fabian waited with the bucket for their reply.

"Ricco here will load your trunks, Lord Carrera. I will return with the extra boat for the ladies. It will take no time at all, sir." Then the first man rowed away.

Every great city had a main street of importance, a place to stroll and be seen, lined with tall trees and ornate spaces. Venice was a city of liquid streets, and the most magnificent of them was the Grand Canal. But instead of being lined with trees and flowerbeds, it was lined with opulent houses trimmed with colorful awnings. In contrast to the vibrant buildings, unadorned gondolas skimmed the water like black shadows across the Venetian rainbow.

Gondolas were the perfect vessels to manage the multitude of canals and watery alleys between the houses and industries. Many privileged Venetians, like the Carrera and Valli families, kept their own flat-bottomed boats at the ready in especially designed docks. But the rest of the city used public gondolas. A daily parade of them transported all classes of people up and down the waterways.

Two such sleek boats paddled the short expanse from the anchored *Margaret* to the entrance of the Grand Canal, carrying the seven visitors.

The Barics and their two servants traveled in a curtained cabin. The shroud was meant to protect the passengers from the weather or unwanted onlookers. At first Resi fretted that she wouldn't be able to see the sights while seated behind a black veil. But the late-afternoon sunshine shone brightly, and the sheer drapes only blocked the view in, not out.

The privacy today was mostly for Mauro's benefit after Resi had not been successful in reviving him right away. Not that it was unusual for a passenger to be passed out on a gondola ride. Just the same, the Barics would be mingling with many influential people in the coming weeks, and gossip traveled in strange ways among the bored elite looking for a scandal. Fabian felt obligated to make sure Mauro's reputation was untainted.

From their cushioned seats, Resi and her servants took in the lavish splendor of the massive Doge Palace looming in front of them. Flanking the extraordinary palace was an expansive public square and the Basilica of San Marco. Their gondola glided past a multitude of columned buildings, statues, and covered promenades. What made the three stare in awe were the people randomly assembled on the plaza in front of the spectacular structures. Mauro had been right about Resi fitting in—it seemed people from all corners of the world and all walks of life called Venice home, if just for a short time.

The fresh breeze had helped Mauro recover, and he pointed out, "Venice was actually built on many islands of sand that were formed by fresh-water streams flowing around them." He explained to his eager listeners, "The early Venetians tamed the shallow rivers to become these canals. As its name suggests, the Grand Canal is the largest in Venice. Some waterways are only the width of a boat."

Verica commented, "There are so many people out and about."

Mauro replied, "San Marco Square is always filled with people, coming and going. It is a good meeting place for all occasions."

"Are there no streets at all, Lord Baric?" Verica asked.

"There are streets through each island, but you might consider them to be more like alleys, even walkways. They connect the shops and bakeries and houses that fill the space," Mauro explained.

Davor studied the rows of houses along the canal and beyond, and he asked, "How can sand support so many buildings, Lord Baric?"

The fog of Idita's drugged tea had cleared, and Mauro answered thoughtfully, "The founders were quite clever, and the sand was reinforced to hold the weight."

"How, sir?" Davor wondered.

"Well, for one, the Venetians had all the forests of Dalmatia at their disposal. It is said that the first builders brought in thousands of logs to pound into the sand, like one does to make a pier. Then they filled the spaces between the logs with rocks to make a foundation. The water laps against the houses like they are swimming, but in fact the buildings stand firmly on a sort of platform."

"Will they not sink one day, sir?" Verica asked with worry.

Mauro shook his head. "They have stood for hundreds of years, Verica. I do not think they will sink now."

Resi peeked through the curtain's opening to see the buildings' true colors and said, "They are so splendid. Even the poles holding the boats are colorful. It is hard to take it all in."

"Not all the houses in Venice are lavish, Resi. These are owned by the ruling class. Everything is luxurious in their world."

"I must admit I do see the appeal of it," Resi said with a chuckle. "I love the hidden porches and the tucked-away balconies. It almost seems like the Venetians are watching the outside world in secret."

"I am not sure there is a clandestine reason for the architecture. The Venetians I know do not mind being seen," Mauro said.

"I find it all so different," Verica remarked. "I have never seen a plastered house."

Mauro reflected, "I have always found the sameness of our stone houses in Solgrad to be comforting. Here people strive to be distinct from their neighbors, to stand out."

"What color is Fabian's house?" Resi asked.

"Believe it or not, it is just plain white. It has some gold trim along the arches, where we will dock our boats, and I think the tile is quite colorful, but, otherwise, it is what you might call 'understated.' There it is. The Carrera villa is up ahead, on the right."

Resi pulled the curtain aside to see it better. Her eyes were wide with surprise. "The one all by itself, with canals on each side?"

Mauro chuckled at her shocked expression. "Maybe my description did not do it justice. It is a beautiful villa."

"Mauro, it is practically a palace," Resi exclaimed.

"There are palaces here and there, but the Carreras are not quite in that league. Lord Carrera is an important man in Venice, so he wanted something stately, I suppose. And a man with six children needs a large house."

Resi looked out the rear window at the gondola behind them, transporting their three companions.

Fabian was in animated conversation with Vilim and Hugo, pointing here and there along the canal.

Clinging to the side of the cushioned bench in nervous anticipation, Resi asked, "How many siblings live at the Carrera villa?"

"Gabriel and Michele have their own homes now, but not too far away. I believe Cristina recently moved with her husband to the other side of Venice. I am sure you will meet them, though. Fabian and Isabella were given a suite on the top floor when they married, and Caterina will stay until she marries Cyro, of course. And then there is Bianca, the youngest. You will see much of her, I am sure."

Mauro tied back the veiling curtains as their gondola approached the Carrera dock. He turned with a smile and said, "Here we are."

Chapter 24

The oarsmen navigated the sleek boats into the slips in front of the arched entrance to the Carrera villa. Gilded columns held up the low roof over the dock where the passengers would disembark.

Waiting there were two servants, dressed in blue-and-gold striped breeches. The men hurried across the shadowed platform to assist the visitors.

Fabian was the first to climb out of the gondola, followed by Hugo and Vilim. He gave the Carrera servants their orders, "The luggage is coming in the boat behind us. The bags are marked and should be brought upstairs." He helped Verica out onto the dock, and Davor stepped out after her.

Mauro offered Resi his hand. Despite the layers of confining fabric, she found her footing on the platform with ease. Just the same, Mauro protectively held her hand until he was sure she was away from the murky water.

A glimpse of green shrubbery and dappled sunlight could be seen ahead through the twists of stylish iron fencing. Fabian cheerfully led the visiting party through the open gate.

The building's true size was revealed when they walked into the welcoming courtyard in the middle of the villa house. The ground was paved with colored mosaic tiles, punctuated by a stone well in the middle of the artful pattern. Exotic trailing flowers and potted lemon trees lined a sunny wall, interspersed with inviting benches. The late-afternoon shadows shaded the rest of the small, lush courtyard.

Looking up, Resi counted the number of balconies built into the walls of the Carrera house that gave each occupant a bit of fresh air and natural light. Under the eaves of the clay roof were tiny windows of the servants' quarters. Resi squeezed Mauro's hand, and he returned her gesture with a smile.

While the visitors looked around, Fabian took charge of the details. "Piero," he called to the servant waiting by the house door. "Show the baron's servants where the Barics will be staying. I believe they will have the room next to mine."

"Yes, my lord," Piero replied. He led Davor and Verica through a hidden door just off the courtyard.

The remaining four followed Fabian up a set of limestone steps to an etched-glass doorway.

A doorman opened it from the other side, and Fabian waved his friends through. "Shall we see who is home?" he asked charmingly.

The impressive entrance hall was efficiently laid out like a plaza. There was a wide staircase in front of them with closed doors on either side. An opulent corridor led to still more doors. Subtle music could be heard from behind the one to the left. Fabian opened it and went in.

The party followed him into the Carrera parlor, big and open, with a tall ceiling and a windowed wall that looked out onto a narrow canal.

Caterina was seated at a gilded table with an elegantly costumed man whose back was to the door. When no one looked up, Fabian announced to the room, "We have visitors."

Caterina's focused expression turned to joyful glee. She tossed her hand of cards onto the table and sprang from her chair.

"Lady Terese! Mauritius! We expected you yesterday!" Her happy outburst prompted the music to stop as the player turned to see who had arrived.

Caterina and the Barics greeted each other with warm embraces. Vilim and Hugo formally bowed over Caterina's graciously outstretched hand before she hooked her elbow in Resi's and guided her to a long sofa in the center of the room.

"I was worried sick, Lady Terese," Caterina blurted out. "We had the most terrible storm here yesterday, and we said to ourselves, 'Well, they must be lost at sea.'"

Fabian interjected, "But here we are, dear sister, safe and sound. We waited for the storm to pass. All disasters were averted."

Caterina held Resi's hand for reassurance and told her brother, "I am relieved you had the forethought, Fabian, but what a shame you arrived so late today. You missed Father and Mother by a mere hour. They are to dine with some ambassador from some Habsburg land tonight. We were just contemplating dressing for dinner ourselves."

"Good, because we are starved," Fabian replied for everyone. He looked around the room and asked, "Where is my lovely Isabella?"

"I told her she should have waited, but she urgently needed a new hat for the party tomorrow," Caterina explained sweetly.

Fabian seemed to forget his role as host and complained, "A new hat? Just ten days ago four new hats were delivered."

Caterina also forgot herself and replied, "She sent them all back, Fabian. None of them would do. I told Isabella I would not spend another moment shopping for her accessories if she cannot make a decision."

The young woman seated in front of the harpsichord stood up and complained, "Good God, you both have terrible manners. Will you not make the introductions?"

All eyes turned to the precocious teenager who stood straight-backed in her corseted gown.

Fabian grinned with amusement and said, "My baby sister speaks the truth. Lady Terese, if you please, this is Bianca. Bianca, this is Mauritius's wife, Lady Baric."

Fabian grinned with pleasure as the debutante curtsied regally to Resi. Then he continued the pompous introductions for his sister's benefit and announced, "Bianca, you remember Mauritius and his cousin Vilim."

They bowed formally for show.

"And this gentleman is our good friend, Captain Hugo Novak."

"At your service, Lady Bianca," Hugo said with a swoop of his hat.

Bianca did not miss a chance to practice her flirting and rewarded Hugo with a coy smile.

Hugo was speechless for once.

With Fabian's lesson to his sister over, Vilim casually remarked, "I think the last time I saw Bianca, she was in pigtails and short skirts. Has it been so long since I was last here, Fabian?"

"It has been so long. Three or four years, I imagine."

Fabian regarded the young man, waiting politely in front of the tabletop instrument. "Did we interrupt your lesson, Bianca?"

"We have just finished," Bianca said with relief.

"Are you a new tutor? Where is Signor Roland?" Fabian asked.

Bianca's teacher opened his mouth to answer, but Bianca was quicker to explain, "Signor Roland was too impatient with me. This is my new teacher, Felix Soranzo. I will see you on Tuesday, then, Felix."

"Yes, Lady Bianca. Good day." Felix Soranzo bowed to the group, collected his hat and jacket, and left the room.

The wigged man at the card table stood up and cleared his throat to be acknowledged.

Fabian found his smile and said, "We have one more guest staying with us. I'd like to introduce Monsieur Vincent from Lyon, in the Kingdom of France." Fabian waved his hand in the direction of the sofa and said, "Monsieur Vincent, this is Lady Baric from Croatia."

The Frenchman crossed the room and bowed over Resi's outstretched hand. In his melodic Latin, he gushed, "Lady Caterina has already told me so much about you. I feel we are practically friends, Lady Baric."

Resi replied in his native tongue, "Je suis enchanté de faire votre connaissance, Monsieur Vincent."

"You speak flawlessly, madam," he acknowledged with astonishment. Then he turned to Caterina and exclaimed, "My dear Lady Caterina, you did not mention that the baroness has lived in my homeland."

Caterina was unaffected by his scolding and replied, "I am sure I told you that her mother is French, Jean-René. Was I not right, though? Is the baroness not stunning? Your new designs would suit her wonderfully."

Jean-René crossed his arms thoughtfully and looked Resi over with an artist's eye. "You are absolutely right, Lady Caterina. I would very much like to dress her."

Mauro moved to Resi's side and warned the foreigner, "I take offense at such overly familiar remarks about my wife, Monsieur Vincent."

Fabian, who had also found the Frenchman's comments about his own wife's charms shocking at first, explained, "Our guest meant no offense, Mauro. Monsieur Vincent is a fashion designer, for women in particular. I think it is a compliment, nothing more. Is that not right, Monsieur Vincent?"

Jean-René dabbed his forehead with a silk handkerchief and said, "Oh, yes, Lord Fabian. Thank you for that."

Mauro held his glare.

Flustered, the Frenchman went on to apologize, "If I offended you in any way, Lord Baric, I am deeply sorry. Sometimes I cannot help myself when I look upon a beautiful woman. It is my art, my passion. I must dress her in my imagination."

His eyes moved to the sofa where the women sat, and he said with a flourish, "In my work, I am like a sculptor. Beautiful fabrics and delicate lace I drape over feminine curves make each woman feel unique. Dressing women is what I do."

Mauro's hand rested on his wife's shoulder, and Resi gave it a light squeeze to signal that she took no offense at the designer's explanation.

Mauro accepted the unusual apology and added, "I will leave it up to my wife whether you shall be allowed to dress her or not, monsieur."

"Well, this is a lovely homecoming," Fabian interjected cheerfully to counter the awkward start to their evening. "Caterina, can you show our guests to their chambers so they can refresh themselves before dinner? I will let the kitchen know that we will be a larger group tonight."

"Of course, Fabian. Will you excuse us a moment, Jean-René?" she said pleasantly.

The Frenchman gathered his hat and gloves. "I must be leaving myself," he said. "I bid you a good evening, Lady Caterina. Until tomorrow." He bowed formally to the others and said, "Lady Baric, Lady Bianca, gentlemen."

"Will you not dine with us, Jean-René?" Caterina asked hopefully.

"I must have neglected to tell you that I have plans for dinner out. I am meeting Claudius."

"Claudius is back in the city?" Caterina asked with visible disappointment. "I was hoping to go with you this time. He is so amusing."

"I will tell him to call on you," Monsieur Vincent assured her.

Caterina held out her hand, and the Frenchman obediently kissed it. "Until tomorrow, Jean-René," she said.

Fabian frowned as he watched their familiarity, but his focus quickly shifted from his sister to the tasks at hand.

"Mauritius, perhaps you could show Vilim and Hugo where their room is. They will be on the first floor, where you normally stay."

Caterina accompanied the group out to the staircase and led the way up. When they reached the first floor, Davor and Verica were there waiting.

"Resi, darling, I will be up in a few moments," Mauro said. He and Davor went with the men down the hallway, and Verica followed the ladies up the stairs.

Caterina took her pregnant friend's arm in her own as they climbed to the top floor. "Mother wanted to give you the best guest room although I thought you might prefer to take a room on the first floor instead. Does it shake the baby too much to climb the stairs?"

"The climb will be invigorating for the baby, as long as I am not wearing these shoes," Resi said, holding up her skirts to show the pointed ivory-heeled pumps she had worn at the ball earlier that summer.

Caterina dreamily said as they continued up the stairs, "Wouldn't it be exciting if you had your baby while you are here?"

Resi let out a surprised laugh. "I will have to disappoint you, Lady Caterina. I am barely seven months along, and we only plan to stay for three weeks."

"Perhaps it is wishful thinking on my part since I will no longer live in Venice when you have your baby, you know." Caterina breathed out an exasperated sigh when she added, "At least I think so. I am not so sure anymore."

Resi stopped in the middle of the staircase. "Have you not heard from Cyro?"

Verica waited by their side, listening with concern as Caterina tearfully admitted, "I have heard nothing at all, Lady Terese. Cyro promised he would write to me every day, and there has been no letter from him for three full weeks. I am beginning to think he has changed his mind after visiting me in Venice."

Resi held her friend's arm closer as they continued up the steps. "I am sure you are wrong about that, Lady Caterina. There must be an explanation."

"Wrong or not, at least I have had company while I suffer through the long wait. Jean-René has been a godsend these past weeks. We have gone to the theater, the opera, to restaurants and parties. He is a wonderful escort."

Resi asked cautiously, "Is it wise to become so familiar with a bachelor while you wait for your beloved Cyro?"

"Oh, no, Lady Terese. Have no worries. Jean-René is not an eligible bachelor. He is in mourning," she said with emphasis. "His wife died earlier this year. He keeps a small portrait of her in his pocket. It is so romantic. She left him her estate when she died, but he cannot bear to stay there without her. That is one reason he came to Venice—to get away from the memories."

Verica walked closely with the two noblewomen as they made their way down the wood-paneled corridor. She had gleaned so much about love affairs this past summer by listening to Lady Caterina and Lady Isabella, and it seemed there were more lessons to be learned.

"How sad for Monsieur Vincent," Resi remarked. "Did he tell you how his wife died?"

Caterina shook her head glumly and said, "He has not been able to talk about it, so it must have been tragic. He said he might be ready to remarry one day but does not think about himself at the present. I shared Salar Nassim's advice about loving again one day. Jean-René said he thought those were the most hopeful words he had heard since her passing."

Caterina took a deep breath to shed her sorrowful mood when they stopped before the last door. "Here we are, Lady Terese. This is your chamber. Fabian and Isabella have the one across from you."

Resi stepped into the light-filled bedroom. It was splendidly appointed with mosaic plaster walls and polished oak floors. A billowing bedcover and many fabric pillows decorated the sizeable canopied bed against the far wall. On the long dressing table that stood along the opposite wall were several pitchers and two basins. Resi looked forward to washing the dried salt spray from her face and stretching out on the inviting bed for an hour before dinner.

Caterina opened the glass-paned door at the back of the room. She pointed out with a wave of her hand. "Your chamber and Fabian's one look over the Grand Canal. You can even nap on the balcony, if you like. It is quite private."

Resi stepped over the threshold to take in the view. It was more of an open-air room than a balcony. The glassless window openings facing the water could be shuttered against the weather. Resi thought it was the perfect sanctuary in the crowded Carrera household.

"I see your trunks have found their way to your chamber. I will leave you to get settled, Lady Terese," Caterina said. "It will just be a small party in the house tonight. With the addition of Isabella, of course. Take your time resting. She may still be an hour or so. Hats can be so difficult to shop for."

Resi realized she was still wearing the one she had traveled in. "Yes," she agreed. "Hats are vexing."

~*~

Fabian made the decision to start without Isabella. "She may have run into an old friend and accepted an invitation to dine elsewhere," he speculated.

"She is very impulsive that way," Caterina added matter-of-factly.

In the middle of their soup course, the dining-room door opened, and Isabella strode in with her lady's maid, Anastasia, who carried two hatboxes in her arms.

"You are all here! Fabian, darling, why did you not send Piero to find me in the shops?" Isabella scolded her husband.

Fabian went to her side to appease her. "Isabella, my love, you have arrived just in time. You do not like soup anyway."

Isabella's mood lightened while she handed her long gloves to Anastasia, who curtsied and left the room.

Fabian kissed his wife squarely on the lips and then raised his glass and toasted, "To the best shopper in Venice!"

The others held theirs in the air, too, and Isabella blushed with amusement and said, "You are forgiven, my darling Fabian." Looking around the table, she continued, "You all look splendidly well. I am so delighted to see you again. What stories have I missed?"

The group of friends fell quickly into a conversation again.

~*~

Hours later, intoxicated and sleepy from the wine and good food, the ladies went to their chambers while the men lingered over after-dinner drinks.

Verica had finished unpinning her mistress's intricate coils when Mauro quietly opened the door.

"I thought you would be asleep already," he said.

Resi turned from the grooming table and said, "How could I sleep without telling you how much I am enjoying myself. Will we have time to explore Venice tomorrow?"

"We will have plenty of time, but not tomorrow, I am afraid. I have already accepted an invitation to go hunting," Mauro groggily answered.

"Hunting?"

He looked through his trunk to see whether his valet had thought to pack his leather breeches.

Verica took her mistress's visible annoyance as her cue to leave the couple to their private conversation. "If there is nothing else you need, Lady Baric, then I will go to my chamber."

"Where are you sleeping, Verica? Lady Caterina did not show me," Resi said with concern.

Verica lit a candlestick from the candelabra and replied, "On the floor above this one. I am sharing a bedchamber with Lady Bianca's maid."

Resi smiled contentedly and said, "Well, if it is with Lady Bianca's maid, I am sure you will be comfortable. I will see you in the morning, Verica."

"Good night, Lady Baric. Lord Baric." Verica curtsied and closed the door behind her.

Resi had not forgotten her interrupted conversation with Mauro. "Where does one hunt in Venice?"

"We will be on one of the uninhabited islands close by. There are plenty of deer and waterfowl to hunt," he explained.

"So you must go by boat then?" she asked provokingly.

She opened the door to the balcony. The noises of the canal floated into their room as she wandered out.

Mauro called over, "I know you drugged me for the journey today. Or was it Fabian's doing? He looked quite guilty when I told him at dinner that my head was splitting."

Mauro was in his sleep shirt when he joined Resi at the railing. He wrapped his arms around her, and she relaxed in his embrace. "I know that you could have managed without my help, or Fabian's," she told him.

"I will put it to the test tomorrow without your tea. It will be no worse than the gondola ride from the harbor."

Mauro kissed her forehead and stepped back into the room. He contemplated the bed and then began tossing pillows onto the floor. There would be no way to get under the covers otherwise.

Resi watched him with amusement from the balcony door. "Must you leave early tomorrow?" she asked.

"Not too early," he said thoughtfully. "The true Venetians do not rise with the sun like we do in Solgrad."

"Would you like to sit on the balcony for a little while, or are you too tired?"

Mauro was tired and drunk. Still, he followed her out the door and remarked, "Why only sit, Resi, when there is a couch here?"

"Do you think of nothing else, Mauro?" she asked with a laugh. "Besides, we could be seen by any boat on the water, don't you think?"

Mauro looked over the edge of the railing, then back at his wife and asked, "Since when are you so modest, my dear?"

The moonlight and glowing candles twinkled in his green eyes. He lifted Resi's hair and whispered in her ear, "May I undress you, Lady Baric?"

"And leave the dressing to Monsieur Vincent?" she teased.

Mauro slipped the robe off her shoulders and let it drop. He nuzzled her neck and said, "You may be his model if you wish, as long as I am the only one who undresses you."

"You will always be the only one, Mauro."

The candles flickered as the breeze touched them.

Mauro kissed her. "I am not bothered if a passerby sees us making love on our balcony. But if it makes you feel more at ease, I do not need the candlelight."

"I don't mind," she whispered.

He tugged on the ties that held her summer shift on her shoulders. It fell to the ground.

"We will leave the candle glowing then. I want to be the lucky man looking at you."

Chapter 25

Long shadows followed her candlelight down the dim hallway. Seemingly alone in the big house, Verica found her way to the stairs that would take her to the attic bedrooms. She counted the doors after the landing. Her assigned chamber was the third one on the right. Davor had been given a private room two doors farther down, but no light came from under his. Verica was extra quiet coming into the room to not wake Carla, but her roommate's bed was empty.

Verica had met Bianca's lady's maid earlier at dinner in the kitchen. She liked her easy style right away—friendly and chatty by nature. Verica was two years younger, but Carla latched onto her like they were old friends suddenly reunited.

Just like Verica had never been away from Solgrad, Carla had never left her island city. When she helped Verica unpack her belongings after dinner, Carla had asked question after question about her life in the territories. Finding Verica's experience lacking, she then explained everything the Croatian had missed in life by never having lived in Venice.

The Baric's maid was glad to be alone for a little while. She was exhausted from her long day of travel and her duties late into the evening. She hurriedly undressed, washed up, hung her gown carefully on a peg for the morning, and then crawled under the covers of her small bed. Her head fell on her pillow with a heavy thud. The candle was wastefully burning, but it was across the room on the stand by the door, and Carla would need the light shortly when she returned from helping her own mistress.

After only what seemed like a few minutes of sleep, Verica was startled awake by two women talking in rapid Venetian next to her bed. It was Carla with her mistress.

In the heat of the stuffy attic room, Bianca unclipped her fur-trimmed shoulder cloak, revealing a stunning beaded gown of silvery blue silk. Her hair was pinned high and her lips rouged. She was dressed for a night out.

Lady Bianca held a candlestick over Verica's bed, and the maid's eyes sleepily met the young aristocrat's.

"She is quite pretty," Bianca said to Carla.

"I told you so, my lady. She will be a fine escort for you tonight."

Carla went to the wardrobe and pulled out the gown that she had helped Verica unpack earlier. "See, Lady Bianca? She has a party dress, and I can help her fix her hair. It will take but a few minutes."

Bianca acquiesced. "All right, Carla. She will do, but be quick about it. Pasquale is waiting at the bridge, and you know how he hates to wait."

In the fog of waking, the Baric maid hadn't followed what was being said about her or why Carla was holding the special gown she had sewn. "Am I going somewhere?" she asked the Carrera's youngest daughter.

"We are going out, Verica, you and I and some friends of mine. I will meet you downstairs. Hurry along, now," was all Bianca explained before she took her candle and left the attic chamber.

Carla lit more light and immediately went to work finding the pieces of wardrobe Verica would need. "I am very sorry to put you in this spot the first night." Carla began to chatter, "Lady Bianca was very insistent that she meets her lover tonight, but I finally put my foot down with her. The mistress already knows that I go with her daughter to her late-night parties, and I will lose my position if I disobey her ladyship again. She made it very clear that I am to tell her when her daughter goes out with him. But if you go in my place, I won't have to say a word, and Lady Bianca will not throw a fit, and I get to keep my employment. Do you have a corset?"

Verica tried to piece together the rambling explanation. "Uh, no," she replied.

Carla sized her up and said, "You are shapely enough without one, I suppose."

Carla pulled Verica's new gown over the shift the Baric maid had worn to bed and tugged at the stays. When Verica was hooked and buttoned, Carla told her, "Come sit down, and I will twist your hair with these combs to make it pretty." She efficiently pinned Verica's dark tresses, leaving long locks spiraling down her back.

Verica finally protested, "Carla, I cannot just leave. It is the middle of the night. What will Lady Baric say?"

"Lady Bianca and I checked the doors, and everyone is in their chambers. You will not be missed. Now stand up and let me look at you."

Verica turned around as she was asked.

Carla smiled at her efforts and said, "You look quite presentable. Do you have a cloak?"

Verica pointed to the peg.

"Ugh. That is so dreary. Is that how you dress in Croatia?" Carla went to her wardrobe and took out a wrap. "Lady Bianca gave me this for our nights out. You can wear it. It will keep off the chill."

Verica took the heeled shoes the other maid held out for her. "Where am I going?" she implored Carla.

Carla beamed and said, "To a party, silly."

Verica found her best stockings and tied the garters that held them above her knees. "Who is this man, Pasquale?" she asked.

"Lord Pasquale Passini is Lady Bianca's new admirer. Lady Carrera has forbidden Lady Bianca from meeting him, so she sneaks out in secret," Carla said in a low voice, although they were alone in the room.

Verica suddenly understood the weight of her assignment. "Isn't Lady Bianca too young to meet a man in secret? I don't know what I can do to protect her."

Carla put the wrap around Verica's shoulders. "Lady Bianca has come out in society, and it is not uncommon to have a favorite suitor that your mother doesn't approve. Besides, Lady Bianca is playing coy with Lord Pasquale. She understands that her virtue is not to be given away, so I don't think she needs much protecting."

"Why does her mother not approve of him?"

Carla was well-informed and eager to share what she knew. "Well, Lord Pasquale has come of age but has not yet chosen a profession. I overheard some of their conversations, and I don't think he is so concerned about ever finding one. He will inherit his father's fortune, and he lives on a large allowance already. In most circumstances, that would not be a reason to be taken out of consideration. He's rich! The truth is, Lady Carrera doesn't like the Passini family, and she has other ideas for a match for her last daughter."

Carla put a candlestick in Verica's hand and opened the door. She peered up and down the hall and whispered, "All is clear!"

Verica held her ground and shut the door in a panic, dripping hot wax onto the floor. "I cannot just go to a party with Lady Bianca and her lover."

"Of course, you can! Lord Pasquale will not come alone. They run in packs, like feral dogs."

"What!"

"Don't worry, Verica. Her clique of socialites is harmless, mostly. You will not be expected to join in their follies—they will hardly notice you. Just keep near Lady Bianca," Carla instructed.

Verica argued, "Baroness Baric will not like that I am out at night with strange men."

"And women," Carla corrected her. "Besides, your mistress doesn't need to know that you were ever gone."

Verica tried to make Carla understand, "I cannot lie to her."

"You can and you will. I need this position," Carla pleaded. "It is not so hard, Verica. Now, take this candle and off you go." Carla opened the chamber door again, and this time Verica ventured out.

Then she looked back and whispered, "I do not know where the front door is."

Carla pointed at something in the dark and said, "Take that stairwell, eight turns to the red door. That is the main foyer, and it leads to the street side. She will be waiting there, just nearby."

"Where will we be going?" Verica whispered urgently.

"She said something about dancing earlier. Hurry now," Carla whispered back before she shut the door.

The candle shook in Verica's hand, but she did not drop it. She found the stairway. Holding her light in one hand and her heavy skirts in the other, she found her footing on the narrow wooden steps. Five steps down, turn the corner, five more steps, then another corner. Two turns out of eight.

It seemed the stairs would never end in the still darkness. Finally, the red door marking the foyer entrance was ahead of her. She took a deep breath and opened it.

An ornate panel discreetly hid this particular access near the edge of the grand marble staircase. Verica saw Bianca seated on the cushioned bench by the door, flicking her fan open and shut as she waited. The doorman stood statue-like at his post across from her.

When Verica approached, Bianca looked her new escort up and down. "I suppose it is not your fault you do not know the current fashion," she said, "but it is too late to change now."

The debutante picked up her fur cloak and smiled at the handsome doorman, warning him, "Not a word, Enrico."

"No, my lady," Enrico promised. He showed no judgment when he opened the front door for the two mischievous girls.

~*~

Verica had only seen Venice from the water, and Baron Baric had not convinced her earlier that the city was indeed webbed with tiny streets.

Once leaving the Carrera house, the two girls walked a labyrinth of paved walkways that connected the villas perched on the Grand Canal to the smaller homes and shops built up behind them. Verica could barely keep up with Bianca's quick pace in her unaccustomed shoes on the slick pavers.

Around the next corner, two lanterns came into view. Bianca took Verica's hand and pulled her along in the direction of the dark figures holding them.

The taller of the two men was wearing a cloak that did not reach the white glow of his stockings and golden ribbons on his heeled shoes. Verica's first thought was of Lord Fabian when she saw the outline of the erect plumes decorating the man's broad hat.

"We almost gave up on you, Bianca. What was the delay?" the cloaked man asked.

Bianca offered her cheek, and he kissed it in greeting before she explained, "My mother has Carla spying on me, so I had to find a different escort. Where are the others?"

"Ferdinando and Carolina were tired of waiting and have already gone ahead. Ruggero took a wrong turn somewhere on the last canal, and we lost track of him. Being drunk does not mix well with rowing."

"Even sober, Ruggero is not good at directions," Bianca remarked with a laugh.

When Pasquale took her gloved hand in his, she asked, "Are we walking?"

"Yes, darling. We left the boat docked at the Ricci house. I did not want to risk being seen at your father's dock again."

"Is that where the party is tonight?" Bianca asked.

"Yes, Caesar's parents have gone for the month. He has a week of mayhem planned while the family is away."

"Your friends are very naughty, Pasquale."

The second man scoffed at Bianca's remark, and she leaned in to ask, "Why is Felix here? He is such a bore."

Pasquale whispered, "You would be glum, too, if you just lost your entire fortune. Still, he is my cousin, and my mother says I cannot leave him to rot with his books."

"He would prefer it, you know," Bianca shot back.

"Do not worry about Felix spoiling your evening, darling," Pasquale reassured her, then asked loudly for the others to hear, "Who have you brought with you tonight?"

"This is Verica. She is Lady Baric's handmaiden."

At being spoken about, Verica curtsied in the slow, elegant way she had learned with her mistress and had practiced a dozen times. "Good evening, sir," she said.

Pasquale was openly amused and declared, "She is charming! What a delightful accent. And pretty, too. Don't you think so, Felix?" he asked with a roguish wink. "She is a much better choice than Carla."

"Behave yourself, Pasquale!" Bianca warned.

Pasquale inquired, "I have heard of the Barics. They are from the territories, are they not, Verica?"

"Yes, sir," she answered timidly.

"Well, this will be fun for you, then. Not like your harvest dances, or whatever else you do to amuse yourself in the countryside." Pasquale laughed to himself as he seemed to conjure the image.

Openly annoyed at their continued delay, Felix asked his cousin, "Shall we go now?"

Bianca locked her elbow in Pasquale's as she told him, "I can only stay a few hours. My mother will lock me up if I am caught again."

Pasquale repeated an earlier promise, "I will ask your father for your hand, Bianca, and then we can play every night without sneaking about."

"You know he will not grant it," she said with a pout.

"Because I have not yet come into my money?" he asked without really caring to know the answer.

She laughed and said, "Because my father thinks you are a lazy drunk, and you have yet to prove to him otherwise."

Pasquale feigned heartbreak and clasped his chest, saying, "Felix, defend my honor to pretty Verica here or she will get the wrong impression."

"I have no defense for you, Cousin," Felix declared unsympathetically.

Pasquale countered, "Felix is not always so disagreeable, Verica. After a few drinks, he might smile."

Verica didn't know what to make of her temporary companions, but she was grateful when Pasquale focused all his attention on Bianca after that.

As they made their way through the cobbled alleyways to the party, Verica glanced at Felix by her side. He wore no hat, and his short, black hair curled at the base of his lace collar. His complexion was pale, like that of a man who unnaturally spent too much time indoors. Not a sickly sort of pale, though. Rather, his features reminded her of a marble statue—chiseled and handsome.

They turned onto a narrow walkway at the edge of an even smaller canal. Felix politely waved Verica on ahead of him to follow Bianca and Pasquale. Then he took his place behind her.

The fog had begun to settle in, and Verica felt dizzy walking so close to the water in the faint lamplight. She paused for a moment to find her nerve again.

"Allow me," Felix said kindly. He stood on the water side of the narrow walkway and offered her his arm in reassurance.

Verica put her hand on his sleeve and focused on the clicking heels of their companions ahead. She was trapped between these strangers, heading toward what could only be trouble for her.

Chapter 26

As Carla had predicted, the young lords and ladies hardly gave Verica a second glance while they ladled spiked punch into their crystal glasses and danced drunkenly to the music.

Verica kept close to Bianca as her chaperone, although the responsibility was more unnerving than Verica had expected. She was equally fascinated and alarmed watching the forbidden couple play their game of cat and mouse. Lady Bianca was the clever mouse that knew how to keep the pawing predator from locking lips with her. And Pasquale openly enjoyed her artful flirtation while making small strides in his conquest.

~*~

In the wee hours of the predawn, the energy of the crowd of partiers began to wane. Alone and in pairs, some underage aristocrats stumbled to the door to find their way home, and some claimed an empty bedroom to sleep off their drunkenness.

Verica had briefly dozed off in a stuffed chair. She only came back to her senses when the music began to play loudly again. However long she had been asleep had been too long because Bianca and her groping partner danced among the remaining couples in a scandalous fashion. Not knowing how best to intervene, Verica sought Felix's help.

He, like her, did not fit into this reveling group of future nobles. Pasquale mentioned that Felix had just lost his fortune, and Verica decided she could speak directly since they were of the same standing.

She found Felix sitting slumped over near the musicians in the corner of the grand parlor. His elbows braced on his thighs; his head hung low; a glass of port teetered between two fingers.

Verica approached his chair, unsure whether Felix was even awake. She cleared her throat to get his attention. When he did not look up, she tapped his shoulder and said, "I am sorry to disturb you, Lord Felix, but we must be leaving now."

Felix's grip on his glass noticeably tightened, but he did not open his eyes. So Verica tried again to make him listen. "Please, sir. Lady Bianca must be home before dawn. Will you tell your cousin that we must be on our way?"

He stayed as he was, awake but not awake, and Verica was at a loss how to rouse him. "Lord Felix, sir. Did you hear me?" she asked one last time.

Felix raised one hand but gave no reply.

Not knowing what that meant, to leave or to stay with him, Verica waited impatiently.

When the music ended, Felix opened his eyes. He smiled up at Verica with such unanticipated warmth and joy that she could not help but smile sweetly back.

"What did you think of the song?" Felix asked unexpectedly.

Verica said the first thing that came to her mind, "The people danced nicely to it."

"Because of the rhythm, or the complexity of the harmonies?"

There was a surprising seriousness to his question, and his expression told her he expected she would have an answer. In truth, Verica had not even listened to the music while she waited for Felix to wake up.

"I do recall one thing," she finally said. "The violin solo stood out to me."

"Yes! It was brilliant!" Felix exclaimed, rewarding her with a smile, like a stern teacher praising a student's correct answer.

She shrugged and maintained, "I am afraid I am ignorant as to what makes music brilliant or even good. But I did like it."

He curiously regarded her and said, "I do not need to know about fashion to find your dress brilliantly assembled. The layering of the fabric is unique and somehow essential to its beauty. The drape of the skirts is subtly balanced with the lace that stands out vividly. The colors and textures are pleasing to the eye." Felix touched the delicate embroidery on the front of her gown as she stood stone-still before him.

Verica felt like he had undressed her as he took her gown apart, piece by piece. His stroke scared her, and she took a step back. "You are drunk," she said.

He shook his head, and his trance was gone. "I simply wanted to explain my view of music in terms that you might understand, Verica. I love music, and the song that just played is layered but well-balanced, meant to be enjoyed by its audience. Just like what I see before me."

She thought he was teasing her, and her cheeks burned red with embarrassment. Still, Verica found she could meet his unsettling stare when she said, "I know I am not dressed fashionably like the ladies here tonight, but I would rather you not point it out."

"I meant my comparison to be a compliment, Verica. Truly, I did. Your dress has an Ottoman influence, does it not? I suppose that comes from your mistress."

"Yes, sir. I suppose it does."

The moody Felix that Verica had first encountered by the canal surfaced again, and he said with irritation, "Do not call me 'sir.' I am no longer a lord but a beggar. It would seem more honest if I called you 'madam.'"

"You seem a gentleman to me," she said.

He held back a laugh. "Looks can be deceiving in any level of society."

Looking across the room, Verica was reminded again why she had sought Felix out. Pasquale and Bianca were still entwined on the dance floor.

"It is very late, and I need to get Lady Bianca home, Felix. Will you please help me?"

Felix stood up in full command of his movements, not drunk like she had accused him. He set his glass down, took Verica's hand, and led her across the room.

The amorous couple they sought was practically sleepwalking on the dance floor, holding each other up.

Felix unpeeled his cousin's heavy arms from his partner and tipped his drooping chin to look at him. His eyes were closed.

"Pasquale!" Felix said in a loud voice to wake him. "I am taking the ladies home. Are you coming?"

"You spoil everything, Felix," Pasquale slurred.

Ignoring his cousin's drunken insult, Felix guided Pasquale to a nearby chair and leaned him against it until the man slid down onto it with a thud.

Felix turned his attention to Bianca. "Are you ready to go, my lady?"

Lady Bianca was just as drunk, and her answer came in a mumble, "Carla put you up to this, didn't she?"

"Carla is not here," he replied. "The streaks of dawn told me to find you."

"Shit," Bianca grumbled in an unladylike way. "Late again."

Verica had set their cloaks aside in the foyer earlier, and she grabbed them on her way out.

Felix paused long enough to cover Bianca's shoulders with her fur.

"Hold me tight, darling," Bianca muttered half-coherently as the blast of fresh air hit them.

Felix wrapped his arm around the pretty teen and led her toward the entrance; then he and Verica pushed Bianca along between them.

"Do you do this often?" Verica asked with a chuckle.

"About once a week," he replied just as lightheartedly.

As they progressed toward the Carrera villa in the fog, Felix asked, "Do you like working for the Barics?"

It was an easy question, and Verica answered, "I could not imagine doing anything different. I love helping my mistress, and Lord Baric is a kind master to everyone."

They turned a corner and guided Bianca along the water's edge before Felix continued his train of thought. "I have never been to Croatia, but I hear it is beautiful there."

"I think so," Verica agreed while watching her footing on the uneven stones.

"How do you like Venice?" Felix asked.

"We have only just arrived today."

They were back at the spot where the men had waited for the ladies earlier that night. "I suppose Venice is quite different, though," he remarked.

Felix stopped and gave Verica his full attention when she told him, "Indeed, I have never seen any place like it. We came in on Lord Baric's ship and just the view from the harbor was already enough to make me fall in love with the city. When I was sitting in the shrouded gondola I felt like I was spying on a fictional world. Lord Baric explained the history of the monuments and pointed out things like the two bronze men ringing the bell on the top of the clock tower. He told us how two columns were brought here from the far reaches of the Mediterranean, plundered just to display to the Venetians, but only one survived." She laughed when she recalled Lord Baric's story. Then she said, "Imagine, bringing something so large across the sea only to have it fall into the water and be lost to you. His lordship said they had not been able to recover it, and there it remains, on the harbor floor."

Her description entranced Felix. "How old are you, Verica?" he asked out of the blue.

She cocked her head. "Why do you want to know?"

Felix adjusted his grip on Bianca, limp between them, and said, "I guessed your age when I first saw you, but after hearing you talk, I think I was wrong. So I am curious now."

Verica laughed and said, "You have a strange way of explaining yourself, Felix. All right. I will be seventeen in November. And you?"

He answered in the same augmented way, "I will be twenty in December."

The tall windows of the Carrera villa came into view, and Verica had little time to satisfy her own curiosity. "Lady Bianca said you are her music tutor," she remarked.

"For the moment, yes, but I will need to secure a real profession soon. I thought maybe I would sign on with an army to train as an officer."

"That is a fine profession, Felix," Verica agreed cheerfully. "Lord Baric was an officer in Count Toth's Army for many years before he became Baron Baric. He trains his own guardsmen at his castle now."

Felix asked, "Count Toth is Lord Baric's uncle, is he not?"

"He is," she said, "and a very good man. I have met him."

"Is Lord Baric staying long in Venice?"

She replied, "Until the end of September, I believe."

Felix nodded. They were at the gate to the Carrera courtyard, and he asked, "Can you take her from here, Verica?"

Bianca came to life again when Verica gripped her under her arm.

"Will I see you again?" Verica asked Felix impulsively.

Felix thought for a moment. "Tomorrow is Caesar's birthday," he said. "Pasquale will surely come around to take Lady Bianca to that party."

Verica remembered the rowdy toasts to a man named Caesar and asked, "Didn't we celebrate his birthday tonight?"

"That was the pre-celebration," he told her with a chuckle.

Felix's genuine smile softened his dark features, and the sparkle in his eyes caught Verica off guard. She had the urge to start the night over again, beginning right now. Instead, she bowed her head and said, "Good night."

Enrico, the doorman from earlier, opened the front entrance for the two women.

Felix gracefully bowed before they were out of sight, like a lord who had escorted noble ladies home from parties his whole young life.

His expression blank, Enrico shut the door between them.

~*~

Bianca's chamber was thankfully on the first floor, and with the help of the doorman, Verica left her sprawled on her bed. Verica had done enough for one night and wanted nothing more than to crawl into her own bed and close her eyes. She climbed the sets of stairs without encountering a soul. She liked that the Venetians were not early risers.

Carla was in front of her washbasin in a wrinkled shift when Verica entered the room. She dropped her linen and rushed to close the door.

"Oh, thank God. I was worried you would not get her home."

Verica took off her wrap and kicked her new shoes off her aching feet. "Do I have time to sleep a few minutes?" she asked.

Carla, who began to untie the stays of Verica's gown, said thoughtfully, "It depends on your mistress. I have to help Lady Bianca undress, but after that I can bring Lady Baric her breakfast for you."

Verica let her gown drop to the floor and collapsed onto her bed. "Thank you, Carla. I would like that very much."

Carla sat on the edge of the bed next to her and asked eagerly, "Was it so terrible?"

Verica thought about the night's events, and a smile unwittingly grew across her face.

Carla grinned, too, and said, "Ho, ho! Then you did have some fun."

Staring up at the beams in the ceiling, Verica declared, "It was the best night I have ever had, Carla." She curled up and explained, "Not that I was asked to dance, or anything remotely like that, but I loved being with the lords and ladies as a person and not to serve them."

Carla carefully pulled the combs from Verica's hair and asked, "And what did you think of my mistress and her admirer?"

Verica shook out her locks and then plopped back down on her pillow. "I think you are right, Carla. Lady Bianca is smarter than she appears, and Lord Pasquale is quite the rogue."

Carla laughed and wondered, "Didn't you find him appealing, though?"

"He has a handsome face, is trim and tall, and he smelled nicer than the ladies. Do you think she might marry him?"

"I doubt it." Carla fastened the bodice of her starched uniform while she continued, "Most young ladies find Lord Pasquale dashing, but he says ungentlemanly things in front of them. And when he drinks too much, well, Lady Bianca will tire of his ways soon enough." Carla then slipped her full skirt over her head and hooked the waistband to her top.

"His cousin Felix was with us. What do you think of him, Carla?"

Carla shook her head as she laced her shoes. "Felix is dreary. But in his defense, I heard he was not always so dull. He was at the university when his father died and only just came back to Venice. He moved in with the Passinis."

"How did he die?" Verica asked with concern.

Carla eagerly told her, "He drowned in the canal on his way to prison. Prison, mind you!"

Verica rewarded Carla with a look of wide-eyed shock.

Carla continued, "They had Felix's father in shackles. The rumor is that the man slid off the side of the boat of his own free will. Suicide," Carla said with emphasis. "After his funeral, they called in Lord Soranzo's debts, and Felix's family was ruined."

"Then he is a beggar," Verica said under her breath.

"Lord Pasquale's mother is Felix's maternal aunt. Thanks to her, he has a place to stay, at least for now. There were some noble families who supported his father's innocence and questioned whether it really was suicide. Those families let Felix teach their daughters music. But not many, I hear."

Verica was too tired for gossip but asked, "How do you know all the goings-on, Carla?"

"The Carreras speak freely in this house. Keep your ears open, and you will see what I mean."

Carla stepped over Verica's dress but thought better of it. "I am going to hang it nicely in my wardrobe. You might need it again tonight."

"I won't," Verica insisted before shutting her eyes.

"Yes, you will," Carla whispered.
Dawn was breaking over the rooftops, and Carla closed the shutters for Verica to sleep without being disturbed. She took her candle and went to check on the other party girl.

Chapter 27

Carla had been a servant in the Carrera household since she was a girl of twelve, when she was put in charge of lighting the hearths. Bianca was only nine then, and Carla became her favorite among the maids to talk to or sometimes play dolls with when her sisters would not entertain her.

When Bianca was introduced into society in the spring, she needed a handmaiden to dress her, and she asked if Carla could be promoted. Her mother, Lady Carrera, had agreed.

After years of real toil as a common housemaid, Carla for once had idle time on her hands while waiting on and for Lady Bianca. She spent much of that extra free time lost in daydreams.

Of the three Carrera brothers, Carla had always had a secret crush on Fabian. Over the years, the youngest son had brought equally fascinating companions with him on his leaves of absence from the army. She had fantasized that one day one of them would notice her, and they would fall in love. Carla was delighted that two of his bachelor guests this visit had been given the room across from Lady Bianca's chamber.

With Lady Bianca now in her nightclothes and sound asleep in bed, Carla headed to the kitchen for Lady Baric's breakfast tray. Her heart skipped a beat when Lord Fabian cheerfully bid Carla a good morning as he and Lord Baric knocked on Hugo and Vilim's door.

Carla dutifully curtsied at the side of the corridor and followed them with her eyes until Lord Fabian and his rugged friend, the married baron, disappeared into the chamber. The men were on their way to play their sporting games, clad casually in leather breeches and tall boots. The masculine wardrobes of these visiting lords only fueled Carla's girlish infatuation with them.

Her brief encounter with Lord Fabian was an excellent way to start her morning, and she hummed to herself as she hurried down the stairwell to the kitchen on the ground floor. Carla would gladly do this favor for Verica, who had saved her job last night. She collected a breakfast tray for the visiting baroness and then climbed the flights of wooden stairs to deliver her ladyship's meal.

The Carrera lady's maid had only caught a glimpse of Lady Baric when she peeked into the dining room yesterday. Carla had heard that foreign lady had been matched to the handsome baron when he was still a boy and she a young girl in a faraway land. The baroness's fairy-tale beginning made Carla even more in awe of Lady Baric and envious of the dream that lady was living.

When Carla entered, Baroness Baric was already at her grooming table, brushing out her braid.

"Good morning, Lady Baric," Carla said merrily. Seeing her up close, Carla understood why the baron had wanted her for his wife: she was beautiful, even in her nightdress. "I have brought your breakfast, madam."

"Thank you, but I was expecting Verica this morning."

"I am sorry to tell you that Verica is not well today, Lady Baric," the young maid explained solemnly. "My name is Carla," she continued to say, "and I will help you get ready this morning if that is to your liking, madam."

Carla efficiently cleared the table of the baron's breakfast dishes and unpacked the plate and teacup for his wife. She wanted to make a good impression so she would not be turned down as Verica's replacement.

"Not well?" the baroness repeated with genuine concern. "Verica seemed fine when she left here last night."

"Yes, my lady, she was. But she felt queasy in the night. I did, too, but I was not fully overcome like she was. I think the cream sauce on our dinner might have been curdled," she lied. "Verica asks your forgiveness, madam. She wishes to stay in bed just a while longer."

Lady Baric said, "Tell her she can take the whole day to recover. The Carrera ladies have a full schedule planned for me. We will hardly be here today."

"Would you like to eat your breakfast first, Lady Baric, or shall I help you dress?"

"I will help myself to what you brought, and then you can come back in a half hour to help me with my gown," the baroness said kindly.

Happy to have been accepted as a surrogate, Carla replied with a curtsy, "Very good, my lady."

Carla shut the chamber door and blew out a sigh of relief at Verica's luck today. She clambered up the narrow stairs to tell her new friend the news. It had been a good start to the day all around.

~*~

Isabella and Resi descended the marble staircase together to fetch Caterina, who was in the parlor, drinking tea with her mother and Jean-René.

"Are you ready, Caterina?" Isabella asked as she pulled on her lace gloves for the outing.

"Yes, my cloak is at the door."

Caterina abandoned her tea and joined the two ladies to leave. "I am so looking forward to our morning in the Basilica, Lady Terese," she said. "We have arranged a private tour with the curator."

"Perhaps you have changed your mind, Mother Carrera, and would like to join us," Isabella said to her mother-in-law, who was seated at the table.

Felicita Carrera was an early riser, and this was her second breakfast. She looked up from her cup and explained, "Isabella darling, the Catholic Charity Group meets this morning, and I am leading the discussion today. We ladies must do something for the nuns, and we cannot put it off another month. They are overwhelmed with new arrivals at the foundling hospital. September is always a busy month for babies."

Caterina fastened her cloak and remarked casually, "I am surprised how women can just give up a child."

"Yes, Caterina, it makes no sense," her mother agreed. She nodded to the servant girl pouring her more tea, then took a sip of the hot drink and concluded, "The work never ends at the orphanage. These poor souls need our guidance, and the nuns need our charitable funding."

Jean-René put his teacup down and declared, "You are so generous, Lady Carrera. If only the wretched poor in Lyon had charitable Christian ladies like you to find places for their bastard children."

Lady Carrera acknowledged his presumed compliment with a pleasant nod.

In farewell, Caterina gave her mother a peck on her cheek and said to Resi, "If you had not been expecting your baby, Lady Terese, my mother would have packed one in your trunk to take home. She is giving Isabella until Christmas to become pregnant, after which she plans to assign her one of the little strays."

"Caterina, my dear, Lady Baric may not realize that you are joking," her mother warned. Turning to Isabella, she added, "But I do hope Fabian is not shirking his responsibilities."

"I assure you, Mother Carrera, your son puts his best effort in whenever he is at home. You have two grandchildren and a third on the way. I think there is no need for any intervention," Isabella said.

Resi rescued Isabella from further scrutiny by interjecting, "I had a chance to admire the art adorning your halls, Lady Carrera. The sculptures and paintings are splendid. I would love to know the history behind them."

The Carrera matriarch replied, "It would be my pleasure, Lady Baric." She turned to Caterina and remarked, "Cyrano said the same when he visited, did he not?"

"Cyro studied the arts, Mother, so of course he complimented our collection. Jean-René also compliments you daily on your exquisite taste," Caterina said with uncharacteristic edginess.

Jean-René smiled and nodded to the Carrera daughter.

Lady Carrera ignored their exchange and said, "Speaking of your betrothed, Caterina, I cannot wait to hear all about young Lord Duarte from the baroness's perspective." She said to Resi, "You certainly left an impression on Caterina's future husband, Lady Baric."

Caterina's tone remained combative. "One is always impressed by something, but it must not be the main topic of discussion. The Barics' gardens left an impression on me, but you have not asked her about that."

Lady Carrera was unfazed by her daughter's moodiness. "Thank you for reminding me, Caterina, darling."

Again, she turned to the baroness and explained, "The last memory I have of Baric Castle was when Lady Margaret was alive. I cannot recall whether Lorenc's second wife ever invited me."

"Then I would like to extend an invitation, Lady Carrera. I am sure you will want to visit Fabian and Isabella at their new home, and I would enjoy showing you the Baric gardens when you do visit."

"Oh, Lady Baric, that is very kind of you, is it not, Isabella?" her mother-in-law said.

"Yes, very kind indeed," Isabella agreed with feigned interest.

"It would have to be in the summer," Lady Carrera went on to say, "or perhaps when the theater season is over and Carnival wraps up."

"Spring is a lovely time of year, Mother Carrera. We should be settled in our new home by then," Isabella remarked.

"Roberto will join me, of course, if the council is not in session. But then again, spring is so charming here in Venice. I think, perhaps, summertime would be best, when it is so dreadfully hot in the city. Yes," Lady Carrera said emphatically, "we will plan on that."

Jean-René added his nod of agreement as though he, too, would put it on his calendar.

"Then it is all decided, Mother Carrera," Isabella said. "Enjoy your visit to the nuns. Shall we, Terese?"

She took Resi's hand and guided her out of the parlor before her mother-in-law could delay them more. Caterina followed closely behind them.

The doorman opened the courtyard gate, and the ladies crossed to the arched boat landing. The groomsmen assisted them into the Carrera's private gondola.

"We only have a few hours until Mira's reception at four," Isabella fretted.

Caterina whispered to Resi, "Mira will never expect us to be on time. Isabella is notoriously late to parties."

"I heard that," Isabella said. "But wouldn't it be a wonderful shock if we were on time today?" Isabella looked up at the darkening sky and told the oarsman, "Hurry now, Leonius, before it rains again."

~*~

Davor had been told about Verica's unfortunate reaction to her meal last night and subsequent confinement to bed. In her place, Davor prepared the Barics' room: he remade the bed, carefully folded away yesterday's clean clothes, replenished the used linens, and brought clean basins. All would be ready for Lord and Lady Baric when they returned.

Davor had been introduced to most of the staff at dinner, and they seemed welcoming and helpful to the visiting valet. As he carried the empty water pitchers down the hallway, he hoped to bump into one of the servants who could remind him where he could find water.

Just as he was about to give up his search, a woman came out of Fabian and Isabella's chamber. Her more refined version of the Carrera servant's uniform, with a high lace collar and straight buttoned sleeves, made the petite woman seem taller than she was. The servant's severe dress was not enough to detract from her striking features. Her expression when coming from her mistress's room was cheerful and pleasant, a smile almost gracing her full pink lips. That is, until she noticed Davor standing there.

The pretty maid had not taken dinner with the others in the kitchen, but Davor was sure she was Lady Isabella's handmaid, Anastasia. Davor strode toward her in the empty hallway with his pitchers and said, "Excuse me, miss."

Her cheerful mood turned sour at his interruption. "I am busy," she replied and walked away, her starched skirt swaying stiffly with her movement.

Davor followed her toward the stairwell. "I only have a quick question regarding the water for the basins."

She turned abruptly and said, "You get fresh water in the closet. If there is none left, you must be patient. The boys will bring more from the well when they have a chance."

Davor tried to smile at the disagreeable woman. "Yes, so it was explained to me last night, miss. But where exactly is this closet? I have opened all the doors on this floor and found only chamber pots and linens."

Anastasia gave him a stern look and replied, "The pails are kept at the other end of the corridor."

Davor took a long breath for patience and asked, "Would you mind taking me to the exact door?"

Her heels melodically tapped as she marched to the end of the hallway, where she pulled a metal ring hidden in the paneling just beyond the main staircase. She pointed to the filled buckets of water on shelves.

"Thank you, miss." Davor bowed gracefully and added, "We have not yet met. I am Davor, Lord Baric's valet."

"I am Anastasia, Lady Isabella's maid. Raffaello is the manservant in charge of the chambermaids and water boys. If you need anything else, you should consult him."

Davor nodded agreeably and said, "I do hope that during your stay at Baric Castle you will not hesitate to ask for my assistance, Anastasia."

Her look of confusion was genuine, and Davor asked, "Are you not coming with your mistress at the end of the month?"

Anastasia explained what she believed to be true: "Lady Isabella isn't moving until next spring, when her house is in order. I will decide then whether I will go with her. If it is any of your business, Davor."

His effort to be friendly was not rewarded, and Davor's voice lost its charm when he said, "I heard incorrectly, then. Forgive me for intruding on your privacy, Anastasia. Good day."

"Good day to you, Davor." She turned on her heels and went down the corridor again.

Chapter 28

Unlike Resi's beloved Thessaloniki, a place that walled itself off from the threat of the sea, Venice's lagoon was held back by the city itself, and the Piazza San Marco was its chief defender.

The immense plaza was the heart of the city's shopping and administration. To one side of San Marco square was a promenade of elegant boutiques and restaurants. On the other side, lawyers and financiers kept the city's commerce going in their discreet offices. Interspersed with the splendid shops and merchant storefronts were stalls of specialized vendors, hawking useful wares and trinkets for the common folk and upper crust alike. On the watery fringe of the square, next to bobbing boats at the public docks, fish handlers noisily hustled customers to buy their fresh catch.

The Carrera's gondola stopped at a pier next to the seawall promenade. Resi longed to venture out where the fishermen, thrifty shoppers, sailors, and dockhands did their business. She had marveled at this scene from their anchored ship when they had arrived yesterday.

In vain, Resi looked back across the harbor for a glimpse of the *Margaret*. It seemed Branislav had already sailed home.

Isabella and Caterina were oblivious to the bustle of entertaining activity along the pier as they exited their little boat. The two linked their arms with the baroness, and together, they sashayed in the direction of the enormous Doge Palace.

Standing alongside the thousand-year-old monoliths, one could see and be seen by all of Venice there. Both ordinary and elite men dressed in ethnic robes or stylish jackets crossed the open square with urgent and not-so-urgent strides. Resi's attention followed industrious street sweepers moving between the well-bred gentry shopping along the piazza. This one walk from the gondola seemed to reveal the breadth of the Venetian world, and Resi's companions forged their way through clusters of people on the square with a haughty entitlement.

Venice had a remarkable history. Resi could see that the same ancient cultures that had a hand in designing every structure in Thessaloniki had also been hard at work building Venice. What seemed different from her beloved home city was the last lavish layer on the buildings here. Venice was uniquely Venetian.

Resi soaked it all in. The mix of Gothic, Renaissance and over-the-top Baroque inlays, archways, and statues were candy to her eyes. The pure gold on the buildings, the intricate tiled detailing, and the Empire's victorious looting were proudly displayed and magnificent to behold.

Isabella and Caterina walked past the massive artwork with only the briefest of explanations to their guest. They had seen Venice's outdoor museum hundreds of times before. Today, they wanted to show the baroness what was on display inside their most famous building of all.

~*~

Resi's hostesses guided her through the golden mosaic portal of the Basilica, Venice's oldest and most revered church. Its opulence was beyond capture during one hurried walk-by, but the ladies were already late for their meeting, so Resi was rushed along into the church.

Beyond the main entrance, a holy man dressed in black robes greeted the three solemnly. He would be their guide through the expanse of the Basilica. Without direction, Resi could get lost there for days and never regret it. More artists had created more masterpieces in this one building than Resi had seen in all her art books back in Solgrad.

But their time flew by quickly, and, to Resi's regret, they had to bid their host a grateful farewell. After only a few short hours, they went back out onto the rain-soaked San Marco Square. To brighten her guest's mood, Isabella pointed out a book handler near the church that specialized in the history and artwork of the Basilica. Resi took note and would be sure to fill a trunk with books to take back with her.

The recent downpour had inspired many pedestrians to seek shelter and refreshments at the small tables under the long arched walkway of the plaza. Caterina suggested that they, too, stop for a quick treat before heading back to change their gowns for Mira's reception. She pointed to an empty table in front of a pastry shop.

"May I order for you, Lady Terese?" Caterina insisted, "You must try my favorite: fried cakes with milk pudding."

The waitress brought enough for the three of them as well as a pot of steaming tea.

Isabella had taken a seat at the edge of the arched cover next to the open plaza. Her tall feathered hat caught the last of the raindrops.

A woman crossing the plaza noticed the tall Venetian with the exceptional hat and called out to her with a wave of her gloved hand. "Isabella!"

Isabella turned to see the elegant lady approaching and said under her breath, "Oh, dear."

Caterina looked up from her tea. "Is that—?"

"I am afraid it is."

Trapped, Isabella and Caterina could only hope she would merely wave and walk on.

The elegant lady was dressed all in black, although the color was the only modest part of her attire. Her gown sparkled with black crystals, strings of black pearls adorned her exposed throat, and long black gloves met her mink wrap that covered her low bodice.

Three children and their nannies accompanied the woman, and the young stragglers jumped across the puddles on the plaza's pavers as they followed their mother to the Carrera table.

Resi looked at her friends with a questioning expression, but there was no time to explain.

Because of their age difference, Caterina had become acquainted with Lady Rosella Bertolino only recently, but Isabella and Rosella had known each other since their youth. Their long friendship was not from their chemistry but from the social events they mutually attended. Rosella had been a capricious nineteen-year-old when she married her middle-aged husband. Afterward, she continued to go to the same parties and festivals that Isabella also found so entertaining.

Isabella offered her cheek in greeting and returned the kiss.

Rosella sweetly remarked, "Dear Isabella, what a fortunate coincidence that we are all caught in the same rainstorm. It has been ages since I have seen you."

"It has been ages, Rosella, but I have been traveling this year. I missed the whole summer party season while I was away in the countryside," Isabella explained. "I did hear the news about your husband's tragic passing. How are you managing, dear Rosella?"

The woman in black sighed dramatically and said, "One does not realize how accustomed one is to a husband until he is gone."

Wanting to be noticed by her mother, her little girl tugged at her gown. The child's nursemaid efficiently scooped the toddler into her arms and carried her to her siblings, who played nearby with a hoop and ball.

Rosella waved off the interruption and said, "At least I have my four little ones for comfort."

"Such heartbreak," Caterina remarked. "Children truly are a gift for widows. But I did not know you had four."

Rosella said, "God has blessed me. The baby is too little for an outing in this weather. She is at home with the wet nurse. These are my oldest darlings."

Then she called over, "Children! Come and meet the Carrera ladies."

Ushered by their caretakers, the well-mannered siblings obeyed their mother's request.

Rosella tenderly patted her youngest girl's cheek. "My precious Carmen is already three. Giosetta is my oldest. She is nine," Rosella said with a smile.

The dark-haired girl stepped forward, held out the stiff layers of her knee-high dress, and curtsied to the ladies at the table.

"And this is Sebastiano, my only son. He is seven," his mother said proudly.

Isabella put her hand out for the little boy to bow over, testing whether he had already learned the manners he would need as a future lord. She eyed him with approval. He was tall for his age, with a curly mop of light brown hair and vibrant green eyes, quite different from his mother's dark features.

"Go play, children," Rosella commanded lightheartedly.

Once unburdened of her motherly duties, she chirped, "I hear congratulations are in order, Isabella. I have always liked Fabian."

"Have you?" Isabella said with a laugh.

Rosella placated her onetime rival, saying, "Darling Isabella, you know that was long ago. Besides, I never had a chance to know him as well as his brothers. As a matter of fact, I was just talking to Gabriel about your plans to move to *terra firma*."

"Are you still friends with my brother?" Caterina asked protectively.

"We happened to be at the same dinner party a short time ago," Rosella said casually. "I don't have to tell you, Caterina, that the Carrera men are very conversational."

"Gabriel is quite happily married, too," Isabella pointed out.

Rosella cocked her head innocently and said, "I am not interested in pursuing married men with so many eligible bachelors knocking on my door."

"Yes, well, I am glad you can find distractions in your grief," Isabella reflected. "I am truly sorry for your loss, and so soon after your baby was born."

"Thank you, Isabella. Considering we were together for almost ten years, I find I actually miss him. It has been two months now, but I am settling into my life as a widow, and a wealthy one at that. I will not need to secure a new husband so quickly," Rosella said.

"Then you are lucky in your circumstances. It must be comforting to have been well provided for, Rosella," Isabella said.

"Sebastiano inherits everything when he comes of age, of course, but I was left a generous yearly allowance," she divulged.

Caterina smiled with understanding and noted, "Who would have thought your husband was such a modern man to have planned ahead?"

"Indeed," Rosella agreed.

Isabella was anxious to cut their conversation short. She stood up and asked, "Will you be at Mira's reception this afternoon? Perhaps we can catch up more then."

"I planned to, but my mother advised against it. She said one cannot wear black to a wedding reception. It is bad luck for the new bride to have a new widow congratulating her."

"Your mother is right," Caterina confirmed.

Abruptly, Rosella turned to Resi, who sat quietly, holding her tea in utter panic while the Venetian ladies chatted around her.

"I do not remember meeting your charming companion. Will you introduce us?" Rosella asked expectantly.

Realizing it could not be avoided, Isabella took an audible breath and met the impending discomfort with a smile. "Of course, where are my manners? Lady Rosella Bertolino, this is Lady Terese Baric. Mauritius Baric's new wife."

Rosella adeptly covered her brief surprise at meeting the baroness and said sweetly, "I am delighted to know you, Lady Baric. I hope you are finding Venice to your liking."

"Very much so, thank you, Lady Bertolino," Resi replied with as much confidence as she could muster. The woman was eight years her senior, mother of four young children, and still, she looked like a goddess draped in all black.

Isabella and Caterina noticed how the encounter affected their friend, but Rosella had never met the baroness before, so she could not know the difference. Rosella did know her history, though. During their brief courtship, Mauro had told Rosella about his lengthy betrothal to an Ottoman girl.

Curiosity got the best of Rosella, and she said, "I sense a slight accent, Lady Baric. Are you not Venetian?"

"No, I am Thessalonian," Resi told her.

Isabella added, "They are living in Solgrad at Baric Castle, of course."

"Yes, of course. I heard that Mauritius inherited the barony there," Rosella replied. "Perhaps you did not know, Lady Baric, but your husband and I are old friends."

Rosella noticed that Resi focused on her son playing nearby with his sisters. With a sly satisfaction, Rosella tightened her wrap and abruptly bid them farewell.

"I have so enjoyed seeing you again, but I must be on my way. The children are expected for their gallery tour. My husband wanted all his children to be well-rounded in the arts, just like he was."

"He must have been a good father," Resi found herself saying, although she still had the image of a bloated toad-man in her mind.

"Considering his small role in conceiving them, he did take an active part in his children's lives."

"I am sure you will have no problem finding a man who can take on that role again," Isabella said.

Rosella cocked her head and said thoughtfully, "I think I can be choosy about my next mate; test the waters again, so to speak."

The deliberate bathing innuendo was not lost on Resi, and her composure nearly faltered as Rosella's eyes locked with hers.

Giosetta came to her rescue. "Mama! It is beginning to rain again," the girl cried.

The lady in black sighed and said to the table, "This unseasonable rain has been hard on the children. They just want to play outdoors."

Resi wondered how children could freely play in such confining adult outfits. The little boy was dressed like a miniature nobleman in a long jacket, buttoned waistcoat, and short breeches. He was missing a ribbon that should have held up one of his stockings. Resi smiled to herself at the thought of Mauro's little boy snagging this ribbon while climbing a tree, as all little boys should learn to do.

Rosella bent to kiss Isabella farewell, then embraced Caterina. "Perhaps we can have tea before you leave the city," she suggested to the table.

Isabella agreed, "Yes, dear Rosella. We shall plan on it."

"It was a pleasure to make your acquaintance, Lady Baric."

"And yours, Lady Bertolino."

Rosella leaned into Resi as if to kiss her lightly on the cheek. The scent of her powdered face was intoxicatingly sweet, making Resi dizzy at this sudden nearness. "Tell your husband hello from me," Rosella whispered before stepping back again.

When the Bertolino entourage was out of earshot, Caterina said, "You look very pale, Lady Terese. Are you all right? Take a drink of tea, my dear."

Resi blurted out, "It is all so unsettling. Mauro had an affair with her almost eight years ago. He told me about it himself."

Isabella took Resi's hand in hers across the table and advised, "Do not presume to make any connection, Terese. In those days, Rosella went from one lover to another quite frequently."

"But his eyes, his hair."

"Green eyes are more common than you think," Caterina insisted.

Resi disagreed, "Not in Venice."

Isabella pointed out, "You have light eyes, Terese, and you come from a land of brown-eyed Greeks."

"Yes, because my mother is French and I got them from her. Where did little Sebastiano get his green eyes if not from his father?"

Isabella insisted, "The boy only has one father, and he is now dead. His mother will remarry in time, and Sebastiano will have a new father. That is all that counts, Terese."

Caterina warned, "Do not complicate your life by mentioning any of this to Mauritius."

Resi protested, "Not tell him that I met Lady Rosella today?"

Isabella explained, "All men have lovers before they marry, and they do not like it when old lovers and current wives meet. It makes them nervous."

"Portraits of the Baric sons hang on our walls in Solgrad. There is a reason her son looks so familiar," Resi argued.

Isabella countered, "Many courting men unintentionally plant bastards in their wake, Terese. These offspring are only pointed out when there is something to gain from it. If Rosella had wanted to, she could have named Mauritius as her son's father. She never has and she never will because it does not matter. My advice is to forget all about meeting them today."

"Mauritius will have his rightful heir from you, Lady Terese," Caterina reminded her.

Resi took a deep breath and let it out. "You are right, ladies. I will not think about it again."

Chapter 29

The noble House of Padovi was a deep-rooted Venetian family, but not of Venice. Their estate was on *terra firma*, north of the lagoon.

The Padovis and their neighbors considered the uninhabited islands across from their estates to be their private hunting grounds. Today, the male counterparts of Mira and Stephan's wedding party took advantage of this connection and gathered there for a day of sport.

More than a dozen soldiering friends from the Toth regiment had been given leave to celebrate the bachelor's final days of freedom. Along with cousins and family friends, Stephan and his soldiering friends docked their shallow-bottomed boats on a narrow island after a morning of serious shooting in small groups.

Servants had readied several blazing fires to warm the men, tapped casks of house-brewed ale, and turned roasts over sputtering coals for a communal meal. The off-and-on showers did not dampen their competitive festivities, and the conversation was lively while the men waited for their hot lunch.

Fabian arrived from pheasant hunting on an adjacent island and joined a circle of his old comrades for the first time. He shook off his rain-soaked cape and listened in on a story being told by an army captain named Horatius Martino.

"My father warned me not to take another man's seconds, but she has proved to be quite a satisfying match," Horatius bragged with a confident laugh. "Cornelius would never set foot in a whorehouse, but he sure taught his fiancée a few tricks before he met his end. Who is the lucky second now? Me!"

His friends hooted at his brazen commentary.

Horatius's buddy, Ignazio, held up his cup and cried, "You cannot truly know a man until you take his woman to bed, gentlemen."

The group roared with drunken laughter.

Fabian was not laughing along with them. In fact, he was uncharacteristically serious when he asked, "What are you talking about, Horatius? Did you marry Cornelius's bride?"

"I did indeed, Fabian! I sent both you and Mauritius an invitation last year. You must not have gotten it."

"No," Fabian answered under his breath, still reeling from the news.

Horatius continued to boast about his good fortune, "And to think I almost married Jovanna. I could barely get a kiss out of her."

"Careful, Horatius. Sergio is courting Jovanna now," another called over good-naturedly.

Sergio was conversing nearby, and he turned and asked, "What about me?"

Horatius hollered, "Just explaining why you can be seen coming from the brothel on payday!"

Sergio made an obscene gesture to Horatius and then laughed along with the others.

Horatius went on to proclaim, "Marrying Octavia has saved me my entertainment money, that's for sure."

Fabian could no longer keep silent. "Jesus Christ, Horatius! You should not go on about your wife like you do about your favorite whore. Have some regard for her good name, man."

Half-drunk on ale and still high on the adrenaline of the hunt, the gathered friends bombarded Fabian with their well-meant objections:

"Did you join the clergy, Fabian?" asked one.

"Since when are you such a puritan?" asked another.

"Did you not hear? Fabian got married last month! Tying the knot changes a man's sense of humor," another chimed in.

"Tying the noose, you mean," added another.

"Holy shit, Fabian. Congratulations! Who is the lucky bride?" one asked.

"Isabella Valli!" another replied.

"How did you manage that, Fabian?" someone called over.

"Word is, she was at Baric Castle just before they married," another said.

The group rumbled with speculation, and one dared to ask, "Did you knock her up while she was there?"

"That's one way to secure a rich bride!" someone shouted over the laughter.

"That is the worst thing I did so far," Horatius said too solemnly, and the jesting mood was stifled.

"Who did you knock up, Horatius?" Ignazio asked, puzzled by his comment.

"My own wife!" he bellowed with a renewed liveliness.

"You'll be joining Sergio at the brothel upon our return," someone joked.

"Why wait? We'll find a good whorehouse tonight in the city!" Ignazio said merrily. "The girls can help us celebrate the loss of our bachelors and the father-to-be!"

The lively group raised their mugs in agreement and then returned to quieter conversations.

"Excuse me," Fabian said to no one in particular. He sought out their host.

Stephan had not joined the gossiping men around the fire but had been cleaning his musket with his cousins.

"Stephan, may I talk to you?" Fabian asked. "In private," he added.

Stephan left his weapon leaning against a log, and they walked a few paces away before he said, "You don't look happy. Did something happen during the hunt?"

"Happen? Not today, no," Fabian said, but his expression remained gloomy.

Stephan looked around at the groups of contented friends and asked, "You were fine this morning, what is the matter?"

Fabian said in a hushed voice, "You could have warned me."

"Warned you about what?" Stephan whispered back.

Anger flashed in Fabian's eyes when he said, "You could have told me Horatius married Octavia."

Stephan seemed relieved to hear it was only Fabian's pride rearing its ugly head. Nothing really tragic.

Octavia had been engaged to a fellow officer and friend, who had everything to offer a wife, except personality and a sex drive. While at Toth Castle, Octavia was casually introduced to Fabian by her then-fiancé, Cornelius. Their mutual attraction was instantaneous.

Fabian's secret affair with Octavia lasted many months until the summer of 1647 when Mauro became Baron Baric, and Fabian left the Toth Army to join his friend in Solgrad. He did not visit or even write to Octavia after that. It would have been pointless; her wedding to Cornelius was later that year.

Fabian was cursed with wanting the woman he could never have. With deep regret, he had let her go.

"Is that your trauma?" Stephan asked.

Fabian crossed his arms in displeasure that his best friend was not more sympathetic.

"She was special to me, Stephan."

"You have not seen Octavia for two years, Fabian. You never even heard from her after leaving the army. I think she is over your love affair."

"Yes, but—Horatius?" Fabian demanded in dismay.

"Why would you care if she married Horatius? You are married to Isabella."

"I care because Horatius is a fucking prick. He treats his women like he treats his dogs, probably worse."

Then Stephan finally understood, and he said, "You truly loved her, didn't you?"

Stephan held his questioning stare.

"If you must know, yes, I never quite got over Octavia."

"Would you have sought her out had you known Cornelius had been killed?" Stephan asked his troubled friend.

Fabian rubbed his temples to get a grip on his thoughts. "Maybe. I don't know. I had made peace with her marrying Cornelius, but it might have made a difference at the time."

With clenched fists, Fabian groaned, "Ah, it kills me to know that Horatius takes her to bed each night, Stephan. Octavia deserves better."

"Horatius can be an asshole, but he can be a decent fellow, too. We know worse men who have contented wives."

When Fabian did not answer, Stephan continued, "Did you consider Octavia might be happy, like you are happy with Isabella? You are happy, aren't you?"

"Of course, Stephan. I am very happy with Isabella."

"Can't you ignore Horatius, just for today?"

Fabian nodded.

"Then shake it off, Fabian. This is a party. My wedding party!" Stephan pointed out for good measure.

Fabian's smile blossomed into a grin. "Have I ever ruined a party?" he said.

"Join my group after lunch, Fabian. We will shoot together, like old times."

"Yes, like old times."

Then Stephan pointed to the shore and said, "Look who just arrived. I wonder how he did."

Mauro climbed out of a boat with his catch from the hunt.

"Hmm. That seems far less than what I bagged this morning," Fabian remarked.

Stephan seized the chance to reset Fabian's mood. He called over to Mauro, "That looks like a good string of pheasants, Mauritius. I don't think Fabian got close to that."

Mauro waved, holding up his trophy. "Can you best this, Fabian?"

"Of course, I can!"

Fabian crossed the camp to inspect Mauro's haul, and Horatius was forgotten.

Chapter 30

The ladies of the wedding party had their own reception that afternoon, hosted by Mira's best friend, Ernestina. She was newly married, and it would be her first party at her husband's new house.

Since Ernestina lived on the opposite side of Venice, the ladies had planned for the long boat ride, but they had not anticipated getting caught in a downpour on the way home from San Marco Square.

Cristina, the eldest Carrera daughter, had been invited to the party as well, and she waited in the parlor while the three soggy ladies changed their clothes and primped.

Like the other Carrera siblings, Cristina was a raven-haired beauty. Unlike her sisters, though, she was modest in her appearance. Her finely made satin gown had no lace or embroidered ornamentation. Her hair was twisted and pinned with a simple ebony comb near her high collar, and a pearl necklace with a gold cross at her throat was her only jewelry besides her wedding ring.

Isabella had told Resi that she and Cristina had been friends for years, and Resi wondered if it had been a case of opposite attraction. Isabella confided that marriage had changed her old friend, and Resi wondered by how much.

Cristina had married an up-and-coming new senator her father had mentored as a law clerk. She was already a mother to a toddler, and she suspected she was pregnant again. Resi had not met Cristina before that day, but after only a short time in her company, Resi liked her and her straightforward outlook.

~*~

Sitting next to the baroness in the gondola, Cristina asked, "I was curious to hear your opinion of Cyrano Duarte, Lady Terese. I understand you got to know him almost as well as my sister."

Resi smiled as she thought about Cyro's unsuspected courtship with Caterina earlier that summer. "I did get to know him, Lady Cristina, and I recommend the match. He was a thoughtful and intelligent man, and he seemed to have truly fallen in love with your sister."

After Cristina saw that Caterina was conversing with Isabella, she whispered, "It is encouraging to hear that from you. Without letters of affirmation, Caterina suspects that his love has faltered. She thinks he has changed his mind about taking a Venetian bride."

"I watched Cyro, the humble sellsword, court your sister over the week they were together. The two would walk in the garden, and he charmed her with his wit and stories. He convinced me that she had stolen his heart. I am certain Cyrano, the nobleman, has a very good reason for not writing. The distance is great, and Caterina must give him time to settle their plans." Resi thought about her own complex marriage arrangement and added, "Such matches take time."

"Will you talk to Caterina, Lady Terese? There is a rumor that her affection is already being given to another."

"To Monsieur Vincent, you mean?"

Cristina sighed and said, "Unfortunately, Caterina must be in love to be happy. It takes very little to sway her, and Monsieur Vincent is an eligible man. I am worried she will do something she later regrets."

"I will talk to her."

The oarsman interrupted their quiet conversation when he announced, "The Garzone residence just ahead, my ladies."

He steered the boat down a narrow waterway and docked at a communal pier that led to a footpath between the houses. They could see colorful splotches of movement in the opaque glow of the paned windows.

"Well, this is a delightful little house," Caterina said as their driver helped her out of the boat.

"It seems we are the last ones to arrive but not as late as usual," Isabella remarked optimistically.

The boatman told Isabella politely, "I will need to find a better place to secure the boat, Lady Carrera."

Isabella shrugged and said, "I suppose not every house can have its own boat dock, Leonius. We will be at least three hours. Why don't you come back then?"

"Very good, Lady Carrera." He steered the boat back into the central canal and left them to their own devices to find the front door.

The humble outside appearance of the house hid the refined elegance of its refurbished interior. A doorman took their cloaks, and a timid servant girl added their gifts to the center entrance table, already piled high with colorful boxes and tied paper wrappings. A second girl led the four ladies into the center of the house, where the others were waiting.

Resi was amazed that so much velvet furniture, gilded paintings, Oriental carpets, and candelabras on polished tables could be stuffed into Ernestina's parlor and still have standing room for twenty gowned guests. A flurry of colorful skirts swayed one against the next, hovering near the future bride, seated on a settee at the far edge of the room.

Heads turned when the Carrera group confidently entered their realm.

The Carrera sisters and Isabella were well-known, but the newcomer incited a hum of urgent comments. The wave of hushed chatter rolled across the room from the rouged lips of one lady to the gem-studded ear of the next:

"Is that Mauritius's wife?"

"I thought he married an Ottoman peasant."

"Can she even understand us?"

"She is enormous with child."

"Why would Isabella bring her?"

"Mauritius is Stephan's best friend."

"Have you seen Mauritius lately?"

"He was always gorgeous."

"I could have had him."

"I heard he married her for a debt."

"Her gown is fabulous."

"Probably borrowed."

"Shhh."

"Shhh."

"Quiet."

"Isabella!" Ernestina called out. "So good to see you again!"

Isabella and her companions made their way through the whispering ladies to reach their hostess. The pretty Ernestina hugged Isabella, who returned the embrace and said with restrained politeness, "So wonderful to see you, Ernestina. What a lovely home you have."

"Yes, delightful," Caterina added cheerfully. "It has been a while since we last met. You are looking well."

"As do you, Caterina," Ernestina replied. "And Cristina! How good to see you again."

Cristina exchanged a quick peck on the cheek with her hostess, saying, "I never got a chance to congratulate you, Ernestina. How long have you been married now? A year?"

"Yes, it will be a year next week."

Isabella turned her attention to the pretty blonde sitting on the sofa and said, "There are so many congratulations in order, beginning with our friend Mira."

Resi did not mind that she had been neglected in the introductions. It was better that no one noticed she could not keep her eyes off the guest of honor. Stephan's bride was out of place in the room of dark-haired ladies and was not at all what Resi had expected. Meeting her, Resi was reminded of Davor, with his aquamarine eyes and fine blond hair. Mira's was piled high in cascading ringlets, tied back with little bows around her temples. Her creamy complexion was on display in the low-cut bodice of her splendid white gown. On the lap of her taffeta skirt, she held a sleeping dog on a velvet pillow.

Mira turned to Isabella when she heard her name. "We had almost given up on you, dear Isabella, but then I remembered that you always like to arrive last."

Not being the object of her criticism, Cristina kissed Mira's cheek in greeting and said, "Do not hold it against us, Mira dear."

Caterina greeted the young bride and added, "The boatman did his best, but the rain and wind were against us on the ride here."

"No matter, Caterina," Mira told her sweetly, "we will still have plenty of time to talk about your new betrothal. Is it true that you are to marry a Genoese nobleman? Are you not afraid of such a union?"

"That practically makes you a traitor," Ernestina said in a hushed voice.

"It makes her a patriot," Cristina clarified. "Her marriage will help bridge a void in Venice's complicated relationship with Genoa. Besides, dear Ernestina, the war is over."

Isabella asked, "Is that your view, Ernestina, or your husband's? Is he not willing to move ahead with negotiations like the rest of the senate?"

"Ladies! Must we talk politics at my party?" Mira scolded. "Venice's affairs should be left to the men. The dinner table conversation must be quite dull at the Carrera house." Mira looked around at her attentive friends and asked, "Would you not agree?"

Through the nods and giggles of the tightly clustered room, Resi spoke up, "I find the conversation at the Carrera house most enlightening."

The room went quiet. Mira's bright eyes flashed when noticing the stranger for the first time. "You must be Mauritius Baric's new wife," she exclaimed.

Isabella took charge of the introductions and said, "Forgive me, Mira. Of course, she is. Lady Terese Baric, this is Stephan's bride-to-be, Mira da Monte."

Resi curtsied as well as she could in the small space allotted her.

"Lady Terese. May I call you that?" Mira asked, not expecting an answer. "Stephan has spoken so much about you that I feel I already know you. You look exactly as he described: ethnic and exotic. He said your Greek companion also made an impression on him." Mira scanned the room and asked, "Is she here today?"

"No, unfortunately Ruby was not back in time to join us. She left for Thessaloniki earlier in the summer. Mauro's brother, Jero, and Ruby were to be married there," Resi explained cheerfully.

Mira stroked her silky dog, dozing on her lap, and remarked, "Keeping it in the family. How nice for the Barics."

Caterina interjected, "Lady Ruby and Jero make an adorable pair, Mira. I am sure you will meet them soon enough."

Mira contemplated Resi. "Stephan said you wore robes and veils and such. Today you look almost Venetian."

Resi was tongue-tied at the unwanted attention, and Isabella came to her rescue, saying, "Lady Terese is so well-bred that she fits into any society, Mira. When in Venice, she is Venetian."

Seated next to Mira was a pretty, ginger-haired lady. When she inquired in her thick Tuscan accent, heads turned again, "Speaking of society, Lady Isabella. Did I hear correctly that you will not be staying in Venice much longer?"

"Yes, Gessica, the rumors are true this time. Our new estate is in the Croatian territories, near the Barics, actually. Fabian is having our house renovated, and we will live there beginning next spring."

"What on earth will you do there?" a squat woman in a red ruffled dress interjected. She was Gessica's spinster sister, Giada.

Caterina replied, "I had the loveliest summer at Baric Castle, Giada dear. The countryside can be very romantic and entertaining. If Isabella becomes bored, Venice is only a day away by sea."

"I cannot recommend a long stay in the territories," Mira warned. "Each time Stephan returned from the Barics, he was dramatically changed. Living in the territories was a bad influence on him."

Eager to confirm her suspicions, Giada asked, "How so, Mira? Did he lose all manners? Was he intolerable in conversation?"

"Not totally intolerable, but I did have to put my foot down on a few things."

"Like what, Mira?" Ernestina asked.

"His manner of dress was the first thing I changed when he finally settled back in Venice. No more tall boots and drab leather doublets. Stephan has such shapely legs. I insisted he show them off. Tight stockings and heeled shoes are what real men should wear. It makes them so much more appealing."

The partygoers mumbled their agreement.

Resi could not disagree more. Their dress was one reason the soldiers were a delight to watch riding off through the gate. She wanted to correct her hostess on her flawed notion of good taste, but Isabella suddenly asked, "Was there tea, Mira? Or have we missed it?"

Ernestina took this as her cue and announced, "We can move into the dining room, ladies, now that we are all finally here."

Isabella took Resi's elbow to hold her back a moment.

"Drink a little wine, Terese, and the conversation won't seem so jarring," Isabella told her quietly.

Resi gave Isabella's hand a friendly squeeze as they followed the line of dresses into the dining room. "Do not leave me, or I am afraid I will say something too contrary for the company," she whispered back.

Isabella chuckled and said, "Do not worry about offending these ladies. They love controversy. It is practically required."

~*~

The dining room was tightly furnished with several round tables brought in for the occasion, each with eight chairs. Ernestina directed Isabella to a table by the front window and then took it upon herself to help the baroness find her assigned place.

Ernestina cheerfully introduced Resi to an equally pregnant woman at her table. She, too, was a visitor, accompanying her cousin who had already been seated with Mira's elite clique at the window.

"Lady Baric, this is Signora Martino," Ernestina pointed out. "Her husband was in the Toth Army with yours. She was a lady in your aunt's court at one time, were you not, my dear?"

"I was indeed," the striking woman answered with a slightly Slavic accent. She wore her long black hair in two thick curls prettily draped over her heart. Her cheeks glowed with the room's heat, and her smile was welcoming.

Resi was thrilled at the prospect of having something tangible to talk about while confined to the table and said, "I am delighted to meet you, Signora Martino. I have not had the occasion to visit my new relations in the North, and I would love to hear your news of them."

"I hope you can find the occasion, Lady Baric. Lady Toth is one of my favorite women and most admirable."

"The countess has been very good to me without me even meeting her, so I imagine she is worthy of your praise. And do you know my husband?" Resi asked.

"I met your husband on several occasions, Lady Baric. We were even on a first-name basis."

"That sounds almost scandalous, Signora Martino," interjected Giada, seated on the other side of her.

Signora Martino chuckled at Giada's reaction and said to Resi, "Be assured, Lady Baric, I had no romantic inclination, although Mauritius is a charming man. I was more acquainted with Fabian Carrera at one time a few years back. I am sure he would not have mentioned me. Octavia?"

"Fabian has told us many stories, but unless you were wielding a sword, I am afraid he did not mention your name," Resi informed her kindly.

Octavia held back a laugh. "That would be true. Fabian talked to me about many important people in his life, but I do not remember him ever mentioning his new wife's name. Has he known her long?"

Resi noticed Giada leaned in to listen again. Still, she answered Octavia openly, "Fabian has known Lady Isabella since they were children, and he has loved her almost that long. I hear there were years when their love seemed impossible, and they devoted their attention to others. Chivalrous men do not kiss and tell so quickly, which is why I am sure Fabian did not mention his former love interests to you, Signora Martino—even in intimate conversation."

Resi looked directly at Giada and said, "Fabian values his privacy."

"Well said, Lady Baric," Octavia replied.

Giada turned and struck up a conversation with the lady on the other side of her. With the ice broken, the two misfits became easy friends at their table of cold shoulders.

The room hummed with chatter while servants carried a multitude of platters and trays to each table. There was the usual cured ham, marinated eel, salted sardines, and fried squid that Resi enjoyed in Solgrad. The servants also brought polenta with eggplant and risotto steamed with cuttlefish, blackened by their ink. Peas in aspic and greens with garlic were offered. Small pigeons stuffed with rice, as well as liver pâté molded as a Roman goddess, added to the overwhelming choices. With the baby pressing against her stomach now, Resi tried not to be greedy.

After the main meal was cleared, the ladies retired to the parlor again for a glass of sweet wine to accompany their plates of almond cakes, candied pistachios, and fresh figs.

Mira held the room's attention as she drunkenly gushed with admiration about her Stephan. She surprised everyone when she suggested: "Let's play a little game, ladies! I would love to know what my best friends think is most admirable about my future husband. I will start."

She set her glass down and demurely announced, "Stephan is the most handsome of all my past suitors."

The ladies applauded her answer.

Satisfied with the reaction, Mira said, "Julietta, darling, you go next!"

Caught off guard, Julietta chose a safe compliment. "I like talking to Stephan. He is so well-spoken," she said with a contented smile.

The lady seated next to Julietta chimed in, "Stephan has always been extremely polite to me."

And on they went, around the room, with the next lady offering, "He comes from a prominent family. That is better than being handsome for me."

The others nodded and giggled at her answer.

Octavia's cousin, Roberta, spoke up next, "He is a war hero with no missing parts." With a wink to Mira, she added, "That we know of!"

When the laughter died down, it was Cristina's turn, and she said matter-of-factly, "Stephan is an excellent kisser."

"Cristina! When did you kiss Stephan?" Mira wanted to know.

She thought a moment and said, "I think everyone has kissed everyone at Carnival. I only knew it was Stephan because he put his mask on at our house."

"That is why I love Carnival," Gessica proclaimed. "You can taste forbidden fruit incognito. I am afraid to say it, Mira, but I may have also kissed your fiancé."

While the women whispered among themselves about whom they had kissed while masked, Mira brought the room to silence when she boasted, "I must say, I am lucky that Stephan never pressed me to kiss him."

After the gasps of disbelief settled, Caterina asked what was on everyone's mind, "Are you saying, Mira, that you have never kissed Stephan? Ever?"

"How could I have kissed him? We have never really been alone, and Mother never let me go out during Carnival season."

Isabella remarked, "You can steal a kiss in the open without a mask. It is not forbidden if you desired it."

"It is not a matter of desire. Stephan has shown me complete adoration in many ways, and we are waiting until we are married before we share physical love," Mira declared.

A tipsy Ernestina asked, "Are you not the least bit curious, Mira?"

Giada interjected, "I find it completely admirable. Stephan is like an old-fashioned knight in shining armor, holding his love and affection contained until Mira is truly his. Not one of those hands-on, good-for-nothing sorts of men," she concluded under her breath.

"That is exactly it, Giada. Stephan loves and adores me, and that is far more romantic than stealing kisses," Mira explained.

"You are an inspiration to all of us unmarried women," Giada toasted.

Again, the mood became festive, and the other hopeful bachelorettes raised their crystal glasses to Mira, who had won her prized husband on her terms.

~*~

The bridal party concluded shortly thereafter with a parade of shrouded gondolas leaving the congested waterway in front of Ernestina's house.

After a few minutes, the Carrera boat paddled alone along the Grand Canal back home. Clouds had descended over the water, and the ladies were glad for the wool blankets to warm their legs against the growing mist.

For a time, they remained quiet, listening to the rhythmic splashing of water against the gondolier's long paddle. This hush felt welcome after the hours of thrumming chitchat that had saturated their minds.

Isabella finally broke their silence. "Did you enjoy the party, Terese?" she asked.

"I did very much. I was happy to finally meet Mira. I had pictured her to be different somehow."

Isabella agreed, "Stephan was always spellbound by her unique beauty. The other girls at court practically lined up for him, but he only focused his admiration on Mira when she was there."

Caterina commented, "I was surprised to learn the two did nothing more than dance at those parties. Stephan's devotion is remarkable, really."

Isabella was blunter in her assessment, "Mira has the hair of an angel and the breasts of a goddess—what man would not be swayed by that? I like Mira, I really do, but she is a prude. For her sake, I hope she overcomes that."

Cristina pointed out, "She kissed her dog a dozen times at the party, so I am sure she will be able to kiss her husband satisfactorily."

Isabella reminded them, "Despite all his good qualities, Stephan is still just a man, and not an inexperienced one at that. I just hope he is not disenchanted once her beauty fades."

Chapter 31

Hugo and Vilim scraped their muddy boots across an iron grate near the door and then shook off their dripping hats before stepping into the Carrera house from the courtyard.

The two tired hunters gave their wet cloaks to the doormen. Vilim noticed the clock by the wall: a quarter to eleven. The house should be asleep. They came quietly into the foyer, worried their echoing voices would rise up the open stairwell and disturb their hosts.

Bianca could have used a little noise as a warning. She was nearly down the stairs when the two visitors came around the corner. She could not guess how long Fabian's friends would linger before going up to their rooms, so she played as though her late-night departure was perfectly normal.

"Good evening," Bianca said to Hugo and Vilim and then continued past them to the front door.

The two men exchanged knowing looks.

Bianca said to the doorman in a low voice, "Tell Verica I will be waiting for her outside."

Before he could agree, that same door opened, and her brother and Mauro walked into the foyer.

Fabian handed over his cloak to the startled doorman, and then his eyes met his sister's.

Bianca had the guilty look of a dog caught stealing a haunch from its master's table. It was clear that she was dressed for a night out—her thin arms were covered with satin gloves, and her best cape was already buckled at her throat.

Fabian exchanged a quick nod of "I told you so" with Mauro but managed to keep his expression stern for his sister.

"Hello, Bianca," he greeted her.

"Hello, Fabian. Gentlemen."

She was surrounded on all sides when he took a step closer, although the three bystanders would not complicate Fabian's sting with unnecessary conversation.

"You have had a long day, Brother," Bianca said sweetly. "Do not let me detain you." She took a step forward, and the men closed their circle.

Fabian went straight to the point, "It is I who will detain you, dear Bianca. Where are you going?"

"I came down looking for a book," she said almost believably.

He managed to challenge his sister's lie without laughing. "You need a book at this hour?" he asked.

"Yes, Fabian. It helps me fall asleep," she asserted with growing irritation.

He took her hand and held it as though he were inspecting the quality of her gloves. "Is it so cold in the library?"

Bianca was defiant. "As a man, you cannot know how chilled one gets in a lady's gown."

"And what a pretty gown it is," Fabian remarked. He pulled her hand closer, like he would a dance partner's, and asked, "Were you going to take your book out dancing tonight?"

Fabian was a head taller than his youngest sister. Her confidence faltered with his looming closeness. She answered, "Do not be ridiculous."

"I am ridiculous?" Her brother repeated her story, "You are going to the library, getting a book, then going back upstairs to your chamber to read it and fall asleep in your new gown. Do I have it right?"

Bianca scowled at the patronizing interrogation. "I guess you are not as drunk as you smell," she said. "Now, if you will excuse me." She pushed her way through to the door.

Fabian said, "Enjoy your book, then. I just wanted to be certain that it was right of me to tell Pasquale Passini to go home. I saw his boat docked at the side canal and went to have a look. He and his friends were waiting near the footbridge. Perhaps he was waiting for a book?"

When Bianca finally understood she had been caught, the three spectators could not hold back their amusement and began to laugh.

Fabian was enjoying his win until Bianca let loose on him. "You didn't!" she cried.

Fabian became just as livid and said, "What are you doing sneaking around with that man, Bianca?"

"I am not sneaking," she said through gritted teeth.

"Were you going to meet him alone? With no chaperone?"

Bianca crossed her arms in defiance.

Fabian asked again, "Well, were you?"

"I have a chaperone, but your shouting scared her off."

"Carla again? Bianca, you know—"

Bianca shouted over him, "I know what Mother said. I have a better one."

"Who?"

"None of your business."

"Pasquale will never be a good match for you, Bianca. You need to give him up."

"I like Pasquale," Bianca protested. "He is fun and handsome and—"

"There are plenty of handsome men Mother approves of who can take you to parties at normal hours," Fabian growled.

Bianca shouted back, "Do not lecture me!"

"I will lecture you, and I will pass this conversation on if you do not run upstairs and lock yourself in your chamber right now."

"You are so cruel, Fabian. I hate you!" she cried.

Fabian pointed toward the stairs and ordered, "Go!"

Bianca lifted her full skirts and noisily ran up the steps, sobbing.

Fabian waited to hear the expected door slam. He was not disappointed.

"My God, Fabian," Vilim said with a chuckle, "you are going to make a wonderful father one day."

"You are so cruel, Fabian," Hugo repeated in a mocking feminine voice.

"We should not be laughing, really," Fabian told them. "If my sister does not begin behaving like a lady, she might do something regrettable."

"I would be glad to be Bianca's chaperone if she needs a proper escort," Hugo said eagerly.

Fabian was surprised by the offer. "Do you fancy my baby sister, Hugo?"

"I did not see a baby, Fabian. I saw a grown woman, and a spirited beauty at that," Hugo stated.

Fabian gave a questioning look to Mauro and Vilim, who shrugged in reply. They followed Fabian as he started up the stairs.

"Knowing that you want to take my little sister dancing does not sit well with me, Hugo. She is only sixteen."

Mauro came to Hugo's defense and said, "Hugo is only twenty-two. That is a good age to chaperone your sister."

Fabian warned, "I have seen you dance with girls, Hugo. As a brother, I am supposed to protect my sister."

"She needs no protection from me, Fabian. You have seen me well-behaved, too," Hugo insisted.

"I have witnessed it," Vilim said good-naturedly. "Besides, Hugo does not have to marry your sister, Fabian, but perhaps he can keep her entertained for a few nights. You know, distract her from this Passini fellow."

Fabian remained pessimistic. "I will still have to disappoint you, Hugo. After I talk to my mother, Bianca will most likely be sequestered for a while."

The four reached the broad landing on the first floor.

"Mention me to your mother," Hugo said. "She might like the idea."

Vilim and Hugo lit candles from the sideboard table before bidding their friends good night and retreating to their chamber.

Fabian noticed the crack of light coming from under Bianca's closed door.

Mauro did, too, and suggested, "Give your sister one more chance, Fabian. After your warning tonight, Bianca will not meet her suitor in secret again."

As they trudged up the flight of stairs, Fabian asked, "Do you think I properly scared her?"

"You scared me," Mauro teased. "Do you always talk to your sisters so heatedly?"

Fabian frowned and asked, "Would you not react the same if you had a sister?"

"I guess I will never know," Mauro said.

Their leather boots loudly clacked as they rounded the last set of marble steps, holding their dripping candles steady.

"I want to protect my sister," Fabian said, "but maybe you have a point. I will not turn her in this time."

They stopped at Mauro's door. There was no light coming from under it. Not wanting to wake his wife with echoing voices, Mauro patted Fabian on the shoulder and acknowledged his good decision with a nod.

~*~

Across the hallway, Fabian's room was illuminated, and Isabella was sitting up in bed with her sketch pad.

"Did you wait up for me, my love?" Fabian asked as he closed the door behind him.

"I could not sleep," she said from across the room. "Drawing my day helps to clear my mind."

He began to unbutton his jacket. "Do you want to tell me about it while I undress?"

"All right, Fabian, if you are interested."

"Of course, I am interested."

He dropped his jacket on the chair next to the bed and bent over his wife to kiss her.

Isabella licked her lips, tasting the remnants of cognac. "Perhaps my evening was not as enjoyable as yours. You seem to be in a very good mood."

He sat down on the bed beside her and unwound his cravat. "My day was immensely enjoyable," he said slowly, looking over her shoulder at what she had drawn in her notebook. "All my old chums from the Toth regiment are in town for the occasion. We shot four bucks and enough pheasant to feed the entire wedding party. Then we returned to the city and had dinner and some drinks at the Seven Sabers."

"Ah, now I understand why you reek of alcohol."

"Do I? You are the second person to say that. We were toasting Stephan, and I might have spilled more on my jacket than went in me."

Fabian went to the basin to wash the cognac off; then he splashed his face to revive himself. "There were many new weddings to celebrate," he continued to explain. "Mine, Mauro's, Stephan's, Horatius's. Do you remember me telling you about Horatius? He got married about the same time as Mauritius."

"No, I am sorry, darling. I do not recall the name," Isabella answered honestly.

Fabian dried his face and said casually, "His wife was at Mira's reception. I think he said Octavia is her name. She lived at Toth Castle for a time until she married. Did you happen to talk to her at your party?"

Late in the party, Giada had gossiped to Isabella that Octavia had asked about Fabian. Isabella knew now what her husband was doing, and a pang hit her heart like a chisel to a stone.

"Octavia? Let me think," Isabella stalled. Should she give Fabian the satisfaction of learning what he wanted to know about his former lover?

Fabian unbuttoned his waistcoat. The linen shirt beneath it clung to his back. He went to his wardrobe for a fresh one. "Martino is Horatius's surname," he said to the stack of shirts.

Isabella acquiesced, "I did meet a Signora Martino. She was at Lady Terese's table."

"How did she look? I mean, Horatius could not stop talking about her tonight. It would surprise me that he had been matched with such a beauty as he claimed."

Fabian had not been as slick in his questioning as he imagined. Isabella frowned at his continued prodding and told him, "I did not find her especially attractive. She was quite pregnant, for one. Not with that pleasant glow that Terese has. Octavia had more of a pasty, bloated look."

"Hmm. That is a shame. But did you talk to her?" Fabian asked.

"Why are you so interested?" she finally asked.

"I am not interested, darling. I am drunk and am just rattling on, as I always do."

"Well, I found we had little in common," she said, ending the discussion.

Fabian came back to the bedside. There was an uncomfortable silence that lingered while Isabella regarded him suspiciously. Fabian reached out and gently stroked her cheek the way she liked. She shut her eyes at the pleasure and forgave him.

"So, did you have a nice outing to San Marco?" he asked quietly. "The rain did not spoil your visit this morning?"

"Luckily, we missed the showers while we were in the Basilica. We spent hours looking at the art and architecture. We could have stayed longer if the party were not today."

Feeling suddenly overcome with sleep, he nudged his way next to her on the pillow. "I am sure Terese was happy to see it, and Mauritius will thank you heartily for helping him avoid the chore."

"It was not a chore, darling. And while we were there, I had a chance to talk with Signor Gaspari about my painting."

"Gaspari?" Fabian shook his head, not recognizing the name. "Should I know him?"

"Perhaps not. He is the curator there and a friend of my father. I asked him about the tinting powder I need for my paints."

Fabian stretched out and pulled off the cord binding his hair. He shut his eyes as Isabella combed out his locks with her fingers. "Are you going ahead with your painting, then?" he asked sleepily.

Isabella took a chance that he would be too tired to argue against her plan. "Yes, my love, but I will need to go to the Jewish Quarter for the ingredients."

He had indeed listened and opened his eyes in surprise. "Can you not find your powders in a reputable place? Give me the list, and I will send someone to procure them."

She smoothed his hair again and nuzzled his cheek. "I want to pick out what I need myself, Fabian. The Jewish Quarter is very safe to visit. I have been there before."

He regarded her curiously. "Have you? When was that?"

"I just want you to know I shall be going there. Tomorrow, perhaps."

"I would go with you, my darling, but tomorrow I actually have to work. The senate is finally in session."

"I was not planning to go alone. Terese is coming with me."

In his relaxed state, Fabian still protested, "You need a male chaperone, Isabella. Perhaps Mauritius will go with you."

"Do not worry, darling. You forget that I roamed Venice quite well without your supervision all these years."

Fabian yawned and said, "Hold that thought for tomorrow. We will discuss it in the morning."

She playfully slid the buckle of his belt open. "Are you really going to sleep, Fabian? I wore your favorite nightgown."

"I didn't think I had drunk so much, but my head is spinning, my love. Can I enjoy you in it in the morning?"

Isabella straddled him on the bed and slowly unhooked the ivory buttons that held the sheer bodice closed.

"I wore this to test you, darling. I was worried your gang of revelers might have stopped at a brothel. Did you?"

"You must trust me, Isabella," he whispered.

She cocked her head and said, "The question requires a yes or no."

He opened his eyes and told her, "No is my answer. Mauritius and I left before the others headed there. He and I are happily wedded men. We do not need entertainment outside our own bedrooms."

She kissed him leisurely on the mouth, then asked, "Shall I entertain you?"

Fabian said with a moan, "In my mind I would make love to you right now, but I cannot even finish undressing." He stretched out on the bed completely and asked, "Before you ravage me, my darling, can you first do one thing?"

She kissed his lips again and whispered, "Anything you want."

Fabian sighed groggily. "Can you pull off my boots?"

Isabella shoved him over in disappointment. She fastened her bodice buttons again and got off the bed.

"You are worthless as a drunk," she said with a chuckle.

"And you are a wonderful woman. Thank you, my love. The belt, too, please," he added drowsily.

It took several tugs to get the grimy boots off his feet. Isabella set them aside and wiped her dirty hands at the dressing table. She then went back to her sleeping husband and pulled at his leather breeches, inching them down his heavy legs. Fabian snored softly while his wife worked to make him comfortable. She left his shirt in place and stared affectionately at him before covering him with a blanket.

She curled up next to Fabian on the sliver of mattress unencumbered by his sprawling limbs. She smiled to herself at how fortunate she had been to marry her first love, her true love, and not an old Hungarian in a mossy castle somewhere far away.

Isabella loved her new husband, and she knew at her core that he loved her in return. Perhaps one day, they might trust each other enough and tell the truth.

Chapter 32

Fabian's bare feet protested the cold parquet floor when he climbed out from under the covers. From their warm bed, Isabella watched her husband rummage through his wardrobe until he found his black stockings and pulled them on. He unfolded his favorite black-and-red-striped breeches and slipped them on next, then tied red ribbons to hold them both in place.

The morning rays were just reaching their third-floor balcony windows, and Fabian opened the shutters fully before he finished his task dressing.

"May I unlock the door now?" he asked Isabella with noticeable annoyance.

Isabella and Fabian had discussed this thoroughly before. Isabella reminded him, "Anastasia only asks that you wear bottoms when she is in the room, Fabian. Not every woman is comfortable seeing a man fully naked."

"And when we want our hearth lit early on a cold morning, how is the chambermaid to get in if the door is locked?" Fabian argued again. "I cannot live under these silly constraints in my own bedchamber. Anastasia is not going to work out, Isabella."

"She cannot help it if she has never been a lady's maid to a married woman. I like Anastasia, and I want you to give her a chance. She was a lady's maid to one of the Passini daughters and came highly recommended to my mother. If you could just dress behind the screen, darling, that would solve everything."

"And how do I get to the screen? Shall I put a pillow in front of my objectionable parts when I crawl out of bed? You are asking too much of a man."

Isabella laughed at his unfounded criticism. "I did try to get Daria back when I returned from Solgrad. She was a good maid, but she is settled nicely with Lady Cassinello on the mainland now." A sly smile spread over her lips, and she confided, "I think Daria would have been eager to see you without your breeches on."

"Daria was pretty, too," Fabian teased.

"You are such a hypocrite, Fabian. Your manservant isn't allowed in the room until I am dressed."

"Yes, well, I do not want you distracting him from his duties."

She smoothed the velvet of her crumpled cover and said coyly, "I would never distract him on purpose. I like Christian. He is a sweet young man."

"Sweet, you say? Hmm, maybe I will have to hire a different valet—perhaps a eunuch can fill the job."

"Since when are you so jealous, Fabian?"

"Since I discovered how fantastic you are in bed."

Fabian came back to his wife's side and kissed her greedily. "Right now, I am tempted to make them all wait outside a little while longer."

"Did you not get enough this morning?" she asked.

"I am very satisfied, my love. You are quite generous with your attention to a man's weaknesses. Your father should have sent you on to Hungary after all. You would have been a fantastic assassin against the Habsburg bluebloods. Think of all the happy deaths you would have caused among the old bastards of the Hungarian court, stopping hearts with your energetic lovemaking."

"Must they be old men?"

"From now on, there will be no other men at all. Just me, forever and ever."

"Just you, my love," Isabella agreed sweetly.

As she watched him at the basin, she said, "Fabian, I have a question."

"Hmm?" he absently replied as he shaved the stubble above his groomed beard.

"We were having tea at an outdoor table along the plaza when Rosella Bertolino happened by with her gaggle of children," Isabella began.

"Does she have so many already?" Fabian interjected.

"That is not my point."

"Sorry, darling. Tell me your point."

"Well, Terese was at the table with us, and of course I could not avoid an introduction."

"Of course," he said distractedly.

"But the whole encounter got me thinking."

Fabian wound his lace cravat in front of his looking glass. "Go on," he urged.

"All right, I was wondering, do you think you might have made any little Fabians in this world?"

He considered her odd question. "No one has knocked on my door to say so."

"But you have been with other women. Have you ever wondered?"

"No, I do not give it a second thought."

"But a woman can get pregnant after just one encounter with a man, is that not true?"

"That is what they say. But maybe my seed is not so potent."

"Have you ever tried to, um, prevent your seed from being potent?"

"Prevent it? With a prophylactic, you mean? It is not done, Isabella. It goes against the Church."

She chuckled at his sudden ethics. "I know that, darling. Fornication also goes against the Church, but you only married for the first time six weeks ago."

"*Touché*, Isabella!" He indulged her jab with a smug smile.

She raised her brow in demand of an answer. "So? Have you?"

"All right, Signora Inquisitor. To be honest, I have used a sheath once, maybe twice or so. But it was more for fear of a disease rather than fear of making a bastard."

"So, perhaps it works for both," she said purposefully.

He stopped his primping and gave her his full attention. "Why this sudden interest, Isabella?"

"I told you. Rosella was with some of her children. One was a handsome, fair-haired little boy of seven. With greenish eyes," she added with emphasis.

"Ah, and you believe the rumor that Mauritius fathered her son."

"Has Mauritius ever mentioned the boy?"

"No," Fabian replied with finality. "He does not listen to rumors, and you should not either."

"I suppose it does not matter for him anyway. Rosella's son inherits Lord Bertolino's fortune, and she is content with her yearly allowance as a widow. I think I would be content not to remarry so quickly, as well."

"Even with children? Surely, you would want a protector, Isabella."

"I do not plan to have four children in eight years, like she has."

Fabian asked, "Why not? My mother did. Who knows, I might have just now impregnated you."

"Would you like that? Do you want to be a father so soon?" she cautiously asked.

"To be honest, I could wait a while. I like fucking you," Fabian said with a mischievous wink.

It was hard for Fabian to shock his wife, but she countered with a pout and asked, "Is that what you call it now? What happened to the romantic courtier I married?"

He sat down by her on the bed and smoothed the hair on her temples. "Do you still need the romantic overtures?"

She frowned. "I sometimes wonder—is that how you think of me when we are in bed together?"

"Please, do not be so hard on me, Isabella. If it seems I desire you without the poetic nuances of a new lover, it is only because I know you are finally mine. You know that I love you." He kissed her cheek. "I adore you." He kissed her the nape of her neck, lifting her long braid, caressing his way to her throat. "You are divine." He nuzzled her open bodice, cupping her breasts with a soft moan, saying, "We have come full circle, darling."

She raised her brows and asked, "To the fucking part?"

"You don't want to?"

Isabella playfully shoved him off the bed. She retied the ribbon of her gown as she steadily shook her head no. She pulled the covers up to her chin and said, "I suppose I will have to accept that my summer lover has been downgraded to my husband. Husbands have obligations that lovers do not. It is opening session, darling, and your father does not like to wait. Put on your shoes, Senator Carrera. I will not be blamed for making you tardy."

Fabian begrudgingly did.

"If I was not certain that my father was pacing in the foyer right now, I would stay and prove to you how truly romantic I can be as a husband," Fabian told her.

"Show me tonight, my love. Now, let my maid in and be on your way."

~*~

Across the hall from Fabian, Mauro was also mindful of the late morning hour. He secured the buckles on his low-heeled shoes and checked his look in the mirror. Davor had a knack for dressing him, and Mauro was pleased that he was not overly ruffled to meet with his banker.

"Why the hurry, Mauro? Can't you stay and have breakfast with me?" Resi asked from the cradling blankets.

"I am meeting Signor Salvatore for breakfast, did I not mention that?"

"No. I have hardly seen you since we arrived. We did not even talk last night."

"Tonight I am all yours, my dear. I promise."

"Will we be going alone to the opera?"

"Yes, just the two of us. And we will have dinner at one of Venice's finest restaurants afterward."

She toyed with him and asked, "Is this the courtship you promised?"

"If you want it to be," he said.

"I know you so well now, Mauro. I cannot imagine there is anything left to discover in a courtship."

"I discover something new about you every day, Resi, and I am better for it."

"Have I changed you, Mauro?"

He said thoughtfully, "One cannot live so closely with another and not be changed."

"I liked you from the beginning, you know. I never wanted to change you. I have always liked the way you dressed in your soldiering clothes, with muddy boots and smelling of horses; I like how the sweat from the day makes the ends of your hair curl—your real hair, not a fancy wig. I know what your legs look like, even hidden under your tall boots, and you don't need tight stockings and high shoes to show how masculine they are. And, well . . ." She stifled a sniffle that betrayed her. "I don't even mind just fish stew for dinner, with water instead of wine, and apple slices instead of fancy marzipan fruit."

Mauro sat down next to her with worry. "Resi, what is bothering you?"

She took a deep breath and let it out. "It is just that Mira talked of how she must change everything about Stephan, and how living in Solgrad was bad for him. She said some harsh things, Mauro. Stephan had only kind and loving things to say about her. I just expected a different sort of bride for him, after he had described her so glowingly."

"Did you not like Mira?" he asked earnestly.

"Of course, I liked her. How could I not like her, with her pretty blonde curls and piercing blue eyes? What is there not to like about a woman who shows more affection to a little lap dog than to her future husband? And her comments about my dress, and her disdain for Croatia did not bother me at all. And the other ladies, well—" Unintended tears leaked from the corners of her eyes.

"Shhh. Quiet now," Mauro whispered. He wiped her tears with the back of his fingers as she sobbed against him. "Do not be upset, my love. I am sorry you did not enjoy the party."

After a gulp of air, she said, "I will never fit in, Mauro. I can put on the gowns and the jewels, but I do not know what to say, what to do, how to gossip and pass judgment like the Venetian women."

Angry that his wife's first dinner alone with the Venetian upper crust had revealed its ugly side, Mauro insisted, "Do not strive to match their pettiness, Resi. You were worthy of being there. Isabella and Caterina adore you. Lady Nikolina is a good friend to you, and she is a lady with a noble upbringing."

"Yes, but I did not have that upbringing. I wore your beautiful cross, but it does not prove I am Catholic, like the Venetian ladies. I had on my favorite gown designed by Venetians, yet Mira described me as ethnic. Are you ashamed to have an Ottoman wife, Mauro? Would you not have been happier with a Venetian one?"

"Resi, how could you still think that? You know I regret ever questioning our betrothal. Now, dry your tears, my love. You did too much yesterday. Stay in today and regain your confidence. You can read your books on the balcony in the sunshine."

Resi wiped the last tears on her billowing sleeves and sputtered, "Isabella asked me to go shopping with her for her painting supplies this morning. She wants to start my portrait while I am here."

"That sounds like an even better idea. Shopping should not be too strenuous." He kissed her tenderly on her mouth, and she rewarded him with a smile that showed she would be fine. "Enjoy your outing with her, my dear. I have to go now. I will see you this afternoon."

~*~

After breakfast, when Isabella came to Resi's room, Resi told her, "I thought Verica might join us today. She has not left the house since coming here."

Isabella gave no objection as the three left the Barics' room. "You are very welcome, Verica. One more woman along is a good compromise in case I cannot find a man to join us. I promised Fabian I would take an escort, but it seems all the men have already gone out this morning. We may have to settle for Christian, if I can track him down. I sent Anastasia to find him."

Resi slid her gloved hand along the smooth railing for support as they slowly descended the stairs in their wide skirts.

As they passed the second floor, maids scurried up and down the hallway, carrying breakfast trays, linens, and washing basins. Verica watched them at their hurried work.

The muffled sound of Bianca's harpsichord playing in the parlor reached the foyer. The music lifted Resi's mood, and she asked, "Do we even need an escort into the city, Isabella? We did not have one yesterday, and I felt perfectly safe."

"We are not going into the city," Isabella disclosed. "I am getting pigments for my paints from a Jewish chemist in the ghetto. He has the best quality at a good price and will grind the minerals for me before they are delivered. He came highly recommended."

Resi was intrigued by their destination. "Is that what you were consulting with Signor Gaspari about yesterday?"

"I asked him to recommend a tutor for me. This chemist is also a fine painter, albeit a Jew. I can draw with charcoal and pencils, and have studied the arts, but I do not know how to work with paints, or even how to make them. Signor Gaspari could not think of anyone who might show a woman these techniques. Then he thought of Signor Morgenstern. He was not sure if the

Jew would be willing to teach me, but Signor Gaspari thought at least he would understand the bias against me and sell me the supplies."

"If Signor Morgenstern agrees to it, must you go to the ghetto for your lessons?" Resi asked.

"No, he can come here to me. Fabian has already granted permission to bring in an instructor. But you must not say anything about who the man is or how I arranged this," she whispered back.

"You need an alias for him."

"An alias?" Isabella asked, puzzled. "For the Jew?"

"Yes. To quell any rumors, you should introduce him as . . ."A name came into her head from a book she had recently finished. "Signor Morgante."

"That is brilliant. I will let Signor Morgenstern know his new Italian name. Morgante," Isabella said with satisfaction.

The parlor door swung open, and Felix came face to face with the three women standing in the middle of the entryway. "Oh! Please excuse me, ladies," he said with a hasty bow.

"Are you in a hurry to go somewhere, Felix?" Isabella asked with more than a polite interest.

"No, Lady Carrera. I apologize. I was distracted coming from the lesson. Music does that to me. I bid you a good morning." He bowed again and put on his hat.

The Carrera servant opened the front door for him.

"Felix. Wait!" Isabella called out.

Felix came back to her side.

"If you have no other lessons this morning, I need an escort," Isabella said.

"To where, my lady?"

"We are heading across the city. The boat is waiting for us. I would be happy if you could accompany the three of us on my errand. I imagine we will be gone a few hours, though."

In the foyer, Verica stood next to the baroness. Felix could not read her downcast eyes, but he could see her hopeful smile.

Felix smiled, too, and replied, "I am at your service, Lady Carrera."

Chapter 33

In the Middle Ages, the Jewish Quarter was home to Venice's copper foundries. Before the growing, prosperous city expanded its boundaries, the foundry island was considered safely outside Venice in case of explosions and fires. As the copper industry waned, the foundry island was deemed far enough outside Venice for another reason: To allow for a unique settlement known as the ghetto.

A century ago, The Serene Republic mandated that all people practicing the Jewish faith must reside within their confined community. The ghetto was set apart from the rest of Venice by the deep waterways surrounding the island sanctuary.

Word spread, and Jews from all around Europe learned about the unique island where they could openly worship, school their children in their faith, and live in relative safety within the narrow confines of the island. The Jews were free to come and go about their business in the city during the day, but at twilight, the Venetian police locked their one gate and barred their movement outside their island until the next dawn. The community accepted the harsh restrictions in exchange for a peaceful place to carry on their traditions.

Efrem Morgenstern's grandparents had migrated from Germany in those early years and had opened the chemist shop that Efrem now ran with his sons. From gunpowder to lacquer, one could buy minerals, powders, and solvents needed for many useful purposes. Isabella needed his wares to make oil paints.

~*~

The Carrera oarsman steered their boat past neighboring villas and modest houses of middle-class merchants and shopkeepers. Yesterday's storm had blown inland, and the cloudless September sky reflected brightly on the murky water of the Grand Canal.

The gondolier maneuvered around low barges loaded with goods and garbage near the industrial docks of Venice's ragtag warehouses. From there, the Grand Canal parted with the city, and the Carrera boat entered an open waterway where Venice's real commerce happened.

Resi and the others gawked at the unfamiliar world with its billowing smokestacks and grating noises until their boat turned down yet another liquid avenue, finally arriving at the entrance to the ghetto.

Isabella instructed their oarsman to return to the same dock in one hour. She imagined it would not take longer than that to pick out a few stones to be ground and finalize the plan for Signor Morgenstern's visits.

Isabella took Felix by the sleeve and warned him, "You do understand that I am counting on your complete confidentiality. My business here is a private affair."

Felix had nothing to gain from gossiping, and he promised, "You can trust me to be discreet, Lady Carrera. In truth, I have never had a reason to come to the Jewish Quarter, and I thank you for the opportunity."

His enthusiasm heartened Isabella. "Well then, we will call it an adventure for everyone. I just hope I can remember the way."

Isabella led them through the claustrophobic alleyways. Canopied tables stretched along every wall. Looking overhead at the odd rooflines, it was evident that the owners had added new floors to the tops of old houses. From those four stories of apartment windows, women hung wet linens and hemp shirts on lines strung between the tall buildings. Isabella had been through these narrow streets before, but she never had to find the way by herself. She was glad when she spotted Morgenstern's sign hanging above a door. "Here we are," she announced happily.

Felix opened the shop's entrance for the ladies. A few other male clients were browsing and making purchases. A clerk approached the young man, but Felix graciously directed him to Lady Isabella.

"I am here to meet Efrem Morgenstern," Isabella confidently stated.

A middle-aged man from behind the counter said, "You must be Lady Carrera. Welcome."

He wiped his hands on the dusty black apron he wore over his equally dusty shirt and came around to the smartly dressed group of Venetians. "Signor Gaspari sent a message this morning telling me to expect you, madam. I must say, his request took me by surprise."

"Are you in agreement, Signor Morgenstern?" Her tone was practically a challenge, and the Jew met her eyes, studying his challenger. "Are you willing to teach a woman to paint?" Isabella asked him point-blank.

Felix seemed surprised by her question, but he said nothing, clearly remembering his promise not to pass judgment on her business here. Next to him, Resi and Verica stood by in suspense of the chemist's answer.

Signor Morgenstern's expression was unreadable when he said, "I have taught my skills to many people of my community. I have also been asked by

Venetian Christians to show them how the craft is done. But in all those years, Lady Carrera, I have never taught a woman."

"So, you are against teaching me?" she asked.

A smile spread across Morgenstern's face, making his dark eyes glint. "It is not that I am against it. It has just never occurred to me that a woman would want to paint. Signor Gaspari praises your natural talents, Lady Carrera. If he took the trouble to write to me, madam, then who am I to deny helping someone merely because God decided to make that artist female?"

Isabella was not sure whether it was a compliment or an insult, but in his roundabout way, she had heard him say yes. "Thank you," she replied.

"Signor Gaspari wrote that I should equip you with paints, canvases, and an easel," Morgenstern said.

"Yes, that is why I came in person, sir. To discuss the details."

Morgenstern was not accustomed to speaking to ladies, and he said frankly, "I understand you want to paint portraits, madam, but blending the colors and learning the strokes will use costly paint. You must first learn how to work a brush and be prepared to make wasteful mistakes. I would like to start with something simple, like painting a piece of fruit or a flower."

Isabella was just as candid in her reply, "I understand that it will take time. I am not afraid of failing at first, Signor Morgenstern. I want to learn, and I will work hard at it."

Satisfied with her answer, he nodded and said, "For any painting, one needs blue, red, yellow, white, green, brown, and black pigments. The question is, madam, how much do you want to invest?"

"I have brought lire for the purchases. What do you mean by invest?"

"Let us take blue, for example. The boldest color comes from ground lapis. That is a rare stone, madam, and my price is nearly that of pure gold. You can stretch the lapis pigment with other powders, but the color will not be as vibrant. So, if you are painting a large canvas, you should limit the color blue. I can prepare a list of what I think you should start with and the cheaper alternatives."

"Whatever you recommend, Signor Morgenstern."

"If you come with me, Lady Carrera, I will show you the materials."

Isabella turned to Resi and whispered urgently, "I did not imagine arranging paints would be so complicated, Terese. Do you mind waiting?"

"Perhaps Verica and I can have a look around the vendor stalls along the street," Resi suggested.

Isabella had a better idea. "If you are interested in herbs and spices, there is an apothecary next door. I was planning to stop by to get a few ingredients for a tonic I needed. It would save time if you could purchase the herbs for me while I pick out the pigments with Signor Morgenstern."

"Yes, of course, Isabella. What do you need from the shop?"

Isabella asked the waiting chemist, "Do you have an extra parchment, sir?"

She took the offered quill and paper and told Resi, "The shopkeeper will know what I need from this."

~*~

The sign over the apothecary door across from the chemist had the word "Herbalist" scrolled in Hebrew and Latin. Below the lettering was a picture of a woman in a skirt, indicating that the tiny shop specialized in curing the specific ills of the female sex. Generations of healing women had worked in this same shop, now run by a midwife and her daughters.

A brass bell jingled when Felix opened the door for the ladies, and he reluctantly accompanied the baroness and Verica inside. The smells in the overstuffed store were both pleasant and pungent to their senses. They looked around the small room. The narrow display shelves across the middle of the shop were filled with blown-glass jars of dried flowers, weeds, bark, and roots used for making teas and tonics. Stacked on a table were various-sized baskets for sale like the one Idita used to keep her medicines handy.

Resi wandered ahead through an aisle to the front counter. The opaque containers lined on the shelf there were labeled in Hebrew. She studied the letters to decipher the names of the contents.

Verica stayed near the entrance. She took a random container down to examine it and then returned it to the shelf. She went to the next row of goods and did the same.

Felix followed her. "Did you get any sleep yesterday?" he asked quietly.

Verica opened one of the baskets on the table and shut it again without looking in it. "A few hours. Did you go to Caesar's birthday party?"

"I did, unfortunately. It went on until dawn. I planned to get some sleep after Lady Bianca's music lesson. She was in a foul mood this morning." He took down a jar of colorful petals and breathed in their scent. It made him smile, and he handed the jar to Verica.

"Lady Bianca's brother caught her leaving the house last night," Verica quickly said before giving the jar of dried flowers back.

Felix opened a second jar and said, "Her brother came up to us outside last night. He told Pasquale not to come around."

Verica strolled along the next short row of items. "Well then, that explains it," she said.

At the counter, Resi noticed Felix following her maid down the aisle. She watched Verica lift lids and put them back in an attempt not to look like the two were in a conversation. Before Resi could intervene on her maid's behalf, she was startled by the sudden appearance of the shopkeeper.

The grandmotherly woman dressed all in black was Rachel, the matriarch of her family of healing women. She had come through the small door built into the back wall across from where Resi was standing. The herbalist quickly sized up her new customer's predicament.

"Good day, Signora," she said in Latin. "How are you feeling today? Are you having early pains? Pressure on your legs, perhaps? Trouble with your digestion?"

Flustered, Resi replied, "Oh, thank you for your concern, good lady. Some days are harder than others, but I am well. I have not come for myself, though. My lady friend is just next door finishing some business, and she wrote down what she needs from your shop." Resi gave the folded note to the woman and asked, "Will it take long to fill her recipe?"

Rachel tucked a loose strand of graying hair under her cap and adjusted her spectacles to read what Isabella had written. "This will not take long to put together. Will your friend come herself, or should I write the instructions for her?"

Resi could not say for sure. "My friend said she has used this tonic before, but perhaps you could refresh her memory and write the instructions down."

"Of course, Signora. I will use this same parchment if that is agreeable."

Resi saw nothing wrong with saving paper and nodded.

Rachel called out in Hebrew, and a young assistant came from the backroom to help gather the herbs needed from the jars behind the counter.

Rachel laid the paper down again before finding her quill and ink in a drawer, and Resi casually glanced at what Isabella had written: "To provoke the menses. Four weeks."

Four weeks? Resi forced herself not to speculate on the meaning of this. The cryptic instructions seemed clear enough to the healing woman because she asked for no clarification. Resi would not have been able to clarify it even if she had wanted to.

While waiting for Isabella's herbs, Resi watched Verica and Felix through the shelf that separated them. They were speaking directly to each other now, but Resi could not hear their hushed words.

~*~

"Pasquale has been coddled by his three sisters his whole life. He can be a bit overconfident around women," Felix explained to Verica.

"Lady Bianca does not seem to mind his ways. But what I don't understand is why he doesn't come to the door, like a gentleman."

Felix became suddenly serious, explaining, "Lady Bianca is below what Pasquale could potentially marry. She might have told you her mother does not approve of the match, but my aunt says the same about Lady Bianca. The Carrera daughter cannot offer as large a dowry as other young ladies with fewer siblings can."

"You know quite a lot about matchmaking, Felix. Has your marriage been arranged?" Verica asked bluntly.

He replied just as directly, "I was once considered to be a desirable match. Until this summer, I even had a fiancée from a good family. A contract had been drafted, and we were to marry next year. But my family has fallen in status, so I am no longer a desirable suitor within the Venetian upper crust."

Verica objected, "Are people so shallow in Venice? Can this girl never be matched with you? Perhaps she loves you already."

Felix held back his laugh. "You are kind to say that, Verica. But I no longer have an inheritance, and that has changed her affection for me," he explained.

"Does money always count more than love with the Venetians?" she asked.

"Usually, yes. No one takes the time to fall in love here," he said.

"Lady Bianca is in love," Verica retorted. "That is why she risks everything to meet Pasquale."

Felix did chuckle this time. "That is not love. She only knows Pasquale through parties and dancing. Lady Bianca is entertained and flattered and caressed. She will change her mind when the music stops and she faces the real Pasquale. Still, like with the other girls, his future inheritance might be enough to keep her interested."

The little bell rang, and Isabella came through the door. "Felix," she said when she spotted him. "Can you please get my new easel from Signor Morgenstern next door? I will take it with us today."

Felix bowed obediently and left the shop on Isabella's errand without glancing back to Verica.

The young maid seemed to understand that she meant little to him beyond a simple distraction. But just the same, Verica watched Felix through the window panes as he crossed the narrow street and disappeared in the chemist's shop.

Isabella joined Resi at the counter, and the healing woman went over her remedy, "The red willow root should be cooked in a low pot of wine for one hour with the parsley, oregano, and rue. The dried fennel will make it more palatable. Be faithful to the proportions I have written and drink it all."

Isabella was unusually serious when she asked the midwife, "How long until it takes effect?"

"You might feel the flow begin as soon as an hour later, but sometimes it takes as long as a day. Eat a raw egg after the purging. It will strengthen your womb again."

Isabella took some coins from her purse and paid the woman. "Thank you, Rachel."

"May God go with you, Lady Valli," the healing woman said in Hebrew as the three left the shop.

"Isabella," Resi said reluctantly, "I did not tell Rachel your name."

"Rachel and her daughters are very good at remembering people. I have been to her shop with a friend before. They have a following among my acquaintances."

"What makes her shop special?" Resi asked.

"They offer medicine a woman would not get from a Venetian physician. At your castle, you have your Idita, and here I have my Jewish healer."

Felix emerged from Morgenstern's shop with the folded wooden easel and a tied paper bundle of brushes and small spatulas.

"Thank you, Felix," Isabella said, cheerful again. "This went better than I expected. We can go home now."

~*~

The short adventure to the Jewish ghetto had taken most of the afternoon. When the Carreras' gondola entered the central canal again, it was one small boat paddling among barges and flat-bottomed vessels hauling goods into and away from the city. Now and then, another passenger gondola floated along the edge of the industrial waterway. One such boat was transporting a group of young lords when it caught up to Isabella and her companions' gondola. It became apparent that the passengers were trying to get Felix's attention.

"Are these people friends of yours, Felix?" Isabella asked with annoyance.

"I know them, madam, but I would not call them friends."

"Then we will not be bothered with their juvenile merrymaking. Leonius! Stop the boat and let the hooligans pass us," she ordered her oarsman.

Their driver dug in his paddle, and their gondola came to an abrupt halt in the water.

The three men waved to Felix and laughed as they continued past. One could be heard yelling, "Don't fall in, Felix."

Isabella signaled Leonius to continue on, but she kept her inquisitive glare on Felix.

Though noticeably embarrassed, he said, "I am sorry that happened, and I beg your pardon, ladies. I went to the academy with them when we were boys. Circumstances change and so do friends."

"They were yelling about your father, weren't they?" Isabella asked but then reconsidered, adding, "It is a private matter, I am sure."

Felix stared at the passing boats, saying, "The story is very public, Lady Carrera, and people have not been kind in their judgment. They called my father a coward. They said that he flung himself over the side of a boat, that he was guilty of treachery and did not want to face his accusers."

The ladies were speechless as Felix told his sympathetic audience, "He was being transported to stand trial. My mother said he had been ready to testify against the men who framed him, and she was certain he would have been acquitted. I believe someone pushed him overboard so he could not reveal the truth in court. His wrists and ankles were shackled. He sank to the bottom of the canal."

Verica covered her gasp.

Isabella, who had already heard bits and pieces of this tragic story, asked, "Where is your mother living now, Felix?"

"She is in Bologna, with my two sisters. Her brother, my uncle, was generous enough to take them all in. They have been there for four months now."

Sitting next to Felix in the gondola, Resi was compelled to ask, "Why did you not go to Bologna with them, Felix?"

"There is nothing for me there. I had begun studying at the university in Florence before my father's arrest, and I would have preferred to stay there. But after our estate was sold and my father's debts settled, academia was no longer an option for me. I decided to come back to Venice, where it is familiar, until I could secure a commission somewhere."

"You plan to join the army?" Resi asked with surprise.

"Soldiering can be a good profession, Lady Baric, but I want to sign on as an officer, not a foot soldier. It has been more of a struggle than I imagined since our family no longer has the right connections."

"There must be someone who can connect you to a regiment," Isabella said.

Felix politely nodded, replying, "I am hopeful, Lady Carrera."

Resi voiced the obvious solution, "If it might help you, Felix, I could talk to my husband about your situation. He trained as an officer in his uncle's army."

"Of course," Isabella interjected. "Why did I not think of that? Fabian knows a lot of people, although Mauritius would have the most influence in securing a commission with Count Toth."

The prospect transformed Felix's grim expression.

"I thank you for your confidence in me, Lady Baric. Merely arranging a meeting with Lord Baric would already be more than generous."

"I am certain he will agree to talk with you." Resi then promised, "I will send a note tomorrow to say when you should come."

Chapter 34

Anastasia had suspected that her mistress might be pregnant. Since her wedding, Lady Isabella never used any of the squares of rags and wool set aside in her wardrobe for her lady's days. When her mistress asked her to brew the packet of herbs she had brought home, Anastasia questioned its reason. Isabella explained it was to purge any bad humors, but Anastasia was skeptical.

Being new to the Carrera household, Isabella's maid did not know who she could turn to in order to stop her mistress from purposely sickening herself. Anastasia was not going to speak up to her new employer. She had done that before, and it had not gone well.

Under duress, Anastasia lit the coal in the brazier and boiled the pot of wine with the measured bark and herbs. The odd-smelling steam made her nauseated as she tended the bubbling brew for the required hour. Then Anastasia helped Lady Isabella change into her nightclothes, even though it was only nearing the dinner hour. She watched in alarm as her mistress drank the foul wine. All of it.

Lady Isabella lay back against the sofa pillows to wait for something to happen.

"Will you want a tray for your dinner tonight, Lady Carrera?" Anastasia asked.

"I cannot eat until the tonic takes effect," Isabella replied. "Perhaps you can bring me some broth and bread in a few hours."

Anastasia nodded obediently. She hesitated at the door before asking, "Is this tonic for purging the stomach, my lady? Should I have a clean pot at the ready? Perhaps two?"

"You can bring those now, Anastasia." Isabella groaned and shut her eyes as the potion began to work.

After Anastasia brought the chamber pots, she stood by and helplessly watched her mistress double over in pain, waiting for her body to give up something. "Perhaps you have drunk too much, madam. Let me call a physician for you. Please."

Isabella had no patience for her maid's unwelcome advice. "The purging is known to be painful, Anastasia, but it will pass. Leave me now," she moaned miserably.

Tearfully, the new Carrera maid followed the order but remained outside the door in case her mistress called out for help.

~*~

For the last hour, Anastasia had been so focused on the noises from the other side of the Carrera chamber door that she did not notice Fabian coming down the hall after his day in the senate. She jumped with fright when he stood directly in front of her.

"Why are you so startled, Anastasia?" Fabian asked. "Are you spying on my wife?"

She found her voice and said, "I would never listen in through the door, my lord. I am sorry if it appears that way, but your wife is not well. You might want to send for a physician."

"If she is ill, then why are you out here and not by her side?" Fabian demanded to know.

Anastasia was stricken with guilt when she told him, "Her ladyship sent me away, sir."

Fabian's uplifted mood was gone, and anger replaced it. "Why would my wife send you away? What did you do?"

Anastasia shook her head, not knowing what to say. She wanted him to help Lady Isabella but did not want to be disloyal to her. With her master staring down at her accusingly, she chose to be helpful over loyalty to her mistress's secret.

"Your wife drank a tonic, my lord, and then she asked to be left alone. I followed her orders, sir, but I think she drank too much."

"What sort of tonic?" Fabian asked.

"I believe it purges the womb, sir," Anastasia said fearfully.

"Purges the womb?" Fabian repeated under his breath.

"Yes, my lord. It is supposed to benefit a lady's health when the bad humors do not bleed out on their own. Sometimes the potion does not make it that far down and there is terrible vomiting instead."

Fabian grasped the actual problem that Anastasia had avoided saying. "And you left her to bleed?"

"I don't know, sir."

"Step aside, Anastasia," he ordered. He rushed past the distraught maid and into his bedroom, where Fabian found Isabella collapsed on the sofa. He crouched down next to her while Anastasia watched from the open door.

"Isabella? Wake up, my love. Tell me you are all right," Fabian cried.

"I am awake," Isabella said weakly. "I will be fine."

The shock that he could have lost her washed over him, and Fabian breathed out in relief. He looked in the chamber pots on the floor. "I know what you are doing, Isabella," he said.

"I told you I am feeling better, my love. Just leave me in peace a while."

"Is this how it will be?" he pleaded. "You would rather poison yourself than do the one thing that is asked of you? Why, Isabella?"

She sat up unsteadily and leaned back against the pillows. "I knew you would not understand, Fabian."

He walked away from her, rubbing his temples in frustration. The maid was still waiting at the open door, and he shouted, "Out!"

Anastasia whimpered and shut the door between them.

Isabella clutched a pillow, her knees folded against her to endure the continued cramping.

There was no pity in Fabian's voice when he said, "You are right, Isabella. I do not understand. I give you everything as my wife, why would you not give me this one thing in return?"

"Everything, Fabian?" she sniffled. "All I want is a little time. Can you give me that? One year to be just a married signora? To paint and ride and love the man who makes me happy?"

"And what do I do during this time? Not touch you for a year so you can gallop through a fucking meadow on a horse? What about my love for you, Isabella? My desire for you?" he pleaded. "Whatever comes from that desire, my darling, is God's will. You cannot change that with a tonic."

She met his anger with growing irritation. "We can have it both ways, Fabian. You must know that."

He argued, "It is my right as your husband to demand children of you, Isabella. I can force you, you know."

She fired back, "Would you like that, Fabian? Hold me down until I spread my legs and submit to your seed?"

He knelt down next her. "Please, darling. You know I love you. Why is it so hard for you to do anything anyone asks of you?"

The next wave of pain washed over her, and he watched her battle through it.

When the cramping passed, she wiped her tears and made her case, "I do everything that is asked of me. I do it willingly, and you know it. I am sorry if I cannot feel joy when everything ends after only one month of marriage."

"You are a selfish woman, Isabella. My seed takes root and you purge it."

"Perhaps you should have married Octavia Martino when you had the chance. I know she was your lover, Fabian. Do not lie and deny it," Isabella said with a sudden fury. "She is round with someone else's child, but it could have been yours. Is that what you wanted? Do you regret that?"

Fabian chose his words carefully: "You were my first love, Isabella. Always the one my heart desired. Octavia means nothing to me. I wanted to marry you ever since I can remember."

"I want to be married to you, Fabian, but I want to live a little, too."

"You are twenty-four, Isabella. You have lived all those years freely. Will you never be satisfied?"

"Grant me this one consolation, Fabian. One year of freedom is all I ask."

"How will you maintain that freedom?" he shouted. "Lock me out of my own bedchamber each night? I will not agree to such constraints just so you can have a corseted figure at this year's Carnival!"

Her head was spinning again, and she retched into the chamber pot. She wiped her mouth with the back of her hand and said, "We talked once about this, Fabian."

"We did not talk about you purging yourself with poison, Isabella," he exclaimed. "What a foolish thing to do. I can barely look at you right now!"

"Then get out," she moaned, leaning over the pot again.

"With pleasure," he spat back. "You are selfish and inconsiderate, Isabella. I hope you enjoy your misery."

Anastasia was still outside the chamber door, and she lowered her eyes in shame when Fabian walked out.

"Throw the last of the tonic out and bring my wife a pitcher of water," Fabian ordered.

"Water, sir?" Anastasia repeated.

"Make her drink it all or you will be dismissed."

"Yes, my lord." She began to sob loudly as she rushed down the hallway for water.

Fabian went down the stairs, grabbed his cloak from the stand by the door, and left the house.

Chapter 35

Fabian strolled aimlessly for a time as the setting sun left the narrow passageways of the neighboring island in shadow. Fabian's meandering led him toward the city center. The small cafés had opened their doors and windows to the warm evening air, and relaxed patrons enjoyed steaming platters and refreshing drinks at small tables along the alleyway. Fabian's empty stomach conquered his reeling thoughts, and he took a seat at a random table for a plate of dinner.

His quick meal did not fortify him enough to face Isabella again. He continued past music-filled taverns and darkened shop windows, with their canopies drawn tight for the night, until he saw the red lacquered door. He rapped on it and gave the welcoming doorman his name.

Fabian was led into a lamplit sitting room lined with settees and lounging sofas. Two of them were occupied. After his brisk walk in the fresh night air, the heavy flowery perfume mixed with burning tobacco assaulted his senses. He waited for one of the ladies on duty to acknowledge his arrival.

After a moment, a scantily clad woman gingerly slipped off the lap of a half-conscious patron. The petite whore wore a tall, powdered wig decorated with red bows. The satin robe she hastily tied closed did not completely cover the corset that lifted her full bosom or the frilly skirt that revealed her silk stockings tied above her knees. She was called Angelica for a reason. Even the dim lamplight could not hide the creases on her powdered face, but it did not diminish her appeal. Skillful experience in her job was prized as much as a youthful complexion.

Angelica was the brothel's hostess that night. The drunken man she had been entertaining hardly noticed that she had left him to cross the room to Fabian, who still stood at the doorway. Her seductive smile grew into a merry grin when she recognized the new guest.

"Fabian Carrera! It has been a while, sweetie." She took his hand in hers and leaned in to kiss his cheek like she would welcome a friend. "What is your pleasure tonight?" she asked playfully. "I have two girls available. I will take you upstairs and you can have your pick."

Fabian would have eagerly followed her upstairs as a bachelor, but he barely smiled at her suggestion tonight. "I am not here for pleasure, Angelica. I was hoping Fiametta was available."

"Fiametta?" the hostess asked with surprise. "She is in her apartment with clients. Is there something wrong, sweetie?"

"No worries, Angelica. I wanted to talk to her about something. Perhaps she can spare a few moments?"

"For Roberto Carrera's son, perhaps she can. I will tell her you are asking for her."

He gallantly kissed the top of her hand before replying, "Thank you."

While Fabian waited for Angelica to return, he paced in front of the cold fireplace. The drunken man that Angelica had been toying with had fallen fully asleep, but the two lovers on the sofa across the room were absorbed in lustful foreplay. The man's pretty partner straddled his hips in her lacy petticoat, and the two kissed hungrily. Fabian paid them no notice as they progressed with their unapologetic coupling.

Fabian seemed lost in his troubled thoughts when Angelica returned to the sitting room. "Fiametta said I am to bring you up," she merrily proclaimed.

Fabian followed her through two sets of doors to a staircase that led to the matron's private quarters. Fiametta's luxury apartment spanned the entire third floor of the narrow villa. The other floors housed the prostitutes that worked at Fiametta's exclusive bordello. She herself no longer welcomed random clients. She was a courtesan and entertained a select group of men at her pleasure in her apartment above the girls she managed.

Still alluringly beautiful in her late thirties, Fiametta was not paid for just sexual encounters with the wealthy gentry of Venice. The shrewd businesswoman played other roles for her clients: she was an entertainer who would sing and perform for their amusement; she was a surrogate wife who eagerly listened to their complaints; she was a counselor who gave advice on topics a man could not confide about to another man. And when she could not lift her client's mood with sex or theatrics or a sympathetic ear, Fiametta offered a refuge for her patrons. Sometimes several could be found there at once.

Roberto Carrera had been her client for nearly a decade. It was not that he did not love and cherish his wife of thirty years, but there were things he could tell Fiametta that Felicita Carrera no longer pretended to be interested in. Unlike a mistress, a courtesan expected little emotional commitment from her patrons, and she did not burden them with her own. She only expected to be paid for her precious time.

The clients Angelica had mentioned earlier were two middle-aged politicians. They sat across from each other at a chess table, deep in concentration. Fabian recognized the two men, and they acknowledged his arrival with brief nods and then returned to their competition.

Fabian had first patronized Fiametta's bordello on his eighteenth birthday—a gift from his father. Fabian had only called directly on the courtesan once in the past for her unique, matronly advice. She knew him by sight, though, since he looked like a younger Roberto Carrera.

Fiametta embraced Fabian warmly and asked with concern, "What brings you here tonight, darling Fabian? Is your father unwell?"

"He is very well, thank you. I am here on my own account, Fiametta." He motioned toward the two players at the table and asked, "I hope I am not imposing?"

"This is a good time, darling. My guests have a serious wager going. They will not notice my absence until someone wins. Come, let us go into the other room and hear what is troubling you."

The other room was Fiametta's private bedroom. Fabian did not take in the opulent details, like the gilded canopied bed trimmed with velvet curtains and handmade lace panels. He was interested in advice, not seduction. Fabian understood her time was short, and he began explaining the purpose of his visit straight away, "You might know I am recently married."

"Yes, your father told me. Congratulations, darling! I know exactly who your bride is. She is a lovely girl. You must feel very fortunate." The courtesan could not help but stroke his masculine ego with her soft voice.

"I do feel fortunate, except . . ."

Fabian hesitated, searching for the right words to explain his problem, while Fiametta patiently waited.

He nodded to himself as if he had solved his inner conflict and then said, "I am telling you this in the strictest of confidence. My father should not hear of what I would like you to help me with."

She cocked her head. "Now I am intrigued," she cooed. "You can trust me to keep your confidence, darling. What sort of help do you need tonight?"

"I love my new wife, Fiametta, but I need to keep her from getting pregnant," Fabian told her bluntly.

"You can do many pleasurable things without actual coitus, darling. Shall I have one of the girls show you the best ones?"

"I think I know all the ways around intercourse, but I wish to love my wife fully," he said.

"Of course, you do, Fabian."

"Isabella is very independent, and she wants a year without the burden of, well, how do I say it?"

"Pregnancy," she leaned in and whispered slyly.

"It is wrong of her, which is why it is not something one can just ask about."

"I am flattered that you thought of me, Fabian dear," Fiametta purred. "Of course, I can help you and your lovely, modern wife. There are several things a woman can do to avoid becoming pregnant: sponges and other barriers that are not obvious to the man."

"What do you mean by obvious?" Fabian asked.

"I mean her lover cannot feel these barriers when a man is in the heat of the moment. My girls use these methods themselves with rarely a complaint of displeasure."

"I see."

"And then there are the various things a man can wear to keep his juices contained. Nothing is foolproof, of course, and they have their risks for the lady's delicate anatomy."

"Yes, I can imagine," Fabian agreed. "Can you show me some of these barriers?"

Fiametta decisively regarded Roberto Carrera's handsome son, standing vulnerably in the flickering light. "I would love to explore this with you, darling, truly I would. But I sense I will be needed in a few minutes when my guests finish their game. Someone is always a poor loser."

Fabian could not hide his disappointment, but Fiametta had an easy solution. "Camilla does not have a client booked this evening. Go to her room, Fabian. She is an excellent teacher. Follow what she shows you, and both you and your wife will be satisfied. Tell her I said to give you a few gadgets to take to your lovely bride."

Fabian bowed over the courtesan's scented hand and kissed it lightly. Looking up at her perfectly powdered face, he said, "Thank you for your help tonight, Fiametta. I knew I could count on your counsel."

"I am always glad to help a Carrera. Now, let me show you to her room."

Chapter 36

Camilla remembered the dashing soldier when she opened her door and saw him standing with Fiametta. Fabian smiled when he recognized her, too.

Years ago, Fabian had shared a night, or two or three, with Camilla after Fiametta had rescued the pretty teen from the workhouse. Her stern stepfather had abandoned the inquisitive debutante there for disobeying his strict parenting rules.

Camilla was now a pampered prostitute in Fiametta's fold and seemed amused at Fabian's predicament as a married man. She gladly tutored him in the art of inserting honeyed sponges, squares of fat-coated cloth, and hollowed-out lemon rinds for a lady's safety and a man's pleasure.

Fabian was a good student and took an active role in her erotic demonstrations. In Fabian's mind, the tutoring session was necessary to save his relationship with his stubborn wife, not for his own gratification. Just the same, he tested both the sheep bladder sheath and the infused linen one to determine his preference in comfort and functioning effectiveness. Fabian paid Camilla generously for her intimate advice and the extra sheaths, small lemons, crystal vials of vinegar and honey, and the pieces of perfectly sized sea sponges.

~*~

The cobbled alleyway magnified Fabian's heavy footsteps when the young man left the brothel. He had been gone most of the night, but it had been worth it to find a tolerable answer to Isabella's intolerable plea. With a borrowed lantern swaying in his grip, Fabian's instinct took over as he zigzagged past tiny houses and closed shops: first left, then right, then left again. His route home took him over arched footbridges that crossed narrow waterways through the sleeping neighborhoods until he reached the Carrera villa.

From the final bridge, Fabian noticed a light from the porch shining in the surrounding darkness. The front door closed again, but Fabian could still make out two figures leaving. He knew who to expect to encounter, and Fabian was in the right mood to set the young playboy straight.

As the talkative men approached, Fabian blocked their way on the step of his family's bridge. He had left without his signature hat earlier, and his black cloak with its high collar disguised Fabian's features. He was only a shadowed man when he said, "The hour is late, gentlemen. What are you doing on this path?"

Pasquale stopped and called out, "Late or not, it is none of your business, sir. Move aside. Let us pass." There was a distinct tremble in his voice.

"I will let you pass, but I will have my say first, Pasquale Passini," Fabian replied.

"If you know me, then reveal yourself," Pasquale demanded.

Fabian held his lantern up to show his face. "I am the man who told you yesterday to not play games with my sister."

Pasquale scoffed. "You dare criticize another for playing the courting games you so infamously took part in yourself, Fabian Carrera? Rumor has it, you were just like me at twenty."

Fabian stepped into the moonlight and faced his opponent directly. "Do not flatter yourself, Pasquale Passini. I may have frequented the best parties and sweet-talked the prettiest ladies, but I followed the rules of courtship. I never put a lady in a compromising position. I was not a prick like you. You may not care about your reputation, but a young woman's reputation is all she has. So, unless you plan to marry Bianca, do not ruin her by enticing her out on your midnight strolls, or worse."

Pasquale seemed unmoved by Fabian's commentary and countered, "Your accusation is insulting, Fabian Carrera. I have not touched your sister."

"Yet," Fabian asserted.

Pasquale began to walk away, but Fabian grabbed his arm. "I will give you this last warning, Pasquale Passini, and you should commit it to memory. If I find you have been alone with my sister again, I will personally castrate you with my sword."

Pasquale let out the breath he had been holding. "I am not afraid of your hollow threats, Fabian Carrera. My family name is just as powerful as yours in this city."

"I will not dispute that, Lord Passini. But if you believe any court would fault me for doing my duty as a protector of my sister's good name and virtue, then you do not understand the politics of this city."

Fabian stepped away from the bridge and waved his arm to let the two pass.

Pasquale hurried through without a glance back, but Felix tipped his hat in Fabian's direction.

Fabian did not hold Felix culpable as a co-conspirator. He understood the loyalty of cousins and Felix's need to keep a roof over his head.

When Fabian reached the front door a few moments later, he found it was locked. After waiting for Bianca all night, the doorman seemed to have finally retired from his post. No one would be answering a knock for the next few hours.

Fabian went around the villa, and the door for deliveries was unlocked. Even at this early hour, torches brightly lit the windowless hallway leading to the pantries. Fabian heard metal pots clanging in the kitchen around the corner as the cooks started breakfast.

Fabian went up the servants' stairwell. It was not yet dawn but not too early to stop on the second floor to share his troubling news. When he emerged from the winding staircase, Fabian saw the thin beam of light under his mother's door that he had hoped for. Fabian rapped quietly on her door and then went in.

Lady Carrera was in her dressing gown, kneeling in front of her small altar. Fabian's mother rose early each day to devote an hour to her morning prayers. She looked up from her meditation and waved him toward her breakfast table. The maid had already left a pot of steaming tea there, and Fabian poured himself a cup while his mother finished reciting the psalm.

Lady Carrera rose from her cushion and joined Fabian at the table. "What brings you to my room at this hour? Is it Isabella? She did not come down to dinner last night."

Fabian ran his finger over the top of the cup distractedly and replied, "If Isabella is ill, it is because of me. In truth, I was out all night trying to sort out her contrived demands," he said, pouting.

"You are not used to being a husband yet, my dear. You will learn how to read your wife soon enough."

"I was hoping for a little more sympathy on your part," he said.

"Of course, you have my sympathy, Fabian, but I know you can be stubborn. Did you succeed in your sorting-out?"

Fabian finished the tea and replied, "I decided I am going to apologize."

"That is good of you, my son. Keep Isabella happy." She poured hot tea for herself into the cup Fabian had just emptied and said, "Was that so urgent that you must interrupt my morning prayers?"

He got the point and said, "I just had a conversation with Bianca's suitor outside our house—again."

Lady Carrera shook her head in disappointment. "She can be vexing, that last girl of mine. But, if it is any comfort to you, Fabian, my dear, I am not in the dark about Bianca's behavior. Enrico would have told me the same news this morning."

"I thought you should know I had a talk with Bianca just two nights ago. Her recklessness will continue until she ruins her good name, Mother. Neither she nor Pasquale seem to be discouraged by my warnings."

"I suppose I should have allowed the Passini boy to call on Bianca like the other suitors. I did at first consider him a plausible match since your father and Lord Passini are longtime friends. But Lady Passini's tongue has grown forked ever since the Doge sent her husband to Paris as his special envoy."

"Forked? What did she say exactly?"

Lady Carrera chuckled and explained, "It is not what she said, but how she said it. Now that the Passinis have the supposed favor of the Doge, she believes her status in society has risen. She told Lady Norina and Lady Marquesa on several occasions that my Bianca is not good enough for her socialite son."

"I always thought Lady Norina and Lady Marquesa adored Bianca."

"Oh, they do, my dear. But then Marquesa told the entire Catholic Ladies Committee that her youngest daughter is favored as a match for the Passini son, which is laughable, since Lady Marquesa's daughter has not even come out in society."

"And because of that, you will not allow Pasquale to court Bianca?"

Her eyes narrowed when she said, "In truth, I do not like the young man. He may outgrow the all-night parties and drunkenness, but for a while there has been gossip that he has a questionable disposition. Anastasia was recently employed in the Passini household, and I believe she had good reason to leave."

"Does he have a temper? Bianca can certainly show hers," Fabian remarked.

"I hear it is more than a temper. It is best not to put the two together from the start. I think my decision is clear now," Lady Carrera told her son with finality.

"Bianca will make a terrible nun, Mother."

She laughed. "You are not wrong, Fabian. Yesterday I spent my entire day with the nuns, and I heartily agree that Bianca is not suited for a life of penance and poverty."

"Then what is your decision, if not the nunnery?"

She refilled her gilded cup with a smile and assured him, "There are other options, Fabian dear. I wrote to Lady Renate Toth last month when this whole late-night theatrics began. The countess has agreed to take Bianca into her house for a year as a lady-in-waiting. If that does not help her to gracefully rejoin society in Venice, perhaps at least she will meet a suitable husband there."

Fabian considered his mother's plan. "That sounds reasonable. By winter, all your children will be out of the house and then you will have no one to worry about."

"Oh, I doubt that very much. Now, go check on Isabella so I do not have to."

Fabian left his mother's chamber and climbed the marble staircase to his room on the next floor. Only the clicking of his leather heels disturbed the quiet. It was still too early for the maids to be bringing breakfast trays.

The candles in his chamber had burned out sometime in the night, but the lantern Fabian held was enough to see Isabella's figure sprawled out on the lounge chair across the room. On the floor beside her drooping arm was a porcelain pot half full with Isabella's purging. Blood-soaked linens were stuffed into a second pot.

Fabian moved the two vessels to the side and crouched on the floor in front of his wife. Guilt washed over him as he studied her pale, serene face. He stroked the wisps of hair that fell over her eyes, and then she opened them. A scowl flitted across her features when Isabella saw him there, but she did not attempt to get up.

Fabian whispered, "I should never have left you when you were so ill. Can you forgive me, Isabella?"

"I sent you away, remember?" Her voice was raspy. She reached out for the cup of water on the table beside the sofa, and Fabian helped her take a drink. "Where have you been all night?" she asked.

"Wandering Venice and thinking," he said.

She accepted his answer with a drowsy nod.

"Are you all right now, Isabella? Did the tonic work?"

"It took several hours, but it did what I expected."

Fabian stroked her temple lovingly when he asked, "How did you know what you needed, Isabella?"

She hesitated.

Fabian raised his brows and pressed her, "Is this method commonly known?"

Isabella lowered her eyes when explaining, "The tonic was first prescribed to a friend to balance her humors. Because she was an unmarried lady, her physician did not dare suggest she might be pregnant."

"A friend?"

"You would not know her," Isabella added.

Fabian asked, "Did you consult this physician?"

"I did not need to. Midwives know these remedies," she replied.

Fabian considered her answer. "Is it worth almost poisoning yourself? You are not an unmarried lady."

She moaned, "It is not poison, Fabian. The side effects have nearly passed. I just need to sleep it off."

"Do you know what I did after I left you?"

"Wandered, you said."

"Yes, and in my wandering, I found myself at the door of an old friend of mine as well as my father's: Fiametta."

Isabella slumped against the cushion. "Oh, Fabian, tell me you did not sleep with her."

"No! I sought her advice."

"And what advice did a courtesan give you?" Isabella asked hoarsely.

"Feminine advice."

She looked up hopefully.

Fabian gently stroked her cheek and said, "I will grant you your wish, Isabella. I will give you your time."

"My year?"

"Yes."

"Truly? Even though it will be hardest on you, my love?" Despite her victory, her voice was laced with remorse. "Maybe I was being selfish."

Fabian chuckled at her quick change of heart. "You will want to hear Fiametta's counsel before deciding who the selfish one is."

He reached into his jacket pockets and pulled out the items Camilla had given him, setting them on the sofa's edge for Isabella to see.

She sat up with curiosity. "What is all this?"

He held up the first item and said, "This is a little lemon." Her laugh lifted his spirits.

"Fruit, Fabian?" she asked.

"Of the prophylactic kind! When you are well again, I will demonstrate how useful a hollowed-out lemon can be," he said with a renewed playfulness.

"Is this what I think it is?" She held up the fashioned sheep's intestine.

"All of it is," he told her eagerly. "You shall have your year of being a signora, and I shall continue to enjoy being your husband. I have been given expert instructions on the placement and usefulness of each item. Some of it will seem unusual, so you will have to trust me."

She handled the sponges and asked, "Are these what the prostitutes use?"

"I suppose they are tools of their trade. But if God wills that you become pregnant despite these whorish tricks, then you must accept what comes of it. No more tonics."

He wagged the sheath in front of her and said, "This is my offer, and those are my terms."

"I don't know what to say, Fabian. I am stunned. And grateful."

"You are the wife of my dreams, Isabella. I can wait a little longer to see you become the mother of my children, but you must do your duty for us one day."

"One year. I promise."

The outside world could be heard emerging from its slumber through the open terrace windows. In the morning stillness, the inside of the Carrera house came to life, too. Angry feminine voices carried with the wind into their room.

"That sounds like Bianca!" Isabella exclaimed in alarm.

"I am sure it is," Fabian said with a chuckle. "My mother must have just shared some bad news with her."

"Oh dear, Fabian! Do you know what the bad news is?"

"I actually do know. I stopped by my mother's bedroom before I came here. She told me she has arranged for Bianca to be a lady-in-waiting at Toth Castle. It is all settled, and I expect my little sister is not happy about it."

Isabella's worried frown left her when she said, "Do you know what I love about you, Fabian?"

"What?" Fabian asked playfully.

"It is barely dawn and yet you know what your mother and your sister are fighting over."

He asked mischievously, "Is that an accusation?"

"It is a comfort. You care deeply about the women in your life." Isabella leaned into him on the cushion and said, "I will never feel neglected with you as my husband."

He kissed her and said, "You have my total devotion, Isabella. Now and forever."

Chapter 37

In her anger, Bianca dismissed Carla for the morning, preferring to spend the day in bed, reliving her misery. She sobbed over her tragic situation. Bianca could not believe her mother had plotted to send her away to the wretched isolation of Toth Castle in the northern Empire. In the end, though, her tears gave way to reason.

Bianca had not bothered to finish dressing before going downstairs to find some parchment in the parlor. Determined to stay in Venice, she saw no way around it. She would end it with Pasquale and then choose a boring suitor from her mother's list.

Caterina was in the parlor that morning, as she was every morning since Monsieur Vincent had come to stay with the Carreras. Today she sat alone by the sunny window that overlooked the quiet canal. She watched the occasional gondola float by while she waited for Jean-René to join her for tea.

The two had sat together every morning at nine before he left for his appointments for the day. Maybe he had an early engagement that he had forgotten to mention. Perhaps he was ill in bed, she worried. Caterina was about to ask a groom to check on him when the man himself appeared at the doorway with an overstuffed bag in each hand.

"Jean-René, are you going somewhere?" she asked.

"I am afraid I am, Lady Caterina. My business here in Venice is complete, and I have lingered too long," he said with the somberness of an undertaker.

"But this is so sudden," Caterina protested. "Why did you not tell me you were leaving today? At least we could have had our tea together."

"My trunks are already loaded in the gondola, my lady. Your father made it clear last night that a long goodbye would be too upsetting to you."

"What are you saying, Jean-René? Did my father tell you to leave?"

The Frenchman reflected on Lord Carrera's explicit request but softened it for Lady Caterina's delicate mood. "He might have brought up the subject."

"Then I will talk to my mother. She would welcome your continued séjour at our home."

He shook his head and gently explained the situation as he would to a child. "In the end, I believe it is your father's choice in who is welcome in his home, sweet Lady Caterina, and I have overstayed that generous offer. It is time I go."

The gravity of his words hit Caterina like a sudden blast of wind. "But you can stay on in Venice, and we can still meet for dinner or a show or—"

"No, Lady Caterina. We have spent more time together than is proper for an eligible man to spend with a beautiful woman. If I had my way, I would ask you to come with me to Lyon. But, regrettably, you are bound to another."

"Jean-René! Are you proposing something?"

Caterina stepped toward the door. One part of her said she should accept his goodbye, and one part wanted to go with him.

He seemed emboldened by her indecision and said, "If only you were free to accept!"

"Accept what, Jean-René?" Caterina asked breathlessly.

He came two steps closer and said, "Marriage, of course, dear Lady Caterina! You must know that I adore you. Imagine what fun we could have in France together. I would take you to Lyon and parade you on my arm for all to see what a beautiful bride I found in Venice. I would design the most glamorous gowns for you to wear in Paris. What an adventure that would be! What a delight!"

He had described their life together with such bravado that Caterina felt herself swooning.

He took her hands in his and brought her back to reality when he reflected, "But alas, sweet Lady Caterina. It was not meant to be." A single tear marred his powdered cheek, and his rouged lips quivered.

"I am speechless, Jean-René," she whispered, looking into his coal-lined eyes. "I have never enjoyed myself more than in your delightful company. What laughs we have had together. And all the people you know, all the parties you were invited to. I know I would have the most wonderful time in Lyon and in Paris with you. I dared not consider it before today, but perhaps that is my destiny: France."

Jean-René sighed dramatically. "Then today is a dark day for me, my sweet and dearest Lady Caterina. It would be my greatest desire to take you back with me as my wife, but your father is fully against it. So, I will leave you now before I make a complete fool of myself in your presence."

He put her hand to his lips and then picked up his satchels again. "I say to you: Adieu, ma chère. Adieu!" He turned on his high heels and closed the parlor door behind him.

Caterina stood at the edge of the grand room in shock that he, too, would leave her. "No, Jean-René!" she said to the solid door. She sank to the spot where he had just stood and began to sob in grief.

"Oh, gracious God," Bianca exclaimed from the corner desk across the room. "You didn't seriously fall in love with Jean-René, did you?"

Caterina had forgotten that Bianca had been writing her letter the whole time. She pulled herself up and smoothed her crumpled skirts. "You are one to talk, Bianca," Caterina muttered through her loud sniffles. "You woke the entire house with your wailing over your own hopeless love affair with that undeserving Pasquale Passini."

Bianca argued back, "At least Pasquale is a real man to shed tears over, Cat. When you returned from Croatia, you cried for days over your phantom fiancé until Papa agreed to meet with him. How is my agony over Pasquale any different?"

Caterina twirled the engagement ring Cyro had given her and answered, "For one, Bianca, I am older and it is expected that I marry soon. You have barely been launched into society, and Pasquale hardly seems like a serious suitor. Cyro is an exceptional match."

"Exceptional?" Bianca challenged. "Your fictional husband-to-be has not even written you since leaving here, and that was a month ago."

Caterina remained defensive of her engagement despite her uncertain outlook. "I am bound to Cyro, and he to me."

Bianca fueled Caterina's doubt when she remarked, "Perhaps Monsieur Vincent was a godsend. At least you got out of the house, had some fun, and did not waste the summer party season. You got to know another man, another view of life, and it was exciting. Think about it, Cat. What did Cyro do to entertain you while he was here? Take a stroll along the canal? Visit an art gallery?"

Caterina sat down on the overstuffed chair across from her sister, thinking about it.

Her expression suddenly brightened as her doubts cleared. "You are right, Bianca. God sent Jean-René to me at the right time for a reason. God is telling me I am to leave Venice but not for Corsica."

Bianca encouraged her with a steady nod.

"Yes! I have always wanted to see Paris," Caterina dreamily exclaimed. "Perhaps I was meant to be in Venice waiting for Cyro only so that I could fall in love with Jean-René."

"Indeed!" Bianca agreed. "And your ticket to Paris is floating down the canal right now, Caterina. Is God going to stop him? No, you must go after him, dear sister."

"Jean-René cannot depart Venice so abruptly. He will have to settle his affairs with Michele and the other merchants." Caterina stood up with a renewed determination. "Yes, I will go to the warehouse and stop him."

Bianca warned her sister, "That will do you no good without Papa's blessing. You must tell Father about your change of heart. Only he can keep your new lover here since he was the one who sent him away."

Caterina clenched her fists, ready to battle to save her heart from another assault. "Yes! Papa must hear me out and bring Jean-René back. I will tell him right now." She walked out, slamming the door behind her.

~*~

Bianca folded her penned letter of regret. As she melted the wax and pressed her seal onto the addressed note, she said a word of thanks to God. Caterina's decision would cause uproar in the house and be the perfect distraction. When their father arrived home that evening with Caterina's rebellion on his mind, Bianca was sure he would not be interested in hearing about her troublesome behavior. Bianca would give up Pasquale, but she would find a way out of going to Toth Castle.

She hopped off her gilded chair, seemingly content with the new turn of events. Rushing out the parlor door, Bianca nearly ran into Hugo at the bottom of the stairs.

Hugo waved her onto the steps with a formal bow. "I beg your pardon, Lady Bianca. Please, do not let me add to your difficult morning."

It was apparent to everyone that Bianca had never made it to bed before her mother called her to her chamber. The teen still wore her satin dressing gown over her linen shift, and her flat slippers covered her stockingless feet. Bianca's high hairdo, styled for the night out on the town, had come unpinned in places, and random curls hung loose over her shoulders. At least she had already washed off the dusting of chalk and hints of rouge on her cheeks, but her soft brown eyes were puffy from crying through the morning. Hugo thought she looked absolutely enchanting, standing face to face with the youngest Carrera daughter.

Although Bianca was in a hurry to get her letter into Carla's hands to be delivered, she took a moment to defend her reputation. "I know what you are thinking, Hugo. I was a bit overcome with some bad news earlier this morning, but I am not so frazzled any longer. I may have found a way around it," she said stubbornly.

Hugo enjoyed a challenge, and he decided he would try to sway her opinion on his favorite place. "I am glad to hear that, my lady. Living at Toth Castle should not be taken as a punishment, especially as a lady-in-waiting to the countess. That should be considered an honor."

Bianca scowled at his interference. "Does the entire house know my business, or are you especially nosy?"

Hugo held back his laugh but not his charming smile. "I apologize if I seem meddlesome, but the level of yours and your mother's voices made it impossible to keep from hearing what was said. My chamber is right below your mother's, you know, and the windows were open."

Her cheeks burned with uncharacteristic embarrassment. Inexplicably, Bianca wanted Hugo to think better of her. Covering her distress with a practiced smile, the debutante said, "You must think very badly of me. I am not normally hysterical, but since you have lived at Toth Castle, Hugo, you must know how horrible it will be for me there."

Hugo leaned casually against the banister and contemplated his memory of life in the North.

Then he shook his head and said, "I would have to disagree, Lady Bianca. I never lived within the castle, but it would have been a pleasure compared to living in the army barracks outside its walls."

"That is exactly what bothers me: the suffocating castle walls, the gloom of the damp stone fortress, being isolated in the dark of the forest."

Hugo laughed at her description. "It is not that way at all, my lady. The castle is in the forest, yes, but it is not so isolated. Count and Countess Toth have a lively schedule of dignitaries coming and going from all points in the region. I daresay the visitors seem to enjoy their stay."

Bianca considered his argument. "Do they have parties there, Hugo?"

"They have dinner parties with dancing, of course, and an occasional ball. I was just a simple soldier at the time, so I was not invited to the festivities. I believe your brother attended a dinner party or two."

"Hmm," she said with a frown. "I will ask Fabian."

Hugo went on to say, "I agree, it is not the same society one would have in Venice, but it is not uncivilized either. And such a charming, attractive young woman, such as yourself, will no doubt be courted by all the eligible suitors."

"You disappoint me, Hugo," she said with a feigned pout. "Do you think I am only concerned with finding a husband? I have other interests and reasons to stay in Venice besides working through the list of bachelors my mother compiles."

Hugo saw in her sparkling eyes that he had not truly insulted her. Just the same, he apologized, "Please, take no offense, Lady Bianca. It is clear to me that you have many talents, and I am sure you would have more opportunities in Venice to pursue those interests."

"I am not saying that I could not enjoy myself in another place, Hugo. But Venice is all I know."

"Ah, but wouldn't you want to see more of the world?" Hugo asked earnestly.

"I suppose it would be an education to live somewhere else for a time. And my mother said I would be away for only a year."

"Only a year? That is no time at all," Hugo said encouragingly.

"But I hardly remember meeting Countess Toth, and I will be given duties and have obligations in her court," she said with genuine concern.

Hugo assured her, "I hardly think you will be washing the countess's clothes and cleaning her hearth. You should visit and find out whether it suits you. And if Baron Baric sends me on an errand to his uncle's castle, I hope you would allow me to call on you, to check on your wellbeing."

"You are a friend of the family, and I would be glad for your visit."

Hugo's directness, combined with his youthful good looks, had Bianca unexpectedly bending to his charms. She maintained, "I won't be leaving for another week or so—if I even must leave, which is not yet certain. In the meantime, perhaps we can talk more about what I should look forward to there. That is, if you have time in your busy schedule, Hugo."

"Time is one thing I have in Venice, my lady. And I would gladly spend it with you."

"Well then, perhaps tomorrow we can sit together and talk."

"It would be my pleasure to talk to you about life in the North, or whatever else you want to talk about. I am at your service, Lady Bianca." He tipped his hat.

"Until then, I bid you a good day, Hugo." A smile remained on Bianca's rouge-stained lips while she clutched her words of rejection to Pasquale in her fist. She went slowly up the stairs with a new resolve, her slippers clomping loudly with each step.

Chapter 38

Piero apologetically explained to Caterina that all the Carrera boats had been taken that morning. The servant tried to make amends for the inconvenience, saying, "Allow me to hail a public gondola, Lady Caterina. It will only take a few minutes."

Caterina brushed him off impatiently. "I do not have a few minutes, Piero. My errand is extremely urgent today. I will go on foot."

Piero seemed to consider the delicate balance between the will of the young Carrera daughter and what his employer, Lord Carrera, would want for her. "Of course, your errand is urgent, Lady Caterina," the doorman said soothingly, "but please allow me to find a groom to walk with you to your destination, madam."

"I am not in the mood for company, Piero. I will be fine on my own." Caterina went back into the house and out through the front door alone.

~*~

Since she was a little girl, Caterina had walked the alleyways and cobbled streets that led to her father's office at the Doge's Palace. This morning she practically jogged, weaving her way toward the tall bell tower of San Marco Square. A quarter-hour later, she arrived at the Doge's Palace.

As Caterina stood in front of the sprawling building that housed the lawmakers' offices, she realized that she had never arrived unescorted at her father's workplace. She was confident that his office was on the second floor but had no idea which of the many staircases would take her there.

Caterina ignored the shocked stares of the dignified men in their black senator robes whom she passed as she roamed the opulent foyer, looking for something that would spark her memory. She found the familiar statues that flanked the proper staircase and recognized the paintings hanging on the walls. She climbed those steps.

Cornelio Oldani, her father's clerk, sat on his tall chair outside Senator Carrera's office. He was hunched over his desk, diligently focused on copying a document onto a blank parchment. Escaping Oldani's notice, Caterina lifted the latch on the carved wooden door and let herself into her father's chamber.

Sunlight poured through the tall windows inside the office, blurring Caterina's small figure in a beam of lighted dust at the threshold. Roberto Carrera sat behind his long oak desk and squinted to make out who had just entered.

The fashionably dressed man sitting across from Lord Carrera turned around to see what the senator was scowling at.

The brisk walk had not calmed Caterina's anger at her father's interference in her happiness. She cried emphatically, "Papa, how dare you send Jean-René away!"

Roberto Carrera stood up from his high-backed chair and asked accusingly, "Who let you in, Caterina?"

"I need to talk to you, Father. Urgently."

Signor Oldani was at the door, having heard the shouting. He shook his head at his employer and said, "I am so sorry, sir."

Caterina was beyond Oldani's reach when she sat down on a sofa in front of a wall of shelved leather-bound documents. She crossed her arms over her chest in defiance and waited for her father's attention.

Roberto Carrera understood how this would go, but he chose not to make a scene in front of his honored guest. Instead, he graciously explained, "Ambassador Krottendorf, this is one of my three daughters, Caterina. Caterina, this is the ambassador of Bavaria. I would prefer for you to leave us now, my dear, and wait outside the door until we are finished. Cornelio!"

Roberto ordered her removal with a nod toward his clerk. Cornelio Oldani stood aside from the entrance and waved her out.

Caterina had come this far, so she held her ground. "This will only take a minute," she asserted.

"I have two grown daughters of my own, Lord Carrera," the Bavarian ambassador acknowledged. "I understand their needs are urgent at times." He smiled at Caterina in a grandfatherly way. He had sympathetic blue eyes and rosy cheeks above his coarse, graying whiskers. He rose from his chair and collected his dossier. "I have an appointment on this same floor, Lord Carrera. I could arrange that now if it is convenient for you, sir. Perhaps we can continue our conversation over lunch."

Lord Carrera remained diplomatic. "Thank you for your understanding, Ambassador Krottendorf. If it is not an imposition, I will meet you at the restaurant in an hour."

The ambassador bowed formally to each of the Carreras and left through the door that Signor Oldani still held open.

"You may shut the door behind you, Cornelio," Roberto Carrera said.

When they were alone, Caterina's father turned his stern focus on his daughter. "Let me guess," he began. "You have come because Monsieur Vincent is returning home today. Is that it?"

She held her head high and proclaimed, "You are sending him home because of me, Papa. That is wrong of you."

His stare was fierce, but his voice was calm. "The only thing wrong is that you interrupted my work for some emotional rant that can only be endured at home."

Her confidence faltered, and she slumped in her seat. "I just needed to understand—why so sudden, Papa?" She felt small under the tall beamed ceiling, with the golden dome of the Basilica looming in the windows behind her.

Roberto sighed at his daughter's naïve innocence and explained, "You and he have made a spectacle of your new friendship, Caterina. I did ask Monsieur Vincent to leave, and now I am certain it was the right thing to do."

"But he brings joy to my day," she argued meekly. "He entertains me while I wait for Cyro. And Jean-René adores me."

"He adores you?" her father repeated with an ironic laugh. "Of course, he does, Caterina. And you probably think you love him now that he has confessed that to you."

"I am not sure what I think, Papa."

Her father grew serious again. "Do you want to marry a man who might adore you but will never bed you?" he asked.

"Papa! What a thing to say!"

Roberto Carrera leaned back in his chair and said, "I hold no grudge against Monsieur Vincent. I find him extraordinarily knowledgeable in the silk trade, and his business sense is commendable. He is agreeable and well-mannered, in a French sort of way. But I do not think he is husband material, at least not for my daughter."

"How he can be a good man but not a good husband?" Caterina said disapprovingly. "I do not understand."

Her father came to sit with her on the sofa. He took Caterina's hand and cradled it gently before awkwardly announcing, "Monsieur Vincent is a homosexual, my dear."

Her expression went blank at the blunt declaration. She shook her head and insisted, "You are mistaken, Papa. He has been married before. Jean-René showed me the picture of his dearly departed wife. She was lovely, and he adored her."

"Caterina, I do not doubt that he was indeed married to a beautiful woman once. Many homosexuals love women and do marry, my dear. But Michele has confirmed that Monsieur Vincent did not try to hide his preferences, although he spoke openly of his desire to remarry."

Caterina stood up, furious again. "Is that why you sent him away, Papa? Because of a little gossip from Michele? He does not like anyone!"

Her father soothingly said, "I asked Monsieur Vincent to find another place to stay because he has set his sights on you as the new woman he will marry. And you, my dear daughter, are already betrothed to Lord Cyrano Duarte."

Sobbing, she asked her father, "Are you sure?"

He tipped her chin to look up into his eyes and warned, "Hear me now, daughter. At your request, I have negotiated an excellent marriage contract with the Duarte family, or have you already forgotten?"

Her lip trembled when she explained, "It is Cyro who has forgotten, Papa. He has not written one letter, and I can no longer believe that he will return to finally marry me."

Her father frowned. "You must show a little patience for once."

"How do you expect me to wait so long, Papa? My heart is breaking."

Her father stood up. "I am done discussing this, Caterina," he said. "As soon as your betrothed arrives, I will call for the priest and you will marry Lord Duarte before you can find another worthless man to seduce you."

Caterina bowed her head in her hands and began to weep in self-pity.

Roberto returned to his desk, opened a side drawer, and took out a tightly packed bundle. The suede wrapping was secured with thin leather straps. He brought it to her on the sofa and held it out. The package had her name on it.

"What is this?" Caterina asked.

"The courier delivered it here at my office yesterday, instead of our home. I have not had a chance to bring it to you."

"This is all for me?" She touched the familiar script on the wrapping. "From Cyro?"

"I have not opened it. The bundle was with the correspondence from Viscount Flores, Cyrano's grandfather. Cyrano is on his way to Venice, my dear."

"Why didn't you say he was coming?" she muttered.

"I hardly had a chance before your visit today. But he is, and when he arrives, Caterina, you will not mention Monsieur Vincent's adoration for you, or the joy you say the Frenchman brought you while you waited for your new husband. Do not ruin what I have worked so hard these last weeks to arrange. Heed my words, daughter: I will not tolerate making yet another contract for you unless it is with the nunnery. Is that understood?"

She assured him, "There will be no need, Papa." She turned her attention to the bundle in her lap. "Do you think there are letters in here?"

Her father looked over her shoulder. "Why don't you have a look? You are welcome to stay as long as you need, but I have important business to attend to this morning."

Nervous now, Caterina untied the leather straps and opened the flap of the wrapping. Her father watched her as she laid the folded squares on the table next to her.

"It seems that Cyrano Duarte also adores you, Caterina."

"He wrote to me every day," she said, beaming. "How could I have doubted Cyro's love?"

As she opened the oldest of the dated notes and drank in her fiancé's loving words, Caterina did not notice that her father took his hat from the side table and placed it on his graying hair. Roberto Carrera took one long glance at his favorite girl before he walked out his office door. She would soon be leaving him and her family home in Venice forever. He had burned her happy expression into his memory.

Chapter 39

That same morning, while the Carrera sisters were in the parlor, Resi leaned on her balcony railing and watched the boats float by on the Grand Canal. It promised to be another glorious day, and she soaked it in contently.

Mauro was dressed to leave and came out onto their private terrace to say goodbye. He wrapped his arms around her waist and could feel his tiny son kicking as he affectionately stroked her belly across the smooth fabric of her tunic.

"What is going through that pretty head of yours?" he asked.

"I am still thinking about the orchestra and singers last night. I don't think I have ever heard such profoundly moving music."

"There will be a different performance next week. I can take you again, if you like."

She leaned into him and breathed out, "I would like it very much."

Mauro looked out onto the busy canal as he held her close. "Do you have plans with the ladies today?" he asked.

"Isabella said she expects to spend most of the day with her painting instructor, and Caterina and Monsieur Vincent were meeting some friends for lunch. I thought I might just stay here in the room today."

"Is that why you are wearing your robes instead of a dress?" Mauro asked.

"I like wearing them, and I thought it would not matter."

He kissed her cheek and said, "I like them, too. I can touch you closer that way." He stroked her middle again for good measure, then asked, "And what will you do with your day with no company?"

"I found a wonderful novel in the Carrera library, and I am content to sit out here on the balcony and read. If I do get bored, Verica and I will take a walk."

"Stephan will be married in three days, and then the festivities will be over. I will have no other obligations after that," Mauro told her.

"No more bachelor retreats, no more luncheons?" she asked playfully.

"Nothing," he mischievously said as he nuzzled her neck.

She stepped back and adjusted the pin in his fashionable cravat. "I cannot imagine a day when you have no battles to wage, no dawn training to lead, no rejected shipments to protest, no looming ambushes threatening you. Something always takes you away from me."

"Nothing will come between us after Thursday. I will be a man of leisure for the rest of the month. I can lie in bed with my wife all day if I wanted. Would you like that, Resi?"

"I relish the idea, but won't the Carreras think we are poor guests if we stay locked away all day?"

"Fabian will make an excuse for us. He understands things like that." He kissed her smiling lips and said, "I will see you later."

She called out, "One more thing, Mauro."

He stopped at the door.

"I was wondering if you considered my request. Will you take some time from your doing nothing to meet with Felix?"

"I already sent Davor with my reply. I will talk to the young man tomorrow afternoon."

"Thank you, Mauro. And when can I expect you to return today? Will we have dinner together again?"

"We can have dinner with the Carreras, or we can go out again. Oh, and I am expecting a delivery," he added. "If you are bored, you may open it when it arrives."

"Did you buy a new hat, Mauro? I always thought Fabian's hats were extraordinarily showy, and then I walked San Marco Square and saw even more extravagant hats on the fashionable Venetian men."

He tipped his simple hat at her. "I like my style and will keep to that," he said playfully. "I was shopping for something else yesterday."

"Then I will be curious to see what you bought. Perhaps I will get my own delivery today: a letter from Ruby. Nestor would forward her letter to me here, wouldn't he?"

"Yes, my dear. Nestor knows how much you are missing your friend, and he would expedite it to you."

"I do miss Ruby," Resi reflected, "and I miss Jero, too. I wonder why we haven't heard from them."

"They are newlyweds, Resi. I am sure coming to Venice is not the first thing on their minds," Mauro replied. "They are having a wonderful time wherever they are."

He kissed her goodbye and said, "Enjoy your book, my dear. I will see you tonight."

~*~

Verica was in her shared bedroom in the attic, mending a seam in her mistress's gown, when Carla came into the room. She hung her apron on a peg and sat down on her bed to change into her walking shoes.

"I have an errand to run for Lady Bianca. Do you want to come along, Verica?" Carla cheerfully asked. "It is a lovely day outside."

"I would need to ask permission, but Lady Baric is napping right now. I will just stay here and finish this." Verica had avoided going out with Lady Bianca last night and didn't want to do anything else her mistress would disapprove of.

Carla argued, "Pregnant ladies nap for hours, Verica. You won't be missed at all." She took the dress from Verica's lap and set it over a chair. "Come out with me. The fresh air will do you good. The sewing can wait until tonight."

Verica wanted to go out in the sunshine, and it was true that Lady Baric would likely be asleep for a while. Smiling, she set her needle and thread down and asked, "What is your errand, Carla?"

Carla sat down next to Verica on the bed and excitedly whispered, "Lady Bianca is breaking it off with Lord Pasquale. She wrote a letter saying so. She does not trust the groomsmen to keep it from her mother, so I have to deliver it."

Drawn in by the secret, Verica asked in a whisper, "So, she is not in love with him?"

"My mistress is more in love with Venice than with any man. Did you hear that her mother plans to send her away? Lady Bianca thinks she can convince her father that she can behave and he will let her stay." Carla rolled her eyes in disbelief. "I am not so sure, though. I have never known Lord Carrera to contradict her ladyship in those matters."

She stood up and tugged Verica's hand. "Tidy up a bit if you like first. You might want to look pretty going out."

"How long will we be gone?"

"An hour, at the most. It is not far."

The girls re-pinned their caps to their smoothed hair to make themselves presentable for their outing. Carla tucked the letter in her skirt pocket, and the two descended the winding wooden staircase.

The Passini villa was only a short distance away by boat, but one could reach it through the narrow side streets and over a few low bridges that linked their small island to the others.

A few minutes into their walk, Carla came across a childhood friend from another noble house that she seemed to need to talk with desperately.

Verica agreed to go the rest of the way to the Passini door without her. The directions from that point were simple enough, and Verica did not mind giving Carla the time she needed to catch up with her old friend.

Verica knocked on the entrance door to the impressive Passini villa. An elderly servant dressed in a fashionable uniform answered her knock with a friendly greeting.

"I have a message for Lord Pasquale Passini," Verica told him formally.

The servant invited her to step inside and shut the door behind her. He took the sealed envelope she held out and asked, "Will you wait for a reply? His lordship is in the parlor."

It had not been discussed whether Verica should wait or not, but she thought that was reasonable. "Yes, I will."

The doorman pointed to a cushioned bench across from the door she had just come through, and Verica took a seat. She looked around the ornate entryway with its marble statue of an unknown goddess in the center of the space and gilded paintings adorning every wall. The Passini family's wealth was on display for their visitors.

It wasn't long before the parlor door opened, and Pasquale crossed the foyer, looking for the messenger. "Oh, it is you, Verica. Come in, come in." He waved her to follow him back into the room.

She had spent one wonderful evening with Lord Pasquale and his friends, and she followed the familiar man without hesitation.

He shut the door and said, "I was expecting Carla, but you are a pretty substitute."

"Do you have a reply for me to take back to Lady Bianca, sir?" she politely asked.

He threw back the last of the brandy in his glass and refilled it. He focused his drunken stare on Verica and asked, "Do you know what the note said?"

"No, sir," she lied.

"Well, let me assure you that there is no reply needed when a lady tells you to go to hell." He took another swallow from his glass.

"Sir, I am sorry I was the bearer of bad news. I will be leaving, then."

She curtsied dutifully and went to the door to be on her way. But Pasquale's hand was against it before she could turn the latch. She had not remembered him being so big, and she took a step back.

"Have a drink with me, Verica," he kindly offered like he would to an old friend. "Do you like brandy, or perhaps a little sweet wine?"

He poured her a glass from the decanter on the table. Pasquale's looming closeness gave her a sudden urge to flee. Verica obediently took the offered wine while looking around the room for another way out.

The parlor was a large space used for welcoming groups of guests. In the middle of the room were upholstered chairs and sofas for conversation, like those in the Carrera parlor, and the opposite wall had tall, curtained windows that looked out onto a canal. The adjoining library door was open, and Verica could see bookshelves and clusters of colorful chairs in that room. She decided she would escape through there and instinctively backed up toward the door.

Pasquale grabbed her hand and pulled her back to him. "Stay a moment, Verica," he said smoothly. "It is rude not to finish your drink."

Not knowing what else to do, the maid took a sip from the glass and let him keep her hand in his. He brought it to his lips and kissed it gallantly like she had seen him do to Lady Bianca. Pasquale guided her back to a row of chairs.

His penetrating eyes made her skin tingle like that of the prey who knew its predator had caught it in its sight. Verica shook her hand free. "I need to be going, sir," she said.

He stroked the sleeve of her bodice and said, "It is too bad your mistress has you wear such a drab dress. The gown you wore to the party was so alluring, and your hair was much prettier with the curls loose. Take off your cap, Verica. Let me see your pretty hair again."

A sense of peril washed over her, but she did as he asked.

Pasquale reached out and lifted a strand of her hair between his fingers and openly contemplated her. "Much better," he said.

To her shock, he grabbed her by the waist and pulled her close to him. Pasquale's deliberate caressing and tugging at her skirt made her cry out, "What are you doing, sir?"

Ignoring her plea, Pasquale leaned down and forced her lips open with his own. She could taste the alcohol as he invaded her mouth with his tongue.

Verica wiggled free from his grip and slapped him across his cheek. She immediately realized her mistake and covered her mouth in horror.

Angered by her defiance, Pasquale grabbed the arm he had just been caressing and pinned it behind her. His breath was hot on her face when he hissed, "You are a feisty girl, Verica. I like that."

"I did not mean to strike you, sir. Please, let me go," she begged.

Pasquale twisted Verica's arm to force her around and then folded her like a rag doll, face-first over the back of a chair. She fought to free herself, but she was immobilized as he tightened his grip on her.

"You are breaking my arm!" she cried.

"Are all Croatian bitches so lively?" he whispered in her ear. "I bet I will enjoy this." He gave her arm a sharp tug that convinced Verica to relent in her struggle.

Pasquale's size and weight were too much for her to defend herself. Verica began to sob as her fate became clear.

The drunken lord worked to lift her layers of skirts from behind her with his free hand. She felt the air on her bare hips as he succeeded in his quest. He gathered the folds over her back while talking in her ear, "How many men have you been with, Verica? Two? Three?" he asked.

She kicked and squirmed against the assaulting probe. "Leave me alone," she shouted. "Stop it!"

His free hand slid between her thighs, and Pasquale chuckled when he learned what he wanted to know. "You have been a good girl, Verica. I expected a farm boy would have already had his pleasure with you in some haystack back in Croatia. All the better for me," he said lewdly in her ear. "I like being the first."

"No!"

She stomped her heel where she hoped his foot was, and he cried out in pain. But it was not enough. She could feel the cold metal of his buckle against her exposed skin as he fumbled with one hand to open his belt.

"There we go." His breathing turned to a pant against her neck. His stiff cock slid against her, and he forced her leg out to one side with his knee. "Play nice, Verica, and you might even enjoy it."

He pressed his heavy body against hers. His conquest was inevitable. Still, she cried out in vain, "Stop!"

Despite her terror, she heard the thud of something heavy falling at her feet.

Pasquale mercifully took a step back, shouting, "God damn you, Felix! That fucking hurt!"

Felix stood at the edge of the parlor with a thick book in his hand. "A book to your head is less painful than what you are doing to that girl. Let her go, Pasquale."

Still hovering in front of Verica's doubled-over figure, Pasquale warned, "Mind your own business, Felix, and let me finish mine."

Verica took the chance and straightened up. Wiggling away from Pasquale's hold, she came around the other side of the chair from him. The adrenaline coursing through her made her lightheaded, and she struggled not to collapse from the shock of everything happening.

~*~

Felix had not recognized that the molested girl was Verica—sweet, dear Verica, whose eyes were wide with fear. An urge to hurt her molester overwhelmed

Felix, but he knew better than to use his fists against his cousin to champion her cause.

"Why this one, Pasquale?" he asked. "Think about the trouble this will cause you. Verica is Lady Baric's handmaiden, not a scullery maid," Felix argued.

Pasquale tucked his shirt into his breeches and closed the buckle on his belt. He took another drink from his nearly empty glass, laughing at his cousin's remark.

"I know why you stopped me, Felix. You are worried about the trouble it will cause you," Pasquale said suspiciously. "You need the favor from Lord Baric, isn't that it? Well, do not fret, Cousin. Verica will not tell her master about her visit here, will you, Verica?" He blew her a puckered kiss to seal her promise.

Humiliated, Verica somehow managed to lower her bunched skirts back to her ankles before her eyes met Felix's pleading ones. He came toward her, but she recoiled in alarm, holding her arm against her side.

"Are you hurt, Verica?" he asked with genuine concern.

She stepped away and then walked backwards to the door. "Yes, I am hurt! He nearly twisted my arm off if you care to know. I understand why you are worried, Felix. You are brutes, both of you!" Verica squeezed the heavy latch despite her handicap and ran out of the room.

Felix stared after her blankly as she continued past the surprised doorman and out of the house. Her words had stung, and he was ashamed that he had not done more for her.

Her insult did not touch Pasquale, though. He picked up the heavy book Felix had thrown at him and jiggled it in his hand to perhaps guess at the weight. Then he put on the jacket he had left on a chairback earlier and looked for his hat.

"Are you leaving?" Felix asked.

His cousin replied, "I did not get the satisfaction I crave. I am going to find a suitable replacement while I am still in the mood."

"Then I stopped you in time?" Felix needed to know.

Pasquale seemed amused by Felix's serious expression. "She left as pure as she came if it makes any difference to you."

Felix cautioned, "Your drinking is fogging your common sense, Pasquale. The Barics are honored guests at Bianca's house. You will not gain Lord Carrera's favor if Verica tells her mistress what happened."

"Fuck the Carreras!" He held up Bianca's letter and threw it in Felix's direction. "Read it if you like. Bianca refuses to see me again. I needed something to clear my mind of that, and wine was not enough."

Felix finished reading the short note and asked, "Did Verica deliver this?"

Pasquale nodded. "Carla usually brings Bianca's notes. Just as well. Verica is more to my liking." He found his hat and added, "You have exceptionally bad timing, Felix. I would have liked to finish the job."

"Do not touch her again, Pasquale," Felix warned.

Pasquale studied his cousin with renewed insight and then began to chuckle. "Now I understand the reason for the interference. You have taken a fancy to her, haven't you?"

Felix did not find it amusing and said, "I am not in a position to fancy anyone at the moment."

"How ironic is that? A lady's maid is now too lofty a pursuit for a man of your diminished means." Pasquale contemplated his cousin again and concluded, "But she might be well-matched for an army officer."

Felix pointed out, "Since there will be no chance of me encountering Verica again, your point is irrelevant. But if you find yourself in her company again, promise me that you will not trouble her."

Pasquale put his somber cousin at ease, saying, "My fleeting interest in your little girlfriend has passed, Felix." With renewed buoyancy, he added, "I am heading out for more willing entertainment. Do you care to join me?"

"No," Felix answered flatly. "I have two lessons this afternoon, and I need to practice before that."

"You work too much, Felix. If you are not practicing your own music all day, then you are teaching it to someone's hopeless daughter. You need to learn to have fun, Cousin."

Felix held his anger in check when he replied, "I will keep my obligations, Pasquale. I do not have such deep pockets to pay for your sort of fun."

"If money is all you need, then let me put this on my tab. Come along, Felix. It will do you good to let off a little steam. You are so uptight sometimes."

It was Felix's turn to laugh. "Even if I had the money, I would not spend it on whores. I am saving for a new bow, remember?"

"You are indeed peculiar," Pasquale replied as he walked out the parlor door.

"It runs in the family," Felix called back before he disappeared through the library door and into the music room again.

Chapter 40

When Verica didn't come back to the bridge where Carla and her friend had been chatting, Carla assumed Verica had taken a different street home after her delivery. The Carrera maid was in their attic chamber, putting on her apron again, when Verica opened the door and fell onto her corner bed without a word. The flood of tears she had so bravely held back on the walk home flowed in fits of sobs.

Carla was scared to know what had happened to her new companion. She sat down on the bed and stroked Verica's back to calm her. "What is it, Verica? Did you get lost on the way home? It is easy to do with all the little alleyways. There is no need to cry over it," she said soothingly.

Verica could not turn from her pillow without causing stabbing pain in her shoulder. But more painful than the injury to her arm was the hurt she felt from her friend's betrayal.

Verica asked Carla the question she asked herself repeatedly on the way back: "Why did you insist I come with you? It wasn't to get some air, was it?"

"I, um," Carla stalled, "I don't like to meet Lord Pasquale alone, is all."

"But you sent me on alone, Carla. Why didn't you warn me?" she groaned.

Carla's eyes welled with tears. She brought her hand to her lips to hold back a whimper and said, "I am so sorry. You are new, and I . . . I didn't think he would keep you there."

Verica demanded, "Did he try to rape you, too?"

"No!"

Carla touched Verica's arm gently and asked, "What did he do?"

"He nearly broke my arm holding me down over a chair. He had my skirts up and—" Verica could not go on.

Carla shook her head. "He never hurt me," she said.

"I tried to fight him off. If it had not been for Felix coming into the room, he would have had his way."

"Lord Pasquale was never violent."

Verica trembled as she relived the horrible details in her mind. "He attacked me, Carla. He held me down." When Carla shook her head again, Verica asked, "What did you do to fend him off?"

Carla stared blankly across the room as she thought about it. "I never had to. He, um, sort of courted me. He told me I was pretty. We shared some wine, and then he took my hand and led me to the sofa."

Verica was stunned. "Led you to the sofa? Did you let him bed you, Carla?"

"It wasn't a matter of letting him. I had been with a man before. Raul was my first. But Raul now seems like a boy after knowing how different it can be." Carla admitted, "He did scare me at first."

"Then he was violent?"

"No, no, it was my fault it didn't go well. The second time was easier." Carla covered her mouth at the slip.

"Carla! How many times did you meet Lord Pasquale alone?"

"Twice, maybe. He said I should never tell Lady Bianca what we had done, but he did not say it with regret. I regretted it. I betrayed my mistress, and I did not want to tempt him again. That is why I asked you to come today," she confessed.

Verica rolled back onto her pillow in disgust. "He does not care about you, Carla, or which girl shows up. You, me—" Verica yelped from pain when she accidentally moved on the bed.

Carla went to the basin. "The water is still cold," she said. "A wet linen might help your arm feel better."

"What am I to do, Carla? Maybe my arm is broken. It hurts so badly."

Carla was wringing out the linen when an unexpected knock startled them both. They exchanged worried glances before Carla cracked the door open. "Davor?" she said in surprise.

Davor said through the crack, "I am sorry to interrupt your privacy, Carla. Is Verica here? Lady Baric has been looking for her."

"Wait just a moment." Carla shut the door again and said in a panic, "What should I tell him?"

"There is nothing to tell," Verica replied more calmly than her roommate. She gingerly got up from the bed and took her apron off the peg. She dried her tears with a corner of the apron and asked, "Can you tie this for me?"

After Carla quickly helped her, Verica opened the door and said with false cheerfulness, "Hello, Davor. I was just napping. I must have lost track of time."

Davor quickly told her, "Lady Baric is eager for you to come to her chamber, Verica. The baron sent her a gift of new clothes—Ottoman robes— and she needs your help to dress in them."

"Robes? Not a gown?" she asked.

Davor chuckled. "Your expression is the same as Lady Baric's when she opened the box I brought her. The shopkeeper is from Constantinople, it seems. Lord Baric sought him out."

"How wonderful for the baroness. I will come right away," Verica said, but a wave of lightheadedness washed over her when she turned too suddenly. She began to sway.

Davor saw her teeter and reached out to hold her steady. He guided her back through the door to her bed to sit down.

"Are you ill, Verica? You look so pale," he said anxiously.

Verica wanted to tell Davor that she was sick to her stomach from having her arm twisted while a man she had thought she trusted tried to rape her. She wanted Davor to convince her that everything was fine now and that she was safe.

From the corner of her eye, Verica saw Carla shake her head and knew the Carrera maid was right.

With a smile on her trembling lips, she lied to the man she loved like a brother, "I will be fine now, Davor. Just give me a moment to freshen up a bit."

Davor seemed to doubt that she was okay. Verica had been acting oddly since they arrived at the Carrera house, but he did not press his concerns in front of Carla. Instead, Davor nodded agreeably and assured her, "I will let the baroness know. I hope to see you at dinner, Verica." He leaned in close and whispered, "If you need to talk, you know where to find me."

"I know. Thank you," Verica said guiltily, and then he left the room.

Verica splashed her face with cool water from the basin, wincing in pain as she tried to dry her hand.

"This is bad," Carla said with a grimace. "You will not be able to help the baroness dress. Let me go in your place, Verica."

"You have already gone in my place once. I will tell Lady Baric the truth about what happened."

"No, no, no! You cannot tell your mistress what happened," Carla pleaded.

"I must," Verica insisted.

"Think about the consequences, Verica. Lord Pasquale will deny it, and Lady Bianca will be devastated when she hears about it—which she will," Carla hissed.

Verica argued, "But Felix was there. Lord Pasquale cannot deny he attacked me. I have a witness."

"Felix is his cousin. He will stand by Lord Pasquale and whatever story he decides on."

Carla paced the small room. "I have it!" she exclaimed. "Here is your story: we went out for some air, and you slipped on the wet stones."

Verica groaned at the absurdity of it. "It isn't even raining, Carla."

Carla invented a better version they would tell: "We were by the canal. There was a puddle, you slipped . . . and I had to grab your arm to keep you from falling into the water."

"I don't like lying to the baroness," Verica said. "I have never lied to her, and now that is all I do."

"For Lady Bianca's sake, please stick to the puddle story. I will come with you to help Lady Baric dress in case you cannot."

Verica reluctantly nodded.

"Good!" Carla said with relief. "Now, where is your cap?"

Verica touched her head and remembered Lord Pasquale's sickening touch. "It is lost, but Lady Baric will not mind. She will mind me taking so much time, though. Let us go."

~*~

By the time the two maids arrived at the Barics' chamber, Resi had already unpacked the tunic, robes, short waistcoat, and long embroidered jacket. She laid them out on her big bed and was holding a colorful robe against her when Verica came through the door.

"I know I gave you the afternoon off, Verica, but look what has arrived," the baroness said excitedly. "Have you ever seen such beautiful embroidery? Imagine having such a shop in Venice. I have never seen anything so lovely, even in Thessaloniki."

Verica crossed the room with sincere fascination. She loved the layering of the Ottoman dresses. "It is stunning work, my lady," she said with admiration, but she dared not take the offered garment in her hands.

Carla was at the door, and Resi looked to Verica for an explanation.

"If it is all right, Lady Baric, Carla will help you fasten everything." Verica attempted to lift her swollen forearm and explained, "I am sorry I am so clumsy lately, my lady. Carla and I went out for some air, and I slipped in a puddle. I am afraid I cannot use my arm." Then Verica began to cry despite her brave attempt not to.

Resi dropped the beautiful jacket on the bed and said, "Sit down, Verica. Let me have a look."

Verica did, and Resi apprehensively examined her maid's arm. The wrist was swollen twice the size of the other and was purple. "I don't want to hurt you by rolling up your sleeve, so I am going to cut the fabric. Carla, bring the blade from my husband's dressing table, please."

The cotton sleeve easily gave way.

A steady stream of tears ran down Verica's cheeks when she repeated the invented story, "Carla tried to stop me from falling into the canal and grabbed my arm. It is nothing really, madam."

Resi said with alarm, "You must have the grip of Atlas, Carla! The arm is black and blue! Let me check if anything is broken."

Resi gingerly felt for a reaction. "Does anything hurt here, Verica? How about here?"

"I just, . . . I don't feel well, my lady," she moaned. "I think I might vomit."

Carla rushed a basin under Verica's chin.

Resi wrapped her arms around her young maid's shoulders to comfort her and said, "Carla, find a messenger to bring a physician. Tell him to hurry."

"I will find Piero, Lady Baric." Carla ran from the chamber.

Resi rocked Verica in her arms. "Shhh. It will be all right," she told her. "The physician will check it all out. I don't think it is broken, but it might need to be wrapped."

Verica took a deep breath to stop her tears. "I wish Idita were here, Lady Baric. She would know how to make it better."

"Yes, she would." Resi held Verica close and stroked her like she would a child.

As her sobs subsided, Verica whispered, "It is not that I am ungrateful, Lady Baric, but I miss home. I miss all the friendly faces. I miss taking walks without getting hurt."

"I know what you mean, Verica," Resi whispered back. "I am missing Ruby, just like you are missing your friends. You had some bad luck this week: first you were ill, now you injured your arm. In a few days, when you are feeling better, I will take you out myself and show you everything the ladies have shown me. After a while, you won't wonder any more about what's going on with the girls in the kitchen or your brother in the stables." Resi sighed as she tried to believe her own words.

Verica straightened from the baroness's calming embrace and wiped her cheeks with the back of her good hand. "You are right, Lady Baric," she said. "They will be there when we return to the castle, and I will love them all the more for having missed them."

"That is what happens when people leave on a journey. They learn what is really important in their lives and who matters the most. Give Venice another chance, Verica. You can make some good memories here, too."

Meanwhile . . .

Chapter 41

Baric Castle, 1 September 1649

In Mauro's absence, Eduard was the ranking officer in charge of the Baric Guard and their daily duties. With no real experience leading tactical training, Eduard kept the guardsmen busy with other vital tasks, like filling the Keep's storerooms with provisions for the coming winter.

Eduard split the men into four groups: chop and gather firewood; hunt and butcher game to hang and preserve; clean and inventory the stockpile of weapons and uniforms in the armory. At Mauro's request, the fourth group was to assist Nela's kitchen with the harvest duties.

The following two months would be busy in the orchards collecting enough apples, pears, almonds, and walnuts to stock the manor house cellar for the year. The olive crop looked promising, and Nela wanted the other staples to be barreled and stored before the olive brining and pressing season.

Cook did her best to set her priorities, and that morning she sent the delegated soldiers with her kitchen maids out mushroom hunting. To her satisfaction, they returned with filled baskets.

Ivana uncovered her basket for Nela to see the delicate fungi, proclaiming, "Daniel and Teodor found the perfect spot while they were deer hunting yesterday. Look at all the mushrooms I collected."

Natalija and Marija followed Ivana to the kitchen table and set down their baskets.

"Last week's rain was good for something, then," Nela said, looking over the mushrooms.

"Do not worry, Nela. We didn't pick any poison ones," Natalija said. "Idita showed us what to look for last year. I like these fat ones. Daniel says they are toadstools."

"Some toadstools are poisonous, and they look almost the same," Nela said kindly. "Bring them up to the nursery and lay them out for Idita to double-check."

"But the linens are hanging there under the rafters," Ivana reminded her.

Nela looked out the kitchen window. "The sun will be out all day. The linens can finish drying outside. The rest of the washing needs to be done tomorrow," Nela ordered.

Brigita picked up her basket to carry upstairs and complained, "Louisa said we have weeks to finish the bedding, Nela."

"Until his lordship returns, yes, but this sunshine may not last for weeks to dry the bedding so nicely," Nela pointed out. "Now, go knock on Idita's door to tell her you are back."

Marija asked worriedly, "Is Idita ill, Nela? We have not seen her since yesterday."

"Idita is fine, Marija," Nela assured her. "Her leg is bothering her, is all, so she is taking her meals in her room. Hurry now, girls. I have other chores for you when you are finished with the mushrooms."

The young maids didn't get a chance to grumble about Nela's next chore. The back kitchen door flew open at that moment, and Geoff came running into the kitchen. "Where is Franja?"

Nela plopped down on her stool and fanned herself with her apron. "I have told you not to burst into my kitchen yelling like that, Geoff! If you do that one more time, you will be the death of me."

"I am sorry, Nela, but this time it's important. They have the pulley rigged up! Simeon has decided to try it! He's coming outside!"

"Well, don't just stand there, Geoff. Franja is in the cellar!" Nela shooed him on his way with a happy grin.

"Can we go watch, too, Nela?" Natalija asked hopefully.

Marija asked, "Can we?"

Ivana and Brigita set their baskets down again with the same pleading expressions.

Nela could not refuse the four hopeful maids. "Oh, all right, girls. But only for a few minutes."

Ivana stayed long enough to ask, "Do you not want to come see what Simeon looks like without a leg?"

Nela wiped her hands on her linen towel and took off her apron. "I suppose I should see firsthand if he is even alive."

~*~

It had been two months since Idita amputated Simeon's leg after his injured horse had crushed it. Weeks passed before Simeon could forgive Mauro for ordering the gruesome task. At first, Simeon wanted to die rather than live as a cripple. But later, his will to live won out over his grief.

Simeon had not been happy when Mauro moved him from his private chamber to the guardsmen's sleeping quarters on the main floor. As a sergeant in the Toth Army, Simeon had gladly bunked with his squadron. But this was different. He needed his subordinates' help.

To Simeon's surprise, Mauro's soldiers did not think less of him. In fact, they encouraged Simeon, beginning with getting himself out of bed, dressing, washing, feeding himself, and getting around with his new crutches. The soldiers understood Simeon would never be the same man again, and they'd finally convinced him that he could still be a soldier. Simeon had turned his bleak existence into a hopeful one as he mastered these everyday chores with one leg. Today Simeon would finally take the biggest step in his recovery: He would go outside.

Eduard opened the dining hall door for Simeon. The recluse squinted in the bright sunshine. It was the first time since the accident that Simeon felt the warm sun on his face. He gave Eduard a nod of approval; his self-imposed imprisonment had been too long.

But his courage slipped when he saw his audience. Simeon had not expected the entire Baric household to be in the courtyard. Fear washed over him, and he hastily turned to leave.

Eduard stopped him. "If I were in your place and you in mine, Simeon, you would tell me there is not one person here who does not want to see you succeed. But if you want, Simeon, I will send them all away."

Simeon took a deep breath and blew it out. Only his arms needed to work, and they were strong from pacing with his new crutches over the last few weeks. With determination, Simeon said, "If I have to make a fool of myself, Eduard, I might as well get it over with."

Eduard praised his decision with an encouraging slap on the back. He then said, "Teodor, are you ready to show the captain how to get down from here?"

The soldiers had drawn straws, and Teo grinned from ear to ear at having won the privilege to demonstrate the chair. The eager soldier took hold of the wooden seat at the top of the stairs and explained, "We drilled a hole here where you can keep your crutches, Captain. They go in like this." Teodor's finger pretended to be a stick through the plank, and Simeon nodded.

Then Teo sat on the plank seat and found his balance along the edge. "It's simple, Captain. Just push off with your foot like this," he said, giving one good kick against the side of the landing. Teodor was now dangling in midair by the pulley bolted to the tower wall above them.

The crowd below him cried, "Oooh!"

Teodor took his role seriously. He called over, "Now, these ropes in front of me move the chair up and down. It can go pretty quickly, but I will do it slowly so you can see, sir." He gripped the looped rope and tugged it on one side. Jolt by jolt, the seat descended to the ground, where Teodor stopped himself with his foot.

"And then you just pull the other side like this, and it lifts you back up," he shouted up to Simeon.

Teodor worked the ropes and pulled the chair back toward the landing. He reached the solid ledge with his outstretched foot, energetically hopped out of the sling chair, and held it still for Simeon to try.

Simeon took an audible breath and sat down.

"Just give it a little kick, sir," Teodor said encouragingly.

Simeon shoved his rope-held chair over the edge of the landing with his good leg and was suspended two stories above the courtyard. He gripped the downward loop of rope and tugged it hand over hand. His pace was cautious and slow at first, lurching with each release. But by the end of his descent, Simeon had the hang of it and smoothly let himself down the rest of the way.

The crowd cheered when his good leg was firmly on the cobblestones below.

"Well, I did not fall on my face," he told everyone with satisfaction. "Now go about your business. There is no more show here."

The servants began to disperse back to their housework and garden duties, chatting noisily amongst themselves.

~*~

Franja stayed behind at the well. She slowly turned the handle to draw the wooden bucket and filled her smaller pail. She pushed her sleeves above her elbows and washed off the fine flour coating her arms.

Alone in the center of the courtyard, Franja pretended not to notice Simeon's shadow growing over her as he hobbled to her side. "I have missed your baking," he said.

She looked up and replied matter-of-factly, "I didn't bake today. I was weighing flour for tomorrow. As you can see, it makes quite a mess." She splashed her arms in the cool water, glad to have something to do during the awkward silence.

Simeon leaned against the well to take the weight off his crutches. "You look well, Franja," he began again.

"And you look like they have not been feeding you," she retorted.

Simeon chuckled at her remark. "Yeah, well, I suppose that is my own fault. I have not had an appetite." He looked up at the intense sun. "I feel like a bear crawling out of hibernation. The sun is too bright, my limbs are too weak, but suddenly I find I am starving."

Franja chuckled. That was her Simeon. "Come by the kitchen, and Nela will fill you up with good things to make you strong again."

"Just Nela?"

Her wet arms dripped onto the hot stones, and she dried them and her face on her apron. Simeon watched her with amusement. Franja smiled back and asked, "What is so funny?"

"Your apron put more flour on your face than you took off," he said. "Here, let me try."

He pulled a clean handkerchief from his pocket and leaned on his crutches to wipe her cheek. He held his hand there longer than needed. "The smudge is gone," he said.

Franja buckled under the weight of so much unspoken between them. "Why didn't you let me see you, Simeon?" she blurted out.

Simeon had a ready answer: "I was not brave enough to let you in. I will never be a whole man again, Franja. You realize that, don't you?"

"Do you think I would hold that against you? I prayed to God every night that He would make you well again, not whole. It does not matter if you have only one leg or one arm. I just want you to be Simeon again. Were my prayers answered?"

Simeon bit at his lip to keep from showing his hurt. Since the beginning of his stay with the guardsmen, he had not shed a tear, but self-pity surged through him again. "Two months ago, I was a soldier, a horseman, a musketeer who trained men to do the things I loved doing. Now I am none of those. No, Franja. I do not think God has answered your prayers."

"There will be something for you to do, Simeon. What did the baron say? Will he make you a cook, perhaps?" Simeon laughed, and Franja understood her mistake. "Did the men vote against it?" she asked, smiling again.

"It has been decided that I should not cook for them. Besides, I cannot stand on my one leg unsupported," he said.

"I heard they are making a peg leg for you."

"Is that so? No one told me about that."

"I overheard Idita tell the baron you can be fitted as soon as your wound is healed." Franja added, "She also said there is no reason you cannot ride again. And you have not lost your voice, so you could probably train soldiers, too, Simeon. I know the baron will give you a chance to prove yourself."

His stump throbbed, his wrists hurt from supporting himself, and Simeon's earlier good mood melted on the sunbaked cobblestones. "You are very generous in your optimism, Franja. But I might disappoint everyone."

Disheartened, Franja shook her head and said, "Then give up, Simeon. Don't try at all. Crawl back into the Keep like an old bear." She picked up her pail to leave, and Simeon attempted to follow her.

"Do you think it is so easy for me, Franja?" he demanded.

"Nobody said it would be easy losing a leg, Simeon. But if you are willing to risk your pride and be Simeon again—my Simeon, the man I was going to marry—then you know where to find me."

Simeon did not let himself believe that "yes" would be her answer. Dumbfounded, he let her walk away.

~*~

Idita watched the former lovers by the well from the nursery window, and nostalgia washed over her. She imagined herself in Franja's place; Ezra took Simeon's. So much time had passed since she lost her lover. What would she say to Ezra now?

Idita's daydream faded when Franja walked away, and Idita's lamenting thoughts went back to the here and now. She would check on Simeon's recovery when her own leg felt stronger, and she could give him encouragement. His forlorn expression told her that he desperately needed some.

Idita returned her attention to the industrious girls who had emptied their baskets onto the drying mats. She looked through their harvest as the maids brushed the soil off the damp mushrooms. "This is a good amount for one day. You did well, girls."

Natalija eagerly told her, "Daniel said he would keep an eye out in the woods and let us know when he sees more clumps sprouting."

"What is he doing in the woods?" Marija asked.

"The men are shooting deer, Marija. They even trapped a bear this week. He said they will leave again tonight to trap a second one."

Brigita said, "Nela will be happy to have some bear meat."

"That will make a lovely winter coat for someone, too," Ivana remarked busily.

"Daniel says the wild asparagus is growing again near the pond," Natalija continued. "When they come back from their hunt in a few days, he said he would show me the exact spot. Not alone, of course, but I think that is very nice of him, actually. If the Barics were home, I wouldn't even be allowed to go to the pond, would I, Idita? But Daniel said that he is Lord Baric's trusted captain and would not let any harm come to us at the water, so I told him—"

"Goodness, Natalija," Brigita interrupted, "never in my life have I heard Daniel talk so much. How did you fix him?"

"I don't know, Brigita. Do you think I somehow fixed him, Idita?" Natalija asked the Baric nurse skeptically.

Idita replied, "Daniel's thoughts get hung up when he talks, Natalija, but I do not think he is broken. A man will do many things to impress a young woman. He might even manage to find his words."

Marija asked, "Does he want to impress you?" She giggled at the possibility.

Natalija pondered her sister's question. "Well, Daniel did give me a little clump of violets he had picked while we were mushroom hunting. But that is just being kind, isn't it, Idita?"

The other girls looked to their mentor for validation.

"I do not know if it means he favors you, but it is definitely a kind gesture," Idita assured her.

Brigita added fuel to the speculation, saying, "Perhaps he thinks he loves you, Natalija."

Natalija shook her head. "That would be very peculiar if he did. I have known Daniel for years. Why would he be in love with me now?"

Their combined innocence cheered Idita's mood, and she counseled, "Men change their minds about many things, including love. Daniel will make his feelings clear about you, Natalija, or any other girl when he is ready. It takes courage for a man to tell a woman he loves her." She said to all the maids, "Until then, we need more mushrooms for the winter, and the baron would enjoy fresh asparagus at his dinner table when he returns."

Idita continued her sorting through the big and small fungi until she finally spotted what she had hoped for. "You did well, girls, but this one should have been left in the woods."

The girls gathered around her to see what Idita was holding.

"One little nibble of this white cap will make you dream strange dreams. Too much of it will stop your heart. Memorize the difference between the good ones here on the table and this one. We do not want to be poisoning ourselves, now do we?"

The girls emphatically shook their heads.

Idita slipped the fungus into her apron pocket. "I will throw it into the fire. Finish cleaning the caps and then go see what Nela needs your help with next."

"Can I help you to your room, Idita?" Marija asked.

"I have my cane, my dear. I can make it back on my own. Thank you."

Idita left the nursery and slowly hobbled toward the stairway. Standing had been bearable after that morning's treatment, but her leg pulsed painfully now.

After making it to her chamber, Idita sat down with a groan at her small table. She opened the cover of her medicine chest and put the toxic mushroom carefully into a linen pouch for later.

A small crock was on the table next to her basket. She examined the wormy creatures at the bottom of their watery home and picked out four thin leeches among the already engorged ones. After unrolling her stocking, she set the blood-sucking parasites on her swollen calf.

Idita understood this was the beginning of her demise. No treatment could cure the pooling of blood in her leg. Every night at Baric Castle, she had thanked God that she lived a prosperous life, more than had first been allotted her. Now, in each nightly prayer, she asked God for a favor: Let her wake up one more time.

Chapter 42

It was just after sundown when Denis knocked on Nestor's door. Mauro's steward was in the habit of retiring early while the baron was away. He enjoyed reading in his comfortable chair by the window, and that was where Mauro's scout found him that evening.

"Come in," Nestor shouted to the closed door.

Denis stuck his head in and said, "I would not disturb you like this, sir, if it were not urgent."

Nestor set his book down and brushed off the intrusion. "I have not even dressed for bed, so you are not disturbing me. What is it, Denis?"

Denis shut the door and took a few steps into the room. "Well, sir, Latif and I were scouting on the southern border when we encountered two soldiers from Lord Raneri's guard. They were bringing an urgent message for Lord Baric. When I told them that the baron was away, they asked to give the message to you instead. They are downstairs, sir."

Nestor frowned and asked, "Why didn't you just bring me the note?"

"Lord Raneri wanted Lord Baric to hear the details surrounding it. The scouts must tell you in person."

"That is odd," Nestor said under his breath. "All right. I will come down." Nestor put on his wig and house shoes and followed Denis down the stairs.

The two anxious soldiers stood dutifully at attention again when the Baric men arrived in the foyer.

"We will talk in the study," Nestor announced without a greeting. He unlocked the door and waved in the scouts.

"I am Lord Baric's steward," he declared when they were behind closed doors. "Denis said you have come with a message from Lord Raneri."

"Yes, sir. I am Cicero, and this is Eligio," the lead soldier said. "Baron Raneri's message is for Lord Baric, you understand."

"Yes, and as Denis told you, Lord Baric is away. Tell me your urgent news."

Eligio took a stained letter from his pouch and set it on the table in front of Nestor. He spoke his rehearsed message: "Lord Raneri sends his greetings to Lord Baric and regrets that he must be the bearer of bad news, sir."

On the tattered envelope was written: "To the hands of Lord Mauritius Baric, Solgrad Castle, Dalmatia, The Serene Republic of Venice."

Nestor demanded, "And did your lordship ask you to explain why the seal on Lord Baric's letter is already broken?"

Cicero had a scripted reply, "He did, sir—with apologies. Baron Raneri understands the message was meant to be delivered confidentially, but the original messenger had been dead for some time. Lord Raneri decided to open the letter to determine its urgency, as it fell into his hands under unusual circumstances."

"What circumstances were those?" Nestor asked.

"Well, sir," Cicero continued, "the letter was found on an Ottoman courier in my lord's woods. Since he was found near a known popular shortcut that couriers take from the border, we suspect he was robbed. His body was left in the underbrush, and his satchel held nothing of value except this and a few other papers. His horse must have been stolen, too."

"I accept Lord Raneri's decision, and I am sure Lord Baric will take no offense."

Cicero nodded.

Nestor unfolded the parchment and read the lengthy note. He set it down with trembling hands and said, "This was indeed urgent, but I am afraid it comes too late."

Cicero told Nestor, "The body was not a pretty sight, sir. It is hard to know, after the scavengers found him, but the rider must have been dead at least a month."

"The fate of the messenger is unfortunate, but this news is still important to Lord Baric. Please, thank Lord Raneri for sending it." Nestor folded the parchment again and added, "It is late. Denis will find you beds in the Keep for the night."

The men stood up and bowed their thanks. They followed Denis out of the study.

"Oh, and Denis . . ." Nestor motioned for him to come out of earshot of the others. "One more thing."

Denis asked, "Yes, sir?"

"Did Branislav leave today?"

Denis considered Nestor's odd question. "He did, sir. I saw the *Margaret* on the sea earlier this morning."

Nestor groaned unhappily. "That is what I thought." He paced in contemplation and asked, "Is Ivanoslav settled at the old inn?"

Denis rubbed his brow, pondering. "I think for about a week now, sir. They are working on the renovations for Lord Baric."

"And does the old sailor seem fit?" Nestor asked.

Denis reflected, "Fit, sir? I would say so. I saw Ivanoslav giving orders just yesterday."

"Very good. That is what I was hoping to hear. First thing in the morning, Denis, you are to bring him here," Nestor ordered.

"Ivanoslav, sir? Here to the castle?"

"Yes, to the castle, Denis. I want to talk to him. But have him already pack whatever he needs for a trip to Venice. He will be sailing there as soon as he can prepare the ship."

Denis did not argue this time. "I will leave at first light to tell him, sir."

When Nestor continued to tap his fingers on the table, Denis asked, "Shall I bring the Raneri guards to the Keep now?"

"Yes, be on your way, and while you are there, Denis, tell Eduard I need to see him."

Denis hesitated. "Now, sir?"

Nestor lowered his spectacles to meet the soldier's stare. "Are you hard of hearing, Denis?" he asked with annoyance.

"Um, Captain Eduard always takes the first shift, sir, and he will be sound asleep at this hour."

Nestor sighed at the growing complexity of his burden.

Denis added, "Knowing the captain, he will ask if it can wait until morning."

"Tell Captain Eduard it cannot wait. I need his advice on who is seaworthy enough to crew a ship to bring Lord Baric home."

Chapter 43

Thessaloniki, 25 August 1649

Ruby had marked the days until Jero's trial. When Patrik's message arrived at the Spiros residence, he and Soren had been gone more than two weeks. His news only fueled Ruby's despair.

"What am I to do, Mama?" Ruby cried after reading it aloud. "If what the innkeeper told them is true, and Jero got away on his horse, then he should be here by now."

Ruby's mother held her weeping daughter and said, "Thessaloniki is still far from Tirana. Give Jero time."

Ruby moaned, "But it has been weeks since his escape."

Her father pointed out, "I see three possible conclusions from Patricius's letter: Jero went back to Solgrad without you, he was hunted down by the police, or he is still coming for you here."

Tears streamed down Ruby's cheeks as she wailed, "It can only be the third, Papa!"

He took her hand in his and held it tightly. "Escaped prisoners are always chased down, Ruby. You have to accept that he might be dead. I will allow you to wait one more week, but then you must get on with your life, my daughter."

Her mother cradled Ruby's shaking shoulders and cooed, "There, there, Ruby dear. You wait for your Jero as long as you like."

Angelos gave his wife a stern glare of disagreement, but she argued, "We will find something to tell Kallisto, Angelos. She is still young to be marrying and can wait a little while longer, too."

~*~

Kallisto and Ruby lay on top of the blanket in their shared bed. They had left the shutters open, and the waning moon in front of the window cast a long beam of moonlight across the room. The stars were clear and bright, and Ruby wondered if Jero was looking at the same sky that night.

It had been ten days since Patrik's message arrived, and Kallisto had not made Ruby's wait any easier. Tradition required that the eldest daughter would marry first, but now that Kallisto had a husband promised to her, she was eager to marry ahead of her sister.

As she lay awake next to Ruby, she said, "I saw Nikko at the market today. He asked to come visit me tomorrow. Do you mind, Ruby? I mean, you could have married him, but now I will be his bride—after you find someone to marry first, of course."

"I don't care if he visits."

"He wants to bring his friend Basil along. Basil is a nice man, Ruby. He is a fisherman with his own boat. He has a nice smile, too, with all his teeth."

"What are you getting at, Kallisto? Why should I care about his teeth?"

"Because more than a week has passed since Patricius's letter arrived. You said it had only taken you five days to ride here from Tirana. I would also wait forever if Nikko were lost to me. But I cannot wait much longer. It isn't fair to me, Ruby."

Ruby looked at her sister in the starlight. "You are right, Kallisto. Why should you have to wait? Marry Nikko—you deserve to start your life," Ruby said in defeat.

Her sister whispered, "But what about you, Ruby?"

"Me? I will stay a spinster and be the auntie who cares for all my nieces and nephews."

"Don't give up, Ruby. Castor will ask about Jero when he meets the Barics' ship. When he returns, you will know whether you should find a husband here."

"I don't want a—wait!" Ruby sat up suddenly. She looked out the window at the sliver of moon in the night sky. "Is Castor still here?" she asked urgently.

"What has come over you, Ruby?"

Ruby calmed her racing heart. "I am just trying to sort out my future, is all. Castor leaves on the quarter moon and that was today, right? Or is it tomorrow?"

Kallisto reflected, "I think he sails tomorrow morning. I talked to Alexis at the market, and she said he was preparing his ship today."

"That is my answer," Ruby whispered.

"I know," Kallisto said with a yawn. "I already told you that Castor will ask the Barics' captain for you, and then you will have your answer."

"No, I—" Ruby began to explain but changed her mind. She lay back down on her pillow and smiled hopefully. "Like you said, Castor will help me."

"And then we can all be married," Kallisto said dreamily. She rolled over again and mumbled, "Good night, Ruby."

"Good night, Kallisto. I am sure you will make a beautiful bride." Ruby whispered to the peaceful girl, "I am sorry I won't be here to see it."

Ruby stayed frozen on her bed until she felt the tremble of soft snores next to her. Then Ruby tiptoed to her wardrobe and contemplated what she would need. Despite the warm night air, she put on an extra change of tunics and then covered her loose hair with a dark scarf. She took one last look at her sleeping sister.

"Goodbye, Kallisto," she said. "Do not worry about me." Then Ruby crawled out their bedroom window and into the quiet night.

~*~

Ruby knew all the back ways to get to the harbor where her father and Demetrius Kokkinos moored their merchant ships. She was anxious that she would be stopped on the docks, but no one was working at that late hour.

The seawater lapped against the pillars of the wooden walkway, making her look around suspiciously with each splash. She spotted Castor's ship, still tied to a loading wharf. To her relief, a gangplank still connected the ship to the dock. Next to it, a man leaned against the side of the hulking ship. His chin was tipped toward his chest. He was the ship's watchman for the few hours between the loading and the crew's return to cast off with the morning tide. Ruby watched him from the shadows until she was confident he was asleep.

Looking up and down the pier from her hiding place, Ruby told herself, "Now or never."

She dashed to the gangway but suddenly had a second thought. Ruby eyed the sleeping guard. A water jug rested at his side, and a round of bread was on the ground next to it. Ruby tucked them into her robe pockets. She took a deep breath for courage and then scurried up the narrow plank.

Her worry of encountering sleeping sailors on board was short-lived; the ship's deck was empty. Pushed on by adrenaline, Ruby crossed the dark open space and disappeared into the belly of the Kokkinos ship.

~*~

The rendezvous point with Lord Baric's ship was where the Adriatic and Mediterranean seas met. The Venetian Navy did not patrol this far south, and the Ottoman Navy was rarely spotted along that length of the Greek coastline.

Castor lit the all-clear signal, and Branislav's crew rowed the *Margaret* alongside the Kokkinos ship in the dark to transfer their black market cargo to Castor's crew.

Only half of the Kokkinoses' cargo hold had been loaded with goods destined for customers across the Mediterranean. The second half was reserved for the barrels and bundles the Kokkinos crew would acquire along the way, some from Baron Baric's ship, some goods from other customers during the three-week tour.

Castor and Branislav had met many times at sea, and their routine was swift. Some Venetian sailors walked goods across the planks; others hoisted the heavy salt urns by overhead ropes as the two ships rocked side by side.

Castor was supervising the exchange on deck when his first mate, Riginos, reported: "You need to see what the men found below, Captain."

"Found?" Castor repeated.

"You have a stowaway, Captain. They found her asleep on the bales of silk."

"A woman? Bring me the sailor who smuggled her in," Castor ordered.

"No one smuggled her in. We think it's Angelos Spiros's daughter Ruby. When they woke her up, she wanted to know when we would meet the Barics' ship."

Castor let out an exasperated cry, "Damn that girl!"

Riginos looked across the deck of the ship. "Yorgos was getting her some water. Here they come."

An empty cup in hand, Ruby stood sheepishly by when the sailors left her alone with Castor.

"How did you get on my ship, Ruby?" Castor demanded angrily. "Did you tell anyone what you were doing?"

"I . . . no, Castor. It was sort of an impulse," she confessed glumly.

Castor was livid. "An impulse? Your parents must be worried sick wondering where you disappeared to! Do you know how much trouble this will cause?"

Ruby began to tremble. She was weak from the two days in the dark hold and panicked at Castor's words. She had indeed not thought it through.

"Please, don't yell at me. I have to go back to Solgrad, and there is no other way to get there. Jero has not come for me, and I have to know why." She put her hand up to her mouth to hold back a sob.

"I will not be a part of your foolishness, Ruby. I am taking you home."

The hour was closer to the morning than midnight, and Castor was not in a negotiating mood. He called out, "Yorgos, take Ruby to my cabin and don't let her out until the Baric ship has sailed again."

"No! Please, Castor. I beg of you!"

The Kokkinos sailor dragged Ruby away.

Having finished their side of the exchange, Branislav and two of his crew approached Castor on the lamplit deck.

"Did I hear a woman just now?" Branislav asked.

Castor shook off his anger and grumbled, "You heard Ruby Spiros yelling."

Branislav didn't seem surprised that she was on board. "Am I to take her back with me?" he asked.

"That is exactly what she wants, Branislav. She somehow got below deck before we sailed. She wants to go back to confront Jero."

Branislav looked to his crewmen, but the two only shrugged. "Jero is not in Solgrad," Branislav told the Greek captain. "He is supposed to be in Thessaloniki with Lady Ruby. I was actually told that they might be on your ship this voyage, ready to come home with me, together."

"I don't understand. Did the baron not get my brother's news?" Castor asked urgently. "Patricius couriered a message to Baron Baric explaining what happened in Tirana."

Branislav shook his head gravely. "I know nothing about that. I am not privileged to all the news at the castle, but most does make it to us at the docks. There has been no message from your brother, or from Jero."

Castor rubbed his temples that were rapidly filling with a budding headache. "Then I will need your promise as a gentleman."

"As a gentleman?" Branislav repeated with a chuckle. "What are you talking about?"

"I am going to let Ruby sail back with you," Castor announced. "She is a stubborn girl, and if I don't let her go with you tonight, she will find another way to get to Solgrad."

Branislav became suddenly serious. "I cannot take her unchaperoned— who will watch out for her? We have two more deliveries after yours, Castor. We will be at least a week at sea."

Castor held his stare. "I know that, and I would not ask if it was not urgent. Lock her in your quarters if you must."

"Do I get a choice in the matter?"

Castor argued, "My sister, your baroness, would want Ruby to come to Solgrad once she learns the tragic news about Jero."

The three Venetian sailors mumbled in unison, "Tragic news?"

"Tell us what you know," Branislav said with alarm.

"Well, it seems there was a fateful incident with three thieves along the way to Tirana. When they arrived in the city, Jero was arrested. For murder."

The sailors reeled with shock.

"Murder?" one cried.

"Jero was jailed, but he did not murder anyone. That is not my news, though." Castor explained, "Patricius and Soren took Ruby home, and during that time, Jero somehow escaped his imprisonment. No one has heard anything since then. There is no report of his capture, he has not made it to Thessaloniki, and you say he has not returned to Solgrad, either."

Branislav asked, "Am I to report that Jero is dead?"

Castor shook his head. "Not yet. Ruby holds out hope that Jero is riding to Solgrad instead of Thessaloniki. Maybe he has already arrived while we've been out at sea. Report what I told you to Baron Baric, and he can come to his own conclusions."

Branislav ran his fingers through his unkempt hair in despair. "That is bad news, Castor. I like Jero. I spent time with him and so has my crew. I hope it is some grave miscommunication and he has found his way home."

"Maybe he has."

Branislav reluctantly came around to Castor's request. "I will take Lady Ruby with me, then. She will be safe on my ship with my crew. Do not worry."

"I don't expect she will be any trouble to you. Thank you, Branislav."

Riginos joined the two captains and announced, "We are finished loading the Baric goods below deck. We can shove off now."

"All right, but first bring Ruby across to Baron Baric's ship," Castor ordered. "She is going with Captain Branislav back to Solgrad."

"Alone?" Riginos asked. "With the Venetian sailors?"

"Take her over the plank," Castor said, frowning. "That is an order."

After his first mate left to get Ruby, Castor took a sealed envelope from his jacket and handed it to Branislav, who tucked the payment into his inside pocket.

Castor reminded him, "If news comes that Jero is lost to us, bring Ruby with you for our next rendezvous. Her father will want her back in Thessaloniki."

"Lord Baric will do what her father wants, I am sure," Branislav replied. "But let us hold out hope for a while. Jero is a good man. God may show him a way home."

Chapter 44

Balkans, 18 August 1649

The gypsies had covered little distance at their slow pace. Jero rode alongside the walking children on the dusty trade route as they made their way east. His borrowed hat shaded him from the hot noon sunshine. Sasho sat unhappily in front of Jero on his horse. The Romani patriarch, Chavdar, had agreed to a lenient punishment for Sasho's crime. Instead of cutting off the boy's hand for stealing bread, he and Jero had agreed to three days of labor as payment.

Sasho didn't like traveling with the group of strangers. When he and Jero were out of earshot of the gypsy children, the boy said, "I don't trust the old man."

"We have no choice, Sasho. We have no food and no money," Jero whispered back.

"I don't like them," the boy complained under his breath.

"You should have thought about that before you stole from them."

"I am sorry, Jero," he whispered guiltily.

"It is all right, Sasho. It is only three days. Besides, they gave us clean clothes and our bellies are filled. This may not be so bad. We will get to Thessaloniki soon enough."

"I suppose princes don't know how to harvest grain," the boy said with worry.

"I told you I am not a prince. And we have harvests on our land, too. It will be hard work, Sasho, but we will get through it just fine."

"We will, Jero. And I promise I will not make any trouble for you again."

From the high bench of his caravan wagon, Chavdar called out, "Isaak!"

Jero had forgotten his new alias until Sasho poked him with his elbow to remind him it was his new name.

Jero slowed his horse until the gypsy's wagon caught up to him. "Yes, Chavdar," Jero said pleasantly.

"Isaak. Is that a Jewish name?" Chavdar inquired.

Ottoman law did not restrict Jews in their Empire, although they were often watched with suspicion. It was more out of curiosity than concern that Jero asked, "Would that be a problem for you if I were Jewish?"

The gypsy scoffed. "I am Romani. I trade with all peoples and live in harmony with everyone in these lands. I just like to know what sort of a man is riding with my clan."

Sasho held the horse's mane tightly and listened to what his new guardian would answer.

"Isaak is sometimes a Jewish name, Chavdar. But I am a Christian, not a Jew."

Chavdar approvingly nodded. "You are a stranger to these parts. What is your business here, so deep in the Balkans?"

"I am traveling through on my way to Thessaloniki."

Chavdar asked pointedly, "Traveling from where, my friend?"

"From different places," Jero replied.

Chavdar continued his smooth inquisition, "You have an odd sort of speech, Isaak. You speak Slavic fluently, yet I cannot place the accent."

"You have a stupid accent!" Sasho interjected.

Jero squeezed Sasho's arm to remind him of his manners.

Chavdar did not hide his disdain and said, "I can clearly hear that you are a gutter rat from Tirana, Boy. But you, Isaak, are not from Tirana."

"No, Chavdar. I am from Dalmatia," Jero divulged.

"Ah! A Venetian! I would not have guessed that."

Jero corrected him, "That is because I am a Croatian, not from the capital."

"Venetian, Croatian," the Romani said with an indifferent shrug, "either way, you are a long way from home, Isaak."

"And how much farther will we travel today?" Jero asked.

Chavdar said, "Not far. Maybe another hour."

"Whose farm is this we are going to?" Jero asked.

"It is a communal field," the Romani explained. "The villagers grew the grain, and the village will benefit from it. My cousin lives in this village."

"Does the Empire own the farm, or do you have landlords, like we do?"

"The sultan owns everything, of course, but he delegates the overseeing of his lands to men in his favor. The overseer in my cousin's village is a man called Ludvik. He takes a cut of everything produced and is in charge of managing the harvest. We will be camping on Ludvik's land."

"Can the harvest even be completed in three days?"

"It doesn't matter to us, my friend," Chavdar said merrily. His bench seat rocked when his wagon wheels hit a pothole in the road. "I owe Ludvik a debt from last year, and three days of my family's labor will settle it."

"Like it settles Sasho's debt?" Jero said, holding his stare.

Jero had inherited his father's unyielding glare, and Chavdar shook off the chill it gave him. "Yes, my Venetian friend," he replied, "As promised, I will take you to the crossroads when the debt is paid in three days."

Chavdar flicked the reins in his grip and moved his caravan ahead of Jero before letting his contemptuous scowl show.

~*~

The rye fields looked endless to Jero, but at least it was not his problem whether the rain came too early or the market price was not enough to get the farmers through this year. His only job was to rise each morning and do what he was told.

Jero figured there must have been more than a hundred peasants at Ludvik's barn at daybreak to be assigned their chores for the day. The men toiled in the fields with long-handled sickles to cut the stalks of ripe rye. If a child was old enough to leave its mother, it was put to work during harvest time. Sasho and the other boys beat the grain from the stalks that the women carried in bundles on their backs from the fields. Girls brought water and the noon meals out to the men in buckets and baskets dangling from poles held across their thin shoulders.

The work was hot and dusty under the late summer sun. Jero put his vest beneath the ragged hat to keep his neck from burning. He toiled next to the villagers with his borrowed tools, but Jero found it was easy to keep to himself during the monotonous work.

Not all the laborers were locals, and they needed a place to bed down each night. Jero and the other hired hands were allowed to sleep in the overseer's big barn. There was no shared camaraderie; the men collapsed exhausted onto their bedrolls with hardly a word between them.

The Romani boys slept together at their family camp, and Sasho stayed with them after their long day thrashing the harvest. The camp women kept track of the children and took care that they were fed. Jero did not talk to Sasho in all that time, but he made peace that the boy was being treated well enough without his supervision.

The third day was the easiest for Jero. His muscles had memorized the swift dance of the sickle: One foot forward, a hard pull of the blade, then the other foot followed, then repeat. With that motion, he crept up his assigned row of rye.

Lost in the rhythm, Jero hardly noticed a petite water girl stop next to him. She carried her two buckets on a thick yoke.

"One ladle only," she had told the thirsty laborers in her girlish voice; Jero was sure she could be no more than ten. She would come around several times during the day, and her reasonable request of only one ladle made Jero smile with each passing.

On this go by, the girl set her pails down next to Jero and proclaimed, "You are the last on my rounds, Mister Isaak. You may drink the rest, and then I will not have such a burden to carry back."

"Thank you, little lady," he told her in his improved Turkish.

Jero tipped the bucket up to his mouth and drank the rest of the tepid water. He picked up his sickle again, but the little water bearer remained by his side. "Was there something else?" he asked.

"The older girls said you are dangerous. Are you?" she inquired boldly.

"No, little one," Jero assured her. "You should not always believe what others are saying."

"Your boy told the girls the same thing. I like him," she added sweetly.

Jero chuckled at her surprise admission. "You like Sasho, huh?"

"Yes," she said with a bright smile. "I might marry him one day since he is the cutest boy I have met so far."

Jero laughed at her innocence. "You are a bit young to already be choosing a mate."

"Boys pick girls all the time. If we keep him, I will tell Sasho what I think of him before he picks another over me," she reasoned.

Jero thought he misunderstood her. "Keep him?" Jero repeated. "Sasho will be back in Tirana by the time he is old enough to pick you or any girl."

She hung her empty buckets on her yoke again and said, "Maybe not, Mister Isaak."

Her naïve comment should have been an amusing distraction in his day of drudgery, but Jero could not deny the odd feeling that came over him as the girl skipped away with her empty pails. Protectively, Jero scouted the line of women carrying the unbeaten stalks to the older boys in the distance. Where was Sasho? Jero was too far away to pick him out among the blur of faces.

But something else clearly caught his attention across the field. Chavdar's daughter Jasmina was walking alone through the tall, uncut rye. A young man walked in the opposite direction, only a few steps from her. Jasmina was a pretty girl of marrying age, Jero reflected, and it was not unusual for matches to be sealed during harvest time. That was the way of things everywhere, and Jero gave it no more thought.

He wiped the sweat from his forehead and repositioned his hat when he noticed the overseer watching him. Jero picked up his sickle and returned to his work before the man could complain. Only a few more hours of daylight remained, and then his debt to Chavdar would be repaid.

Chapter 45

The mood was merry that evening. It wasn't just Jero's last day, but many of the other hired hands would also be moving on. The rye was cut, the fields gleaned, and the villagers would finish the last of the thrashing in the coming days. In celebration, Ludvik tapped a cask of house-brewed barley ale for the laborers who lingered around the fire that night.

Strong ale was a powerful agent to loosen tongues. Men who had hardly said three sentences in the last few days now bragged to the group of their bold adventures over the years; others told of peculiar happenings they had witnessed in their travels. The captivated audience was eager to be entertained, and the focus eventually turned to Jero, who sat sleepily against a crate, listening to the boastful tales of everyone else.

A jovial man named Talip tapped Jero's leg with his boot and said, "It is too early to sleep, Venetian! You must have a story or two from your travels. Any tragedies to share? Delights even?" Talip winked to the group, and the dozen companions around the fire egged Jero on.

Jero replied, "I have led an ordinary life. There is nothing unusual to tell, really."

Boris insisted, "A wandering Venetian is cutting grain from dawn to dark to pay a debt to a gypsy deep in Ottoman lands. There is a story you can tell, Isaak!"

"How did you get into this mess, Isaak?" Talip asked him.

Jero was not a natural storyteller, but he accepted that reciprocation for the night's ale and entertainment was required. Jero stood in the center of the circle to be heard better and drew himself up to mimic the storytellers he had enjoyed back at home. He decided he would tell his true tale that was too incredible to be believed.

"Until a week ago," Jero began, "I was traveling with a Persian from the southern lands, a Salonikan tribute who had escaped his recruiters, a Portuguese half-breed Jesuit from Ethiopia, and a yellow-haired Dane who had once sailed with pirates past the edge of the world. All fearless sellswords I was proud to call my friends. And with them was the woman I planned to marry."

The group came to life at this last detail.

"What happened to all of them?" a man called Rinor asked.

Jero looked around at his audience and said, "What happened to them all, you ask?"

The men nodded in suspense.

"I do not know," Jero answered honestly.

His audience stirred and rustled in their places.

Jero continued, "I can tell you this much. We had crossed from Ragusa on our warhorses and took our chances on a shortcut through the swampland. There, we were met by miserable swarms of mosquitoes all day and prowling boars at night."

"Boars?" someone repeated.

"Yes, boars. Packs of feral dogs and man-eating snakes found us there, too. My mercenary friends are sharpshooters, and that is how we survived the marshes."

Rinor wondered, "With bows and arrows?"

Talip pointed out, "Isaak said they were mercenaries. They must have used muskets."

"Pistols, as a matter of fact," Jero said. "The hazards of the marshes should have been our last worry, but our luck ran low again when we crossed onto solid roads." Jero paused, looking from face to bearded face in the flickering firelight, the way Fabian would tease an audience.

"Is that when you lost your friends?" one man asked.

"And your woman?" asked another.

"My woman is the reason I am here tonight."

Jero's comment was met with the grumbling of hushed speculation.

"Not that she caused me any wrong," he clarified. "But unbeknownst to us, a group of thieves had stalked us through the lowlands. My sellsword friends carried expensive weapons and bags of coins slung over their saddles that those lowlifes sought to steal. And the one time we were at the river away from our horses, the robbers slunk into our camp. But they stole more than our silver."

"What did they steal, Isaak?" Talip asked.

Jero took his time. "I do not need to tell you how enticing a beautiful woman is to a pack of lowly bandits," he said.

Chavdar's son Andrei was seated among the others around the flickering fire. He asked wide-eyed, "Were your friends killed trying to protect her?"

"My friends are too fierce to be killed," Jero told the boy.

A man in the circle asked, "Did the thieves get away with your woman, Isaak?"

Jero laughed. "Ruby, my bride-to-be, is as tough as the gem she is named for. She dug in her heels and fought them off until we could rescue her. Only two of the thieves got away."

The group exchanged nervous glances. Rinor asked Jero point-blank: "Did you kill one, Isaak?"

"No," Jero answered too quickly to quell their doubts. "His death was not at my hands. But after that day, my friends and I were separated."

"You lost your companions?" the man tapping a new cask of ale asked.

"They lost me, actually. I am on my way to Thessaloniki, where I hope to find them again and marry the woman I love. If God wills it."

The men mumbled their condolences and raised their mugs, repeating, "If God wills it."

"There is one part of your story you left out," Boris said accusingly. "How did you meet this Ottoman woman and these mercenaries in the first place?"

Here Jero veered from the facts, adding bits and pieces from other truths, "I am from an old family of traders. We have business with a sea merchant in Thessaloniki, and my betrothed is his eldest daughter."

"Sea traders?" Boris asked with interest.

"What does your family trade?" Talip prodded.

"We trade almost anything," Jero replied frankly. "Salt, olives, wine, dried fruits, skins, leather, salted fish; whatever is in surplus that can be sold."

"With such a family business, why marry this Salonikan woman?" Rinor asked. "Do Venetians not have beautiful women to choose from?"

Lounging at the fire, Chavdar had quietly listened to Jero's unfolding story and interjected, "Traders need loyalty, Rinor. Isaak's father must have needed to seal an alliance. Marriage is the easiest way to keep trust."

Jero remained silent while the men speculated back and forth whether Venetians could even be loyal allies in business.

Having heard enough, Chavdar suddenly announced, "My clan will be leaving tonight. Gather your things, Isaak. Boris, Andrei—hitch the caravans."

The others around the fire shifted noisily at his hasty announcement.

"It's fully dark, Chavdar. Why leave now?" Talip asked.

Boris wondered the same. "Are you sure, Brother? Irina must have already put the children to bed. She will be angry at me for waking them," he protested.

"Are you afraid of your wife?" Chavdar said with a chuckle. "The stars are bright and the road is good, Boris. We can travel faster with the women and children sleeping in the wagon than walking beside it. I have a daughter to marry, and we have many miles to go for the wedding. We will leave now," he proclaimed.

Jero was bone-tired, but he followed Chavdar's order and gathered his bedroll in the barn after saying his goodbyes to the men around the fire.

When Jero brought his meager supplies to the parked caravans, Boris and his nephew were hitching the horses.

"Is Sasho with the other children?" he asked.

The three gypsies exchanged glances.

"All the boys are asleep in my wagon," Boris told Jero.

"I'll just go get him," Jero said.

"Don't bother to wake him, Isaak. Sasho is fine where he is. He can ride with you in the morning," Boris reassured him.

Chavdar added another piece to the charade, saying, "You've worked hard today, my friend. I saw you can barely keep your eyes open. Why don't you hitch your horse to one of the wagons and sleep in Granny's bunk a while? She can share Irina's bed tonight while Boris drives. Andrei will drive Granny's wagon."

Jero objected, "I am tired, but I could not take your mother's bed. I can ride horseback until the turnoff. It won't take all night, will it?"

The gypsy argued, "It might, but I can drive as long as needed. I did not wield a sickle all day like you, Isaak. Take my offer! My mother will not mind."

And so they hitched Jero's horse to Boris's wagon for extra speed, and Jero climbed into the small room on wheels. He was asleep as soon as his head hit Granny's mattress.

An hour or so down the road, the Romani caravans passed the large sign showing the way to Thessaloniki. Sitting perched on Granny's wagon, Andrei pointed to it, but Chavdar waved his son on. They were not going to say goodbye to Isaak at the crossroads. He would come east with them to Bulgaria.

~*~

Irina and Granny had woken the younger girls early to gather firewood to cook their breakfast the next morning. The older girls set up the plank tables and aired out the many blankets in the sunshine. The boys were climbing sleepily from Boris's caravan while Granny hollered orders for them to fetch water from the stream that ran through the woods. Jero climbed out and watched the scene but noticed something was wrong.

"Toma," Jero called to the last boy disappearing into the underbrush, "is Sasho still sleeping?"

The boy stopped long enough to say, "Sasho didn't sleep with us."

Jero was dumbfounded. "Why not?" he called out.

"My uncle said you want him to be a farmer now," Toma answered before running after Dragan to find the stream.

Boris, Chavdar, and Andrei were stretched out on blankets on the ground under a wagon. They had been driving until near dawn before pulling off the road for a bit of sleep.

Jero leaned under the wagon and shouted, "Chavdar, I need to speak to you."

Chavdar rubbed his eyes. "You are very agitated for such an early hour, Isaak. Did you not sleep well in Granny's bed? I would have been grateful to have it."

Jero ignored his host's banter and demanded, "Why have you left Sasho behind?"

"Maybe he is with the boys, Isaak. Go look for him there."

Jero said, fuming, "He is not with the boys, and he never was. Boris's son told me he was left behind."

Chavdar asked, "Boris, did you not fetch Sasho from the camp?"

"Of course I did, but Sasho didn't want to come," Boris replied groggily.

"You are both lying!" Jero shouted.

"Those are strong words, Isaak. Perhaps you want to take them back," Boris threatened.

Chavdar shot his brother a look of warning and calmly explained, "The boy is thirteen, Isaak, and he made that choice himself. I did not want to delay our departure last night, so I did not argue with him. We had to be moving on."

"According to Toma, I made the decision that he stay behind. What kind of lies did you tell Sasho?"

Chavdar crawled out from under the wagon and brushed the dirt from his breeches. "You are not even his kin, Isaak," he said. "Why is the boy so important to you?"

Jero shot back, "Because his mother asked me to watch over him. I am to take him back to her, and I always keep my word."

The Romani shook his head with a pitying expression. "A mother never lets a son grow up. It was time she let him go. The boy wanted his freedom."

"Freedom?" Jero shouted loudly enough for the women by the fire to look his way. "You sold him! Do not deny it!"

"You are our guest, but your tone is unfriendly, Isaak," Boris warned. "Sasho decided to stay on as a farmhand—a good job for any young lad. He already made friends and seemed happy with the work."

Jero argued, "He was happy coming with me."

"He changed his mind!" Boris insisted before walking away.

Jero turned to Chavdar. "Our debt is settled," he said firmly. "How far is it to the crossroads from here?"

Chavdar considered his dwindling options and quickly invented a new one. "Our debt is settled, Isaak, and you may leave us at any time," he acknowledged. "But then again, you might as well stay on another day. We did not travel long in the night, so it is still a good way to the road you want."

Jero saw that Cairo was still hitched to Boris's wagon, and he said, "I'll take my horse now."

Chavdar remained diplomatic. "Listen, Isaak. Boris's horse began limping in the night. It needs a day's rest from the yoke, but we need to keep moving today if we are to make it to my daughter's wedding on time."

"You cannot have my horse," Jero said firmly.

Standing next to Jero, Chavdar's eldest son offered, "You can hitch your horse to Granny's wagon and drive it yourself. I will walk with the others."

"Yes, Isaak," Chavdar added smoothly, "let us use your horse until the turnoff. In payment for that, Granny will pack you a sack of food to take along with you. It is a three-day ride to Thessaloniki from the turnoff. You will get hungry along the way. Do us a small kindness, Isaak, and we will do you one in return."

Jero was trapped, and the realization of that showed on his face. Traveling an unfamiliar road with no food and no means to hunt was also a risky journey.

"Just for today," he reluctantly agreed. "Tomorrow I will leave with my horse and your generous supplies. My bride is waiting for me."

Chavdar smugly patted Jero on the back and said, "That is good of you to do us this service, Isaak. Surely, your woman will not mind waiting one more day."

"Perhaps she will not mind waiting one more day, but I do," Jero said and then walked away to hitch his horse.

Chapter 46

After a hurried breakfast, the Romani clan rolled down the road just as the sky began to thunder. They piled the children inside the three caravans with Irina and Granny while Boris and Chavdar drove their wagons in hooded wool capes to shield them from the downpour.

With only a tattered jacket and a borrowed hat, Jero sat high on the driver's seat of Granny's caravan and shivered. He was soaked to the bone, had lost Sasho to Ludvik, and had gained one more day bound to the gypsies. His desolation was complete.

The gypsies pushed on through the storm that eventually blew west. When the rain subsided, they found a good spot to stop to eat and dry off. Irina sent the children to find firewood, and the girls set up tables for lunch. Chavdar and Boris whispered by the horses while sharing a pipe of tobacco. Jero kept to himself, trying to warm up in the bright sunshine.

While Jasmina and Violeta set out the dishes around him, Granny came to the table and sat down across from Jero.

"Chavdar said you are leaving us tomorrow," Granny remarked. "Would you like me to see what is in store for you?"

The old woman's offer piqued his curiosity. She was a small figure, but to Jero, she embodied the aura of witches from the tales he loved to read in the Baric library.

"Do you have special powers to see the future?" he asked nervously, believing that she might.

She took out an ebony box from her wide apron pocket and set it in front of Jero. "I don't have powers, but the cards do. They can tell the future, but only if you are willing to see it."

Jero nodded that he was.

Granny opened her little box and took out the stack of stiff cards, perfectly sized to fit in the palm of her hand. The deck of cards looked ordinary from the back until she fanned them out and turned them over.

Jero was spellbound by the beautiful and magical figures depicted holding objects or surrounded by unusual symbols; each was a miniature work of art.

"How do the cards work?" Jero asked apprehensively.

Granny scooped them up into a stack and held them out before Jero, facing them down again. "Place your hand on the top," she said.

Jero put his right palm over the deck. They felt warm to the touch.

After a moment, Granny took them back and shut her eyes. She shuffled the cards while repeating a phrase three times in a language Jero didn't recognize. When she opened her eyes again, she proclaimed, "I will read you your future now. Turn the first card over."

When Jero did, she announced suspiciously, "The Knave on his horse."

Jero was drawn in. "Is that good or bad?" he inquired.

"If you need a warrior or a champion, it is a good sign. Still, a knight on a horse can do you harm, cut you down." Her dark eyes focused intensely on Jero when she confirmed, "This card reveals either a hunter or a protector will come your way."

"Does the card tell me who will come?" Jero asked anxiously.

Granny did not answer but tapped on the second card.

Jero turned it over. A tower.

Granny stared at the card before explaining, "The Tower means danger."

Jero released an audible sigh.

"It can be conquered, though. Do you see how the symbol is facing down in the pile? That signals it is possible to overcome it."

"How?" Jero asked.

"The past always bleeds into the present, Isaak. If the danger can be beaten, the card that follows it will tell me how."

She pointed to the deck, and Jero carefully flipped the next card. "The Empress," she announced optimistically.

"Is she a good sign?"

"An Empress in this order is hopeful. She brings abundance and encourages possibilities."

"Could the empress be Ruby?" Jero asked hopefully. "She is the woman I am going to marry."

"This card can be a sign for marriage, yes. Let us see what follows," Granny replied thoughtfully.

Jero cautiously turned the next card, and Granny looked up in surprise.

Jero groaned. "A noose? Does that mean death?"

Granny considered the cards in their order. "Not always. The Hangman can mean punishment or torment, instead. It comes after the Empress, which is not favorable to a man. She might be the danger here."

"Can you be certain?"

"The meaning of each card is certain, but together they do not reveal specific outcomes. They show possibilities," Granny explained. "Shall we see if something changes this omen for the better?"

Jero held his breath and flipped the next card.

Granny shook her head, frowning.

"A sun cannot be a bad sign," Jero insisted.

She put the card at the end of the row of pictures. "The Sun is many things. It can nurture. It brings warmth and light to your world when it rises. But like the Tower card, this card was upside down when you turned it. That tells me the Sun can also set, or the Sun can scorch you. It is difficult to be sure which it is in this order," Granny admitted.

Jero held his stare and asked, "Are there any good cards in your pile?"

The old woman shrugged. "Do you want to see one more?"

"I have seen enough," Jero said. "Thank you for the enlightenment, Granny, but now I would rather not know." Jero got up from the table and walked away.

Granny watched him disappear behind the wagons before she turned the next card over. A smile spread across her wrinkled face at the revelation. She collected the line of Jero's exposed fates and stacked them with the other untold fortunes. Then she returned them to the shiny black box.

Lilyana came to the table with the first platters of food. "Were you reading Isaak's fortune, Granny? He did not look happy."

"He did not have the courage to see it to the end," Granny told her. "But you look happy, child. What has put a smile on your face?"

"Baba said this is our last day on the road. Tomorrow I will finally marry."

"That wedding and your happiness are foretold, Lilyana. But I expect surprises are in store for others among us."

~*~

The three caravan wagons and nine walking children moved steadily toward their destination. When it was apparent that they would not arrive at the gypsy festival before nightfall, they found a clearing off the road and efficiently set up camp once again.

Jero was not interested in hearing the wedding details over dinner—he was leaving in the morning—so after politely acknowledging Irina for her delicious offerings, Jero excused himself for the night.

Chavdar did not object to his snub and even suggested, "There is a nice clearing through the trees where our voices won't bother you. Sleep well, my Venetian friend."

Jero took his bedroll to the secluded spot the patriarch had pointed to. The day's wet start had steamed away into a muggy evening, and Jero lay on top of his blanket, listening to the murmurs of the Romani voices. Before long, a lute could be heard through the trees, and the voices changed to a harmonic rhythm. He drifted into a restless sleep surrounded by melodic songs that joined the chirps of crickets floating on the evening breeze.

Jero hadn't dreamed so vividly in years. Sparked by his unsettling séance with Granny, he saw visions of towers burning from the sun's rays while he struggled to free himself from a choking noose, only to be cut down by a knight on a white horse.

And then there was the empress. Her auburn hair blew in the breeze as she held her arms open to Jero's desires. In his dream, the woman was alone on a ship in the middle of the sea. A man was suddenly with her in a romantic embrace. The sails tore, and the mast cracked in the howling wind, but the two lovers did not care about their perilous fate. Jero was a part of the storm raging overhead, and he watched the bodies of the empress and her lover entwined on the deck of the sinking ship below him.

The vision was powerful, and he was physically overcome by it. He felt the beautiful woman press against his own body, her lips on his neck, and her flowing hair against his cheek. He ached for her as she unfastened the tie of his breeches and caressed his nakedness. Her hot thighs straddled his, and the empress pressed down on him with a groan of pleasure.

"I love you, Ruby," he cried out in his dream.

"Jasmina," a voice panted in his ear.

He knew that voice. The breath on his neck was hot and real. The sensation he thought he had only dreamed about was real. The empress was on him. He was in her. And Jero panicked.

"What are you doing!" Jero pushed Jasmina off him as if she were a venomous snake. He clambered to his feet and defensively stepped out of her reach.

The gypsy girl brushed the pine needles off her clothes and smoothed her skirts. "I was just doing what you wanted, Isaak," she said, pouting.

"I gave you no cause to think that!" he exclaimed.

"I . . . it is done," Jasmina whimpered. Frazzled and crying, she ran away through the trees, back to the wagons.

Jero trembled, trying to close his breeches and tuck in his shirt again. He gathered his blanket and wrapped it around himself, leaning up against a tree, trying to make sense of the encounter. It was still fully night, but he would leave now and put this behind him.

Jero searched the black ground for his vest and hat. Then he crept back to where the horses were hobbled. The campfire still glowed, and Jero could see feet sticking out of the canopy shelter where the children were sleeping. The caravan windows were shuttered and dark except for Chavdar's. There, a lamp was lit, and he could hear muffled voices.

Jero crept past the wagons and untied his horse's bindings, but the bridle wasn't where Jero had left it. Frustrated, he searched for the critical tack without luck. He would improvise.

As Jero fastened a loose leather strap onto Cairo, he heard the unmistakable click of a pistol being cocked. He turned to face his assailant.

Chavdar stepped forward in the moonlight. "Are you leaving without saying goodbye, Isaak?"

"My debt is paid. It is my right to leave," Jero replied steadily.

The old gypsy pointed the gun at Jero's chest. "My daughter just woke me, accusing you of a despicable act. You are not going anywhere until you answer for that."

"I do not know what possessed Jasmina to come to me in my sleep, but I had done nothing to tempt her."

"Ah! So you know which daughter I am referring to. She said you raped her!"

"She is lying!"

"I think we have heard that accusation from you before. You are the liar, Isaak."

"I did nothing to the girl. Let me leave."

Chavdar said, "I took Jasmina to Granny. She will confirm her story and tell us if you did nothing to my daughter."

Everyone was now awake. Chavdar shoved Jero with the tip of his pistol into the open, where the camp glowed with their lamplights. Granny came down the steps of her caravan with Jasmina, whose head was lowered in shame. Boris threw open his door and stomped down his short stairs while he buttoned his shirt. Irina stood at their caravan doorway in her night shift, clutching a blanket around her shoulders, uncertain what the shouting had been about.

Granny stood directly in front of Jero and said, "I looked at your next card in the stack, Isaak. Do you want to know what it was?"

Jero remained silent.

"It was the Fool," she said with a smirk.

Chavdar asked the old woman, "Is Jasmina telling the truth?"

"The girl is no longer a virgin," Granny reported. "She told me Isaak took his pleasure with her in the woods tonight."

A loud gasp rang across the camp. Jero turned to see the alarmed faces of Jasmina's sisters peeking out of their tent.

Andrei ran to Jero, shouting, "I will rip you limb for limb."

Boris held his nephew back, saying, "We should have watched the Venetian better, but the damage is done. What will you do with Isaak, Chavdar?"

Chavdar paced around Jero and contemplated the punishment.

Jero continued to protest, "I did nothing to your daughter! I was sleeping!"

Chavdar roared at the presumed insult, "Now you call my mother a liar!"

"I do not know why your mother would say it was I who deflowered your daughter, but I think I would know if I did."

Boris took a menacing step toward Jero and growled, "We welcomed you. We fed you. We gave you the shirt off our back. If you wanted to marry one of our daughters, I would expect you to ask like a man and not just lure her in the night."

"She came to me!"

Andrei shouted, "So you admit you were alone with my sister?"

"Tell them the truth, Jasmina!" Jero begged her.

"Come here, Daughter," Chavdar ordered.

Jasmina wiped the tears from her cheeks as she stood trembling in front of her father.

"Did the Venetian seduce you to come to him in the night?" he asked point-blank.

She took a deep breath and said, "He did, Baba. He said if I lay with him, he would marry me. So I did as he asked."

"Do you want to marry this man?" Chavdar asked his daughter.

Jero shook his head repeatedly to answer for her, but her eyes remained downcast. "Yes," she whispered.

"There you have it! If you wanted to marry my daughter, Isaak, you should have just said so!"

Jero was dizzy at the onslaught of lies. "No! You are wrong!"

"I understand your ways are different, Isaak. The Venetians are known to be violent and ungodly people—you take what you want," Chavdar declared. "If that is your tradition, I suppose you cannot help yourself."

The accusation was indefensible, like in Tirana, and Jero was outnumbered.

"Is there nothing I can say to convince you?" Jero pleaded. "I have only wanted to find my way south. I have a bride waiting for me. You know that!"

"Your actions tonight speak for your real desire, Isaak," Chavdar concluded.

The clan waited impatiently for their patriarch to decree a punishment for Jero's crime.

"What will you do, Brother?" Boris finally asked.

Chavdar threw up his arms in defeat. "I will let him marry my daughter," he proclaimed to surprised gasps. "But properly—tomorrow, with Lilyana and the others."

Jero stepped back in shock, looking for a gap in the mob surrounding him. "Jasmina is a liar! I will not marry her!"

Chavdar pointed his pistol at Jero again. "This is not a good way to start family relations, but I will forgive your outburst. You will pay for your crime, Isaak, and you will learn to be happy with my lenient sentence. Andrei, Boris, tie the Venetian up."

The two men rushed Jero before he could run.

As Andrei forced Jero's wrists behind his back to bind them, he hissed, "I would cut off more than your hands for what you did to my sister."

"This is your new brother you are talking to, Andrei," Boris reminded him. "Your father is making a wrong into a right, and you should not contradict him. Accept it. Do you hear me?"

"I will accept it, Uncle, after we hear what the clan elders say tomorrow." Andrei finished the bindings, shoved Jero to the ground, and strode away.

Boris hollered for calm in the camp, "Quiet now, children. Everyone back to your beds!"

"We will get a few more hours of sleep," Boris told Jero. "Try to do the same." He nodded approvingly to Chavdar and then went back up the short steps into his caravan. Jero was left squatting in the dirt next to the woodpile.

"Jasmina can sleep safely in my bed tonight," Granny offered.

"Let me talk to my daughter alone first," Chavdar said.

Granny reluctantly nodded and climbed back into her small quarters.

"Did I do all right, Baba?" Jasmina quietly asked when she and her father were alone behind the wagon.

"Yes, Jasmina," Chavdar whispered.

"You are no longer angry at me?"

"No. Isaak will be a fine husband for you."

"But Gustof loves me," she whined.

"Gustof is a peasant, a farmhand. Isaak is the son of a tradesman, a sea merchant. There will be rewards for us with his connections in Dalmatia."

"Will Isaak take me back with him?" Jasmina asked worriedly.

"I expect he will. But first we must be sure he will remain loyal to us."

"And what if I am pregnant with Gustof's child? If the baby has dark hair with dark eyes, my new husband will know it is not his."

"Men do not pay attention to those particulars. You give Isaak a son, and all will be forgiven. Just as I have forgiven you for your shameful behavior."

Jasmina's courage faltered. "Does Granny know?" she asked pitifully.

"Boris is the only one who knows. He saw you in the field with your farm boy. You should thank him for finding a solution to your unfortunate mistake before you were branded a slut," her father admonished her.

"I am sorry," she whispered. "Will you still punish me?"

"Your punishment is the burden of what you have done tonight."

"Yes, Baba. I will keep it secret."

"Good. Now hurry off to Granny's bed and get some sleep. We have a busy day tomorrow, and the night is wearing thin."

~*~

Chavdar locked Jero in Granny's wagon for the rest of the trip. With his wrists bound together and locked in the stuffy, shuttered caravan, Jero could do nothing to save himself.

When the door finally opened, Chavdar woke Jero and told him, "The council has met, and it has been decided that you may marry into our clan. But you cannot wed Jasmina looking like that! A man must have a proper costume and a good washing to take a wife. Come!" With his wrists still tied, Jero nearly fell on his face, stepping unsteadily down the wagon's stairs to the dirt below.

It was dusk. Granny's wagon was surrounded by dozens of other ones just like it. Fire pits were lit among the clusters of caravans, and children ran gleefully between them. Jero followed the gypsy into his new nightmare. After a short walk, Chavdar passed him off to two waiting men, saying, "This is my late wife's cousin, Kuzman, and my oldest son, Chedomir. They will find you something more fitting for a wedding than the rags you have on, Isaak."

Chedomir looked Jero over and scoffed at his new in-law. He took a knife from the sheath on his belt and cut the cords on Jero's wrists. "We will take good care of him, Father. Come with us, Venetian!"

Jero rubbed his raw wrists and did as he was told.

The men guided Jero through the maze of campers spread across a vast field. Kuzman and his cousin waved friendly hellos from time to time at people they passed. To Jero's relief, no one seemed to take special notice of the stranger walking with them.

The dried stubble of cut hay covered the harvested field, and Jero carefully trod on the uneven ground in the dark.

"What is this gathering? Some sort of festival?" Jero asked.

Kuzman chuckled and said, "You are far from home, aren't you?"

Chedomir was not amused by Jero's curious accent like his cousin was. "Tell me, Isaak," he said, "what sort of a Venetian spell did you put on my father?"

"Spell?" Jero repeated warily.

Chedomir surmised, "What else could it be? He let you join his caravan, marry one of his daughters, and is making you a clansman. Many men here have spent years setting themselves up to be in your position. What is so special about you?"

Kuzman laughed and pointed out, "He fucked your sister before the others could."

"Shut up, Cousin," Chedomir said with annoyance. Again, he focused on Jero, asking, "Did you promise him something in return? Some sort of a deal you want to let me in on?"

"There is no deal," Jero said defiantly, "and I am not marrying your sister."

The two cousins laughed.

"It doesn't matter what you say," Chedomir replied. "My father went out of his way with the council to let you marry Jasmina. I will eventually learn why, but until then, we are obligated to make you into a presentable husband. You are indeed marrying tomorrow."

The men stopped in front of a large canvas tent, and Kuzman said, "Here we are, Isaak. The Romani have extra special wedding clothes, but I found you something that might work. Leave your old clothes here after you bathe. The other grooms are already at the river."

"How many weddings are there?" Jero wondered out loud.

"I believe you are number six tomorrow."

"Six!" Jero exclaimed. "Aren't I lucky?"

Kuzman explained, "No worries. The ceremonies will go quickly, but the toasts will go on all night!"

"All the grooms will sleep in this tent tonight while the brides get ready on the other side of the camp," Chedomir said. "Oh, and my father said I am to shave you myself. He doesn't trust you with a blade."

"And am I to trust you?" Jero asked.

"Ah! He is a clever one," Kuzman said, laughing.

Chedomir told Jero, "My little brother thinks I should slit your throat and be done with you. But I think I will just bind your wrists again, just in case."

"I am not dangerous," Jero tried to assure him.

Chedomir looked him up and down with a shake of his head. "Perhaps not, but let me give you this fair warning, Venetian. I am dangerous."

Granny had shown Jero his fate in the cards, and Jero was ready to let it happen. Undaunted, he said with a shrug, "I am glad we understand each other."

Through clenched teeth, Chedomir said, "Let's get you ready for your wedding."

Chapter 47

Stephan and Mira were married that morning in a centuries-old church in the center of a well-to-do neighborhood across the lagoon from the Padovi estate.

The stucco building was not much larger than the stone church Mauro's grandfather had built in Solgrad, but its conspicuous affluence put any country church to shame. A kaleidoscope of expensive, colorful glass adorned the high windows. Life-sized frescos depicting dramatic, biblical scenes decorated the walls, interspersed with paintings of the Empire's victories through the centuries.

In contrast to the vibrantly decorated chapel, the ceremony was solemn and reserved, presided over by an equally somber priest robed in black. Resi sat among the modestly dressed spectators who filled the pews. While repeating the priest's sacrament prayers, their blended voices resonated around the sanctuary. The harmonious sound was almost as delightful to Resi as her night at the opera had been.

Dressed demurely for the holy occasion, the bride and groom knelt before the carved altarpiece of the Virgin Mary. Here Jesus' mother was depicted as a jeweled, medieval princess adorned with a golden halo. An hour-long Mass followed the marriage vows, and then voices of an angelic choir echoed in the domed room as the newlyweds departed as man and wife.

The Padovi couple and their guests would meet again that evening for a livelier reception to celebrate their matrimony with a festive banquet at a luxurious restaurant in the city. That was hours away, though, and the Carrera group headed home for a quick lunch and some rest before the long night of toasting and dancing ahead.

As evening approached, Mauro and Fabian took refuge in Vilim and Hugo's room to dress, leaving the entire third floor to the women to primp and prepare for the big wedding party. When the ladies were sure they had done enough to impress their fellow partygoers, they were expected to meet the men in the parlor. Resi sent Verica down to get her husband instead.

Dressed in his finery, Mauro answered the knock on Vilim's door. "Hello, Verica," he said with surprise. "Does my wife want me to escort her down?"

Verica explained anxiously, "There is a bit of a dilemma that requires your attention, sir."

Fabian shook his head and said, "It is never good when a woman uses the word 'dilemma.'"

"Well, Fabian, a woman's choice of words cannot be helped," Mauro said cheerfully. "Shall we fetch our wives and see what the trouble is?"

Verica pointed out, "Lady Isabella and Lady Caterina are coming directly, sir. Lady Baric asked that you come alone."

Mauro exchanged questioning glances with the other men.

"Take your time, Mauro," Vilim said. "We will meet you downstairs."

His three friends descended the staircase, and Mauro went up the steps with Verica at his side.

"How is your arm, Verica? Is it feeling better?" Mauro asked.

Verica moved it back and forth to show him. "It is a little stiff, my lord, but I am happy I do not need the sling any longer."

Isabella and Caterina came around the corner of the staircase, and Mauro complimented them, "You look splendid, ladies. My wife and I will be down shortly."

"We will be having a drink in the parlor until Terese is ready. We don't mind waiting if she decides to change," Isabella said pleasantly.

"Yes, Mauritius. Let your wife take as long as she needs. We are plenty early," Caterina added as they continued down the stairs and out of sight on the next landing.

Shaken by their remarks, Mauro hurried up the last steps, leaving Verica to wait outside the chamber door. He burst into the room, asking, "Is something the matter, Resi?"

His wife sat on the edge of the bed. She smoothed the expensive fabric of her robes with her jeweled fingers. "It's just . . . I'm unsure." She stood up. "I don't know, Mauro. What do you think?"

She was wearing the ensemble Mauro had seen in the Constantinople dressmaker's window that first day. There were no fewer than five layers of silk and gauze and embroidered satin to make the draping perfect, and the effect on his wife's feminine figure made him stare in appreciation. The rich blues and gold and rose-colored decorations on the cream chiffon suited her beautifully. Master tailors had trimmed each layer with threads of contrasting colors. The mother-of-pearl buttons were strategically placed at the bottom of Resi's bosom to lift its fullness, and a wide satin sash met the last button at her waist. A sheer fabric showed on the corners of her cleavage. It flowed airily down the length of her slender arms to the cuffs of her brocade robe. The last showy layer peeking out below the robe was a pale green fabric gathered at her ankles like blooming breeches. The velvet slippers Resi had packed from home were a perfect complement, and the blue coat swept the floor behind her.

"Say something, Mauro," she urged him anxiously.

He touched the strand of golden ribbon Verica had woven through her loosely piled hair, held secure by her favorite jeweled pins. "You look stunning, Resi. Do you not like my gift?"

"Oh, Mauro, it is sumptuous and grand. Lady Caterina said I look like an Ottoman princess. I feel like one, too. I have never worn anything so extraordinary."

He tilted her chin so that she would look into his worried eyes and asked, "Then why will you not come downstairs?"

"Don't you think I will be distracting? I look like a foreigner and not like a Venetian baroness."

He took her hand and assured her, "A newcomer is always distracting at parties, especially a beautiful one. You have worn Ottoman costumes in public before, Resi. What is really troubling you?"

She awkwardly explained, "I suppose I am dreading the whispers: Look at Baron Baric with his Ottoman wife."

Mauro frowned and tried to soothe her worry, "No one will say that."

"But, Mauro, you yourself said that you wanted to look across the room and see me as a baroness. I want to be sure you won't be ashamed if I don't look like the other noble ladies this evening."

"No one is expecting me to have a Venetian lady on my arm tonight. I bought you the costume because I wanted you to wear it."

"It is hard for me to keep up with your contradictions, Mauro," she said tearfully.

"This is who you are, Resi. You will turn heads tonight, but for all the right reasons."

"What if they don't like the real me?" she asked with doubt.

Mauro's smile was bright, and his eyes twinkled when he declared, "I like you, and that is all that counts tonight."

She cocked her head and managed a smile. "You like me, Mauro?"

He touched her rouged cheek before gliding his fingers down to the cross at her throat. He brushed by her heart and then down the five buttons of her waistcoat. Mauro affectionately stroked her round middle before pulling her closer, saying, "I like you just as you are, Baroness Baric. In fact, I love you very much."

She melted into him as he kissed the last of her worries away. "I am sure that I love you more, Baron Baric. And thank you."

"For what, my love?"

"You know how to say the right thing at the right time."

"Do you still want to change your dress?" he asked.

"No," she replied. "I am ready to go now."

Verica was outside the door awaiting instructions when they opened it.

"I will not need your help after all, Verica," Resi told her maid cheerfully.

Mauro added, "We will be gone until quite late. The baroness will not wake you when we return. You may retire for the night."

Verica wished them a good evening before the couple walked arm in arm down the stairs. In front of the last step, Fabian was waiting for them, anxiously pacing.

"We weren't upstairs too long, were we, Fabian?" Mauro asked jovially.

"Long enough for visitors to arrive, Mauro," Fabian replied.

"Has Cyro arrived?" Resi asked hopefully.

"I wish it were Cyro, Terese. He would be a welcomed addition to our evening."

"Be out with it, Fabian. Who is here?" Mauro demanded.

"Denis and Teodor," Fabian said.

"My soldiers? Here?"

Fabian confirmed, "They brought you an urgent message from Nestor. He said you would want to know right away. They are waiting in the parlor."

"You know I hate drawn-out explanations. Tell me, Fabian. Who has died?"

"No one has died, Mauro, but you should hear it directly from them."

Holding Resi's hand, Mauro followed Fabian into the parlor, where the others sat around the room, looking stricken.

Teodor took a step forward to greet the baron. "I am very sorry to interrupt your festive evening, Lord Baric. We came directly from the harbor."

"Thank you, Teodor. I hear you bring difficult news."

"Yes, sir," Teodor said solemnly. "We have brought a letter addressed to you, Lord Baric. Lord Raneri's scouts said it was on the body of an Ottoman courier they found rotting on his land. The letter is from her ladyship's brother, Patrik. He wrote it after Jero was imprisoned in Tirana."

Resi gasped, "Imprisoned?"

Mauro guided her to a chair before opening the letter Denis held out for him.

"Read it aloud, Mauro," Resi whispered.

With a tremble in his voice, Mauro read, "The 3rd of August. Tirana. To my brother Mauritius and my dearest sister Resi, I deeply regret I must write to you about the trouble we have encountered here. What happened was unpreventable and unjust, but our hope is that it will be fairly resolved.

Specifically, Jero has been jailed in Tirana. The crime he is accused of is murder."

The blood drained from Mauro's face, and he sat down to catch his breath. He dared not look at his wife, or he would have faltered in finishing the message. He held the letter on his lap to not shake and continued, "A man did die at our hands while the bastard attempted to rob our camp and kidnap Ruby."

Despite the shocked cries from the ladies, Mauro read on, "Do not worry! Ruby was unharmed and is safe with us. We are still shaken that Jero was arrested when we arrived in the city. We nearly succeeded in buying his freedom today, but the prison's commander thinks he knows your father and, to our dismay, has accused your father of killing one of this commander's own family in cold blood. To everyone's distress, Jero will stand trial for this war crime that no one witnessed. We are confident that Jero will be acquitted, but the magistrate will not hold court in Tirana again until the 21st of August. It pains all of us to write you, and, moreover, we ask you not to come yourself, for you are a son of Lorenc Baric and your safety is not guaranteed. Bem and Salar Nassim will remain in Tirana to assure Jero is treated well enough while Soren and I bring Ruby home. Please, know that we will resolve this, but it will take time. I send my sister my love, and I ask you, Mauro, to be patient with our efforts. Yours truly, Patrik."

Mauro folded the weathered note again and clenched it in his fist as he began to pace the room's length.

Resi clutched her kicking middle and walked away to a window in need of air. "The 21st of August was two weeks ago, Mauro," she said from across the room.

Mauro tucked the letter into his pocket and said unconvincingly, "It is resolved, Resi. This explains why they missed Castor's last voyage. Jero and Ruby will be with him on his next sailing, and when we return home, my love, they will be waiting for us."

Mauro looked around the parlor for someone to support his theory. Isabella and Caterina nodded weakly, but the soldiers in the room remained uncommitted to his optimism as they thought it through.

Resi said what no one else would: "Why didn't Jero write to us when he was released, Mauro? He would have known Patricius sent that message. Why is there no other correspondence?" She turned to Denis and asked, "Has any other news arrived?"

Denis lowered his eyes. "No, Lady Baric. This is all we know."

Teodor explained, "Nestor thought it was important we come in person, Lord Baric. He sent us on your ship, sir, in case you wanted to return early to Solgrad."

Mauro asked, "Did Branislav already sail with the next cargo delivery?"

"Three days ago, as scheduled," Teo replied. "Ivanoslav Tomsic captained your transporter, sir."

"Who crewed the ship, then?" Fabian asked.

Denis straightened up and answered proudly, "Teodor and I, along with six of the guardsmen, sailed with Ivanoslav this morning. We learned on the job, so to speak. The others are still onboard awaiting your instructions, Lord Baric."

"We will sail back to Solgrad immediately," Mauro said decidedly.

Vilim spoke against it, "What is your hurry to go home, Mauro? Patrik wrote that Jero would be released. You said yourself it is old news, and Jero will return with Branislav on the next tour."

Hugo agreed, "According to the letter, Bem and Salar Nassim stayed with him. Maybe it was later than intended, but I am sure the sellswords got him to Thessaloniki to marry Ruby."

Mauro shook his head. "I want to believe it, too, but I cannot shake this growing doubt." He turned to his soldiers and asked, "Why did Nestor not simply courier a message, Denis? Why did he send you to me, Teodor? What else did he tell you?"

Teodor looked to Denis, who shrugged before answering, "There is nothing more to tell, Lord Baric, except Nestor wanted you and the baroness to have the opportunity to return ahead of schedule if you wanted. Otherwise, he instructed that we sail back tomorrow, and Branislav will come for you in a few weeks, as arranged, sir."

Vilim reflected, "I think we should go to Stephan's party. But if you decide otherwise, Mauro, then I will leave with you tonight."

"I have not heard your opinion, Fabian," Mauro said. "What would you do if it were your brother held in an Ottoman jail for murder, and you found out that you were three weeks too late to help him?"

"I would sail my ship down the coast and storm the jailhouse because my brother would not have Ottoman sellswords there protecting him. Jero has that protection, Mauro." When Mauro still seemed doubtful, Fabian unflinchingly advised, "Listen to your brother-in-law. He said they were taking care of him, and Jero will be found not guilty of this fabricated charge. Patrik wrote specifically to tell you not to come."

Mauro said, "I thought you had little faith in Patrik and his opinions."

Fabian shrugged, asserting, "I have tremendous faith in greater things. Patrik wrote to you because he wanted you to know why Jero's return would be delayed. If you had gotten the note from the courier last month, would you have skipped Stephan's wedding to stay in Solgrad, worrying about something you could not change?"

"I am not sure," Mauro said quietly.

Fabian looked across the room at his wife, Isabella, dressed so beautifully for a wonderful evening out with friends. "If you want my opinion, Mauritius, here it is: Nothing can be decided tonight. Send Denis and Teodor to tell the captain to wait until the morning. Isabella, my darling, shall I get your cloak?"

Mauro could not let it go and insisted, "How can I celebrate tonight?"

Hugo added weight to Fabian's advice, saying, "Jero was released from jail weeks ago, Mauro. You said it yourself; he will be home with Branislav next week."

"The ladies are looking forward to the party, Mauro," Vilim said. "It would be a shame to keep such beauty at home tonight."

Fabian asserted, "We all have to eat tonight, and we might as well do that at Stephan's expense. If you do not escort your wife to the banquet, then I will. Come with us, Mauritius. Dance, get drunk, and yell at the top of your lungs in the middle of the canal, if you like—God knows I have done that before. Decide in the morning," Fabian urged.

With a frustrated sigh, Mauro agreed and said to his guardsmen, "Tell Ivanoslav to hold anchor. Come back again in the morning."

"As you wish, Lord Baric," Denis said dutifully.

"Not too early in the morning," Fabian warned. "We have a long night ahead of us." Then Fabian took a pouch of coins from his jacket pocket and said, "I suggest you enjoy yourselves in the city tonight, too. Share this with the others, all right?"

"Thank you, sir!" Denis and Teodor said in unison.

They all left the house together. The guardsmen took the waiting gondola back to the harbor, and the partygoers took three of their own boats into the city.

Isabella and Fabian were alone in their boat, their legs warmly wrapped with a wool blanket. Isabella leaned into her husband and asked, "Do you think the Barics will leave for Solgrad tomorrow?"

"No," Fabian said. "Jero's situation has resolved itself or else the Barics would have heard differently by now. After a few drinks, Mauritius will have forgotten why he was ever so concerned."

Isabella took her husband's hand in hers under the blanket and said, "You have given me new insight tonight, Fabian."

Stroking her hand in return, he asked, "In my advice to Mauritius?"

"No, in rewarding the guardsmen like you did. Do you often buy your men a night out with gambling and women?" she asked.

Fabian chuckled, trying to make light of it. "What makes you think they won't use the money to merely get drunk after a good meal?"

"Because earlier I saw how much lire was in that pouch," she said with raised brows. "I dare you to deny it."

Fabian considered his wife's accusation. "Would that be so terrible?" he asked. "If you are honest, Isabella, is that not what you want on an evening out? A little gambling and seduction."

"Fabian! How can you even suggest that? I have never sat drunk in a tavern gambling, and I definitely never paid for sex."

"Is that so, my darling?" he cheerfully refuted. "Every time you dressed for a party, wondering if you had chosen the right gown to win attention, you gambled. I always admired how you could hold your wine better than any woman I drank with, my little lush. And perhaps no one directly paid for the seduction, but sex was exchanged, even if you left your suitor wanting more."

"Hmm," she murmured. "I always thought of you as a player, Fabian, not as a wallflower, watching the room."

"One can watch and participate," Fabian corrected her lightheartedly.

"And do you expect to participate tonight, darling?" she asked with a renewed seriousness. "You are a married man now. Or should I play the wallflower and keep my eye on you at the party?"

"I hope you will allow me some fun flirting tonight, but I am not seeking a reward from it. I have my prize. She is sitting right next to me, and I need nothing else."

Isabella relaxed against her husband as she stared ahead at the sun setting over Venice. "You are a charmer, Fabian," she said. "I think Stephan and Mira will be content in their marriage, but I suspect they can never be as happy as I am with you."

Chapter 48

The servants moved the heavy trunks down the delivery stairs to the waiting gondolas at the dock. Resi was saying her farewell to the women of the Carrera house when Fabian ran through the front door in time to intercept Mauro.

"I thought I had convinced you to stay this morning!" Fabian cried. "Were you going to just slip away without saying goodbye?"

"That is why I sent a messenger to your office, Fabian. We only have a few hours to make this tide," Mauro explained calmly.

But Fabian was not calm; he was openly agitated after his dash across the city to meet his departing friends.

"You had agreed to wait another day, or two or three," Fabian insisted. "Why hurry for today's tide?"

Mauro shook his head and said, "I know what I said, but I also know it will be impossible for me to enjoy myself here."

"Think about your wife, Mauritius, and all that you promised to show her in Venice," Fabian argued.

"The truth of it is, Resi is just as worried as I am. She thinks Patrik would never have written to me unless something was gravely wrong. I need to be at home when Jero and Ruby arrive, and she agrees."

"Nestor would send a courier when Jero is back. You can return to Solgrad then."

"Nestor knows me too well, Fabian. That is why he sent my ship for us. Hugo and Vilim have decided to return today, too. And the young man I agreed to train is coming on short notice as well. It is all arranged."

Fabian rubbed his temples in frustration. "I feel guilty that I cannot somehow offer more help. I have three more weeks here and then I can continue my senate duties from the territories."

"By then it will all be resolved, Fabian, so do not worry yourself. Isabella also offered to come along to keep Resi company, but my wife convinced her that Caterina needs her support while she waits for Cyro."

"According to my father, Cyro's entourage should arrive any day now. Once Caterina is on her way to her new life as a Genoese lady, I will arrange Isabella's passage to Croatia. I know she needs to be involved somewhere."

"Will Bianca not need her encouragement here at home?"

"Mother has decided Bianca will leave directly after Caterina's wedding. She will join Countess Toth's court before she can get into more trouble."

"Then perhaps it is better that we are not a distraction, with everything else going on next week."

"You would never be a distraction, but I know there is no talking you out of it."

Mauro chuckled at his friend's expression. "Do not be so full of regret," he told Fabian. "I had a fantastic week in Venice, a memorable reunion that was long overdue, and I got to see Stephan off with fanfare. You have been a wonderful host to us."

"Since you admit you owe me a debt, will you check on the renovations at my new villa? Put a little pressure on them to get it finished."

"You know I will. Goodbye, Fabian. We will see you in a few weeks."

"Goodbye, Mauritius. Send word when you hear from Jero."

~*~

That noon, a message arrived telling Felix that the Barics were leaving weeks ahead of schedule on the evening tide. Not wanting to miss his chance to start over, Felix quickly penned notes of regret to his few remaining music students and thanked his aunt for her generosity these past months.

Most of Felix's worldly possessions were still packed in trunks at the Passini house, so it was easy to decide what to take in a hurry. And hurry he did, but not before Pasquale gave him one of the Passini swords from the display wall and told him not to get his head shot off by the Habsburgs.

When the Barics' gondola arrived at the harbor later that afternoon, Felix was waiting with two stuffed bags, a sword, and a black case in hand.

Mauro nodded his approval when Felix climbed into one of the gondolas to be rowed to the Barics' anchored ship. He had not yet told Vilim and Hugo about his recruit. Seated together with them in the first boat, Mauro explained, "Lord Felix Soranzo is coming with us. He would like a commission in my uncle's army, and I have agreed to train him in preparation. If Felix shows potential, I will recommend him. Alternatively, if he is a quick learner and works well with the men, I might offer him a place in my guard."

As they approached the ship, Latif could be seen climbing the rungs of the tall mast. "Who trained your soldiers to be sailors, Mauro?" Hugo asked, chuckling at the sight of his latest recruit.

"Let's go aboard and find out," said Mauro.

~*~

Ivanoslav came across the deck to greet the baron. "Your trunks are loaded, and the ship is ready to lift anchor upon your command, Lord Baric."

"You once told me your sailing days were behind you, Captain Tomsic. I am glad you changed your mind."

Ivanoslav scratched under his canvas cap and reflected, "I thought they were too, sir, until Nestor made a very convincing argument that there are some things you never forget. I have done this crossing in the dark of night and foulest of storms more times than I can count."

"I hope we do not have to test that today, Captain."

The seaman nodded slowly. "I agree, my lord. I agree."

"And how is my crew?"

"We made it here, sir," Ivanoslav said with a low rattle in his voice. "That is to say, they are hardworking and seaworthy. Your men listen to orders, and I am hoarse from giving them, but they are a disciplined group, Lord Baric, and I expect smooth sailing back home."

"I have brought you three more. Hugo and Vilim lent a hand at the ropes while sailing here, and this is our newest soldier, Felix."

Ivanoslav looked Felix over. The banished aristocrat had dressed in his most unassuming clothes for the trip, but those were still finer than anything Mauro's other soldiers owned.

Felix sensed the old sailor's scrutiny and stated, "I have never crossed the open sea, Captain Tomsic, but I have been on boats all my life. Just tell me where I should go."

Ivanoslav asked, "How is your voice, young man? Can you holler over the wind?"

"I think so, sir," Felix asserted loudly.

"Then you shall be one of our lookouts. Go to the bow and Vic will explain what to do."

Hugo went with Felix to make the introduction.

Vilim stayed behind to talk to Mauro. "This Lord Soranzo is an odd choice, Mauro. I thought he was a music teacher. Is he trying to prove something to his father in his change of profession?"

"He has something to prove, I am sure, but not to his father. His father died recently in what could be called dishonorable circumstances. Felix is trying to find his place after his family lost theirs in society."

"Ah, I see. A man of my own history," Vilim acknowledged.

"My wife introduced us a few days ago. She has an affinity for strays, and it was her suggestion to give him this chance. He seems to be a serious and dedicated young man. You know what my uncle expects from his officers, so I would like you to mentor him."

Vilim nodded. "I will make the music teacher into a soldier."

"Thank you, Vilim. Now, I think I will go to the cabin. You can find me there if you need me."

Mauro passed his wife at a side railing. She was looking out onto San Marco Square one last time. He asked, "Would you like to come inside with me?"

"I will in a few minutes," Resi replied. "I know you don't feel the same, but I wanted to watch us sail out of the harbor."

"As you wish, my dear." He gave her an affectionate peck on the cheek and added, "One thing, though."

"Yes, Mauro?"

"With our late start, we will be sailing through the night. Tell Verica she should join us in the cabin before it gets dark."

"I will let her know," she assured Mauro.

Resi walked the length of the small ship to find her young maid. She lingered to watch the familiar faces in their unfamiliar duties.

Tucked away out of the breeze, Verica sat on a coil of rope. She was wrapped in her warm cloak, reading one of the books Resi had given her, and hardly noticed when her mistress walked up to her side.

"You are quite enthralled, Verica. Which story are you reading today?" Resi asked.

Verica made room for the baroness to sit with her and replied, "*The Adventures of Guzman de Alfarache*. It is the one about the street urchins and all the trouble they get into. It is a terrible story," she said with a nervous laugh.

Resi chuckled as she thought about it. "It is, but told in an entertaining way, don't you think?"

Verica shrugged under her flapping cape. "I am only halfway through, so I have not quite decided, my lady."

"I must compliment you," Resi said. "You have come a long way in a short time. You should be very proud of yourself."

"Thank you for teaching me, Lady Baric. You have opened up a whole world to me." She pulled her cloak tighter and shifted on her rope seat.

"Are you too cold sitting here? You can come into the cabin and sit with me and the baron. I see Davor has already given up on the breeze and is going below deck."

"I am content to sit here a while, my lady. I'll keep my back to the wind."

Resi maintained, "The baron is feeling protective of you, and he does not want you sitting here alone after the sun goes down."

"I have known all of these men for years, Lady Baric. They will not bother me, but I will gladly come inside for the lamplight."

Resi took a chance to ask about Felix. "There is one man you have only just met, Verica, and yet you seem to know him quite well already. He has been looking your way ever since I've been sitting here."

Verica looked over at Felix, standing on a platform near the railing. She shook her head and said, "He is looking past me to the sea, not at me, Lady Baric."

"Hmm. I see what you mean now." Resi went on to say, "I never had a chance to ask what the two of you were talking about in the shop last week."

Verica made light of her pleasing encounter with Felix, explaining, "We talked about the things for sale in the shop, is all. As the son of a nobleman, he is well-trained in small talk, I think."

Resi remarked, "That is what I like about gentlemen like Felix. You can trust them to say the right thing to a lady."

Verica winced at her assessment, but Resi didn't notice that as she stood up and gathered her cloak tightly around her.

"Come in for some hot tea when you get cold, all right, Verica?"

"I will soon," Verica promised.

~*~

The baroness left her maid to her reading, but Verica's attention was no longer on her book.

Felix had moved to the starboard side, her side, in his job as a lookout for obstacles in the sea. Now and then, he looked across the deck to Verica. This last time, their glances finally locked.

A hundred different things traveled through Verica's thoughts when their eyes met. She wanted to forgive Felix, to believe he was a man of noble intentions, and to rush to stand next to him in the cold wind. But her rational side reminded her that Felix was not to be trusted. His motives to help her at the Passini's had been calculated for his own gain, and he got what he wanted. Felix was a reminder of how treacherous the world outside Solgrad was to a girl like her. She could avoid him at the castle, she thought. She was a house servant, and he would live and work at the Keep. Their paths would not have to cross before he moved on to Toth Castle.

With those thoughts in her head, Verica picked up her book, found her marked page, and went back to the troubled lives of the characters in her story.

Felix continued to watch Verica from the railing for another long moment. When she did not look up from her book again, he returned his focus to the rushing sea.

Chapter 49

Baric Castle, 9 September 1649

Davor was waiting outside the baron's chamber door when Mauro came out. "Here is your bag, sir."

Mauro took it from his outstretched arms with a nod and continued down the corridor with Davor by his side.

"Is Nestor up?" Mauro asked.

"Yes, my lord. He is at his desk in the study."

Mauro hurried down the stairs alone.

The study door was open, and Nestor was right where Davor had said he would be. Mauro stood by the door and asked impatiently, "Is there any news this morning? Is Branislav back?"

Nestor looked up from his ledgers and adjusted his spectacles. "It is too early, Mauro," he said kindly.

"I suppose so," Mauro said under his breath. "Send someone to find me if news comes. I am going to Fabian's estate, and then we will do a quick loop around the farms, beginning in the north."

"I know how to find you. You told me last night."

Mauro nodded distractedly. "So I did."

Nestor asked, "Did you make a decision about the harvest celebration? It has been a good summer, and your tenants have worked hard to give you a good crop."

Mauro considered the idea with a groan.

"You avoided it last year, Mauro, but it is an expected reward for the villagers."

"This is hardly the time for a celebration."

Nestor assured him, "Jero will be back before then, and you will be ready to celebrate." Nestor held the baron's gaze and waited for him to agree.

"All right, then," Mauro conceded. "I will let the farmers know they can plan on it. What should I tell them, Nestor? Mid-October? Out on the hay field?"

"The second week of October is when we have held it in the past years." Nestor scanned the calendar. "You should plan it for the fourteenth."

Mauro slung his pack on his shoulder, impatient to be on his way. "Whatever you think is best. I will leave the details to you. And did you send a note for the surgeon to come?"

Nestor shook his head. "Idita told me not to bother. She won't let him examine her."

"Send for him anyway," Mauro insisted. "She is ill, and he might know how to cure her."

Nestor reminded the baron, "She is nearly seventy, Mauro. I regret saying this, but there is no cure for old age."

Mauro frowned at the thought of losing Idita. "She told me the same thing when I talked to her last night. Her leg aches and she has a cough. She is otherwise as fit as any woman here. I am sure there is a remedy for those isolated ailments."

Nestor agreed, "She told me her cough comes and goes. I myself took medicine for that."

"Then what are you waiting for?" Mauro protested.

"I will make her see the physician today," Nestor promised.

"And when the crew returns, I think we can evaporate one more pool of saltwater before the weather turns for the winter."

"I have already talked to Jakov," Nestor informed him.

"Excellent. Thank you, Nestor. I can see you have thought of everything. I will be back in a few days, then."

"Safe travels, Mauro."

Mauro hurried across the courtyard and met Vilim, Daniel, and Denis by the stables.

The three men greeted their commander cheerfully.

"Did Simeon take the men out to the shooting field?" Mauro asked while he strapped his bag onto Janus's saddle.

"All went as planned for Simeon's first morning," Vilim confirmed optimistically.

Denis added, "He did confide that he was nervous to start training again."

"Simeon could load and shoot a musket in his sleep. He will do fine," Mauro said.

"He wants to do better than fine," Vilim asserted.

"That is already a good sign, isn't it? Stubborn man," Mauro said.

Vilim remarked, "There is more than one stubborn man here today."

Mauro confirmed his cousin's accusation by ignoring it. "Denis, Daniel, are you ready?"

"Yes, sir," they answered in unison.

Mauro gave the order, and the four sped away from the castle to their new neighbor's house.

~*~

Resi poured her morning tea and asked, "What shall we do today, Verica? Does Nela need any help with the preserving?"

While choosing her mistress's ensemble, Verica answered toward the wardrobe, "I am sorry, Lady Baric, but I was told not to let you help in the cellar."

"Is that what he said?" Resi grumbled. "All right, then. I will wear the linen gown today and work in the garden with Danica."

Verica shook her head and held out two choices for the baroness—a delicate taffeta gown and a set of soft robes. "His lordship told me specifically to keep you out of the garden, madam." She cocked her head to entice her mistress to choose the pretty gown.

Resi put her cup down and went to the window, fuming in frustration. "This is so vexing! Mauro has told everyone in the castle to reject all my plans."

When Verica nodded, it added to Resi's annoyance. "He gets to be sour and moody and ride across the countryside until he feels better. But I am left sequestered in the house just because I am a little pregnant. It is hardly fair, don't you agree, Verica? Danica works every day in the garden, and she is as round as I am."

Verica put her hand over her mouth to stifle a chuckle. "Begging your pardon, madam, but I saw Danica yesterday. I am sorry to say she is not nearly as round as you, Lady Baric."

Resi stood sideways before her looking glass and rubbed her bulging middle. "I am finally enormous, aren't I, Verica?"

"Remember how the constable's wife thought she, too, was so huge and then how tiny her baby was when it was born? You might get even bigger before it is over, my lady. That is the way of it," Verica said sympathetically.

Resi slipped off her dressing gown and took the tunic from Verica's arm. She slid it over her cotton shift. "I know it is unreasonable of me," Resi said, "but I will not sit in my chamber for the next two months waiting to grow fatter. I must have something to do."

Verica helped her mistress secure the fashionable sash of her robe and said, "Today is market day, Lady Baric."

"Oh, it is, isn't it?" Resi replied. "I've lost track of the days since coming back. We shall go into the village, then." Resi lifted her long braid so Verica could adjust the collar on the final layer of her ensemble.

"It is the third week of the month and the trinket man will be there," Verica mentioned offhandedly. "I thought I might buy some new buttons for my jacket."

Resi pondered the ribbons on her grooming table. "I do not really need anything, so perhaps I will stop in at the constable's house while you pick out your buttons and such."

Verica remarked, "You are always in a good mood after you visit the constable's wife, madam."

Resi sat down in front of her mirror for Verica to unbraid her hair. "Are you thinking of visiting Natalija's brother? Did she mention anything about him since our return?"

"Luka? No, Lady Baric," Verica replied.

"Are you still fond of him?"

"Um, yes, madam. I am."

"I was just thinking you hadn't mentioned your tanner friend since returning," Resi said. "Perhaps Natalija would like to join us today, and you could visit him."

Verica looked hopeful in the reflection. "Could I, my lady?"

Resi smiled at her eager innocence. "I insist. If you could ask Nela to pack a basket with cakes for my visit with Elizabeta, you and Natalija can go visit Luka for an hour. Is that long enough to gaze at your future husband?"

While Verica brushed the baroness's hair, she pondered, "He has not asked me to marry him yet, but if he does, should I say yes, Lady Baric?"

"Do you want to say yes, Verica? Do you want to marry this young man?"

"I think so. His parents like me, and they think I would make a good wife for him, and Luka is so very, well, grown-up now."

Resi had only seen Luka a few times over the last year. The young man was indeed tall with strong arms and a burgeoning beard, but 'grown-up' was not how she would describe this nineteen-year-old. "How long have you known Luka? Since you were children?"

Verica shook her head. "No, my lady, I only really met him when I became friends with Natalija. That was after she came to work for the baron's mother."

"And now that you are both grown-up, as you call it, you want to marry him? I am surprised you are so swayed by a little facial hair," the baroness said playfully. "What does Luka dream about for the future, Verica? Will he be a good provider for you? Where will you live?"

"To be honest, Lady Baric, we have never really talked about anything other than what he was working on. He is very talented with leather, though, and his father thinks he can open his own shop in a few years."

Resi looked at her maid in the reflection and asked, "Does he love you?"

Verica replied, "I think he does. Luka always talks to me after Mass. When we were together at Radic's party, he told me how much he liked dancing with me. Natalija even said he asks about me when she visits her family on Sundays."

The maid put the final touches on her mistress's pinned curls while the baroness watched her pensively.

Resi finally said, "It makes me happy to know you are in love, Verica, but I would say wait a year before marrying your tanner. I will need that long to get over losing you."

Verica laughed at her mistress's roundabout approval. "Thank you, Lady Baric. I heard whispers in the kitchen that he is openly talking about marrying. Maybe he will ask me today."

~*~

The soldiers were unsaddling their horses in the confinement of the stalls after their morning on the training fields.

Josip took the tack from them and hung it on the designated pegs. The stable groom casually asked the lingering soldiers, "Did you hear that the baron is organizing a harvest dance next month?"

"When did the baron announce that?" Neno asked with interest. He slid his horse's damp blanket over the stall's railing to dry.

Josip carried Neno's saddle away, saying, "I heard the baron tell Eduard just this morning."

"This is excellent timing! I am thinking about taking a bride before winter sets in," Neno announced to the group.

Vik raised his brows in surprise and asked, "Have you already picked out a bride?"

Neno shrugged, saying, "I thought I could do that at the harvest dance. All the eligible girls should be there."

"Well, Neno, you should join our bet, then," Teodor said jovially.

"I will!"

Felix had been listening to the conversation with a look of puzzlement, so Bruno explained to him, "The men of the Keep have a running bet since the New Year—who will be the first to marry? Daniel and Teodor are favored."

"Even though it is already September," Neno added.

"My money is on Teo," Vik said with a nod to Teodor in the next stall. "He has a new sweetheart in the village that seems willing to marry him."

"That is true," Teodor asserted.

Vik explained to Felix, "Daniel has set his eye on one of the Baric maids, but she doesn't seem to be in a hurry to take a husband."

Felix asked, "Has this maid turned him down?"

Vik cocked his head and replied, "Come to think of it, I don't think Daniel has even asked her yet."

Latif pointed out, "A farmer's daughter is your best choice if you want to get married in a hurry. She is most eager to get out from under her pa's roof, and she usually knows how to cook and care for a man."

Neno agreed with Latif's assessment, "Beware of the castle girls, Felix. They make you court them. I am looking for a girl who is ready for a husband. I think I will only dance with farmers' daughters at the party to help my chances."

It dawned on Felix that he shared their plight. He asked the soldiers, "How do you even get to court one of the house servants? I have not seen them around the castle grounds."

The group of men nodded knowingly, and Vik explained, "The manor house is designed so the servant girls come and go from the other side. The kitchen is at the back of the house, and so are the gardens and the wash yard. They send Aron to fetch the well water, so there is no reason for them to come into the courtyard for their chores."

Neno chuckled at Felix's sudden gloominess and asked, "Why so disappointed? Do you have someone in mind already, Felix?"

Felix confided to his new comrades, "I met one of the Baric servants in Venice."

The men began to murmur.

Teodor remarked, "You must be talking about Verica. She is a pretty girl, but I think Luka is courting her."

"Is Luka a guardsman or one of the servants?" Felix was eager to know his competition.

"Luka is the tanner's son," Vik explained. "Nice enough fellow, but you don't owe a villager the same consideration as your fellow soldiers."

Latif added, "A man of the Keep is allowed a fair chance with a maid who shows interest before another can try his luck."

Josip had overheard bits and pieces of their gossip while he led the horses one by one to the corral. He told the men, "Luka isn't interested in Verica any longer. The tanner delivered some goods this week and mentioned that Luka is going to marry the butcher's daughter from the neighboring village. It has been decided."

Bruno asked, "Do you mean Carmen? Since when has he been courting her?"

"Well, Luka's pa told my pa that they met earlier this summer, but Luka got a little too close, if you know what I mean. The butcher is forcing the wedding to take place pretty soon. Now that Verica is back, someone needs to tell her," Josip said.

"Ha! Luka's lack of self-control is our good fortune. Everyone will have a chance to catch Verica's eye at the harvest dance," Vik exclaimed.

"I will get my chance before that," Teo bragged. "I am a part of the baroness's escort this afternoon."

"You already have a girl!" Vik protested.

Neno told Felix, "Lady Baric goes to the village each market day, and she usually takes two maids with her. That is how Daniel got to know Natalija better. She is a lady's maid."

"Verica always accompanies Lady Baric, and whoever drives the wagon also escorts them through the market," Teodor said.

"And how do I get the honor of escorting the baroness?" Felix asked Teo.

Teo explained, "It goes by ranking. Hugo and Daniel are usually given the duty, but now that Captain Padovi and Captain Carrera are gone, they have more responsibilities here at the castle. Captain Eduard assigned me to drive the wagon today, but, come to think of it, I did not hear who the second is."

"So, I should talk to Eduard?" Felix asked eagerly.

"Or talk to Geoff," Vik advised with a chuckle. "He is your quickest way to Verica."

Geoff and Alberto had arrived at the stalls to take the saddles to their stands. Geoff asked, "Talk to me about what?"

Vik handed him his saddle and said, "There are a few of us who want to try our luck gaining your sister's favor, especially our new man, Felix."

"I won't help him," Geoff mumbled as he carried the saddle away.

"What do you have against Lord Baric's new recruit, Geoff?" Teodor asked with a friendly wink in Felix's direction.

Geoff eyed the newcomer and said, "My sister told me all about you and what happened in Venice."

A wave of chuckles and *oohs* came from the enlightened group before Vik asked Felix, "How well do you know Verica already?"

Neno added to the speculation, "Why has she complained to her brother about you?"

Felix could not hide the blush burning on his cheeks as all eyes were upon him, but he insisted, "I cannot imagine what she might have said, Geoff, but there is no story to tell. I escorted Lady Baric and Lady Carrera on an outing. Verica was with them, and we talked, but that is all."

"That is all?" Geoff spat back. "You are a liar! You keep away from Verica."

Alberto had not paid the soldiers' conversation much attention until he heard Geoff's raised voice. "Mind your place, Geoff," he warned him in a fatherly fashion.

Teo told the boy, "She is very pretty, Geoff. You should be proud to have a nice sister like Verica."

"All of you! Leave my sister alone!" Geoff shouted.

The stunned guardsmen were quiet while Alberto took hold of Geoff's collar and pulled him wordlessly away from the stalls.

The soldiers eyed their new comrade suspiciously.

Latif was the first to confront him, "Whatever happened on your outing, Felix, must not have been agreeable with our Verica."

Teo challenged, "Why would Geoff point you out like that, Felix?

Their remarks shook Felix to his core. "I really don't know, Teodor. I actually thought Verica liked me," he said in his defense.

At that moment, Eduard strutted into the stables and roared, "There you are, you bunch of milkmaids! You can't even put some horses away! Be done now, lads. I need the muskets cleaned and counted. Come on! Out you go!"

~*~

The men came out of the stables as Hugo and Simeon drove up in the musket-filled wagon. Hugo hopped down, put a wooden crate down for Simeon to step on with his good leg, then gave the wagon's reins to Josip and headed toward the Keep.

Hugo had been friendly and helpful toward Felix since their Adriatic crossing earlier in the week. Felix ran after him, calling out, "Can I ask a favor, Hugo?"

"If there is something in it for me," Hugo answered cheerfully.

Felix was caught off guard and gave him a questioning look.

Hugo had taken a liking to Felix. He saw something in the serious young Venetian that reminded him of the baron a few years back. "Ask your favor, Felix, and I will tell you what it is worth," he said heartily.

Felix took an audible breath and said, "Fair enough. I need to talk to Verica, but I don't know how. I cannot wait for my turn to escort the baroness to the village, and if the maids never come through the courtyard, then, well, I don't know where I can find her."

Hugo chuckled at his predicament. "You have not joined the priesthood here, Felix," he said. "You are not forbidden from knocking on the manor door and asking to talk to her. Well, not the front door, in your case."

Felix grinned at the simplicity of Hugo's solution. "You mean I can just go in and visit?"

"Sure, if you are not on duty," Hugo said lightheartedly. "The best time is just before or after dinner. Most days, Verica eats in the kitchen with the other servants. Take the delivery path to the kitchen door before sundown and ask to talk to her there."

"Can I go tonight?" Felix asked hopefully.

Hugo thought a moment. "We don't have you assigned to gate duty yet, so yes, I believe you can."

"So, I just go to the kitchen door?" Felix confirmed.

"It is not a scary place. Nela won't roast you for dinner, although she might look you over and decide to send you away." Hugo continued, "Oh, and, Felix . . ."

"Yes?"

"That favor will cost you a lunch." Hugo tilted his head toward the Keep and said, "Come on. I'm starved."

~*~

After Geoff's outburst, Alberto took the groom to his private quarters at the back of the stables and sat him down. "What's biting at you, son?" he asked.

Geoff clenched his fists and told him, "The baron's new man has his eye on my sister."

"Is that all, Geoff?" Alberto shook his head at the boy's ignorance and warned, "You are going to have to get used to more of that. Verica is of marrying age, and you cannot fight every man who starts looking at your sister with that in mind."

"I don't like Felix," Geoff grumbled unhappily. "And Verica doesn't think much of him, either."

"Verica has good instincts. When your sister does decide she likes a man enough to court him, you have to let her, even if you might not have picked that mate. I have enough daughters to know it is better to let them choose," Alberto said with a sigh.

Geoff slumped down and said to the dirt floor, "Verica is the only family I have."

"You have all of us, Geoff. You are like one of my own boys, and Josip is as close as a brother to you. We will always be your family."

"But I only have one sister. What if she leaves me?"

"Cheer up, Geoff! Chances are Verica will find a husband among the castle guards. Still, it is not your choice."

Geoff hung his head in shame. "I am sorry, Alberto. I promise I will do better," he said. "Are you going to punish me?"

"For protecting your sister? No. But you must promise me something else."

The boy looked up from his gloom.

"You must never challenge one of the baron's guardsmen in my stables again."

"Yes, sir. I promise."

Chapter 50

Felix took a deep breath and opened the kitchen door at the servants' pathway. He was welcomed by the clanking noise of utensils being set on silver trays. When no one noticed him standing at the entrance, he announced with a bow, "I am sorry to interrupt you, ladies."

Franja looked up from her work. "Hello, you must be the baron's new recruit," she said with a quick curtsy.

Nela waved Felix in with a motherly smile. "Come in, young man, and introduce yourself properly."

"Yes, ma'am."

Felix came closer to the long table in the center of the room and confidently said, "I am Felix Soranzo. I have come to ask whether I could talk to Verica for a moment. Perhaps I am too late or too early to find her in the kitchen?"

Nela and Franja exchanged curious glances.

"You are looking for Verica? She will be down shortly," Nela said with a critical eye.

Felix felt the scrutiny and asked, "Should I wait outside?"

"Have you had your dinner, Felix? You are welcome to join us at the table if you like," Nela offered.

"Thank you, ma'am, but I have eaten in the Keep."

Cook grinned at his refined accent and aristocratic formality. "Please, call me Nela. I am Lord Baric's cook. And this is Franja. She is the one to thank for the bread you eat."

"It is delicious. Thank you, Franja," he acknowledged sincerely. "Um, perhaps you could tell Verica I will be waiting for her outside?"

"I will do that, Felix," Nela assured him merrily.

Franja waited until Felix closed the back door before remarking, "That was awkward."

Nela shook her head and told Franja, "He reminds me of someone a few years back who came courting someone else in this room for the first time. When will we see Simeon at our kitchen door again, or is that too awkward now?"

"That is up to Simeon," Franja said curtly.

The door to the foyer opened, and the chatting maids came noisily into the kitchen for their dinner.

"Are there any trays to go upstairs tonight?" Ivana asked Nela dutifully.

"Yes, Idita and the baroness are eating their dinners in their rooms."

"Add Nestor to that list," Davor told Nela as he came into the kitchen with Verica.

"You had an easy day without the baron here, Davor. How about you bring Nestor his dinner tray tonight?"

"With pleasure, Nela," the valet said with a grin.

"Verica dear, let Brigita bring the baroness her dinner tray. There is someone outside who would like to talk to you. A young man," Nela said with emphasis.

Verica looked just as surprised by the announcement as her friends around her. "Why doesn't he come in?" she asked hesitantly.

"I imagine he has something private to say. Come here first, Verica. Let me fix the hair falling over your eyes," Nela said kindly. She smoothed the loose locks with a bit of spit on her fingers.

Nela would not try to make Verica look pretty if it were not for Luka waiting outside for her, and Verica could not keep from grinning when she left out the back door, expecting to find him.

"Why didn't you tell her who was waiting?" Franja asked when Verica was gone.

Nela whispered, "I hear Luka did not break the news to her today, and I'd like to avoid being the one who explains that she needs to forget about him. Maybe this new man can help her with that."

~*~

When Verica saw no one outside the kitchen door, she wandered down the path. She had almost given up on finding Luka when Felix stepped out from the arbor. "You?" she said with surprise.

"I am sorry if you were expecting someone else," Felix replied nervously.

"I was, as a matter of fact. What do you want, Felix?"

Her words hit him like a slap across the face. "What do I want?" he asked pitifully. "I have been here four days, and all I can think about is why you avoided me on the ship and how I could see you again."

"We have no reason to see each other, Felix," she said coolly. "I have my work, and I am busy all day. You have a job here, and you are busy. That is all we have in common now. Good evening to you." She turned and walked down the path.

"Wait!"

She stopped, and he hurried toward her. "I never got a chance to tell you I am sorry for what had happened. Pasquale was drunk that day. He did not realize what he was doing."

"He knew exactly what he was doing, Felix."

"But I stopped him," he said.

The nightmare played fresh in her mind again, and her anger rose as she relived the scene. "What reward do you want for throwing a book at a man raping a girl?" she asked with disgust.

"Let me right this wrong. I want to be your friend, Verica."

"Friends trust each other, Felix, and I do not trust you."

She started for the kitchen again.

"Please!" he called to her. "I remember when you first stepped into the lamplight with Lady Bianca. You were afraid of falling into the canal, do you remember?"

She turned and defiantly pointed out, "I was not afraid of falling in."

He breathed out with relief to have gained her attention again. Walking toward her, Felix said, "That night at the party I asked you about the music, and you picked out the violin in the piece played. Right then, I knew I wanted to know you better. And then at the ghetto, I wanted to ask what else you liked, but there was no time to talk. That is why I wanted to see you again, Verica, to get to know you, to be your friend."

Her scowl told him she wasn't convinced.

"I know enough about you already, Felix, and I don't want to know any more. You used me to get the meeting with Lord Baric. Do not deny it."

Felix took a step closer. "Is that why you won't talk to me? Is that my transgression?"

"It is one of them." She took a step back and held her ground.

"The last thing I ever intended was to use you, Verica," Felix said. "Why else do you find me so intolerable?"

She crossed her arms defiantly and replied, "I don't have to explain anything more to you. I don't have to like you, Felix, and I don't want to."

But Felix would not give up. When his honest plea failed to win her over, he tried a different approach.

"I have found only one fault in you, Verica. Shall I name it?"

Curiosity got the best of her, and she indulged him, saying, "All right. Tell me what you dislike about me."

"You are shallow-minded, specifically in your judgment of me," he asserted.

Verica's jaw dropped at his insult. "That is a self-serving observation."

"It is an observation, but not self-serving. From mere association with my cousin, you have judged me untrustworthy and, by your own words, a brute. Yet, all I did was walk into a room and stop Pasquale from assaulting you."

She angrily pointed out, "And then you told him the only reason for him to stop was because I would cause him trouble. Did you not think of the trouble and pain he caused me? You gave him immunity for it, Felix."

He took a step closer. "There you are wrong. I was trapped at that moment, just like you, and had to think of a way to stop him without making him angry at me."

"See, there you go making selfish excuses again," Verica retorted. "You did not seem trapped to me."

"Hear me out," he pleaded.

Her curiosity won out again. "Make it quick," she said, "I must get back."

He hastily insisted, "I'd like to pose a question."

"I am listening."

"What would you do if Lady Baric came to you today and told you to pack your bags and leave?"

"This has nothing to do with what happened in Venice, Felix."

"I need to hear your answer. Where would you go, Verica, if the Barics no longer welcomed you in their house?"

She bit her lip, deciding.

"And what if your mistress would not give you a reference? What would you do if no one would hire you and the little money you had ran out?"

"Lady Baric would never do that," she said firmly.

"Many employers do. Those questions haunted me daily."

Verica scoffed at his outrageous statement. "My guess is you have never been at the mercy of an employer. You have money and ties to society to keep you housed and clothed."

"I wish you were right, Verica, but I am the son of an accused criminal who they say drowned himself to save his neck from the gallows. What is left of my father's estate is barely enough for my mother and sisters to live on. My aunt took pity on me until I could figure out a way to support myself. Her husband was against taking me in. I lived there solely at the mercy of my aunt's generosity. If my cousin had turned against me, she could have been swayed to turn me out."

"Then why live with such terrible people?" she asked.

Felix laughed at her flawed logic. "Because it was the only choice I had. I sought a profession, but no gentleman would answer the solicitations of a criminal's son. I tried for months, Verica. Then I saw a possibility through the

Barics. I did not use you, like you believe, but I was desperate to get out of Venice."

"Your story is indeed sad and pitiful, Felix. But why do you even care what I think?"

Felix stared at her in disbelief. "Is that not clear to you already?"

"I have never met anyone like you, Felix. Your ways are very unclear to me. I have to go."

"Wait. You like books, right? Stories?"

She was pulled in again and nodded.

"Some stories tell about being swept off your feet, but I never understood what it really meant until I encountered you. You are like music to me, Verica. There is something about you I am drawn to," he confessed.

He thought he had convinced her. He saw understanding in her eyes. But then Verica crossed her arms, and Felix heard her say, "My dinner is waiting." He swallowed the lump in his throat and nodded in defeat.

"Yes, of course," he told her. "You have my sincerest apologies for my part in your troubles, and I will not bother you again. I bid you a good evening." He tipped his hat and walked away from her.

A few moments later, Verica was back in the kitchen, where four of the servants were seated around the long table.

"Sit yourself down next to me. We are ready to eat," Nela said.

"It seems your visitor had a lot to say," Franja remarked when Verica was settled across from her.

Ivana asked, "What did he talk to you about for so long?"

"Does this new soldier fancy you, Verica?" Louisa asked with a giggle.

Verica replied with an unexpected seriousness, "I don't know what he fancies, Louisa. He is very confusing."

"What makes him confusing?" Franja asked with sincere interest.

Verica did not have to think long to answer, "He is like a complicated poem. I understand each word, but I cannot really understand the meaning of the words strung together. I feel like I need to read it again and again to appreciate it."

Franja asked, "Appreciate the poem or the man?"

Ivana and Louisa merely giggled at the confusing talk of poems.

Davor came into the room, followed by Brigita. Sitting down next to Ivana, Brigita asked, "Did we miss something funny?"

Still watching Verica, Nela told her, "No, dear, there is nothing funny here."

~*~

Felix returned to the Keep through the armory, but he did not go upstairs to the common room. He was too agitated to sleep, and his mind was racing too wildly for a simple conversation with the other soldiers. He needed a release from his frustrating encounter, and there was only one thing that could do that.

He stood alone in the torchlit space. The shields and chainmail hung on the pegs along the tall stone wall. Then Felix noticed a dim corridor away from the main armory. He took a torch from the wall and followed it to the Keep's storerooms. He decided this could be the perfect refuge and would spend hours there that night.

Exhausted, Felix later crept back to his cot among the sleeping soldiers. He peeled off his sweat-soaked shirt and finally slept deeply like he had not slept in days.

Chapter 51

In front of her looking glass, Resi watched her maid absently brush the same strand of hair over and over again. "Is something the matter, Verica? You seem distracted this morning," she said.

Verica set the brush down with a sigh. Natalija had finally broken the news about Luka's engagement to Carmen. That and Felix's sudden confession last night had left her nerves frayed.

"May I ask a personal question, Lady Baric?"

Resi nodded.

"Have you ever felt that if you gave into a feeling, you might be consumed by it?"

Resi chuckled and said, "I think you have seen me let my emotions take over reason more than a few times. Is that what you are asking?"

"I admire you for the choices you have made, Lady Baric, so I wondered if it is normal to feel so confused. My thoughts are going round and round and, well—"

"Has Luka finally asked you to marry him?" Resi was in suspense to know.

"He hasn't, my lady, and he won't." Verica took a deep breath; her lip quivered as she explained, "I talked to Natalija after breakfast. Luka will marry a girl in the next village. He met her at Radic's party, and he likes her better."

Resi embraced the brave girl before she burst into tears. "I am so sorry, Verica," she said. "I thought you were distracted from love, but it is loss that you are feeling."

Verica admitted, "I feel numb, Lady Baric. But the odd thing is . . ."

"Yes?" Resi said encouragingly.

"Well, I think I am relieved."

Resi squeezed her tightly at the unexpected confession. "And so am I, Verica. You are not ready to be a tanner's wife, or anyone else's."

The sadness in Verica's eyes showed lingering doubt, but she agreed, "It seems I am not, my lady."

"We will find something to get your mind off Luka. How about washing him away with a long soaking in my bathhouse?"

Before it could be decided, footsteps running down the hallway made them turn toward the open door.

Davor came through the doorway, breathless, and exclaimed, "The *Margaret* is back, Lady Baric. Vik brought word that Lady Ruby is onboard. Lord Baric is bringing the wagon to meet her."

"Thank you, God," Resi whispered to the rafters, and the two women embraced.

Then Resi turned to Davor and asked, "Why didn't my husband come get me? I want to meet them at the pier."

Davor's expression was tense when he explained, "Yes, madam, it seems Lord Baric left quite hastily because Lady Ruby arrived alone. Without Jero."

Resi sat down to steady herself. "Where is Jero?" she asked no one in particular.

"Lady Ruby will certainly be able to tell you, madam." He bowed politely and left the two women alone again.

"How long will it take for my husband to bring Ruby? Thirty minutes? An hour?" Resi wondered aloud.

"At least that, my lady," Verica agreed.

Resi took her wool wrap from the window seat. "I know it is wretched weather outside, but I need some air. Would you like to walk the garden with me while we wait, Verica? I don't think I can stay walled-in right now."

"I will get my cape, madam."

~*~

Natalija opened the door to Idita's chamber, where the old woman was sitting by the window, looking out.

"Good morning, Idita. I've brought your tea and some hot stones," Natalija cheerfully announced as she crossed the room. "Are you feeling better?"

"Thank you, child. I think a little tea will help," Idita replied. She gripped her cane and moved with effort to sit on the soft chair next to the breakfast tray. Idita lifted the lid off the iron pot that held glowing hot rocks. "Does the surgeon recommend I eat these for breakfast?"

Natalija stared into the pot and wrinkled her nose at the thought. "Nela said that Nestor said that the surgeon said that you have bad spirits living in your leg, Idita. The surgeon told Nestor that your cough is not strong enough to push the spirits out, so the burning stones should do the trick. I don't think he intended that you eat them, but I cannot say for certain."

Idita scoffed at his prescription, but it only prompted a wave of coughing. When she caught her breath again, she asked, "Did Nela say that she believes the nonsense about spirits causing my leg to swell?"

"Not directly, no. But Signor Gilberto does seem nicer than Signor Santiago, so she thinks that he would not prescribe anything that could hurt. But maybe you should let the stones cool a little first."

"You can take his scorching rocks back to the kitchen, child. I will use my own medicine this morning. Could you bring my basket to me? I am settled so nicely here in my chair." Idita pointed to the shelf by her wardrobe, and Natalija brought the basket over.

"Oh, I didn't realize it was so heavy, Idita. What do you keep in it?" Natalija asked with a renewed cheerfulness.

"You can open it, and while you are having a look, find me the gray linen pouch. It should be in a side pocket."

Natalija looked through compartments but did not find what Idita asked for. "You have so many little bottles and jars in here. Is it all medicine?" she inquired curiously.

"It is. Every ailment has a different cure, Natalija, and I am prepared to heal it."

The maid continued to look for the cloth pouch among the many neat bundles. "How long have you been curing people?" Natalija asked.

"A long time, my child. I brought this exact basket with me when I came to Baric Castle fifty years ago, although I did not use it much at first as a nurse for Lady Anika."

"If I weren't a lady's maid, I would have liked to be a wet nurse," Natalija remarked. "I like rocking babies. Do you think Lady Baric will hire a nurse for her new baby? Maybe she will use me."

"Even if she does hire one, Natalija, you cannot be a wet nurse for the new baby without having a baby of your own first."

"Oh, right. I forgot."

Natalija watched Idita find the correct pouch in her basket. "How did you come to be the nurse for the Barics if you did not have your own baby, Idita?"

The old woman smiled and replied, "I did once, Natalija, but that is a long story."

"Will you tell it to me? I could sit with you and listen while you eat your breakfast."

"If you had brought my breakfast, I could, but you only brought me stones."

Natalija looked at the contents on the silver tray again and counted, "Teapot, stone pot—oh! You are right, Idita. I forgot to add your porridge and toast with honey. I will come right back with it."

"There is no hurry, child. I am not so hungry after all."

"You might be once you smell the toasted bread. I'll make it fresh for you over the fire, and then you can tell me about your baby and what happened to it."

"It was long ago," Idita said.

"Can you not remember?" the girl asked kindly.

"A woman never forgets her baby," Idita said softly.

"Did your baby die, Idita?"

"No, but she was lost to me, which is the same for a mother."

"It was a girl? How sad for you, Idita. What was her name?"

Idita had not said that name in fifty years, but she could today. "I called her Magdalena."

"Magdalena. That is a beautiful name. Magdalena," the maid repeated as she went to the door, shutting it behind her.

Alone now, the old nanny held the small linen bag in her crooked fingers and sighed with indecision. She finally opened the pouch and pinched a corner from the shriveled mushroom the girls had collected earlier in the week. "What has become of you, Magdalena?" whispered Idita before she bit down on the leathery medicine.

She leaned back in her chair to wait for the expected release. Almost immediately, the pain in her lungs waned, and she drifted into a vision of a man crossing the room. The sight of him made her sit up, alert again. She was dreaming, or was she?

She rose to greet him. "Is it really you, Ezra? It has been so long."

The man cocked his head at her remark and said good-naturedly, "It has only been three days, Idita. I know I usually don't come on a Saturday, but I promised your father I would finish the grinding after the Sabbath."

He took off his cap and jacket and hung them on a hook on the wall with casual familiarity, then took an apron down and tied it around his waist.

"My father did not mention you were coming. He is not here right now."

"All the better," Ezra said with a flirtatious wink. "Then you can help me today. You know as much about mixing this recipe as I do—probably more."

Idita settled into her role as the object of the young clerk's infatuation. In her father's shop, she was light again, happy to be with the man who made her feel attractive and smart.

"I know no more than what my father taught me," she humbly said.

"And what your mother taught you when she was alive. You are a clever girl, Idita. I like that."

"Most men don't."

"I am not most men."

She held his stare and smiled. "What will you do now that your apprenticeship is done?" she asked. "What will we do, Ezra?"

"I have thought a lot about it lately. There are already two chemists in the ghetto, so it is out of the question to open my own shop there."

"You could work here for my father. There is so much to do; you could be his partner one day."

"As a Jew? I was lucky he let me work in the back of his shop. I could never work as an equal in this part of Venice."

"The law is unfair."

"Fair or unfair, I do have a plan," he said encouragingly. "I have written to my uncle in Bari. He has a profitable shop but no sons, and he is getting on in age. It would be a good start."

Idita pleaded, "Don't leave Venice, Ezra."

"Come with me, Idita. You will like it there. Bari is also on the sea."

"I cannot leave. My father needs me."

"I need you, Idita. And I love you. You know that." He took her in his arms and kissed her like he had a dozen times already.

She melted into his embrace before she remembered they were not hidden in the back storeroom. She took a step away and whispered, "The shutters are open, Ezra. We will be seen."

"You are too practical. I love that about you!" He kissed her quickly for good measure and took her hand in his. "Come on, then—help me mix this last jar and we can contemplate our life in Bari."

"I've come back with your breakfast, Idita," Natalija announced when she came through the door with the refilled tray.

The old nurse was sitting where Natalija had left her. Her eyes were open, seeming to watch something out the window.

"I'm not hungry, Auntie."

Idita was no longer in her father's shop. She was across town, in her Aunt Leona's apartment above the herbal shop Leona had managed with Idita's mother. Idita was sitting in bed with her aunt by her side. She stroked Idita's brow with a kind touch.

"You must keep up your strength, sweet Idita," Leona advised.

"How could you take my Magdalena?"

"I told you not to name her."

"She was mine for four days, Auntie. How could I not give her a name? Every person needs a name, even the youngest of souls."

"She will get a name at the foundling hospital."

"Idita? Are you alright?" Natalija looked into the old woman's blank stare with fear. "Please, tell me you are not dead, Idita!" The maid touched her shoulder, and Idita turned in Natalija's direction but looked right through the girl.

Natalija wrung her hands, deciding what to do next. "I'll go get Nela," she told herself. "Nela will know if you are dying, Idita. Wait right here!" Natalija ran out of the room and down the stairs to the kitchen while Idita stayed in Venice.

"You are young and attractive, Idita. You can still find a husband and have more children," Leona consoled her.

"But I love Ezra."

"You must forget about him."

"Did you even post my letter, Auntie?"

She shook her head and said, "What would be the point, dear girl? He has been gone for seven months without a word. He knows you cannot marry a Jew. Why can you not accept that, Idita, when Ezra has?"

"I wrote to tell him he has a daughter. He would want to know that he has a child, Auntie."

"He has no daughter, and neither do you. She belongs to the Sisters at the orphanage now. They will find a home for her with a new father and a new mother."

"I should be the one to care for her. I can, you know. I love her. You had no right to take her away."

"Do you want to bring shame to your father? You will if he learns you were pregnant. You must put this all behind you, Idita."

"Does my father not suspect already? You took me away four months ago."

"He didn't know your condition then. It was always planned that I would mentor you in the art of healing. That is your path, and your father agreed to it, my child. You will fill the void your mother left when she died."

"I have no strength to heal anyone now, not even myself."

"You must carry on, Idita. Now, eat your breakfast and you will feel better."

Idita eyed the porridge and honey-smeared toast on the table. "No," she told her aunt in her dream.

"See what I mean, Nela?" Natalija whispered. She and Cook had tiptoed into Idita's chamber and watched her from a distance.

Nela saw the mushroom lying on the table and said, "Idita is not dead. She took some strong medicine to ease her pain, and it makes her dream deeply."

"Then why are her eyes open, Nela?"

"Not all dreams come as sleep. Let us leave her in peace for a few hours. You can ask her to tell you her story over supper instead."

The two crept back out and shut the door behind them.

In the back of her consciousness, Idita heard the door close. She floated in her thoughts until she landed in another room, a room where the door had also just closed. She was in her aunt's house again, but a different woman appeared before her.

"Who are you?" Idita asked.

"You know me, Idita. I am Orsa. I was a friend of your mother's. I have brought you some special broth. Drink it, and you will feel better."

"Broth will not sate my grief."

"I have something for your grief. A gift."

"Did you bring my Magdalena back? That is the only cure for my grief."

"There is a baby who needs you more than Magdalena. I just came from a noble house where I treated a visiting lady. She is very ill, but I expect she will recover. Her son needs a nurse to feed him while she is weak. Will you care for him, Idita?"

"A baby boy? I don't know, Orsa. I still imagine my little girl's hand touching me, touching my heart as I fed her. How can I replace that with someone else's baby?"

"You can add his touch to it."

"And forget her? No."

"I will give you something to keep her memory alive, but you must also learn to live without her." Idita's hopeful expression assured Orsa, and she said, "Show me where Magdalena touched your heart."

Idita achingly undid the tie to her shift while the woman unpacked the small case she had brought with her.

"I have seen this before," Idita said of the box Orsa had laid out on the table.

"Your mother was the one who taught me this art. It is a painful remedy at first, but it eases your longing for a lifetime. Do you trust me, Idita?"

"If this was my mother's art, then I suppose I must."

Orsa lit two candles on the table to help her see her work ahead. She then opened the decorated box she had taken out of the basket and unpacked its contents: a small wooden mallet; several thin, sharpened sticks; two jars; and a golden plate. Orsa opened one jar, sifted the dark powder onto the plate, and then mixed it carefully with spirits from the other jar. "This remedy is reserved for those who are consumed by loss. Your mother left you a box just like this one with her supplies, should you meet someone who needs this special gift."

"How does it work?" Idita asked with fascination.

"It is old medicine. Lie down, Idita, and think of your last memory of Magdalena. Listen to my words carefully and learn them."

Orsa proceeded to ink her sticks in the plate of black liquid. "Do not focus on the pain, Idita, but on the memory. You must stay very still. Can you do that?"

"I can," Idita breathed out.

The healing woman took over an hour to tap the design into the flesh above Idita's heart. It burned, and then became numb, but Idita did not flinch, and she memorized the words the wise woman chanted repeatedly.

"It is done," Orsa finally said. "How do you feel?"

Idita dried the tears that had silently fallen on her cheeks. They were not tears of pain but from letting go of her loss. "I feel warm and cold all at once," she replied.

"That is the medicine in the ink. You need to drink the broth I brought. It will revive you."

Idita lifted the lid from the covered pot and took a spoonful of the tepid soup. "I will never see her again, will I, Orsa?"

"I am a healing woman, not a fortune-teller, Idita. But I do know that you were meant for something different in this world. Will you come with me to this noble house now?"

"How many days will I be gone? Aunt Leona says my father is waiting for my help."

"Your father will not miss you for three or four days. That is all that is asked of you. Her husband wants to sail home when Lady Baric is well enough to travel."

"All right, Orsa. I will help Lady Baric and her baby boy."

~*~

Mauro set the candelabra on the table and sat down at Idita's bedside. He took her hand in his and rubbed it gently. "Idita? Are you awake?" he whispered to her.

She opened her eyes and smiled when she saw him.

"I wanted to check on you. I heard you had a difficult day."

"Did Nela send you?"

"She did. She was worried about you."

"Sometimes old women have difficult days, Mauro. I slept well for the first time in a long time and am feeling better."

"That is good to hear, Idita. You have always been there for everyone who is sick, but you will not let us be there for you."

"Do not waste too much worry on me. You have other things on your mind. Nela told me that Ruby is back at the castle, but Jero is missing. I am so sorry, Mauro."

"I have decided to go after him, Idita. I am leaving first thing in the morning. Vilim and Hugo are coming with me. It is all arranged."

"You will be gone a long time, no doubt."

"Not so long. We are going by ship. Ivanoslav knows all the ports along the Ottoman coastline, and he will take us as close as he can to Tirana. That is the last place where they saw Jero, so we will start there first."

"Be careful, Mauro. You have responsibilities here, too."

"I know, Idita, but Jero is my brother, and I must know what has become of him. If he is dead, it is my responsibility to bring him home to bury him with his ancestors."

Still holding his hand, Idita whispered, "Do you know how many Barics I have seen buried under this castle?"

Mauro thought about it and said, "My grandparents, my father, his wives, their children . . ."

She nodded weakly. "I saw all the babies born and grow and live happily until their time came. And with God's help, I will see the next Baric baby come into this world. The time is close for your wife, Mauro. You should be here."

"I have time, Idita. I must find Jero first. He is lost."

"You are thinking of Mateo now, aren't you? Maybe you cannot save Jero, either."

"Maybe I can. At the very least, I must know the truth about what happened to him."

She squeezed his hand. "Of course, you must go. Someone there will point you to Jero so you can bring him home, where he belongs, like you said. But if you cannot find him, Mauritius, Jero would want you to be strong for those who also need you."

Mauro swallowed hard to find his voice. "You said those same words once before, when I was just a boy."

"And you have been strong ever since."

He shook off his self-doubt and told her, "I plan to be back in a few weeks. If I am not back in time, will you help bring my son into the world?"

"You know I will."

Tucked in her bed, she looked small. Mauro kissed her lightly on her soft, wrinkled cheek. He had never done that before.

"Sleep well, Idita," he told her, "and I will see you when I return."

Chapter 52

Resi had waited all morning and could wait no longer. She went down the hall and carefully opened the door. "Do you want it so dark in here?" Resi asked from the threshold.

"Is it morning already?" Ruby groaned into her pillow.

Resi crossed the dim room to open the shutters. "It is almost lunchtime. You've slept all morning."

Ruby rubbed her eyes in protest to the bright sunlight and stretched her long limbs. "I didn't sleep much while stowing away. It is nice to be in a bed."

"Where did you even sleep on the ship?" Resi asked.

Ruby thought about it through a long yawn. "Well, at first I hid in Castor's cargo hold among the bundles. It wasn't easy to find a place to sit, let alone sleep. Branislav was then kind enough to give up his cabin, but there was a lot going on at all hours: bells ringing and voices outside the door. It must take practice to ignore it all."

"I am glad you sneaked onboard my father's ship, Ruby. It was the right thing to do."

"Your brother would disagree with you."

"Mauro is grateful to you, you know. He left early this morning for the coast of Albania. They will find out what happened to Jero."

Ruby wondered out loud, "Have you heard from Patricius again? I hope he and Soren are all right."

"As long as he wasn't jailed, Patricius can take care of himself. His next letter was probably lost somewhere, too." Resi took Ruby's hands in hers and said, "We will stay positive and not let the wait for more news eat at us."

"Speaking of eating—missing dinner last night was a mistake. Can you hear my belly growling?" Ruby asked with a chuckle.

"The maids are setting the table for lunch. I came to ask if you wanted to join me."

"Gladly." Ruby went to her wardrobe. Her clothes were still where she had left them. "You didn't pack my things yet," she said contentedly.

Resi explained, "I had planned to send them to your new house, but then we packed for Venice, and, well, I am glad I forgot."

A loud, rumbling noise from the courtyard reached Ruby's open window. Voices from the ramparts rose with it, and Resi eagerly went to the open window to see who could be visiting. "It is the Leopolds' carriage!" she said with surprise.

They watched the driver open the door, and Lady Nikolina stepped out with a bounce. The neighboring baroness noticed the two women hanging out of Ruby's window across the courtyard and waved in their direction. Resi waved back with a welcoming grin.

"How delightful!" Resi said. "I have not seen Lady Nikolina since the ball. Now you really should get dressed, Ruby. I will see you on the terrace."

Davor came up the stairs as Resi was going down. "Lady Leopold has just arrived, madam. Shall I show her to the sitting room?"

"I saw her carriage out the window, Davor. I will greet her myself, but if you can tell the kitchen to set one more plate for lunch and have the maids ready the green room."

"Right away, Lady Baric."

Resi met her friend out on the front steps. "Welcome, Lady Nikolina! This is a pleasure, and the timing is perfect."

"My dear Lady Terese, I did worry I might be imposing," she said sweetly. "Neven got Mauritius's note this morning that he has gone looking for his brother. Your husband was concise, if not limited in his choice of words. He only wrote he was sailing down the coast to Ottoman territories. I had to come see that you are well and not frantic with worry." She stepped back and added, "Oh, my. Look how you have grown, Lady Terese. Are you not yet in confinement?"

"I still have a while before anyone confines me. And I am not alone, Lady Nikolina. Ruby is here again. But I am truly glad you made the trip to check on me. Come in."

Nestor stepped out of the study when he heard feminine voices in the foyer and said with a bow, "A pleasure to see you again, Lady Leopold."

"The pleasure is mine, Signor Nestor. I must congratulate you. My mother-in-law still talks about her wonderful evening in your company. She is even contemplating a ball at our house now. That is quite a feat of persuasion."

Nestor replied, "Your mother-in-law is a delightful woman. She charmed everyone at the party."

"Was it charm?" Lady Nikolina reflected mischievously. "That is kind of you to say."

"Will we see you at dinner, Nestor?" Resi interjected to spare him more small talk.

"Yes, madam," he said and retreated into the study with a bow.

Resi hooked her arm in her guest's and led Nikolina up the stairs. "I thought you might like to refresh yourself after the long carriage ride. You will stay the night, won't you, Lady Nikolina?"

"I have not been away from my children in months, but I thought I could spend one night away. The little one is grown enough to not need me every day."

"Is this your first outing since your new baby?" Resi asked.

"It is, as a matter of fact," Nikolina said with a relieved sigh. "I recovered quicker than I expected after number four. Julius's delivery was no trouble at all, and he is a perfectly happy little babe."

"Has it already been two months? You look very well, Lady Nikolina."

Lady Nikolina rambled on, "I have a fantastic nurse just for the baby. The other children have their favorite nannies, and I do so love to watch them interact." At the top of the stairs, Nikolina eyed Resi and counseled, "I do not pretend to be an expert on maternal figures, but perhaps you have miscalculated your conception like I did."

"It is my choice of clothes that gives me away, I think. It cannot hide my middle as well as a corseted dress can."

"That could be true," the guest agreed pleasantly. "You should still have a wet nurse at the ready, just in case. It takes time to find a new mother in good health ready to wean her own."

Resi explained, "I am going to feed the baby myself."

Lady Nikolina diplomatically warned, "I suppose you could in a pinch—some ladies do. I would not recommend it for the long term, though. That would take all your free time, and your husband would suffer from it. A woman must consider a husband's needs, and if you have a daughter, you will want to try again as soon as possible."

"I suppose." Resi opened the door to the green room and smoothly changed the subject, "Here we are, Lady Nikolina."

The maids had already brought water pitchers and a vase of flowers to the bedchamber. The guest untied her hat and set it down with a contented smile, saying, "It is such a bright, charming room. Oh, and I see my trunk is already here."

"Whenever you are ready, lunch will be on the terrace through the great hall. Take your time, Lady Nikolina."

"Thank you, dear Lady Terese."

Resi waved to Ruby coming down the corridor as Resi shut the door. "Lady Nikolina will meet—," she began to explain, but a loud shriek stopped her.

Ruby jumped in surprise. "Was that the baroness?"

After rushing into the guest room, the two women found the visitor sitting on a chair, wildly fanning herself.

"Lady Nikolina! Are you hurt?" Resi asked breathlessly.

"Just my pride, Lady Terese. I know I should not be afraid of a little mouse, but two of them skittered across the bedcover and caught me quite by surprise. I have a tremendous fear of little crawling creatures."

"I am so sorry, Lady Nikolina! The girls were supposed to sweep out the room. With the cooler weather, we get a surge of mice this time of year."

"There is nothing to explain, Lady Terese. I have cats roaming my halls right now for the same reason. If you have a good mouser you could spare, I would not mind the company of a cat in my chamber."

Resi agreed, "That is a perfect solution. Our barn cats are very tame. I will have one brought up right away, and that should solve the problem."

"Oh, and . . . if you could spare one of your maids, Lady Terese. I want to change out of my traveling clothes, but I will need a little help. The hooks on this dress are so tedious."

"Natalija has very nimble fingers for just such a task," Resi said.

"I will find her," Ruby offered, "and I know the perfect cat to keep you company, Lady Nikolina."

The house servants were in the kitchen together, eating their noon meal, when Ruby came in looking for Natalija.

Nela sprang to her feet to greet her. "Lady Ruby, it is so good to have you back. Are you well, dear? Are you hungry?" She held out a platter of sliced bread.

Ruby nodded and took one. She said after a big bite, "I will join the baroness for lunch, but first, I am on an errand for Lady Leopold."

"Davor just told us Lady Leopold arrived," Nela said.

"Yes, and she needs Natalija's help to change for lunch."

Natalija wiped her mouth on her apron and took a quick swig from her cup. "I would love being her lady's maid. I will be right there."

"Well, that chore was easily solved," Nela remarked as Natalija hurried out.

"Also, Lady Leopold saw two mice running across her bed," Ruby said grimly. "Lady Baric thought we could bring a barn cat to her room to catch them."

"Hmm," said Nela. "The mice will just be chased into another chamber. Better to let several cats roam the halls to be rid of the pests before winter sets in."

Verica reminded Nela, "The baron does not like animals in the house."

"That includes mice, Verica. Besides, the cats will be back in the barn before his lordship returns," Nela asserted.

Verica stood up, saying, "I am finished with my lunch. I'll go tell Geoff to catch a few cats for you."

"It will still be a while before Lady Leopold is dressed for lunch. I wouldn't mind helping Geoff find the cats," Ruby offered.

~*~

Around the courtyard, soldiers were returning from the fields and changing guards on the ramparts when Ruby and Verica came looking for Geoff. News of Ruby's return yesterday had spread throughout the castle, and the familiar faces greeted her with friendly nods and waves.

One soldier looked new, though, and she asked Verica, "Who is that man at the well?"

Verica, who had hoped to avoid meeting Felix so soon after yesterday's strange encounter, begrudgingly explained, "Oh, that is Felix. Lord Baric is training him for Count Toth's regiment. He has only been here a week."

Ruby stopped at the stable door, saying, "He keeps looking this way, and his eyes are not on me."

Verica turned away from him and stammered, "Yes, well, um, he asked me a question the other day, and I suppose he expects me to answer."

Ruby brightened with curiosity and asked, "What sort of question?"

Verica shrugged convincingly. "Oh, nothing really," she replied. "I just didn't have time before to tell him."

"Go on, then, and answer your soldier's question, and I will find Geoff. I know exactly which cats the baroness would like upstairs."

Ruby walked into the stables, leaving Verica with no choice but to set Felix straight once and for all.

~*~

The courtyard had emptied, and those not assigned duties were in the dining hall for their noon meal. Felix lingered at the well and did not seem to be in a hurry to go anywhere. He dipped the ladle into the drawn water as Verica approached.

"Did you come for a drink?" he asked.

She shook her head. "I came to tell you something."

He dropped the dipper into the bucket and asked, "That you have a better opinion of me?"

"It's not about last night," she said. "It is about what I said back in Venice at the party. I lied."

Felix lifted the edge of his broad hat and looked up at the ramparts. The three guardsmen on duty stopped pacing and stared down at him. He lowered his voice and asked, "What did you lie about?"

She wavered for a moment. Her throat was suddenly dry, but she had to get this over. "Well, you see, I was not listening to the music while I waited for you to pay attention to my request," she began.

Felix pointed up at their audience, and Verica continued in a whisper, "My focus was on leaving the party, and when you were so intent on having an answer about the song, well, you put me on the spot, Felix, so I made up an answer to hurry you along."

He began to laugh with relief. "That seems rather trivial, Verica. Is there nothing else bothering you since we last spoke?"

"It is not trivial," she said defensively. "You said you liked me for my answer. It must change your opinion of me to know I had no opinion on the music at all."

His voice was low and calm when he asked her, "You do like violin music, though, don't you? That will affect my opinion of you."

His unconventional criterion of friendship was unexpected. "Of course, I do, Felix," she assured him. "Violin music is beautiful, which is why it was the first thing that came into my head when you asked."

His exhaled relief was audible. "I thank you for clarifying that, Verica. I bid you a good day." He bowed in the regal way that was second nature to a man of his upbringing and then walked away from the well.

"Wait!" Verica called out.

He stopped and said, "I beg your pardon. I thought you had finished what you came to say." Felix pointed up to his comrades again and explained, "I am late for my shift guarding the wall."

Verica looked up at the snickering spectators and whispered urgently, "Do you not have anything to say, Felix? I just told you I lied to you. I would understand if you wanted to take back what you said outside the kitchen yesterday. You don't have to like me."

Gossip had reached the Keep about Verica now knowing Luka would marry Carmen. Felix took her continued conversation as an opening for him.

"I still mean what I said, but until you decide that you like me in return, I will keep my promise and not impose on your time, Verica."

He tipped his hat, and she watched him walk away.

~*~

Ruby and Geoff broke Verica's gloomy trance when they came up to her at the well with three squirming cats between the two of them.

"Hold out your apron," Geoff told his sister. He dropped the felines into the bunched fabric. The cats hammocked there were her two favorites.

Ruby stroked the tomcat she held in her arms. He was an old fellow and the friendliest cat in the barn.

"You didn't need my help after all," Verica told them. Her mood was light again.

Geoff pointed out, "The spotted one is pregnant again, but she is still a good mouser."

"I will leave her in Lady Baric's room, then. The soon-to-be mothers will be a good match," Verica remarked.

Ruby suggested, "The little ginger will be good in the visitor's room. She is very gentle."

Geoff stroked the head of the cat Ruby held, adding, "And old Blacky here eats his weight in mice. You should let him roam the halls."

"I see the baronesses are coming outside now. Why don't you carry the old tom upstairs, Geoff, so Lady Ruby can go ahead to lunch?"

Ruby handed off the cat and strode across the courtyard to the terrace. Verica and Geoff carried their purring burden down the shady path to the front door of the manor house.

On their way, Geoff grumbled to his sister, "I thought you were avoiding Felix."

"I never said I was avoiding him, did I?"

"Yes. Yes, you did, Verica," Geoff said too sternly.

"Well, that was when I thought I would marry Luka, and I didn't want to offend him by talking to other men," Verica reasoned. "But now it doesn't matter."

Geoff reminded her, "You said Felix was intolerable."

Holding her apron of cats closer for comfort, she admitted, "I might have been wrong about Felix. To be fair, he has gone out of his way to be kind to me. I still don't know why, though."

Their footstep crunched on the pebble. Geoff glared at his sister as they walked.

"I defended you in the stables," he pointed out. "Alberto was mad that I had done that, and he gave me a harsh talking to."

"What did Alberto say?"

They stopped in front of the manor's front door, and Geoff replied, "He said that I shouldn't interfere if you decide you like someone, even if I don't like the man."

Her tone softened when she explained, "I don't mind you interfering or standing up for me. But remember, you are the only one I can really talk to, Geoff, and I cannot promise I won't change my mind. And when I do, like this time, you should also change your mind."

Geoff scowled with puzzlement. "Josip told me girls are fickle," he said. "Since you are a girl, I suppose I should expect that from you. Just one thing, though, Verica."

"What, Geoff?"

"Even if you think you like this Felix fellow, do I really have to like him, too?"

She smiled brightly. "You are my one and only brother, Geoff, and I value your opinion."

"All right, Sister. I will keep my eye on him and let you know."

~*~

Lady Nikolina reclined against the cushions of her chair. "Your terrace is so peaceful for a lunch, Lady Terese. I simply adore your garden. You must love the calm of your castle after the bustle of Venice."

Resi agreed, "Venice is a marvelous city, but I never realized how the simple sounds of birds tweeting and rustling could be so missed."

"I have not been to the capital in years, but I was never seduced by its frivolity. But you went for a wedding at one of the noble houses if I remember correctly."

"Indeed, we were quite busy in our short time there, with the wedding parties and seeing the sights. We had planned to stay a few more weeks before the news of Jero reached us."

"How exhausting for you to have to return under such stress," Lady Nikolina said gravely. "Neven is friends with Lord Raneri, and we heard about the dead courier."

Resi was surprised the Leopolds had been told such private information. "Were the contents of the letter shared?" she asked.

"Oh, no, I doubt it. Lord Raneri is a man of confidence, and Neven did not share any more than that with me. But your heroic story, my dear Lady Ruby, is spreading across the countryside. Sailors have no scruples when it comes to gossip."

"I hope that is not true," Ruby fretted. "I am not so proud of my impulsive act."

"Nonsense," Lady Nikolina assured her. "It was incredibly brave of you to stow away with Greek pirates and demand they sail you to Solgrad to find your missing Jero. The tale is just like a romance novel. And when Mauritius brings your lost love back, you and he will marry and have a happy life together," she said with a genuine smile.

Ruby's stunned expression made it clear to Resi that Lady Nikolina's ramblings were not met as positively as the visiting baroness had intended.

Resi quickly intervened, "Ruby's story is not as dramatic as others might have told you, Lady Nikolina. The Greek ship was captained by my eldest brother, and he is merely a merchant trader, not a pirate. His ship was scheduled to meet my husband's ship in the Adriatic, and he willingly returned Ruby safely home. That is all there is to it. No pirates or coercing."

Lady Nikolina nodded politely at the revised version of Ruby's escape but asked, "How did you happen to become separated from Jero, Lady Ruby?"

If a story were to spread across the countryside, Ruby would make it her version. "There is not much to it, really. There was a misunderstanding in a restaurant in Tirana because Jero did not speak Turkish. He was detained, but we were not told for how long. Since lodgings for an unmarried woman are not always convenient, as you might appreciate, my escorts took me directly home. I have not heard from any of them for weeks, and I thought they must have come back here. So I came back myself."

"Detained?" Lady Nikolina repeated the one critical word. "The Ottomans are a brutal people, so we can only pray for Jero's safety." She backpedaled when she noticed their wide-eyed expressions. "Oh, ladies! I did not mean you and your families. We are all in agreement that the Thessalonians are from a very enlightened society. I was speaking of the uncivilized fringes of the Ottoman Empire. It is known that those places hold danger for outsiders."

Resi took her apology in stride and maintained, "Our hope is that Jero is not in danger, and Mauro can resolve any misunderstanding and bring him home. Would you like more tea?"

"Thank you." Lady Nikolina held out her cup and added, "Men like your husband know how to resolve these conflicts with civility. Time is not on his side, though."

"We are hopeful," Resi assured her firmly.

Ruby dabbed her eyes with her napkin and stood up abruptly. "If you will excuse me," she whimpered and ran from the terrace.

Nikolina shook her head sadly. "Such a pretty girl to have such heartache. Is there something we can do to cheer her up today?" she asked Resi.

"I think only Jero can do that."

~*~

The eventful few days had been hard for Resi. The grim news about Jero, Ruby's sudden return, Mauro leaving on his ship that morning and Lady Nikolina's unannounced visit that afternoon were too much, even for her. Resi made her excuses to her guest at dinner and retired to the comfort of her chamber. Before Verica could take the sharp pins from her mistress's piled curls, Resi plopped against her pillow in exhaustion and fell fast asleep with her new furry companion purring at her side.

Verica slid the shoes off the baroness's feet before covering her with a blanket and closing the shutters. She was not yet tired, so she borrowed the candelabra her mistress would not need that evening and took it to her room next door. There, Verica took out her ink and quill to practice penning her letters on the parchment the baroness had given her. Her methodical writing exercise was meant to clear her mind of Felix, but when Verica got to the letter F, she carefully wrote it across the page several times and found herself adding the letters e, l, i, and x.

This would not do. With obstinate resolve, Verica buckled her shoes, found her shawl, and went out of the quiet house into the courtyard. It was dusk, but the torches were already lit on the corners of the gated entrance. Guard duty went from noon until midnight, and Verica was confident Felix would still be on the wall. The maid couldn't see the men who walked the ramparts above her, but the four men would see her. She didn't need to call out a name, only to wait for the right man to join her.

Verica set her lantern down on the edge of the well. The rhythmic echo of the boots that sounded above her became shuffled. After a brief few minutes, a tall shadow descended the stairs along the side of the wall. It crossed the courtyard and stood in front of her.

She met his eyes, saying, "You can bother me again. Come to Mass on Sunday with the others, and we can talk on the walk home."

"Have you changed your opinion of me?" the cloaked soldier whispered.

"I don't know yet, but I do know I would like to start over, perhaps where we left off in the herbal shop."

"I would like that," he breathed out.

"Until Sunday, then. Good night, Felix."

"Good night, Verica."

Her lamplight disappeared down the path, and Felix practically floated back up the stone steps to his post.

Chapter 53

Baric Castle, 15 September 1649

Lazar opened the storeroom door. "What are you doing in here?" he asked the intruder curled up on the stone floor.

Felix jumped up from his slumber. His note-filled parchments flew from where he had propped them up to scribble on. That was hours ago. "What do you want, Lazar?" he demanded in return.

Lazar stepped over the papers scattered in his way. "I am getting a shank of ham for my pa, like I do every Monday," he said.

The servant boy had seen the odd Venetian coming and going from the Keep's pantry and reminded the newcomer, "You know, Lord Felix, there is food by the fire if you get hungry at night."

"Yes, thank you, Lazar. I will look there next time. Is it already morning?" Felix asked impatiently.

"Of course, it is morning, sir. Why else would I be fetching ham for breakfast?"

Lazar was just tall enough to reach the hanging shank, and he lifted the weighty joint from its hook with a grunt. At the same time, Felix stooped and carefully arranged the loose papers of his precious creation. "What is that funny writing on your parchment?" Lazar asked suspiciously.

"Funny writing?" Felix repeated. "Can you read, Lazar?"

"I memorized a few words Eduard puts on a list for me, like cheese and wood and what the names of the captains look like."

Felix invented a story to keep the boy from giving away his secret. "The writing on my papers is French, Lazar. They like neat lines when they mark their letters. It looks very different from ours."

The boy's face lit up with understanding, and then he took down a second ham.

Felix packed his notes in the case he kept hidden behind a basket on the pantry shelf, and Lazar asked, "Is that your sword case, sir?"

"Yes. It is my sword case," Felix lied. "You must never touch it."

He shrugged indifferently. "I won't, sir. But it looks kind of small for a proper sword. Lord Baric has a much longer sword case, and he and the baroness's brother fought over it. They were all bloody. I saw them myself," Lazar bragged.

"Is that right?" Felix asked with genuine interest. "Who won the fight?"

Lazar impressively heaved a sizable ham under each arm and said as he walked out the door, "The baron, of course."

Felix smiled to himself and said, "Of course."

The Venetian hid his music case away and pondered when he might sneak back again. He shut the solid pantry door with regret. Tonight was the start of gate duty for two days. If he had not fallen asleep, he might have finished the last part of the piece that Verica had inspired.

The armory was unmanned at that early hour, and Felix left without being noticed. He hurried up the spiral stairs to the shared bunk room. The rising sun had not yet found the narrow openings in the thick Keep walls. He climbed into his bed for five minutes of shut-eye to quell any talk of his absence as the men around him began to wake.

~*~

Nela looked up from her chopping as the door across from the kitchen table opened. "Ivana dear, I thought you were helping Idita this morning," she said.

"I helped her dress and walked with her down the stairs. She dismissed me until she is done with her patient."

"If you need a chore, there are bundles of leeks to wash and chop."

"Alright, Nela," Ivana said. She picked up the pungent vegetables by their stems, but her stare was fixed on Franja.

Nela asked the girl, "If you would you rather work with Franja, I know she has plenty you could lend a hand with, don't you, dear?"

Franja replied, "Biscuits smell better than leeks. Come help me with the trays, Ivana."

The girl perked up. "Leeks do not bother me, but I was just thinking . . ."

"Spit it out, girl," Nela said.

"I know you said we should not gossip about what the others do in the manor house, Nela, and I never would, but Simeon hasn't come by since his accident, and well, he is in the sitting room right now. I thought Franja might want to know that."

Franja put her mound of dough to the side and wiped her dusty hands on her apron. "Does he want to see me?"

"He didn't say. Idita is wrapping his stump to fit his new peg leg, so maybe after."

"Why don't you go see if Idita needs any help, Franja?" Nela suggested.

Franja took up her dough again and murmured, "Simeon could have told me he was coming by today. He could have asked that I be there."

"You are a stubborn girl, Franja. Ivana, I will trust that you will be careful with my sharp knife. I need these sliced thin." Cook turned to Franja and said, "I will go see."

Ivana took up Nela's chore and asked Franja, "Should I have told her that the baroness is helping Idita?"

~*~

Davor announced, "I am sorry to interrupt, Lady Baric, but the post came, and there are two letters for you, madam."

Resi and Ruby exchanged eager glances. "Thank you, Davor. Set them on the table there, please."

As Davor left again, he passed Nela at the door. She watched Idita, sitting in front of Simeon's amputated leg, adjusting the buckle on the leather strap that held the wooden leg in place.

Simeon looked up toward the door, and the women's eyes followed his.

At the threshold, Nela said cheerfully, "I hope I am not intruding, Lady Baric. I was worried Idita might need help."

"We are actually just finished, Nela. How does that feel, Simeon?" Idita asked her patient.

Simeon carefully pushed himself against the arms of the chair to stand. He picked up one crutch and leaned on it as he moved around.

"Is the padding thick enough?" Idita asked with concern.

"For now, I think so." He stood up straighter and said, "I can put my weight on it. It feels good, I think."

"Come back this evening, Simeon, and I will check the stump for redness. If it is rubbing too much, come back earlier," Idita ordered.

"I will. Thank you," Simeon said.

Nela held his stare as he came toward her. "There are fresh biscuits on the kitchen table if you need a little something before lunch, Simeon," she said.

The many feminine eyes upon him made him stutter with discomfort, "Oh, I, uh, am already late for the field training."

Nela crossed her arms over her bright apron. "Come with me to the kitchen door, and I will put one or two in your pocket for later, huh?"

The ladies in the room smiled encouragingly at Simeon, and he replied, "Well, that might be all right." With his second crutch, he walked steadily on his new leg to the kitchen, followed by Nela.

Idita said, "Lady Ruby, if you would not mind taking my arm on the stairs, I think I will go back to my room now."

"Of course. I was just going upstairs myself."

Idita stood with effort and nodded goodbye to her mistress. She took Ruby's offered elbow as they left the sitting room.

Alone now, Resi picked up the two letters Davor had delivered. One had Lady Isabella's seal stamped in blue wax on the seam, and the other envelope was tied with twine and stamped with several ink markings. "France" could be deciphered, and she cut the cord and opened the tattered parchment with growing curiosity. On the inside envelope, her brother's hand was more recognizable.

"What are you doing in France?" she mumbled to herself and then read the answer:

Dearest Sister, I hope this letter finds you and all those around you well and happy. What I am about to write, dear Resi, will not add to your happiness. I imagine it will bring you sorrow, and I am sorry for that. I am, however, certain of my decision.

As I write this, I am looking out over the Marseille harbor from my lodgings here. Soren and I sailed from Ragusa to France to start a new adventure. With good fortune on our side, we will leave in two days for the New World.

I know what you are thinking, dearest Terese, and I would be grateful if you would believe me that crossing the ocean is no more perilous than what I have already experienced. By the time this reaches you, we will be on a French ship, sailing to the West Indies. I already wrote to Pa, and I hope he is proud that I will finally be a sailor. Who knows, I might come back as a captain!

You must have learned Jero's fate by now. He was already gone, escaped, as you know, when we arrived in Tirana for the second time. I do not pray often, but I did ask God to keep Jero safe. God owes me no favors, but maybe he will grant this one request.

Along with Jero and Ruby, you and your new family are in my thoughts and heart. You will have your baby soon and many more before my eventual return. I will return one day, and when I do, I will play the doting uncle, as I promised you.

I do not know whether my next letter will reach you from the West Indies, but I will send one with a ship sailing back at the first chance.

I miss your sweet smile already. Your devoted brother,

Patricius

Resi set the parchment down and dabbed her eyes with the sleeve of her tunic. She took a deep breath to stop her sobbing. "You foolish man," she whispered. "I cannot lose you, too."

She looked at the second letter on the table and prayed it held happy news. She carefully cracked the sealing wax and read the flowing Latin script. She read it a second time to be sure she had deciphered Isabella's flowing script correctly.

The letter reported that Caterina and Cyro had married the day Isabella wrote the note, and despite the hurried wedding reception, all were blissfully happy. The two were to depart for Genoa at the end of the week, and Isabella would take the ferry to join Resi in Solgrad.

"Some prayers were heard," Resi whispered.

Resi put both letters in her pocket. She would answer Isabella when her mood lightened and she was no longer sad over Patricius's departure. She went with her letters to find Ruby in her room.

~*~

Meanwhile, Ruby waited with Idita at the top of the stairs for her to catch her breath. Strangely overwhelmed by the climb she had made daily for fifty years, Idita leaned on her sturdy cane. "You are very patient with an old woman," she said, "but I can walk the rest of the way now."

Ruby opened Idita's door, telling her, "You are the patient one, Idita, especially with Simeon today. I am glad you got him to agree to be fitted."

"It was my responsibility to make sure he had a leg to replace the one I took from him."

Ruby squeezed her hand as they crossed the room. "You saved his life by taking his leg, Idita."

"I did, didn't I?" The old nurse smiled and frowned all at once.

"Are you sure I cannot bring you anything? Some hot tea for your cough, perhaps?" Ruby asked.

Idita eased herself onto her cushioned chair by the window. "Ivana is bringing some later."

"I will tell her you are in your room now. Rest well, Idita," Ruby said and quietly shut the chamber door behind her.

Sitting in her chair, Idita sucked in one ragged breath. The next was more difficult, and she winced at the painful effort. Breathe in and breathe out, she thought, struggling through the pain.

When her breathing calmed, Idita looked around for her medicine basket. It held her remedy but was out of reach on the other side of her table. She stood up to get it but was startled by a man at the door.

"Ezra!" she cried out in surprise. "Is that you?"

"Shut your eyes, and you will know it is me."

With closed eyes, Idita saw Ezra clearly. Her lost lover stood in front of her, dressed in his apprentice apron, young and handsome like the last time she saw him in Venice. He smiled at her with a playfulness she found so lovable.

"I thought you had forgotten me," she said to the empty room. A wave of pain shot through her chest.

"I could never forget you, my dearest Idita, my one and only love."

"Then you got my letters? I sent them to you in Bari."

"I did not make it to Bari."

"Oh, Ezra. Where did you go?"

"Away. I have been waiting for you."

"You have a daughter, Ezra, but she is lost to both of us."

"Come away with me. We will find her together."

"Not yet. There is a new baby coming. I am needed here."

"Your work here is done, my love."

"They need my help, Ezra."

He reached out and said, "Take my hand, Idita."

"I cannot leave. There is still so much to do."

"You have done enough, my darling."

"Was it enough?"

"Let go of your worries, Idita. Are you ready?"

His warm smile drew her in, and she rose from her chair. Her movement was light and effortless. She held his outstretched hand in hers. "I am ready now."

Ivana hummed a song as she opened the door and entered Idita's chamber with her tray of hot tea and little cakes. "I brought an extra treat to go with your tea, Idita. Franja just finished baking them. Shall I put the plate on your table?"

The young maid didn't wait for an answer before setting the tray down next to Idita's chair. The overturned basket was on the floor at Idita's feet, and Ivana picked it up again.

"Oh, one of your jars broke," Ivana said. "I will bring a broom to clean it up. Shall I pour your tea first?"

When Idita did not answer, Ivana took a step closer to the old woman. Her hands were outstretched on her lap, her eyes closed, and the corners of her mouth turned up in a sweet smile.

The maid tapped Idita's hand gently to rouse her. "Wake up, Idita," Ivana said.

The nurse's hand was cold, and Ivana stepped back in fear, whispering, "I'll get the baroness. She will know what to do."

Ivana rushed out of Idita's room, and her cry rang through the house, "Lady Baric! Come quick!" The doors along the corridor began to open as the distraught girl wailed, "Idita is dead!"

Chapter 54

Tirana, 15 September 1649

Drifters and hustlers tried their luck with anyone who would stop and watch their tricks for a few coins on market day. Roman was merely one of the entertaining scammers who gathered an audience now and then among the stalls. He had been released back onto the streets after arguing his innocence at his trial in August. Broke, homeless, and friendless again, Roman did the only thing he could: get back into the business.

Going solo was more complicated than working a crowd with partners, but the money Roman earned was all his to keep. No one remembered that Roman's ill-concocted potion had landed him and his unlucky companions in jail a few months ago. He would soon have enough to move on from Tirana, to find a better place to play his hustle.

It had been a good morning on the plaza, despite the threat of heavy rain. Mauro, Hugo, and Vilim were among the shoppers walking through the stalls. Even in their simple traveling clothes, the outsiders drew attention as they walked beside their horses on the street. Their horses were what caught Roman's eye, and he went to see if they were the Venetians that Jero had expected to save him.

Roman jogged up alongside the passing trio, got a good look at the taller man's face, and decided he could be Jero's brother. The conman held up cards and called out in broken Slovenian, "Allow me to tell your fortune, sir. It will only take a minute."

Mauro snubbed the peddler's offer and kept walking. "Not today, good man," he muttered.

Roman insisted, "Today is all you have, my lord, if you want to find your brother."

Mauro stopped on the spot. "What did you say?"

Roman took a chance. "I knew your brother," he said, barely audible, worried who else was looking their way.

"Where is he now?" Mauro demanded.

Roman scanned the nearby stalls and warned, "The streets have many eyes and ears, sir. There is an inn at the western edge of town called The Pelican. I have a room there, and we can talk privately."

Vilim suspiciously said, "We were told to ask for information at a different inn."

Roman said to the second stranger, "Of course, you were, sir. The inn you are looking for is run by Isaak Linos, the old Greek. Isaak can tell you some things, but I can tell you what you want to know."

The three Venetians surrounded him, and Mauro asked, "Why should we take your word, Fortune-teller?"

Roman nearly backed down at the threat, but a flash of Jero's soft eyes showed in the stern glare of the baron's. He spoke directly to Mauro and hastily whispered, "I was a prisoner with your brother. My name is Roman. Jero helped me in my time of need, and I want to return the favor . . . Baron Baric."

Mauro nodded to Vilim and Hugo, and they stepped aside. "We will find The Pelican after we talk to this Isaak Linos. Where is his inn?"

"You are nearly there, sir. His lodging house is across from the red canopy at the end of the market." Then Roman cautioned, "Do not linger with your horses on the main street. The police might decide they want to talk to you. There is a stable next door to Isaak's place."

Mauro frowned at the possibility of being interrogated and thanked the hustler, "You have been very helpful, Roman. We will find you shortly."

~*~

No one paid Vilim and Mauro any attention when they took seats at a dirty table in the back corner of the restaurant. The waiter on duty was a young man with a stained apron tied over his billowing trousers. "I am Iason, at your service, sirs. Our plate of the day is roasted kid, or we have grilled sardines. What can I bring you?"

"Do you serve ale?" Vilim asked.

The waiter did not pretend to approve. "We do, sir," he replied.

Mauro ordered for the two, "Just drinks for now. Is the innkeeper around?"

The waiter pointed to the bar where a gray-haired man was talking intently to an unhappy serving girl.

"Can you tell him we would like a word with him?" Mauro said.

The waiter shrugged. He was new to this job and didn't know all that had transpired in this same dining room that summer. He left and went to the bar.

A few moments later, the patron greeted the Venetians, "Welcome, gentlemen. Iason thought you might need lodging for the night?"

"Are you Isaak Linos?"

"I am," he said with a diplomatic smile. "How can I help you?"

The girl Isaak had been scolding by the counter brought Mauro and Vilim their drinks. She watched the two skeptically until Isaak dismissed her.

"That will be all, Galena."

After Galena left, Mauro told the innkeeper, "Patrik Kokkinos left a note in your care. I have come to retrieve it."

The old Greek's eyes widened, and his smile faded as he stammered, "Oh, yes, yes, um, you must be the Venetian they expected. I have two messages for you, sir. The Persian left a letter as well."

Vilim asked, "Salar Nassim?"

"Yes, that was his name," Isaak said. He went quickly across the room for a man his age and rummaged through a box behind the counter. "It has been a while, gentlemen. Just give me a moment," he called over.

Isaak scratched his head in his forgetfulness. He sorted through a cabinet with bottles and extra glassware before taking down a locked chest from the highest shelf. He smiled with satisfaction and brought the two sealed letters to the table, setting them in front of Mauro. The baron's name was on the front of each.

"When your friends left and your brother disappeared, trouble found my door, as well," Isaak said in a hushed voice. "They took my serving girl in for questioning, and I was certain they would call me in, too, so I hid these in my lockbox, just in case. I swore to your friends I would keep their letters in confidence. I kept my word, sir."

"Your continued confidence will, of course, be rewarded. But we have a few questions first," Mauro said.

Vilim nodded and asked, "You said 'they.' Who took your serving girl?"

"The police," Isaak replied. "When Captain Poljani couldn't find your brother, they arrested Zerina, suspecting she had something to do with it."

"Where is she now? Can we talk to her?" Mauro asked hopefully.

Isaak shook his head pitifully. "Zerina is dead."

The Venetians exchanged troubled glances. "I am sorry to hear that," Vilim mumbled.

"Yes, well, so am I. She was a good worker, but bad luck always followed Zerina. They say she committed suicide."

The news seemed to catch them by surprise. "When was this?" Mauro asked.

"After they jailed her, she hung herself with her apron," Isaak grimly explained. "I didn't believe them, but they gave me her body with the ties still wrapped around her neck. They said that proved her guilt."

"Guilt over what? Did she help Jero escape?" Vilim asked.

Isaak shrugged and said, "No one will ever know. The dead do not talk."

Mauro listened to the disturbing tale with one nagging thought: "Would my brother have gotten a fair trial had he not escaped?"

"He was accused of murder, you know. Or, I should say, that your father was accused, and Poljani wanted your brother to hang for it. If I were you, sir, I would not linger in Tirana to find out whether anyone would get a fair trial for that crime."

"We will heed your advice," Mauro said. His bag was at his feet, and he reached into it for coins to pay the innkeeper for his troubles. His hand touched something familiar next to the purse of silver he sought, giving him a nudge of hope.

Mauro put a small linen pouch on the table before Isaak, saying, "This should cover your losses. Thank you for keeping your word to our friends."

Picking it up, Isaak felt its ample weight and said, "I thank you, sir. I am sorry that you had to come all this way for nothing. Your brother is long gone."

Mauro stood up to leave, but Vilim said, "One more question, Isaak. The name Roman was mentioned to us. Do you know a man by this name?"

"Roman, the entertainer?"

Vilim said, "Perhaps."

"I have seen him about, and he's had a few meals in my establishment. I believe he was in jail the same time as Jero."

"What for?" Mauro asked.

Isaak smiled as he recalled the circumstances. "Roman got caught cheating the wrong person. If I remember right, his two partners died in jail, but Roman has a knack for talking his way out of things. As I recall, he was finally released with only a fine."

Mauro patted the two sealed papers he had put into his pocket and said, "Thank you for everything."

After leaving Isaak's lodging house, the two met up with Hugo in the stables around the corner.

"That didn't take long. Was the innkeeper helpful?" Hugo asked.

"Somewhat," Mauro answered. "Both Patrik and Salar Nassim left letters behind."

"What did they write?" Hugo wanted to know.

"I have not opened them, but whatever they had to say, I fear their advice comes too late."

"Do you still want to hear what the fortune-teller has to say?" Vilim asked Mauro. "I am sort of curious whether his story matches Isaak's."

"I am anxious to leave this town, but I think we can risk a visit."

~*~

Roman was pacing impatiently when a knock on his door rattled the thin walls of the small room. He eagerly invited the three men in. "Have a seat wherever you want, gentlemen."

Mauro got right to the reason for their meeting. "You were in jail with my brother. What happened to him there?"

Roman sat down in his nervousness, with the three staring at him. "Yes, well, we shared a cell in the beginning. Then the jail commander, Captain Poljani, moved me into another cell to punish Jero."

"He moved you to punish him?" Mauro asked.

Roman explained, "Poljani thought your brother was being defiant and isolating him would weaken Jero's will. Or at least the commander believed that."

"Why was Jero arrested in the first place? Do you know?" Vilim asked.

"Yes, yes, yes," Roman said with a steady nod. "Jero's friends figured the scam out from the start. One of the sergeants wanted to extort some quick money from Jero's friends for the death of his cousin, whom they had crossed paths with a few days before. But when the captain learned Jero's name, he charged him with a different murder. He thought Jero owed him a blood debt. Jero's father, your father, killed his brother after a battle."

"That is absurd," Hugo asserted.

"War is war, and soldiers get killed in every battle," Vilim maintained.

Mauro was more sedate than his companions, pointing out, "My father never fought the Ottomans."

Roman agreed eagerly, "Of course, that is what Jero said all along, and his friends were convinced that he could easily defend that to the magistrate."

"Salar Nassim and Bem?" Vilim interrupted. "Did you talk to them?"

"Not directly, no, but they came to our cell every day for a while. They thought if Jero could just wait it out until the trial, he would be set free, and they would be on their way. But after his companions left, Poljani wanted the debt paid."

"Do you know how Jero escaped?" Mauro asked. "Did you help him plan it out?"

"Jero never talked about escaping, even after the first round of torture."

"He was tortured?" Hugo exclaimed.

"Was he hurt badly?" Mauro wanted to know.

"Not badly, no," Roman assured him. "Poljani cares more about breaking a man's spirit than causing him lasting harm. But the captain mistook your brother's kindness for weakness. Jero was not broken by the torture."

Mauro looked at his companions with relief.

Roman clarified, "Still, Poljani was not going to let him go to trial. After Jero recovered from the second round, the captain was angered. The guards let it slip that he was planning an accident for your brother."

Hugo surmised, "Jero learned about that and had to escape to save himself. But how?"

Roman shrugged, telling them, "That is where facts get murky. Your friends paid a servant girl to bring him food each night. Zerina would have heard the rumors and might have helped him."

Mauro nodded with understanding, and Roman remarked, "So you talked to Isaak, then."

"He said the police had charged her for helping Jero," Vilim answered.

Roman scoffed. "The guards admitted that Zerina had been there, sure, but she couldn't have stolen the key, let him out, and put the key back again without anyone seeing something."

"So why did they arrest her if it was so unlikely?" Mauro asked.

"I heard she was charged with prostitution, but she was able to argue her way out of it, despite the facts."

Hugo pointed out, "You said the guards admitted she was with them the night Jero escaped."

"Yes, well, but that is not a crime. They all agreed she wasn't paid for sex that night. It might have been immoral, but agreeing to sex is not prostitution. And since she was not a married woman, it was not adultery either. The magistrate is not interested in enforcing a citizen's morality. That is a matter left for the holy men."

"Why did she kill herself, then?" Vilim asked.

"Kill herself? Ha! She was strangled! We prisoners were practically witnesses. We could hear Zerina arguing with Poljani from her cell, insisting she go free. Then the argument turned to muffled cries, and then silence. Shortly thereafter, the captain walked past our cell, and we all knew what he had done. Two guards came by, and they must have hung her from the window bars. It would have been impossible for her to hang herself."

"It is all very tragic, indeed," Mauro murmured.

"But what about Jero?" Vilim pressed Roman. "Did they not search for him?"

"Of course," Roman said. "They even offered a reward. If someone had found Jero's body, they would have told the authorities for the money. No one came forward. Jero is gone, sir; that is for sure."

The three exchanged nods.

"Thank you for your insight, Roman. Is there something I can do for you?" Mauro asked.

"Your brother's charity saved my life, Lord Baric. My help to you today pales in comparison to the kindness he showed me."

"Then you really did meet Jero," Mauro reflected.

At the door, Roman asked, "If Jero does find his way home, will you let him know I cleared my name?"

Mauro assured him, "I will be sure to tell him."

Once outside The Pelican, Vilim asked, "Where to now, Mauro?"

Mauro said what the other two would not, "There is no reason to go any farther. There is nothing more we can do for Jero."

~*~

The port city of Dirac was only a few hours away. Ivanoslav and his crew were waiting there, docked at a crowded pier, when the three returned. They walked their horses up the makeshift bridge onto the ship.

"Make ready to sail home, Ivanoslav. I will be below deck," Mauro told his captain.

Ivanoslav did not ask for any details about the baron's search. He merely nodded and replied, "Yes, Lord Baric."

Most of the sailors followed their baron below deck and sat at the long oar handles to direct the ship into the open Adriatic. Above deck, the remaining crewmen set the sails to catch the wind home.

Mauro plopped down on a bale of hay loaded for the horses. He leaned against a thick beam as the vessel lurched forward. They were underway, and the oarsmen left the baron alone in the dimly lit belly of his ship. He was both relieved to be heading home and panicked that he had to travel again over the depths that still filled him with dread.

Troubled thoughts washed over Mauro like the water slapping on the sides of his ship until he remembered the talisman his wife had hidden in his bag. He felt for his grandmother's cross. Green sparks flickered in the cut emerald when he pulled it out and passed it over the lamplight.

Mauro recalled seeing his mother holding this same cross in prayer. Had it worked for her? Clutching it, he shut his eyes and whispered in defeat, "Am I to give up on another brother, God? I beg of you: bring Jero home to me."

He opened his eyes again before he tucked the crucifix back into his bag and took out the two letters Isaak had given him. The words on the parchment were blurry when he unsealed the first envelope. He wiped his tearing eyes to read them.

Patrik had penned this letter after they returned to Tirana from Thessaloniki. Along with explaining Jero's escape they already knew about, his brother-in-law wrote that he was crossing the Atlantic with Soren to the New World. There were no other clues in the note to help Mauro in his search for Jero.

The letter from Salar Nassim was more rewarding. The Persian had done his best to protect Jero until Bem learned the news about his wife, Fatina. The tone of Salar Nassim's final letter was upbeat, and his words reflected his belief that all would end well for everyone, even Jero. Reading it, Mauro could not know that the author of the uplifting note was now dead and buried in an unmarked grave, and Bem was miserable in the company of the one woman he had thought would make him happy.

Chapter 55

Ottoman Territory, 17 August 1649

Alone on the deserted bank of the shallow river, Bem silently struggled to come to terms with Salar Nassim's death. In his grief, he walked the riverbank until he found just the right place for his friend.

The small cave was not far from where the bullet from Sadik's soldier had found its mark on Salar Nassim's back. Bem carried Nassim's body to a soft pit he had dug in the sandy floor. He placed the Persian's sword in his friend's right hand and laid Nassim's battered shield over his still heart.

Freed from the bond of Sadik's house but traumatized from losing her baby boy to gain that freedom, Fatina sobbed in sporadic fits while she helped her husband bury his friend. Bem sent her to gather stones from the cave's entrance to line the final resting place while he scooped sand into the shallow grave. He said a Muslim prayer over his friend and mentor; then Bem and Fatina went out into the daylight again.

"We only have a few hours before nightfall, but I don't want to sleep here. Can you ride my horse alone, Fatina?" he asked.

Fatina had not said a word since they entered the cave. Her guilt over the warrior's death was overwhelming, and her husband was still a stranger to her. She replied with a weak nod.

~*~

It was not far from Skopje to the gates of Thessaloniki, only three days on horseback. Each day together was a little easier than the last as the couple became reacquainted. Bem had been so desperate to find his wife, and he ached for Fatina to love him again. But instead of forcing her love, Bem remembered his broken friend Soren. He had come back to life with time, and Bem would give Fatina the time she needed to put her painful past behind her.

Their unexpected arrival in Thessaloniki was celebrated as a welcome diversion. The Kokinnos family drew strength from the stories Bem could tell them about his adventures with their son over the years and their last, fateful journey together.

Bem was eager to introduce his wife to the Kokkinoses, and they embraced her as family. For Bem's sake, Fatina pretended that all was well. Concealing her unhappiness was made easier with the news that Ruby would indeed wed Jero when he arrived in Thessaloniki. Patrik's fateful letter explaining his escape would not come for another week.

The couple stayed in Thessaloniki long enough to settle Bem's affairs and plan the next leg of their journey. They would travel by ship to spare Fatina the strenuous ride to Athens on horseback. Bem sold his horses to Angelos Spiros and hawked all of his and Salar Nassim's gear, except his favorite pistol and sword.

The Greek women insisted Fatina shop with them for new clothes to start her new life. Bem was grateful for the help and encouragement they gave his wife. After a tearful farewell to the Kokkinos and Spiros families, the couple pressed on to Athens to deliver the sorrowful news of Salar Nassim's death to Nassim's second wife, the love of his life, Emine.

~*~

In Athens, Bem and Fatina were met with tragic news. The houses on the street where Emine lived had been destroyed in a fire since Bem had last visited. Rubble covered the lot where her home had once stood, and the new neighbors didn't know if Emine had even survived the fire. With no alternative place to look, Bem left a letter of regret with the neighbors in case she returned to her burned-out house. He could do no more than that for Salar Nassim's widow.

From there, Bem and Fatina booked passage on a ship to Salar Nassim's second home in Rhodes. Bem restlessly watched the sailors maneuver the large vessel around the archipelago of rocky islands from the fringes of the deck. Fatina insisted he ask the ship's captain if he could lend an idle hand, and the amused captain obliged him.

Fatina kept off the deck and out of the baking sun. She had been trained in whiling away a long day of nothingness as a handmaiden. Fatina had purchased spools of colorful thread, and she passed the time embroidering decorative details on the simple robes she had bought on her shopping spree. Fatina was good at games of skill and chance from her years entertaining her mistress, Alimah, and she and Bem would play a quiet game to pass the evening.

On one particular day, as the ship sailed uneventfully on the open sea, Bem came back to their tiny cabin to see how Fatina amused herself. The shutter was closed, and Bem cautiously entered, thinking Fatina might be sleeping. She wasn't. She was trying on the new robe she had been busily sewing.

"You've finished," Bem said from the doorway.

She gasped, embarrassed at being caught relishing her new creation. "You startled me!"

"Show me what you are working on," Bem said kindly, and she turned around for him. "I had no idea you were so skilled with the needle. Your work is beautiful."

She held her arms out to show him the full effect of the stitched sleeves and the embroidered sash. "Do you really like it? I still need to stitch the hem."

"You look very pretty," Bem said. He closed the space between them and stroked her cheek. He felt her tremble. "Now, will you take it off for me, Fatina?"

She stiffened under his gentle touch.

"Only if you want to, Fatina," he added.

"What do you desire?"

Bem sat down on their shared bed and beckoned her to join him. He stroked her cheek again and touched her hair. "Do you remember how I used to touch you like this? You would shut your eyes and sigh with anticipation. I could feel you melting into me when I made love to you. That is what I desire again, Fatina. I am not Sadik, my love. I will not hurt you."

She locked her fingers in her lap and bowed her head in shame. "I cannot overcome my dread."

"Whatever you endured in Sadik's bed is in the past, Fatina. I am the same Chidubem you married. I will always cherish you, always treat you with love."

"I want to feel that again," she whimpered. "I just need a little more time." It was the same request every night: just a little more time.

Bem nodded solemnly. "May I give you a kiss, Fatina?"

"You are my husband. It is your right," she said and braced herself.

Bem took one clenched hand from her lap and touched it lightly to his lips. Then Bem left her sitting on the edge of the bed and closed the cabin door.

Fatina fell back onto her pillow and began to weep.

~*~

Leaning on the railing, Bem could barely contain his eagerness to be off the ship. After a week at sea, stopping at small ports along the way, Bem and Fatina, at last, watched the grand island of Rhodes grow on the horizon. Like Thessaloniki, the prized, ancient harbor had been conquered by every powerful navy since history began. Its dominance showed in the architecture of the many castles and villas that loomed above the port.

Bem took Fatina's hand and kissed it excitedly. She did not flinch or squirm at his loving gesture but smiled back at her husband with the same enthusiasm. "It looks inviting, Bem, even promising."

"Just this one last visit, Fatina, and then we can finally make our own plans."

Bem gathered their meager belongings, and the two followed the other passengers off the crowded deck. Once they left the bustling harbor, Bem hired a donkey to carry their baggage and speed their walk to their destination a few miles beyond the city.

The cobbled road to Salar Nassim's family home meandered by another fishing village outside the port. There, the small boats were done for the day; the nets hung neatly onshore, readied for another outing on the sea. Beyond the weathered fishing docks, the road straddled the gentle hillside, and vibrant colors splashed the suntanned earth under the blue September sky.

The planted fields and colorful houses were a feast for their eyes after the liquid monotony of the azure sea. Purple grapes hung fat on the vines growing along the pale stone fences dividing the fields they passed. Farther up the road, pomegranates reddened lazily on a row of trees while little birds pecked at the sticky remains of black figs dangling from a neighboring tree along a wall.

"I think this is the house up ahead," Bem announced. "The man in the village said it was the one with the blue shutters."

He helped Fatina down from the back of the donkey and drew strength from her encouraging smile. Salar Nassim's last possessions were strapped on the pack animal. Bem took the bulky satchel in one hand and his wife's hand in the other to face his last duty to his friend.

The stone blocks of the modest house matched the low wall that surrounded its large garden. Chickens pecked below the pink oleander that reached over the creaking gate. Bem shut it just as a barking dog bounded toward them.

Fatina smiled enviously at the idyllic home, with its laundry blowing on the line in front of the Aegean Sea they had just come from. She petted the friendly hound that followed them to the blue front door, and Bem knocked confidently on it.

A servant girl answered. "Yes?" she said to the strangers.

"My name is Bem Tavares. I have come to talk to Hafza on behalf of her husband. Is your mistress at home?"

"Wait here."

The servant left them standing in the open doorway. The afternoon sea breeze drifted up the long hallway, which ended at a bank of opened windows in a sitting room. Bem tried to recall whether Salar Nassim had ever lived in the house he had bought for his first wife and her parents to raise his little girl. But Shirin was no longer little, although she was not much older than the skeptical servant girl who accompanied her to the door.

Nassim's daughter entered the hallway, tall and beautiful in her gauzy robe and a sheer veil. Without a welcome, the girl said, "Harmonia tells me you came to speak to Hafza."

Bem bowed politely to the pretty hostess. "I am Bem Tavares, a friend of Hafza's husband, Salar Nassim. Is she home?"

"She is dead," the veiled girl said flatly. "I am her daughter. What can I help you with?"

The unexpected announcement jolted Bem as he tried to decide how to proceed.

Fatina came to his rescue, saying, "I am sorry for your loss. You must be Shirin. The news my husband brings for your mother is for you as well. May we come in?"

She begrudgingly offered, "We can sit on the terrace out front. Harmonia, will you bring our guests refreshments?"

When they were seated, Bem asked, "Your father did not know your mother had died. Was it recent?"

"It has been a year now," Shirin told him. She studied Bem's grave expression and said, "You came to tell me my father is dead, didn't you?"

"I am sorry. He was on his way here to see you when he was killed. His dying wish was that I bring you his treasured possessions." Bem set the bag he carried over his shoulder on the table and said, "I knew your father well. He spoke often of you, Shirin, and about how much he loved and missed you."

Shirin pushed the bag away. "Whatever you brought, you can give to his other wife. We did just fine without him all these years."

Bem did not tell her Emine was most likely dead. Instead, he insisted, "Everything your father did was for a better life for his family. He wanted these to go to you."

"There is no more family," Shirin contended, "and I don't need whatever you have brought."

"Do you live alone here?" Fatina asked.

Shirin replied coolly, "I take care of my grandmother. She is in the house."

Harmonia brought the steaming tea, glasses, and a pot of crystal sugar on a tray. Shirin set the bag on the ground to make room for it and asked indifferently, "Can I pour you some tea, sir?"

Bem did not care about tea. He only cared about finishing what he had come there for. He reached into his pocket and set two rings next to the tea tray on the table. Shirin stared at them.

"Your father wanted you to have his rings. He said they were to remind him of the love he was fighting for."

"I don't want them. I don't want anything."

"Do as you wish with these and everything else I have brought. I have done what Salar Nassim asked, and I thank you for your hospitality, Shirin."

He stood up, and Fatina followed his lead.

"Before I go," he said, "I am bound by a promise to leave you with a message. When your father knew he was dying, he had me write it down in a letter to you."

Bem took the folded parchment from his breast pocket and set the small square on the table next to the rings. "Read it when you are ready to forgive him," Bem counseled. "May peace be with you, Shirin."

When Fatina and Bem returned to the gate and their waiting donkey, Fatina asked, "Will you tell me what was in the letter?"

Bem led the beast down the cobbled hillside and pondered aloud, "Did I ever tell you about my father, Fatina?"

"Bits and pieces."

"Yes, well, Nassim and I had a lot of time to talk while we were looking for you. In one conversation, I told him what I most remembered about my father was that he had left me when I was eleven."

"He left you with the Jesuits, at a Portuguese settlement, right?"

"That's right. But I probably never told you how angry I was at him for leaving me there. The longer I waited for him, the more I hated him for abandoning me. And after a time, I convinced myself that my father was happier without the burden of a needy son. Salar Nassim defended my father. He told me everything the angry boy still deep within me needed to hear. And on the riverbank, before he took his last breath, Salar Nassim reminded me of our conversation. He asked that I tell Shirin what I had wanted to hear as a boy. So, I wrote exactly that. In time, she will forgive Salar Nassim for not being there, like I forgave my father."

Bem shook off his melancholy, looked up at his beautiful wife on the donkey's back, and said, "But that is all in the past, Fatina. We are starting anew today."

"I have been thinking about the future, Bem," Fatina said warily. "As I listened to Shirin and saw how alone and empty she seemed when we parted, I realized I have everything I need now to fill my emptiness. I was wrong to shun you these past weeks."

Bem stopped walking, but his heart raced when he asked, "Are you saying you can love me again?"

Her voice trembled. "That is what I am trying to say. I want to start again. Maybe we can stay here," she said hopefully. "You can buy a small boat and learn to fish, and I can tend our goats and grow a garden. Maybe we can have a baby or two."

Bem laughed with delight. "I want all that with you, Fatina, but why here?"

"Why not? This is far enough away, and Rhodes is big enough to get lost in. I am ready to be on solid ground, Bem, not packing and moving from place to place any longer."

Bem tugged the rope of the beast and began to walk with Fatina again. He led them past the moored boats at the village dock, toward the city, thinking about her choice.

Finally, he admitted, "I have roamed without a home and lived from a saddlebag for years. I want to settle somewhere, but not in Ottoman lands."

She frowned and asked, "Where else would we go?"

A smile brightened Bem's handsome features when he said, "What if we took one more ship to a place with sunbaked castles and endless views of the sea?"

Fatina laughed and pointed at the tall fortress across the harbor. "If that is what you seek, then we do not have to travel far."

Bem's certainty grew when he saw the ships loading in the harbor. "I am not a fisherman, Fatina, and I cannot do what I truly want to in this Empire."

She stroked the gentle beast carrying her and asked, "Where do you want to go, then? Portugal?"

"Did I tell you about my friend Cyro?" he asked with budding enthusiasm.

"The one who helped you find me?" she recalled.

"Cyro is a good man and a good friend. He told me there would always be a place for me in Corsica. His family owns horses and has a small army. That is what I know, Fatina, and that is what makes me happy—after you, of course."

Fatina stared out over the city on the hillside that she would never call home. "I will go wherever you go, Bem."

Bem quickened his pace, telling her, "I promise we will plant roots and grow our family."

"When can we leave?" she asked with renewed courage.

At the harbor, the ship they had arrived on was reloading supplies for the journey back to Athens. Bem pointed to the pier and said, "The captain told me they will sail on the evening wind."

"I like the sound of that. Then let us be on our way."

~*~

Alone at the table, Shirin tapped her father's two rings in front of her. She recognized them from her spotty memories. She gave in and slid one ring on each hand. The sun had heated the gold, and she took comfort in their warmth.

Shirin then opened the satchel and moaned at the burden of the inheritance. There were pouches of coins—gold and silver—a fortune for anyone, especially a solitary teen.

She closed the bag again. She didn't want his treasure; she wanted her father back. She bowed her head in her hands and wept. In her sorrow, Shirin searched her memory. What did her pa even look like? How did he sound? She remembered how he would carry her on his strong shoulders to the village while she pretended she was a sultana, riding on her fine steed. They would laugh and laugh. What else?

Her mother had always served her father's tea, never coffee, and the sweeter, the better. Mother made sure she had enough sugar when he was home. Her mother preferred honey, but honey wasn't the same to him. Her parents disagreed on that and many other things.

Shirin put three spoonfuls of sugar into a cup and poured the hot tea how he liked it. She fought back the tears for a man she barely remembered but must have once loved.

Then she picked up the letter on the table. She gripped it, pondering while she drank her soothing drink. When the cup was empty, she broke the wax seal and opened the folded page, penned in Bem's neat handwriting, the way the Jesuits had taught him. She stared at the Turkish words meant to make up for a lifetime of loss. There were only four lines on the parchment, and Shirin read the last one over and over: "I should have stayed."

Chapter 56

Ivana leaned her weight on the handle of the apple press before rotating it. "I love the smell of apples, but I wish we were finally done with the juicing," she said.

"It looks like my husband is going to spoil your wish," Danica told her, pointing to Krsto wheeling a cart up the walkway.

He said, "This is the last load from the orchard."

The maids moaned in reply.

"Ah, don't be glum, girls," Krsto said. "Just think about the extra cider we will have at Christmastime."

Danica eyed the basket slung over his back. "Leave us what you are carrying, Krsto, but the cartload can go into the barrels in the cellar."

Krsto set the basket down with a thud. He kissed his wife on her forehead and patted her protruding middle with a smile before rolling the heavy cart away.

Looking into the sack, Marija groaned, "There must still be hundreds of apples to press."

"Cheer up, Marija," Brigitte said, "Franja will make some nice apple pockets with the pulp."

"Sprinkled with cinnamon and honey?" Marija asked hungrily.

"Maybe even with thick cream on top," Ivana added.

Their culinary fantasies were interrupted by Geoff. He ran up to the maid under the grape arbor, panting, and asked, "Is the baroness out here?"

"She is in the house," Danica said.

"I looked there. I didn't see Verica, either."

"What do you need her for?" Ivana called out.

He shouted back as he ran off, "A carriage is coming!"

~*~

Nestor heard the clip-clopping of hooves coming closer to the house and looked out the study window. A red and gold carriage stopped on the driveway at the front door. Bags were strapped to the low roof, and a bulky trunk was tied to the rack of the regal vehicle. The driver jumped down from his perch and opened the small door for two ladies who awkwardly descended the iron steps.

Nestor recognized the unlikely passengers and called out, "Davor!" Mauro's valet stood just beyond the door. "Tell Lady Baric that Lady Isabella and her companion have arrived."

Running down the foyer from the kitchen, Geoff stopped in his tracks when he saw Nestor's scolding scowl. "I am sorry, Nestor, but a strange carriage is coming!"

"I can see that, but since you are here, *walk* upstairs and tell the baroness that Lady Isabella has arrived. Her ladyship is in Idita's room. Davor, you can help with the luggage," Nestor said with authority.

Davor followed Nestor out the front door, and Geoff ran up the marble staircase, Nestor's scolding already forgotten.

In Idita's chamber, Verica and Natalija were turning the feather mattress, and the baroness and Ruby were crouched over an open trunk.

"I wonder whose baby gown this was," Ruby thoughtfully said as she admired the faded ivory lacework.

They had pulled Idita's trunk into the middle of the room and unpacked the many gifts given to her by generations of Barics. There were pocket pictures of the children she had raised and memorabilia of her former life. Resi and Ruby unhappily sorted through the items.

Geoff poked his head in and broke the solemn mood hanging heavily over the room. "Lady Baric?" he said.

The startled women turned in the direction of the stable boy.

"Oh, I, um," he stuttered with sudden embarrassment, "Nestor sent me to find you. Lady Isabella is here, madam. In a big, red carriage!"

Resi stood up with effort from having kneeled for so long. "Are you sure it is Lady Isabella?" she asked the boy.

He nodded excitedly.

"Her letter did say she would arrive at the end of the week," Ruby reminded her friend.

"In a carriage?" Resi wondered, then turned to Natalija and asked, "Is her room ready?"

"Everything is ready, my lady," Natalija replied. "I will find Aron to fill the pitchers."

"I'll tell him. I know where he is," Geoff said before disappearing from the doorway.

Verica put the pillows back onto the remade bed and took off her apron. "Shall I bring tea to the sitting room, Lady Baric?" she asked.

Resi said with a fresh glow of excitement, "Tea with Lady Isabella is just the remedy for our low spirits."

~*~

Isabella set her cup down on the low table in front of her. "I am glad I won't have to make the crossing again anytime soon. I had no idea how awful traveling by sea is."

Resi was taken aback by her comment: "We had rather pleasant weather here the last few days. I am sorry the sea was so rough, Isabella."

Isabella's velvet hat quivered as she shook her head. "The sea was calm enough, Terese, but the ship itself was intolerable."

Resi's questioning expression prompted Isabella to clarify, "I suppose traveling on one's own ship could be pleasant. Mauritius has everything in order, I am sure. But the ferry to Croatia is not exactly a luxury voyage, which is why Fabian reserved a room for me on board." She took a sip of her tea and added, "It was the least he could do since he could not escort me himself."

"What a pity you had to travel without him," Ruby said mournfully, dwelling on her own missing mate.

Isabella replied, "It all might have been acceptable if Anastasia and I were not invaded."

"Invaded?" Resi and Ruby cried in unison.

"There is no other word for it," Isabella said, taking her teacup. "Fabian had already helped us settle in before the ship set sail and said his goodbyes when, quite unannounced, the captain himself escorted a lady into the room and introduced her as Signora Mirabella. It seemed this awful woman claimed to have booked the one cabin on board and would not budge from her opinion. The captain feigned an excuse of having to keep to his schedule, and he left the four of us crammed in the tiny box of a room like a fat lady in a corset."

Intrigued, Ruby leaned closer and asked, "What did you do?"

"What could I do? I held my ground. The cabin was mine."

"What did the lady say when you didn't leave?" Resi asked.

Isabella rolled her eyes and shivered at the memory. "It's not what she said, but what she did. Right from the start, her maid opened a basket, and the horrible matron began eating the most odorous haunch of roasted lamb. She said eating fatty flesh would help her avoid seasickness, but I think she planned it to cause my own sickness. I could not stay in the stuffy room after that, of course, and the witch knew it." Isabella picked up a biscuit from the porcelain plate and added, "I spent most of the journey in the open air."

"Fresh air is always calming for me," Resi remarked kindly.

"I had hoped so, too, dear Terese, but to my shock, the ship's deck was overloaded with people leaning on the railings and sitting in every corner. It was all quite different from when I had boarded the ship. It felt more like the crowd on market day than a sea voyage. Stacked crates of squawking animals were piled high everywhere. Now I understand your husband's aversion to the whole crossing ordeal."

The sailors' daughters exchanged knowing looks.

Resi told her guest, "I see how that must have been dreadful for you."

Isabella agreed breathlessly, "Indeed, it was, but the strain of the voyage was forgotten when I arrived and saw what was waiting at the harbor."

"Geoff said you came in a carriage. That was thoughtful of Fabian," Resi remarked.

"Fabian did not arrange my ride. It was divine intervention."

Chuckling, Resi set her teacup down. "God arranged a carriage at the harbor?" she asked.

"Well, Fabian did hire a wagon for the rest of the way to Solgrad, but when I told the driver my name, he led me to the carriage instead. Now, is it my fault the Croatians cannot understand proper Venetian?"

Ruby was puzzled. "What do you mean?"

Isabella said with a smirk, "He only listened to my first name and mistook Isabella for Mirabella."

"Oh! There is a Mirabella family in Dalmatia," Resi recalled. "Lord Mirabella was at our ball this summer."

"And his sister was in my cabin," Isabella said with a laugh.

"You took her carriage?" Resi asked.

"Of course, I did. She sat warm and dry in my cabin, so why shouldn't I ride warm and dry in her carriage? I did have a difficult time persuading the driver to leave me at Baric Castle instead of her brother's manor house."

Ruby covered her open mouth to keep from laughing, and Resi asked what they both were thinking, "How will she get there, Isabella? Lord Mirabella will worry over his missing sister when she doesn't arrive."

"She is not lost, Terese. As we drove away, they were loading her things into my hired wagon. The beast of a woman will arrive eventually and with all her luggage. I, on the other hand, will have to wait until tomorrow before they can deliver the rest of my things." Her lips curled into a broad smile when she added, "I am quite satisfied, though. It was a very elegant ride."

There was a noticeable droop to Ruby's bright smile when she remarked, "It has been a long day for you, Lady Isabella."

Resi asked, "Would you like to freshen up? We ourselves have been sorting all afternoon and will need to change for dinner."

Isabella's cheerful expression turned gloomy at the reminder. "Oh, ladies, do forgive me for going on about my plight," she said as she fretted, "I forgot I am arriving in the midst of such sorrowful times. Poor Jero, lost in Ottoman lands, and Idita's sudden passing . . . such a sweet woman and so helpful to everyone. What will you do now, Terese, without your midwife?"

"I have not thought beyond planning the funeral."

Isabella cocked her head in surprise. "Is she not buried yet?"

Resi's eyes filled with tears when she explained, "She is laid out in the crypt. I thought Mauro should decide on her final resting place. Father David said we could wait a few more days, but if my husband isn't back by the end of the week, I will have to make the choice myself. I would like to bury her with the Barics," she confided.

Isabella seemed to ponder such a choice and advised, "You must follow your heart, of course, despite protocol."

Anastasia came stealthily into the sitting room and stood by the door. Isabella noticed her and said, "Terese, my dear, I am so happy to be here finally, but perhaps I will retire for a short time."

"Oh, but the wedding! We are in suspense how it all turned out."

Ruby added, "I am sure Lady Caterina was a beautiful bride."

Isabella retook her seat with a grin and explained, "She was indeed dressed beautifully, but like my own rushed ceremony, hers was attended only by family. However, their reception made up for it. Caterina's party did not have the glamour of Mira's reception, but the number of official dignitaries who had sought an invitation was impressive. Of course, with so little time to plan a proper banquet, it was held at the Carrera villa and not at a venue in the city. Still, Mother Carrera knows how to throw a grand party on short notice."

Resi was enthralled and said, "I wish we could have stayed for it."

"You would have loved it, Terese, but Caterina was somewhat overwhelmed by all the fuss. The Duartes' gifts showered on the Carreras were impressive, and Cyro convinced me that he truly loves Caterina. She will have her devoted husband wrapped around her needy fingers in no time," Isabella maintained.

"I imagine she was happy to finally be on her way to Corsica," Resi said.

Isabella shook her head, telling them, "Caterina cried over it all of the next morning until I promised her I would visit in the spring. Her mother said I could take Bianca with me."

"Is Bianca not going to Toth Castle?"

"Oh, yes, she left Venice the day I did, but with the promise of a break in her service now and then." Isabella explained with renewed enthusiasm, "No one is sad about Bianca any longer. I sensed a new determination in the stubborn girl. Oh, and I have my own news."

"You are pregnant!" Resi guessed.

Anastasia noticeably shifted. Her stiff skirts rustled loudly across the room.

Isabella continued without remorse, "Goodness, no! Not yet, at least. I have been too busy with another man."

"I hope you mean Signor Morgenstern," said Resi.

"With your alias, he is now Signor Morgante! He faithfully visited every day these past weeks, and I am ready to start painting."

"That is fantastic, Isabella! Did you bring canvas with you?"

"That is what had to be left behind for the wagon delivery. But as soon as my supplies arrive, we can begin your portrait, Terese."

"I am delighted," Resi replied as she struggled to stand up from the embrace of the settee. She held out her hand to Ruby, and her friend tugged on it.

Isabella stared curiously at the baroness's figure. "Dear Terese, how did you disguise your swollen middle so well in Venice? I do not remember you being so burdened. Can you manage to move about?"

Resi hooked her arm in Isabella's with a grin and assured her, "I was nearly this large the last time you saw me. As long as I don't sit in deep cushions, I still manage just fine."

Isabella admiringly said, "You have such a lovely maternal glow about you, Terese. I cannot wait to put that on canvas."

Chapter 57

Anastasia closed her mistress's door behind her and immediately regretted not asking Lady Carrera for directions.

A servant boy came from the landing of the small staircase carrying two pails. "Are you the water boy?" Anastasia asked.

"Yes, ma'am. I am Aron. I already filled the pitchers in your lady's room. Does she need more?"

"No. She has plenty. But tell me: who is in charge of the servants here?"

Considering all the changes in the house, the boy had to think about it. "Well, we were told the baroness is in charge of everyone. Jero used to be in charge of me, but he is gone now. He left to get married, and he hasn't come back."

Anastasia sympathized with the boy, but he had not answered her question. "I heard about Jero. I am very sorry he is gone. Who do you answer to now, Aron?"

Aron panicked at the pretty maid's prying and asked, "Did I do something wrong, ma'am?"

Anastasia smiled sweetly. "You did well. It is not about the water, I just wanted to know who might answer my question without bothering the baroness, is all."

Aron nodded. "You probably shouldn't bother her ladyship since she is always busy. If Idita didn't die this week, she would have been the one to ask. Nestor knows a lot, but he is always in the baron's study." Aron smiled as he pointed to the green-clad man poised at the top of the stairs. "Davor would be the one to ask! He knows everything that's going on, just like Jero did." Aron bowed and went away with his pails of water.

Anastasia frowned at her predicament. She smoothed an imagined strand of loose hair with a steady hand and walked down the corridor to where Davor stood at attention. With her head held high, she said, "I don't know if you remember me, Davor. I am Lady Carrera's maid."

"I do remember you," Davor said with a forced smile. "You are the maid who was so helpful to me in Venice. How can I return the favor, Anastasia?"

Anastasia felt she deserved the mocking tone since she had brushed him off when Davor had searched for water for his master's chamber. "I just had a question about where my room might be," she said.

"Ah, yes. Natalija has been assigned to show you where everything is in the servants' quarters. I will go find her for you." He turned to go down the marble staircase.

Anastasia asked disapprovingly, "Do the servants use the master's stairs?"

Davor considered her question. "We are not as formal here as you are accustomed to in Venice, and Lord Baric does not mind his valet using his stairs. For your duties, the servant staircase is the lacquered door at either end of the corridor. If you wait there, I will send Natalija to you."

~*~

That evening, Davor was lighting the sconces in the foyer when Neno came to the front door. He was the scout sent to relay the news that the *Margaret* had arrived in the harbor.

"We thought the baroness would like to know the baron's ship has docked," Neno told him.

"Is Jero with the baron?" Davor asked.

Neno shook his head. "I am not sure. I rode on before they disembarked. I just thought the servants might want to prepare for his lordship's early return. I have already told Captain Eduard."

"Thank you, Neno."

~*~

The sun was setting over the Adriatic as the weary travelers arrived at the castle gates. The baron's soldiers were assembled in the torchlit courtyard when the three horsemen rode in. It was clear that they had not found Jero.

Vilim shook his head in a preemptive warning to the questioning crowd, but Mauro was ready to talk.

"Thank you for coming out to welcome us home, but I bring no news of my brother. We could not confirm his death, and no one has seen him. Until I learn otherwise, Jero is still alive, and we will keep the hope that he will return home," Mauro announced.

The muttering voices of the soldiers stirred the crisp air as they made their way back up the Keep's stone steps. Eduard waited while the baron handed his reins over to Josip.

"There is something you should know, Mauro," Eduard said.

"Can it wait until morning, Eduard?"

"To save the baroness the pain, I think you should hear it from me," he said gravely.

Hugo and Vilim shook their heads in anticipation of more bad news.

Mauro locked his gaze with Eduard's. "Tell me."

"Idita died suddenly a few days ago."

The words penetrated Mauro's fragile defenses, but he masterfully steadied himself. He nodded to Eduard, slung his saddlebag over his shoulder, then crossed the empty courtyard and disappeared through the immense oak door of his ancestors.

Davor was dutifully waiting at the bottom of the stairs.

"Is my wife up?" Mauro asked him.

"Verica left your chamber a while ago, sir. Lady Baric is sleeping. Lady Carrera arrived yesterday. And there is one more thing, sir."

"Idita is dead," Mauro said point-blank. "I know. Eduard told me."

"Yes, my lord," Davor whispered.

"Was she buried already?"

"No, sir. Her ladyship had her laid out, but no funeral has taken place."

"Thank you, Davor. That will be all for tonight."

Mauro shuffled up the stairs, one heavy step at a time. The only light glowing under a doorway in the corridor was from Nestor's chamber; Mauro would talk to him in the morning. He lit a candlestick from those on the sideboard in the hallway and opened his dark room. Resi was nearly hidden under her billowing blankets, and a cat was curled up next to her. Mauro moved the purring animal to the floor. He leaned down and kissed his wife's soft cheek, the only thing exposed by the blankets. He had hoped that would stir her, but she was sound asleep.

In the quiet, he stripped off his dusty clothes. Pitchers of water and a clean shirt had been set out next to his toiletries. Davor knew him too well, he thought.

Mauro was under the warm covers next to his wife in no time. He breathed in her scent, glad to be home again, and fell into a deep sleep.

~*~

The dawning light from the unshuttered windows reached the bed, and Resi woke with a start. "Mauro?" she gasped.

Her husband opened his eyes. "Yes, my love. I am home."

"I dreamed I felt you next to me, but I couldn't convince myself that it was real." She curled up closer and asked, "Why did you not wake me?"

"You were sleeping so nicely, and I brought no news worth waking you for."

"I am sorry, Mauro," she whispered.

"It is a big world, Resi, and I was foolish to think my brother would be waiting in Tirana."

"Did you learn anything new?"

"We talked to a few people, and they confirmed what Patrik had written. Jero escaped, that is certain, but there was no trace of him, no sighting. He had a horse, at least, and maybe even help." Staring up at the oak beams above him brought back memories of lying in his childhood bedchamber, worrying about another missing brother.

Resi broke his trance when she asked, "So what will you do, Mauro?"

"What can I do? I have a castle to run, and I have a wife I left alone in a time of tragedy." He stroked her brow and said, "I am sorry, my love. I heard about Idita."

Resi could no longer stay strong and choked back a sob. "It was so sudden, Mauro. She was dead before we could send for help."

Mauro breathed deeply and recalled, "I visited her the night before we sailed. I think she knew she was not long for this world. She practically told me so before I left, but I did not want to hear it."

"I was going to bury her with the Barics," Resi told him. "I thought you would want that."

Mauro nodded softly against the pillow. "That is what we will do. She was mother and grandmother to all of us, and we will honor that."

"Father David will be waiting to hear from you today."

"I will ride down to the village and make arrangements after lunch," he replied before rolling out from under the covers and striding across the room.

Resi watched him as he bolted the door and returned to her side. She lifted the covers for him to slide back into bed.

"I hope you are not wanting breakfast today," he whispered, "because I plan to spend the whole morning in bed with you."

Chapter 58

"Mauro!" Simeon called out. He tied the reins of his horse to the post and slid his crutches from the saddle.

Mauro rode up next to him. "Were you just riding, Simeon?"

"Since yesterday," Simeon said, beaming proudly. "I need a little help getting up, but getting off, I can manage."

"And you have a leg!"

The significance of it hit Simeon, and he hung his head. "It was the last thing Idita did. I am truly sorry, Mauro."

Mauro agreed, "We are all sorry to lose her. I have just returned from talking to Father David. We will hold her funeral in the village church tomorrow. All the men will have the day off to pay their respects."

"Of course, Mauro," Simeon said with a nod.

Josip came up to the riders, took the reins from the two, and led the horses away.

Mauro walked with Simeon to the Keep and asked, "How did the men do without their captains while we were away?"

Simeon chuckled, telling him, "Eduard was shouting orders right and left, and Daniel, well, not shouting orders, but he is taking charge, more and more. With me just getting back out there, the men haven't gotten the attention they usually do."

"Hmm," Mauro said pensively. "And is my new recruit working out?"

"He is a quick learner and is doing well. I approve of him although there is a funny rumor going around."

"About Felix?"

"Lazar told a few of the men that Felix sleeps in one of the storerooms because he gets hungry for ham at night."

Mauro laughed. "The boy has been known to tell tales."

"Yeah, but since then a few noticed that Felix's bed is empty most nights, even when he's not guarding the wall."

"That is strange. Is he a loner?" Mauro asked.

"Not at all. The group I put him in charge of seems to like him, even respect him. He seems to lead them with confidence, too. He doesn't sleep in a bed, is all."

"I would like to dispel this rumor before it takes hold. Let's go have a look," Mauro said with a cock of his head, and Simeon kept up with Mauro with the aid of his crutches.

The two went into the open armory, past the shields and swords. Mauro grabbed a torch from the wall to take down the corridor. The chill of the pantry was noticeable as the door closed behind them. Reed baskets lined the shelves of the wide hallway, where colorful carrots and apples could be seen through the weaving. Braids of onions and garlic hung between the shelved wheels of hard cheeses in neat rows. After a quick look, they found no blanket or anything out of the ordinary in the Keep's stores. Still, at the end of the long hallway were two more doors. One room stored the ale, and the other was for cured meats. Mauro opened one, and a smoky deliciousness hit their senses.

Simeon commented, "Lazar said Felix was sleeping in here when he was getting supplies for his pa the other day. I can see the attraction if you are hungry." He patted a smoked venison haunch, and it swung lazily on the hook.

Mauro remarked, "I certainly would not choose sleeping on the cold floor over a warm bed in the Keep, hungry or not." He peered through the stacks of coiled sausages on the slotted shelf and said, "There is no blanket tucked away here to sleep on, either."

Simeon pointed his crutch to a dark shadow on a lower shelf. "Since when are sausages kept in sword cases?"

Mauro slid the long box out into the torchlight and opened the latch on the leather case. "It seems Felix brought a different tool of his trade with him."

Simeon let out a low whistle. "I've never seen one of those up close. Did you know he played?"

Mauro plucked a taut string on the narrow neck and replied, "Felix taught the harpsichord to the Carrera daughter, but I have no idea how far his training goes." The baron unfurled the tight roll of parchment next to the delicate instrument. "Look at all the notes," he remarked. "This is for an orchestra."

"I don't know anything about music, but it looks fucking impressive," Simeon said.

Mauro returned the roll of sheets in the case and latched it again. He took up the torch, and Simeon followed him out of the pantry and back into the light of the armory. "I will be in the house. Send Felix to me when you see him, and he can claim this."

Simeon nodded. "I will look for him."

~*~

Anastasia and Verica stayed behind in the bathhouse to gather their mistresses' discarded clothing.

"This seems like a nice estate," Anastasia remarked pleasantly. "Do you like working here, Verica?"

Verica didn't have to think long and replied, "I have lived here all my life. I like it very much."

"How about the other servants?" Anastasia asked as she rolled Isabella's stockings and set them on the stack to take back.

"Have you met the kitchen maids and the cooks? They are the sisters and mother that I never had."

Anastasia picked up her pile and asked, "How are the male servants? Do they leave you in peace?"

"What do you mean, Anastasia?"

The Carrera maid asked point-blank, "Do they try to court you, or worse?"

Verica knew now what 'worse' meant. "There is nothing like that going on here," she replied.

Anastasia raised her brows. "Davor, too? He is always watching in the corridor. He makes my skin crawl."

Verica laughed at her unfounded remark. "He is not watching you, Anastasia. The baron wants to know what is going on in his house, and Davor tells him."

"So he is the baron's spy?"

"No!" Verica insisted. "It is not like that here. Davor is a friend to all us servants. I like him a lot, actually."

Anastasia choked with surprise. "Is he your lover?"

Verica recoiled at her question and asked, "Have you never been friends with any male servants where you've worked? It is possible, you know."

"That is not my experience." Anastasia sat down on the bench with her bundle in her arms and told Verica, "I left two posts because of *friendship*. One was with a valet and the other with the master of the house. I should never have trusted either. I was lucky to get this new employment with Lady Carrera before being marked as difficult."

Verica's tone softened when she asked, "How long have you worked for the Carreras?"

Anastasia's reply was softer, too, "Only since August."

"Have you always been a house servant?"

"When I was old enough to be on my own, my mother found me employment as a nanny for two beautiful little boys. I felt fortunate to work in such an important noble house. But one summer, a new valet was hired, and I had my first lesson in the treachery of men."

Verica's heart sank. "Oh, Anastasia."

"My mistress was kind, and she found me employment as a lady's maid for the eldest Passini daughter. It was a good change from being a nanny, and I worked in their house for a few happy years until her brother returned from his schooling."

Verica gasped. "Pasquale Passini?"

Anastasia's cold stare into the steam rising from the water answered her question.

"I met him and couldn't wait to get away," Verica confided.

"I have learned it is the same in every noble house: Never trust men who take a friendly interest in you. In the end, men are not friendly at all."

Verica promised, "I would trust any man here with my safety or my virtue. You can be at ease at the House of Baric, Anastasia."

Anastasia tucked her mistress's garments under her arm and said, "I wish I could believe you."

~*~

Arriving at the top of the stairs, Mauro noticed Isabella's door swing shut, and a thought crossed his mind. He knocked, and Isabella opened it with a flourish of energy.

"Ah, Mauritius! Come in. We were just talking about you in your delightful bathhouse." Isabella shut the door behind him and motioned for Mauro to sit down.

Mauro stayed poised by the door and remarked, "I hope your gossip was all good."

She sat down on a chair and shot him a coy smile. "I would never gossip about you, dear Mauritius. I was simply telling your wife how much I would love to ride one of your horses out to my new estate. It is not far, I hear, and Lady Ruby desperately needs an outing, too. Could that be arranged for tomorrow?"

Mauro said thoughtfully, "Not tomorrow, Isabella, but I might ride out with you myself the day after."

Isabella beamed at her victory. "I hope you will." She cocked her head and added, "You came here to ask me something, Mauritius. What can I help you with?"

"It is about Felix Soranzo."

"Oh, I had forgotten he was here. Such a helpful young man. How is he getting along?" she asked.

"He seems to be a quick learner. I understand he was a university student before becoming a music tutor. Do you know anything about that?"

Isabella considered his question and shook her head. "I did not personally know the Soranzos. I did hear Felix was talented, though, and showed potential in his music studies before his family was tainted in society."

"That is what I am curious about, Isabella. He taught the harpsichord to Bianca. Did he teach any other instruments?"

"The harpsichord is really the only instrument a lady needs to learn. It is very social, you know, and draws attention to a girl at parties."

"Indeed. Well, thank you for that clarification. I will not keep you from your day," Mauro said with a polite bow.

"I will tell Lady Ruby about our plans, Mauritius," Isabella cheerfully added before he closed the door again.

Anastasia and Verica were coming from the servants' stairwell, holding colorful skirts and glimpses of lace in their arms. Mauro passed them with a kind nod and continued down the grand staircase.

At the bottom of the steps, Davor said, "I was just looking for you, sir. Lord Felix is in the great hall. He was sent to talk to you?"

Without missing a stride, Mauro ordered, "There is a black case on the table in my study. Can you bring it to me, please?" Mauro then opened the door to the expansive hall and found Felix in front of the large canvas set up by the windows. An outline of the baroness was drawn on it in charcoal. "It is lifelike, isn't it?" Mauro said as he approached the young nobleman.

"Who is the artist, sir?"

"Lady Carrera," he said with emphasis. "She is painting a portrait of my wife."

Felix grinned at the revelation. "I am impressed. I could already see it was Lady Baric on the canvas. Might I ask, Lord Baric, if I could have a look as the painting progresses?"

"Are you a student of art, Felix?"

"I suppose I am, and how one creates it is especially fascinating to me."

Mauro waved him to the chairs next to the canvas and said, "You probably wonder why I asked you to come to the house today."

Felix took a seat. "I hoped it was to talk about when I might leave for the Toth Army."

Mauro had not spent time with the man sitting across from him, and he studied Felix for a moment before asking, "Do you like being a soldier? Do you think it will be the right profession for you?"

"I do, sir."

Mauro watched him for clues and asked, "Eduard isn't overworking you, is he? You look a bit tired."

"No, sir. I enjoy the pace of the work."

"Let me see your hands, Felix," Mauro asked unexpectedly.

Felix's confidence seemed to wane under the scrutiny of his superior. He begrudgingly held out his hands for the baron to examine them.

Mauro turned Felix's palms up to see his fingers. "Archers have calluses on the tips of their fingers like this," he remarked. "I did not know you were a bowman, Felix."

Davor cleared his throat as he approached the baron.

Mauro let Felix's hands go and said, "Set the case on the table, Davor. That will be all."

Felix nodded with understanding as Davor left them. "I see why you have called me here," Felix began. "Please, forgive my impertinence for using your storeroom, Lord Baric. This is a hobby of mine. I like to play from time to time to clear my thoughts. I did not think I would be breaking any rules."

Mauro went to open the case. "I encourage my men to entertain themselves, but I also encourage my men to sleep. This is more than a hobby, Felix. Did *you* write the music on these pages?"

Felix shifted in his seat. "Does it make a difference, Lord Baric?"

"It does."

Felix sat up a little taller and replied with renewed confidence, "I started writing this piece in Venice and wanted to finish it. When it is done, I will put it away."

Mauro held Felix's gaze. "Can you, really?"

Felix lowered his eyes.

Mauro took out the polished instrument from the velvet-lined case and examined it. "What else do you play, Felix?"

Felix guardedly watched the baron holding his prized possession. "The cello, the harpsichord, the harp—anything with strings," he rattled off. "But the violin is my favorite."

He handed Felix the instrument. "Will you play something for me?"

Felix was caught off guard. "I . . . um . . ." He shrugged.

"Play this." Mauro unrolled the parchment, set it on the table, and practically dared him.

Felix accepted the challenge. He lightly plucked the violin while fine-tuning the strings, then took up the bow from the case. Felix didn't need the notes in front of him; the music was engraved in his thoughts and fingers.

Mauro kept his eyes fixed on Felix as his mournful song resounded through the room. Felix, the violinist, bloomed in front of him as he flexed and dived with the same complexity as the marks on the page.

When the young man had played the last heartbreaking chord and opened his eyes, the room echoed with applause. Along the back wall of the great hall, the House of Baric residents clapped in admiration.

Mauro joined in their delight. "That was remarkable!" he said. "Why have you been hiding this talent?"

Felix wiped the sweat from his brow with his sleeve. "That life is behind me, Lord Baric. I just, um, had inspiration to finish my piece."

"I insist you continue, but your music needs a bigger space than my storeroom." Mauro offered, "I will release you from your training in the afternoon, Felix, if you want to practice and finish your composition here, in the great hall."

Felix bowed and said, "I am grateful, sir."

Mauro concluded their meeting, "Today I have other business to attend to, Felix, but we can talk later about your position with my uncle."

The baron left, and the servants dispersed to their duties while Felix carefully packed up his precious violin.

Verica was waiting for him in the foyer when he walked out of the great hall, deep in thought. Before he could ask if she liked the music he had written for her, she heatedly demanded, "Why didn't you tell me, Felix?"

Confused by her outcry, he asked, "Why are you angry?"

She mocked him in a hushed voice, "Do you like music, Verica? Do you like the violin, Verica? You were not honest with me!"

He looked around them to see that they were alone and whispered back, "They were simple questions to know you better. I was not trying to hide anything. I was trying to move on from what could not be."

"Could not be?"

"It costs money to study music, Verica, and I have none. I don't want to be a pauper, teaching girls simple tunes on the harpsichord or playing at drunken parties for the rest of my life. I already told you I need a real profession. That is why I wanted to come here."

She slumped against the wall. "Maybe you didn't lie to me, but you are lying to yourself. You could never stay a music tutor when you are so obviously talented. Why give up so readily?"

He leaned over her. His face was inches from hers when he again explained his plight, "We cannot all get what we want in life just because we want it. One needs money and connections. You should know that as well as I do."

"So you quit trying when they took away your money? I thought you were different, Felix." She slipped out from under his arm and hurried up the stairs.

Miserable again, Felix rushed out the front door and back to his assigned place on the wall.

Chapter 59

Resi stretched in bed, looking at Mauro. "I am still thinking about Felix's composition. It was so different from anything I had heard before. Haunting. It bored a hole in my soul and set root there."

Mauro stood in front of the open window and said into the night, "When I asked him to play I was not expecting such a concert. I am torn about what to do for him."

Resi sat up against her pillow, wondering, "What do you mean, 'torn'?"

He came back to her side and admitted, "I cannot in good conscience recommend him to my uncle."

"What do you propose he do instead?" she asked.

"I don't know, but a lifetime of soldiering does not seem the right choice."

"You should sponsor him. That is what you are considering, aren't you?"

Mauro rubbed his brow pensively. "It crossed my mind, but I am doing more for him than I would for any stranger already. There are others closer to me who need my charity."

"This is not charity, Mauro. It is art. You know very well the piece he wrote is nothing less than magical. The world needs more music in it."

He shook his head. "That is what I love about you, Resi." He was tired but rewarded her with a smile and said, "How about I watch him practice for a while and then I can decide how I might best help him."

"Fair enough, Mauro. Now, why don't you undress and come to bed?"

Mauro bent to kiss her, then picked up his cloak off the chair and said, "I wanted to visit the crypt before the funeral. I will be back shortly." He opened the door to leave.

"Mauro, wait!"

"Yes, my love?"

"Um, there is something about Idita you might want to know. Ruby and I thought if Idita hadn't told you herself, then perhaps she wouldn't want you to know, but, well, now I am not so sure."

His wife's nervous declaration made Mauro anxious, too, and he asked impatiently, "What should I know?"

Resi sank deeper into her bed and bemoaned her dilemma, "I wish I could have asked her to explain it, and I don't want to add to your troubles."

Mauro took a breath and let it out. "Just say it, Resi. Or don't. I am not in the mood for riddles."

"Well," she began, "Ruby and I dressed Idita for the burial, and just there, she has the same tattoo as you, Mauro." Resi tapped herself above her heart and added, "The marking is still clear and beautiful—a letter 'M' with a little hand in black ink."

"An 'M'? Scrolled above her heart?" Mauro repeated in dismay.

Resi nodded. "Just like yours on your shoulder."

Mauro closed the door again. His expression, tired just a moment ago, was now alert, dark and piercing. "You know how much the mark has puzzled me my whole life. Did you plan to keep this news from me?"

Surprised by his anger, Resi countered, "I did not plan anything, Mauro. I just felt I should respect her secret as it seemed so private and, well, almost a burden she chose to carry alone. But then I wanted you to know she shared that with you in her own way. She gave you what was hers."

His resentment faded, but his decision renewed. He opened the door and said, "I must see it for myself."

"Wait! Let me get dressed and go with you."

"No, Resi."

"It isn't proper, Mauro! You should not disturb the dead," she cried.

A strange smile crossed his lips, and he scoffed. "You think she will haunt me for it? She is my Idita. She will not mind."

~*~

Inside the whitewashed chapel, Mauro dipped his fingers in the holy water and said a prayer for his departed nanny. He buckled the collar of his cloak against the impending cold of the crypt and descended the dark stairs, lighting the torches as he went.

Near the arched entrance into the cavern of Baric tombs was a marble table for the newly dead. A shroud covered the body that lay there, ready to be interred. Idita's draped figure seemed surprisingly small without her layers of skirts or the tall cap that had always covered her piled gray hair.

Mauro gingerly pulled the linen cloth back from Idita's face and choked on the breath he tried to take. She was dead, alright. Her face was as white as the gauze gown his wife had dressed her in. Mauro had never seen her hair left long down her sides as Resi had combed it for the burial, and her delicate features seemed youthful for a woman of nearly seventy.

His nanny's cold hands were folded across her chest, and Mauro took one in his. "Idita," he whispered. He stared at her closed eyes, expecting them to open. He told her, "Thank you for always being there for me, Idita. Was it only out of duty that you took care of us troubled boys—Jero, Mateo, me? We felt your love, Idita. The love of a mother."

He placed her hand back at her side and began to untie the satin ribbon holding the throat of her simple gown closed. His hand trembled. Maybe it shook from the cold or from the wrongness of what he wanted, but Mauro had to know her secret. He undid each pearl button on the bodice until he saw the black ink on her white skin. He took a deep breath of courage and undid two more buttons to expose the elegant letter. It was his.

Mauro cried out, "Why did I not know this? You knew my whole life's story—every pain, every happiness—yet I know nothing about yours." He shook his head in anger at his failure. "Who was the 'M' that broke your heart, Idita? Did you ever fully recover?" He begged to know, "Will I one day?"Mauro bowed his head and sobbed miserably over her.

When his tears ran out and his sorrowful stupor faded, Mauro closed the tiny buttons again and tied the ribbon below her chin. His cold hands placed hers back over her heart, and he said to her peaceful face, "I did not bring Jero home, Idita. It is just like Mateo all over again. If you see Jero in heaven, tell him I tried. Tell him I love him. Tell Mateo, too, that I love him, just like I love you."

He pulled the end of the shroud over her and whispered, "I know what you would say to me; that I must keep living and carry on for the Barics. I am trying, Idita, but I need someone to tell me it will be all right." Then Mauro kissed her on her veiled cheek and said, "Until we meet again, sweet Idita, rest in peace."

Mauro climbed the worn steps and snuffed out the torches on his way out. After leaving the chapel, he knew he could not face the living. Instead, he crossed the courtyard to the armory and climbed the spiral steps to the tower roof. Clouds had rolled in from the sea, and no stars shone above him.

Standing on the edge, he waited for the blackness to envelope him. It would, eventually. Mauro knew that from the times he had felt lost in the weighty world as a boy and came here to unburden that weight. The young Mauro would sit hidden in the corner, where the massive blocks of the tower met, invisible to the guards on the ramparts.

Mauro sat down there again, his thoughts heavy with grief and guilt, and the question he had asked the void on that same spot a dozen years ago crossed his lips again: "Where are you, Brother?"

Chapter 60

Bulgaria, 26 August 1649

Dressed in borrowed linen trousers, tucked neatly into his polished Venetian boots, Jero choked out the dreaded words, "I will."

Standing next to him in a matching embroidered waistcoat, Jasmina repeated them. With that promise, the two were joined, and Jero's new family clapped and danced around them in celebration.

Jasmina was pulled to the center of their circle and danced for her new husband. She was especially pretty in her brightly colored skirts, which caught the air and lifted around her ankles as she twirled under her sisters' linked arms.

Six marriage ceremonies were held that day on the expansive hayfield. Open wagons, caravans, and makeshift tents glowed with oil lamps, and fire pits lit up the continuing celebration. The Romani men of all ages assembled away from the women to dance and drink to the future fortunes of the newly joined couples. Jero hardly heard the music as his mind raced to find a way out.

"Join us, Isaak!" one man shouted.

"He is anxious to start his wedding night," another yelled drunkenly.

"Your woman will wait, but the brew might not! More drinks for everyone!" an onlooker hollered.

Still another voice across the fire pit rang out: "More music!"

The drums picked up their beat, and two gypsies locked elbows with Jero, pulling him into their circle of dancers.

Jero's head was spinning, and he convinced himself that the nightmare would never end, that the people would never tire. But eventually, the dancing dwindled and men slumped over, falling into a drunken slumber where they sat, and no one relit the torches as they flickered out.

Chedomir and his cousin Kuzman stumbled with Jero through the various camps to his wedding tent on the edge of the field.

"Here you are, Isaak. My sister awaits you!" his new brother-in-law announced.

Jero surveyed the field one last time. "Where is your camp, Chedomir?"

He laughed at the odd question, telling Jero, "We're well out of earshot, Isaak, so don't worry about us."

"Maybe he'll need to ask for help," Kuzman said with a bellowing laugh.

Chedomir swayed and laughed with his cousin. "Isaak has proven he knows what to do with a woman, Kuz, remember?"

"Well, enjoy yourself, Isaak!" Kuzman added, and the two staggered away, leaving the new groom in front of the glowing flap.

Jero took a breath of courage and stooped through the makeshift door, past the sturdy pole there. Someone had laid a carpet over the rough stubble of the harvested ground. His bride was stretched out on blanketed cushions. The oil lamp next to Jasmina flickered as Jero's movement stirred the air in the tent. As Jero came closer, she opened her eyes and sat up, straightening her thin veil.

Jero crouched down next to her. "Go back to sleep," he said.

"It is our wedding night. It is my duty to serve you," she said through a yawn.

Jero looked at her pitifully. "You have done your duty, Jasmina. You found a father for your bastard baby."

"All our children will be yours. I promise you, Husband."

Jero cringed at the word. "I do not want to be your husband."

She inched closer, promising, "I will be a good wife, Isaak." She leaned in and whispered, "Let me show you how good I can be. Shall I undress for you?"

Their eyes met in the lamplight, and Jero made his choice. "Yes," he said. "Take off your veil."

She was suddenly timid and lifted it shyly off her braided hair.

Jero took it and set the sheer cloth off to the side. "That is nice. Now, your bangles," Jero said.

She pulled the gold hoops off her thin wrists and gave them to her new husband.

He felt their weight. "Is this real gold?" he asked.

Jasmina shrugged at the odd question. "They were a gift from my dead mother."

Jero smiled, saying, "And now they belong to your husband." He put them into his vest pocket and held out his hand. "I'll take the earrings, too."

Jasmina lifted the cascade of little interlocking loops from each lobe and hesitantly dropped them into Jero's open palm. "Don't you want me to look pretty for you?" she asked.

Jero shook his head. "It doesn't matter. I am going to blow out the lamp."

"Why? Don't you want to see me?" she pouted.

"Venetians do things differently," he answered.

Jero took Jasmina's veil and playfully tied one corner to her wrist.

She coyly smiled as he fingered the other end of the long veil. To her surprise, Jero pulled it tightly around her other wrist.

Jasmina began to struggle. "Are you going to punish me?"

Jero whispered into her ear, "Who was the man in the field, Jasmina? Someone your father did not approve of?"

"I am sorry," she whimpered. "I thought my father would merely be angry, maybe send you away. I didn't know he would make you marry me, Isaak."

"Do you love this other man?"

Jasmina hung her head to avoid Jero's demanding glare.

"Tell me the truth, or I will punish you."

Terrified, she shivered at her new husband's threat. "Will you promise not to strike me?"

Jero held his stare.

Jasmina's chin quivered as she explained, "Gustof is not a good match in my father's eyes, but he is to me. Since we were little, we were together at every harvest. We are grown now, and I wanted him."

"And now you have me," Jero muttered. He touched Jasmina's chin, then brushed his fingers along her throat, toying with one last decision.

She sobbed. "You promised you wouldn't hurt me."

"I did, didn't I?" He then lifted the gold chains from her neck and put them in his trouser pocket.

"Those are mine," she said.

Ignoring her protest, Jero took the sash from his waist and bound her mouth before she could yell out. He held her tightly and did his best to soothe her fear. "Shhh. I don't want to hurt you, but you need to stay quiet."

She choked back a muffled moan and nodded that she would not struggle against him.

Jero held her chin and made her look at him. "When they find you, tell them whatever lie works best," he said. "You will have plenty of time to think of one."

Her questioning eyes told him she did not understand what was happening.

"I will be dead to you soon. Do not let them follow me." He lifted her light frame and propped her against the tent pole. Then he tied the ends of the veil to it to hold her fast by her wrists. "I am sorry to make you a widow on your wedding night."

Her eyes widened.

"Ha! I thought you would understand. I am freeing you to marry the man you want, Jasmina. Use my gift well, and I will use yours to marry the woman I love." He patted his pocket filled with her gold.

Before he blew out the lamp, Jero put his finger to his lips, and the bound and gagged girl nodded. He ducked through the low opening and waited a moment outside the tent to ensure Jasmina would not cry out. She didn't.

He scanned the shadowy field. Chedomir had said their caravans lay straight ahead, and that was where Jero found Cairo. The unhappy horse had been left bridled and tied outside Boris's caravan. Those windows were shuttered and dark.

Jero whispered soothing words as he led the horse away from the other animals. If anyone was awake at that late hour, they did not notice the lone rider in the moonlight. Once away from the encampment, Jero ran Cairo hard through the night until he was confident he had a good enough lead and couldn't be followed.

The morning broke dull and cloudy. Other travelers on the highway stared openly at the odd rider, dressed in his wedding outfit. Jero did not dare ask any he passed where the road led for fear of being remembered.

Fortunately, Jero remembered that the gypsies had made hardly any turns getting to the Romani reunion. He was confident this road would take him to the turnoff to Thessaloniki.

~*~

The next day, hungry and desperate after a short night of rest and a long morning of riding, Jero met up with a peddler's cart, slowly coming toward him. It was loaded with trinkets and fabrics and pots and pans, but what caught Jero's attention were the wheels of bread and coils of sausages stacked at the front of the trader's wagon.

With renewed energy, Jero called out, "You there! Sir! Are you selling your bread?"

The driver stopped his donkey and smiled at the stranger. "I am indeed. Do you need more provisions, Friend? I have boiled eggs, smoked trout, and freshly picked pears to go with the bread. I have a few gourds of fermented goat's milk, too, if that is to your liking."

"I do need provisions, but I have no money, only trinkets to trade."

"Show me what you have, my friend, and I will tell you what your trinkets are worth."

Jero pulled the gold chains and hoops from his pockets. "I believe they are real," he said.

The peddler could not hide his surprise at the beauty of the gleaming bracelets. "You want to sell these?" He looked around, although they were alone on the side of the road. "Are they stolen?" he asked.

"No, no. They are mine. My wife wanted me to use them to pay my way to Thessaloniki and then beyond, if I can get a good price."

The peddler looked Jero up and down. "Did you just marry this wife?"

Jero asked cautiously, "How did you know?"

The man laughed. "Most men don't wear such an extravagant costume except on their wedding day."

Jero looked down at his clothes as if he were seeing them for the first time. "Oh, yes, well, I did not have my other jacket to change into after the rush of the wedding night and all."

"Hmm." The man pondered Jero's story. "I may have a solution for you, my friend."

The peddler jumped down from his cart for a closer look at Jero's boiled wool vest. He admired the red and blue stitching on the interlaid squares that created its hypnotic pattern. "I will tell you what," the trader began. "I have a customer who might want to buy such a fine waistcoat, and I happen to have a warm jacket here to trade for it. Straight across, of course."

When Jero frowned at the offer, the skilled negotiator smoothly countered, "But because I am feeling generous today, I will throw in a nice felt hat, too. You will be happy to have it for your ride. Rain is coming."

Jero considered the warm coat and hat offer but asked, "What about the jewelry? The bracelets are gold, and the earrings and chains are well-crafted. Will you give me a fair price for those?"

The man shook his head with a grimace and said, "I can't pay you all in cash, my friend. Jewelry isn't easy to resell."

Jero replied, "Well, then, I will have to ask elsewhere. I need money for my journey."

"Ah, but I have a solution!" the man eagerly offered. "I can give you a week's worth of provisions along with ten silver coins for all of it."

"This is gold, sir!"

"Maybe it is, but I do not have the market for it," the man lied.

Jero put the earrings back in his trouser pocket, held out the rest, and said, "Make it twelve silver coins, and you have a deal."

The man agreed.

Jero turned over his borrowed vest and slipped on the patched wool jacket. As promised, it was a satisfactory fit for Jero, and he already felt warmer. As the peddler began to pack the food, Jero asked, "How far is it to the road to Thessaloniki?"

The man chuckled and pointed ahead of them. "You are practically there, my friend. The turnoff is no farther than what you can see on the horizon."

In his self-pity, Jero had not surveyed the surrounding landscape, but now that he did, he recognized the familiar mountain in the distance, the one that flanked the valley where he had labored for Sasho's punishment. "I'm so close."

The jovial trader laughed, not understanding Jero's reaction. "Close indeed, Friend, but still a good distance to Thessaloniki."

But Jero had another destination in mind, and he asked, "Do you know of a farm run by a man called Ludvik?"

"Indeed, I have customers in the village there. It is only a few miles west of the crossroads." The merchant handed Jero his two sacks of food and counted out his coins. "This will keep you fed, my friend! Have a safe journey and a happy marriage," the old trader said.

Jero dropped the coins into his empty pocket and replied with a smile, "I will, sir. Thank you." He pulled off a chunk of the bread before he tied the bags together and slung them over Cairo's neck.

Renewed by the uplifting information and a little food in his belly, Jero rode west, past the sign to Thessaloniki, to make good on his debt to Zerina.

~*~

It was only a week ago that Jero had slept in this barn. He trotted Cairo directly to the building and looked around. He saw Ludvik's right-hand man, Tahir, coming down the path from the main house nearby.

Tahir called over, "The work is done. We don't need any more help."

"I have come for the boy," Jero said.

A second man joined Tahir by the barn. Jero did not recognize him, but the man remembered Jero. "He's the Venetian," he told his boss.

Jero said, "That's right. I am Isaak. I came with Chavdar's clan. I want to speak to Ludvik."

"Ludvik is busy. Be on your way," Tahir replied.

"Tell your master I have come to buy Sasho back." Jero dismounted and stood by his horse. "I will wait," he said.

Tahir nodded to the worker, and the man ran back up the path. Moments later, the overseer himself came around the corner of the barn.

"What are you doing here, Venetian?" Ludvik said with a sneer.

Tahir told his boss, "He wants Chavdar's boy."

Ludvik crossed his arms over his dusty vest and threw back his head with a laugh. "You can't have him. The boy signed on, and he owes me five years."

As the Venetian pondered his play, Ludvik watched Jero stroke Cairo's smooth hide.

"Chavdar sold Sasho to you," Jero maintained. "How much will it cost me to buy him back?"

The two Ottomans laughed like Jero had told a joke. "The boy is not for sale," Ludvik said. "He is my apprentice now."

"Find another boy," Jero asserted. Adding to his demand, he mounted Cairo and trotted the warhorse around the two men, stopping again in front of the boss.

"I will trade my horse for Sasho," Jero said.

Ludvik scoffed. "Why do you want the boy so badly? I heard he barely knows you."

"That is my business."

"This horse for the boy?" Ludvik asked, frowning.

The conman walked the length of Jero's horse, taking his time to inspect the tired beast.

Tahir shifted in anticipation of what his boss would do.

Ludvik nodded to Tahir, and a smile grew across his face. "A good horse is harder to pass up than another scrawny boy."

"Do we have a deal, then?" Jero asked.

Ludvik said with amusement, "You will have a long walk home, Venetian."

The Ottoman held out his hand to take the horse, but Jero gripped the reins. "First bring Sasho to me."

The old Ottoman waved his hand, and Tahir ran through the barn door to find the boy.

It seemed an especially long wait before Tahir returned with Sasho walking behind him.

The boy's face lit up when he realized it was Jero on the horse with Ludvik.

Tahir gripped the boy's thin arm to keep him back.

Ludvik called over, "Let him go!"

Jero slid off the horse, and Sasho ran to Jero's side and hugged him tightly. He was smaller than Jero remembered, and his lament over losing Cairo melted in the boy's arms.

When his little friend loosened his hold, Jero stepped away and handed his horse's reins over to Tahir. "The boy came with shoes and a jacket. He will take those with him."

With a victorious smile, Ludvik called over to a second man, "Demir, get the boy's things."

Sasho stood dumbfounded. "Are you taking me away?"

Jero took his bags off Cairo and said, "You didn't think I would leave you here, did you?" He gave his faithful horse a final pat before Tahir led the animal away.

Wiping a tear, Sasho asked, "Why is he taking Cairo?"

Jero ruffled the boy's already messy hair and replied, "The man is coming with your shoes, Sasho. Put them on. We have a long walk ahead of us."

Sasho wasted no time and did what Jero asked. Then Jero took the boy by the hand, and they walked away from Ludvik's farm.

~*~

Jero and Sasho trudged along a dusty road. Neither had realized before how much they needed each other right then. Sasho rubbed his eyes and said, "I am not crying, in case you are wondering. The dust makes my eyes water."

"I have the same problem," Jero told him.

They walked along in silence for another long moment before Jero asked, "Did they treat you well, Sasho?"

The boy sniffled. "The work was hard, but they only beat me once. Why did you change your mind, Jero?"

Jero looked down at his little companion and asked, "Change my mind about what?"

Sasho hung his head and replied, "They said you wanted me to stay behind."

Jero stopped walking and explained, "They lied to you, Sasho. I didn't know Chavdar left you behind until we were long gone."

Sasho wiped a tear with his dirty fingers and took a needed gulp of air. "I never believed them, not really," he said.

Jero lifted the boy's chin and said, "We are friends, and friends look out for each other. I just got a bit delayed in getting you." Jero took Sasho's hand in his, and they began walking again.

Sasho asked, "Did you go to Thessaloniki?"

"No, I have not made it that far yet. They took me with them to Bulgaria, to Lilyana's wedding, remember?"

Sasho perked up at that. "Did they have lots of pastries and endless food?" he asked. "Violeta said that they would."

He looked down at the boy and replied, "Yes, endless." Jero shook off a shiver as he thought back on his nightmare, but Sasho didn't notice.

Becoming chatty again, the boy remarked, "My mother was married once, but it didn't work out. She was too pretty, and afterward she was too ugly to marry again. She told me to marry a girl in between. Is your lady pretty, Jero?"

"Yes, Sasho. Ruby is beautiful."

Sasho thought about Jero's predicament. "Oh, well, I guess if you don't take a second wife who is prettier than her, then it will work out with Ruby."

"I think I will only have one wife," Jero told him.

"Me, too," Sasho agreed.

The boy began to skip to keep up with Jero's long strides. "Are you mad that you had to give up your horse for me?"

"Cairo was a good horse, but we will manage. We can take our time now that no one is following us." Those words were for his reassurance.

"How far do we have to walk? For days and days?" Sasho asked.

"Probably."

"What is in the bags?"

"Are you hungry?" Jero stopped and opened them. "I met a peddler on the way here and bought some provisions." He reached into one and handed Sasho an apple. "Or do you want a boiled egg?"

"You have eggs?"

Sasho held out his other dirty hand, and Jero filled it.

"Did Chavdar give you money to buy food?" the boy asked.

"Jasmina did. I helped her with something," Jero said and took a bite of an apple.

"That was nice of her. My mother would give me money for helping her," Sasho said before he stuffed the egg into his mouth.

"I will take you back to your mother after I see my family first."

The boy took the news in stride. "Will we have to walk all the way there, too?"

Jero bit his egg and said, "From Thessaloniki we will take a ship. Have you ever been on a ship, Sasho?"

The boy looked terrified. "I have never even seen the sea."

"I bet you will like the water. I do, and my home is right near the sea."

"What is your city called?" Sasho asked as he finished his apple.

"Solgrad, but it is just a village."

"Solgrad," Sasho repeated thoughtfully. "Like salt? Is there lots of salt there?"

Jero chuckled. "As a matter of fact, there is. My brother gleans it from the sea to sell."

Sasho raised his brows in surprise. "I'd like to see how he does that."

"You will. You can stay in Solgrad as long as you like. And when you are ready, I will take you back to Tirana."

They walked another mile, lost in their thoughts until they came to the crossroads.

Jero pointed and said, "There is that peddler." Jero waved.

"Hello, Friend! I didn't expect to see you again," the trader called out. "You have lost your fine horse! Are you no longer going to Thessaloniki?"

Jero answered with a renewed cheerfulness, "We will go by foot now, but the boy and I are in no hurry. Thessaloniki isn't going anywhere."

The man chuckled and said, "That is a good way to look at life, my friend. Your road is just ahead. May God go with you."

With a wave, the peddler and his cart rolled on.

~*~

It took two weeks to reach the formidable walls of Thessaloniki. Along the way, Jero had traded Jasmine's earrings for a wool blanket and spent his coins to keep them fed, but they could not have gone much longer without means or better shelter.

Jero and Sasho looked around the city in awe, wondering where they should start. Ruby had talked about her home and the neighborhood she grew up in, but the city was dense, and the streets were unmarked. Jero decided to find the harbor and start their search there.

Thessaloniki's port was bustling; without Sasho, Jero would not have learned what he needed to know. The boy was fearless in a crowd, and he darted in and out of open shack doors and up gangways, asking anyone who looked like a local where he could find Angelos Spiros. The dockhands talked to the boy without suspicion, but the news was disappointing.

A warehouse supervisor told him, "You missed him. Angelos's ship sailed yesterday, boy."

"Can you direct me to his house? It is about his daughter Ruby," Sasho told him.

The boy could not have anticipated that mentioning this name would bring such a reaction. "Do you know where Ruby Spiros is?" the warehouseman demanded.

Sasho answered, "I think so."

"Larisa will want to talk to you," the man said. He went to the door and called out, "Damon."

A boy about the same age as Sasho, barefoot in a belted tunic, came around the corner of the building.

"Do you know where Angelos Spiros lives?" the warehouseman asked. Damon nodded, and the man instructed him, "Show this boy where it is, and then hurry back."

Jero was waiting for Sasho on the pier, and they met up with hardly a chance to explain what was going on. Damon didn't look back to see whether his companion was following, but Sasho took it upon himself to keep up with the ragged boy. Sasho and Jero tracked him through the city gate, past the market filled with shoppers, then down a quiet side street again.

Damon stopped in front of a low garden wall. "This is it," he said, then turned and jogged away.

The two stood in front of a gate that looked like all the others in the row of houses on the tranquil street. Jero hesitated, but Sasho nodded encouragingly. Jero lifted the latch, and the two went up the stone path to the brightly painted front door. Jero knocked.

After a moment, a young servant woman opened the door partway and asked, "What do you want? Food?"

Jero had not considered that they might look like beggars. "No, miss," he said in Turkish. "I am Jero Baric. I have come for Ruby."

The woman closed the door, and they stood numbly at the threshold.

"Try again," Sasho said.

After Jero knocked the second time, they heard muffled voices behind the door. Then it opened, and an older woman stood before him this time. She had Ruby's hair, but a shade darker, and the same fair skin and soft eyes, with wrinkles at the edges.

Larisa Spiros stared at Jero with an expression of disbelief. "You are Jero?" she asked.

Jero held his head high despite how crushing her tone was to him. "I apologize for my appearance, madam, but I have not had an easy time getting here," he said. "I would like to see Ruby if I could."

Ruby's mother studied Jero's bearded face, searching for the young aristocrat her daughter had described in such detail. His patched peasant's jacket and dirt-streaked Romani trousers were oddly mismatched with his tall, black riding boots. "Ruby is gone," she said.

Jero slumped in response, which was all it took for Larisa to believe it was really him.

"Has she already married?" Jero managed to ask.

"No, Jero. That is not what happened. Come in, and I will explain everything." She stepped inside and hollered, "Kallisto! Run and get Celine. Tell her Jero is here!"

~*~

By the time Resi's mother arrived with Alexis and several of her grandchildren, Jero had already washed up and changed into the clean clothes Larisa had given him.

Sasho sat quietly on a stool in the kitchen, eating a bowl of warm stew with an audience of young children curiously watching him.

Larisa told Jero the story of Ruby's escape on Castor's ship and what they knew about what had happened to his other friends. The ill-timing of the Spiros and Kokkinos ships being out at sea did not help Jero's situation, and the women tried to convince him to stay.

"They will be back in a week or two. Surely, you can wait that long, Jero," Celine said.

Feeling a little stronger from the news and the warm food, Jero insisted, "I cannot wait one more day. Now that I know I have your husband's blessing to marry your daughter, all I can think about is seeing her."

Larisa replied, "It warms my heart to hear the love in your voice, but you have been through quite an ordeal, Jero, and Angelos will want to meet his new son-in-law. Stay with us and rest. Castor will take you to meet the Baric ship next month."

Jero lowered his eyes, ashamed to decline this offer of hospitality, but he was sure of what he needed to do. "I am grateful for your invitation, Mother Spiros, and I promise that Ruby and I will come back to Thessaloniki. But I have been in motion for a long time now, and I cannot stay still until I am finally home."

Chapter 61

Baric Castle, 1 October 1649

Mauro spent the morning in his study, his mind clouded with indecision. He was pacing in front of the long table when Fabian came through the open doorway.

"Did you call me in to discipline me, Mauro?"

Mauro looked over and asked, "Do you need disciplining, Fabian?"

Fabian took off his broad hat, plopped it on the table, and then sat down on the end chair. "Then no one from the Keep talked to you this morning?" he asked casually.

Mauro frowned.

"Ah, it is rather early for news." Fabian reached for the wine bottle and poured himself a glass of it.

Mauro contemplated his friend's sly smile. "Fabian, you've only been back from Venice for two days. What scandal have you brought into my house?"

Fabian shrugged, changing the subject, "Sometimes I have no idea what rolls off my tongue before I have had my breakfast. Do you have time to ride out with me to check on the progress at my villa?"

"I would not mind an excuse to get out from these walls today." Mauro then insisted, "But only after you tell me what I haven't yet heard."

Fabian downed the rest of his wine. "It was impulsive, and I am sure it will sound quite silly when I tell you."

Mauro crossed his arms over his buttoned waistcoat, waiting.

"All right, then," Fabian began awkwardly. "I wanted to sleep in my old chamber one more time before I am the master of my own house. I have always liked that corner room in the Keep, so quiet, and the bed is very comfortable. But then, I have my new wife to keep me warm and, well, I could not choose between them," he concluded with a shrug.

Mauro tried to keep a straight expression when he said, "You didn't?"

"I did." Fabian added a pout for good measure.

"Did anyone see her?" Mauro asked, knowing what the answer would be.

"Just Vilim. And Daniel. And, um, maybe Lazar."

The old friends locked stares, and Fabian explained, "It was just one night, Mauro—one fabulous dream-of-a-night. Isabella thanks you for the experience. She has never slept in an old tower before."

"Fabian! I have rules in the Keep."

"We won't do it again! We will sleep in the manor house for the rest of our stay," Fabian agreed readily.

"Thank you," Mauro said, going back to his desk.

"So, what did you call me in so early to talk about if not that tiny indiscretion?"

Mauro searched the papers and handed Fabian a folded parchment. "I received a reply from the music director at the university in Florence. Felix Soranzo's former mentor will take him back as a student right away. Signor Grado writes that he is very much looking forward to the young man's return. I am deciding whether to accept their terms and sponsor Felix."

Fabian picked at a cluster of grapes on a platter and remarked, "Isabella told me about Felix's impromptu violin concert."

"I asked him to play that day because I was curious why he would secretly practice in a pantry. I did not expect Felix to be any good, really. But he was good, too good."

Fabian poured more wine. "That is a big commitment to sponsor a traitor's son."

"Do you believe a son should be penalized for a father's crime, even if it was true?" Mauro asked skeptically.

Fabian shook his head ambivalently. "Either way, it is a grand gesture on your part to help him. You are far more charitable than I would be."

Their conversation was interrupted by Davor knocking on the open door. "Lord Felix is here, sir," he announced and waited.

Fabian said, "I thought you were asking for my opinion. Have you already decided, then?"

Mauro told his friend, "I have, but I wanted you to sit in with us when I tell him the news." Mauro then said to Davor, "You may send Felix in."

~*~

Fabian's presence initially jolted Felix, but the baron's friend might be a positive indication. He had, after all, been an officer in the Toth regiment. Felix bowed to each gentleman.

"Have a seat, Felix," Mauro said, smiling encouragingly.

"Thank you, sir." He took the first chair in front of him.

"I have some good news for you," Mauro announced straight away.

The soldier-in-training sat poised and asked, "Has my commission been granted, sir?"

After two glasses of wine, Fabian ambiguously interjected, "Would you be disappointed if it had not been granted?"

Felix looked to his mentor and asked, "Have I not proven myself worthy, Lord Baric? What more can I do, sir?"

"I have not yet forwarded my recommendation, Felix. Instead, I asked Signor Grado to have you reinstated at the university. You do know the gentleman, don't you?"

Felix was confused. "He was my teacher, yes, but Lord Baric, sir . . . I cannot go back to Florence."

"I think you can, Felix, and you should. My wife thinks the world needs more music and less fighting, and I happen to agree."

Felix hung his head and said, "You do not understand, Lord Baric. My mother has no means to pay for it, nor do I."

"Talents should be fostered regardless of one's lack of funds. The opening is yours if you want it. I will pay your fees and give you a stipend for two years. What you do after that is up to you and your own motivation."

Felix hopped up from his seat. "Oh, Lord Baric. You have no idea how happy this news makes me. I will repay every lira. I promise you, sir."

Mauro shot a glance at Fabian, who chuckled at Felix's enthusiasm.

"I do not expect repayment," Mauro said, "but I do expect great things from you."

"When can I leave, sir?" Felix blurted out. "Not that I am ungrateful for all that you have done for me, but, well, I am overjoyed and would like to start in Florence as soon as possible."

"And I would agree, except I need you to wait until after the harvest festival," Mauro said.

Fabian cocked his head at Mauro's odd provision.

Mauro went on, "We are short a musician, Felix, and you would be doing me a favor if you could help the band out. I trust you know a few traditional melodies for dancing."

"Indeed, I do. I would be honored to help where I can, sir."

"Excellent." Mauro walked with Felix to the door and said, "You can get your things in order and write to Signor Grado directly. Tell him he should expect your arrival at the end of October."

"Thank you, Lord Baric."

"Oh, and join us in the manor house for dinner tonight. I am inviting all the officers, and I will make the announcement then."

"I will be there, sir. Thank you again, Lord Baric." Felix turned back to Fabian at the table and tipped his hat. "Good day, Lord Carrera."

Fabian strolled to the door and shut it. "Well, Mauro," he said with a grin, "you have earned another notch on your staff of good deeds. Well done."

"It does feel good somehow to help the man. But now I need to find my wife and cancel our lunch together."

"Ah, damn! Lunch!" Fabian exclaimed. "I keep forgetting I need to check in for things like meals with Isabella. She thinks I am a man of leisure now that we have left Venice."

"I will ask Resi to tell Isabella we have pressing business away. A grand dinner in the great hall should make up for a missed lunch with you."

"Thank you, Mauro, and I will make myself useful and let the officers know about dinner. I will meet you at the stables."

Fabian left out the front door, and Mauro went up the stairs.

Verica was coming out of the Barics' chamber and said, "Her ladyship is taking a nap, my lord. She wasn't feeling well after her breakfast."

Mauro stopped in front of the door and asked, "She is ill?"

"She seemed more tired than ill, sir. I have heard pregnant women are often tired."

Mauro nodded. "Then I won't disturb her. I am riding out with Lord Fabian to his estate, but we will be back for dinner in the great hall. Lady Isabella should be told that as well."

"I will tell them, my lord."

"Oh, and perhaps you can save me a trip to the kitchen. My officers will join us for dinner tonight, and I would like a special dessert for the occasion."

Verica perked up. "Is there a birthday to celebrate, my lord?"

"We will be celebrating Felix's departure," the baron said pleasantly.

Verica stifled her gasp. "Is he leaving for Toth Castle, Lord Baric?"

"There has been a change of plans, Verica. Felix is going to Florence to continue his music studies."

"Florence," Verica mumbled under her breath.

"If you could tell Nela about tonight," Mauro confirmed.

"Of course. I will go right now, sir." She hurried to the servants' stairwell.

Mauro tiptoed into his chamber and changed into his riding breeches and boots. He watched his wife shift uncomfortably as she slept across the room. The barn cat was stretched out at Resi's side, and Mauro gathered the lazy feline in his arms to bring to the stables with him.

"You have overstayed your welcome, old girl," he whispered to the cat, noticing for the first time how enormous with unborn kittens her middle was.

Mauro sat down next to his wife. As she slept on, he watched with fascination while his own offspring kicked and moved under the silk of her loose tunic. He covered Resi and kissed her cheek; then, he changed his mind about the pregnant cat and put her back in her place at Resi's side before he went back downstairs.

~*~

Having finished her errand to the kitchen, Verica was in the foyer as the baron came down the stairs. She curtsied and said, "Have a good ride today, Lord Baric."

Not answering, Mauro stared at the maid in contemplation.

Verica cheerfully added, "I gave Nela your message, sir. Was there something else?"

Frowning, he said, "Tell me, Verica, has my wife arranged for a midwife yet?"

Verica thought about it and replied, "She met with Lady Leopold's midwife, sir, but I believe she decided against her help."

"Who is coming to help, then? Did the baroness reconsider Elizabeta Radic's suggestion?"

"She interviewed her midwife, my lord, but I believe the baroness has decided against her, too," Verica said.

"Were you with her during the interviews? Was confinement mentioned?"

Verica treaded lightly, not wanting to cause her mistress trouble. "It was mentioned, sir, but her ladyship discussed it with Nela and Lady Ruby. They both know about childbirth and agreed that the baroness still has time."

She waited for her master to leave, but the baron merely tapped the baluster with his fingers. "Is something the matter, sir?" she asked.

He stopped his tapping and told her, "When the birthing begins, Verica, I am to be informed immediately, no matter where I am. Do you understand?"

She did not understand. Men were never called until after the baby was born, but she agreed, "Yes, my lord. You will be the first to know, sir."

"Do not leave my wife unattended. Not in the chapel, not in the bathhouse," he ordered.

His anxious tone frightened Verica, and she said, "I will go sit with the baroness right now, sir." She hurried up the stairs.

Mauro brightened at having saved his wife from the fate his mother had suffered. He strode out the front door and crossed the courtyard.

Fabian was at the gatehouse, holding the reins of Mauro's horse. He was talking intently to Denis and Latif.

Mauro quickened his pace, anxious to hear why his scouts had returned early from their rounds. "What is it?" he asked.

"A ship is anchored just offshore, sir," Denis reported. "It is flying an Ottoman flag."

"Is it the Kokkinos ship?" Mauro inquired hopefully.

"We don't think so, sir," Dennis replied.

"We saw them lowering a skiff into the water as we left," Latif reported. "They might be coming ashore at your harbor."

"It could be Jero," Fabian exclaimed.

Mauro took his reins from Fabian's grasp and was in his saddle in seconds. "It has to be Jero!" he cried as he rode out the gates.

~*~

Branislav and his crew were not back from their monthly deliveries, and the pier where the *Margaret* usually docked was vacant. Mauro and Fabian stood together on the plank walkway and watched as the Ottoman oarsmen maneuvered their small boat into the inlet. The faces of the men sitting on the benches grew clearer with each stroke. The pair of black-haired sailors manned the oars in efficient synchrony. Both passengers were dressed in Ottoman garb. The smaller of the two wore a black cap on his curly dark hair that lifted in the wind. The taller man's brown hair was tied back, but his belted tunic fluttered in the breeze.

The progress of the skiff felt painfully slow, and Mauro began to pace. "That must be Zerina's boy," he remarked.

Fabian warned his friend, "Jero will be changed, you know. All prisoners are. He will need time."

Mauro was unfazed by the possibility and replied, "I will take him any way he comes, whole or broken."

Jero stood up in the middle of the boat, not waving a greeting, not smiling at the reunion. He had the same troubled expression as Mauro, as though neither believed the other was real.

"God give me strength," Mauro whispered.

~*~

Jero climbed out before the rowers could tie the ropes and ran to Mauro's embrace.

Clutching onto what he feared was a dream that would dissolve in his arms, Mauro told Jero, "I thought you were lost to us."

Jero loosened his grip and whispered, "I almost was, but here I am."

"We were so worried. Let me look at you. Are you well? Are you whole?" Tears rolled down Mauro's cheeks.

Jero stepped back from his brother and said, "It has been a long journey."

"Where did you sail from?" Mauro anxiously wanted to know.

"From Thessaloniki," Jero managed to answer. He took a needed breath and dried his nose and wet cheeks.

Mauro looked out toward the shoreline. "That is not Castor's ship, is it?"

"It is a merchant ship on its way to Venice," Jero said. "They agreed to stop first in Solgrad because of Celine Kokkinos. Resi's mother is very much like her daughter. Or the other way around, I suppose."

"You met Resi's family?" Mauro asked, although he shouldn't have been surprised.

"I met all the Spiros and Kokkinos women; the men were at sea. They took good care of me, but I did not want to take their money when I could settle the voyage myself." Jero smiled for the first time when he said, "Or you could, Mauro. That is why the sailors are waiting. Celine convinced the captain that you would pay a good price for delivering me home."

Mauro's laughter turned to sobs again. "That is the least I can do." He called over to his friend, who had waited with the scouts. "Fabian! Join us!"

Fabian embraced Jero tightly and said, "Welcome home!"

"Thank you, Fabian. It is good to be home," Jero said, looking around the familiar harbor.

Mauro explained to Fabian, "Jakov keeps a money box to pay the crew in his office. Can you go get that from him? It seems I need to settle the voyage with these sailors, Fabian."

"I can do better," Fabian said. "I was supposed to pay my masons today, but I can pay the sailors from that purse." Fabian strode to the rowboat to negotiate the fee.

Mauro turned his attention to Jero's companion, standing a few steps away on the pier. "I see you have brought someone with you. Is he Zerina's boy?"

Jero gave a questioning look and replied, "Indeed, he is."

Jero waved the boy over and said, "Mauro, this is Sasho. He helped me get back home." Then Jero said in Slavic so the boy would understand, "And this is my brother, Lord Baric. He is the prince we talked about."

Mauro told Sasho, "I know who you are, young man. I went to Tirana looking for Jero and was at Isaak's inn. They wondered what had happened to you."

"My mother knew where I was. Did you talk to her?"

The boy's question caught him off guard, but Mauro hastily fibbed, "I did not get a chance. I will explain later, but for now, why don't we get you to your new home?"

Sasho turned to Jero and asked excitedly, "To the castle?"

Jero nodded. "Yes."

Mauro looked curiously at the two unlikely friends, but their complicated story would have to wait. A cloud of dust swelled above the harbor and broke their focus.

"She is here," Jero whispered.

A horse charged down the hill to the salt flats, and Ruby was riding it.

Sasho followed the red-haired beauty with his eyes as she stopped at the top of the pier. "She is as pretty as you said, Jero, and she rides like a man. I like her!"

Mauro said, "Come with me, Sasho." He put his arm around the boy's shoulder and led him to join Fabian at the end of the dock.

Ruby slid off the back of the horse and ran straight into Jero's open arms. "Where have you been, Jero?" she cried.

"Trying to get back to you," Jero breathed out as the two embraced.

Ruby sobbed into his warm chest as he held her close. "I am sorry I didn't believe you would come for me," she told him. "I should have waited."

"I myself almost stopped believing I would make it there. I am sorry I caused so much grief," he cried on her shoulder.

"I dreamed every night that we would finally be together again," Ruby exclaimed, "and here we are!"

Jero stepped back from her, his expression serene. He touched her wet cheeks and brushed a strand of hair from her brow. "I need to ask you something," he said softly.

"Yes, Jero?"

"We have been apart a long time," he told her.

"Three long months," she said.

"You have not changed your mind, have you, Ruby? Do you still want to marry me?" His eyes were pleading.

Ruby understood she needed to convince him to believe her and not let any doubt fester. Her eyes met his when she said, "I learned something important during our time apart."

He waited.

She continued, "My heart was aching until I laid eyes on you again today. There was a void I never knew needed filling. I am no longer whole without you, Jero."

Jero took her hand in his and said aloud the words that had sustained him through his journey, "I love you so much, Ruby Spiros."

"And I love you, Jero Baric." She tugged at his hand and said, "Let's go home."

Chapter 62

The next day, Jero rode to Solgrad on an urgent errand. Sitting on the hard bench behind the closed drape, he waited for the priest to take his place on the other side of the panel.

"You may begin, my son," Father David said with gentle authority.

"I have sinned, Father, and I ask God's forgiveness."

"Tell me your sins, my son, and I will absolve you in the eyes of God."

Jero inhaled deeply and breathed out the dreaded words, "I am married, Father."

The silence from the other side was audible. Not a fidget on the polished bench or a ruffling of the priest's robes could be heard.

"Did you hear me, Father David?"

"Yes, my son." Then the priest asked in a steady voice, "Did you mean to say you want to marry?"

"I want to marry Ruby Spiros, but I do not think I can," Jero mourned. "Through no desire of my own, I agreed to marry a different Ottoman woman."

"How did you happen to make this agreement?" the priest asked with genuine surprise.

"It is a long story, Father, but I married her when her Romani clan took me to Bulgaria."

"You married a gypsy woman?"

"I know it sounds unlikely but, well, yes. It was a real wedding, in front of her kin and everything, and I said I would have her as my wife."

Father David considered the sinner's confession. "Were you married in a church before God?" he asked pointedly.

"Um, no. It was not in a church. But they spoke of God and our sacred union, so I am sure it was binding in His eyes."

"Is the gypsy woman a Christian?"

"I do not know."

"And yet you agreed to take her as your wife?" Father David inquired disapprovingly.

Jero leaned his head against the wooden panel holding the screen between them. His eyes were shut in shame when he answered, "I did agree."

Jero waited for his condemnation, but instead, the priest asked, "Did you consummate your union, my son?"

"No, Father," Jero answered too quickly.

Father David pressed him, "Not even on your wedding night?"

"No, I left on our wedding night."

The holy man pondered some more while Jero sat in silence on his side of the wall. "Well, my son, if she is not a Christian, and you did not consummate the union, then your marriage is not valid in the tradition of our Catholic faith."

Jero sat up tall on the narrow bench and asked, "Then I am free to marry Ruby?"

"Yes, but your confession raises a point I had not considered," the priest acknowledged. "It was my discretion to give the Church's blessing for you to marry Ruby Spiros in her native land. But I cannot perform the sacrament for you here."

Jero was puzzled. "Why not, Father?"

"Ruby is not a Catholic, my son. For you to marry her, the rules are clear: She must receive the Holy Spirit and be purified of her sins before I can join you in matrimony. Above all else, she must be baptized."

"Baptized? Will she also have to study catechism and prayers and such?" Jero wanted to know.

"It would be helpful for the lady to know the expectations God has for her. And, of course, she must be willing to accept Jesus as her savior and take the sacrament of communion."

Jero sighed in frustration. "I am sure she would be willing," he said. "How long will it take to prepare for her baptism? We thought we would marry next week."

Father David's low laugh rumbled in the boxy confessional. "That is a bit rushed, even for the Barics."

Jero sat anxiously through another long silence before the priest declared, "Since I know Ruby to be a moral woman, and she is marrying into a fine Catholic family, I think we can forgo many of the usual preparations. The rites can be made in the small chapel as long as your intended understands the devotion expected of her. I will come by the castle later to discuss the details with Ruby."

Jero leaned back against the wall in relief. "That would be most kind of you, Father David. I think that solves all my worries."

"You have been away a long time, Jero. Is there more you wish to repent? A sin on your conscience is a burden on your soul, my son."

"I understand, Father, but that is all I have on my conscience today." Jero then bowed his head and recited humbly, "For the sins of taking a wife outside the Church and abandoning her on her wedding night, I beg God's forgiveness and ask for penance for my failings."

Through the screen, the priest declared in a clear voice, "For these sins, you are forgiven. In the name of the Father, the Son, and the Holy Spirit, I absolve you of your sins. As for penance, I believe God has put an orphan in your care. You are to do right by him, as others did right by you as a boy."

Jero crossed himself and said, "I will, Father. God is good."

"May God bless you, my son."

"Amen. Thank you, Father."

Jero opened the velvet curtain. His new boots clicked on the polished stone with a renewed lightness at finding a solution to his marriage dilemma.

When he left the quiet sanctuary of the empty church, he found Mauro sitting on the stoop, watching the villagers go about their morning in the main square. Their two horses were tethered to the railing at the bottom of the steps.

Jero paused outside the door and said, "I did not expect to find you here, Mauro. I thought you were leaving with Fabian."

Mauro stood up and brushed the dust from his breeches. "Isabella convinced Fabian that she should accompany him instead. Something about lemons," he said.

"They are nicely suited," Jero remarked. "I am glad they were able to marry."

"Did you talk to Father David about your ceremony next week?"

"I did, but there is an important detail we overlooked."

Mauro scowled at the news of another hurdle.

"The Ottomans would have allowed Ruby to marry a Catholic," Jero said, "but it seems the Catholic Church will not let me marry an Ottoman."

"What does the priest propose? That we find a Protestant minister to perform the ceremony?"

Jero appreciated his brother's attempt at humor. "Now that I think about it, what he asks will be a bit overwhelming for my bride."

"What did he say?"

"Ruby has to become a Catholic. And she must agree to be baptized," Jero said doubtfully.

Mauro scoffed and said, "A baptismal is easy. The smallest babies receive the sacrament, so I am sure that is quickly accomplished."

"Father David will visit later and let Ruby know what is expected. It might take a while to fulfill all his requirements."

Mauro took the delay in stride. "I am sure Ruby will try her best. In the meantime, we can still celebrate your upcoming nuptials tonight. If you are up to it, that is." Mauro untied the horses' reins and passed the straps of the one he had ridden to Jero, keeping Janus to ride home.

Jero patted the unfamiliar horse's neck. "I am sorry I ruined your plans yesterday," he said absently.

Mauro shrugged good-naturedly. "Plans are easily changed, Jero, and you needed the sleep more than a party. Nela told me she will make an even grander dinner tonight."

Jero told him, "You should have seen the loaded tray she brought for my breakfast. Nela said I look half-starved, so she sat with me and watched me eat. It was the most delicious breakfast I can remember."

Mauro hopped in the saddle and declared, "You can ride it off. I thought we might go out to your new home and have a look. It is all ready for you."

Jero followed Mauro's lead, and the two rode their horses out of the town square, side by side, past the villagers' shops and stone houses. Women and men alike stopped their business to wave and bow to their baron and his brother. The Barics smiled and tipped their hats in greeting as they trotted toward the highway.

When they were alone again, Jero contentedly said, "I don't know how to thank you for your generous gift, Mauro."

"There is nothing to thank me for, Jero. By birth and by measure of courage, you should have been the heir to the House of Baric. You saved it, after all."

"I can still say my humble thank you. You changed my life from being an orphan to belonging to a family. With my own house!"

"Speaking of orphans, has the boy made up his mind?"

Jero shifted uncomfortably in the saddle. "Sasho wanted to return home, mostly to see for himself that his mother is dead. I think I finally convinced him it would still be too dangerous for him there. He will stay here for a while."

"How old did you say he was?"

"He said thirteen to try to impress me, but I think he is younger. Maybe ten or eleven," Jero replied.

"That is a good age to start learning a skill. Why don't you arrange an apprenticeship for him in the village?" When Jero stalled, Mauro suggested, "Or send him to a city where a young lad has many apprentice choices."

Jero looked beyond his brother to their castle on the hill. "I am going to make him my ward," he said firmly.

Mauro stopped his horse and shook his head. "How will that help him, Jero? He is a foreigner, remember? Let Sasho learn a skill that he can use later in Tirana."

"There will be no later for him. No one cares what happens to him there. I care, though. I will look after him."

"He is practically feral, Jero," Mauro pointed out.

"I would not call him that," Jero said more optimistically. "He is a little rough around the edges, but he is smart and capable. I think he can be trained and molded to be a gentleman. I thought I might hire a tutor for him once we are settled." Jero flicked his reins, and his horse trotted ahead.

Mauro caught up and insisted, "You hardly know the boy, Jero. Give yourself more time to decide."

"I do not need more time. His mother would still be alive if she hadn't stuck her neck out to help me. If he wants to return to Tirana when he comes of age, I will make sure he returns as a man of means. Sasho and Zerina saved my life, and I will repay him for it. That is my decision."

Mauro backed down. "I will not question it again," he said.

Jero stroked the strong neck of the mare he sat on and asked, "When did you get this horse, Mauro?"

Mauro smiled slyly, answering, "She is a beauty, isn't she? I brought her and two more mares into my herd before we went to Venice."

"Does she have a name?" Jero asked.

"Alberto calls her Siren. She seems placid and sweet until the rider takes her out of the paddock. Then her disposition is a bit, well, erratic."

Jero laughed. "And you wanted me to ride her through the countryside?"

"Yes," Mauro said just as cheerfully. "You will need a new horse to take with you when you move. If she suits you, she is yours."

"Really?" Jero stroked her again with growing admiration. "Thank you, Mauro."

"Thank Fabian. He sees something special in her, like he saw in Bacchus. With a little more training, he thinks she will be a fine horse for you."

They continued riding south, past the turnoff leading to the castle, and Jero remarked, "Siren seems to be minding her manners well enough. Can she run?"

Mauro thought about it. "Only Josip has been riding her, but he seems to think so."

"Faster than Janus?"

Mauro saw the unmistakable twinkle in his brother's eyes and asked, "Do I hear a challenge?"

Jero matched his playful tone. "Her trot is steady. She is lean and long. I'd like to let her loose and see."

Mauro halted Janus and asked, "From here to the harbor road?"

"On three," Jero said.

"Two, One!" Mauro shouted.

The horses took off sprinting while the brothers hooted and laughed like they had not done in months, each holding on tight as their horses raced down the empty road.

~*~

Verica searched the marble bench, between the linens and among the piled clothes. "I seem to have forgotten your comb, Lady Baric. I would go get it, but I should not leave you alone."

Resi ran her fingers through her wet hair and said, "Ruby is with me, Verica. If I swoon and sink, she can fish me out."

"Of course," Verica agreed hesitantly.

After the maid left the bathhouse, Resi confided to Ruby, "Verica has been acting strangely the last few days. I can hardly use the chamber pot without her waiting by the screen, asking if I am all right." Resi leaned back to take the weight off her heavy middle, and her mood lifted with it.

"But then again," she continued, "I don't think I could get through the day without Verica now. When you are married, Ruby, you will want to find a handmaiden. She should be someone you like and trust. Maybe Mauro will let one of our maids move in with you. Would you like that, Ruby? Ruby," Resi said, "are you even listening to me?"

"I am listening." Ruby let a handful of water run through her fingers and pondered, "Do you really think the wedding should coincide with the harvest party?"

"Why not? Everyone will want to celebrate your wedding with you, and the fine weather won't hold much longer to have a reception outdoors."

"You don't think maybe it is too soon?"

"Did Jero say something to make you change your mind?" Resi asked with worry.

"He said he wants to marry me still, but . . ." Ruby hesitated.

"What is bothering you, Ruby? Tell me."

Ruby sank into the water and groaned, "There is nothing to tell. We haven't had any time alone to talk yet. I don't know what happened in those months, but he doesn't seem happy to be home."

Resi scooted to her side in the pool and exclaimed, "Think about how you felt the first day coming back, Ruby. The reception yesterday was overwhelming. I would have felt smothered by all the attention and retired early, too. Have you seen Jero today?"

Ruby sobbed, "I haven't, and when I asked Davor if Jero was in his chamber, he said he had left for the village. I thought for sure he would stop by my room to say good morning."

"Don't be sad, Ruby dear. Give him time to settle in. Once you are married, you will get to know each other again."

"My mind is reeling. There is so much to think about."

Resi tried brightening her outlook and asked, "Have you decided what you will wear at your wedding?"

"That too!" Ruby fretted.

Resi chuckled at her friend's sudden panic. "Then I will decide that for you. You must wear your pink gown."

Ruby floated along the pool's edge, thinking aloud, "I do love that gown, but it isn't exactly modest for a wedding."

"If you don't wear a corset, like at the ball, it can be more modest, and Verica can add some lace to the bodice. You will make a beautiful bride."

~*~

Marija openly stared at Sasho as he stuffed more pastry into his mouth. "Don't you have cakes where you come from?" she asked across the kitchen table.

Sasho wiped the crumbs from his face with the back of his sleeve and asked in broken Croatian, "Is that what they are called?"

"Maybe you didn't get much food at all, where you were," Brigita surmised as she cleared off her plate.

"Food? Yes. We have food. My mother and I had meat and bread every day. Old Isaak would smack me when I took too much from his kitchen, but only once in a while. If I could steal a fish, my ma would cook that special, just for us."

Aron scooted his chair away from the young criminal sitting next to him. "We don't steal food here," he pointed out. "That is wrong."

"When you are very hungry, it isn't wrong. Jero said so himself when we stole from the farmer's orchard."

"Jero would never steal," Ivana protested.

Natalija wondered, "Why didn't you just ask the farmer to give a hungry boy a handout?"

"Jero did ask, miss. But the farmer's wife began crying that we would murder her, and the farmer tried to kill us with his sickle because the soldiers had already been there and told them to watch out for us, but we only wanted a little broth and bread, not to kill anyone. Especially not Jero since he didn't kill the man like they said he did, but he buried the other two men, and he didn't have to do that, except the captain would have beaten him again, and so he thought digging graves was better than being strung out to blister in the hot sun."

Around the communal table, the young servants were speechless. Their mouths hung open as they contemplated Sasho's rushed and rambling story that he could only have made up.

Franja ignored the children's open disapproval, put another plate of honeyed bread in front of the boy, and explained, "Jero has not had a chance to tell us his stories about farmers with sickles and burying dead men. But be assured, there will be no one chasing you here. And when you are hungry, Sasho, you come to the kitchen, and we will find you a treat to eat."

Aron shook his head, doubting that getting a treat between meals was that simple.

Nela noticed his pout and told the water boy, "Sasho is our guest, and he has a lot of eating to make up for. Why don't you take the last of the sliced bread with you, Aron, and show him the stables? Run along, now."

"Come on, Sasho," Aron said with a new authority, and Sasho followed him out the back door, each carrying a sticky piece of bread.

"Girls," Nela went on to say, "hurry with your lunch now. The baroness and Lady Ruby will want theirs shortly."

Glancing out the window, Nela noticed Verica walking the path from the bathhouse, and it jogged her memory. "Natalija," she called over.

"Yes, Nela?" Natalija stood up and brushed the crumbs from her apron.

"I just saw Verica heading toward the stairs. Can you tell her that Lord Felix was looking for her? He might still be practicing in the great hall."

"He asks to talk to her a lot, doesn't he?" Natalija casually commented.

"And so does your Daniel," Ivana pointed out.

"He is not my Daniel," Natalija corrected her.

Brigita remarked, "He would be yours if you let him ask you."

Natalija cocked her head and inquired, "Ask me what?"

The girls giggled, and Ivana blurted out, "Ask you to marry him, silly."

"Oh, that." As she left the kitchen, Natalija turned to say, "He already has."

~*~

With the comb tucked in her apron pocket, Verica hurried down the grand staircase. "Hello, Natalija," she said in passing.

"Hello, Verica," Natalija replied, and then she remembered her errand. "Wait! I was to give you a message."

"For her ladyship?"

"No, for you, Verica. Nela said Lord Felix is in the great hall and wanted to tell you something."

Verica took a second to listen at the door. "I don't hear him playing."

"It might have been a while ago, actually," Natalija admitted.

"Why didn't you tell me earlier?" Verica asked.

Unfazed by her disappointment, Natalija replied, "I didn't know earlier." She continued up the stairs.

Verica went to the door and found herself face to face with a startled Felix, who was just leaving.

"Verica! Hello."

"I got your message, Felix, but I am on my way to help my mistress."

"I will be quick." He waved her to a quiet corner of the foyer and said, "Maybe you have already heard this, but Lord Baric has offered to sponsor my studies in Florence. I will learn from the masters at the Baroque School of Music again."

Verica forced a smile and offered her congratulations, "That is great news, Felix, and very generous of Lord Baric. You will soon forget you ever wanted to become a soldier." Her chin began to quiver.

"I will not forget you, Verica, if that is what you are thinking. You are very special to me."

She struggled to hold his gaze when she said, "I am sure you will meet many special girls in Florence."

"The last time I was there, I hardly left my music. I doubt I will have time to meet anyone." Then he noticed her looking down and added, "I won't even want to."

Verica reminded him, "The last time you were in Florence, you were engaged to be married, Felix. Now you are a bachelor with a bright future." She brushed the back of her finger across her cheek and asked, "When are you leaving?"

Felix took a step closer. He leaned against the wall to close the space between them. "Not right away. Lord Baric asked me to play with the band at the harvest celebration. Maybe you will save me a dance?"

"Maybe." She shoved her hands into her apron pockets to keep from reaching out. The sharp poke of the comb reminded her she was needed elsewhere. "I have to go," she said.

He touched her sleeve to stop her. "Lord Baric has invited me and the other officers to dinner tonight. Will you be there?" he asked.

She frowned at his ignorance. "I eat in the kitchen. I am a servant, or have you forgotten?"

Felix backpedaled. "I know you will not dine with us, but just the same—will I see you?"

"You might. Lord Baric will probably invite the servants to toast Jero and Lady Ruby's marriage."

"Then I look forward to seeing you again. Good day, Verica."

His elegant bow made Verica feel like a lady, and her smile finally broke through. "Good day, Felix," she mumbled and hurried away.

~*~

Resi lay back on her pillows in bed and contemplated her happiness. "That was the perfect evening, Mauro. I think Ruby feels better about the sudden wedding plans now."

Mauro pulled the covers over the two of them and asked, "Did she have her doubts?"

"Jero was gone for a long time. Ruby imagined he would be the same, but circumstances change people."

"Hardships change people," Mauro corrected her.

Resi stroked the curls around his temple and wondered, "Did Jero talk to you about what happened?"

"He started to, but it all seems too painful still. Jero told me a little about his escape, but not why he broke out of prison in the first place. Then he told me how he and Sasho spent days hiding and hungry until they ended up with a clan of gypsies who promised to lead them to the right road to Thessaloniki. All I know is that they tricked him."

"Poor Jero," Resi said. "I think we will only hear bits and pieces for a while."

"We did take a nice ride out to the old manor house—Jero's new manor house," Mauro told her. "He seemed better after our visit. His thoughts were clearer. I believed him when he said he was truly looking forward to starting his life there with Ruby."

"That makes me happy to—ahhh!" Resi winced with a twinge of pain.

Mauro was on his feet at once. "Is it the baby?"

She moaned loudly, "It is . . . oohhh," she breathed out. "Stabbing sharpness . . . ahh . . . but it will pass."

"How long have you been having these pains?"

"Just this week. Mmm," Resi grunted. "Ruby says false labor pains happen often in the last month."

Mauro argued, "Yes, but you have more than a month to go. Why not bring in a midwife, just to be ready?"

She reached her hand out to soothe his alarm, and he slid beside her in bed again.

"Ahh," she moaned softly. "A midwife will put me in confinement. You promised . . . oohhh . . . no dark room."

"No one will lock you up, Resi, but childbirth is a dangerous undertaking, my love. If you are having pains, then maybe—"

"We've discussed this," she said with a flash of irritation and then took a long breath to ease the pang. "Every day is a dangerous undertaking for you, Mauro, and you don't allow me to worry."

Mauro stroked her furrowed brow and reasoned, "This is different, and you know it, my dear. Just let me bring in someone to check on you."

He planted tiny kisses on her brow and then down the point of her nose to rouse her sensibility. Resi relaxed under his touch and shut her eyes as the last of the pain subsided.

"Lady Nikolina had four good outcomes with her midwife," Mauro reminded her. "Let me send for her, and she will be able to tell you if the pains are serious."

Mauro's patience with his wife paid off because Resi reluctantly agreed, "The midwife can come and check on me. But not until after the wedding."

Mauro grinned at her predictable defiance. "You are a stubborn woman, Terese Baric. After the wedding, then."

Chapter 63

Solgrad, 14 October 1649

The Barics, their tenants, the villagers, and noble guests filled the church to give thanks to God for a bountiful harvest and to witness the marriage of Jero Baric and Ruby Spiros.

Since Father David's visit, Ruby had spent all her free hours cramming for the rituals ahead. Her required baptism had taken place in the chapel a few days ago, without an audience or a script to memorize. But the Catholic prayers and replies in a wedding ceremony took a lifetime to commit to memory. Ruby rehearsed and repeated the lines of the coming sacrament, but time had run out—ten days was not enough. In the end, Ruby's veil hid her forgetfulness as she stumbled through her part in the ceremony to become the second Greek Lady Baric.

On that day, the Barics broke their tradition in another way. The harvest celebration, which had always taken place on the fields outside Baric Castle, was held at the newly renovated villa at the far edge of the barony. Under the waning sun in the October sky, the parade of people arrived in carriages, wagons, carts, and on foot down the eastern road. With his beautiful new wife on the wagon bench beside him, Jero led the long line of well-wishers through the valley. They were Jero's friends he had known since he was a boy, loyal neighbors he had barely met, and loved ones Jero briefly thought he would never see again. Jero felt like he was in a dream, riding over the last hill to a new life. He squeezed Ruby's hand for assurance that it was actually happening.

Jero's adopted servant, Ervin, lowered the drawbridge over the marshy moat and readied the torches along the mossy entrance in advance of the coming darkness. Boughs of fragrant evergreens, yellow and orange gourds, and the last of the summer flowers had transformed the courtyard into a festive, outdoor dining hall.

Beyond the circular courtyard, the wagons and carts emptied their passengers, who joined those arriving on foot to add their crocks of homemade specialties and baskets of baked goods to feed the hungry party. Long spits had been turning over sputtering logs all morning, and the aroma of roasting fowl and sizzling skewered pigs filled the afternoon air. Men unloaded and tapped kegs of ale and cider, and the eager congregation sat down to feast.

Plank tables, decorated with the Barics' banner colors, had been assembled for the communal meal. The Barics and their honored guests took their places at the elevated table in front, exchanging stories and memories exuberantly as they and the others, seated in rows below, stuffed themselves from the lavish banquet.

When the platters were empty and no one rose to refill them, the Baron of Baric stood up to continue the tradition of his ancestors. He signaled his guardsmen to bring out the readied baskets, proudly displaying a sampling of everything harvested that season.

The dozen tenant farmers and their families, villagers with their children, and the castle's residents and servants turned their attention to their lord. Mauro began his speech with a humble familiarity: "People of Solgrad and welcomed guests! Our cellars are full with this year's bounty. It was a banner year for apricots and cherries, and the figs and grapes drying in our barns will sweeten our winter meals. The last of the apples and chestnuts are being picked, and the men will start shaking the olives in a few weeks. This year, the rye and barley fields filled each farmer's stores, and the leftover grain was sold for a good profit. I thank all the farmers and their families who toiled in the fields and orchards with success!"

The applause echoed across the yard.

Mauro went on, "Your goats, sheep, and cows have given us milk and meat to feed our growing children, wool to weave, and hides to tan. Thank you for your hard work this year, shepherds. Many of you work as woodsmen, as well, tirelessly cutting and splitting all summer, so our hearths will glow warm all winter. And I thank you!"

The partygoers raised their mugs with renewed cheers.

"But there are others who help keep our houses stocked and our hearths warm. Even today, the coopers are working long hours, making barrels to hold your bounty. The tradesmen take your surpluses of grain and wool and cheese to the markets in Venice. I thank you, villagers of Solgrad, for your dedicated work!"

Mauro continued to talk above the hoots and applause, "God provides fish along our shores for our fishermen who bring their catch to market each week, and I thank them! The sea provides more than fish for your table. It holds the salt that seasons your meals, preserves your game, and sustains the House of Baric. It takes hard work to glean it, and the Kuzjak men managed to collect one extra harvest this October." Mauro tipped his hat to Jakov. "I thank you!"

Mauro pointed to the dozen baskets that lined the cobbled ground below him. "This is your triumph! This harvest nourishes and sustains our lives! But even such a bounty cannot ward off death forever, and we mourn the passing of several of our loved ones this year. Especially heartbreaking at Baric Castle was the loss of our healing woman and maternal figure to many over generations: Idita of the House of Baric."

The faithful bowed their heads and made the sign of the cross.

Mauro took a deep breath and continued, "As Idita would have pointed out, death and life are inseparable, and happily we celebrate the babies born into our village this year as well." Mauro looked down at his wife next to him and added, "My own child will be born very soon."

The applause and gleeful hollers made Mauro smile when he said, "And with each passing harvest, children will grow up, marry, and start families of their own. Three weddings were held in Solgrad this year, among them my own brother's, whose marriage we celebrate today." Mauro turned to Jero, sitting at his side, and joined the others in their ovation.

The musicians were taking their places on low stools set up in the corner of the crowded courtyard when Mauro finally concluded, "There is indeed much to be grateful for this year and much to celebrate." He hollered above the noise of shuffling feet and murmurs, "Clear the tables, and let the dancing begin!"

The musicians began to play.

~*~

Isabella moved down the table to sit at Resi's side. She whispered, "I feel a bit overwhelmed by the day, Terese. Perhaps my corset is laced too tight."

"Isabella, are you—?"

"I am not," Isabella interrupted before Resi could ask the obvious.

"Whether you are or you are not, it has been quite a long day." Resi rose and linked arms with her new best friend. "Why don't we go into the house and make some adjustments?"

Resi stopped Mauro, who was helping to carry the plank tables away, and asked, "Will you save me a dance?"

"With pleasure," her husband replied distractedly.

Resi led Isabella past the table where the Leopold ladies lingered, watching the young men and women partnering up to dance. Resi announced, "We are going into the house to refresh ourselves."

The entire table of ladies perked up at Resi's general offer of refuge. Joining Lady Nikolina and her mother-in-law, Lady Eleonora, were Lady Raneri, her spinster daughter, and the wives of three of Mauro's Croatian council colleagues with their eligible daughters in tow.

Ruby had already slipped away before her new sitting room was taken over by colorfully skirted ladies and their maids, who were retying stockings and fanning themselves on the sofas. They were surprised to see the bride coming down the staircase.

"Are you here alone, Lady Ruby?" Lady Eleonora wanted to know.

"Perhaps she has already slunk off with her new man," one of the visiting ladies teased.

"Geltrude," Lady Raneri scolded, "do not put your wicked ideas into Lady Ruby's sweet thoughts. She was overwhelmed, is all, weren't you, Lady Ruby?"

"Weddings are very stressful for a bride," Lady Nikolina remarked.

Ruby explained to the room, "To be honest, I haven't had a moment to myself all day. Jero is waiting for me in the courtyard. I think there will be more toasts and then dancing."

"I believe the dancing has already begun," Resi told her.

Lady Raneri asserted, "Lady Baric, you should let your maids join the dancing, and they could take my Ester with them. She was not able to come to your ball, but she dances so beautifully."

"I do not want to, Mother," Ester mumbled in reply.

"Such a delightful girl," Lady Eleonora said as she headed up the steps. "Is there a servant girl upstairs, my dear?" the old matriarch asked Ruby.

"Lucija is the chambermaid. She will help you, Lady Leopold."

Old Lord Zoric's new wife joined the conversation: "I wanted to tell you how much I admire your lovely gown, Lady Ruby. The color is perfect for your complexion, and the lace is so delicate."

"Ah, but you were not at the Barics' ball to see the dress before the lace was added, Lady Zoric. When Lady Ruby arrived for the dancing there, she turned every man's head," Lady Nikolina recounted.

Isabella, who had been fanning herself, came to life again in her overstuffed chair. "Verica!" she called out.

Verica dutifully stepped to her side. "Is something the matter, Lady Isabella?"

"It just occurred to me that the lace has served its purpose. Lady Ruby owes her husband the full effect of her gown again. Can you snip the lace?"

Verica turned to Ruby and said, "If you will allow me, I left a few loose strings in case you changed your mind."

With a strategic tug on the tucked thread, Verica left the square bodice of Ruby's dress unadorned again.

Isabella made her inspection, saying, "You do the dress justice that way." Isabella then unpinned the veil that covered the bride's fashionably twisted hair to reveal the ivory combs Resi had lent her.

Sitting against some pillows to relieve her aching back, Resi watched as Isabella fussed over Ruby, fixing the rouge on her lips and cheeks.

Ruby could not hide her growing nervousness with everyone's attention on her appearance. She asked Isabella, "When the time comes, how will I get out of the gown?"

Isabella smiled mischievously and said, "That is part of the foreplay, my dear. All men love to undress a woman."

Lady Raneri laughed and remarked, "I doubt there will be any foreplay on her wedding night, Lady Carrera. A newly married man can barely get his breeches off, especially with everything exposed. Perhaps she should leave some lace in place to keep him wondering."

Ruby looked to Isabella, who insisted good-naturedly, "What would be the point, Lady Raneri? She is married now."

Lady Raneri countered, "Yes, but a lady only has one wedding night. If I had one piece of advice . . ."

The assembly of ladies pelted Ruby with their advice faster than a squad of bowmen could shoot arrows:

"Do not forget to unpin your curls."

"Yes, men love long hair in bed."

"Never undress all the way. A man needs a little mystery."

"Nonsense! A man will want to see what is under her shift."

"On such a chilly night? Keep under the covers, Lady Ruby. Goose bumps are most unattractive."

"That is a good point! A cold room is a disaster for a wedding night."

"You should send your maid to light the fireplace right away."

"No, no, Lady Ruby. Keep the room cold and let him chase you a little. That will heat things up."

At that moment, Lady Eleonora descended the stairs and said with authority, "Jero is a gentleman, not some horny farm boy. Whatever Jero does choose to do, dear Lady Ruby, remember to be agreeable."

"Yes, be agreeable," another agreed.

"Flatter him, however it may turn out," Lady Eleonora concluded, and the genteel ladies, young and old, all concurred with nods and whispers at that last piece of advice.

Ruby looked to Resi, who merely shrugged with an amused smile at the conflicting opinions.

Natalja startled the gossiping group when she opened the sitting room door and announced, "They are starting the toasts for the bride and groom, my ladies!"

Resi shifted and wiggled herself off the comfortable sofa. She took Ruby's arm in hers and said, "Just this one last chore, dear Ruby, and then you will be left alone with your new husband." They joined the line of ladies who gracefully emptied the room.

Anastasia stayed behind. She tapped Verica on the shoulder and said, "I was wondering if you might help me with my lace, too?"

"Do you have a thread you need fixed?" Verica asked.

"I would actually, um, like to cut some away. I am ready to draw a little attention to myself."

"Oh, I see," Verica said, hiding her surprise.

She studied the design of Anastasia's high collar. "Well, if I cut along the pattern and fold it under, you can easily stitch the lace back together again if you wanted. Wait here and I find a blade in the kitchen."

Verica returned with a paring knife, and Anastasia stood still while the maid carefully cut through the tight threads of the intricate lace and folded it open. "There, that looks like it was made for a party."

With no looking glass in the room, Anastasia ran her fingers over her exposed cleavage. "It is not too revealing?"

Verica considered her dilemma and assured her, "It is still modest enough. Whose eye are you trying to catch?"

"I was thinking I would not mind dancing with Davor," Anastasia admitted.

"Davor?" Verica could not hide her surprise.

"I know what I said before, but I find I am indeed attracted to him somehow."

With a raised brow, Verica agreed, "Of course, you are. What is not to like about Davor? Can I make one suggestion, though?"

Anastasia nodded eagerly.

"It's your hair."

The Venetian touched her tight bun and asked, "Is something out of place?"

"Not a wisp! It is as stiff and tight as an old matron's. That will not do for a party, Anastasia. Sit down and let me fix it."

Anastasia had not had her hair down in public in years. She shut her eyes anxiously and did as she was asked.

Verica pulled the combs and pins holding Anastasia's long hair tight against her scalp, then loosened the locks with her fingers, lifting them until they floated down her back. Verica smiled at the change. The young handmaid looked her age again. "The knot has made pretty spirals. I'll leave the rest pinned as you had it but let the length fall."

When Verica was done, Anastasia asked, "Is it good?"

"It is perfect. Let's go join the party."

~*~

"Jero, Jero!" Sasho tugged at Jero's jacket and said, "The boys are playing a game outside the wall. Can I go with them?"

"Yes, go play," was Jero's hasty answer until he looked down at the boy. "Wait! Where are your stockings?" he asked.

Sasho stared down at his skinny bare legs above his new leather shoes. "Um, they are in my jacket pocket, Jero."

Mauro had overheard his brother's new ward and joined the inquisition, "Where is your jacket, young man?"

Sasho still could not look the baron-prince in the eye. "Oh, right, sir," he mumbled to his feet. "I took the coat off when I went in the moat. I didn't want to risk spoiling it."

"You went in the water in your breeches?" Jero asked.

"Not in the deep part! I was mostly in the mud and didn't get my fine clothes wet. See, Jero?" Sasho held out the billowing fabric of his new pants.

Jero let the argument go. "Have you eaten?" he asked the boy.

Sasho assured Jero, "Oh, yes, lots. Can I go now?" He was eager to join his new friends.

"Go!" Jero ordered, grinning. "But don't fall asleep on the wall or something stupid like that. You are going home with the baron tonight, and I don't want to hear that they had to look for you."

"We can go on the wall?" Sasho asked excitedly.

"No!" Mauro interjected.

Sasho took that as his cue to head off before Lord Baric forbade leaving the courtyard altogether.

Jero called out, "Mind what I said!"

"He is quite a handful, Jero," Mauro warned. "Are you sure he will be able to sit still and learn with Signor Ulysses?"

Jero shook his head and chuckled. "I am not sure at all, but you and Mateo managed to sit long enough at that age. I remember you were out the door the second you were released."

"To find you polishing my boots," Mauro remarked with a frown.

"Yes, and you pulled them from my hands, and we ran outside together," Jero said. "I told you a hundred times, Mauro: I have no regrets."

A waving motion from across the terrace caught Mauro's eye, and he remarked, "I think Hugo and Teodor are trying to get your attention. Not to spoil it for you, but they have something planned before you go upstairs."

Jero nodded with a laugh. "Teo hinted at it earlier. I better go."

Fabian passed Jero as he strolled toward the eager bachelors. The Venetian was carrying two mugs and offered one to Mauro. "That was a wonderful speech earlier, Mauritius. People were practically blushing with pride."

"They should be proud! With no war to fight, it has been an exceptional year for them, and for me."

Fabian raised his brows and reminded Mauro, "Except when you nearly died—twice. Your ship was taken and your castle invaded. Your brother was almost executed in a foreign land, and—"

"And still," Mauro interjected, "I settled a feud with the navy, rid myself of a stalker, regained a brother, fell madly in love with my wife, made a baby, witnessed my two best friends marry, made peace with my dead mother and father—"

"Alright, alright," Fabian conceded. "There is certainly reason to celebrate, old friend, and I do love how the folks in your part of the Empire throw a party." Fabian asked thoughtfully, "Why didn't you have a party after your wedding, Mauritius?"

"My uncle called us away, remember?"

"Ah, yes. Those were trying days, the last year of war with the Habsburgs. It seems so long ago now."

"Terrible times," Mauro agreed, taking a swig from his cup.

"Sleeping in the rain, chewing the last scraps of meat off a bone, wondering if this would be the day an arrow finally found you," Fabian said distractedly.

"You miss it, don't you?" Mauro asked.

Fabian sighed. "I do. Well, not war itself, of course. But I miss the camaraderie of being a soldier and the impulsiveness of the fight."

"That is why I keep my castle guard trained and ready, instead of releasing them to be farmers and tradesmen." Mauro remarked, "You should recruit some guardsmen for your new estate. This peace may not last."

"I was thinking maybe I could take a few of yours."

"Never," Mauro said with a laugh.

"Not Hugo or Daniel?"

"Maybe a year ago, but not now. Look at Denis and Latif and Teo over there. I watched them grow from gangly boys into capable warriors, and I would trust them with my life now. And Daniel could hardly say a sentence a few years ago. Tonight he is flirting with a girl while dancing." Mauro sighed.

"I expect to lose Hugo and Vilim when they finally settle down, but they will always be family to me."

"Another beautiful speech," Fabian proclaimed. "I think I am going to cry."

Mauro shoved him good-naturedly and said, "I was being serious, Fabian."

"So was I," Fabian replied.

"I am glad to have your company again, Fabian." Mauro wrapped his arm around his friend's shoulders, and the two weaved their way through the crowd.

~*~

The musicians played a favorite jig, and a dozen or so flirtatious couples skipped through linked arms, laughing at those too drunk or clumsy to clear the arch of dancers before their arms fell.

Verica was making small talk with a hopeful dance partner while she watched Davor's eyes follow the pretty girl who danced with Denis.

When the music ended, she excused herself from the farmer's son and strolled across the dance floor to Davor's side. "Why aren't you dancing?" she asked.

"Did you want to dance?" He set his mug down to take her arm.

"Not with you," she replied with a friendly wink. "I think you should cut in on Denis and his partner."

Davor searched the colorful dancers assembling again. "Who is Denis's partner?" he asked.

"Don't you recognize Lady Carrera's maid?"

The music had started, and Davor watched Anastasia on Denis's arm.

Verica watched, too. "She looks very pretty tonight. You should ask her to dance."

"She'll say no. She hates me," Davor said bluntly.

Verica shot him a questioning glance. "I doubt that," she said.

Davor rattled off his proof: "I greet Anastasia in the corridor, and she walks the other way. I smiled at her in the foyer, and she turned up her nose. I can barely get her to pass me the butter dish at the kitchen table, so what else would you call that, Verica?"

"Men make her nervous," Verica insisted.

Davor followed Anastasia with his eyes. "She doesn't seem nervous with Denis."

"Maybe it's just servants who make her nervous, then. I shouldn't, but I will let you in on a secret."

Davor turned his attention back to Verica. "About Anastasia?"

"She told me she has never met a kind manservant. As a matter of fact, she thought they were mostly unkind. You should prove her wrong."

Davor considered the challenge. "Do you really think she would say yes if I asked her to dance?"

Verica watched Denis's happy expression as he chatted with the receptive Venetian maid.

"Well," Verica said pensively, "maybe you had better cut in before she finds she favors soldiers."

"I see your point." Davor excused himself and hurried through the bystanders. As the music stopped, he brushed past Simeon, talking to Franja.

Simeon leaned on his crutches and asked, "Why aren't you dancing tonight?"

Franja answered cheerfully, "I don't have a partner."

"There are plenty of men waiting for a pretty dance partner like you."

Her expression brightened. "I guess I am waiting for the right one, Simeon."

"If you are looking at me, my dancing days are over," Simeon said.

She glared at her former lover, reminding him, "A few weeks ago, you said that about walking, and later about riding. I bet you could dance if you tried."

Simeon watched the tide of flowing skirts and billowing sleeves of jacket-less men and shook his head. "Hobbling around with my crutch is hardly dancing unless you want to see me make a fool of myself."

Franja frowned and remarked, "Take a good look, Simeon. Half your chums can barely stand. Who will remember in the morning how you danced?"

He pulled himself up from his self-doubt and said, "Why are you always right, Franja?"

"So, will you dance tonight?" Franja pointed toward the torchlit barn and said, "We can practice there. I am sure the horses won't laugh. I certainly won't." She put out her arm for him to take, and they crossed the shadowed courtyard to the big barn.

~*~

Mauro smiled to himself when he noticed Simeon and Franja leaving the group. He looked around for his wife for their promised dance, but instead, his eyes found Jero's tall frame. There was still something Mauro needed to tell his brother before ringing the bell to send the newlyweds off to bed. He came up to Jero's side and said, "Can I have a word?"

Jero excused himself from the group of men. "Is it time?" he asked.

Mauro shook his head with amusement. "The party has gone on too long for you, I know, but since you have married my wife's best friend, I am compelled to give you some advice."

Jero's bright eyes were questioning. "I think I already know what you will say, Mauro."

"Let me say it anyway."

Mauro put his hand on Jero's shoulder and counseled, "Treat your new bride with care, dear brother. She should be the one person you would give your life to make happy."

Jero replied, "I would not dream of making Ruby unhappy."

"I know that, Jero, but I am speaking about tonight, specifically," Mauro said with emphasis. "The only advice I got before my wedding night was to hurry and seal the marriage contract. But, Jero, a woman expects more from tonight than a man—romance and such. I did not take that into consideration, and I wish I would have taken more time. Am I making myself clear?"

Jero bashfully replied, "You are, Mauro, and I shall heed your sage advice."

Mauro grinned and said, "Then, dear brother, it is time."

A large handbell had been left on a table, and Mauro began to ring it. The drummer from the band struck a beat, and the people clapped to the rhythm. Jero knew his cue from other wedding celebrations, and he and Ruby found each other in the parting crowd. Hand in hand, the newlyweds walked to the front door of their new home through the throng of well-wishers lining the path. Through the singing and cheering, drunken words of encouragement could be heard:

"Hope you remember how it's done, Jero!" someone shouted.

Another added, "Holler down if you have any questions!"

"Don't pass out before you get to the end," a voice in the crowd warned.

"She'll know how to keep him awake," retorted another.

The ceremonial taunting became muffled as the bride and groom climbed the dark staircase with their candelabra. The door to their bedchamber was open, but the house upstairs was quiet and empty. Someone had already turned down the covers and lit the obligatory candle on the window ledge in front of the closed shutters.

Jero smiled shyly at his new wife. "So, here we are."

He shut the chamber door behind her, and Ruby glanced around her new bedroom. "Yes. Here we are," she repeated.

Jero noticed someone had brought a crock of wine and two glasses, and he filled them. "Would you like some?"

"No, thank you. I have had too much already."

He left the glasses on the table and asked, "Did I tell you how pretty you look in your gown?"

"I suppose I should take it off," Ruby said as she reached behind her to fiddle with the closure.

"Do you need help undressing? I mean, there must be many hooks and such."

Ruby turned away from Jero and said, "I do need your help. It unfastens in back." Then Ruby remembered what the ladies had advised earlier, and she pulled the combs from her hair to let her long tresses drop. The locks fell over her shoulder and cascaded down her back.

Jero gathered her soft curls. Her new husband needed no instruction and nimbly unhooked each loop while breathing in Ruby's perfumed scent.

Kissing the nape of her neck, Jero lifted the dress's straps and let the garment slide onto the floor. After his wife stepped out from the billowing cloud of pink and white piled at her feet, the servant in Jero gingerly picked up the precious gown and draped it carefully over the open armoire door.

When he turned back to her and saw her disrobed figure, his mouth curled into a grin. "That is nearly as pretty as your gown," he remarked. "Can you breathe in it?"

Ruby nervously touched the satin corset that she wore over her ruffled shift. Its slats of wrapped ivory pressed against her barely-covered breasts and cinched her already narrow waist.

"I don't normally wear one," Ruby assured him, "but Lady Isabella insisted the Venetian dress needs a corset. She also said it would please you."

"Did Lady Isabella tell you what my reaction would be?"

Ruby's cheeks burned with a blush. "There was some talk of that," she admitted. "She thought you might enjoy helping me out of it. Or I can leave it on for you and help you undress first."

"Leave it on," he nervously replied as he began unfastening his waistcoat. "In general, men do not require help undressing," he remarked. His fingers quickly moved down the long row of silver buttons, and Ruby sat on the bed and watched.

"Why does the baron have a valet if he doesn't need help with his costume?" she asked.

Jero laughed at the truth of it as he unwound his cravat and peeled off his damp linen shirt. He set them aside and said, "Undressing is easy for a man. Dressing, on the other hand, with the proper collars, cravats, and pins, needs an extra hand sometimes."

Dressed only in his breeches now, Jero considered how to honor his promise to his brother. He knelt in front of Ruby, sitting in her layered shift on the edge of the mattress. He slipped her shoes off, setting each down under the bed. He stroked her calf and asked, "Shall I help you with your stockings?"

Ruby bit her lower lip and answered with more of a quiver than a nod.

She lifted her hem to her knees, and Jero's hands lightly explored above the folded fabric until he found the ribbon that held up her stocking. Their eyes met.

"May I?" he asked before lifting the skirt above the ribbon. He unrolled the cotton stocking and set it on the floor with the tie. He touched her second thigh with his fingertips, loosened the other ribbon, and rolled the second stocking down.

While Jero paid her this loving attention, Ruby was lost in the sensation of his closeness. His hand quivered as she unwittingly parted her legs. Emboldened by her response, Jero caressed her thigh at the fringe of her lifted skirt.

Looking up, he whispered, "Can you take off the rest?"

"I will need your help again. It starts at the top," Ruby replied.

She kneeled on the mattress and showed him the laces down the back of her corset. Ruby clutched the bedcover as he patiently tugged each tie free and lifted the stiff corset away.

"Are you cold?" he asked when he noticed how she held onto the covers.

"Not at all. I, um . . . Shouldn't we blow out the candles first?"

"I would rather see you in the light. Does that make you nervous?" He took the blanket from her fists.

"It does, in the candlelight or the dark."

Jero touched her cheek. "Don't be nervous."

"I can't help it. I have been given such conflicting advice about tonight."

He stroked her arm lovingly, across her bare shoulder, then down her neck with his fingertips. He asked in a soothing whisper, "What advice were you given, my love?"

She swallowed hard and replied, "Well, for one, that I should stay dressed in bed. Also, I should completely undress but keep hidden under the covers. That is, unless I let you chase me around the room."

Jero chuckled in surprise. "Why would I chase you?"

"To warm up after undressing?" she guessed with a giggle.

"I am not undressed," he reminded her.

Then he sat down on a chair across from her and unceremoniously shed his shoes and stockings.

Ruby admired his muscular shoulders when he turned around modestly and unbelted his breeches. She had not seen the baked scars on his back until then. She was focused on that alarming sight when he turned around again.

Ruby caught her breath. She had seen glimpses of naked men before but never aroused like this. Her shiver was noticeable, but Jero's shy smile made her relax again. This was supposed to happen just this way, she thought.

Standing before her, Jero toyed with the ribbon that closed the linen shift against her ribs. "You can leave it on if you prefer," he said.

Her shyness melted. She stroked Jero's chest, twirling the soft hairs covering his muscular frame. "Undress me," she whispered.

Jero pulled the ribbon, and the bodice sprung loose. He lifted the gown over her head and admired her youthful body. He ran his finger from her lips, down between her breasts, and to her parted thighs.

"How should we do this, Ruby? I, too, am conflicted because of the ladies' advice."

Her answer became apparent as she fought the impulse to explore her lover's body. "I will take my mother's advice," she whispered as he brushed his lips against her neck.

Breathlessly, Jero asked, "What advice was that, my love?"

"She told me: Sex is easy, so don't overthink it."

"I guarantee you, Ruby, I cannot think at all right now."

Jero leaned her back onto the bed and straddled her nude body. Ruby's hands wandered down his warm back, pulling him closer. She arched her hips to meet his searching fingers while their lips locked in passionate exploration. Ruby moaned with pleasure, whispering, "I understand what she meant now."

Hovering over her welcoming nakedness, Jero asked, "Shall we first send the partygoers home?"

"Don't blow out the candle just yet. I want to see everything."

~*~

The lewd banter from the villagers lightened once again after Jero and Ruby went up to their newlyweds' chamber.

Some families had already loaded their sleeping children into carts and wagons to begin the long walk home. The out-of-town gentry were settling into their carriages to return to Baric Castle, where they would sleep off the filling banquet and indulgent drinking. Mauro and Resi stayed with the lingering villagers and castle servants. They held to the tradition of waiting for the groom's signal that all had gone well in their marriage bed.

With renewed encouragement from their dwindling audience, the musicians took up their instruments again with one less player. Felix made his way through the burgeoning courtships dotting the dance floor to find Verica.

"We never had our dance," he said over her shoulder.

The girls she was talking to giggled when Verica jumped in surprise.

She turned to Felix and replied, "You seemed happy playing with the band, so I didn't think you wanted to dance."

The musicians chose a lively song to wake the hovering partners, and Verica asked, "Are you not needed?"

"They will be fine without my strings. Besides, I need to talk to you." He eyed the group of maids and added, "In private."

Verica's companions whispered amongst themselves and eyed him suspiciously.

"Can we go over by the fire?" Felix asked.

Verica scanned the crowd for her mistress and told him, "The baroness is leaving soon."

"Please, Verica. I will not keep you long."

He held out his hand, and she reluctantly took it. He guided her away from the music and dancing to where the boys had tended the spits earlier. The logs had burned down to mere piles of glowing coal.

"It is quite dark here," Verica said.

"It is not my intention to be improper. I just . . ."

He still held her hand, and she did not pull away.

"What did you want to tell me, Felix?"

"What I wanted to tell you was . . ." He took a needed breath. "The truth is, I think about you every day, Verica, and you flood my thoughts each night."

She searched his eyes and waited for him to continue.

"Um, while I played, I watched you dance."

Verica asked with nervousness, "You watched me?"

"I am sorry. I did and, well, I realized that I cannot bear to see you in the arms of another man."

He took a step closer, and Verica held him at arm's length. "Are you drunk, Felix?" she asked.

"No! But I fear my heart is drunk on my love for you. I think it is called swooning."

"Did you read that in a book?" Her voice rang with doubt.

He shrugged pitifully, insisting, "It is the truth, Verica. I am dizzy with love."

"If one swoons when kissed, then it is love, indeed," Verica recited. "That line is from one of my favorite stories Lady Baric read to us."

Felix brought her hand to his lips and lightly kissed it. "Have you tested this theory, Verica? Did you swoon when the tanner kissed you?"

She pulled her hand away and tucked it into her pocket, saying, "We never kissed."

Felix crossed his arms in mocking disapproval. "The man courted you and never asked to kiss you? That is impossible to believe. I have wanted to kiss you since leaving Venice."

"Well, that is because you are Venetian," she said with certainty. "We are not as indulgent in Solgrad as you are in Venice. A kiss means something here."

"So, I would be the first to kiss you?"

"I have been kissed," she said sharply. "You were in the next room. Remember?"

His heart sank. "Forgive me," he said. "Of course, I remember."

Verica reflected, "It is in the past. I don't count that, anyway."

Felix clumsily digressed. "My reason for taking you aside was not to ask for a kiss, Verica, but to ask you a question. If it is all the same, I would like to hold your hand again while I ask it." He added with a roguish grin, "You did promise me a dance, and holding hands sort of makes up for it."

Warily, she extended her hands as she would to a dance partner. "You want to dance without music?"

He chuckled. "There is always music playing in my head. Shall I hum something?" He pulled her closer and began humming a mesmerizing tune.

"I like dancing without music," she said, spellbound.

"My heart is racing," he whispered. "Perhaps I am swooning."

Verica laughed softly. "Now I do believe you've had too much ale."

He stepped back from her and declared, "It is not the ale, Verica. It is love. *When love's arrow strikes, a man falls hard.* That is also from a story."

A lock of hair had blown free from her ribbon, and Felix gently brushed it off her cheek. His gaze told her he loved her, but her instinct was to pull away, and she did.

"Why are you teasing me with your talk of love, Felix? You are leaving for Florence, or have you forgotten?"

Suddenly serious, Felix pleaded, "Come with me, Verica."

"To Florence? You are just caught up in the moment, Felix." Verica covered her gasp when Felix knelt in front of her.

"You are right. I was caught up. I should have gotten down on one knee like this and asked you properly. Does this convince you of my sincerity, Verica? May I finally kiss you and make you swoon?"

She took his hands in hers and pulled him to stand up again. "I will not be toyed with," she said defiantly.

Felix gave her no chance to reject him and kissed her parted lips.

Verica melted from the undeniable pleasure of his urgent embrace. When Felix stepped back, she breathlessly said, "Oh, Felix. What do we do now?"

"Marry me!"

Her thoughts were reeling, swayed by the pull of love but grounded in reason. "Doesn't someone have to organize our match or do something official?"

"Matches can make themselves. Please, say yes, Verica, for my heart is bursting."

She let herself believe it and hastily answered, "Yes, Felix. I will marry you."

A roar of applause startled the two lovers. The cheers came from the direction of the dance floor. Jero had blown out the candle in the window. Their marriage was sealed.

"I am so overjoyed, I feel like that was for us," Felix said, laughing. "Who should I ask for your hand, dear Verica?"

Verica suddenly panicked. "No one! I cannot go to Florence with you. Lady Baric needs me right now."

"I understand your devotion, Verica, but you are not indentured to her. Lady Baric knows you will fall in love and marry one day. This is that day, my love."

The shuffling of footsteps brought them back to the present. Brigita and Marija appeared in the glow at the fire pit. Verica dropped Felix's hand she was holding, but the girls didn't notice her sudden movement.

"Are we leaving?" Verica asked.

"The wagon is packed. We have been looking all over for you," Brigita said.

Marija turned her attention to Felix. "The soldiers are leaving, too. Those too drunk to ride are sleeping in the hay loft. Are you drunk?" she asked.

"Not at all," he said with a wink to Verica. "I will be riding back."

"You don't have to wait for me," Verica told the girls.

Brigita raised her brow skeptically, but Marija was already gone. After some hesitation, she, too, disappeared into the blackness.

"What happens now, Felix?" Verica asked.

He took her hand in his again and pressed it to his lips. "We go back to the castle knowing that we love each other. I will look for you in the morning. You should leave now."

Verica hurried off toward the courtyard torches where the horses and wagons were gathering.

Felix counted to ten and then followed her.

Chapter 64

After a sleep-deprived night, Resi and Mauro waved goodbye to the last of their overnight guests. The carriage rolled through the gate, and the puffy-eyed Barics walked back toward the manor.

"Do you think Isabella is still sleeping?" Resi asked through a yawn.

"That would be my guess, my dear," Mauro replied. "I have not seen Fabian, either. Are you going back to bed?"

"No, I think I'll take a stroll around the garden before it rains."

"Alone?" Mauro asked abruptly. "I mean, where is Verica?"

Resi leaned into him with a laugh. "I can be without her for an hour."

Mauro acquiesced, "Very well, but I will have her find you when Signora Volanti arrives."

"Who?"

Mauro hesitated. His wife would be angry, but it was inevitable. "She is the midwife Lady Leopold recommended," he said as they continued across the courtyard.

Resi's scowl was warranted. "Lady Nikolina did not mention that name to me."

Mauro said soothingly, "She is not the one who assisted Lady Nikolina, but she is the best in the region, and she can start immediately."

Resi grumbled, "You promised I could decide."

"You promised you would let a midwife look at you after the wedding. Please, Resi. Let her make sure everything is as it should be."

Resi's voice went up an octave, "Would I be standing here if it were not as it should be?"

"I just want this to go well for you."

"And you think I don't?" Resi said with irritation. "You greet the midwife yourself, Mauro. I am taking my walk now. Alone."

Mauro's temper slipped, and he called out, "You won't get far with swollen ankles and an aching back."

Resi hollered back, "I am pregnant, Mauro, not an invalid."

~*~

Nestor was putting his account log back on the shelf when Mauro strode through the study door and plopped down on a chair. He poured a glass of wine and swallowed it in one gulp.

"Is everything all right, Mauro?" Nestor asked.

"It could be better."

"What is there to be glum about?" Nestor asked encouragingly. "You fulfilled two obligations with one party, and everyone seemed fully satisfied."

Mauro slapped his thigh and shook his mood off. "I did indeed, thanks to your efforts, Nestor," he said kindly.

"It was no effort at all, Mauro," Nestor replied. "Now, shall we continue the winter inventory, or do you have other plans for the afternoon?" Nestor straightened the spectacles perched on his nose and reached for a different account book.

"It is already noon, isn't it?" Mauro squeezed his tired eyes and agreed, "Now is as good a time as any. Shall we start in the Keep's pantry?"

"I will get my jacket." Nestor set the book down and left the study.

Mauro grabbed his jacket from the back of his chair just as Davor knocked on the door and announced, "Lord Felix is here to speak to you, my lord. It is the second time this morning."

Mauro murmured, "All right. Show him in."

Felix came to the threshold, and Mauro waved the young Venetian to sit across from him.

"Good morning, Lord Baric. I would not have interrupted your busy day if it were not urgent."

"Urgent?" Mauro said with surprise. "What has happened between last night and this morning?"

"Well, if I may be direct, sir, I asked a girl to marry me."

Mauro choked back his laugh. "Felix, you have been here less than two months. I hope this girl is in Florence."

"No, um, she was at the party, sir," he stammered.

Mauro was no longer amused. "Are you talking about Verica?" He drummed his fingers on the table and said, "I hope you have nothing ungentlemanly to confess."

"On my word, no! I have fallen in love, sir, and I want Verica to be my wife."

Mauro gazed at him suspiciously. "How urgent can this be? She is a girl, Felix, and you yourself are barely of age."

Felix sat up taller and replied, "I am nearly twenty, Lord Baric, and Verica will be seventeen in a week. We are of marrying age, sir, and I intend to take her for my bride."

"Yes, perhaps in a year or two, if you are still certain she is the one you love, but not today, Felix. I forbid it."

"With all due respect, Lord Baric, Verica is free to choose her husband, and she said yes to my proposal last night."

"Is that right?" Mauro stood up and paced along the table with impatience. "I do not think you have thought this through, Felix," he maintained. "My offer to sponsor you is for a single room in a lodging house at the university. By your own words, you plan to eat, drink, and sleep music. Signor Grado already plans to take you with him to Vienna next spring. What will you do with a wife?"

"What will I do with her? I will love her and treasure our time together."

Mauro leaned over the table and demanded, "And how will you feed her? Clothe her? What will Verica do while you are gone for days or months at a time? What if she has a child before you are on your own financially? You will need money to support a family. There is more to a marriage than love, Felix."

Felix leaned back in defeat. "I know all of that, sir, but I cannot leave knowing that she will slip away from me into the arms of another. There is something special about Verica. Can you understand my dilemma, Lord Baric?"

Mauro filled two glasses and handed one to Felix before sitting back down. "Of course, I understand," Mauro sympathized. "I would have never chosen her as my wife's companion if I did not think Verica had something special about her. She is well-mannered and has an uncanny knack for learning. Still, she has lived as a servant and is not self-sufficient. You cannot just abandon her in a room in Florence while you pursue your profession. Do you think that would be fair to Verica?"

Felix asserted, "You are thinking about your wife, Lord Baric, and Verica's service to her."

Mauro downed his drink. "I am thinking how crushed my wife would be, knowing that her dear maid is living in poverty alone in a lodging house. I dare you to think beyond satisfying your urge to have Verica as your own, Felix. Find a whore if your needs are so urgent."

Felix was on his feet, protesting, "Sir, I never—"

Mauro was unmoved by Felix's outrage and motioned him to sit down again. "Go to Florence, Felix, and become the marvelous musician you were meant to be. I will remain your patron, but Verica stays here." Felix opened his mouth to argue, but Mauro held up his hand to silence him. "Here is what I will agree to: If after a time away you still feel the same *urgency*, I will allow your continued courtship."

Felix sat back down and asked, "Does Verica have no say in the matter?"

"Those are my terms, Felix. You are free to choose not to accept them."

Felix put his head in his hands and breathed in and out deeply. He begrudgingly remarked, "I planned to take the ferry from Zadar at the end of the week, but there is one leaving tomorrow, as well. I think I should be on it."

Mauro's tone reflected his exhaustion when he said, "It is better to sever these things quickly."

"I will not forget her," Felix declared with renewed conviction.

"I am not asking you to. But a man of twenty and a maiden of seventeen can wait for the right time to marry."

"Then, may I at least have your blessing to honor my intention to make her my wife one day?"

The plea was so genuine that Mauro had no choice but to agree, "You have my blessing, Felix. But understand that breaking Verica's heart will break my wife's, and that might affect our agreement."

Felix breathed an audible sigh of relief. "My eyes will not wander, Lord Baric. There is more risk of Verica falling in love with someone else first."

"You might very well be right, Felix." Mauro opened the door and said, "Ask Davor to find Verica for you. You may use my sitting room to say your goodbyes in private."

"Thank you for everything, Lord Baric. I won't let you down."

"Goodbye, Felix. Tell Eduard I said you may have two escorts to Zadar today. Write when you get to Florence, and especially to Verica."

"I will. Goodbye, Lord Baric."

~*~

Resi crossed paths with Marija and Louisa, carrying baskets filled with fresh eggs. "Are there so many today, girls?" she asked.

"Good day, my lady," Louisa said with a curtsy.

Marija curtsied, too, and almost tipped her heavy basket. "With the wedding and harvest party yesterday, no one thought to collect the eggs, Lady Baric," she explained.

Louisa added, "The last batch of chicks is grown, and the young hens have all started laying this week."

Marija told the baroness, "Nela was hoping there were some cocks mixed with the hens. She wanted us to bring a few to the kitchen for a nice meal of chicken pie."

"We couldn't find any boy birds in the coop. We might have already eaten them all," Louisa concluded.

The girls' innocent exchange brightened Resi's gray disposition. "Well then, at least we will have a good store of eggs for the winter months. Are there more to collect?" the baroness asked.

The girls looked at each other. "Um, we have one empty basket left to fill. But, Lady Baric, Lord Baric said—"

"I am sure I know what Lord Baric said, Louisa, but I do not think it will do me much harm to carry a basket of eggs."

Louisa could not disagree with her. She held out her filled basket for the baroness.

Resi remarked, "You said there is one empty basket. I'll take that and see firsthand how the flock has grown."

The maids reluctantly left their mistress to her own devices, and Resi went down the path to the fenced chicken yard. She waded through the hens while they were scratching the dirt for worms and grubs, and then went into their low house. Feathers floated around her as skittish young birds squawked and flew off their perches at the intrusion. Resi laughed as her old favorites stepped over the young chickens, expecting scraps of something good from her pocket.

A fat hen flew up onto Resi's shoulder. She petted the bird, saying, "I have no treats for you today, girl, but I bet you have eggs for me."

As she checked under the feathers of the few brooding hens, Resi heard the distant crunching sound of wagon wheels over the cobblestones. She grumbled to the chickens, "The midwife can wait, but your eggs cannot."

~*~

The visiting wagon stopped in front of the manor house. The wagon's driver helped his passenger down, and the woman sternly looked around.

Nestor stood outside the front door with the baron and looked to his employer for an explanation. "Who is she, Mauro? A nun?" he asked.

Mauro wondered that, too. "Neven did say something along those lines. She is the midwife I hired."

Nestor took the logbook from Mauro's grip and said, "I suppose you will need some time to make the introductions to your wife. I will start the inventory and check in with you later." Nestor nodded politely to the woman as he passed her on his way to the Keep.

Mauro greeted the midwife with a stiff bow. "Sister Donata, I am Baron Baric," he said.

She pursed her lips in distaste. "It may not have been explained, Lord Baric, but I am a laywoman with the Church. I did not take the vows, sir. You may call me by my surname."

"Of course, Signora Volanti. Thank you for coming on short notice."

"Is your wife already in confinement?" the woman wanted to know.

"No. My wife still feels quite well."

"Hmm. Your letter said Lady Baric's midwife recently passed away. Did she not recommend confinement?"

"Her midwife was monitoring her."

"Is that so?"

Mauro maintained his composure at her curtness and explained, "My wife is a foreigner, you see, and they do things differently where she comes from."

"A foreigner? Well, Lord Baric, I do require that the women I assist—be they low-born, high-born, or foreign-born—follow the modern rules of confinement to settle the humors for a successful birth. I insist—"

Mauro caught a glimpse of Resi's bright orange robe on the path and interjected, "Here comes Lady Baric now. She was walking the garden for some air before going to her chamber to rest."

As Resi approached, Mauro held out his hand for her to join them but struggled to hold back his smile. His wife had downy feathers on her shoulder and in her hair. She looked almost comical to anyone who didn't adore her.

"Resi, my dear, this is Signora Volanti. She is the midwife I was telling you about."

Resi said, "It is a pleasure to meet you, Signora Volanti." She took a moment to assess the midwife. With her coiled hair covered with a simple veil, and her figure robed from throat to shoe, one could not guess her age and actual appearance.

The midwife seemed to decide right away what sort of a woman the baroness was in her colorful silk robes and chains of gold. "I will need to examine you, Lady Baric," she proclaimed.

Mauro noticed Felix crossing the courtyard from the manor house. He acknowledged him with a wave when Felix stopped and shook his head glumly before continuing to the Keep. It had not gone well.

"Lord Baric, sir. Did you hear what I said?" the midwife asked.

Mauro turned his attention back to the women. "No, I am sorry. What was that?"

"We are going inside, Mauro," Resi answered. "To be examined," she added with emphasis.

The midwife scrutinized the baroness's appearance and asked, "Did birds attack you on your walk, Lady Baric?"

Mauro knew where his wife had been and raised his brow when Resi replied, "Birds swarm here often, Signora Volanti." She stroked her middle and said in response to the woman's frown, "It did not disturb the baby or me."

"I will be the judge of that, Lady Baric."

Mauro ignored Resi's startled expression and motioned to the midwife. "Right this way, Signora," he said pleasantly.

Davor held the front door open for them, and the visitor glanced around the grand foyer. "Lord Baric, since this is your first child, you may not know that husbands remain outside the bedchamber at this point."

Mauro nodded stiffly, biting his tongue, even though his wife was visibly unhappy at the rule.

Resi turned to Mauro and said, "I would like Verica to come."

Mauro patted her hand and said, "I will find her, my dear, and send her right up."

When the two women went up the stairs, Mauro asked Davor, "Have you seen Verica?"

"She is in the sitting room, my lord."

"Are you sure?" Mauro asked, puzzled. "I saw Felix outside."

"Lord Felix did leave a while ago, sir. But unless Verica went out the terrace door, she has not come out of the sitting room."

Mauro suppressed a groan and went in. Verica was indeed still in the room, sitting at her mistress's writing desk with a dozen words penned on parchment. She turned in her chair when the heavy door closed.

Mauro stayed by the hearth and said, "The baroness is asking for you upstairs, but I thought we might talk first."

She stood up dutifully, her gaze directed downward.

"You have been at the House of Baric your whole life, Verica, and I feel a great deal of responsibility for your wellbeing," Mauro told her.

She could not look at her master when she acknowledged, "I consider the Barics my family, and I owe you everything, my lord. But you are not my father, sir."

He calmly replied, "I am not."

"Felix asked me to marry him. I want to marry him, but Felix said you forbid it. Why, my lord?" Her eyes shifted, and she held the baron's formidable stare.

"It takes more than infatuation and good intentions to make a marriage work, Verica. You are better off here," Mauro declared.

"How dare you decide that!"

Verica went past him to the door and grabbed the handle, but Mauro grabbed her arm to stop her from leaving. "I will tell you how I dare, Verica."

The maid turned to him, quivering with emotion. Still, Mauro kept his resolve and said, "I have agreed to sponsor the son of a disgraced nobleman who I believe will go far with his talent. But he needs to do it alone, Verica. You have seen how he works. You know that composing will always come first. He will have no time for a wife right now, and he has no income to support you in a lifestyle that you might admit you have grown accustomed to."

He released her arm, and she released her grip on the latch. Her voice trembled when she replied, "I do not need much to be happy, Lord Baric."

Mauro clenched his hands behind his back to keep from taking the pitiful girl in his arms. "Let him find his place in the world, Verica, and then he will come for you."

Her welling tears betrayed her underlying fear.

"You think you will lose him, don't you?" Mauro asked.

She searched her apron pocket for her kerchief to wipe her wet eyes and said, "I am just a simple girl in a faraway land. He will find someone better in Florence, and my heart cannot take that."

When she regained her composure, Mauro asked, "Do you want to know what Felix said to me earlier?"

"What, sir?" she sniffled.

"Felix worries that you will forget him while he is away. He thinks you will marry someone else."

She whispered to the floor, "I would never do that."

"You must believe the same about Felix, Verica." Mauro raised her chin to look into her eyes and said, "Have patience. If he wants to marry you now, he will want you even more in a year or two."

"I want to believe that, Lord Baric, but I cannot." Verica opened the door, crying, "You have ruined all my hopes for love."

Nestor was returning from the Keep just as Verica ran up the marble steps. "What was that all about, Mauro? Should I reprimand the girl for her insolence?"

Mauro stared up after her and shook his head. "Verica has every right to be upset with me, Nestor. I will deal with her again later." He took a deep breath to shake off the encounter and asked, "How are our winter stores?"

Nestor quickly pivoted back to his accounting and reported, "We have nearly the same provision count as this time last year, but last year the men were away half the winter, fighting. Not that I hope for war, but it does feed your soldiers."

Mauro walked the length of the foyer. His troubled thoughts wrestled with that and everything else going on.

Nestor offered a solution, "I will inventory the stores in the manor's cellar and maybe shift a few things between the Keep and the manor pantries."

Mauro agreed with a nod. "We'll reconcile the two tomorrow. For now, I need to check on my wife."

~*~

Mauro knocked on his chamber door, and Signora Volanti came out of the blackened room, closing the door behind her.

"How is my wife?" he asked.

"I have finished my examination. It is my opinion that she could give birth any time."

Mauro stared blankly. "Are you sure? She is barely in her eighth month."

The midwife's eyes narrowed. "Are *you* sure, Lord Baric? Your wife said that you were away at war the first part of the year."

"What do you mean by that, Signora Volanti?"

"Nothing, sir, except if she indeed conceived in March, the baby should be much smaller than it is."

Worriedly, Mauro asked, "Could she be carrying twins?"

The matron frowned. "I examined her for that, of course, and there is only one baby. Lady Baric said the movement has slowed, so I have put her in immediate confinement."

Mauro clenched his teeth with regret and asked, "What does that entail exactly?"

"I have already instructed Lady Baric that she is not to leave her bed or bathe or have any disruptions until after the birth."

Mauro asked the question he already knew the answer to, "Including myself?"

The midwife's attempted smile resembled a grimace. She explained, "Visitors are distracting at this critical time, Lord Baric. I think there is an urgency that I move in straightaway. I require my own room and will take my meals alone there. I will give your cook a list of foods the baroness may eat until she delivers."

"If you do not mind, Signora Volanti, I would like a moment with my wife before the sequestering begins."

She shook her head disapprovingly, but Mauro opened the door. "One moment," he said and shut it again.

Mauro made his way to the shutters in the darkened room. When he opened them completely, sunlight spilled over Resi, lying in bed. Mauro leaned over his wife and kissed her tear-stained cheek. "I came to ask if I should employ her, but I think I know your opinion."

Dressed in her nightclothes, Resi sat up against her pillows and sniffled, "Do you want to hear it?"

"I talked to her, my dear," Mauro said soothingly. "She said you are very close to your time, and you should keep to your bed."

"She also said bathing will make the baby ill, and I am to eat only organs and drink only goat's milk. The woman will allow nothing from the ground, nothing from the trees, and no spring water to pass my lips!"

Mauro stroked her wet cheek and whispered, "Resi, darling, Signora Volanti has delivered hundreds of babies. There must be some wisdom to her counsel."

"I cannot lie unwashed in bed for six weeks eating sheep brains." His wife's eyes were pleading.

Mauro took her hand and divulged, "She thinks you are mistaken with the date, Resi."

Sobbing, Resi said, "She practically called me adulterous, questioning my devotion to you, Mauro. You are the only one who has ever touched me, except for this vile woman today." Her voice was stronger when she asserted, "I will not have her probe me again. She put her fingers inside me until I yelled out for her to stop her mauling."

Mauro moaned in frustration. "I can ask Radic about Elizabeta's midwife," he offered.

"She will do the same," Resi said. "Please, Mauro. Nela has delivered many babies, and Ruby has helped with four already. I trust them. You must, too."

He shut his eyes, and his face betrayed what was in his thoughts.

"They will not let me die. Please, Mauro."

Her solemn plea was too much. "Very well, my love. It is decided, then," he conceded. "But would it hurt you to stay in bed?"

She squeezed her husband's hand with relief. "When you leave, Mauro, could you send Verica to our chamber?"

"Why don't you sleep a bit before I send her to you? I will leave the shutters open for some air."

"Thank you, Mauro. I suppose I am tired." Resi rolled onto her side and shut her eyes.

In the hallway, Mauro told the midwife, "If you would come with me, Signora Volanti, I will introduce you to my steward, Signor Nestor. He is in charge of my household staff."

They descended the stairs in silence, and Mauro brought her into the study, where Nestor sat behind the desk.

Mauro asked, "Could you please settle Signora Volanti's fee for the day, Nestor, and arrange a wagon back for her? I will not need her services after all."

Signora Volanti's mouth dropped open. "But, Lord Baric—"

"I changed my mind," Mauro said, interrupting her protest. He took his hat from the table and concluded, "I thank you for coming. Good day, Signora."

Mauro told Davor in the foyer, "Watch my chamber door. No one is to disturb my wife until I return."

"Yes, sir."

Davor went up the stairs, and Mauro strode across the courtyard to the stables. He saddled Janus and led him to the gate.

Latif asked his commander, "Do you need an escort, Lord Baric?"

Mauro mounted his horse. "I will not be long," he said before he took off galloping down the castle road. He didn't slow at the crossroads but turned left and rode on, beyond the salt flats, until he found himself at the cliffs overlooking the expansive Adriatic.

The seashore was breezy, and the azure water rippled in the inlet below him. He shut his eyes and imagined a different day, one far darker and stormier. He kicked off his boots and peeled off his jacket, wishing the gray clouds overhead would release their showers and wash his troubles away.

The wind swirled on the cliff's edge, whipping Mauro's hair and inflating his shirt. He shouted to the wind: "It has been a long time since you were here, Mateo! How I yearn for one simple day with you again! If you were baron, and I was only a brother, what would you do differently in my place?" And then, as if summoned, Mauro jumped.

Chapter 65

Baric Castle, 1 November 1649

Isabella left Resi's chamber door open to let more light into the room. She came to the bedside and twirled for Resi to admire her. "How do I look?"

Propped against her pillows, Resi set her book aside with a smile. "Is that a new gown, Isabella? You look beautiful."

"Thank you, Terese. My mother sent it. I wasn't sure if off-white would be appropriate for honoring the saints, but they are dead, so I am sure they do not have an opinion." Isabella sat down on the chair next to the bed. She pulled on the lambskin gloves she held and straightened her fur wrap.

Resi remarked, "It looks blustery outside. I thought you didn't ride in the rain."

"Did you not hear the news?" Isabella said with excitement. "My carriage from Venice finally arrived! My father is so kind. When I told him I rode in open wagons, he insisted on buying one for me."

Resi shared her enthusiasm. "I cannot wait to ride in it. I am sure it is spectacular."

Isabella grinned. "It is, actually. When your baby finally arrives, we will go for a ride together to visit Lady Ruby." She gave Resi an encouraging embrace and added, "I wasn't supposed to linger. Fabian is waiting downstairs."

"Will you open my shutters before you leave, Isabella? I want to hear the rain on the shingles."

Isabella cocked her head with a frown and warned, "The breeze will come in, Terese, and that is not good for you."

Resi sank back against her pillows. "That is what Mauro said before he left for the church, but the room is so stale."

"It won't be too much longer," Isabella said and went to open one shutter. "Send word right away when your baby comes."

"I am sad to see you leave, Isabella, but I am sure you will be happy to sleep in your new home tonight."

Isabella watched the rain out the window and remarked, "Such a dreary day to move into an empty house. It dawned on me this morning how dull it will be without your company, Terese. And I will lose my riding partner, although Lady Ruby has hardly been here since her wedding."

Resi corrected her with a chuckle, "She has come three times already, and it has only been two weeks since she moved."

In a more upbeat tone, Isabella said, "Anastasia is willing to learn to ride. I had to give her Sundays off in exchange. I think your husband's valet is to blame for that."

"Verica told me their courtship is blooming. Davor certainly seems cheerful this week."

Isabella pouted, "Yes, and then they will want to marry, and I will be out a good lady's maid."

Resi picked at her coverlet. "I know the feeling, Isabella."

Isabella came back to the bedside, frowning. "I am sorry. I forgot Verica is leaving you."

"Not soon, at least. Mauro forbade it, you know. Verica is quite heartsick over his interference," Resi said glumly.

Isabella took her hand in sympathy. "Well, someone had to step in. You cannot have your best servant running off with the first boy who kisses her at a party."

"It was more than a drunken infatuation. She told me Felix confessed his love to her."

Isabella perked up at the romantic notion. "Of course, he fell in love with her. She is very pretty for a common girl and has an extraordinary sense of style. Both are a bit eccentric—in a good way, of course. Old souls, perhaps."

"Even Mauro agrees they are a good match, but he still stands by his decision."

"Your servants have an unusual familiarity with their master. That is why they are surprised when he enforces his authority."

Resi shifted uncomfortably against her stack of pillows. "I think Verica understands Mauro's misgivings. Still, she has barely said more than a few words to my husband since Felix left."

Isabella suggested, "Mauritius should buy her a new hat or something pretty. That always helps change a woman's opinion of a man."

Resi chuckled at her Venetian friend's take on the world. "I don't think Solgrad has the selection that Venice does. Tomorrow is Verica's birthday, and I have already asked Franja and Nela to make a special meal for all the servants in the great hall. If that doesn't cheer her up, I will suggest the hat."

Isabella noticed Anastasia standing at the open door. "Is my husband pacing?" she asked her maid.

"He is, madam."

Anastasia's appearance took Resi by surprise. The maid's long black hair draped prettily under her fashionable hat, and she was an attractive companion for her elegant mistress.

Isabella noticed her friend's reaction and whispered, "Anastasia has come out of her shell." Then Isabella kissed Resi on the cheek and said, "I am off to mourn the dead. Be brave in your confinement, dear Terese. When the weather clears, I will ride out to see how you are doing."

~*~

It wasn't long after Isabella had left for church that Verica checked on her mistress. "Can I bring you anything, Lady Baric?"

Resi rolled over with effort and asked, "Are you the only one left in this big house?"

"Nela is in the kitchen with Ivana. It is usually a long service for the Saints, so they stayed behind to tend the roast. Everyone will be hungry when they return." Verica shifted the grip on her apron, holding it up at the corners.

"What do you have there? Another cat?" Resi asked.

Verica smiled brightly. "No, my lady, I brought candles. I thought we might have our own little ceremony and light them for the Barics who have passed, and for Idita. I brought the prayer book from the library, too."

"That is a wonderful suggestion, Verica." Resi threw her covers back and swung her legs over the side of the bed with a groan.

"Shall I bring the chamber pot to the bed, Lady Baric?"

Resi dismissed her maid's help: "I can do it myself. I need to stretch my legs." Resi went behind the screen. "Is Aron here? I would love some hot water to wash up."

"He went to Mass with the other servants, but Nela will have some water boiling over the fire. I will bring up a pitcher." Verica checked the two dressing tables for cool water to mix with the hot water and fretted, "Empty. Let me see if Aron left a pail of cold water in the hall closet. Otherwise, I can run to the well and—"

"Forget the pitchers, Verica. I need to move about for a while. I was thinking a quick dip in the bathhouse might feel good."

Verica had been given specific instructions, and she protested, "Lord Baric said—"

Resi moved the screen aside again. "Lord Baric doesn't need to know, Verica. My back aches from lying in bed all day. I would love to float a while and take the weight off everything."

Resi put on her flat slippers while Verica looked through the wardrobe for fresh robes. The baroness filled her deep pockets with the candles and prayer book, saying, "We will have our celebration of the saints in the bathhouse."

~*~

The gurgling of the cascading fountain at the room's entrance stirred the misty air in the bathhouse. Resi hovered in the deep center of the pool while Verica set the short candles along the tiled edge and lit them.

"It is like a watery chapel," the maid said dreamily. "Shall I read from the book, Lady Baric? I have been practicing."

"Yes, I'd like to hear you read," Resi replied. She came to the edge, leaning back against the warmed tile, and listened to her maid sound out the words from the little prayer book:

"And God, the Father of heaven, have mercy on us. God, the Son, Redeemer of the world, God the Holy Ghost, Holy Trinity, one God, have mercy on us. Holy Mary, pray for us. Holy Mother of God, Holy Virgin of virgins, Saint Michael, Saint Gabriel, Saint Raphael. All ye holy angels and archangels, all ye holy order of blessed spirits, Saint John the Baptist, Saint Joseph. All ye holy patriarchs and prophets." Verica looked up from her book. "There is a whole list here, my lady. It goes on and on for pages."

Resi shut her eyes and said encouragingly, "That's all right. It is good practice to read the names."

Verica found her place again and continued, "Saint Peter, Saint Paul, Saint Andrew, Saint . . ."

Lulled by her maid's melodic reading and the warm water lifting her, Resi nodded off on the pool's step. She had not felt this relaxed in days.

When Verica looked up from her page and saw her mistress's closed eyes, she panicked that the baroness might drown. "Lady Baric," she called over, "I have finished the prayer. Perhaps you want to dry off now."

Resi breathed deeply and came to life at hearing her name. She looked at her puckered fingertips and said, "Oh, you are right. I have been in too long."

Verica helped the baroness gain her footing on the slippery tile and held out a cloth for her to wrap herself in. A puddle of warm water grew beneath her feet.

"Oh, dear God, no," Resi cried.

Verica brought another drape for the baroness's hair. "What's the matter, Lady Baric?" she asked when she saw her mistress's frightened expression.

Resi stepped out of the puddle, and the stabbing pain hit her. She grabbed Verica's arm and cried, "Ahh! The baby is pushing hard. I think it is time."

"Now?" exclaimed Verica. "Sit down, my lady! Let me get you dressed and back into the house!"

Resi leaned on the girl and panted, "No, no, no. I can't. I have to stand. Oh, God!" She doubled over in pain.

"Maybe if you lie flat, Lady Baric?" Verica piled linens on the floor for her. "Oh, you are shivering!" The maid moved quickly to wrap her mistress's wet locks and pull a tunic over her while Resi moaned and grunted.

"I will try lying down now," Resi said.

Verica helped her mistress and then walked to and fro with indecision. "I'll get Nela. Yes. It will only take a moment. Stay on the floor, Lady Baric. Do not move!" The maid didn't wait for an answer and ran out of the bathhouse.

~*~

Verica startled Nela when she bolted into the kitchen, shouting, "Hurry, hurry! The baby is coming!"

Nela set her knife down. "Baby? Why are you so wet, Verica?"

"We were in the bathhouse, and, and, and—"

"Calm down, girl, and tell me slowly," Nela demanded.

Verica took a deep breath and rattled off, "Well, the baroness was dozing, and then there was a puddle of water, and then she wailed with pain, so I left her on the floor to get you, and I am wet because it is raining!"

"You left her ladyship on the floor? Good God, what will the baron say when he finds out?" Then it finally sank in. "The baron!" Nela looked around for her helper and called out, "Ivana!"

The kitchen maid came out of the pantry, unaware of the alarm. "Yes, Nela?"

"Go find someone who can ride with a message to the church. Lord Baric needs to come right away. Lady Baric is having her baby!"

"Her baby?" Ivana repeated.

"Quick, girl!"

All three left the kitchen. Ivana ran to the gatehouse, and Nela and Verica to the bathhouse, holding their aprons over their heads against the downpour.

When the two crossed the sultry domed room, they found the baroness squatting in front of the bench.

"Lady Baric! Let us help you up!" cried Nela.

"No," Resi grunted. "I can feel something happening."

"If it is all right with you, madam, we will take a look."

Resi bit her lip and said, "Go ahead."

"Verica, dear, you'll have to do it for me. These old bones don't like marble floors."

"What am I looking for, Nela?" Verica asked anxiously.

"A head!" Nela quickly answered.

Resi let out a wail, and Verica was on her feet as though bitten. "There is something! I think the baby is going to birth itself!"

"Ahhh!" Resi bawled as the next contraction flowed through her. "I couldn't stop the birth if I tried."

"Then let it happen. Bear down, like on a pot, Lady Baric," Nela coached her. "Verica! Put those linens under the baroness. Quickly now!"

"I need to push!" Resi yelled.

"Yes, yes, that is good, Lady Baric! Push!"

In a flash, Nela sprang into action and knelt on the floor in front of her mistress's wide-open hips. "The head is out, Lady Baric," she told her excitedly. "Oh, such a pretty sight! Keep pushing, my lady! You are almost there."

"I need to catch my breath," Resi panted.

"Do that now, Lady Baric. Have a good, deep breath and a little rest." Nela wiped her mistress's brow with a cloth and said soothingly, "When the next pain comes, bear down with all you have, and I will catch the babe."

Resi gripped Verica's hand as the next wave of contractions urged her body to push, and the tiny baby slipped out and into Nela's waiting hands. Its gurgling cry echoed under the high ceiling.

Nela swiftly patted the newborn dry, praising her mistress's success, "Isn't she a beauty? Look at your new little girl, Lady Baric." Nela held her close to her mother.

"A girl," Resi said with a tired moan.

Nela shook her head and insisted, "I know what you are thinking, Lady Baric, but do not worry yourself. The baron will be proud that you have given him a healthy daughter." Cook unwrapped the newborn and showed her to the baroness, saying, "All her parts are perfect, and she has a strong cry for such a wee babe. Oh, Lady Baric. Look how she is looking right at you."

Tears fell from Resi's eyes. "She is perfect, isn't she?"

From then on, instinct took over, and Nela went to work finishing her duty. "You can let your little one suckle a bit, madam. That helps with the afterbirth. I'll tie the cord, and then we'll get you all cleaned up, Lady Baric, and move you to the house." The old servant chattered on, "Who would have thought such a sweet little babe could come so easily? Aren't you the perfect little girl?"

Resi hardly heard Nela. She was transfixed by the newborn at her breast.

"How do you feel, Lady Baric?" Verica leaned down to ask. "Can I bring you a drink of water?"

"I don't know. I feel a little queasy, Verica, but maybe water will help."

Nela assured the baroness, "You will feel much better when you purge the rest, my lady. Why don't you give the baby to Verica now, and she'll get her all tidied up. Do you want to use the pot, madam? Sometimes that helps all the extra parts drop out."

Nela helped the baroness onto her feet, but Resi stayed doubled over.

"My back," Resi groaned. "There is a pressure. Uhhh!"

Nela crossed herself and whispered, "Virgin Mary, Mother of Jesus."

Resi looked over in alarm. "Something is wrong, isn't it?"

"Wrong? No, Lady Baric. Sit down, sit down! Just let me have a feel around your middle."

Resi sat on the cold floor with her knees spread and her head back, tensing from agony, while Nela pressed and prodded.

Finally, Cook smiled, but her lips trembled. "Do not worry, madam, but I think a second baby is waiting to be born. With luck, it will slide out just like the first one."

Resi nodded, holding her breath to keep from crying out. "I am ready to push, Nela."

"Not yet, Lady Baric!" Nela warned her. "Verica, swaddle the baby and set her on the bench. I need your help."

When Verica was at Nela's side, the old cook suggested, "Now that everything is opened up, let us try this standing. Squat down and we will hold your arms to brace you, madam."

"Oww! I can't! I can't!" Resi cried out after a moment.

"You can, madam. You have done this already. You can do it again!" Nela urged patiently.

Resi sank down with the next contraction, and Verica prepared to catch the arrival.

"It hurts terribly," Resi whimpered. "Something is wrong."

Nela took a deep breath to keep her wits about her. "Here is what we will do," she said calmly. "Lay back down and I will feel for the baby."

It took both women's help to get the baroness down on the floor again. As Nela prodded her mistress, Resi wailed in pain.

Mauro shouted from the fountain, "What are you doing to her?"

No one had heard the baron come into the bathhouse, and Nela was on her feet quicker than a woman of her girth should be.

"Lord Baric! Oh, thank God! Did you bring Lady Ruby with you?" Nela wanted to know.

Caught off guard, Mauro answered, "Um, no, I came alone. Mass isn't over, and . . . how is she doing, Nela?"

"She is doing great, my lord. We had a little setback, is all."

Mauro leaned over his wife and stroked her sweat-beaded brow. "I am here, my love," he whispered.

"It's not working, Mauro," she sobbed in reply.

Mauro looked at Nela and asked, "What is not working?"

Nela gently handed him the swaddled baby. "Keep your daughter warm, Lord Baric. We will get the other one born soon."

"Other one?" Mauro asked in a daze.

Nela was back at his wife's feet and said, "Tuck your baby into your doublet, sir. Her twin is coming, but it is breech. One leg is doing a little dance in and out of its mother. The foot is moving, so that is a good sign."

Verica asked Nela, "How can I help?"

"Find the second leg and pull it down with the other. Gentle now!"

Resi gritted her teeth at the new invasion and squeezed Mauro's hand. "You wanted a boy, Mauro. It is a girl, but she is perfect," Resi moaned.

Mauro had followed Nela's order and packed the linen bundle in his doublet without a glance. Tears ran down Mauro's cheeks when he opened his shirt and realized a baby was curled up against him. "How did you do that already? She is beautiful, my love."

Resi had no time for sentiment. She gripped his hand like a vise and cried, "I need to push!"

"No, no, no. Not yet!" Nela urged.

Verica cried, "Both legs are out and the water, too. What else, Nela?"

"All right," Nela breathed. "We must do this slowly, Lady Baric. A little push. Very little, please."

Resi panted, "I can't do it, Nela. The pain keeps cresting like waves in a storm."

Nela turned her eyes to the ceiling and mouthed the words, "God in heaven, please help us."

The urgency finally sank in, and Mauro told Nela, "Find the arms first. It's like with horses. Limbs can break."

"You are right, my lord. Verica!"

Verica retook her place on the floor. "I wish Idita were here," she sobbed.

"You can do this, Verica," Nela assured her.

While the women huddled on the floor, Resi reached for Mauro's hand. "Promise me something," she groaned.

Mauro leaned in closely, clutching the bundle against his chest.

Resi whispered, "If I die, you must marry Lady Rosella."

"Why are you saying that, my darling? You are not dying," he soothed her.

"I met her, Mauro. On the plaza."

Mauro shook his head. "Shhh. Do not worry about her."

She panted through the next contraction, "Her boy. Sebastiano. Green eyes. Fair hair."

Mauro nuzzled her neck and whispered, "I know, my love. Why are you telling me this?"

"She thinks you are his father." Tears streamed down her cheeks.

Mauro grimaced. "You will not die, Resi. I will not let you."

Resi's chin quivered when she told him, "It feels like I am. It hurts so badly, Mauro. I cannot finish this."

Nela caught Mauro's eye. "We are ready, my lord," she said.

Mauro took Resi's hand again. His tears streamed down unchecked, and he trembled when he whispered, "Listen to Nela now, and you will have two babies with one try. Don't you want to see if your daughter has a brother or a sister?"

"I do, Mauro." Resi sat up again. "I will try."

"There you go, Resi. Be brave," he said for her and himself.

Nela said, "All right, Lady Baric, just one small push. Be careful, Verica."

Resi shut her eyes and squeezed them as she breathed out with a grunt.

Nela cried, "Good, Lady Baric. There is a little back to go with the little legs. Stop pushing now! We don't want to hurt him."

Mauro gasped at her warning. *Him.* It was a boy.

Nela announced, "Verica is going to help free the arms now."

"There is so much blood," the maid whimpered.

"There is always some blood, girl, so put that out of your mind." Nela handed Verica a cloth and instructed, "Ease one arm out and then the other, just like you fashion the lady's curls. Quickly!"

Mauro held Resi's hand with his right and cradled his baby with his left. "Don't push," he warned her when he saw her teeth clench.

"Just the head now!" Nela exclaimed. "Find the little chin, Verica, and hold it still so Lady Baric can do her part."

Kneeling between the baroness's legs, Verica looked up at her mistress and nodded that she had it. "Whenever you are ready, madam."

"Here it comes!" Resi gritted her teeth through the wave of pain and pushed with all she had.

"It is born!" Nela cried.

Spent and aching, Resi fell back against Mauro.

"I'll just cut the cord, my lady, and then you can see him," Nela said. She rubbed the limp baby to rouse it, then sucked its nostrils and nudged its chest to take a breath.

Mauro was on his feet. "He's turning blue."

Cook was white with fear. "It may have been too much for the babe," she said softly. Nela held it to her broad chest and rocked it. The baby let out a stifled squeak. "Come on, little one," she pleaded.

Mauro said in a calm and steady voice, "Give him to me."

Nela unwittingly clutched the baby tighter when she saw his dazed stare. The words "No, my lord!" left her lips.

"If he dies, Nela, he will die in my arms, and his sister will know her brother one time in this world."

Nela handed the baby over, and Mauro put the naked boy against his skin.

"Take care of my wife, Nela," he ordered and then took refuge behind the panel by the fountain.

Alone there, Mauro was overwrought with grief. He rocked and swayed as he held the tiny bundles against his chest, uttering, "What is the matter, little man? Is it so bad to be second? Will you not stay with us, my sweet little son?"

Cradled close in their father's shirt, the two babes found each other, and the girl began to suck on her brother's arm.

Mesmerized, Mauro stroked the tiny boy. "Is that how it was in your mother's belly? Your sister was always playing, and you wanted quiet. I had a brother who never gave me peace, and I loved him with all my heart. I would have liked a sister just as much."

Mauro shut his eyes and rocked his two babies to the rhythm of the percolating water until Nela tapped him on his shoulder.

"Lord Baric," she said quietly, "the baroness should also have a chance to say goodbye to her little boy."

Mauro unbuttoned his doublet and handed her the swaddled girl. "I think she is hungry, Nela."

Nela took the baby from him but pleaded, "Let your wife see her son before he passes, my lord."

The baby boy had opened his eyes and looked upward as his father said, "The boy and I are going to have a little talk first."

Nela wiped the tear that rolled down her cheek. "He looks just like you did as a babe, my lord. Light hair and bright eyes."

The baby in Nela's arms began to cry without her father's warm body to comfort her. As if on cue, her little brother let out a squeaking whine. His soft cry became a wail as his lungs finally filled, and the blue tinge of his lips warmed to a rosy pink.

"Well, will you look at that?" Nela said, choking on a sob. She put the baby girl back into Mauro's open shirt, and the cries from the twins subsided as they curled into little balls against each other.

Verica had helped her mistress dress again, and Resi stood at the partition. "May I see them?" she asked, and Nela left them alone.

Mauro regarded his wife adoringly as he held their little family. "How are you feeling, my darling?"

Resi took a needed drink from the fountain. "I feel like I was kicked by a horse, but I am fine. I think." She opened Mauro's collar and admired her rewards. "Two babies, Mauro."

Mauro was giddy with pride. "They are all yours, but I may never let them go."

"I would like to hold them, but I think I need to sit down." She braced herself on the fountain's edge.

"Nela! Verica!" Mauro called out. He put one baby into each servant's arms, then wrapped his cloak around his wife and lifted her into his arms. "Let me take you to bed."

"Are you going to carry me the whole way?" she asked with surprise.

"You just gave birth to two children, my love." Her bare feet were sticking out from his cloak, and he reminded her, "And you have no shoes."

Verica held the door open, clutching her treasure, and the cool air hit them like a slap. They hurried down the garden path and into the warm kitchen.

"My roast is burning. Where is everyone?" Nela asked no one in particular. "You and the mistress enjoy those little ones, my lord. I will come and check on Lady Baric shortly." Then Nela got right to work saving their dinner.

Mauro carried Resi through the foyer to the stairs. They heard rumbling voices from behind the great hall doors.

Resi sunk into her husband's arms. "Please, Mauro. I am so tired. I cannot see anyone just now."

"Do not worry, my love. I will take you and the babies upstairs."

When the three Barics were settled in the big bed and Verica in the chair next to them, Mauro kissed his wife and rushed downstairs to see who was waiting in the great hall.

Behind the door, all of Baric Castle, along with Jero, Ruby, Fabian, and Isabella, was pacing the room.

"There you are!" Fabian bellowed. "We searched the entire house!"

Mauro shrugged dramatically. "Well, you know how fond my wife is of her bathhouse."

"Is it already over?" Isabella asked with astonishment.

Mauro relished telling her, "Terese was amazing. She was almost finished when I arrived."

"Is she still in the bathhouse?" Ruby asked.

"They are all upstairs, resting," Mauro announced.

Ruby rushed past Mauro, stopping first to squeeze her new brother-in-law's hand in gleeful congratulations.

Isabella embraced Mauro at the doorway. "I can hardly believe it, Mauritius. I am very happy for you," she chirped as she hurried after Ruby.

The kitchen maids and other servants said their congratulations with bows and curtsies as they, too, filed past the baron out of the great hall.

Natalija was the first to ask, "Have you picked a name, sir?"

Fabian and Jero handed out glasses of Mauro's best brandy, and the men of the Keep gathered around the baron to hear the name of the newest arrival. The servants paused at the doorway to listen.

Mauro looked around at all those who meant so much to him and reflected, "I had not really thought about a name until just now. But as I look around this great hall my grandfather left for his grandchildren, I think it is time to honor him with another Fredrik or a Fredrika."

The room was silent, each person looking at the other in puzzlement.

Fabian stepped forward and asked what everyone was wondering, "It can only be one, Mauritius. Which shall we toast to?"

Mauro held up his glass and said, "I am still in shock myself when I tell you, we toast to both!"

Chapter 66

Baric Castle, 28 November 1649

Lady Eleonora leaned on her cane in front of the wall of portraits. "I am glad to see Mauritius took my advice. This is a stunning portrait of Lady Terese. Who painted it?" the Leopold matriarch asked Nestor.

Nestor regarded the newly hung painting he had watched Lady Isabella create in this same room and said, "The baron commissioned the portrait to a new artist in Venice. It is an excellent likeness of the baroness, wouldn't you say?"

"I would, indeed. I would also say Mauritius Baric is an unusual man, Silvijo. How he runs his affairs continues to surprise me."

Nestor was unfazed by her criticism but wondered, "How so, Lady Eleonora?"

The dowager arrogantly rattled off, "Letting an unknown painter undertake such an important portrait, for one. Giving away half his estate to a half-brother who did not ask for it; spending money on a nobody composer in Florence; even naming his new heir after a Toth and not a Baric."

Nestor maintained, "Dominik Toth was a well-respected nobleman in the Empire, and Vladimir Baric did inherit Toth Castle. The baron honored the Baric forefathers with the second names for both children."

"I will not contradict you, dear Silvijo. Dominik Toth was a friend of my late husband. You will have to admit, though, that the name *Viviane* is an unexpected choice."

"Baron Baric is a modern man, Lady Eleonora, and he left the naming of the girl to his wife. She thought it matched her daughter's personality," Nestor unapologetically explained.

Eleonora dismissed his logic: "Babies have no personalities."

"Well, I cannot judge that, but I do know the baroness wanted to honor her maternal grandmother from France. The name has sentimental meaning to her."

The dowager pointed out dryly, "Sentiment is not for noble families. Tradition is."

"Ah, but new generations start their own traditions," Nestor remarked.

Lady Eleonora coyly returned his smile and asked, "Are you saying that we are old, Silvijo?"

"I am saying we are of a different time, Lady Eleonora."

~*~

"Nestor and Lady Eleonora seem quite flirtatious today. Do you think she likes him?" Ruby asked Resi.

Resi searched the crowded room to see where her friend was looking. "I suppose widows and widowers can still fall in love, even after decades of pretending they cannot," Resi pointed out.

Ruby leaned back in her upholstered chair and reflected, "Being in love is wonderful."

"Does that surprise you?"

"I suppose not, but what does surprise me is how being married hasn't changed my feelings for Jero. I imagined marriage would tame our passion, but it has heightened it. Somehow, I wasn't expecting that."

Resi laughed. "I miss not having you here each day to talk to, Ruby."

"You still have Verica. When is she leaving?" Ruby asked with concern.

"Oh, didn't I mention it? Her visit to Florence has been postponed. Felix is traveling to Bologna to visit his mother and sisters for Christmas. She will go later, in the spring perhaps. She wants Geoff to chaperone her."

"Jero already agreed to it," Ruby replied. "Geoff is very excited to travel to Italy."

"Can Jero spare him for so long?" Resi asked.

Ruby nodded agreeably and explained, "Jero has nothing but fond memories of Florence, so he is happy to let him go. Besides, Ervin is still our stable master although Geoff knows almost as much as he does. It was kind of Mauro to send Geoff to us."

"Alberto made it clear he would like Josip to take over his role, eventually. Geoff deserves a chance to advance." Resi noticed Ruby's eyes wandered again and asked, "What are you looking at?"

"Lady Isabella," she whispered secretively. "Who would have thought she could be so maternal?"

"Speaking of maternal," Resi said with a groan, "I should collect my babies. My breasts are aching to feed them again."

"How are you managing with twins?" Ruby asked with a chuckle.

"I do have two nurses, remember?"

"Yes, and you should let them do more for the babies."

"I know, but they are so little. Moving the babies upstairs to the nursery was already a big step for me." Resi stood up and looked around the room for whoever was holding Viviane.

Ruby stood up with her. "At least you are able to sleep through the night now," she said.

"I still like them with me as much as possible. And then, well, I might as well feed them when I hold them."

A longing smile crossed Ruby's lips when she said, "I cannot wait to be a mother."

Resi confided quietly, "This last month has been remarkable, really. But having two new babies at once changes everything."

"You seem so happy, Resi."

She spotted her baby. "I am," she said. "Completely. Mauro is a doting father and takes such good care of us, but something has come over him, and maybe over me, too. A sort of, well, I don't know. Maybe it is the taming you mentioned, a deepening in our love." Resi brightly smiled when she told Ruby, "It is everything I could have wished for."

~*~

Fabian sat down on the sofa next to his wife with two glasses. "You have held the baby for a long time, Isabella. Give him to his mother. He might be hungry."

Isabella's focus was on the blanketed bundle in her arms. "You know nothing about babies, Fabian. He cannot be hungry when he is sleeping."

Fabian asked, "Have you changed your mind, darling?"

She took the offered glass with her free hand and took a drink. "Changed my mind about what, my love?"

"Being a mother, of course?"

"That question again? I have been anointed godmother for little Dominik Fredrik Matej Lorenc Baric, which is almost as good as being a mother myself. I can cuddle and spoil my sweet godson, and he will adore his auntie." Isabella cooed at the waking baby and handed the empty glass back to Fabian.

Fabian told her, "You look very natural holding a baby, Isabella. Should we not start trying for our own?"

"With lemons almost in season?" she teased.

Fabian lifted her chin, forcing her to look at him. "I am asking a serious question, my love."

She stared into his chestnut eyes and conceded, "I suppose I wouldn't mind being a mother if I could have a son as sweet as little Dominik."

Fabian took a good look at the baby on her lap for the first time. "He is quite tiny and helpless."

"There, he is waking up now. They say he finally looks like a newborn, all pudgy and pink. Look at that little smile, Fabian. You will soon charm all the girls, won't you, my little lady-killer?" she said to the baby.

Fabian watched the two and admitted, "He is rather appealing." Then Fabian pressed his earlier question, "When we return from visiting Caterina, will you finally put your sponges away?"

"You gave me an entire year, Fabian. Do you want to break our contract? There will be a penalty for that."

Fabian took her playful bait: "I will pay your price, my darling. Just name it."

"Well," she said thoughtfully, "I know you cannot stand to be outdone by another man. Can you make twins, like Mauritius?"

He chuckled at the challenge. "I do not know the trick to it, but if that would please you, I will certainly try my hardest."

~*~

Simeon sat across the kitchen table from Franja. Flour dust covered her apron, and sugar glistened on her cheek.

"You know, when we are married, you won't have to work so hard," he told her.

"Advent is my favorite time to bake, Simeon, and baking is what I do, my love."

He dipped his finger into the sugar bowl sitting between them, and Franja slapped his hand playfully away. "Leave that for the cakes. It will make the icing look like snow," she said.

He licked his powdery finger. "That is better than snow!"

Franja dusted the top of the pastries with a spoonful of the crystals. "I have just a bit more to finish here. Aren't you in charge of the music tonight, or something?"

The view out of the window was dark. "Oh, it is getting late. Alberto, Daniel, and I have been practicing some carols for the mistress. The baron thought we might dance a bit, too."

Franja reached for the last platter to decorate, saying distractedly, "That will be a nice way to end a festive day."

"I have a better way." Simeon leaned across the desserts and whispered, "The baron gave me the key to our new cottage. Will you meet me there tonight?" He snuck a kiss on her sugary cheek.

She shook her head, laughing. "Put the key away, Simeon. You promised we would wait until after the wedding."

He sighed dramatically, propping himself up with his crutches. "I love you so much, Franja. Just one more week, and then I can take you home," he said, limping to the door to leave.

"I know, Simeon. I do, too. Now go join the party!"

~*~

Jero picked up a pastry from the offerings on the adorned table and said to Mauro, "It is strange to be a visitor in this house. All my memories are here."

Mauro found a morsel to his liking on the platter and agreed, "I suppose it would be strange for me, too. You are settled into your new place, aren't you?"

"There was not much to settle, thanks to your help. The servants keep the house, the tenants tend the fields, and Nestor still keeps the books. It is a wonderful place but, for the first time in my life, I have nothing to do."

Mauro walked along the table and added another delicacy to his plate, saying, "I was hoping to hear that."

Jero laughed. "I am not a baron, remember? I need to do something useful every day."

"I know that," Mauro replied. "That is why I am turning the inn over to you, Jero."

"I thought Ivanoslav was overseeing the renovations."

"Just the grounds," Mauro clarified. "The renovations have stalled, and I cannot find time to manage them."

"We could go there together, and you can show me what is left to do," Jero suggested.

"No," Mauro said.

"No?" Jero repeated with concern.

Mauro backpedaled. "Yes, well, I rode out there not too long ago, and I realized something. I am giving the land to you, Jero, so I won't have to go there again. You will know what needs to be done and how to make it profitable."

"That is too generous, Mauro," Jero said, shaking his head in disagreement. "I will get the inn up and running and you can have it back."

"I do not want it back."

Jero didn't question why. He had seen this look in his brother's eyes before and heard that unwavering tone.

Mauro turned away from the table and became upbeat again. "I will be busy in the coming months, actually," he remarked. "I am going with Hugo to

Toth Castle for a visit. Uncle Vladimir has offered him a full commission as a ranking captain.”

“Really?” Jero said with surprise. “I thought Hugo was happy here.”

Mauro explained, “It seems Hugo has been corresponding with Lady Bianca Carrera since leaving Venice. He thinks he will be happier closer to her.”

Jero laughed. “What sort of love potion did you put in your well this year, Mauro?”

Mauro shrugged merrily and said, “It is a little premature for wedding plans, but Hugo is finally smitten, and she seems to return his devotion.”

“When do you leave?” Jero asked.

“After the holidays.”

Jero downed the last of his wine and asked, “Can I get you a glass of something, Mauro?”

“Not right now, thank you,” Mauro said. “I want to get some air first.”

~*~

After the smoky air in the brightly lit great hall, the foyer was already refreshing. Still, Mauro took his cape from the peg and went out into the frigid evening. His boots crunched on the frosted granite path to the chapel. It wasn’t much warmer when he went inside and touched his fingers to the icy holy water. Mauro said a quick prayer to the Virgin Mary before opening the panel door in the sanctuary. He lit the torches as he descended into the crypt.

What Mauro sought was in the middle of the cavernous burial chamber. His parents’ names, along with those of Margaret and her four children, were chiseled on the face of the tomb. He crossed himself and then ran his fingers over the words *Lorenc Jeronim Fredrik Baric.*

Mauro knelt down, and his voice echoed against the stone walls. “I fulfilled my duty, Father,” he said to the empty room. “The Barics will live on. I have a son now. He is a beautiful boy, perfect in every way. Everyone says he looks like a true Baric already. I named him after Grandfather Toth and Grandfather Baric.” Mauro waited in the stillness of the crypt, expecting a reply somehow.

He touched the smooth stone and continued, “I have a daughter, too, Father. Twins! She is a little angel and so pretty, like her mother. She breathed life into little Dominik when we thought we would lose him, so we named her Viviane. Hers is not a Croatian name, I know, but you are to blame for that. You wanted me to marry a foreigner, and I thank God every day that you got what you wanted.” Mauro wiped the corners of his wet eyes and whispered, “I wish you were here to meet them.”

Then Mauro rose again and left the ghosts of his ancestors. He made his way back upstairs to the chapel, snuffing out the torches as he went. The small church seemed brighter and warmer than when Mauro had passed through a short time ago. He left one lamp burning for the dead.

Outside the door, Mauro looked back at the chapel. The light in its opaque window faintly flickered against the whitewash. The steady bootsteps on the rampart above him had paused. They picked up their rhythm again when the soldiers saw it was their baron on the glistening path below. Beyond the courtyard, slits of yellow illuminated the darkness where his loyal guardsmen had retreated for the night.

Mauro followed the path around the old oak. He could hear music playing within the House of Baric. The blurred figures in the great hall windows pulled him from his pensive mood. The shifting colors were dancing. The green reflected in the etched glass could only be Resi. Mauro watched her movement while snowflakes were collecting on his cape. So beautiful. He quickened his stride to join her.

~*~~*~~*~

To learn more about the author and her stories, please visit:
www.JillianBald.com

Books in This Trilogy:

The House of Baric Part One: Shields Down
The House of Baric Part Two: A Brother's Defense
The House of Baric Part Three: Widows and Weddings